"Eggers has done something remarkable with this book. He has managed to cross many barriers, both real and artificial, to tell the story of one man's tragedy and triumph in a way that emphasizes his simple humanity above the drama of his terrible situation. It is a book that shows there is no reason why geographical and cultural divides should prevent us from attempting to understand each other as citizens of this world."

—Uzodinma Iweala, author of *Beasts of No Nation*

"*What is the What* is a novel that possesses the best qualities of a documentary film: the conviction of truthfulness and the constant reminder of the arbitrariness of fate, for worse and for better. By setting his story of African annihilation and survival as a story of American immigration, Eggers insures that it belongs to us all, as it must."

—Philip Gourevitch, author of *We Wish to Inform You That Tomorrow We Will Be Killed with Our Families: Stories from Rwanda*

"Eggers's limpid prose gives Valentino an unaffected, compelling voice and makes his narrative by turns harrowing, funny, bleak and lyrical. The result is a horrific account of the Sudanese tragedy, but also an emblematic saga of modernity—of the search for home and self in a world of unending upheaval."

—*Publishers Weekly* (starred review)

"I have been interacting with the Lost Boys since the late 1980s, from the time they were first displaced in Sudan to their arrival in the United States. I thought I had heard and seen it all. But reading Valentino's story has touched emotions in me I didn't even know I had. Eggers tells the story of Sudan through the eyes of Valentino Achak Deng, but he also elucidates the best and worst of our common humanity."

—John Prendergast,
Senior Advisor, International Crisis Group

"Reworking this powerful tale with both deep feeling and subtlety, Eggers finds humanity and even humor, creating something much greater than a litany of woes or a script for political outrage. *What is the What* does what a novel does best, which is to make us understand the deeper truths of another human being's experience."

—Keir Graff, *Booklist* (starred review)

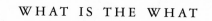

WHAT IS THE WHAT

MCSWEENEY'S

SAN FRANCISCO

For more information about McSweeney's, see www.mcsweeneys.net

Copyright © 2006 Dave Eggers

Cover art by Rachell Sumpter

All rights reserved, including right of reproduction
in whole or part in any form.

McSweeney's and colophon are registered trademarks
of McSweeney's, a privately held company with
wildly fluctuating resources.

ISBN: 1-932416-64-1

Printed in Canada.

What Is the What

THE AUTOBIOGRAPHY
OF VALENTINO ACHAK DENG

A NOVEL

DAVE EGGERS

PREFACE

This book is the soulful account of my life: from the time I was separated from my family in Marial Bai to the thirteen years I spent in Ethiopian and Kenyan refugee camps, to my encounters with vibrant Western cultures, in Atlanta and elsewhere.

As you read this book, you will learn about the two and a half million people who have perished in Sudan's civil war. I was just a boy when the war began. As a helpless human, I survived by trekking across many punishing landscapes while being bombed by Sudanese air forces, while dodging land mines, while being preyed upon by wild beasts and human killers. I fed on unknown fruits, vegetables, leaves, animal carcasses and sometimes went with nothing for days. At certain points, the difficulty was unbearable. I hated myself and attempted to take my own life. Many of my friends, and thousands of my fellow country-men, did not make it through these struggles alive.

This book was born out of the desire on the part of myself and the author to reach out to others to help them understand the atrocities many successive governments of Sudan committed before and during the civil war. To that end, over the course of many years, I told my story orally to the author. He then concocted this novel, approximating my own voice and using the basic events of my life as the foundation. Because many of the passages are fictional, the result is called a novel. It should not be taken as a definitive history of the civil war in Sudan, nor of the Sudanese people, nor even of my brethren, those known as the Lost Boys. This is simply one man's story, subjectively told. And though it is fictionalized, it should be noted that the world I have known is not so different from the one depicted within these pages. We live in a time when even the most horrific events in this book could occur, and in most cases did occur.

Even when my hours were darkest, I believed that some day I could share my experiences with readers, so as to prevent the same horrors from repeating themselves. This book is a form of struggle, and it keeps my spirit alive to struggle. To struggle is to strengthen my faith, my hope, and my belief in humanity. Thank you for reading this book, and I wish you a blessed day.

—Valentino Achak Deng, Atlanta, 2006

BOOK I

I.

I have no reason not to answer the door so I answer the door. I have no tiny round window to inspect visitors so I open the door and before me is a tall, sturdily built African-American woman, a few years older than me, wearing a red nylon sweatsuit. She speaks to me loudly. "You have a phone, sir?"

She looks familiar. I am almost certain that I saw her in the parking lot an hour ago, when I returned from the convenience store. I saw her standing by the stairs, and I smiled at her. I tell her that I do have a phone.

"My car broke down on the street," she says. Behind her, it is nearly night. I have been studying most of the afternoon. "Can you let me use your phone to call the police?" she asks.

I do not know why she wants to call the police for a car in need of repair, but I consent. She steps inside. I begin to close the door but she holds it open. "I'll just be a second," she says. It does not make sense to me to leave the door open but I do so because she desires it. This is her country and not yet mine.

"Where's the phone?" she asks.

I tell her my cell phone is in my bedroom. Before I finish the sentence, she has rushed past me and down the hall, a hulk of swishing nylon. The door to my room closes, then clicks. She has locked herself in my bedroom. I start to follow her when I hear a voice behind me.

"Stay here, Africa."

I turn and see a man, African-American, wearing a vast powder-blue baseball jacket and jeans. His face is not discernible beneath his baseball hat but he has his hand on something near his waist, as if needing to hold up his pants.

"Are you with that woman?" I ask him. I don't understand anything yet and am angry.

"Just sit down, Africa," he says, nodding to my couch.

I stand. "What is she doing in my bedroom?"

"Just sit your ass down," he says, now with venom.

I sit and now he shows me the handle of the gun. He has been holding it all along, and I was supposed to know. But I know nothing; I never know the things I am supposed to know. I do know, now, that I am being robbed, and that I want to be elsewhere.

It is a strange thing, I realize, but what I think at this moment is that I want to be back in Kakuma. In Kakuma there was no rain, the winds blew nine months a year, and eighty thousand war refugees from Sudan and elsewhere lived on one meal a day. But at this moment, when the woman is in my bedroom and the man is guarding me with his gun, I want to be in Kakuma, where I lived in a hut of plastic and sandbags and owned one pair of pants. I am not sure there was evil of this kind in the Kakuma refugee camp, and I want to return. Or even Pinyudo, the Ethiopian camp I lived in before Kakuma; there was nothing there, only one or two meals a day, but it had its small pleasures; I was a boy then and could forget that I was a malnourished refugee a thousand miles from home. In any case, if this is punishment for the hubris of wanting to leave Africa, of harboring dreams of college and solvency in America, I am now chastened and I apologize. I will return with bowed head. Why did I smile at this woman? I smile reflexively and it is a habit I need to break. It invites retribution. I have been humbled so many times since arriving that I am beginning to think someone is trying desperately to send me a message, and that message is "Leave this place."

As soon as I settle on this position of regret and retreat, it is replaced by one of protest. This new posture has me standing up and speaking to the man in the powder-blue coat. "I want you two to leave this place," I say.

The powder man is instantly enraged. I have upset the balance here, have thrown an obstacle, my voice, in the way of their errand.

"Are you telling me what do, motherfucker?"

10

I stare into his small eyes.

"Tell me that, Africa, are you telling me what to do, motherfucker?"

The woman hears our voices and calls from the bedroom: "Will you take care of him?" She is exasperated with her partner, and he with me.

Powder tilts his head to me and raises his eyebrows. He takes a step toward me and again gestures toward the gun in his belt. He seems about to use it, but suddenly his shoulders slacken, and he drops his head. He stares at his shoes and breathes slowly, collecting himself. When he raises his eyes again, he has regained himself.

"You're from Africa, right?"

I nod.

"All right then. That means we're brothers."

I am unwilling to agree.

"And because we're brothers and all, I'll teach you a lesson. Don't you know you shouldn't open your door to strangers?"

The question causes me to wince. The simple robbery had been, in a way, acceptable. I have seen robberies, have been robbed, on scales much smaller than this. Until I arrived in the United States, my most valuable possession was the mattress I slept on, and so the thefts were far smaller: a disposable camera, a pair of sandals, a ream of white typing paper. All of these were valuable, yes, but now I own a television, a VCR, a microwave, an alarm clock, many other conveniences, all provided by the Peachtree United Methodist Church here in Atlanta. Some of the things were used, most were new, and all had been given anonymously. To look at them, to use them daily, provoked in me a shudder—a strange but genuine physical expression of gratitude. And now I assume all of these gifts will be taken in the next few minutes. I stand before Powder and my memory is searching for the time when I last felt this betrayed, when I last felt in the presence of evil so careless.

With one hand still gripping the handle of the gun, he now puts his hand to my chest. "Why don't you sit your ass down and watch how it's done?"

I take two steps backward and sit on the couch, also a gift from the church. An apple-faced white woman wearing a tie-dyed shirt brought it the day Achor Achor and I moved in. She apologized that it hadn't preceded our arrival. The people from the church were often apologizing.

I stare up at Powder and I know who he brings to mind. The soldier, an Ethiopian and a woman, shot two of my companions and almost killed me. She had the same

11

wild light in her eyes, and she first posed as our savior. We were fleeing Ethiopia, chased by hundreds of Ethiopian soldiers shooting at us, the River Gilo full of our blood, and out of the high grasses she appeared. *Come to me, children! I am your mother! Come to me!* She was only a face in the grey grass, her hands outstretched, and I hesitated. Two of the boys I was running with, boys I had found on the bank of the bloody river, they both went to her. And when they drew close enough, she lifted an automatic rifle and shot through the chests and stomachs of the boys. They fell in front of me and I turned and ran. *Come back!* she continued. *Come to your mother!*

I had run that day through the grasses until I found Achor Achor, and with Achor Achor, we found the Quiet Baby, and we saved the Quiet Baby and, for a time, we considered ourselves doctors. This was so many years ago. I was ten years old, perhaps eleven. It's impossible to know. The man before me, Powder, would never know anything of this kind. He would not be interested. Thinking of that day, when we were driven from Ethiopia back to Sudan, thousands dead in the river, gives me strength against this person in my apartment, and again I stand.

The man now looks at me, like a parent about to do something he regrets that his child has forced him to do. He is so close to me I can smell something chemical about him, a smell like bleach.

"Are you— Are you—?" His mouth tightens and he pauses. He takes the gun from his waist and raises it in an upward backhand motion. A blur of black and my teeth crush each other and I watch the ceiling rush over me.

In my life I have been struck in many different ways but never with the barrel of a gun. I have the fortune of having seen more suffering than I have suffered myself, but nevertheless, I have been starved, I have been beaten with sticks, with rods, with brooms and stones and spears. I have ridden five miles on a truckbed loaded with corpses. I have watched too many young boys die in the desert, some as if sitting down to sleep, some after days of madness. I have seen three boys taken by lions, eaten haphazardly. I watched them lifted from their feet, carried off in the animal's jaws and devoured in the high grass, close enough that I could hear the wet snapping sounds of the tearing of flesh. I have watched a close friend die next to me in an overturned truck, his eyes open to me, his life leaking from a hole I could not see. And yet at this moment, as I am strewn across the couch and my hand is wet with blood, I find myself missing all of Africa. I miss Sudan, I miss the howling grey desert of northwest Kenya. I miss the yellow nothing of Ethiopia.

My view of my assailant is now limited to his waist, his hands. He has stored the gun somewhere and now his hands have my shirt and my neck and he is throwing me from the couch to the carpet. The back of my head hits the end table on the way earthward and two glasses and a clock radio fall with me. Once on the carpet, my cheek resting in its own pooling blood, I know a moment of comfort, thinking that in all likelihood he is finished. Already I am so tired. I feel as if I could close my eyes and be done with this.

"Now shut the fuck up," he says.

These words sound unconvincing, and this gives me solace. He is not an angry man, I realize. He does not intend to kill me; perhaps he has been manipulated by this woman, who is now opening the drawers and closets of my bedroom. She seems to be in control. She is focused on whatever is in my room, and the job of her companion is to neutralize me. It seems simple, and he seems disinclined to inflict further harm upon me. So I rest. I close my eyes and rest.

I am tired of this country. I am thankful for it, yes, I have cherished many aspects of it for the three years I have been here, but I am tired of the promises. I came here, four thousand of us came here, contemplating and expecting quiet. Peace and college and safety. We expected a land without war and, I suppose, a land without misery. We were giddy and impatient. We wanted it all immediately—homes, families, college, the ability to send money home, advanced degrees, and finally some influence. But for most of us, the slowness of our transition—after five years I still do not have the necessary credits to apply to a four-year college—has wrought chaos. We waited ten years at Kakuma and I suppose we did not want to start over here. We wanted the next step, and quickly. But this has not happened, not in most cases, and in the interim, we have found ways to spend the time. I have held too many menial jobs, and currently work at the front desk of a health club, on the earliest possible shift, checking in members and explaining the club's benefits to prospective members. This is not glamorous, but it represents a level of stability unknown to some. Too many have fallen, too many feel they have failed. The pressures upon us, the promises we cannot keep with ourselves—these things are making monsters of too many of us. And the one person who I felt could help me transcend the disappointment and mundanity of it, an exemplary Sudanese woman named Tabitha Duany Aker, is gone.

Now they are in the kitchen. Now in Achor Achor's room. Lying here, I begin to calculate what they can take from me. I realize with some satisfaction that my computer is in my car, and will be spared. But Achor Achor's new laptop will be stolen. It will be my fault. Achor Achor is one of the leaders of the young refugees here in Atlanta and I fear all he needs will be gone when his computer is gone. The records of all the meetings, the finances, thousands of emails. I cannot allow so much to be stolen. Achor Achor has been with me since Ethiopia and I bring him nothing but bad luck.

In Ethiopia I stared into the eyes of a lion. I was perhaps ten years old, sent to the forest to retrieve wood, and the animal stepped slowly from behind a tree. I stood for a moment, such a long time, enough for me to memorize its dead-eyed face, before running. He roared after me but did not chase; I like to believe that he found me too formidable a foe. So I have faced this lion, have faced the guns, a dozen times, of armed Arab militiamen on horseback, their white robes gleaming in the sun. And thus I can do this, can stop this petty theft. Once again I raise myself to my knees.

"Get the fuck down, motherfucker!"

And my face meets the floor once more. Now the kicking begins. He kicks me in the stomach, and now the shoulder. It hurts most when my bones strike my bones.

"Fucking Nigerian motherfucker!"

Now he seems to be enjoying himself, and this causes me worry. When there is pleasure, there is often abandon, and mistakes are made. Seven kicks to the ribs, one to the hip, and he rests. I take a breath and assess my damage. It is not great. I curl myself around the corner of the couch and now am determined to stay still. I have never been a fighter, I finally admit to myself. I have survived many oppressions, but have never fought with a man standing in front of me.

"Fucking Nigerian! So stupid!"

He is heaving, his hands on his bent knees.

"No wonder you motherfuckers are in the Stone Age!"

He gives me one more kick, lighter than the others, but this one directly into my temple, and a burst of white light fills my left eye.

In America I have been called Nigerian before—it must be the most familiar of African countries—but I have never been kicked. Again, though, I have seen it happen. I suppose there is little in the way of violence that I have not seen in Sudan, in Kenya. I spent years in a refugee camp in Ethiopia, and there I watched two young boys, perhaps twelve years old, fighting so viciously over rations that one kicked the other to death. He had not intended to kill his foe, of course, but we were young and very weak. You cannot fight when you have not eaten properly for weeks. The dead boy's body was unprepared for any trauma, his skin taut over his brittle ribs that were no longer up to the task of encasing his heart. He was dead before he touched the ground. It was just before lunch, and after the boy was carried off, to be buried in the gravelly soil, we were served stewed beans and corn.

Now I plan to say nothing, to simply wait for Powder and his friend to leave. They cannot stay long; surely soon they will have taken all that they want. I can see the pile they are making on our kitchen table, the things they plan to leave with. The TV is there, Achor Achor's laptop, the VCR, the cordless phones, my cell phone, the microwave.

The sky is darkening, my guests have been in our apartment for twenty minutes or so, and Achor Achor won't be back for many hours, if at all. His job is similar to the one I once had—at a furniture showroom, in the back room, arranging for the shipping of samples to interior decorators. Even when not at work, he's seldom home. After many years without female companionship, Achor Achor has found a girlfriend, an African-American woman named Michelle. She is lovely. They met at the community college, in a class, quilting, which Achor Achor registered for by accident. He walked in, was seated next to Michelle, and he never left. She smells of citrus perfume, a flowery citrus, and I see Achor Achor less and less. There was a time when I harbored thoughts of Tabitha this way. I imagined us planning a wedding and creating a brood of children who would speak English as Americans do, but Tabitha lived in Seattle and those plans were still far away. Perhaps I am romanticizing it now. This happened at Kakuma, too; I lost someone very close to me and afterward I believed I could have saved him had I been a better friend to him. But everyone disappears, no matter who loves them.

Now the process of removing our belongings begins. Powder has made a cradle of his arms and his accomplice is stacking our possessions there—first the microwave, now the laptop, now the stereo. When the pile reaches his chin, the woman walks to the front door and opens it.

"Fuck!" she says, closing the door quickly.

She tells Powder that outside is a police car, parked in our lot. The car is, in fact, blocking their own car's exit.

15

"Fuck fuck fuck!" she spits.

This panic goes on for some time, and soon they take positions on either side of the curtained window that looks out on the courtyard. I gather from their conversation that the cop is talking to a Latino man, but that the officer's body language seems to indicate that the matter is not pressing. The woman and Powder express growing confidence and relief in the fact that the police officer is not there for them. But then why won't he leave? they want to know. "Why doesn't that motherfucker go do his job?" she asks.

They settle in to wait. The bleeding from my forehead seems to have subsided. With my tongue, I explore the damage to my mouth. One of my lower front teeth is chipped, and a molar has been smashed; it feels jagged, a saw-toothed mountain range. But I can't worry about dental matters. We Sudanese are not known for the perfection of our teeth.

I look up to find that the woman and Powder have my backpack, which contains nothing but my homework from Georgia Perimeter College. Imagining the time it will take to reproduce those notebooks, now so close to midterm exams, almost brings me to my feet again. I stare at my visitors with as much hatred as I can muster, as my god will allow.

I am a fool. Why did I open that door? I have an African-American friend here in Atlanta, Mary, a friend only, and she will laugh about this. Not a week ago, she was in this very room, sitting on my couch, and with Achor Achor we were watching *The Exorcist*. Achor Achor and I had long wanted to see it. We have an interest in the concept of evil, I admit it, and the idea of an exorcism had intrigued us. Though we felt that our faith was strong and we had received a thorough Catholic education, we had never heard of an exorcism performed by a Catholic priest. So we watched the film, and it terrified us both. Achor Achor didn't make it past the first twenty minutes. Retreating to his room, he closed the door, turned on his stereo, and worked on his algebra homework. In one scene in the film, there is a knock on the door, boding ill, and a question occurred to me. I paused the movie and Mary sighed patiently; she is accustomed to me stopping while walking or driving to ask a question—*Why do the people ask for money in the highway medians? Are all of the offices in those buildings occupied?*—and at that moment I asked Mary who, in America, answers when there is a knock at the door.

"What do you mean?" she asked.

"Is it the man, or the woman?" I asked.

She scoffed. "The man," she said. "The man. The man is the protector, right?" she said. "Of course the man answers the door. Why?"

"In Sudan," I said, "it cannot be the man. It is always the woman who answers the door, because when there is a knock, someone has come for the man."

Ah, I have found another chipped tooth. My friends are still by the window, periodically parting the curtains, finding the cop still there, and cursing for a few minutes before settling back into their slump-shouldered vigil.

An hour has passed and now I'm curious about the business of the police officer in the parking lot. I begin to harbor hopes that the cop does indeed know about the robbery, and in the interest of avoiding a standoff, is simply waiting for my friends to exit. But why, then, advertise his presence? Perhaps the officer is at the complex to investigate the drug dealers in C4? The men in unit C4 are white, though, and as far as I can ascertain, the man the officer is talking to is Edgardo, who lives in C13, eight doors from my own. Edgardo is a mechanic and is my friend; he has saved me, according to his estimate, $2,200 in car repairs over the two years we have been neighbors. In exchange, I have given him rides to church, to work, to the North DeKalb Mall. He has his own car, but he prefers not to drive it. I have not seen its axles bearing tires in at least six months. He loves to work on his car, and does not mind working on mine, a 2001 Corolla. When he is working on my car, Edgardo insists that I entertain him. "Tell me stories," he says, because he doesn't like the music they play on the radio. "Everywhere in the country they play norte music, but not in Atlanta. What am I doing here? This is no city for a lover of music. Tell me a story, Valentino. Talk to me, talk to me. Tell some stories."

The first time he asked, I began telling him my own story, which began when the rebels, men who would eventually join the Sudan People's Liberation Army, first raided my father's shop in Marial Bai. I was six years old, and the rebel presence seemed to grow in our village every month. They were tolerated by most, discouraged by others. My father was a wealthy man by regional standards, the owner of a general store in our town and another shop a few days' walk away. He had been a rebel himself, years before, but now he was a businessman, and wanted no trouble. He wanted no revolution, he had no quarrel with the Islamists in Khartoum. They were not bothering him, he said, they were half a world away. He wanted only to sell grain, corn, sugar, pots, fabric, candy.

I was in his shop, playing on the floor one day. There was a commotion above my head. Three men, two of them carrying rifles, were demanding to take what they wanted. They claimed it was for the good of the rebellion, that they would bring about a New Sudan.

"No, no," Edgardo said. "No fighting. I don't want all the fighting. I read three newspapers a day." He pointed to the papers spread underneath the car, now brown with grease. "I get enough of that. I know about your war. Tell me some other story. Tell me how you got that name, Valentino. That's a strange name for a guy from Africa, don't you think?"

So I told him the story of my baptism. This was in my hometown. I was about six years old. The baptism was the idea of my Uncle Jok; my parents, who opposed Christian ideas, did not attend. They were believers in the traditional religious ideas of my clan, and the village's experiments with Christianity were limited to the young, like Jok, and those, like me, who they could entice. Conversion was a sacrifice for any man, given that Father Dominic Matong, a Sudanese man who had been ordained by Italian missionaries, forbade polygamy. My father, who had many wives, rejected the new religion on these grounds, and also because to him the Christians seemed preoccupied with written language. My father and mother could not read; not many people his age could. —You go to your Church of Books, he said. —You'll come back when your senses return.

I was wearing a white robe, surrounded by Jok and his wife Adeng, when Father Matong asked his questions. He had walked two days from Aweil to baptize me and three other boys, each of whom followed me. It was the most nervous I had ever been. The other boys I knew said it was nothing compared to facing a beating from their father, but I did not know such a situation; my father never raised his hand to me.

Facing Jok and Adeng, Father Matong held his Bible in one hand and raised his other palm in the air. —Do you, with whole your heart and faith, offer your child to be baptized and to become faithful member of the family of God?

—We do! they said.

I leapt when they said this. It was far louder than I had expected.

—By so doing, have you rejected Satan with all his might, deceit, and unfaithfulness?

—We do!

—Do you believe in Jesus, the son of God, borne by the Virgin Mary, he who

18

suffered and was crucified and who on the third day ascended from the dead to save us from our sins?

—We do!

And then cold and clean water was poured over my head. Father Matong had brought it with him on his two-day walk from Aweil.

With my baptism came my Christian name, Valentino, chosen by Father Matong. Many boys went by their Christian names, but in my case, this name was rarely used, as no one, including myself, could pronounce it. We said Valdino, Baldero, Benedeeno. It was not until I found myself in a refugee camp in Ethiopia that the name was used by anyone who knew me. It was then that, improbably, after years of war, I saw Father Matong again. It was then that he reminded me of my Christian name, told me of its provenance, and demonstrated how to speak it aloud.

Edgardo liked this story a great deal. He had not known until that moment that I was a Catholic like him. We made plans to attend a Mass together some day, but we have not yet done so.

II.

"Look at this guy. Bleeding from his head and looking so mad!"

Powder is addressing me. He is still at the window, but his accomplice is in the bathroom, where she has been for some time. With this development, her use of my bathroom, I now feel sure that this apartment will have to be abandoned. Their violation of it is now complete. I would like to burn this place down the moment they leave.

"Hey Tonya, come out here and look at the Nigerian prince. What's the matter, man? You never been robbed before?"

Now she is staring at me, too. Her name is Tonya.

"Get used to it, Africa," she said.

It occurs to me that the longer the police officer is in the parking lot, the better the chance is that I will be discovered. As long as the cop is there, the chance remains that Achor Achor could return, or Edgardo might knock on my door. He has only knocked on my door a few times before—he prefers the phone—but it is not impossible. If he knocked on the door, there could be no disguising what was happening here.

My cell phone rings. Tonya and Powder let it ring. Minutes later, it rings again. It must be five o'clock.

"Look at this pimp," Powder says, "his phone's ringing every minute. You some kind of pimp, prince?"

If I had not set rules, the phone would ring without end. There is a circle of perhaps three hundred Sudanese in the U.S. who keep in touch, me with them but more often them with me, and we do so in a way that might be considered excessive. They all think I have some kind of direct line to the rebels, the SPLA. They call me to confirm any rumors, to get my opinion on any developments. Before I insisted that any calls to me be limited to between five o'clock and nine, I would get an average of seventy calls a day. I am not one prone to exaggeration. The calls do not stop. Any five-minute conversation can be expected to be interrupted eight or nine times by more calls. Bol will call from Phoenix, and while I talk to him about a visa for his brother who has made it to Cairo, James will call from San Jose, and he will need money. We share information about jobs, car loans, insurance, weddings, events in southern Sudan. When John Garang, the leader of the SPLA and the man who more or less began the civil war, died in a helicopter crash this past July, the calls obeyed no limits or hours. I was on the phone, without break, for four days. Yet I knew nothing more than anyone else.

In many cases, the Lost Boys of Sudan have no one else. The Lost Boys is not a nickname appreciated by many among our ranks, but it is apt enough. We fled or were sent from our homes, many of us orphaned, and thousands of us wandered through deserts and forests for what seemed like years. In many ways we are alone and in most cases we are unsure of where exactly we're going. While in Kakuma, one of the largest and most remote refugee camps in the world, we found new families, or many of us did. I lived with a teacher from my hometown, and when, after two years, he brought his family to the camp, we had what resembled a family. There were five boys and three girls. I called them sisters. We walked to school together, we retrieved water together. But with our relocation to the United States, again it is just boys. There are very few Sudanese women in the U.S., and very few elders, and thus we rely on each other for virtually everything. This has its disadvantages, for very frequently, we are sharing unfounded rumors and abject paranoia.

When we first arrived here, we stayed in our apartments for weeks, venturing out only when necessary. One of our friends, who had been in the U.S. longer than we had, had just been assaulted on his way home. I am sad to say that again it was young African-American men, and this set us wondering how we were being perceived. We felt watched, pursued. We Sudanese are recognizable; we look like no one else on Earth. We do not even look like anyone else from East Africa. The isolation of many parts of southern Sudan has ensured that our bloodline has remained largely unaltered. We stayed inside those weeks, worried not only about predatory young men but also that the U.S. immigration officials would change their minds about us. It's amusing to think about now, how naïve we were, how skewed our perspective was. Anything seemed possible. Should we become too visible, or if a few of us ran into some kind of trouble, it seemed perfectly likely that we would all promptly be returned to Africa. Or perhaps just imprisoned. Achor Achor thought we could be executed if they found out that we had once been affiliated with the SPLA. At Kakuma, many of us lied on our application forms and in our interviews with officials. We knew that if we admitted affiliation with the SPLA, we would not be sent to Atlanta, North Dakota, Detroit. We would remain in Kakuma. So those of us who needed to lie, lied. The SPLA had been a part of our lives from early on, and over half of the young men who call themselves Lost Boys were child soldiers to some degree or another. But this is a part of our history that we have been told not to talk about.

So we stayed inside. We watched television most of the day and night, interrupted only by naps and occasional games of chess. One of the men living with us in those days had never seen television, outside of a few glimpses in Kakuma. I had watched television in Kakuma and in Nairobi, but had never seen anything like the 120 channels we had been provided in that first apartment. It was far too much to absorb in in one day, or two or three. We watched almost without pause for a week, and at the end of that period, we were exhilarated, disheartened, thoroughly confused. One of us would venture out at dusk for food and whatever else we needed, fearing always that we, too, would be victims of an assault by young African-American men.

Though the Sudanese elders had warned us of crime in the United States, this sort of thing was not part of our official orientation. When, after ten years, we finally were told we would be leaving the camp, we were given a two-day course in what we would see and hear in the United States. An American named Sasha told us about American currency, about job training, cars, about paying rent, about air conditioning and public transportation and snow. Many of us were being sent to climates like Fargo and Seattle, and to illustrate, Sasha passed around ice. Many of the members of the class had never held ice. I had, but only because I was a youth leader at the camp, and in the UN compound had seen many things, including the storerooms of food, the athletic equipment donated by Japan and Sweden, the films of Bruce Willis. But while Sasha told us that in America even the most successful men can have but one wife at once—my father had six—and talked about escalators, indoor plumbing, and the various laws of the land, he did not warn us that I would be told by American teenagers

22

that I should go back to Africa. The first time it happened, I was on a bus.

A few months after I arrived, we began venturing out from the apartment, in part because we had been given only enough money to live for three months, and now we needed to find work. This was January of 2002, and I was working at Best Buy, in the storeroom. I was riding home at 8 p.m., after changing buses three times (the job would not last, for it took me ninety minutes to travel eighteen miles). But on that day I was content enough. I was making $8.50 an hour and there were two other Sudanese at that Best Buy, all of us in the storeroom, carting plasma TVs and dishwashing machines. I was exhausted and riding home and looking forward to watching a tape that had been circulating among the Lost Boys in Atlanta; someone had filmed the recent wedding, in Kansas City, of a well-known Sudanese man to a Sudanese woman I had met in Kakuma. I was about to get off at my stop when two African-American teenagers spoke to me.

"Yo," one of the boys said to me. "Yo freak, where you from?" I turned and told him I was from Sudan. This gave him pause. Sudan is not well-known, or was not well-known until the war the Islamists brought to us twenty years ago, with its proxy armies, its untethered militias, was brought, in 2003, to Darfur.

"You know," the teenager said, tilting his head and sizing me up, "you're one of those Africans who sold us out." He went on in this vein for some time, and it became clear that he thought I was responsible for the enslaving of his ancestors. Accordingly, he and his friend followed me for a block, talking to my back, again suggesting that I go back to Africa. This idea has been posed to Achor Achor, too, and now my two guests have said it. Just a moment ago, Powder looked at me with some compassion and asked, "Man, why you even *here?* You coming here to wear your suits and act like you're all educated? Didn't you know you were gonna get *got* here?"

Though I have a low opinion of the teenagers who harassed me, I am more tolerant of this sort of experience than some of my fellow Sudanese. It is a terrible thing, the assumptions that Africans develop about African-Americans. We watch American films and we come to this country assuming that African-Americans are drug dealers and bank robbers. The Sudanese elders in Kakuma told us in no uncertain terms to stay clear of African-Americans, the women in particular. How surprised they would have been to learn that the first and most important person to come to our aid in Atlanta was an African-American woman who wanted only to connect us to more people who could help. We were, it should be noted, confused about this help; in some ways we saw it as our right, even while we questioned others who needed assistance. In Atlanta, when we saw people out of work, homeless people or young men drinking on corners or in cars, we said, "Go to work! You have hands, now work!" But that was before we started looking for jobs ourselves, and certainly before we realized that working at Best Buy would not in any way facilitate our goals of college or beyond.

When we landed at John F. Kennedy International Airport, we were promised enough money to cover our rent and groceries for three months. I was flown to Atlanta, handed a temporary green card and a Medicaid card, and through the International Rescue Committee provided with enough money to pay my rent for exactly three months. My $8.50 an hour at Best Buy was not enough. I took a second job that first fall, this one at a holiday-themed store that opened in November and closed just after January began. I arranged ceramic Santas on shelves, I sprayed synthetic frost on miniature wreaths, I swept the floor seven times a day. Still, between the two jobs, neither of them full-time, I was taking home less than $200 a week after taxes. I knew men in Kakuma who were doing better than that, relatively speaking, selling sneakers made of rope and rubber tires.

Finally, though, a newspaper article about the Sudanese in Atlanta led to many new job offers from well-meaning citizens, and I took one at a furniture showroom, the sort of place designers go, in a suburban complex with many other such showrooms. The job kept me in the back of the store, among the fabric samples. I should not feel shame about this, but somehow I do: my job was to retrieve fabric samples for the designers, and then file them again when they were returned. I did this for almost two years. The thought of all that time wasted, so much time sitting on that wooden stool, cataloging, smiling, thanking, filing—all while I should have been in school—is too much for me to contemplate. My current hours at the Century Club Health and Fitness Centre are superficially pleasant, the gym members smile at me and I at them, but my patience is waning.

Powder and Tonya have been arguing for some time. They are increasingly anxious about the purpose of the police presence in the parking lot. Tonya is blaming Powder for parking the car in the lot; she wanted to park on the street, to facilitate an easier escape. Powder contends that Tonya specifically told him to park in the lot, so they would be able to leave as quickly as possible. This debate has been going on for twenty minutes or so, quick heated exchanges followed by long stretches of silence. They act like brother and sister, and I begin to think they are related. They talk to each other without respect or boundaries, and this is how siblings in America act.

I should be in Ponte Vedra Beach, Florida, right now, with Phil Mays and his family. Phil has been my host, the American sponsor and mentor who agreed to help me transition to life here. A lawyer working in real estate, he bought me clothes, rented my apartment, financed my Toyota Corolla, gave me a floor lamp, a kitchen set and a cell phone, and brought me to the doctor when my headaches would not cease. Now Phil lives in Ponte Vedra Beach and two weeks ago invited me to spend a weekend there and to tour the University of Florida. I declined, thinking the trip was too close to my midterms at Georgia Perimeter College. I have two tests tomorrow.

But I have been thinking for some time of leaving Atlanta.

It need not be Florida where I go, but I can't stay here. I have other friends here, other allies—Mary Williams, and a family called the Newtons—but there is not enough here now to keep me in Georgia. It is very complicated here in the Sudanese community; there is so much suspicion. Each time someone tries to help one of us, the rest of the Sudanese claim that this is unfair, that they need their share. Didn't we all walk across the desert? they ask. Didn't we all eat the hides of hyenas and goats to keep our bellies full? Didn't we all drink our own urine? This last part, of course, is apocryphal, absolutely not true for the vast majority of us, but it impresses people. Along our walk from southern Sudan to Ethiopia, there were a handful of boys who drank their own urine, a few more who ate mud to keep their throats wet, but our experiences were very different, depending on when we crossed Sudan. The later groups had more advantages, more support from the SPLA. There is one group, which passed through the desert just after my own, that rode atop a water tanker. They had soldiers, guns, trucks! And the tanker, which symbolized for us everything that we would never have, and the fact that there would be, always, castes within castes, that within groups of walking boys, still there were hierarchies. Even so, the tales of the Lost Boys have become remarkably similar over the years. Everyone's account includes attacks by lions, hyenas, crocodiles. All have borne witness to attacks by the mura-haleen—government-sponsored militias on horseback—to Antonov bombings, to slave-raiding. But we did not all see the same things. At the height of our journey from southern Sudan to Ethiopia, there were perhaps twenty thousand of us, and our routes were very different. Some arrived with their parents. Others with rebel soldiers. A few thousand traveled alone. But now, sponsors and newspaper reporters and the like expect the stories to have certain elements, and the Lost Boys have been consistent in their willingness to oblige. Survivors tell the stories the sympathetic want, and that means making them as shocking as possible. My own story includes enough small embellishments that I cannot criticize the accounts of others.

I wonder if my friends Tonya and Powder would care if they knew. They know nothing about me, and I wonder if, knowing about my journey here, they would alter the course they've taken against me. I do not expect they would.

They are at the window again, the two of them, cursing the officer. I don't think it's been more than ninety minutes, but still, it is puzzling. I have never seen a police officer spend more than a few minutes in the parking lot of this apartment complex. There was one previous burglary here, but no one was home and it was forgotten in days. This burglary in progress, and the officer's prolonged stay—it seems illogical.

Tonya lets out a shriek.

"Go, pig, go!"

Powder is standing on the kitchen chair, splitting the blinds with his fingers.

"Yeah, you keep driving! Go, motherfucker!"

I am deflated, but at the same time, if the officer does leave, it might mean the quick exit of my two guests. Now they are laughing.

"Oh man, I thought he—"

"I know! He was—"

They cannot stop laughing. Tonya lets out a whoop.

Now they move with urgency. Again Tonya stacks the stereo, VCR, and microwave onto Powder's arms, and once more he walks to the door. She holds it open, and for a moment I have a fear that the cop has indeed laid some sort of trap, feigning his departure. Maybe he's just around the corner? It could mean the arrest of these two, but it also could mean a longer standoff, a hostage, more guns. I find myself improbably hoping that the police officer is long gone, and that these two will disappear just as quickly.

And it seems, for ten minutes or so, that they will. Under the cover of night, they are now brazen—they take two trips each to bring all of the apartment's valuables to the car. And now they are standing above me.

"Well, Africa, I hope this has been educational," Tonya says.

"Thanks for your hospitality, brother," Powder adds.

They are ebullient with the possibility of their clean and imminent getaway. Powder is on his knees now, unplugging the TV.

"Can you get it?" Tonya asks.

"I got it," he answers, heaving as he lifts the set from the shelf. It's a large TV, an older model, bulbous like an anvil, a nineteen-inch screen. Tonya holds the door open for him and Powder backs out. They say nothing to me. They are gone and the door is closed.

I wait a moment on the floor, not believing. The apartment now has an unnatural air to it. For a minute, it is stranger with them gone than it was with them inside.

I sit up. I stand, slowly, and the pain in my head sends rays of white heat down my back. I stagger to my bedroom, to see what sort of damage there is. It looks not unlike how I left it, subtracting my camera, phone, clock, and sneakers. In Achor Achor's room, they have been less kind: all of his drawers are open and have been emptied; his file cabinet, which he keeps with maniacal attention to organization, has been upended and its contents—every piece of paper he ever signed his name to since he was eleven—now cover the floor.

I walk back to the living room and stop. They are here. Tonya and Powder are in my apartment again and now I am scared. They don't want a witness. It had not occurred to me before but now it seems understandable. But how will they shoot me without alerting the fifty-four other residents of the building?

There might be another way to kill me.

I stand in the doorway and watch them. They make no move toward me. If they do, I will have a moment to lock myself in my bedroom. That might buy me enough time to escape through the window. I step slowly back.

"Stay there, Africa. Just stand motherfucking still."

Powder has his hand on his gun. The television is on the floor between them.

"We can repack the trunk," Tonya says to him.

"We're not gonna repack the trunk. We got to get the fuck out of here."

"You're not telling me we're leaving this here."

"What you want to do?"

"Let me think."

I am a fool, as I've said before. Because I am a fool, and because I was taught too many times by good men and women with rigid moral codes, I find strength in asserting what is right. This has rarely served me in situations such as this. Watching them argue, an idea occurs to me, and I again speak.

"It is time you two left. This is over. I've already called the police. They're coming." I say it in an even tone of voice, but while I am uttering the last two words, Powder is heading toward me, and in rapid succession he says, "You haven't called shit, fool," and then swings his arm at me. Thinking he's aiming for my face, I cover my head, leaving my torso unprotected. And for the first time in my life, I am struck in a way that I think might kill me. To be punched in the stomach with all the force of a man like Powder—this can scarcely be borne, much less by someone like me, built with poor engineering, six foot three and 145 pounds. It as if he has removed my lungs from my chest. I gag. I spit. Eventually I list and I fall, and while lunging earthward my head hits something hard and unbreakable, and that is the end, for now, of Valentino Achak Deng.

III.

I open my eyes and the scene has changed. Most of my possessions are gone, yes, but the TV is still here, now on the kitchen table. Someone has turned it on. Someone has plugged it in and there is a boy watching it. The boy can be no more than ten, and he is sitting on one of my kitchen chairs, his feet dangling below. He has a cell phone in his lap, and takes no notice of me.

I could be hallucinating, dreaming, anything. It does not seem possible that there is a young boy at my kitchen table contentedly watching television. But I keep my eyes on him, waiting for him to evaporate. He does not evaporate. There is a ten-year-old boy in my kitchen, watching my television, which has been moved. Someone relocated the set from the living room to the kitchen, and took the time to reattach the cable. My head pulses with a pain far surpassing any of the many headaches I have had since I landed at JFK five years ago.

I lie on the carpet, wondering whether I should make another attempt to move. I do not even know who this boy is; he could be in the same sort of trouble I am. I try to find my arms and realize they are behind me, tied with what I assume is the phone cord.

This, too, is a first for me. I have never been restrained like this, though I have seen men tied by the hands, and I have seen these men executed before me. I was eleven years old when I saw seven such men killed in front of me, in front of ten thousand of us boys in Ethiopia. It was meant to be a lesson to us all.

My mouth is taped closed. It is packing tape, I know, because Achor Achor and I had been using it on the food we were storing in the freezer. Powder and Tonya must have wrapped it across my mouth; now the roll is lying next to my shoulder. My voice and movements are restricted by the things I own.

I am not sure what will happen to me here. I have come to know that shootings happen more as a result of struggle than of planning. Because I have given up my struggle, and because there is a ten-year-old boy at my kitchen table, I believe they do not intend to kill me. But I am, I know, lost in this series of events. I do not know where my assailants are, or if they are coming back. Who are you, TV Boy? My assumption is that they have left you to guard me and the television, and that they will soon come to retrieve both. As a boy I was asked more than once to guard the AK-47 of a soldier of the Sudan People's Liberation Army. For much of the war, it was said that a rebel soldier who lost his gun would be executed by the SPLA, and thus when a soldier was busy in some way he often employed the help of a boy, all of us willing. I once guarded a gun while one particular soldier found pleasure with an Anyuak woman. It was the second time I ran my hands over that kind of gun, and I can remember its heat to this day.

But thinking, bringing forth any memory at all, causes such searing pain in the back of my skull that I close my eyes and soon lose consciousness again. I wake up three or four times and am not sure what time it is, how long I've been lying on my floor, bound. There are no longer clocks in the room, and the night is as dark as it was when I first fell. Each time I wake, the boy is still at the kitchen table, having barely moved. His face is no more than eight inches from the screen, and his eyes do not blink.

As I lie here, my brain grows more lucid, and I begin to wonder more about this boy. He has not once turned to look at me. I cannot see the screen but I hear the laughter bursting from it and it's the saddest sound I have heard since arriving in this country. If I am right, and this boy is guarding me, I think I will definitely leave Atlanta. I might very well leave this country altogether; perhaps I'll go to Canada. I know many Sudanese who have settled in Toronto, Vancouver, Montreal. They tell me to join them, that there is less crime, more job options. They have guaranteed insurance there, for one thing, and as I lie here it occurs to me that I have none. I was insured for a year, until recently, when I allowed it to lapse. Four months ago, I quit my fabric-sample job to become a full-time student, and insurance seemed an inessential expense. I try to guess at my injuries but at this point I have no idea. The fact that I can think at all leads me to believe that either I have escaped a major head wound, or I am already dead.

The Sudanese who are not heading to Canada are moving to the Great Plains, to Nebraska and Kansas—to states where cattle become meat. Meat processing is high paying, they tell me, and it is relatively inexpensive to live in these parts of the country. Omaha now hosts thousands of Sudanese men, Lost Boys and others, a good percentage of whom are paid to divide and carve the animals, cattle, that in many parts of our native Sudan were only to be slaughtered as sacrifices on the most sacred of occasions: weddings, funerals, births. The Sudanese in America have become butchers; it is the single most popular occupation among the men I know. I am unsure whether this is a giant leap forward from our lives in Kakuma. I suppose it is, and the butchers are building a better life for their children, if they have them. To hear young Sudanese children, born of immigrants, speak like Americans! This is how it is now, in 2006. There are few things stranger to me.

I look up to the couch and think of Tabitha. Not long ago, she sat on that couch with me, her legs over mine. We were entwined so tightly that I was afraid to breathe, lest she move at all. TV Boy, I miss her with a growing heat that surprises me and will likely engulf me. She was here with me not long ago for a weekend where we barely left the apartment; it was decadent and quite contrary to the ways in which we were raised. She had come to the United States, to Seattle, from the refugee camp at Kakuma, too, and here we were, two children who grew up in that camp, so many years later living in America and sitting on this couch in this room, shaking our heads at how we came this far and what lay ahead. She giggled about my thin arms, demonstrating that she could touch her thumb and forefinger around my bicep. But there was nothing she could do or say that could offend me or dissuade me from loving her. She had come to Atlanta to visit me and that said everything that mattered. She was sitting on my couch, in my apartment, wearing a very snug pink T-shirt I had bought for her the day before, at the DeKalb Mall. *Shopping is my therapy!* it said, in glittering silver lettering that swung upward from left to right, with a splashy star as the bottom of its exclamation mark. Sitting next to her in that shirt was intoxicating and I loved Tabitha in a way that made me feel like an adult, like I had finally become a man. With her I felt I could escape my childhood, its deprivation and calamity.

* * *

31

The boy is now looking in the refrigerator. He will find nothing palatable to him. Achor Achor and I cook in the Sudanese way, and I have yet to find any Americans who are eager for the results. We are not, I admit, skilled chefs. For our first many weeks here, we did not know which foods belonged in the freezer, which in the refrigerator, which in the cabinets and drawers. To be safe, we placed most items, including milk and peanut butter, in the freezer, and this proved problematic.

The boy finds something he likes and returns to his seat. I am somewhat sure that this boy, now sitting with the TV again, Fanta in hand, knows nothing about what I saw in Africa. I wouldn't expect him to, nor do I fault him. I was far older than he is when I realized that there was a world beyond southern Sudan, that oceans existed. But I was not much older than he is when I began to tell my story, what I had seen. In the years since our journey from our villages to Ethiopia, and then across the bloody river to Kenya, it has helped me and it has helped others to tell our story. When we were proving our case to UN officials in Kakuma, or are now trying to convey the urgency of the situation in Sudan, we tell the most dire stories. Since I have been in the U.S., I have told abridged versions of my story to church congregations, to high school classes, to reporters, to my sponsor, Phil Mays. Perhaps a hundred times at this point I have traced the basic outline. Phil, though, wanted all the details, and I have told him the most complete account. His wife heard the broad strokes and could hear no more. It was Phil and I who, every Tuesday night, after a meal with his wife and young twins, would walk up his spiral stairs and down the hall, to the infants' pink playroom, and there I would tell my story in two-hour stretches. When I know someone is listening, and that person wants to know everything I can remember, I can bring them forward. If you have ever kept a diary of your dreams, you know how the mere recording of them each morning can bring them forth in your mind. Backward from the part you remember best, you can recreate the night's adventures and wishes and terrors, conjuring everything from when you lay your head on your pillow.

When I first came to this country, I would tell silent stories. I would tell them to people who had wronged me. If someone cut in front of me in line, ignored me, bumped me or pushed me, I would glare at them, staring, silently hissing a story to them. *You do not understand,* I would tell them. *You would not add to my suffering if you knew what I have seen.* And until that person left my sight, I would tell them about Deng, who died after eating elephant meat, nearly raw, or about Ahok and Awach Ugieth, twin sisters who were carried off by Arab horsemen and, if they are still alive today, have by now borne children by those men or whomever they sold them to. *Do you have any idea?* Those innocent twins likely remember nothing about me or our town or to whom they were born. *Can you imagine this?* When I was finished talking to that person I would continue my stories, talking to the air, the sky, to all the people of the world and whoever might be listening in heaven. It is wrong to say that I used to tell these stories. I still do, and not only to those I feel have wronged me. The stories emanate from me all the time I am awake and breathing, and I want everyone to hear them. Written words are rare in small villages like mine, and it is my right and obligation to send my stories into the world, even if silently, even if utterly powerless.

I see only the profile of this boy's head, and he is not so different than I was at his age. I do not want to diminish whatever is happening or has happened in his life. Surely his years have not been idyllic; he is currently an accomplice to an armed robbery and is staying up much of the night guarding its victim. I will not speculate about what he is or is not being taught at school and at home. Unlike many of my fellow Africans, I don't take offense at the fact that many young people here in the United States know little about the lives of contemporary Africans. For every young person who is ill informed about such things, though, there are many who know a great deal and have respect for what we face on the continent. And of course, what did I know about the world before high school in Kakuma? I knew nothing. I did not know of the existence of Kenya until I set foot in it.

Look at you, TV Boy, settling into that kitchen chair like it was some kind of bed.

He is using a trio of towels from our closet as a blanket, leaving his small pink toes exposed. I try not to compare his life to mine, but his crouched posture reminds me too much of the way we slept en route to Ethiopia. No doubt if you have heard of the Lost Boys of Sudan, you have heard of the lions. For a long while, the stories of our encounters with lions helped garner sympathy from our sponsors and our adopted country in general. The lions enhanced the newspaper articles and no doubt played a part in the U.S. being interested in us in the first place. But despite the growing doubts of the more cynical, the strangest thing about these accounts is that they were in most cases true. As the hundreds of boys in my own group were walking through Sudan, five of us were taken by lions.

The first incident was two weeks into our walk. The sounds of the open forest at night were beginning to make us crazy. Some could not walk at night any more; there were too many noises, each a possible end of life. We walked through narrow paths in the bush and we felt hunted. When we had had homes and families, we never walked through the forest at night because small people were eaten by animals without any fanfare. But now we were walking away from our homes, our families. We walked in a line of boys, hundreds together, many of us naked, all of us defenseless. In the forest, we boys were food. We walked through forests and through grasslands, through desert country and through the greener regions of southern Sudan, where the earth was often wet beneath our feet.

I remember the first boy who was taken. We were walking single-file, as we always did, and Deng was holding my shirt from behind as he always did. He and I walked in the middle of the line, for we had decided that this was safest. The night was bright, a half-moon high above us. Deng and I had watched it rise, first red then orange and yellow and then white and finally silver as it settled at the uppermost point of the dome of the sky. The grass was high on either side of us as we walked and the night was quieter than most. We first heard the shuffling. It was loud. There was an animal or person moving through the grass near our line, and we continued to walk, for we always continued to walk. When boys yelled out in the night, the eldest among us—Dut Majok, our leader, for better and worse, no more than eighteen or twenty—rebuked them with quick ferocity. Calling out in the night was forbidden, for it brought unwanted attention to the group. Sometimes a message—this boy was injured, this boy has collapsed—could be sent up the line, whispered from one boy to another, until the message reached Dut. But this night, Deng and I assumed that everyone knew about the shuffling in the grass and had decided that this shuffling was common and not a threat.

Soon the sounds in the grass grew louder. Sticks broke. Grass crashed and then went quiet as the creature sped and slowed, running up and down along the line of us. The sounds were with the group for some time. The moon was high when the movement in the grass began and the moon had begun to fall and dim when the shuffling finally stopped.

The lion was a simple black silhouette, broad shoulders, its thick legs outstretched, its mouth open. It jumped from the grass, knocked a boy from his feet. I could not see this part, my vision obscured by the line of boys in front of me. I heard a brief wail. Then I saw the lion clearly again as it trotted to the other side of the path, the boy neatly in its jaws. The animal and its prey disappeared into the high grass and the wailing stopped in a moment. That first boy's name was Ariath.

—Sit down! Dut yelled.

We sat as if the wind had knocked us all down, one by one, from the front of the line to the back. One boy, I remember his name as Angelo, he ran. He thought it was better to run from the lion than to sit, so he ran into the high grass. This is when I saw the lion again. The animal broke across the path once more, leaping, it caught Angelo quickly. In a few moments the lion carried the second boy in his mouth, his teeth settled into Angelo's neck and clavicle. He brought this boy to where he had deposited Ariath.

We heard whimpers but soon the the grass was quiet.

Dut Majok stood for some time. He could not decide if we should walk or sit. A tall boy, Kur Garang Kur, the oldest next to Dut, crawled down the line to Dut, and spoke into his ear. Dut nodded. It was decided that we should continue walking, and we did. It was then that Kur became the principal advisor to Dut Majok, and the leader of the line of boys when Dut would disappear for days at a time. Thank God for Kur; without him we would have lost many more boys, to lions and bombs and thirst.

After the lions, we did not want to stop that night. We were not tired, we said, and could walk until dawn. But Dut said sleep was necessary. He sensed there were government army soldiers in the area; we needed to sleep and learn more in the morning about our whereabouts. We believed nothing Dut said because many of us blamed him for the deaths of Angelo and Ariath. Ignoring our complaints, he gathered us into a clearing and told us to sleep. But for some time, though we had walked since sunrise, no boy could close his eyes. Deng and I sat up, staring into the grass, watching for movement, listening for the pushing or breaking of sticks.

No boy turned his back to the tall grasses. We sat spine to spine, in pairs, so we could warn each other of predators. Soon we were a circle, and those of us who slept, did so with our bodies radiating from the center. I found a place in the middle of the circle and made myself as comfortable as possible. Meanwhile, the boys on the outside of the circle were trying to move into the middle. No one wanted to be at the edge.

I awoke in the night and found I was no longer at the center. I was cold, connected to no one. I looked around, only to find the circle had moved. As I had been sleeping, the boys outside were moving to the inside, so much that the circle had migrated twenty feet to my left, leaving me outside and alone. So I moved back into the middle, accidentally stepping on Deng's hand. Deng slapped my ankle, shot me a look of disapproval, but then went back to sleep. I settled in among the boys and closed my eyes, determined to never again be left outside the circle of sleep.

Each night of our walk, TV Boy, sleep was a problem. Whenever I woke in the dark hours I saw other eyes open, mouths whispering prayers. I tried to forget these sounds and faces and I closed my eyes and thought of home. I had to bring forth my favorite memories and piece together the best of days. This was a method taught to me by Dut, who knew that we boys would walk better, would complain less and require less maintenance if we had slept properly. *Imagine your favorite morning!* he yelled to us. He was always barking, always bursting with energy. *Now your favorite lunch! Your favorite afternoon! Your favorite game of soccer, your favorite evening, the girl you love most!* He said this while walking along our line of sitting boys, talking to our heads. *Now create in your mind the best of days, and memorize these details, place this day center in your mind, and when you are the most frightened, bring forth this day and place yourself within it. Run through this day and I assure you that before you are finished with your dream-breakfast, you will be asleep.* As unconvincing as it sounds, TV Boy, I tell you, this method works. It slows your breathing, it focuses your mind. I still remember the day I made, the best of days, stitched together from so many. I will tell it to you in a way you will understand. It is my day, not yours. It is the day I memorized and the day I still feel more vividly than any here in Atlanta.

IV.

I am six years old, and am required to spend a few hours of each day in a pre-elementary class in the one-room school of Marial Bai. I am here with other boys of my age-set, those within a few years of me, older and younger, learning the alphabet in English and Arabic. The school is tolerable, is not yet tedious, but I would rather be outside, so my dream-day begins when I arrive for school and it is canceled. *You are too brilliant!* the teacher says, and orders us home, to play and make of the day whatever we wish.

I go home to see my mother, who I left only twenty minutes earlier. I sense that she misses me. My mother is my father's first wife, and she lives in the family compound with his other five wives, with whom she is friendly, even sisterly. They are all my mothers, TV Boy, as odd as that sounds. Very young children in southern Sudan are very often unsure who the birth mother is, so integrated are the wives and their children. In my family, the children borne by all six women play together and are considered family without barrier or reservation. My mother is one of the midwives of the village, and has aided in the delivery of all but one of my siblings. My brothers and sisters are as old as sixteen and as young as six months, and our compound is full of the sounds of babies, their screams and their laughs. When I am asked to, I help with the infants, carrying them when they wail, drying their wet clothes near the fire.

I run from the school and sit next to my mother as she repairs a basket partially chewed by one of our goats. I spend a long moment contemplating her beauty. She is taller than most women, at least six feet, and though she is as thin as any woman in the village, she is as strong as any man. She dresses bravely, always in the most glorious yellows and reds and greens, but she favors yellow, a certain yellow dress, the pregnant yellow of a setting sun. I can see her across any land or through any brush, can see her from as far away as my eyes can penetrate: I have only to look for the swishing column of yellow, moving toward me across the field, to know my mother is coming. I often thought I would like nothing better than to live forever under her dress, clinging to her smooth legs, feeling her long fingers resting on the back of my neck.

—What are you staring at, Achak? she asks, laughing at me, using my given name, the name I used until it was overtaken by nicknames in Ethiopia and Kakuma, so many names.

I am frequently caught watching my mother, and am caught this time, too. She shoos me off to play with my friends, and so I run to the giant acacia to find William K and Moses. They are under the twisting acacia near the airstrip, where the ostriches scream and chase the dogs.

Moses was strong, TV Boy, bigger than I was, bigger than you, with muscles carved like a man's, and across his cheek a half-circle scar, a dull pink color, where he'd cut himself running through a thorn bush. William K was smaller, thinner, with a huge mouth that never stopped filling the air with whatever he could think of. He spent every day, from when he woke on, crowding the sky with his thoughts and opinions and, more than anything else, his lies, for William K liked to lie a great deal. He made up stories about people and the objects he possessed or wanted to possess, the things he had seen and heard and that his uncle, an MP, had heard while traveling. His uncle had seen people who had the legs of a crocodile, women who could leap over buildings. His favorite subject of fabrications was William A, the other William in our age-set and so forever the arch-enemy of William K. William K didn't like having the same name as anyone else, and thought, I suppose, that if he harassed the other William enough, he might renounce his name or simply leave town.

Today, in the day I conjure when I need to, William K is in the middle of a story when I arrive at the acacia.

—He drinks his milk straight from the udder. Did you know that? You get diseases that way. That's how you get ringworm. Speaking of ringworm, William A's father is part dog. Did you know that?

Moses and I don't pay William K much attention, hoping he'll tire himself out. This does not happen this day; it never happens. Silence only alerts William K that more words and sounds are needed from the dark, endless cavity of his mouth.

—I guess having the same name should bother me but I don't have to worry because he won't be in my grade next year. Did you hear that he's retarded? He is. He's got the brain of a cat. He won't be in our school next year. He's got to stay home with his sisters. That's what happens when you drink milk from the udder.

In a few years, when they're circumcised and ready, Moses and William K will be sent to the cattle camps with the other boys, to learn to care for the livestock, beginning with goats and graduating to cattle. My older brothers, Arou, Garang, and Adim, are at the cattle camp on this dream-day; it is a place with great appeal to boys: at cattle camp, the boys are unsupervised, and as long as they tend the cattle, they can sleep where they want and can do as they please. But I was being groomed as a businessman to learn my father's trade and to eventually take over the operation of the shops in Marial Bai and Aweil.

Moses is shaping a cow from clay while William K and I watch. Many boys and some young men took cow-shaping as a hobby, but the practice does not intrigue me or William K. My interest in the activity is passive, but William K cannot ever see the point. He can't see the pleasure in making the cows or in keeping them in the hollow of the willow, which is where Moses has stored dozens since he'd begun shaping them a few years earlier.

—Why do you bother? William K asks. —They break so easily.

—They don't. Not always, Moses says quietly, still deeply immersed in the task of forming his cow's horns, long and twisting. —I've had these for months. He nods his head to a small group of clay cattle a few feet away, standing crookedly in the dirt.

—But they can break, William K says.

—Not really, Moses says.

—Sure they can. Watch.

And with that, William K steps on one of the cows, crushing it into dust.

—See?

The word is barely out of his mouth when Moses is upon him, punching William

39

K's head, flailing at him with his thick arms. William K at first is giggling, but his mirth disappears when Moses lands a mighty punch to William K's eye. William K squeals with pain and frustration, and immediately the tone and tenor of his wrestling changes. In a flurry he is atop Moses and lands three quick blows to Moses's arms—crossed in front of his face—before I pull him off.

In my dream day our scuffle is interrupted by the sight of a something so bright we all have to squint to see it. We rise slowly from the dirt and walk toward the market. Light shoots from the trunk of a tree in the market, near Bok's restaurant, and we sleepwalk toward it, our mouths agape. Only as we are upon the source of light we can see that it's not some second sun but is actually a bicycle, absolutely new, polished to a gleam, magnificent.

Where did it come from? Who owns it? It is easily the most spectacular object in all of Marial Bai. Its pedals are the silver of the stars, its handlebars exquisitely shaped. The color of the frame is different from any color previously seen in town, a mixture of blue and green and white, swirled together as in the deepest part of a river.

Jok notices us admiring the bicycle and comes to bask in the glow.

—Nice bike, right? he says.

Jok Nyibek Arou, the owner of the town's tailor shop, has just purchased the bicycle from an Arab trader from over the river, in a truck full of very new and impressive objects, most of them mechanically complex—clocks, bed frames made of steel, a teapot with a top that springs open, on its own, when the water is boiling.

—Cost me quite a bit of money, boys.

We don't doubt him for a moment.

—Would you like to see me ride it? he asks.

We nod gravely.

Then Jok gets on the bike, as gingerly as if he were mounting a mule made of glass, and begins to push the pedals with such care that he barely keeps himself vertical. The other men of the market, happy for Jok and jealous of him and also wanting a joke or two at his expense, greet his very slow rides with a string of insults and rhetorical questions. Jok answers each very calmly.

—That as fast as you're going to go, Jok?

—The bike is new, Joseph. I'm being careful.

—You may break it, Jok. It's fragile!

—I am getting used to it, Gorial.

Gorial, who does not work, drinks most days and borrows money he cannot repay. No one likes him much, but this day, he makes a point of showing Jok how slow he is going on the color-swirled bicycle. As Jok rides by, Gorial walks the path next to him, indicating that he can easily stroll faster than Jok is riding.

—My two legs are faster than that whole beautiful bicycle, Jok.

—I don't care. Someday I might ride it faster. Not yet, though.

—I think you're getting the tires dirty, Jok. Careful!

Jok smiles at Gorial, smiles placidly at all of his spectators, because he has the most beautiful object in Marial Bai and they do not.

When Jok has again parked the bike against the tree, and is admiring it with me and Moses and William K, the talk turns serious. There is debate about the plastic. The bicycle has been delivered covered in plastic, plastic that like a series of transparent socks covers all of the bicycle's metal tubing. Jok examines the bike, his arms crossed before him.

—It's a shame that they don't tell you whether the covering is necessary, he says.

We are afraid to say anything about the plastic, for fear that Jok will send us away.

Jok's brother, John, the tallest man in Marial Bai, angular and with close-set eyes, approaches. —Of course you take off the plastic, Jok. You take the plastic off of anything. It's just for the shipping. Let me help you...

—No!

Jok physically restrains his brother. —Just give me a moment to think about this.

At this point, Kenyang Luol, younger brother of the chief, is standing with us. He strokes his chin and finally offers his opinion.

—Remove the plastic, and the thing rusts the first time it gets wet. The paint will begin to rub off and eventually will fade in the sun.

This helps Jok decide not to do anything. He decides that he will need more opinions before doing anything. Over the course of the day, William and Moses and I canvass the men in the market, and find that after dozens of consultations, the debate is perfectly split: half insist that the plastic is for shipping only and needs to be removed, while the others assert that the plastic remain on the bicycle, to protect it from all sorts of potential damage.

We report the results of our survey to Jok as he continues to stare down at the bike.

—So why remove it at all? Jok muses aloud.

It seems the most cautious route to take, and Jok is nothing if not a man of caution and deliberation; that is, after all, how he came to be in a financial position to buy the bicycle in the first place.

In the late afternoon, William K and Moses and I lobby for and are granted the right to guard the bicycle from all those who would steal, damage, touch, or even look too long upon it. Jok does not actually ask us to guard it, but when we offer to sit by it and keep it from harm or undue scrutiny, he agrees.

—I can't pay you boys for this, he admits. —I can just as easily bring it inside, where it would be very safe.

We don't care about payment. We simply want to sit and stare at the thing, outside Jok's hut, as the sun sets. And so we sit beside the bike, with the sun to our backs, to better see the bike as it stands on its kickstand next to Jok's house. We guard the bicycle for the majority of the afternoon, and though Jok and his wife are inside, we barely move from our spot. Initially, we take turns on patrol, circling the compound, holding a stick on one shoulder to imply some kind of weapon, but finally we decide that it is just as well that we all sit under the bike and stare at it.

So we do this, examining every aspect of the machine. It's far more complex than the other bicycles in the village; it seems to have far more gears, more wires and levers. We debate whether its extravagance will help it go faster, or the weight of it all would slow it down.

TV Boy, you are no doubt thinking that we're absurdly primitive people, that a village that doesn't know whether or not to remove the plastic from a bicycle—that such a place would of course be vulnerable to attack, to famine and any other calamity. And there is some truth to this. In some cases we have been slow to adapt. And yes, the world we lived in was an isolated one. There were no TVs there, I should say to you, and I imagine it would not be difficult for you to imagine what this would do to your own brain, needing as it does steady stimulation.

As my dream-day passes into the afternoon, I lean on my sister Amel as she grinds grain. I did this often, because the leaning and its expected result gave me great joy. As she squats I lean against her, my spine to hers. —I can't work this way, little monkey, she says.

—I can't get up, I say. —I'm asleep.

She smelled so good. You might not know what it's like to have a sweet-smelling sister, but it is sublime. So I am lying against her, pretending to sleep, snoring even, when she thrusts herself backward and I'm sent flying.

—Go see Amath, why don't you? she growls.

Such a good idea! I have certain feelings for Amath. Amath is my sister's age, far too old for me, but visiting her seems a very good suggestion to me, and in a few minutes, in her family's compound, I find her. She is sitting alone, winnowing sorghum. She looks exhausted, not only from the work but from having to do it by herself.

When I see her, I cease to breathe properly. The other girls my sister's age don't care what I say or what I do. To them I am a boy, an infant, a squirrel. But Amath is different. She listens to me as if I am a man of consequence, as if my words might be important. And she is an uncommonly beautiful girl, with a high forehead and small glittering eyes. When she smiles, she does not show her teeth; she is the only girl I know who smiles this way—and her walk! She walks with a strange bounce, resting longer on the balls of her feet than most, resulting in a happy kind of gait, one I have on occasion tried myself. When I imitate her I feel merrier, too, though it makes my calves sore. On most days, Amath wears a brilliant red dress, with a picture of a milk-white bird upon it, English letters splayed around it like flowers thrown into a river. I know that we can never be married, Amath and I, for with her many desirable features, she will be spoken for by the time I am ready. She is almost of age already and will likely be married within the year. But until then she can be mine. Though I have always been too timid to say much to her, there was one day, in a state of heightened courage or carelessness, I simply walked up to her, and so this becomes part of my best day.

—Achak! How are you, young man? she says, brightening.

She often called me young man and when she did I immediately knew what it was, in every way, to be a man. I was very sure I knew.

—I am good, Madam Amath, I say, speaking as formally as possible, which I know from experience will impress Amath. —Can I help you? I have time to help if you need it. If you need help from me in any way...

I know I'm rattling on but cannot help it. I stomp quickly with one foot, wanting to cut my tongue from my mouth. Now I have only to find a way to finish my thought and let it be.

—Can I be your helper in some way? I say.

—You're such a gentleman, she says, treating me, as she always does, with the utmost seriousness. —You may help me indeed. Can you get me some water? I have to cook soon.

—I'll get some from the river! I say, my feet already restless, ready to run.

Amath laughs while still concealing her teeth. Did I love her more than any other? Is it possible that I loved her more than anyone in my own family? Often I knew I would choose her over anyone else, even my mother. She confused me, TV Boy.

—No, no, she said. —That's not necessary. Just…

But already I'm gone. I'm soaring. My grin grows as I run, as I imagine how excited she will be with my speed, the incredible speed with which I will carry out her request, and my grin fades only when I realize, halfway to the river, that I don't have a container to hold the water.

I alter my course, turning into the marketplace, into the mass of traders and shoppers, weaving through a hundred people so fast they feel only my wind. I fly past the smaller shops, past the men drinking wine on the benches, past the old men playing dominoes, past the restaurants and the Arabs selling clothes and rugs and shoes, past the twins my age, Ahok and Awach Ugieth, two very kind and hard-working girls carrying bundles of kindling on their heads, Hello, Hello, we say, and finally I step into the darkness of my father's store, completely out of breath.

—What's the matter? he asks. He is wearing the sunglasses he wears every day, in daylight and most nights. He traded a small goat-calf for the glasses, and so treats them with as much care and reverence as he does his best cow.

—I need a cup, I manage, between gasps. —A big cup. My eyes scan the shop for the proper vessel. It is a large shop for the region, big enough to hold six or seven people, with two walls made of brick and a roof of corrugated steel. There are dozens of objects to choose from, and my eyes race around the shelves like a sparrow caught indoors. Finally I grab a measuring cup from behind the counter.

—At your speed that won't help you, my father says, his eyes amused. —You'll spill half of it before you get back to her.

How did he know?

—You think I'm blind? my father says, and laughs. My father is known for his sense of humor, for finding a reason to smile during any minor calamity. And his laugh! A belly-laugh that rumbles and shakes his shoulders and stomach and brings tears to the corners of his eyes. Deng Arou can find humor in a flood, people say, and they mean this with great affection. His calm and balanced perspective is one of the reasons, people assume, he is so successful. Not for nothing is he the owner of five hundred head of cattle and three shops.

He reaches to his highest shelf and hands me a small plastic jerry can with a cap atop it. —That should hold everything you need, son. Amath will be very pleased, I bet. Now remember—

I hear nothing else. I am running again through the market, past the goats penned at the edge of the market road, past the old women and their chickens, and onward to the river. I fly by the boys playing soccer, past my Aunt Akol's compound—I can't even look her way to see if she is outside—and sprint down the deeply pitted path, the path of hard dirt walled in with the highest grasses.

I make it to the river quicker than I ever have before, and once on the low bluff, I leap past the boys fishing and the women doing their wash, and into the deep middle of the narrow stream.

The women and the boys all look at me like I've lost my mind. Have I? Soaked, I smile back at them and immerse my jerry can in the milky brown water. I fill the container, but am not satisfied with the amount of sediment inside. I have to filter it, but I need two containers for that task.

—Can I please borrow your bowl please? I ask one of the washing women. I am amazed at my own courage. I had never spoken to this woman before, who soon I recognize as the wife of the main teacher in the upper school, a man named Dut Majok I know only by reputation. I have heard the wife of Dut Majok was, like him, educated and very quick with her tongue; she could be cruel. She smiles at me, removes the shirts she is washing, and hands the bowl to me. She seems, more than anything else, curious to see what I—this tiny boy, far smaller than you, TV Boy—want with the bowl, my eyes desperate and my jerry can full of the brown river water.

I know my task and go about it deliberately. I pour the jerry can's contents through my shirt and into the bowl, then, carefully, pour the water back into the jerry can. Having done this once successfully, I can't decide how clean to make the water; what's more crucial, I wonder: to bring the water quickly, or to deliver it in as pure a form as possible? In the end, I filter it three times, screw the cap back onto the jerry can, and return the bowl to the woman, my gratitude whispered through heavy breaths as I climb the bank.

At the top of the riverbank, in the rough grass, I set off again. I am tired, I realize, and now I run around the path's many holes, rather than leaping over them. My breathing becomes loud and labored and I curse my loud breathing. I do not want to bring the water to Amath while running slowly or walking or out of breath. I need to be running with as much speed and agility as I had when I set off. I forbid my breath to pass through my mouth, sending it through my nostrils instead, and pick up my pace as I get closer to the center of town.

This time my aunt sees me as I pass her home.

—Is that Achak? she sings.

—Yes, yes! I say, but then find I don't have enough breath to explain why I'm racing by, unable to stop. Perhaps she, like my father, will guess. I had been momentarily ashamed when my father assumed that my task involved Amath, but quickly I didn't care who knew, because Amath was so uncommon and appreciated by all that I was proud to call her friend and to be caught on any errand for her, this beautiful Madam who refers to me as young man and gentleman and with her closed-mouthed smile and happy walk is the best girl in Marial Bai.

I pass the school and once in the clear, I can see Amath, still sitting in the spot where I left her. Ah! She is watching me, too! Her smile is visible this far away and she doesn't stop smiling as I fly closer and closer, my bare feet touching the dirt with toes only. She is very excited to see me with the water, which perhaps she can see is very clean water, very well filtered and good for anything she can dream of. Look at her! Her eyes are huge, watching me run. She is truly the person who best understands me. She is not too old for me, I decide. Not at all.

But suddenly my face is dust. The ground has risen up to pull me down. My chin is bleeding. I have fallen, taken down by a high gnarled root, the jerry can sent tumbling ahead of me.

I am afraid to look up. I don't want to see her laughing at me. I am a fool; I am sure I have lost her respect and admiration. She will now see me not as an able and fast young man, capable of caring for her and tending to her needs, but as a ridiculous little boy who couldn't run across a field without falling on his wretched face.

The water! I look quickly and it hasn't leaked.

When I raise my head further, though, I see her walking toward me. Her face isn't laughing at all—it's serious, as it is always serious when she looks at me. I jump up quickly to demonstrate how uninjured I am. I stand and feel the great pain in my chin but deny it. As she gets closer, my throat goes coarse and there is no air within me— I am such a fool, I think, and the world is unfair to humiliate me this way. But I suppress everything and stand as straight as I can.

—I was running too fast, I say.

—You were certainly running fast, she marvels.

Then she is close to me, her hands are upon me, dusting off my shirt and pants, patting me down, making *tsk-tsk* sounds as she does so. I love her. She notices how quickly I can run, TV Boy! She notices all the best things about me and no one else notices these things. —You are such a true gentleman, she says, holding my face in her palms, to run like that for me.

I swallow and take a breath and am relieved again to speak clearly and like a man. —It was my pleasure, Madam Amath.

—Are you sure you're okay, Achak?

—I am.

I am. And now, as I turn to walk home—I have planned to lean on my sister two more times before dinner—I can think only of weddings.

There is to be a wedding in a few days, between a man, Francis Akol, who I don't know very well, and a girl, Abital Tong Deng, who I know from church. There will be another calf sacrificed, and I will try to get close enough to see this one, as I saw the last one, when I watched it pass onto the next world. I saw the eye of the calf, watched it as its legs kicked aimlessly. The eye faced straight up into the white sky; it never seemed to look at those who were killing it. I thought this made the killing easier. The calf did not seem to blame the men for ending its life. It endured its early death with courage and resignation. When the next wedding comes, I will again position myself over the dying head of the calf to see how it dies.

I enjoyed the weddings, but there have been too many in recent months. There was too much drinking, and too much jumping, and I was often scared of some of the men when they'd had too much wine. I wonder if this next time, at the wedding of Francis and Abital, I could hide from the festivities, if I could stay inside and not dress in my best clothes and talk to the adults and instead hide under my bed.

But perhaps Amath would be there, and perhaps she would be wearing a new dress. I knew all of her clothes, I knew all four dresses she owned, but the wedding brought the possibility of something new. Amath's father was an important man, owner of three hundred cattle and a judge in many disputes in the region, and thus Amath and her sisters were often wearing new clothes, and even owned a mirror. They kept the mirror in their hut, and they stood before it for long stretches, laughing and arranging their hair. I knew this because I had seen the mirror and heard their laughter many times, from the tree over their compound, the tree in which I found a very secret perch well placed for knowing what happened inside the hut. I could see nothing untoward from my bough, but I could hear them talking, could see occasional flashes as the sun found its way through their thatched roof, catching the reflection of their earrings or bracelets, sending light into their mirror and back out to the unrelenting dust of the village.

V.

TV Boy, there was life in these villages! There *is* life! This was a settlement of about fifteen thousand souls, though it wouldn't look like it to you. If you saw pictures of this village, pictures taken from a plane passing overhead, you would gasp at the seeming dearth of movement, of human settlements. Much of the land is scorched, but southern Sudan is no limitless desert. This is a land of forests and jungles, of river and swamps, of hundreds of tribes, thousands of clans, millions of people.

As I lie here, I realize that the tape over my mouth is loosening. The saliva from my mouth and the perspiration on my face has softened the tape's grip. I begin to accelerate the process, exercising my lips and spreading saliva liberally. The tape continues to break away from my skin. You, TV boy, see none of this. You seem unaware that there is a bound and gagged man on the floor, and that you are watching television in this man's home. But we adapt, all of us, to the most absurd situations.

I know everything one can know about the wasting of youth, about the ways boys can be used. Of those boys with whom I walked, about half became soldiers eventually. And were they all willing? Only a few. They were twelve, thirteen years old, little more, when they were conscripted. We were all used, in different ways. We were used for war, we were used to garner food and the sympathy of the humanitarian-aid organizations. Even when we were going to school, we were being used. It has happened before and has happened in Uganda, in Sierra Leone. Rebels use refugees to attract aid, to create the appearance that what is happening is as simple as twenty thousand lost souls seeking food and shelter while a war plays out at home. But just a few miles away from our civilian camp, the SPLA had their own base, where they trained and planned, and there was a steady pipeline of supplies and recruits that traveled between the two camps. *Aid bait,* we were sometimes called. Twenty thousand unaccompanied boys in the middle of the desert: it is not difficult to see the appeal to the UN, to Save the Children and the Lutheran World Federation. But while the humanitarian world fed us, the Sudan People's Liberation Army, the rebels who fought for the Dinka, were tracking each of us, waiting until we were ripe. They would take those who were old enough, those who were strong and fit and angry enough. These boys would trek over the hill to Bonga, the training camp, and that was the last we would see of them.

I almost cannot believe myself, but at this moment, I am contemplating ways that I might save you, TV Boy. I am envisioning freeing myself, and then freeing you. I could wriggle my way out of my bindings, and then convince you that being with me will serve you better than remaining with Tonya and Powder. I could sneak away with you, and we could leave Atlanta together, both of us looking for a different place. I have an idea that things might be good in Salt Lake City, or San Jose. Or perhaps we need to be away from these cities, any city. I think I am finished with cities, TV Boy, but wherever we go, I have an idea that I could take care of you. It was not so long ago that I was like you.

But first we have to leave Atlanta. You need to move far away from these people who have put you in this situation, and I need to leave what has become an untenable climate.

Things here are too tense, too political. There are eight hundred Sudanese in Atlanta, but there is no harmony. There are seven Sudanese churches, and they are being pitted against each other constantly and with increasing rancor. The Sudanese here have regressed to tribalism, to the same ethnic divisions we gave up long ago. In Ethiopia there were no Nuer, no Dinka, no Fur or Nubians. We were, in many cases, too young to know what these distinctions meant, but even if we were aware, we had been taught and had agreed to set aside our supposed differences. We were all in Ethiopia alone, and had seen hundreds of our own die en route to a place only marginally better than what we'd left.

Almost from the moment we arrived here, it was impossible to return to life in Sudan. I have not been to Khartoum, so I cannot speak for the style of life there. I hear there is some semblance of modernity. But in southern Sudan, we are by any estimation at least a few hundred years behind the industrialized world. Some sociologists, liberal ones, might take issue with the notion that one society is behind another, that there is a first world, a third. But southern Sudan is not of any of these worlds. Sudan is something else, and I cannot find apt comparison. There are few cars in southern Sudan. You can travel hundreds of miles without seeing a vehicle of any kind. There are only a handful of paved roads; I saw none while I lived there. One could fly a straight east-west line across the country and never pass over a home built of anything but grass and dirt. It is a primitive land, and I say that without any sense of shame. I suspect that within the next ten years, if the peace holds, the region will make the sort of progress that might bring us to the standards of other East African nations. I do not know anyone who wishes southern Sudan to remain the way it is. All are ready for what comes next. There are SPLA tanks parading through Juba, the capital of the south. There is pride there now, and all the doubts we've had about the SPLA, and all the suffering they caused, have been largely forgiven. If the south achieves freedom it is through their work, however muddled.

I realize that my mouth is soaked and the tape is no longer firmly attached. I blow, and to my surprise, the left half of the tape flaps away. I can speak if I want to speak.

"Excuse me," I say. My voice is soft, much too quiet. There is no indication he hears me. "Young man," I say, now in a normal volume. I don't want to startle him.

I get no reaction.

"Young man," I say, now louder.

He turns briefly to me, disbelieving, as if he noticed the couch itself talking. He returns to the television.

"Young man, can I speak with you?" I say, louder now, firmer.

He whimpers and stands up, terrified. My only guess is that they told him that I was African, and in his mind he did not think that classification entailed the ability to speak, much less speak English. He takes two steps toward me, stopping in the entranceway to the living room. He is still not sure I will speak again.

"Young man, I need to talk to you. I can help you."

This sends him back to the kitchen, where he takes the cell phone, pushes a button, and brings the phone to his ear. He listens but does not get the desired recipient. He has, I am assuming, been told to call his accomplices if I wake up or anything is amiss, and now that I have, they are not answering. He gives his predicament some thought and finally settles on a solution: he sits again and turns up the volume on the television.

"Please!" I yell.

He leaps in his seat.

"Boy! You must listen to me!"

Now he searches for a solution. He begins to open drawers. I hear the rattle of silverware and worry that he might do something drastic. He opens five, six drawers and cabinets. Finally he emerges from the kitchen with a phone book. He carries it over to me and holds it over my head.

"Young man! What are you doing?"

He drops the book. It is the first time in my life that I have seen something coming toward me and have been unable to properly react. I try to turn my head but still the book lands squarely on my face. The pain is compounded by my existing headache and the ricochet my chin makes against the floor. The phone book slides off, toward my forehead, and rests there, against my temple. Thinking he has accomplished his goal, he returns to the kitchen and the volume goes up again. This boy thinks I am not of his species, that I am some other kind of creature, one that can be crushed under the weight of a phone book.

The pain is not great, but the symbolism is disagreeable.

VI.

I open my eyes, having stumbled into sleep for minutes or hours. The boy is asleep on the couch above me. He has taken his towels-for-blankets and has arranged himself on the end of the couch, his feet neatly stuffed into the cushions. And now he is whimpering. He is having a nightmare, his face contorted like a toddler's, his petulant frown robbing him of years. But I am less sympathetic now.

There are no clocks visible, though it feels like the middle of the night. There are no traffic sounds outside. It could be midnight or later.

Achor Achor, I don't want to curse you but this situation would be much different if you saw fit to come home. I like and admire Michelle, and I am proud of you for having found an American who loves you, but at the moment I think your behavior is irresponsible. At the same time, I wonder how the burglars knew that you would be gone, that they could be sure about leaving their son, their sibling, here. It is hard to understand. They are either brilliant or simply reckless.

I wonder what images are troubling you, TV Boy. I am torn—I could talk to you again, waking you from the troubles, or I could relish, in a small way, that the boy who thinks he can crush an African man with a phone book is now suffering night tremors. It does not seem so cruel to let you whimper on the couch, TV Boy. After all, if I were to speak again, what would you drop on me next? I have an unabridged dictionary in my room, and I do not doubt you would use it.

A phone rings, not mine. My phone is gone. The ringtone is that of a popular song I cannot place. My grasp of American popular music is tenuous, I suppose, even after five years and after most of my friends have embraced it vigorously.

Get up, TV Boy, and answer your phone!

The rings continue. The caller might want to tell you to free me; the caller could be the police. Rouse yourself, boy!

Three rings and there is no sign he will awaken. I have to influence these events. At the risk of bringing more objects onto my head, I make as loud a noise as I can. My desperation brings my voice into the higher register; I produce a loud shriek that makes the boy virtually leap off the couch. The phone rings again and this time he picks it up.

"What?" he says. "This is Michael."

The voice coming through the phone is a man's, resonant and slow.

"She's not here."

A question.

"I don't know. She told me she'd be here by now."

The boy is nodding.

"All right."

"All right."

"Bye."

So, it is Michael. Michael, I am happy to know your name. It is a name with less menace than TV Boy, and further convinces me that you are a victim of those charged with protecting you. Michael is the name of a saint. Michael is the name of a boy who wants to be a boy. Michael was the name of the man who brought the war to Marial Bai. It is natural to assume that a war like ours came one day, the crack of thunder and then war, falling hard like rain. But first, Michael, there was a darkening sky.

Now, perhaps, your mood has turned for the worse. You've been here too long, in this apartment, and what seemed like an adventure is now tedious, even frightening. I am not as innocuous as you first thought, and I'm sure you're dreading the possibility that I might speak again. For now I have nothing to say, not out loud, but you should know about the Michael who in 1983 brought the first portents of war to our village.

William K woke me up, whispering on the other side of the hut wall. —Get up get up get up! he hissed. —Get up and see this.

I had no inclination to follow William K, given that on so many occasions I had been asked to run to this place or that place or climb that tree, only to see some hole dug by a dog, or a nut that resembled the face of William's father. Always the sights were greater in the mind of William K and seldom were they worth the trouble. But as William K whispered through my door, I heard the raised voices of an excited crowd.

—Come! William K urged. —I swear this is something!

I got up, dressed myself, and ran with William K to the mosque, where a curious crowd had gathered. After we crawled through the legs of the adults gathered around the mosque's door, we raised ourselves to our knees and saw the man. He was sitting on a chair, one of the sturdy wood-and-rope chairs that Gorial Bol made and sold in the market and over the river. The sitting man was young, the age of my brother Garang, just old enough to be married and in his own home and with his own cattle. This man had ritual scars on his forehead, which meant he was not from our town. In other regions and other villages, the men, at thirteen years old or so, are given scars across their foreheads upon their entry into manhood.

But this man, whose name we learned was Michael Luol, was missing a hand. Where his right hand should have been, his wrist led nowhere. The crowd, mostly men, were inspecting the missing hand of the young man, and there were many opinions about who was to blame. William and I remained on our knees, where we could be close to the missing hand, waiting to hear how this had happened.

—But they have no right to do this! a man roared.

There were three men central to the argument: Marial Bai's chief, a bull of a man with wide-set eyes, his lean and laconic deputy, and a rotund man whose stomach burst through his shirt and pushed against my back each time he made a point.

—He was caught stealing. He was punished.

—It's an outrage! This is not Sudanese justice.

The handless man sat silently.

—It is now. That's the point. This is sharia.

—We can't live under sharia!

—We're not living under sharia. This was in Khartoum. You go to Khartoum, you live under their law. What were you doing in Khartoum, Michael?

The men soon placed the blame squarely on the shoulders of the handless man, for had he stayed in his own village and kept from thieving, he would still have his right hand and might have a wife, too—for it was generally agreed that he would never have a wife now, no matter what dowry he could offer, and that no woman should be required to have a husband with a missing hand. Michael Luol received little sympathy that day.

After leaving the mosque, I asked William K what had happened to the man. I had heard the word *sharia,* and some derogatory remarks about the Arabs and Islam, but no one had clearly related the events that had led to Michael Luol's hand being removed. As we walked to the great acacia to find Moses, William K related the story.

—He went to Khartoum two years ago. He went as a student, and then ran out of money. Then he was working as a bricklayer. Working for an Arab man. A very rich man. He was living with eleven other Dinka men. They lived in an apartment in a poor part of the city. This is where the Dinka lived, Michael Luol said.

This seemed odd to me, that the Dinka would live anywhere considered poor, while the Arabs lived well. I tell you, Michael of the TV, that the pride of the monyjang, the men among men, was very strong. I have read anthropologists who were amazed at the esteem in which the Dinka held themselves.

—Michael Luol lost his job, William K continued. —Or perhaps the job ended. There was no work. He said he had no more work. And so he couldn't pay for the rent. The other guys kicked him out of the apartment and then he was living in a tent on the outside of the city. He said thousands of Dinka lived there. Very poor people. They live in homes made of plastic and sticks and it's very hot and they have no water or food.

I remember at that moment not liking this handless man. I felt like the man deserved to have his hand missing. To be so poor, living in a plastic house! To be asking for food! To have no water! To live so poor near the Arabs who lived well. I was ashamed. I loathed the men who drank during the day in Marial Bai's market and I loathed this man living in the plastic house. I know this is not an admirable sentiment, to despise the poor, the fallen, but I was too young to feel pity.

William continued. —Michael Luol used to go out looking in the garbage for food. He would go with other men, go through the dump, all the city's garbage. He would go there in the morning and there would be hundreds of people sorting through. But because Michael Luol was a strong man, he did well. He found pots and boxes and chicken bones. He ate what he could and was able to sell other things he found. He found a broken radio once and sold it to a man who fixed them. When he got that money, he bought a new dwelling. He needed something bigger because he had a wife.

—He brought the wife to Khartoum? I asked.

—No, he got the wife there. He got the wife after he lost his job.

William K seemed unsure about this part. It made no sense to either one of us, to marry when one had no money and no home.

—They lived in the new dwelling, something made with sticks and plastic. This is when the man who told his story became very sad. His wife died. She had dysentery because the water they drank was bad water they got from some ditch near the city. So she got malaria and there was no way to get her into any hospital. So she died. When she died her eyes popped out of her head.

I knew William K well enough to know that this last part was fabrication. Whenever possible in William K's stories, someone's eyes popped out of their heads.

—So he had this place he had bought, and he sold it. He didn't need it anymore. So he took the money and he bought some drinks. And then he was taken by the police and they brought him to a hospital and cut off his hand.

—Wait. Why? I asked.

—He took something, I think. He stole something from someone. Maybe from the man he worked for when he was working with bricks. He went back there and stole something. I think it was a brick. Wait. It was a brick but he stole it before. He stole the brick when his wife was alive, because the wind kept blowing his plastic house away. So he took the brick and then they found him. Then he was caught and then the wife died and then he came back down here.

—So who cut off his hand? I asked.

—The police.

—At the hospital?

—He said there were two policemen there and a nurse and a doctor.

The story was enhanced and embellished over the next weeks, by the handless man and by others, but the basic facts remained as William K had conveyed them. Islamic law, sharia, had been imposed in Khartoum and was law in much of Sudan above the Lol and Kiir rivers, and there was growing fear that it would not be long before sharia was brought to us.

This is where it gets complex, or relatively so, Michael TV Boy. The broad strokes of the story of the civil war in Sudan, a story perpetuated by us Lost Boys, in the interest of drama and expediency, tells that one day we were sitting in our villages bathing in the river and grinding grain and the next the Arabs were raiding us, killing and looting and enslaving. And though all of those crimes indeed happened, there is some debate about the provocations. Yes, sharia had been imposed, in a sweeping series of laws called the September Laws. But the new order had not reached our town, and there was doubt that it would. More crucial was the government's tearing up of the 1972 Addis Ababa agreement, which gave the south a degree of self-rule. In its place the south was divided into three regions, which effectively pitted each of them against the others, with no region left with any significant government power at all.

Michael, you're sleeping again, and I am glad for that, but still you sleep with whimpers and kicks. Perhaps you, too, are a child of war. In some way I assume you are. They can come in different shapes and guises, but always wars come in increments. I am convinced there are steps, and that once these events are set in motion, they are virtually impossible to reverse. There were other steps in the country's stumble toward war, and I remember these days clearly now. But again, at the time I did not recognize these days as such, not as steps but as days like any others.

I was running to my father's shop, through the market's thick Saturday crowd. On Saturday the trucks arrived from over the river, and the marketplace doubled with traders and activity. The shoppers came from all over the region; Marial Bai's market was one of the largest within a hundred miles, and so drew far-flung commerce. When I reached my father's store, running as usual at my top speed, I almost collided with the great, unblemished white tunic of Sadiq Aziz.

—Where have you been today? my father said. —Say hello to Sadiq.

Sadiq's hand descended onto the crown of my head, and he let it rest there. Sadiq was of the Baggara, an Arab tribe that lived on the other side of the Ghazal. The Arabs were seen during market days and during the dry season, when they came down to graze their cattle. There had been centuries of tension between the Dinka and the Baggara, largely over grazing lands. The Baggara needed the more fertile southern soil to graze their cattle when the earth of the north cracked with drought. Arrangements were generally made between chiefs, and cooperation had been managed historically through alliances and payments of cattle and other goods. There was balance. During the cattle season, and often on market days, there were Baggara and other Arabs everywhere in Marial Bai. They moved freely among the Dinka, speaking a jumbled mix of Dinka and Arabic, often staying in Dinka homes. There were very good relations between the majority of their people and ours. In many areas there was intermarriage, there was cooperation and mutual respect.

My father was popular among the Baggara and other Arab businessmen; he was known to go out of his way, sometimes comically so, to court and please the Arab traders. He knew that his own success was due in large part to his access to the merchandise in which the northerners specialized, and so he was ever eager that the Arabs knew they were welcome in his shops and homes. Sadiq Aziz, a tall man with large eyes and arms twisted with bone and ropy muscle, was my father's favorite trading partner. Sadiq had an eye for unusual things, could find the most exceptional goods: mechanized farm tools, sewing machines, fishing nets, athletic shoes manufactured in China. More important, Sadiq usually brought something for me.

—Hello, uncle, I said. It is customary to call an older man *uncle,* as a term of familiarity and respect. If the man is older than one's father, he is called *father.*

Sadiq raised his eyebrows conspiratorially and retrieved something from his bag. He tossed it in the air to me and I caught it before I knew what it was. I opened my hands upon some kind of gem. It looked like glass, but inside were radial stripes, yellow and black, like the eye of a cat. It was so beautiful. My eyes watered as I stood, staring at it. I was afraid to blink.

—It's made to look like a gem, Sadiq admitted, —but it's made of glass.

He winked at my father.

—It's like a star! I said.

—Say that in Arabic, Sadiq said.

Sadiq knew I had been learning basic Arabic in school, and he often tested me. I tried to answer. —Biga ze gamar, I stammered.

—Very good! Sadiq said, smiling. —You're the smartest of Deng's sons! I can say that because the rest of them are not here at present. Now say *Allah Akhbar.*

My father laughed. —Sadiq. Please.

—You believe God is great, don't you, Deng?

—Of course I do, my father said. —But please.

Sadiq stared at my father for a long moment and then brightened.

—I'm sorry. I was only joking.

He reached for my father's hand and held it loosely.

—So, he asked. —Can I put Achak on the horse now?

Both men looked down to me.

—Of course, my father said. —Achak, would you like that?

My mother had said Sadiq knew intuitively what a boy likes and wants, because each time he visited, he brought me gifts, and, as long as my mother was not close enough to disapprove, for she did disapprove, he lifted me onto the high saddle of his horse, tied just outside the shop.

—There you are, little horseman.

I looked down at the men.

—He looks very natural up there, Deng.

—I think he looks very afraid, Sadiq.

Though the two men laughed, I barely heard them.

Atop the saddle, my first thought was of power. I was taller than my father, taller than Sadiq, and certainly taller than any boys my age. On the horse I felt fully grown and adopted an imperious look. I could see over the fences of our neighbors and could see as far as the school and could spot a lizard at eye level, scuttling across our rooftop. I was enormous, I was the combination of myself and the animal I could control. My grand thoughts were interrupted by the teeth of the horse, which had found my leg.

—Sadiq! my father yelled. He lunged, grabbed me and removed me from the saddle. —What the hell's wrong with that animal?

Sadiq stammered. —She never does that, he said, seeming genuinely puzzled. —I'm so sorry. Are you okay, Achak?

I looked up and nodded, hiding my trembling hands. Sadiq assessed me.

—That's my fierce boy! Sadiq said, again resting his hand on my head.

—I knew this was a bad idea, my father said. —The Dinka are not horse people.

I stared into the eyes of the horse. I hated that accursed animal.

—Plenty of Dinka have ridden horses, Deng. Wouldn't it be good if Achak here could learn? It would only make him more appealing in the eyes of the girls. Wouldn't it, Achak?

This made my father laugh, breaking the tension. —I don't think he needs help in that area, my father said.

They both roared now, looking down at me. I continued to stare at the horse, and found, to my mild surprise, my anger already gone.

I ate with the men that night, a dozen or so merchants at my father's compound, all of them circled near the fire. I knew a few of the men from the shops but many were new to me. There were other Baggara among the guests, but I stayed close to Sadiq, my foot resting on his leather sandal. The conversation had concerned the price of maize, and raids of cattle by certain Baggara groups north of Marial Bai. It was generally agreed that the regional courts, on which sat representatives of the Baggara, the Dinka, and the government in Khartoum, would settle the matter. For a time, the men ate and drank, and then a Dinka man across from my father, a large wide-grinning man younger than the rest, spoke.

—Deng, you don't worry about this business of the insurrection?

He said this with a brilliant smile; it seemed to be his default expression.

—No, no, my father said. —Not this time. I was part of the last rebellion, as some of you know. But this new one, I don't know.

There were murmurs of approval from the rest of the men, who seemed eager to have the matter settled. But the grinning man persisted.

—But they're in Ethiopia now, Deng. It seems like something is brewing.

Again he smiled.

—No, no, my father said. He waved the back of his hand at the young man, but it seemed more theatrical than convincing.

—They have the support of the Ethiopians, the grinning man added.

This seemed to surprise my father. It was not often that I saw my father learning something before my eyes. Sadiq threw a piece from his stew to one of the goats on the perimeter of the compound and then addressed the young man.

—You think, what, twenty deserters from the Sudanese army are going to come back and make Sudan a Communist nation? That's madness. The government of Sudan would crush Ethiopia. And they'll crush any little insurrection.

—I don't dispute that the deserters would lose, the young man said. —But I don't see a great love of Khartoum in Dinkaland. They could gain some support.

—Never, said Sadiq.

—Not this time, my father added. —We know the cost of that. Of civil war. We do that again and we'll never recover. That would be the end.

The men seemed to approve of this assessment and it was quiet again, with the sounds of eating and drinking and the animals who retake the forest when the night comes.

—How about a story then, my father Arou? Sadiq said. —Tell us the one about the beginning of time. I'm always entertained by this.

—Only because you know it to be true, Sadiq.

—Yes. Exactly. I throw out the Koran and adopt your story.

The men laughed and urged him into the story. My father stood and began, telling the story the way he always told it.

—When God created the earth, he first made us, the monyjang. Yes, first he made the monyjang, the first man, and he made him the tallest and strongest of the people under the sky....

I knew the story well, but had not heard my father tell it in the presence of men who were not Dinka. I scanned the faces of the Arabs, hoping their feelings would not be hurt. All were smiling, as if they were hearing a fable of some kind, and not the true story of creation.

—Yes, God made the monyjang tall and strong, and he made their women beautiful, more beautiful than any of the creatures on the land.

There was a quick burst of approval, this time of a more guttural tone, joined by the Arab men. It was followed by a wave of loud laughter from all. Sadiq nudged me and grinned down to me, and I laughed, too, though I wasn't sure why.

—Yes, my father continued, —and when God was done, and the monyjang were standing on the earth waiting for instruction, God asked the man, "Now that you are here, on the most sacred and fertile land I have, I can give you one more thing. I can give you this creature, which is called the cow..."

My father turned his head quickly, spilling some of his cup into the fire, where it hissed and sent a plume of smoke upward. He turned the other direction and finally found what he was looking for: he pointed to a cow in the distance, one of those waiting to be sold at the market the following day.

—Yes, he continued, God showed man the idea of the cattle, and the cattle were magnificent. They were in every way exactly what the monyjang would want. The man and woman thanked God for such a gift, because they knew that the cattle would bring them milk and meat and prosperity of every kind. But God was not finished.

—He never is, Sadiq said, to a wave of laughter.

—God said, "You can either have these cattle, as my gift to you, or you can have the What." My father waited for the necessary response.

—But... Sadiq said, helping out, —What is the What? he said, with an air of theatrical inquisitiveness.

—Yes, yes. That was the question. So the first man lifted his head to God and asked what this was, this What. "What is the What?" the first man asked. And God said to the man, "I cannot tell you. Still, you have to choose. You have to choose between the cattle and the What." Well then. The man and the woman could see the cattle right there in front of them, and they knew that with cattle they would eat and live with great contentment. They could see the cattle were God's most perfect creation, and that the cattle carried something godlike within themselves. They knew that they would live in peace with the cattle, and that if they helped the cattle eat and drink, the cattle would give man their milk, would multiply every year and keep the monyjang happy and healthy. So the first man and woman knew they would be fools to pass up the cattle for this idea of the What. So the man chose cattle. And God has proven that this was the correct decision. God was testing the man. He was testing the man, to see if he could appreciate what he had been given, if he could take pleasure in the bounty before him, rather than trade it for the unknown. And because the first man was able to see this, God has allowed us to prosper. The Dinka live and grow as the cattle live and grow.

The grinning man tilted his head.

—Yes, but uncle Deng, may I ask something?

My father, noting the man's good manners, sat down and nodded.

—You didn't tell us the answer: What is the What?

My father shrugged. —We don't know. No one knows.

Soon dinner was done and the drinking afterward was done, and the guests were sleeping in the many huts of my father's compound, and I was lying in his hut, pretending to sleep but instead watching Sadiq and holding Sadiq's glass gem tightly in my fist.

I had heard the story of the cattle and the What many times, but never before had it ended this way. In the version my father told to me, God had given the What to the Arabs, and this was why the Arabs were inferior. The Dinka were given the cattle first, and the Arabs had tried to steal them. God had given the Dinka superior land, fertile and rich, and had given them cattle, and though it was unfair, that was how God had intended it and there was no changing it. The Arabs lived in the desert, without water or arable soil, and thus seeking to have some of God's bounty, they had to steal their cattle and then graze them in Dinkaland. They were very bad herdsmen, the Arabs were, and because they didn't understand the value of cattle, they only butchered them. They were confused people, my father often told me, hopeless in many ways.

But none of this was part of my father's story this night, and I was glad. I was proud of my father, for he had altered the story to protect the feelings of Sadiq and the other traders. He was sure that the Arabs knew they were inferior to the Dinka, but he knew it would not be polite to explain this to them at dinner.

The next morning I saw Sadiq Aziz for the last time. It was a church day, and by the time my family rose, Sadiq was outside, preparing his horse. I crawled out of the hut to watch him ride off, and found my father there, too.

—You sure you won't come with us? my father said.

Sadiq smiled. —Maybe next time, he said, grinning. He swung himself onto his saddle and rode off in the direction of the river.

This day was also the last day I would see the soldiers posted in the village. Government-army soldiers had been in Marial Bai for years, ten or so of them at a time, charged with keeping the peace. After church, which lasted past noon, I walked to the Episcopalian chapel and waited outside for William K and Moses. As much as I dreaded the length of our Catholic Masses, I was glad not to be among the congregation of Reverend Paul Akoon, whose sermons had been known to last till nightfall. When William K and Moses were finished and Moses had changed his shirt, we walked to the soccer field as the soldiers and the men of the village were getting situated, warming up with the two balls the soldiers kept in their barracks. The soldiers spent a good deal of their time playing soccer and volleyball, and the rest of their time smoking and, when the afternoon came, drinking wine. No one said anything to them about it; the village was happy to have the soldiers, to protect the market and the cattle nearby from raids from the murahaleen or anyone else. The soldiers stationed in Marial Bai were a cross-section of ethnicities and beliefs: Dinka Christians, Muslims from Darfur, Arab Muslims. They stayed together in the barracks, and led lives of relative ease. They spent their days on minor patrols around town, and otherwise at my father's shop, sitting under the thatched roof, drinking areki, a locally made wine, talking about the lives they intended to build after they finished their stints in the army.

As the game began, William K and Moses and I took our place behind one of the goals, hoping to retrieve any missed shots. All over the field, on every sideline and in every corner, boys too young to play with the men were positioned, waiting for a chance to chase down a stray ball and throw or kick it back into play. As the sun set and the dinner fires were lit all over the village, I was able to retrieve two balls, and each time kicked the ball accurately back onto the field. It was a very successful day for me. The game ended and the men shook hands and scattered.

—Red boy! a soldier yelled.

I turned. I looked down at my own shirt; I was wearing red.

—Come here if you want something good.

I ran toward the soldier, a short man with a broad face and deep Nuer scars across his forehead. He held out a small package of yellow candies. I stared but didn't move.

—Take a few, boy. I'm offering them to you.

I took one and put it quickly into my mouth. Immediately I regretted being so impulsive. I should have saved it in my pocket, saved it for a special occasion. But it was too late. It was in my mouth and it was delicious—like lemon, but not sour like a lemon. More like a lemon-shaped lump of sugar.

—Thank you, uncle, I said.

—Take another, boy, the soldier said. —You have to know when to take what's offered to you. Only a rich boy could be so careful. Is that true, boy? Are you wealthy enough to be choosy?

I was not sure if it was true. I knew my father was prosperous, was an important man, but I couldn't agree that this had made me choosy. I was still trying to think of an answer when the soldier turned and walked away.

The war started, for all intents and purposes, a few weeks later. In fact, the war had already begun in some parts of the country. There were rumors of Arabs being killed by rebels. There were towns that had been cleared of Arabs, mass slaughters of Arab traders, their shops burned. Rebel groups, mostly Dinka, had formed all over the south, and they had sent a clear message to Khartoum that they would not stand for the enforcement of sharia law in Dinkaland. The rebels were yet to organize under the banner of the Sudan People's Liberation Army, and their presence was sporadic throughout the south. The war had yet to come to Marial Bai, but it did soon enough. Our village would be one of the hardest hit, first by the rebel presence and later by the militias empowered by the government to punish the rebels—and those who supported them, actively or otherwise.

I sat in my father's shop, playing on the ground with a hammer, pretending it was the head and neck of a giraffe. I moved it with the giraffe's slow grace, having the neck bend down for water, reach upward to eat from the high boughs of a tree.

I walked the hammer-giraffe silently, slowly over the dirt of the shop floor, and the giraffe looked around. He'd heard a sound. What was it? It was nothing. I decided the giraffe needed a friend. I retrieved another hammer from a low shelf and the second joined the first. The two giraffes glided over the savannah, their necks pushing forward, first the first, then the second, alternating in time.

I pictured myself as a businessman, running my father's affairs, organizing the store, negotiating with the customers, ordering new goods from over the river, adjusting the prices to the nuances of the market, visiting the shop in Aweil, knowing hundreds of traders by name, moving with ease through any village, known and respected by all. I would be an important man, like my father, with many wives of my own. I would build on the success of my father, and would open another store, many more, and perhaps own a greater herd of cattle—six hundred head, a thousand. And as soon as I could manage it, I would have a bicycle of my own, with the plastic still wrapped tightly around it. I would be sure not to tear the plastic anywhere.

A shadow grew over the land of my giraffes.

—Hello! my father said in the sky above.

The greeting in return was not warm. I looked up to see three men, one of whom carried a rifle tied to his back with a white string. I recognized the man. He was the grinning man from the night at the fire. The young man who had raised the question of the What with my father.

—We need sugar, the smallest of the men said. He was unarmed but it was clear he was the leader of the three. He was the only one who spoke.

—Of course, his father said. —How much?

—All of it, uncle. Everything you have.

—That will cost a good deal of money, friend.

—Is this everything you have?

The small man picked up the twenty-pound sisal bag resting in the corner.

—That's everything I have.

—Good, we'll take it.

The small man picked up the sugar and turned to leave. His companions were already outside.

—Wait, his father asked. —You mean you don't intend to pay for it?

The small man was at the door, his eyes already adjusting to the light of the mid-morning sun. —We need to feed the movement. You should be happy to contribute.

—Deng, you were wrong, the smiling man said.

My father came out from behind the counter and met the man at the doorway.

—I can give you some sugar, of course. Of course I will. I remember the struggle. I know the struggle needs to be fed, yes. But I can't give you the entire bag. That would cripple my business—you know this. We all have to do our part, yes, but let's make this fair for both of us. I'll give you as much as I can.

My father reached for a smaller bag.

—No! No, stupid man! the small one yelled. The volume startled me to my feet. —We'll take this bag and you'll be grateful we don't take more.

Now the grinning man and his companion, the man with the gun tied with a string, were back, standing behind the small man. Their eyes held on my father. He stared back at the men, one by one.

—Please. How will we live if you steal from us?

The smiling man wheeled around, almost stepping on me.

—Steal? You're calling us thieves?

—What can I call you? This is the way you—

The smiling man threw a great sweeping punch and my father crumpled to the ground, landing next to me.

—Bring him outside, the man said. —I want everyone to see this.

The men pulled my father out of the shop and into the bright marketplace. Already a crowd had gathered.

—What's going on? said Tong Tong, whose shop was next door.

—You watch and learn from this, the grinning man said.

The three men turned my father onto his stomach, and quickly tied his hands and feet with rope from his own shop. My mother appeared.

—Stop this! she screamed. —You maniacs!

The man with the rifle pointed it at my mother. The small man turned to her with a look of deepest contempt.

—You'll be next, woman.

I turned and ran into the darkness of the shop. I was sure my father would be killed, perhaps my mother, too. I hid under the sacks of grain in the corner and pictured myself living without my mother. Would I be sent to live with my grandmother? I decided it would be my father's mother, Madit, who would take me in. But that was two days' walk away, and I would never see William K and Moses again. I rose from the bags of grain and peered around the corner, into the market. My mother was standing between my father and the three men.

—Please don't kill him, my mother wailed. —Killing him won't help you.

She was a head taller than the small one but the man with the gun had it directed at my mother and I could not breathe. My head rang and rang and I blinked to keep my eyes open.

—You'll have to kill me, too, she said.

The small man's tone was suddenly softer. I looked through the doorway and saw that the man had lowered his gun. And with that, without any sort of passion, he kicked my father in the face. The sound was dull, like a hand slapping the hide of a cow. He kicked him again and the sound was different this time. A crack, precisely like the breaking of a stick under one's knee.

At that moment something in me snapped. I felt it, I could not be mistaken. It was as if there were a handful of taut strings inside me, holding me straight, holding together my brain and heart and legs, and at that moment, one of these strings, thin and delicate, snapped.

And that day, the rebel presence was established and Marial Bai became a town at war with itself—contested by the rebels and the government. The soccer games were forgotten. The rebels came at night, raiding where they could, and during the day, government army soldiers patrolled the village, the market in particular, reeking of menace. They cocked and uncocked their rifles. They were suspicious of anyone unfamiliar; young men were harassed at every opportunity. Who are you? Are you with these rebels? Trust in the army had evaporated. The uninvolved had to choose sides.

I was no longer allowed to play in the market. School was out indefinitely. Our teacher had left and was reportedly training with the rebels somewhere near Juba, in the southeast corner of the country. The discussions among the men of Marial Bai were constant and heated, after church and over dinner and along the paths. My father told me to stay home and my mother tried to keep me at home but I strayed and sometimes Moses and William K and I saw things. We were the ones who saw Kolong Gar run.

It was dark, after dinner. We had gone to the tree where we could hear Amath and her sisters talk. The perch had been my secret until William K had seen me there one day and had threatened to reveal my position unless he were allowed up, too. Since then our nighttime spying had become regular, if not fruitful. If the wind was strong at all, the leaves of our acacia would shake and shush and drown out anything we might hear in the hut below. The night we saw Kolong Gar was a night like that, a starless night with a whirling wind. We could hear nothing of what was being said by Amath and her sisters, and we were bored with trying. We had begun to climb down when Moses, who occupied the highest bough, saw something.

—Wait! he whispered.

William and I waited. Moses pointed toward the barracks and we saw what he saw. Lights, five of them, jumping over the soccer field.

—Soldiers, Moses said.

The flashlights moved slowly over the field, and then spread further. Two disappeared into the school and threw shards of light around the room. Then the school went dark again, and the lights began to run.

That was when Kolong Gar ran directly below our tree. Kolong Gar was a soldier for the government army, but he was also a Dinka, from Aweil, and now he was running, wearing only white shorts—no shoes or shirt. With a flash of muscle and the flicker of the whites of his eyes, he raced under our dangling legs. We watched his back as he flew past Amath's compound and down the main path out of Marial Bai, heading south.

Minutes later two of the lights followed. They stopped short of the tree that held us, and finally they turned and walked back to the barracks. The search was over, at least for that night.

That was how Kolong Gar had left the army. For weeks we were the tellers of the story, which everyone found fascinating and rare, until similar stories became common. Anywhere there were Dinka men in the government army, they were deserting to join the rebels. The government soldiers stationed at Marial Bai had numbered twelve, but soon were ten, then nine. Those remaining were Arabs from points north and two Fur soldiers from Darfur. Public sentiment did not encourage their remaining. Marial Bai was quickly becoming decidedly sympathetic to the cause of the rebels—who wanted, among other things, better representation in Khartoum for southern Sudan—and the soldiers were not blind to this.

And then one day they were all gone. Marial Bai awoke one morning and the soldiers charged with protecting the village from raids and keeping the peace were no more. Their belongings were gone, their trucks, any and all trace of them. They left the south of Sudan for the north, and joining them were many of Marial Bai's more prosperous families. The men who worked for the government in whatever capacity—as judges, clerks, tax collectors—took their families and went to Khartoum. Any family with means left for what they considered safer places, north or east or south. Marial Bai, and much of the region of Bahr al-Ghazal, was no longer safe.

The day the troops disappeared, Moses and I went to the soldiers' barracks, crawling under their beds, looking for money or souvenirs, anything they might have left in haste. Moses found a broken pocketknife and kept it. I found a belt without a buckle. The building still smelled of men, of tobacco and sweat.

The few Arab traders who remained in the market soon packed up their shops and left. In a week, the mosque was closed, and three days later, it burned to the ground. There was no investigation. With the soldiers gone, the rebel presence in Marial Bai increased for a time, and soon the rebels had a new name for themselves: the Sudan People's Liberation Army.

But after a few weeks, the rebels were gone. They weren't in Marial Bai to protect or patrol. They came when passing through, to recruit, to take what they needed from my father's shop. The rebels were not there when the people of Marial Bai reaped what they had sown.

VII.

Michael's phone is ringing again.

The boy slowly rouses himself and jogs over to the kitchen to answer it. I can't hear much of the conversation, but I do hear him say, "You said ten," followed by a series of similar protestations.

The call is over in less than a minute and now I must try again to reason with the boy. Perhaps he is comfortable enough with me now, with my unmoving presence, that he will not fear my voice. And it's evident that he is upset with his accomplices. Perhaps I can forge an alliance, for I still harbor hope that he'll see that he and I are more alike than are he and those who have placed him here.

"Young man," I say.

He is standing between the kitchen and the living room; he had been deciding whether to return to the couch to sleep, or to turn the TV on again. I have his attention for a moment. He looks at me briefly and then away.

"I don't want to scare you. I know this is not your idea to be here with me."

He looks at the phone book now, but it seems that because it's resting against my temple, to retrieve it he would have to get too close to me. He walks past me and disappears down the hall, headed for the bedrooms. My throat goes dry with the thought that he very well might return with the unabridged dictionary after all.

"Young man!" I say, projecting my voice down the hall. "Please don't drop anything on me! I will be quiet if that's what you want."

Now he is above me, and for the first time, he is looking into my eyes. He is holding my geometry textbook in one hand and a towel in the other. I'm not immediately sure which poses the greater threat. The towel—would he suffocate me?

"Do you want me to be quiet? I will stay quiet if you'll stop dropping things on me."

He nods to me, then takes his foot and gently steps on my mouth, pushing the tape back into place. To have this boy pushing my mouth closed with his foot—it is too much to accept.

He disappears from my view but is not finished. When he returns, he begins a construction project in my living room.

He first pushes the coffee table closer to the entertainment center, reducing the space between the three objects: me, the table, and the shelving. Now he drags a chair from the kitchen. He places this near my head. From the couch he brings one of the three large cushions that sit upright. He stands the cushion up against the seat of the chair. Bringing another chair from the kitchen, he places it, with a couch cushion soon resting against it, at my feet. He has effectively eliminated me from his view. My view is now limited to the ceiling above me, and the little I can see between the windows of the coffee table. I lie, finding myself impressed with his architectural vision, until he surprises me with the blanket. The bedspread from my room is carefully spread over the couch cushions until it forms a tent over me, and this is too much. Michael, I have little patience left for you. I am finished with you, and wish you could have seen what I saw. Be grateful, TV Boy. Have respect. Have you seen the beginning of a war? Picture your neighborhood, and now see the women screaming, the babies tossed into wells. Watch your brothers explode. I want you there with me.

I was sitting with my mother, helping her boil water. I had found kindling and was feeding the fire, and she was approving of the help I was providing. It was unusual for a boy of any age to be as helpful as I was. There is an intimacy between mother and son, a son of six or seven. At that age a boy can still be a boy, can be weak and melt into his mother's arms. For me, though, this is the last time, for tomorrow I will not be a boy. I will be something else—an animal desperate only to survive. I know I cannot turn back and so I savor these days, these moments when I can be small, can do small favors, can crawl beneath my mother and blow on the dinner fire. I like to think I was luxuriating in the final moment of childhood when the sound came.

It was like the sound of the planes that flew over occasionally, but this was louder, more dissonant. The sound seemed to be dividing itself, again and again. Chaka-chakka. Chaka-chakka. I stopped and listened. What was that sound? Chaka-chakka. It was like the noise an old lorry might make, but it was coming from above, was spreading itself wide across the sky.

My mother sat still, listening. I went to the door of the hut.

—Achak, come and sit, she said.

Through the doorway I saw a kind of airplane, coming low over the village. It was a fascinating kind of plane, black everywhere and dull, unreflective. The planes I had seen before resembled birds in a rudimentary way, with noses and wings and chests, but this machine looked like nothing so much as a cricket. I watched it as it flew over the village. The sound was rich and black, louder than anything I had ever known, the vibrations shaking my ribs, pulling me apart.

—Achak, come here!

I heard my mother's words, though her voice was like a memory. What was happening now was utterly new. Now there were five or more of these new machines, great black crickets in every direction. I walked out of the hut and into the center of the compound, transfixed. I saw other boys in the village staring up as I was, some of them jumping, laughing and pointing to the crickets with the chopping sound.

But it was strange. Adults were running from the machines, falling, screaming. I looked at the people running, though I was too dazed to move. The volume of the machines held me still. I felt tired in some new way, as I watched mothers grab their young sons and bring them back into their huts. I watched men run into the high grass and throw themselves to the ground. I watched as one of the crickets flew over the soccer field, flying lower than the other machines; I watched as the twenty young men playing on the field ran toward the school, screaming. Then a new sound pumped through the air. It was like the cutting and dividing of the machine, but it was not that.

The men running to the school began to fall. They fell while facing me, as if they were running to my home, to me. Ten men in seconds, their arms reaching skyward. The machine that had shot them came toward me now, and I stood watching as the black cricket grew larger and louder. I could see the turning of the guns, two men sitting in the machine, wearing helmets and sunglasses like my father's. I was unable to move as the machine drew closer, the sound filling my head.

—Achak!

My mother's hands were around my waist, and she pulled me with great force into darkness. I found myself inside the hut with her. The sound roared over us, thumping, chopping, dividing itself.

—You fool! They'll kill you!

—Who? Who are they?

—The army. The helicopters. Oh, Achak, I'm worried. Please pray for us.

I prayed. I flattened myself under her bed and prayed. My mother sat up, rigid, trembling. The machines flew overhead then away and back again, the sound retreating and filling my head once more.

I lay next to my mother, wondering about the fate of my brothers, my sister and stepsisters, my father and friends. I knew that when the helicopters were gone, life would have changed irreversibly in our village. But would it be over? Would the crickets leave? I did not know. My mother did not know. It was the beginning of the end of knowing that life would continue. Do you have a feeling, Michael, that you will wake up tomorrow? That you will eat tomorrow? That the world will not end tomorrow?

It was over in an hour. The helicopters were gone. The men and women of Marial Bai slowly left their homes and walked again under the noon sun. They tended to the wounded and counted the dead.

Thirty had been killed. Twenty men, most of the victims those who had been playing soccer. Eight women and two children, younger than me.

—Stay inside, my mother said. —You don't need to see this.

The next morning, the army's trucks returned. The trucks that had left with the government's soldiers weeks before now returned, again carrying soldiers. They were accompanied by three tanks and ten Land Rovers, which surrounded the town in the early morning. Once there was enough light to function efficiently, the soldiers jumped from the trucks and went about methodically burning down the town of Marial Bai. They started a great fire in the middle of the market, and from this fire they took burning logs and torches, and these they threw onto the roofs of most of the homes within a one-mile radius. The few men who resisted were shot. This was effectively the end of any kind of life in Marial Bai for some time. Again, the rebels for whom this was retribution were nowhere to be found.

VIII.

We left Marial Bai a few days later, Michael. My father and his shop were targets, both of the government and the rebels, so he moved the target. He closed the Marial Bai shop, divided his family, and prepared to move himself and his business interests to Aweil, about one hundred miles north. He brought two wives and seven children with him; I was selected to accompany him, but my mother was not. She and the other wives and their children were to remain in Marial Bai, living in our half-ruined home. They would be safe in the village now, he assured us all; he had gathered us in the compound one Sunday after church and had laid out his plan. The worst of it was over, he said. Khartoum had made their point, punishment had been meted out to those collaborating with the rebels, and now the important thing was to stay neutral and make clear that collaboration with the SPLA was not happening or even possible. If my father had no shop in Marial Bai, he could not aid the SPLA, willingly or not, and thus no retribution could be directed his way, or toward us, from government, rebels, or murahaleen.

My mother was furious to be left behind. But she said nothing.

—I want you to be easy for your stepmothers, she said.

I said I would.

—And to listen to them. Be smart and be helpful.

I said I would.

I was accustomed to traveling with my father. On his business trips to Aweil, to

Wau, I had often been selected to go with him, for I above all was being groomed to run the shops when he was too old to do so. Now my father was moving his operations to this, a larger town on the railway that ran between the north and the south. Aweil was in southern Sudan and its population was primarily Dinka, but it was government-held, acting as a base for Khartoum's army. My father thought it a safe place to run his shop, to stay out of the escalating conflict. He still believed firmly that the rebellion, or whatever it was, would flame out soon enough.

Our lorry arrived in the evening and I was carried, half-sleeping, to a bed in the compound my father had arranged. I awoke in the night to the sounds of men arguing, broken bottles. A scream. A gun blasting open the sky. The noises of the forest were largely gone, replaced by the passing of groups of men, of women singing together in the night, the screams of hyenas and a thousand roosters.

In the morning I explored the market as my father entertained his friends from Aweil. I was without Moses and William K for the first time, and Aweil was vast and much more densely packed than Marial Bai. I had seen only a few brick buildings in Marial Bai, but here there were dozens, and far more structures with corrugated roofs than I had seen before. Aweil seemed far more prosperous and urban than Marial Bai, and to me it held little appeal. I saw many new and largely unhappy things in my first day, including my second handless person. I followed him, an elderly man in a threadbare dashiki of gold and blue, through the market, watching his handless arm sway beneath his cuffs. I never found out how he had lost his hand, but I assumed that there would be more missing limbs here. Aweil was a government town.

I saw a monkey riding a man's back. A small black monkey, skittering from one shoulder to the other, squealing and grabbing at his owner's shoulders. I saw trucks, cars, lorries. More vehicles in one place than I had known possible. In Marial Bai, on market days, there might be two trucks, possibly three. But in Aweil, cars and trucks came and went quickly, a dozen at any time, dust exploding behind them. The soldiers were everywhere and they were tense, suspicious of any new arrivals to the town, particularly young men.

Every day brought an assault, an interrogation. Men were hauled to the barracks with such regularity that it was expected that any young Dinka man in Aweil would be subjected to interrogation sooner or later. He would be brought in, given a beating of varying degrees of severity, would be forced to swear his hatred of the SPLA and to name those he knew who were sympathetic. He would be released that afternoon, and whomever he had named would then be found and interrogated. Staying away from the market ensured freedom from harassment, but because the SPLA moved in the brush, in the shadows, those who lived outside the town were assumed to be SPLA, to be aiding them and plotting against Aweil from the farms and forests.

Though he had been careful, had treated the soldiers well, it was not long before my father was suspected of colluding with the rebels.

—Deng Arou.

—Yes.

Two soldiers were at the door to my father's shop.

—You are the Deng Arou from Marial Bai?

—I am. You know I am.

—We have to take this store.

—You'll do nothing like that.

—Close for today. You can reopen after we talk.

—Talk about what?

—What are you doing here, Deng Arou? Why did you leave Marial Bai?

—I've had a store here for ten years. I have every right—

—You were giving free goods to the SPLA.

—Let me talk to Bol Dut.

—Bol Dut? You know Bol Dut?

My father had tipped the balance. His closest friend, in Marial Bai or anywhere, was Bol Dut, a long-faced man with a grey goatee, a well-known lender of money; he had helped my father open his store in Aweil. He was also a member of the national parliament. In all he was one of the best-known Dinka leaders in Bahr al-Ghazal, and had managed to spend eight years as an MP without alienating the Dinka from his region. This was not easy to do.

—Bol Dut is a rebel, the soldier said.

—Bol Dut? Watch what you're saying. You're talking about an MP.

—An MP who has been heard talking on the radio to Ethiopia. He's with the rebels and if you're his friend you're a rebel too.

I watched as my father was brought in for questioning. He was taller than the boy-soldiers but still he seemed very thin and feminine walking beside them. He was wearing a long pink shirt and his exhausted sandals while they wore thick canvas uniforms, sturdy boots with heavy black heels. That day, I was ashamed of my father, and I was angry. He hadn't told me where he was going. He hadn't told me if he would be jailed or killed or return within an hour.

He returned in the morning. I saw him walking down the road to us, muttering to himself. My stepsister Akol ran to him.

—Where were you? she asked.

He walked past her and into his hut. He emerged a few minutes later.

—Achak, come!

I ran to him and we walked back to the market; he had left his shop unattended when he had been taken. As we walked, I scanned his face and hands for signs of injury or abuse. I checked his sleeves to see if either hand was missing.

—It's a bad time to be a man in this country, he said.

When we arrived, we found the shop unmolested. It was surrounded by businesses run by Arabs, and we assumed they had watched over it. Still, staying in Aweil now seemed impossible.

—Are we leaving Aweil? I asked.

My father leaned against the back wall and closed his eyes.

—I think we'll leave Aweil, yes.

Bol Dut came for dinner. I watched him come down the path. His walk was well-known, a magisterial stride, one foot kicked forward then the other, as if he were shaking water from his shoes. His chest was broad and barrelled, his face always conveying or feigning great interest in everything.

He pushed open the door to our compound and took my father's hands in his.

—I'm sorry about the mix-up with the soldiers, he said.

My father waved it off.

—Normally I would do something.

My father smiled and shook his head. —Of course you would.

—Normally I *could* do something, Bol added.

—I know, I know.

—But now I'm in more trouble than you, Deng Arou.

He was being watched, he said. He had met with the wrong people. His frequent trips in and out of Aweil were looked upon with grave concern. He had declined an invitation to Khartoum, to see the minister of defense. His words were meandering as he looked back to the market, seeming utterly lost.

—Come inside, Bol, my father said, taking Bol's arm.

The men ducked into my father's hut. I crawled quickly in and lay down, pretending to sleep.

—Achak. Out.

I made no sound. My father sighed. He let me be.

—Bol, my father said. —Come back to Marial Bai with us. There are no soldiers there. You'll be protected. You'll have friends. It's not a government town.

—No, no. I have to do *some*thing, I suppose. But...

Bol Dut's voice was broken.

—Bol. Please.

Bol dropped his head. My father placed his hands on Bol's shoulders. It was an intimate gesture. I looked away.

—No, Bol said, now sounding stronger. He raised his head. —I should wait it out. It would be worse if I left. It would look far more suspicious. I have to stay or...

—Then go to Uganda, my father pleaded. —Or Kenya. Please.

The men sat for a time. Bol sat back and lit his pipe. The bitter smoke filled the hut. Bol looked at the wall as if there was a window there, and through this window, a way out of this predicament.

—Fine, he said at last. —I will. I will.

My father grinned, then touched his hand to Bol's. —You will what?

—Marial Bai. We'll go. I'll go with you.

Bol Dut seemed certain. He nodded firmly.

—Good! my father said. —That makes me very happy, Bol. Good.

Bol Dut continued to nod, as if still convincing himself. My father sat silently next to him, smiling unconvincingly. The two men sat together while the animals took over the night and the lights of Aweil threw jagged shadows over the town.

In the morning, there was no doubt what had been done to Bol Dut and who had done it. A group of women had found him on their way to gather kindling. My father was despondent, then methodically went about making arrangements to return to Marial Bai. It was decided we would leave the next day. We would pack up the compound immediately and a lorry would be arranged.

I wanted to see Bol Dut and convinced a local girl I had befriended to come.

—Let's look, I said.

—I don't want to see him, she said.

—He's not there, I lied. —They buried him already. We'll only look at the tracks of the tank.

We followed the treads through the dirt and the mud and into the forest. The tracks penetrated the earth deeper there, and disappeared occasionally where the tank had encountered a thicket or roots.

—Have you seen one of these move? she asked.

I said I had.

—Are they fast or slow?

I couldn't remember. When I thought of the tank, I pictured the helicopters. —Very fast, I told her.

—I want to stop, she said.

She saw the man first, sitting, legs crossed, on a chair where the tracks ended. He sat still, alone, his hands on his knees, his back rigid, as if standing guard. Near his chair, in the mud, was a blanket, some kind of wool material. It was the grey of a river at twilight and was matted into the tracks left by the tank. I told the girl it was nothing, though I knew it was Bol Dut.

She turned from me, and began walking home. I followed.

Early the next morning, the day my family left, bullets sprayed the fence of corrugated steel around our compound. It was a message for my father.

—The government wants us to leave, my father said. He threw our last bag onto the lorry and then climbed in to join us. —On this subject I agree with the government, he said, and laughed for some time. My stepmothers were not amused.

We had been gone three months. When we returned, we found only a series of circles of charred earth. I do not know if any homes were still standing. I suppose there were a few, and the families who remained in Marial Bai had crowded into them. My father's homes were no more. When we left, our compound, though damaged, still comprised three huts and a brick home. Now there was nothing, just rubble, ash. I jumped from the lorry and stood in the frame of the brick house where my father had slept. One wall stood, the chimney intact.

I found my sister Amel, returning from the well.

—The murahaleen just came, she said. —Why are you here?

Her bucket was empty. The well had been contaminated. Dead goats and one half-charred man had been thrown into it.

—It's not safe here, she said. Why did you leave Aweil?

—Father said it would be safe. Safer than Aweil.

—It's not safe here, Achak. Not at all.

—But the rebels are here. They have guns.

I had heard that Manyok Bol's militia, a rebel group based in Bahr al-Ghazal, were occasionally seen in Marial Bai.

—Do you see rebels? she said, raising her voice. —Show me the rebels with guns, monkey. Here comes Mother.

Her yellow dress was a blur sweeping over the land. She was upon me before I could sob. She grabbed me and took me and choked me by accident and I smelled her stomach and let her wash my face with water and the hem of her sun dress. She insisted to me and to my father that we needed to leave Marial, that this was the least safe of places, that the army had targeted this place almost above all other villages. The message from Khartoum was clear: if the rebels chose to continue, their families would be killed, their women raped, their children enslaved, their cattle stolen, their wells poisoned, their homes plundered, the earth scorched.

I ran to the hut of William K. I found him playing in the shadow of his home, which had been burned but otherwise was in better shape than any other hut in the village.

—William!

He lifted his head and squinted.

—Achak! Is it really you?

—It is me. I have returned!

I ran to him and punched him in the chest.

—I heard you were coming back. Are you a big-city boy now?

—I am, I said, and tried to walk like one.

—I think you're probably stupid still. Can you read?

I could not read and neither could William K, and I told him so.

—I can read. I read anything I find, he said.

I wanted to walk with him, to explore the village, to look for Moses.

—I can't, he said. —My mother won't let me leave. Look.

William K showed me a line of sticks, set end to end, encircling his family's compound. —I can't walk over those without her. They killed my brother Joseph.

I didn't know anything about this. I remembered Joseph, much older, dancing at my uncle's wedding. He was a very thin man, small, considered fragile.

—Who killed him?

—The horsemen, the murahaleen. They killed him and four other men. And the old man, the one-eyed man in the market. They killed him for talking too much. He spoke Arabic and was cursing the raiders. So they killed him with a gun first and then with their knives.

This seemed to me a very stupid way to die. Only a very bad warrior would be killed by the murahaleen, by a Baggara raider. My father had told me this many times. The murahaleen were terrible fighters, he'd said.

—I'm sorry your brother is dead, I said.

—Maybe he didn't die. I don't know. They dragged him away. They shot him and then they tied him to the horse and dragged him away. Here.

William brought me to a small tree off the path near his home.

—This is where they shot him. He was over there.

He pointed to the tree.

—The man was on his horse. He yelled at Joseph, "Don't run! Don't run or I'll shoot!" So Joseph stopped there and turned to the man on the horse. And that's when he shot him. Right there.

He pushed his finger deep into the hollow of my throat.

—He fell and they tied him to the horse. Like this.

William K arranged himself on the ground. —Pick up my feet.

I lifted his legs.

—Okay, now pull me.

I pulled William K down the path until he began kicking wildly.

—Stop! That hurts, damn you.

I dropped his feet, knowing the moment I did, William K would leap up and punch me in the chest, which is what he did. I allowed him this because Joseph was dead and I had no idea what was happening anymore.

My mother arranged my bed for me and I rolled left and right to warm myself under the calfskin blanket.

—Don't think about Joseph, she said.

I had not thought about Joseph since dinner, but now I thought about him again. My throat was sore where William K had pushed his finger.

—What did he do to them? Why did they shoot him?

—He did nothing, Achak.

—He must have done something.

—He ran.

—William K said he stopped.

My mother sighed and sat next to me.

—Then I don't know, Achak.

—Are they coming again?

—I don't think so.

—Will they come here? To our part of town?

I harbored the dim hope that the Baggara would attack only the outskirts of Marial Bai, that they would not attack the home of an important man like my father. But they had attacked the home of my father already.

My mother began drawing on my back, triangles within circles. She had been doing this since I could remember, to calm me in my bed when I could not sleep. She hummed quietly while rubbing my back in slow circles. Every other time she circled, using her forefinger, she made a triangle between my waist and shoulders.

—Don't worry, she said. —The SPLA will be here soon.

Circle, circle, triangle within.

—With guns?

—Yes. They have guns just like the horsemen.

Circle, circle, triangle within.

—Are there as many of us as there are Baggara?

—There are just as many of our soldiers. Or more.

I laughed and sat up.

—We'll kill them! We'll kill all of them! If the Dinka have guns we'll kill all the Baggara like they're animals!

I wanted to see it happen. I wanted it more than anything.

—It won't be a battle! I laughed. —It'll end in seconds.

—Yes, Achak. Now sleep. Close your eyes.

I wanted to see the rebels shoot the men who had killed Joseph Kol, William K's brother who had done nothing. I closed my eyes and pictured the Arabs falling from their horses in explosions of blood. If I was near, I would stand over them, beating them with rocks. In my vision there were so many of them, at least one hundred, the Arabs on horseback, and they were all dead. They were shot by the rebels and now William K and I were crushing their faces with our feet. It was glorious.

In the morning I found Moses. He was living with his mother and an uncle in his uncle's half-burned hut. Moses was unsure where his father had gone. He expected them to return any minute, though his uncle did not seem to know his whereabouts. Moses thought that his father was a soldier now.

—For which army? The government or the rebels? I asked.

Moses wasn't sure.

Moses and I wandered through the cool darkness of the schoolhouse. It was empty, the walls punctured by bullet holes. We put our fingers in one, two, three—so many that we gave up counting. Moses fit his fingers, bigger than mine, into five holes at once. The schoolhouse was abandoned. Nothing was happening anywhere in Marial Bai. The market now was a few shops only; for substantial goods, one had to travel to Aweil. That trip could be undertaken by older women only. Any man traveling north to Aweil would be detained, jailed, eliminated.

Most of the men of Marial Bai were gone. The men who remained were very old or very young. Everyone between fourteen and forty was gone.

We watched two ostriches run after each other, pecking and clawing. Moses threw a rock toward them and they stopped, shifting their attention to us. The ostriches were known to the village and were considered tame, but we had been told that they could kill any boy quickly, could disembowel someone our size in seconds. We ducked behind a half-burned tree, its trunk scorched black.

—Ugly birds, Moses said, and then was reminded of something. —Did you hear Joseph was shot?

I told him that I had heard.

—It went through him here, Moses said, and then, as William K had done, he pushed his finger deep into the hollow of my throat.

IX.

Do you want to know when I left that place forever, Michael?

The day was bright, the ceiling of the sky raised high. My father was gone, in Wau for business. This was only one week after we had returned to Marial Bai. Again I was feeding the fire when my mother looked up. She was boiling water and again I had brought kindling. I saw her eyes looking over my shoulder.

Tell me, where is your mother, Michael? Have you ever seen her terrified? No child should see this. It is the end of childhood, when you see your mother's face slacken, her eyes dead. When she is defeated by simply seeing the threat approaching. When she does not believe she can save you.

—Oh my lord, she said. Her shoulders collapsed. She splashed hot water on my hand. I squealed for a moment but then I heard the rumbling.

—What is it? I asked.

—Come! she whispered. Her eyes darted around the compound. —Where are your sisters?

I had not seen what my mother had seen. But there was the sound. A vibration from under our feet. I looked for my sisters, but I knew they were by the river. My brothers were grazing the cattle. Wherever they were, they were either safe from the rumbling or had already been overtaken by it.

—Come! she said again, and pulled me with her. We ran. I held her hand, but I was falling behind. She slowed her running and pulled me up by my arm. She ran, jostling me, finally arranging me over her shoulder. I held my breath and hoped she would stop. It was then, over her shoulder, that I saw what she had seen.

It was like a shadow made by a low cloud. The shadow moved quickly over the land. The rumbling was horses. I saw them now, men on horses, bringing the land into darkness. We slowed and my mother spoke.

—Where are you hiding? she breathed.

—Come to the woods, said a woman's voice.

I was placed on the ground.

—Hide in the grass, the woman told us. —From there we can run to Palang.

We crouched in the grass with the woman, ancient and smelling of meat. I realized we were near my aunt's home, on the way to the river. We were well hidden, in the shade and amid a dense thicket. From our hiding place, we watched the storm overtake the town. All was dust. Some horses carried two men. They rode camels, dragged wheeled carts behind them. I heard the crack of gunfire behind us. Horses burst through the grass to the right and left. They were coming from all sides, converging in the center of the town. This is how the murahaleen took a town, Michael. They encircled it and then squeezed all within.

—There were only twenty last time, the woman said.

There were easily two hundred, three hundred, or more now.

—This is the end, my mother said. —They mean to kill us all. Achak I am so sorry. But we will not make it through this day.

—No, no, the woman scolded. —They want the cattle. The cattle and the food. Then they're gone. We'll stay here.

At that moment, the shooting began. The guns were like those the government army carried, huge and black. The sky broke open with gunfire. The pop-pop-pop came from every corner of the village.

—Oh lord. Oh lord.

Now the woman was crying.

—Shh! my mother said, grabbing for the woman's hand and finally finding it. Now quieter, she soothed the woman. —Shhhhh.

A horse carrying two men galloped past. The second man was riding backward, his gun aiming left and right. —Allah Akhbar! he roared.

A dozen voices answered him. —Allah Akhbar!

A man lit a torch and tossed it onto the roof of the hospital. Another man, riding on the back of a great black horse, prepared some kind of small round weapon and threw it into the Episcopalian church. An explosion splintered the walls and eliminated the roof.

When I thought to look for her, I saw the horsemen circling Amath's hut. Four horses carrying six men. They guarded the hut from every side and then threw a torch. The roof smoldered first and then blackened. Fire finally overtook it and leapt upwards first, then crept down. Brown smoke billowed. A figure emerged, a young man, his hands surrendering. Guns popped from the perimeter and the man's chest burst red. He fell, and no one else left the hut. The screams began soon after.

—Achak.

My mother was behind me. Her mouth was very close to my ear.

—Achak. Turn to me.

I looked into her eyes. It was so hard, Michael. She had no hope. She believed we would die that day. Her eyes had no light.

—I won't be able to carry you fast enough. Do you understand?

I nodded.

—So you'll have to run. Yes? I know you're fast.

I nodded. I believed that we could survive. That I could.

—But if you run with your mother, you'll be seen. Do you agree? Your mother is very tall and the horsemen will see her, yes?

—Yes.

—We're going to run to your aunt's house but I might ask you to run alone, okay? You might be better running alone.

I agreed and we ran from the grass further, toward the river, toward my aunt's compound, far from the town center and far from the cattle camp and anything else the horsemen could want. I ran behind my mother, watching her bare feet slap the ground. I had never seen my mother run this way and I worried. She was a slow runner, and she was too tall when she ran. She would be seen with her yellow dress and her tall slow running and I wanted to hide her quickly.

A burst of hooves and we were met by a single man, gun held high, who looked down at us and held his horse.

—Stand still, Dinka! he barked in Arabic.

My mother stood rigid. I hid behind her legs. The man's gun was still held high, pointing upward. I decided to run if he lowered his gun. The horseman yelled in the direction he had come, pointing to me and my mother. Another horseman galloped toward us, slowing and beginning to dismount. But then something saved us. His foot was entangled, and in his struggle to free it his gun blasted into the front leg of his horse. A howl from the animal as it twisted and pitched forward. The man was thrown over like a doll, still caught in the tangle of reins and the strap of his rifle. The first horseman slid down from his mount to help him and in the moment his back was turned my mother and I were gone.

Soon we reached my aunt Marayin's house. It was quiet. The sounds of the attack were distant, muffled. Marayin was not there.

We ran up the ladder to her grain hut and sat in the kernels, burying each other, pushing the mass onto ourselves, sinking lower. My mother's eyes darted back and forth. —I don't know if this is best for us, Achak.

A scream punched through the silence. It was unmistakably Marayin's.

—Oh lord. Oh lord, my mother whispered.

She buried her head in her hands. Soon she gathered herself.

—Okay. Stay here. I have to see what's happening to her. I won't go far. Okay? If I can't see anything I'll come right back. You stay. Be completely silent, okay?

I nodded.

—Will you promise to barely breathe?

I nodded, holding my breath already.

—Good boy, she said. She held my face in her hand and then slipped backward through the door. I heard her feet on the ladder and felt the hut shake with her descent. Then quiet. A shot burst, close now. Another scream from Marayin. Then silence. As I waited, I dug myself into the grain until I was buried up to my shoulders. I listened and kept ready.

Footsteps scratched through the compound. Someone was very close. But so quiet, so careful. A hope grew within me: it was my mother. I quietly pushed myself from the grain and shifted toward the entrance, to be ready when she reached for me. I peered through the entrance and could see a few inches outside. I saw no movement but still heard the footsteps. Then a smell. It was something like the smell of the barracks, complicated and sweet. I eased my way back into the grain, and Michael, I do not understand why I was so quiet. Why I made no discernible sound. Why that man did not hear me. It was God who decided that the movements of Achak Deng would not produce a sound at that moment.

When the man was gone, Michael, I ran to the church. I had been taught that the church would always be safe. The church's walls were sturdy and so I ran to them. Once inside, I found it to be a safe place, at least for the time being. I hid beneath a hole in the thatched wall, in the cool shadows, and under a broken table, and waited there for hours. I could see the village through a mouse-sized hole and I watched when I could bear it.

In the village, the besieged were learning. Those who ran were shot. Those women and children who stood still were herded onto the soccer field. A grown man made the mistake of joining this herd, and was shot. The besieged learned again: grown men should run, or fight and be killed. The horsemen had no use for the grown men. They wanted the women, the boys, the girls, and these they gathered on the soccer field, penned between two dozen horsemen. Elsewhere, there was a certain order to what the horsemen were doing. There were those who seemed to be charged with burning every dwelling, while others seemed to be riding with abandon, shooting and barking their Arabic and satisfying any urge or inspiration.

The grown man who had tried to join the group of women and children in the soccer field was now dead. He was tied by the feet and then was dragged behind a pair of horses. Many of the Baggara were amused by this and I now could imagine what had been done to Joseph.

A man with a different kind of rifle, leaner, narrow with a longer barrel, jumped from his horse and dropped to one knee. He aimed his rifle at a faraway target and fired. He was satisfied with the result and repositioned himself and fired again. This time it required four shots before he smiled.

A horseman, taller than the others and wearing a white tunic, was carrying a sword as long as I was tall. I watched him run down a woman running for the forest and raise his sword high. I looked away. I buried my head in the earth and counted to ten and when I looked again I saw only her dress, a pale blue, splayed in the dirt.

On the soccer field, a group of horsemen had gathered. Ten men had dismounted and were tying up a group of girls. The moment I thought to look for Amath I saw her. She was standing, her face placid, her hands tied behind her back, her legs tied loosely together. Twenty feet away from her, a young woman was screaming at the militiamen, a curse in Arabic that I knew. She was wearing a bright dress, red-and-white patterned. I had never heard a woman tell a man that he had had sexual relations with a goat, but this is what this woman said loudly to the raiders. And so without any particular relish, one of these men drew his sword and ran it through her. She fell, and the white parts of her dress became red.

One by one the rest of the girls were lifted by pairs of men and fastened onto their horses. They threw each girl onto a saddle and then used rope to secure them, as they would a rug or a bundle of kindling. I watched as they took the twins I knew, Ahok and Awach Ugieth, and tied them to different horses. The girls wailed and reached for each other and when the horses moved, for a moment Ahok and Awach found themselves close enough to hold hands and they did so.

After an hour, the action dissipated. Those Dinka who would fight had fought and were now dead. The rest were being tied together to be taken north. The raid was near its conclusion and was, for the murahaleen, a success. Not one among their ranks had been injured. I looked for Moses and William K but did not see either. I could see Moses's hut, and what looked like a person lying in the entrance.

But then there was a shot from a tree and a horseman, with darker skin than most of the murahaleen, fell forward on his mount, and slid slowly off, his head landing hard on the dirt, his foot still caught in the stirrup. Quickly ten horsemen surrounded the tree. A flurry of words in Arabic, spitting with fury. They aimed their guns and fired, two dozen shots in seconds and a figure fell from the tree, landing heavily on his shoulder, dead. He wore the orange uniform of Manyok Bol's militia. I looked closer. It was Manyok Bol. He was the only rebel this day, Michael. Later I would learn than he was cut into six parts and thrown down my father's well.

—Get up!

I heard a voice I knew. I turned to see a boy standing over the body near his uncle's hut—it was a woman lying on the ground, her hands in fists at her sides.

—Get up!

It was Moses. He was standing over the woman, who was his mother. His mother had been burned in her hut. She had escaped but she was not moving and Moses was angry. He nudged her with his foot. He was not in his right mind. I could see from a distance that she was dead.

—Up! he yelled.

I wanted to run to Moses, to hide him in the church with me, but I was too afraid to leave my hiding spot. There were too many horsemen now and if I ventured out we both would surely be caught. But he was simply standing there, asking to be found, and I knew he had lost track of the dangers around him. I needed to run to him and decided that I would, and would suffer the consequences; we would run together. But at that moment, I saw him turn, and saw what he saw: a horseman coming toward him. A man sat high on the back of a wild black animal, and he was riding toward Moses, who looked no bigger than a toddler in the shadow of the horse. Moses ran, and made a quick turn around the ashes of his home, and the horseman turned, now with a sword raised high over his head. Moses ran and found himself along a fence, without outlet. The horseman bore down and I turned away. I sat down and tried to dig myself into the earth under the church. Moses was gone.

As the darkness approached, many of the raiders left town, some carrying their abductees, others whatever they had scavenged from the homes and from the market. But still hundreds were in the village, eating and resting as the last of the homes smoldered. There were none of my people visible; all had run or were dead.

When night approached I planned my escape. It had to be dark enough to pass under cover of night, and loud enough to hide any sounds I might make. As the animals overtook the forest I knew I would not be heard. I saw the Marial Bai Community Center fifty yards away and needed only to make it that far. When I did, I threw myself onto the ground, in the shadow of the roof, now unhinged. I waited, holding my breath, until I was satisfied no one had seen or heard me. Then I was gone, into the forest.

That was the last time I saw that town, Michael. I leapt into the woods and I ran for an hour and finally found a hollow log and slid into it, backward, legs first. There I lay for some hours, listening, hearing the night overtaken by animals, the distant fires, the occasional pops of automatic gunfire. I had no plan. I could continue running, but I had no ideas about where I was or where I would go. I had never gone farther than the river without my father, and now I was alone and far from any path. I might have continued but I could not decide on even a direction. It seemed possible that I would choose a path and find it taking me directly to the murahaleen. But it was not only them I feared now. The forest was not man's now; it was the lion's, the hyena's.

A loud crackle in the grass sprung me from my log and I ran. But I was too loud. When I ran through the grass I seemed to be begging the world to notice me, to devour me. I tried to make my feet lighter but I could not see where I was placing them. It was black everywhere, there was no moon that night, and I had to run with my hands rigid in front of me.

Michael, you have not seen darkness until you have seen the darkness of southern Sudan. There are no cities in the distance, there are no streetlamps, there are no roads. When there is no moon you fool yourself. You see shapes before you that are not there. You want to believe that you can see, but you see nothing.

After hours of falling through the brush, I saw orange in the distance, a fire. I crawled and slithered toward it. I was beaten now. I was bleeding from all parts of my body and had decided that even if this was a Baggara fire, I would allow myself to be captured. I would be tied up and taken north and I no longer cared. The thicket under me cleared and soon I was on a path. I lifted myself to the form of man and ran toward the orange flames. My throat heaved and my ribs ached and my feet screamed with the pain of thorns and my bones striking the hard path. I ran quietly, thankful for the silence of the hard earth under my feet, and the fire came closer. I had had nothing to drink since the morning but knew I could ask for water when I reached the fire. I slowed to a walk but still my breathing was so loud that I did not hear the sounds of whips and leather straps and men. I was so close I could smell the musty odor of their camels. These men were close to the fire but apart from those who kept the fire.

I crouched and heard their voices, their words spoken in Arabic. I dropped to my knees and inched along the path, hoping to find the fire before the voices found me. But soon I knew that the voices were the keepers of the fire. The voices were so close to the fire that the fire had to be a murahaleen fire.

—Who is there? a voice asked. It was so close I jumped.

There was movement almost directly above me, and now I could see them, two men on camels. The animals were enormous, blocking out the stars. The men wore white and protruding from the back of one man I could see the jagged shape of a gun. I held my breath and made myself a snake and moved backward, away from the path.

—Is that a Dinka boy? said a voice.

I listened and the men listened.

—A Dinka boy, or a rabbit? the same voice asked.

I continued to slither, inches at a time, my feet feeling their way behind me until they encountered a pile of sticks that moved loudly.

—Wait! one hissed.

I stopped and the men listened. I stayed on my stomach, still, breathing into the earth. The men were good at being quiet, too. They stood and listened and their camels stood and listened. It was silent for days and nights.

—Dinka boy! he hissed.

The man was now speaking Dinka.

—Dinka boy, come out and have some water.

I held my breath.

—Or is it a Dinka *girl?* said the other.

—Come have some water, said the first.

I remained there for days and nights more, it seemed, unmoving. I lay watching the silhouette of the men and their camels. One of the camels relieved itself onto the path and that got the men talking again, now in Arabic. Soon after, the men began to move. They moved slowly down the path and I stayed still. After a few steps, the men stopped. They had expected me to move when they moved, but I stayed on my stomach and held my breath and buried my face in the soil.

Finally the men rode off.

But the night would not end.

I knew I had to leave the path, which was a path of the Baggara now. I ran away from the path and thereafter the hours of the night tumbled over each other without shape or order. My eyes saw what they saw and my ears heard my breathing and the sounds that were louder than my breathing. As I ran thoughts came in quick bursts and in the moments between I filled my mind with prayer. *Protect me God. Protect me God of my ancestors.* Go quiet. What is that light? A light from a town? No. Stop now. No light at all. Curse these eyes! Curse this breath! Quiet. Quiet. *God who protects my people I call upon you to send away the murahaleen.* Quiet. Sit now. Breathe quiet. Breathe quiet. *Protect me God protect my family as they run.* Need water. Wait for dew in morning. Sip water from leaves. Need to sleep. *Oh God of the sky, keep me safe tonight. Keep me hidden, keep me quiet.* Run again. No. No. Yes, run. Must run to people. Must run, find people, then rest. Run now. *Oh God of rain, let me find water. Let me not die of thirst.* Quiet. Quiet. *Oh God of the soul, why are you doing this? I have done nothing to ask for this. I'm a boy. I'm a boy. Would you send this to a lamb? You have no right.* Jump log. Ah! Pain. What was that? Stop. No, no. Run always. Keep running. Is that the moon? What is the light? *My ancestors! Nguet, Ariath Makuei, Jokluel, hear me. Arou Aguet, hear me.*

Jokmathiang, hear me. Hear me and have mercy on this boy. Hear Achak Deng and lift him from this. Is that the moon? Where is the light?

My own breathing was too loud, every breath a great wind, a falling tree. I was conscious of my exhalations and how loud they were when I ran and when I sat in the grass waiting and watching. I held my breath to kill the sound but when I opened my mouth again my breathing was louder. It filled my ears and the air around me and I was certain it would be the end of me. When my breath calmed and I could hear other sounds, I soon heard a voice, a Dinka voice, singing a Dinka song.

I ran to the singing.

It was an old man singing, the voice small and coarse. I did not slow down when I came to him and emerged from the forest like an animal, almost knocking him over.

He shrieked. I shrieked. He saw that I was a boy and he held his heart.

—Oh, how you scared me!

The man was panting now. I apologized.

—The crashing of the grass sounded like a hyena. Oh child!

—I'm so sorry, father, I said.

—I am an old man. I can't handle these things.

—I am sorry, I repeated. —So sorry.

—If an animal came through that bush he need only breathe on me and I would be sent to the next world. Oh, my son!

I told him where I had been and what I had seen. The man told me he would bring me home to keep me safe until daylight, when we would decide upon a sensible course of action.

We walked and as we walked I expected to be offered food and water. I needed both, had had neither since the morning, but had been taught never to beg. Now I waited, expecting that because it was night and I was a boy alone, the old man would offer me a meal. But the man only sang quietly and walked slowly along the path. Finally he spoke.

—It has been some time since the lion-people have come here. I was very young when I saw this last. They were on horses?

I nodded.

—Yes. These are Arabs who have fallen to the level of the animal. They are like the lion, with its appetite for raw meat. These are not humans. These lion-creatures love war and blood. They enslave people, which is against the laws of God. They have been transformed into animals.

The man walked in silence for some time.

—I think God is sending us a message through these lion-men. This is obvious. We're being punished by God. Now we need only find what it is that God is angry about. This is the puzzle.

I didn't know where the old man was leading me but after some time I saw a small fire in the distance. We reached the fire and were received kindly by the people there. They knew the old man, and asked me where I came from and what I had seen. I told them, and they told me that they had run, too. They gave me water and I watched their Dinka faces red in the fire and I thought that this night was the end of the world and that the morning would not come again. The red faces in the fire were spirits and I was dead, all were dead, the night was eternal. I was too tired to know or care. I fell asleep among them, their heat and murmurings.

I woke up in the purple light of dawn among four men, all elderly but one, and two women, one of them nursing a baby. The fire was cold and I felt alone.

—You're awake, said one of the old men. —Good. We need to move soon. I am Jok.

Jok was only bones and a threadbare blue gown. He sat with his knees by his ears, his hands resting limply on his knees. One of the women asked me where I was from. She spoke into the face of her suckling child. I told her I had come from Marial Bai.

—Marial Bai! You're far from there. Who is your father?

I told her my father was Deng Nyibek Arou. Now Jok was interested.

—This is your father, the businessman? he said.

I said it was.

—And which son are you? he asked.

I gave my full name, Achak Nyibek Arou Deng. Third son of my father's first wife.

—I'm sorry, Achak Deng, he said. —Someone is dead from your family. A man.

Jok and the two women each said they had heard something about the family of the businessman named Deng Nyibek Arou.

—Either your father or your uncle, a younger man with glasses said. —One is dead.

—I think it was your father, the nursing woman said, still not looking up from her baby. —It was the wealthy man.

—No, said the young man, —I'm almost sure it was the brother.

—You'll find out soon enough, the mother said. —When you go home. Oh don't

95

cry. I'm sorry.

She reached out across the ash of last night's fire to touch me, but she was too far. I decided that I did not believe her, that she knew nothing about my father. I wiped my nose on the back of my hand and asked them if they knew the way back to Marial Bai.

—It's a half-day's walk that direction, Jok said. —But you can't go back there. The horsemen are still there. They're everywhere. Stay with us, or you can go with Dut Majok. He's going to get closer to see what's happening.

The young man with glasses, I learned, was named Dut Majok. I recognized him as the teacher from Marial Bai, the teacher of the older boys, husband to the woman I spoke to in the river. He was not much more than a boy himself.

When the day opened, I chose to walk with Dut Majok. We left after eating some nuts and okra. Dut was a man of no more than twenty or so, shorter than average and a bit round in the stomach. His face was small, his head very close to his shoulders. He picked leaves from the trees we passed, tearing them into small pieces and dropping them into the grass. He had a professorial air about him, and it extended beyond his glasses. He seemed more interested in everything—me, my family, the footprints we occasionally found along the way—than anyone I could recall.

—You were at the cattle camp? he asked.

—No.

—Too young I suppose. Where were you when they came?

—At home. In my house.

—Your father was a smart man. I liked him. Funny, shrewd. I'm very sorry about your loss. Have you heard about your mother?

I shook my head.

—Well. The town was burned to the ground this time. Many women were burned inside their homes. The murahaleen do this now. This is new. The homes in your area, where the wealthier people lived, the big homes—the horsemen like to burn those. It was probably burned the last time, correct? Did she run?

—Yes, I said.

—Maybe she's okay. I bet she is. Is she fast?

I said nothing.

—Well. Come with me, son. We'll see what we can see.

The sun rose as we walked and was high and small when Dut climbed into a tree and lifted me up. From there we could see the distant clearing of Marial Bai. All around was dust.

—Okay. They're still there, he said. —Those are their horses, some of the cattle they've stolen. Where you see dust, Achak, this is the murahaleen. We won't be going back into town for some time. We'll check again tomorrow. Come.

I followed Dut down the tree and back in the direction of the fire where we had slept. We walked for an hour before Dut stopped, looked quizzically in every direction, and then turned around completely. Throughout the afternoon, he stopped frequently and seemed to be making calculations in his head and with his hands. Each time, after his calculations, he would appear decisive and would be off again, confident with his new course, with me following. Then, after some time walking in the diminishing light, the process would begin again. He would stop, look to the sun, look all around him, make his hand calculations, and set off on a new path.

The sun had set by the time we reached the camp again.

—Where were you two? the suckling child's mother asked.

—You left in the morning! laughed Jok.

Dut ignored this. —The Baggara are still there, he said. —We'll check again tomorrow.

—You were lost, the woman said. —You're an educated man, but you have no sense of direction!

He brushed this off angrily. —Where is the food, Maria? How long must we wait? Give us food and water. We've been walking all day.

That night I slept with those men and the women under a shelter they had built. In the small hours I heard the sounds like those I heard outside my stepmother's home when my father spent his nights there. I kept my eyes closed and my body near the fire. In a few moments, it seemed, I was woken and there was a weak light in the sky. My eyes opened on the face of one of the elderly men in the group. He had not spoken before.

—We have to get up now, boy. What is your name again? You are the son of the late Deng Nyibek Arou, bless his soul.

This man's voice was feather-light and quivering.

—Achak, I said.

—I'm sorry, Achak. I should remember. Now we have a plan. You'll come with us. We're joining another group who slept nearby last night. Come see.

—Where is Dut?

—He has wandered off. He does this. Come.

The quivering man brought me to a clearing where a group of perhaps a hundred others had gathered, women and children and elderly men, standing among a mix of livestock—goats, chickens, more than forty head of cattle.

—We're going to Khartoum, he said.

I was so young, Michael, but even then I knew this idea was insane.

—Is Dut coming? I asked.

—Dut is gone. Dut would not like this idea, but Dut cannot find his way out of his own hut. You're safer with us.

—In Khartoum?

I thought of the handless man.

—We'll be safe there, the nursing woman said. —Come with us. You can be my son.

I didn't want to be her son.

—But why Khartoum? I asked. —With the Arabs? How?

—People have already gone to Khartoum, the old man said in his feather-light voice. —This is a well-known path. We'll be protected there from the murahaleen. We'll be given food in the camps. They have safe havens up there for people like us, people uninterested in the fighting. We'll stay there until all this is done.

I had no choice but to walk with them. I worried about their plan, but my legs ached from the running of two nights before, and I was content to be among so many people and not alone. The musty smell of the cattle warmed me and I rested my hand on their haunches as we walked. We traveled until midday, whispering when we needed to, trying to slip quietly out of the region with the cattle. Jok, the leader of this group, believed that once we made it over the river and into the north, we would be safe. It was a very strange strategy.

Soon we encountered a man in the orange uniform of Manyok Bol's militia. He looked incredulous to see us.

—Who are you people? Where are you going?

—To Khartoum, the old man said.

The man in orange now stepped in front of us, blocking the path.

—Are you mad? How will you get to Khartoum with forty head of cattle? Who's the maker of this plan? You'll all be killed. There are murahaleen not far from here.

You'll walk straight into them.

The old man shook his head slowly.

—You're the one who should worry, he said. —You have the gun. We're unarmed. They won't harm us. We have no allegiance to you.

—God help you, said the man in orange.

—I trust he will, the old man said.

Muttering to himself, the man in orange walked away and in the direction we had come. Our group continued along the path for a moment, until the soldier's voice came from far down the path. —You'll see them in one hundred yards. You will die one hundred yards from where you now stand.

At that, the cattle group stood still and the elders argued. Some were of the opinion that we would not be bothered if we were passing in peace, that the only reason there was trouble in Marial Bai was the town's affiliation with the SPLA. If our group denounced the rebels and indicated their intentions to walk to Khartoum, we would be allowed to pass. Another faction thought this senseless, that the murahaleen had no loyalty to the government or grievance against the SPLA—they only wanted the cattle and children. The group remained like this for some time, on the path, the elders arguing and the cattle grazing, when finally the debate was settled by the rumbling of hooves and an advancing veil of dust.

In seconds the murahaleen were upon us.

The group ran in every direction. I followed the man who looked the fastest as he dove into the grass and crawled under a dense bush and settled behind a thatch of logs and sticks. The man beside me was older than my father, very thin, his arms roped by protruding veins. He wore a large soft hat that shielded his eyes.

—Army, the hat man said, nodding at the men on horseback. There were seven horsemen, four in traditional Baggara clothing, three wearing the uniform of the Sudanese army. —I don't understand this, he said.

A large portion of our cattle group had stayed, had not run from the path. They were now being guarded by two of the soldiers in uniform. The group stood, saying nothing. There was a long moment when it did not seem like anything at all would happen. Or perhaps all involved were waiting for something to happen. And it did. Suddenly one of the old men ran into the forest, awkwardly and far too slowly. Two soldiers leapt off their horses and raced after him, laughing. Shots followed and the men returned without the old man.

One of the government soldiers turned and seemed to be looking at me and the hat man. My breathing was again too loud, my eyes too big. We both lowered our heads.

—They see us. Let's go, I whispered.

Without warning, the hat man stood, arms high in surrender.

—Come here, abeed! the soldier said, using the Arabic word for slave. The hat man walked toward them. I watched the man's back, and saw the children and women and cattle herded between the horses. I thought of Amath and the way she stood, accepting her fate, and I became angry very quickly. I should not have moved at that moment but my anger overtook me. *Damn you,* I thought, and ran. I turned and ran as they yelled to me. —Abeed! Abeed! *Damn you,* I thought as I ran. *I damn you with the power of God and of my family.* I expected to be shot at any moment but I ran. *Damn you men. Damn you all.* I would die while damning them and God would understand, and in eternity these men would hear my curse.

They shot twice at me but I escaped and continued to run through the thicket. They did not pursue me. I ran through the waning pink light of the afternoon and into the evening. I ran through the bush, looking for my people or a well-traveled way, finding none, and when the darkness came I had no hope of seeing a road or footpath.

But then, finally, I did find a path. When I found the path I sat behind a tree nearby, resting, watching the path, listening for voices, waiting to make sure it was clear. After some time, I heard the heavy breathing of a man. Even by his breath I could tell it was a large man, a suffering man. From my tree I saw him, a large Dinka man who seemed to be walking with purpose. His back was straight and he seemed young. He wore white shorts and nothing else. I thought I would be saved by this man.

—Uncle! I said, running to him. —Excuse me!

He turned to me, but his face had been ripped from his skull. His skin had melted. It was wet and pink and the whites of his eyes were protruding and unblinking. He had lost the lids that covered them.

He brought his face close to mine, his raw skin crossed everywhere by red veins.

—What? What is it? Don't stare at my face.

I turned to run but the man grabbed my arm.

—Come with me, boy. Take this.

He gave me his sack. It weighed as much as I did. I tried to hold it, but it dropped to the ground. The man struck me on the ear with the back of his hand.

—Carry, it, boy!

—I can't. I don't want to, I said.

I told him I wanted only to get back to Marial Bai.

—For what? To be killed? Where do you think I got this? Where do you think I lost my face, stupid boy?

I now recognized the man. He was the soldier, Kolong Gar, who had deserted the army before the first attack. From the tree of Amath, we had seen him running below, the flashlights following.

—I saw you, I said.

—You saw nothing.

—I saw you when you ran. We were in the tree.

He was not interested in this.

—I want you to stare into my face, boy. I need you to do this. You see this face? This was the face of a man who trusted. Do you see what happens to a man who trusts? Tell me what happens!

—His face is taken.

—Good! Yes! My face was taken. That's a good way to say it. This is what I deserve. I said I was the friend of the Arab and the Arab reminded me that we're not friends and never will be. I served in the army with Arabs but when the rebels rose up the Arabs no longer knew me. They were planning to bring me back north to kill me. This I know. And when I left the army they tracked me down and found me and threw my face into the fire. This face is a lesson to all Dinka who think we can live together with those people—

I dropped the sack and ran again. I knew it was not polite to run from the faceless man but finally I thought *Damn it all.* I had never before cursed aloud or silently but now I did, again and again. I ran as he yelled to me and ran as he cursed me and as I ran I cursed him and everything I could name. *Damn the faceless man and damn the murahaleen and damn the government and damn the land and the Dinka with their useless spears.* I ran over the grass and through a stand of trees and then over a dry riverbed and in the next stand of trees I found a great acacia, like the one I shared with William K and Moses, and in its roots I found a hole and in this hole I crawled and stayed and listened to my breathing. I was now expert at finding sleeping holes. *Damn the dirt and damn the worms and damn the beetles and damn the mosquitos.* I had not turned around as I ran and was not sure until I was in the tree that there was no one behind me. I looked out from the dark of the hole and saw nothing and heard nothing and soon the night's black wings beat down from above and I was in the dark, in the tree, with my eyes and my breath. In the night the animal sounds filled the air and I stuffed my ears with small stones to block out the sound. *Damn you forest and damn you animals, every one.*

I woke in the morning and shook the rocks from my head and got up and walked and ran and when I heard a sound or saw a figure in the distance, I crawled. For a week more I ran and crawled and walked. I found people of my tribe and I asked them the direction to Marial Bai; sometimes they knew and often they knew nothing. *Damn you directionless, helpless people.* Some of the people I found were from the region and others had come from the north, some from the south. Everyone was moving. When I found a village or settlement, I would stop there and ask for water and they would say, "You are safe here, boy, you are safe now," and I would sleep there and know I was not safe. The horses and guns and helicopters always came. I could not get out of this ring, this circle that was squeezing us within, and no one knew when the end would come. I visited an old woman, the oldest woman I have ever known, and she sat cooking with her granddaughter, my age, and the old woman said that this was the end, that the end was coming and that I should simply sit still, with them, and wait. This would be the end of the Dinka, she said in a voice hoarse and reed-thin, but if this was the will of the gods and the Earth, she said, then so be it. I nodded to the grandmother and slept in her arms, but then left in the morning and continued to run. I ran past villages that had been and were no more, ran past buses that were burned from the inside out, hands and faces pressed to the glass. *Damn you all. Damn the living, damn the dead.*

In the first light of dawn I ran past an airfield, where I saw a small white airplane and a family and a man who was serving as their representative. He was wearing a strange garment that I would later learn was a suit, and he carried a small black briefcase. A few feet behind him was the family—a man, a woman, and a girl of five, all of them dressed in fine clothing, the woman and child sitting atop a larger suitcase. The man in the suit, the representative, was talking excitedly to the pilot of the plane, who I could see was a very small man, and with skin much lighter than ours.

—These are important people! the representative was saying.

The pilot was unimpressed.

—This man is an MP! the representative said.

The pilot climbed into the cockpit.

—You must take them! the representative wailed.

But the pilot did not take them. He flew off, away from the sun, and the family and their representative were left on the airfield. No one was important enough to fly away from the war, not in those days.

I continued to run.

X.

Michael is awake and roaming. He believes that he has neutralized me, and now feels at ease to search through the house. He walked past me on his way to the bathroom, and once he was finished there, I heard the whine of Achor Achor's bedroom door. I don't know what Michael might be looking for, but there is not much to see in the room where Achor Achor sleeps. He has decorated his walls with two pictures: a poster of Jesus he was given at his Bible-study class, and a large but grainy snapshot of his sister, who lives in Cairo and cleans restaurants.

Now Michael moves down the hall and into my room. My door makes no sound, only the faint swoosh as it passes over the carpet. I hear the sound of my closet opening, and soon after, the blinds being drawn. I know that he has picked up the two books by my bedside—*The Purpose-Driven Life*, by Rick Warren and *Seeking the Heart of God*, by Mother Teresa and Brother Roger—because I hear them hit the floor, one after the other. I hear the bedsprings gasp, and then go quiet. He opens the drawers to my dresser, and then closes them.

Michael is a curious boy and his searching makes him seem more human to me. My fondness for him grows again, and forgiveness fumbles back into my heart.

"Michael!" I blurt.

I had not expected to say his name but it is too late. Now I have to say it again, and have to decide why I am saying it.

"Michael, I have a proposition for you."

He is still in my room. I hear no sounds of movement.

"Michael, this will be an attractive proposition. I assure you."

He says nothing. He does not emerge from my bedroom.

I hear the sound of my bedside table's drawer being pulled open. My stomach clenches when I realize he will see the pictures of Tabitha. He has no right to look at them. How will I ever forget that this broken boy has handled those pictures? Those photographs are far too important to me for my own sense of equilibrium. I know that I look at them too often; I know it seems self-punishing. Achor Achor has scolded me for this. But they give me comfort; they cause me no pain.

There are ten or so, most of them taken with the camera Michael's companions have stolen. In one, Tabitha is with her brothers, and the four of them are together holding a giant fish in a market in Seattle. She is in the center of them all, and it's very clear how much they adore her. In another, she is with her closest friend, another Sudanese refugee named Veronica, and Veronica's baby, Matthew. In front of the baby—a child born in the United States—is a round brown mess, Tabitha's first attempt at an American-style birthday cake. The baby's face is covered in chocolate, and Tabitha and Veronica are grinning, each holding one of Matthew's cheeks. They are not yet aware that the sugar from Matthew's binge will keep him up for the next twenty-two hours. The best photo is the one she thought I had destroyed, at her insistence. She is in my bedroom and is wearing her glasses, and this fact makes it quite rare, one of a kind. When I took it, before we went to sleep one night, she was livid, and did not speak to me till noon the next day. "Throw it out!" she yelled, and then corrected herself: "Burn it!" I did so, in the sink, but a few days later, when she had returned to Seattle, I printed another from my digital camera. Very few people knew that Tabitha wore contacts, and almost no one had seen her in her glasses, which were huge, ungainly, the lenses as thick as a windshield. She kept them near when she slept, in case she needed to use the bathroom. But I loved her when she wore them, and wanted her to wear them more often. She was less glamorous in those enormous frames, and when she had them on, it seemed more plausible that she was truly mine.

We met at Kakuma, in a home economics class. She was three years younger than me, and was very smart, which is how she and I found ourselves placed together. It was required in the camp, for young men and women both, and this caused much consternation among the Sudanese elders. Men taking cooking classes? It was absurd to them. But most of us didn't mind. I enjoyed the class a great deal, even though I showed no aptitude for cooking or any of the other tasks involved. Tabitha, though, showed no interest in home economics, or even in passing the class. Her attendance was infrequent, and when she was present, she scoffed loudly every time the teacher, a Sudanese woman we called Ms. Spatula, attempted to convince us how useful the lessons of home economics would be in our lives. Ms. Spatula did not appreciate Tabitha's scoffing, or Tabitha's disdainful sighs, or those days when Tabitha read from her paperback novels while Ms. Spatula demonstrated the ways to cook an egg. Ms. Spatula did not at all appreciate Tabitha Duany Aker.

But the boys and young men did appreciate her. It was impossible not to.

There were more girls in classes in Kakuma, more than in Pinyudo, but still they were the minority, one in ten at best. And they would not last. Every year they were removed from school in order to work at home and prepare themselves to be married off. At fourteen, any girl without a deformity would be spoken for—sent back to southern Sudan to become the wife of an SPLA officer who could afford the dowry demanded. And they would in many cases go happily, for it was not a good life for a girl at Kakuma. Girls were worked to the bone, were raped if they left the camp looking for firewood. They had no power at Kakuma, they had no future.

But no one told this to Tabitha. Or they had and she was undaunted.

She lived with three brothers and her mother, an educated woman who was determined to give Tabitha the best life possible under the circumstances. Tabitha's father had been killed very early in the war, and her mother refused to be taken in by her husband's family. In many cases in Sudan, the brother of the deceased will assume the wife and family of his brother, but Tabitha's mother would have none of that. She left her village, Yirol, and made her way to Kakuma, knowing that a life in Kenya, even in a refugee camp, might provide a more enlightened world for her children.

I was thankful for her mother's courage and wisdom. I was thankful each time Tabitha chose to attend home economics and each time she rolled her eyes and every time she smirked. She was the most intriguing young woman at Kakuma.

Eventually we were boyfriend and girlfriend, or as close to that status as was possible for teenagers at Kakuma, and I told her many times I loved her. These words, when I used them then, did not mean what they meant much later in America, when I knew that I loved her as a man loves a woman. At Kakuma we were so young; we were careful and chaste. It is not proper, even in a camp like that, for young people to parade their affections before the community. We met for walks after church, we snuck away when we could. We attended events at the camp together, we ate with friends, we talked while waiting in line for our rations. I stared at her heart-shaped face, her bright eyes and round cheeks, and it was everything to me then. But what was it? Perhaps it was nothing.

She left Kakuma before I did. This was extraordinary, for there were very few girls in the Sudanese resettled in the United States, and almost none who had parents in the camp. Tabitha claims it was luck but I believe her mother was clever throughout the process. When the resettlement rumors became true, her mother was brilliant; she knew the United States was interested in the unaccompanied minors. Anyone with parents at Kakuma would be far less likely to be considered. She allowed her children to lie, and she herself disappeared, went to live in another part of the camp. Tabitha and her three brothers were processed as orphans, and because they were young, younger than most of us, they were chosen, given early passage, and were even kept together once in America.

With their mother still in Kakuma, Tabitha and her brothers settled in a two-bedroom apartment in Burien, a suburb of Seattle, and all attended high school together. Tabitha was happy, was becoming an American very quickly. Her English was American English, not the Kenyan English I learned. When she graduated, she was given a scholarship by the Bill and Melinda Gates Foundation to attend college at the University of Western Washington.

By the time I arrived in the United States, almost two years later, she had forgotten me, and I her. Not entirely, of course, but we knew better than to hold on to such attachments. The Sudanese from Kakuma were being sent all over the globe, and we knew that our fates were not ours to determine. When I settled in Atlanta, I had few thoughts of Tabitha.

One day I was talking on the phone to one of the three hundred Lost Boys who regularly call me, this one living in Seattle. There had been a cease-fire declared in southern Sudan, and he wanted to know my opinion, since he assumed I was very close to the SPLA. I was in the middle of explaining his mistake, that I knew as much as or less than he did, when he said, "You know who's here?" I told him I did not know who was there. "Someone you've met, I think," he said. He handed the phone off and I expected the next voice to be a man's, but it was a woman's voice. "Hello, who is this? Hello? Is it a mouse on the other line?" she said. It was such a voice! Tabitha had become a woman! Her voice was deeper, seemed full of experience, greatly at ease with the world. That sort of easy confidence in a woman is overpowering to me. But I knew it was her.

"Tabitha?"

"Of course, honey," she said in English. Her accent was almost perfectly American. She had learned a great deal in two years of high school. We talked aimlessly for a few minutes before I blurted out the primary question on my mind.

"Do you have a boyfriend?"

I had to know.

"Of course I do, sweetie," she said. "I haven't seen you in three years."

Where had she learned these words, "honey" and "sweetie"? Intoxicating words. We talked for an hour that day, and hours more that week. I was disappointed that she was seeing someone, but I was unsurprised. Tabitha was an astonishing Sudanese woman, and there are few single Sudanese women in the United States, perhaps two hundred, perhaps less. Of the thousands of Sudanese brought over under the auspices of the Lost Boys airlift, only eighty-nine were women. Many of them have married already, and the resulting scarcity makes things difficult for many men like me. And if we look outside the Sudanese community, what can we offer? With our lack of money, our church-donated clothes, the small apartments we share with two, three other refugees, we're not the most desirable of all men, not yet at least. There are countless examples of love found, of course, whether the women are African-American, white American, European. But by and large, Sudanese men in America are looking to meet Sudanese women, and this means, for many, finding one's way back to Kakuma or even southern Sudan.

But Tabitha, coveted by so many here in America, eventually chose me.

"Michael, please," I say.

I want to bring him from my room and back to the kitchen, where I can see him and where I know he will not be alone with the photographs.

"I need to talk to you. I think you will be interested in talking to me."

I am silly to think I might be understood by this boy. But young people are my specialty, in a manner of speaking. At Kakuma, I was a youth leader, overseeing the extracurricular activities for six thousand of the young refugees. I worked for the office of the United Nations High Commissioner for Refugees, helping to devise games, sports leagues, theatrical works. Since arriving in America, I have made a number of friends, but perhaps none as important to me as Allison, the only child of Anne and Gerald Newton.

The Newtons were the first American family to take an interest in me, even before Phil Mays. I had been in the country only a few weeks when I was asked to speak at an Episcopalian church, and when I did so I met Anne, an African-American woman with teardrop eyes and tiny cold hands. She asked if she could help me. I was not sure how she could, but she said we could discuss it over dinner, and so I came to dinner, and ate with Anne and Gerald and Allison. They were a prosperous family living in a large and comfortable house, and they opened it to me; they promised me access to all they had. Allison was twelve then and I was twenty-three but in many ways we seemed to be peers. We played basketball in their driveway, and rode bicycles as children might, and she told me about the questions she had at school about a boy named Alessandro. Allison had a fondness for boys of Italian descent.

"Should I write him a long letter?" she asked me one day. "Do boys like letters, or are they intimidated by too much information, too much enthusiasm?"

I told her a note sounded like a very good idea, if the letter was not too long.

"But even then, a note is so permanent. I won't be able to take it back. The risk is just so incredible, don't you think, Valentino?"

Allison was then and remains still the most intelligent young person I have ever known. She is seventeen now but even at twelve she spoke with an eloquence that was sometimes frightening. Her words then and now come from her mouth in perfect sentences, always as if written first—and in a low voice, her lips scarcely moving. I have been curious to see how she interacts with her peers at school, because she is unlike any teenager I've known. She seems to have decided, at age thirteen, that she was an adult, and wished to be treated as such. Even at twelve and thirteen, she wore conservative clothes and glasses, and with her hair pulled taut behind her head, she looked thirty. Still, she was not immune to adolescent fun. It was Allison who taught me how to program people's birthdays into my cell phone, and so I went about asking everyone I knew what their birthday was; it puzzled some but was a great pleasure to me, a pleasure born of some sense of order. Anne eventually suggested that I might in some way still consider myself an adolescent, having been deprived, as she put it, of a childhood. But I am not sure this is why I feel close to Allison, or why I feel sympathetic to this Michael.

Humans are divided between those who can still look through the eyes of youth and those who cannot. Though it causes me frequent pain, I find it very easy to place myself in the shoes of almost any boy, and can conjure my own youth with an ease that is troublesome.

"Michael," I say again, and am surprised at how tired I sound.

The door to my room closes. I am here and he is there and that is that.

The morning after I passed the airfield, after I had slept for a few hours in the branches of a tree, I awoke and saw them. A large group of boys, not one hundred yards away. I waited for my eyes to adjust to the light and then looked again. There seemed to be about thirty of them, all sitting in a circle. A man stood over them, and was gesturing wildly. I knew the boys were Dinka and they were not running, so I climbed down the tree and walked to the group. It was difficult to believe that there would be such a gathering. When I was close enough I saw that it was Dut Majok, the teacher of older boys from Marial Bai. He seemed unsurprised to see me.

—Achak! Good. I'm so glad to see you alive. Now you're safe. There are other boys from your village here, too. Look.

I looked hard at the man speaking my name. Could it really be Dut Majok? He removed a piece of river-green paper from his pocket and, with a small orange pencil, wrote something down. Then he folded the paper and returned it to his pocket.

—How did you get here? I asked.

—Well I'm not crazy, Achak. I knew enough not to try to walk to Khartoum.

He was indeed Dut Majok, and he was well-dressed and clean. He looked like a university student, or as if he were ready to take an important business trip. He wore clean grey cotton pants and a white button-down shirt, leather sandals on his feet and a floppy cream-colored canvas hat on his head.

I swept my eyes over the group, all boys of my age-set, some older, some younger but all close in size and all of them looking hungry and tired and unhappy to see me. A few had bags with them, but most were like me, carrying nothing, as if they had fled their villages in the night. I knew none of them.

—We're going to Bilpam, Dut said. —You know this place? We're going east to Bilpam and there you'll be safe from all this. We'll walk for a while and then you'll be fed. These boys are like you. They've lost their families and their homes. They need sanctuary. You know this word? An English word. This is where we're going, son.

Bilpam. Right, boys?

The boys looked at Dut sullenly.

—Then when this is all past, you'll come back to your families, your villages. Whatever remains. This is all we can do now.

There was only silence from this mass of boys.

—Is everyone ready? Gather whatever you have and let's go. We're going east.

I walked with them. I had no choice. I didn't want to run alone in the night again, and decided that I would stay with them for one day and one night, and then decide what to do. So we set off, walking toward the rising sun. We walked in pairs and alone, most of us single file, and that first morning—it would never be this way again—we walked with energy and purpose. We walked with the assumption that the walk would be over at any time. We knew nothing about Bilpam or the war or the world. During the walk I heard from the boys near me that Dut had gone to school in Khartoum and had studied economics in Cairo. Dut was the only person over sixteen years old among our group. The other boys' trust in him seemed unwavering. But the farther we walked the more certain I was that I did not belong in this group. These boys seemed sure that their families had been killed, and despite what the old man and the nursing woman had said in the light of the fire, I had convinced myself that this had not happened to mine. As the afternoon waned, I caught up with Dut.

—Dut?

—Yes Achak. Are you hungry?

—No. No, thank you.

—Good. Because we have no food.

He smiled. He frequently found himself amusing.

—Then what is it, Achak? Do you want to walk in front with me?

—No thanks. I'm fine near the back.

—Okay. Because I was going to tell you that only those who I choose can walk near the front with me. And I don't know you very well yet.

—Yes. Thank you.

—So what is it? How can I help you?

I waited for a moment to make sure he was ready to listen to my words.

—I only want to go to Marial Bai. I don't want to go to Bilpam.

—Marial Bai? You saw Marial Bai from the tree! You remember? Marial Bai is now the home of the Baggara. There's nothing there. No homes, no Dinka. Just dust and horses and blood. You saw this. No one lives there now—Achak, stop. Achak.

He saw something in my face. I was exhausted, and I suppose it was then that I finally felt the crush of it. The possibility, the likelihood even, that what had happened to the dead in Marial Bai, to all the families of these sullen boys, had happened to my own family. I pictured all of them torn, punctured, charred. I saw my father falling from a tree, dead before he landed. I heard my mother screaming, trapped in our burning house.

—Achak. Achak. Stop. Don't look like that. Stop.

Dut held me by the shoulders. His eyes were small, hidden beneath a series of overlapping folds, as if he had learned to let in only the smallest quantities of light.

—This group doesn't cry, Achak. Do you see anyone crying? No one is crying. Your family might be alive. Many survive these attacks. You know this. You survived. These boys have survived. Your mother and father are probably running. We might see them. You know this is a possibility. Everyone is running. Where are we all running? We're running in a thousand directions. Everyone is going to where the sun rises. This is Bilpam. We're going to Bilpam because I was told Bilpam would be a safe place for a bunch of boys. So here we are, you and me and these boys. But there isn't a Marial Bai now. If you find your parents, it won't be in Marial Bai. Do you understand?

I did understand.

—Good. You're a good listener, Achak. You listen and you listen to sense. This is important. When I want to talk sensibly to someone, I will find you. Okay. We need to go now. We have a long walk before nightfall.

Now I walked with confidence. I was in the grip of the belief that in a group like this, I would find my family or be found. I walked near the back of a line of three dozen boys, all of them near my age, a handful old enough to have hair under their arms. I considered it a good idea to be with them, so many boys and with a capable leader in Dut. I felt safe with all of these boys, some of them almost men, because if the Arabs came, we could do something. So many boys surely would do something. And if we had guns! I mentioned this to Dut, that we should have guns.

—It would be good, yes, he said. —I had a gun once.

—Did you shoot it?

—I did, yes. I shot it many times.

—Can we get one?

—I don't know, Achak. They are not easy to come by. We'll see. I think we might find some men with guns who will help us. But for now we're safe in our numbers. Our numbers are our weapon.

I was sure the existence of us, so many boys walking in such a line, would become well-known and my parents would come for me. This seemed logical enough and so I shared the idea with the boy walking ahead of me, a boy named Deng. Deng was very small for his age, with a head far too big for his frail construction, his ribs visible and slender like the bones in the wing of a bird. I told Deng that we would be safer, and would likely find our families if we stayed with Dut. Deng laughed.

—Were the Arabs afraid of the boys in your town? he asked.

—No.

—Did they shoot them?

—Yes.

—So why do you think the Arabs will be afraid of so many of us? Don't be stupid. They don't fear our brothers or fathers. If they find us we'll be taken or killed. We're not safer, Achak, just the opposite. We're never safe. No one is easier to kill than boys like us.

Michael, as I have said, I am sure your story is a sad one. I will not discount that. I do not think the man and woman who left you here are your parents. So where, then, are your mother and father? It cannot be a happy story. But you are clothed, and you are well-fed, and you have your health and teeth and surely your own bed.

But these boys were not so blessed. I did not hear many of their stories, because we all assumed we had come from similar circumstances. It was not interesting to us to hear more of violence and loss. I will tell you only Deng's story, or allow Deng to tell it as he told it to me, as we walked in the early evening through a more tropical land than Marial Bai was at that time of year. We were already very far from home.

Deng's village was not much different from mine. He had been at cattle camp, a few miles away, when the murahaleen had come. The shooting began, older boys fell where they stood and soon the cattle camp was overtaken.

—I ran, Deng said. —I ran back to the town, thinking this would be best, but this is where the horsemen were headed. It was a stupid place to go. I ran toward my house but it was already on fire. The Arabs love to burn houses. Did you see them burning houses?

Deng was always asking me these questions.

—I ran to the school, he continued. —It was just a simple building, cement and with a corrugated roof, but it seemed safer, and I knew it wouldn't burn because our teacher had always taught us that, that the way it was built would prevent it from burning. So I ran to the school and I hid there; I stayed in the school the whole day. I crouched in the locker where they keep the supplies.

It seemed a silly place to hide, given that they were usually looking for children to steal. But I didn't say this to Deng. I only asked if the Arabs came looking for people in the school.

—Yes they did! Of course they did. But I was hiding in the cabinet, a metal cabinet. I was in the lower shelf, and I put a sisal bag around me. I was under the bottom shelf covered in the sisal bag, and they didn't see me, though a man did open the locker. I stayed there for two days, as they burned the town.

I asked Deng how he could stay in such a small space for so long.

—Oh I'm ashamed to say that I wet my pants that time. I shat at that moment and I still can't understand why he didn't smell me! I'm still ashamed that I shat in those pants. And I walked in those pants for many days, Achak. Those same pants. I stayed in the locker for two days. I didn't once come out. I saw the day come and the night come through the keyhole in the locker. Twice I saw the day come and go. There were sounds of horses and the Arabs for all that time. Men were sleeping in the school and I could hear them.

—They didn't open the locker again?

—They did! They opened it many times, Achak. But this is where my waste was not my enemy, but my friend! Every time they opened the door they gagged, smelling the waste I'd made! It made me so happy. I was punishing the Arab bastards with my waste and it made me proud. Ten times they opened that locker and every time they gagged and they slammed the locker door closed again and I was safe. They kicked the door every time. Those stupid bastards. They thought an animal had died in there.

I was amazed by the cursing that Deng knew how to do.

—Eventually the Arabs left the school. I didn't hear them anymore so I opened the door slowly. I was so sore from sitting like that and from having no water or food.

When I got out there was no one in the school but there were men outside. Most had left, but some had stayed. Some men on camels and some soldiers. I don't know why they were there, but they were living in our houses, those they had not burned. Two were living in my grandmother's house. It made me very sick to see them coming out of her house as if it were theirs. I hid in the school until night and then I left. It wasn't hard. I was only one boy and the night was very dark. So I left my town and ran and ran and then I was far enough away that I felt safe. I ran until the morning and found a village where two Dinka men took me in and fed me. They were scared when they first heard me. I came out of the grass and one of them raised a gun to me. He had a small gun, one that fit in his hand. Like this.

Deng pointed his small bony finger at me.

—The men were scared but then saw it was only me, a boy. Then they smelled me. They yelled at me for some time about my smell. I apologized. They took me to the stream and they pushed me in. They kicked me and told me to stay there until I was clean. I took off my clothes and scrubbed them and watched all my waste become part of the river.

The funny thing, Michael, is that Deng still smelled—even when he was telling this story about his smell. He truly smelled awful, and the stench could not be cleansed from his clothing. But I should say that we all smelled; it was almost impossible to separate one smell from the other.

—I went with these men for some time, Deng continued. —I didn't know where we were going but I felt so much better being with two able men. But we were hiding all the time. The men were scared of every sound and avoided all people. I asked them why and they said they were afraid of Arabs and soldiers. But they also ran from other Dinka. We walked at night and when we came to a village where there were people, they would tell me to sneak into the village and steal food. I would crawl to a hut and take some nuts or meat or anything I could find. One time I took a goat. I lured the goat into the forest with a mango. It was the men's idea. They said take that goat and lure it with the mango. I had stolen the mango the night before. So I did this and it worked. The goat came to us and they killed the goat with a stone and we ate some of the goat that night and kept the rest. The men were very good at these ideas. They had many ideas and knew a lot of tricks. It was working, my partnership with these men, until we came upon a town that had been captured by the SPLA. My partners immediately turned away from the town and were sneaking away, back into the brush, when we encountered a rebel soldier who seemed to be patrolling the border of the town. The soldier looked like the men. He started asking them questions. What are you doing here? Why aren't you at Kapoeta? Who is that boy? Things like that. I think the soldier knew these men with me. The soldier told the men to wait there, while he went to get his other men. The soldier turned to go back to the camp and that's when one of the men stuck a knife in his back. Just put his knife right there.

Deng pointed to the middle of my back.

—It went in very easily. I was surprised. And the SPLA man just fell forward silently and that was the end of him. Then we were running again. We ran and hid that night and sometime in the night I figured out that these men were supposed to be in the SPLA. They had been rebels and then quit and you're not allowed to quit. If you quit you can be killed by anyone. Have you heard this?

I had not heard this.

—It was then that I decided that I had to leave these men. But the problem was that I was sure that the same thing would happen to me. They were afraid of being shot by the SPLA for leaving, and I was afraid of being killed by these men if I left. They seemed very good at killing people. It was so strange, Achak. I'm so confused. Are you confused?

I said that I too was confused.

—So we walked more and I waited for a chance to run from them. After eight days together, we were walking on the road and I saw a truck. The men ran into the woods and waited for it to pass. When the truck got close I saw that it had rebels on it. This gave me an idea. I jumped out and ran to the truck. I knew the deserters wouldn't shoot me because then the rebels would find them. So I ran to the truck and yelled for them to stop. They stopped and lifted me up. I sat in the truck with all the rebels. It was very scary at first because they all had guns. They were very tired and they looked mean and like they hated me. But I stayed quiet and because I was quiet, they liked me. I rode with them to another village and they let me stay with them. I was a rebel, Achak! I lived at their camp for weeks, staying with a man named Malek Kuach Malek. He was a commander of the SPLA. He was very important. He had a big scar here.

Deng drew a line with his finger from my temple to my ear.

—He said it was from a bomb. He became my father. He said I would be a soldier soon, that he was going to train me. I became his assistant. I fetched water for him and cleaned his sunglasses and turned his radio on and off. He liked to tell me to turn it on instead of doing it himself. Then we would listen to the rebel radio together, and sometimes the BBC World News. He was a good father to me, and I was able to eat the same food he, a commander, ate. I thought I would just be his son forever, Achak. I was happy to live with him as long as I could.

The thought of staying in one place seemed very appealing to me that day.

—Then one day the government army came. Malek was not at home when I heard the tank come. All the rebels scattered and got into position to fight and a second later the tank burst through the trees. Everything exploded and I just ran. I ran alone and ran until I got to a truck that was burned. It was just this truck that had been burned out. So I hid in the truck that night until I didn't hear any more guns. In the morning I saw no one. Malek was gone, the rebels were gone and the government soldiers were gone. So I walked in the direction I thought the rebels would go. And eventually I found a village that had not been attacked and I met a woman there who was very kind and who was going to Wau. So I got on a bus with this woman. I was planning to go to Wau to live there with this woman. She said it would be safe there, and that I could be her son. So I got on the bus and we drove for a time and I was asleep. Then I was woken by yelling. The bus was stopped. I looked out the window and it was rebels. There were ten of them, with guns, and they were yelling at the driver. They made everyone get off the bus. They made everyone explain where they were going. Then they took—

—Where did you get that shirt?

Dut had found his way back to the end of the line near us, and took an interest in Deng. He was amused by Deng's shirt.

—My father gave it to me, Deng said. —He got it in Wau.

—Do you know what that shirt is worn for?

—No, Deng said.

Deng knew Dut was laughing at his shirt.

—My father said it was a very high-quality shirt.

Dut smiled and put his arm around Deng's shoulder.

—It's a shirt they call a tuxedo shirt, son. It's worn when people get married. You're wearing the shirt of a man getting married.

Dut laughed with a snort. —But I have never seen a pink one, he said, and laughed loudly.

Deng did not laugh. It was cruel of Dut to say that, and, realizing this, he tried to brighten the mood. —What a good group we have here! he yelled to all of us. —You really are an exceptional group of walkers. Now keep walking. We have to walk till dark. There's a village we'll reach by nightfall and we'll get some food there.

I forgot then that Deng had been telling me his story, and I forgot to ask him to finish it. Every boy had a story like this, with many places they thought they might stay, many people who helped them but who disappeared, many fires and battles and betrayals. But I never heard the end of Deng's story and have always wondered about it.

It was strange land we passed through. We saw fields that had been scorched, goats disemboweled and headless. We saw the tracks of horses and trucks, beautiful bullet casings in their wake. I had never walked so long in one day. We had not stopped since the morning and we had eaten nothing. What water we had been allowed we shared from one jerry can that Dut had brought and which we took turns carrying.

We had walked all day when we came upon a bustling village I had never seen. It was a perfect village. Everywhere people moved as we used to move in Marial Bai. The women carried kindling and water on their heads, the men sat in the small marketplace playing dominoes and drinking wine. The village seemed utterly untouched by any conflict at all. I followed the group into the center of the town.

—Sit down, everyone, Dut said, and we sat. —Stay here. Do not get up. Do not bother anyone. Do not move.

Dut went off into the village. Women walked by us, slowing for a few moments and then walking on. A dog trailed them and sniffed its way to where we sat. Its fur was short and spotted, strangely colored, almost blue in some areas.

—Blue dog! Deng said and the dog came to him, licking his face and then plunging its nose between Deng's legs. —Blue dog! The blue dog likes us, Achak. Look at the blue dog and its strange spots.

Deng scratched the dog, which truly did seem to be colored blue, behind its ears and soon blue dog was on its back and Deng was rubbing its tummy with great intensity. The dog's legs jerked this way and that. It was strange to be stopped, resting in a village I had never seen, petting a happy blue dog.

A group of older boys approached us. The largest of them immediately chased the dog off and stood over Deng and me, so close that I had to look straight up to see the underside of his wide face. He was wearing brilliant white shoes. They looked like clouds, as if they had never touched the earth.

—Where are you going? he demanded.

—Bilpam, I said.

—Bilpam? What's Bilpam?

I realized I did not know. —It's a big town many days away, I guessed. I had no idea what size it was or how long we would be walking but I wanted our walk to seem definite and important.

—Why? the boy with the cloud shoes demanded.

—Our villages were burned, Deng said.

I did not want to tell this boy about what had happened to Marial Bai. Seeing this village, unaffected by any fighting, I was ashamed anew that we had not fought better against the Arabs, that we had allowed our homes to be burned while this village was unharmed. It was not the end of the world at all. Perhaps, I thought, the Arabs had ravaged only the towns where the men were the weakest.

—Burned? By who? the boy asked. He was skeptical.

—The Baggara, Deng answered.

—The *Baggara?* Why didn't you fight them?

—They had new guns, Deng said. —Fast guns. They could kill ten men in seconds. The boy laughed.

—You can't stay here, another boy said.

—We don't plan to, I said.

—Good. You should keep moving. You're just walking boys. You look like you have diseases. Do you have malaria?

At that point, I was finished with these boys. I didn't want to hear anything else from them. I turned my back to them. Quickly I felt a kick to my back. It was the boy with the cloud-white shoes.

—We don't like beggars here. You hear that? Don't you have a family?

I did not react but Deng now was on his feet. His head reached the cloud-shoe boy's chest. Next to this well-fed older boy, Deng looked like an insect.

—Boys!

It was Dut, booming his voice over us. The boys who were harassing us dispersed and Dut emerged from the market with a large older man dressed in a blood-colored robe. The new man carried a staff and walked with a brisk, contented sort of pace. At the edge of the circle of boys, he stopped, startled. He sighed a long confused sigh.

—I told you we were many, Dut said.

—I know. I know. So this is what's happening? Boys walking to Bilpam?

—This is our hope, uncle.

The chief sighed again and surveyed our group, smiling and shaking his head. After a short while the chief took his staff with both hands and tapped it determinedly into the ground and walked back into the village.

—This is good, boys. The chief has agreed to feed us. Please sit where you are, and don't ask for anything from these people. The chief has some women preparing some manioc for us.

Indeed, very quickly there was a great deal of activity in the huts near our group. Women and girls began to busily prepare food and when they were done, we were given food, portions dropped in our hands; there were not enough plates for the dozens of boys and Dut had insisted it was unnecessary. After we had eaten and the chief had given Dut two bags of nuts and two jerry cans of water, we were back on the trail, for we were not permitted to stay.

I had felt weak and heavy-legged that day, but now I was fortified, and I found myself in a good enough state of mind. I wanted to see what would happen next. Though I worried about my family, I told myself that if I was safe, they were safe, and until we were reunited, I would be on a kind of adventure. There were things I wondered about seeing. I had heard of rivers so wide that birds could not fly across; the birds would drop midway and be subsumed by the limitless water. I had heard of land that rose so high that it was as if the earth was tilted on its side; land that was shaped like the contours of a sleeping person. I wanted to see these things and then to return to my parents, to tell them about my journey. It was when I imagined doing so that the strings inside me felt taut again, and I had to breathe heavily to loosen them.

We walked through the twilight and passed women and men along the path, but when the night fell on them we were alone and the path was erased.

—Walk straight, Dut said. —The path is very new.

I had walked in the dark many times before. I could walk under a moon or in the blackest night. But so far from home, without a path, the strain was extreme. I had to lock my eyes to the back of the boy in front of me, and to maintain my pace. Slowing down for even a few moments would mean losing the group. It happened through the night: a boy would fall off the pace, or would step out of line to urinate, and then would have to call out to find the line again. Those who did this were scorned and sometimes punched or kicked. Making noise could bring attention to the group and this was undesirable when the night had been retaken by the animals.

Deng walked behind me, insisting on holding my shirt. This was a practice favored this night and on later nights by the youngest boys—holding the shirt of the boy ahead. Deng and I were certainly among the smallest of the walking boys. The most accommodating boys would remove an arm from its sleeve and allow those behind them to use the sleeve as a leash. Many boys did this with their younger brothers. There were many pairs of brothers in the group, and in the morning, when roll was called, when I heard their names called I felt such envy. I knew nothing about my brothers now: whether they were alive or dead or at the bottom of a well.

That night we stopped in a clearing and boys were sent to the forest to find wood. But the boys Dut chose did not want to go. The forest was wild with noises, squeals and shifting grasses.

—I won't go, one strong-looking boy said.

—What? Dut barked.

It was clear that he was tired and hungry himself and had little patience.

—You don't want a fire? Dut asked.

—No, the boy said.

—No?

—No. I don't care about any damned fire.

This was the first time Dut hit a boy. He struck him across the face with the back of his fist and the boy fell to the ground whimpering.

—You, you, you! Dut stammered. He seemed as shocked as the boy that he had knocked him down. But he did not retreat. —Now go. Go!

Dut quickly chose three more boys, the fire was built, and when it was strong we sat around it. Quickly most of us fell asleep but Deng and I stayed up, staring at the flames.

—I didn't want to hit that boy, Dut said.

Deng and I realized he was talking to us. We were the only boys still awake. We said nothing, for I could not think of anything proper to say to such a statement. Instead I asked Dut about what the old man had said—that the horsemen had fallen to the level of the animals. No one had yet explained to me why it was that Marial Bai had been attacked in the first place. I told Dut about what the man had said, that the Baggara had dropped to the level of an animal, had been possessed by spirits and were now lion-men.

Dut stared at me, blinking with a hard smile.

—He really said this?

I nodded.

—And you believed this?

I shrugged.

—Achak, he said, and then stared at the fire for a long moment. —I mean no disrespect to this man. But these are not lion-men. They're ordinary Arabs. I'll tell you boys the story of how this happened, though you won't understand all of it. Do you want to hear this?

Deng and I nodded.

—I'm a teacher so this is how I think. I see you sitting like this listening and I want to tell you about this. You're sure you want to hear?

Deng and I insisted we did.

—Okay then. Where should I start? Okay. There is a man named Suwar al-Dahab. He is the minister of defense for the government in Khartoum.

Deng interrupted. —What is Khartoum?

Dut sighed. —Really? You don't know this? That's where the government is, Deng. The central government of the country. Of all of Sudan. You don't know this?

Deng persisted. —But the chief is the head of the country.

—He's the head of your *village,* Deng. Now I'm not sure you'll understand this.

I urged him to try, and so Dut spent some time explaining the structure of the government, of tribes and chiefs and the former parliament, and of the Arabs who ruled Khartoum.

—You boys know about Anyanya, yes? Snake Poison. They're the rebel group that came before the SPLA. Your fathers were probably members of this group. All of your fathers were.

Deng and I nodded. I knew that my father had been an officer in the Anyanya.

—Well, now we have the SPLA. Some of the goals are the same. Some are new. You remember the first attacks of the helicopters?

We said we did.

—Well, the helicopters were the governments. They came in response to the actions of a man named Kerubino Bol. He was in the Sudanese Army. Remember when the army was made of Dinka soldiers and Arabs, too? Achak, you remember this, I know. There were many deployed in Marial Bai.

I said I did remember.

—Kerubino was a major in charge of the 105th Battalion, stationed at a large town called Bor. Bor is in the south of Sudan, the region called the Upper Nile. The people there are like you, but different. We're all Dinka, but their customs vary. Many clans scar themselves when they reach manhood. You probably have heard of this. There's another town where all the men smoke pipes. We all have different customs but we are all Dinka. You see this? This is a vast land, boys, bigger than you could ever imagine, and then twice as big as that.

Deng and I nodded.

—Good. Now, Kerubino and his men had been there in Bor for some time, and they were content there. Giving power like this to a southern Sudanese was part of the peace agreement with the Anyanya. In Bor, Kerubino and his men were among their people, most had moved their families to the town and they were happy there. They didn't have to work too hard. You have seen these soldiers. They don't like to move much. Then one day, rumors came down that they would be transferred to the north, and this didn't sit well with them, to be stationed so far from their families. This was made worse by the fact that Khartoum wasn't paying them what they'd been promised. So things got worse, and finally loyalists to Khartoum, knowing that Kerubino was planning a mutiny, attacked the 105th Battalion. Kerubino Bol took the whole battalion and fled to Ethiopia. This is where we're going, boys. Bilpam is in Ethiopia. Did you know this?

We stopped the story there. Deng and I had not heard the word *Ethiopia* before. We didn't know what an Ethiopia was.

—It's a country like Sudan is a country, Dut said.

—If it's like us, why is it somewhere else? Deng asked.

Dut was a patient man.

—In Ethiopia, he continued, —Kerubino was joined by a man named John Garang, a colonel in the Sudanese army. He had fled, too. And then the 104th Battalion, stationed in Ayod, also fled to Ethiopia. By this time it was a movement. There were hundreds of well-trained soldiers there, mostly Dinka, and this was the new rebel army. This was the SPLA. And so began this stage of the civil war. Do you understand these things so far?

We nodded.

—When John Garang began the rebel movement, General Dahab was very angry, as was the entire government in Khartoum. So they wanted to crush the rebels. But the rebels were many. They were armed well and they had something to fight for. For this reason, they were very dangerous. And Ethiopia was helping them, which made them even more of a threat.

—So the rebels have guns? I asked.

—Guns! Of course. We have guns and artillery and rocket launchers, Achak.

Deng laughed a giddy laugh and I smiled and felt proud. I convinced myself that the men who had beaten my father were different than these rebels. Or perhaps the rebels had learned better manners.

—The government was very angry about this new rebel presence, Dut continued, —so this is when the helicopters came. The government burned the villages to punish them for supporting the rebels. It's very easy to kill a town, yes? Harder to kill an army. So as men left to train in Ethiopia, the SPLA continued to grow and they even won battles. They occupied land. Things were looking bad for the government. They had a problem. So they needed more soldiers, more guns. But raising an army is expensive. A government needs to pay an army, to feed an army, provide the army with weapons. So General Dahab used a strategy familiar to many governments before his: he armed others to do the work of the army. In this case, he provided tens of thousands of Arab men, the Baggara among them, with automatic weapons. Many were from across the Bahr al-Ghazal. Many thousands from Darfur. You saw these men with their guns. These guns shoot a hundred bullets in the time it would take to shoot a rifle twice. We can't defend ourselves against these guns.

—Why didn't the government have to pay these men? I asked.

—Well, that's a good question. These Baggara had long fought with the Dinka over grazing pastures and other matters. You probably know this. For many years there had been relative peace between the southern tribes and the Arab tribes, but it was General Dahab's idea to break this peace, to inspire hatred in the Baggara. When he gave them these weapons, the Baggara knew they had a great advantage over the Dinka. They had AK-47s and we had spears, clubs, leather shields. This upset the balance we've lived with for many years. But how would the government pay all these men? It was simple. They told the horsemen that in exchange for their services, they were authorized to plunder all they wanted along the way. General Dahab told them to visit upon any Dinka villages along the rail lines, and to take what they wished—livestock, food, anything from the markets, and even people. This was the beginning of the resurgence of slavery. This was in 1983.

We had no concept of years.

—Just a few seasons ago, Dut said. —You remember when this began?

We nodded.

—They would descend upon a village, and surround it at night. When the village would wake, they would ride in from all sides, killing and looting as they wished. All cattle would be taken, and any animals not stolen would be shot. Any resistance would bring reprisals. Men would be killed on sight. Women would be raped, the homes burned, the wells poisoned, and children would be abducted. You have seen all this I trust.

We had.

—It's worked very well for the Baggara, because their own farms were suffering from drought. They had lost cattle and their harvests were poor. So they steal our cattle and they sell them in Darfur, and then they're sold again in Khartoum. The profits are tremendous. The supply of cattle in the north has increased dramatically, such that there's a surplus, and the price of beef has declined. These were all Dinka cattle, our dowries and our legacies, the measure of our men. Stealing animals and food from these villages solved a great portion of the Baggara's problems, as did the enslaving of our people. Do you know why, boys?

We did not know.

—While they're away stealing our animals, who's looking after theirs? Aha. This is one reason they steal our women and boys. We watch their herds so they can continue to raid our villages. Can you imagine? It's an ugly thing. The Baggara aren't bad people by their nature, though. Most of them are like us, cattle people. *Baggara* is just the word in Arabic for cowherd, and we use it to talk about other herding peoples—the Rezeigat of Darfur, the Misseriya of Kordofan. They're all Muslims, Sunnis. You've known Muslims, yes?

I thought of Sadiq Aziz. I had not thought of Sadiq since I had seen him last.

—The mosque in our village was burned, I said.

—The militias were mostly young men who are used to accompanying the cattle as they move and graze. In their language, *murahaleen* means *traveler*—and this is what they were, men on horseback who knew the land and were used to carrying guns to protect themselves and their cattle against animal attacks. It wasn't until the war began that these murahaleen became more of a militia, more heavily armed and no longer watching cattle, but raiding.

—But why couldn't we get the guns, too? Deng asked.

—From who? The Arabs? From Khartoum?

Deng bowed his head.

—We do have some guns now, Deng, yes. But it wasn't easy. And it took quite a long time. We have the guns that the 104th and 105th left Sudan with, and we have what the Ethiopians have given us.

Dut stoked the fire and put some nuts in his mouth.

—But the men in Marial Bai had uniforms, too, Deng asked. —Who were they?

—Government army. Khartoum is getting lazy. They now send the army with the murahaleen. They don't care. Everyone goes now. Anyone. The strategy is to send all they can to destroy the Dinka. Have you heard the expression, *Drain a pond to catch a fish?* They are draining the pond in which the rebels might be born or supported. They are ruining Dinkaland so that no rebels can ever again rise from this region. And when the murahaleen raid, they displace the people, and when the people are gone, when Dinka like us are gone, they move into the land we've vacated. They win on many levels. They have our cattle. They have our land. They have our people to mind the cattle they have stolen from us. And our world is upended. We wander the country, we're away from our livelihoods, our farms and homes and hospitals. Khartoum wants to ruin Dinkaland, to make it uninhabitable. Then we'll need them to restore order, we'll need them for everything.

—So that is the What, I said.

Dut looked long at me, and then stoked the fire again.

—Perhaps, Achak. Maybe it is. I don't know. I don't know what the What is.

We were nodding off, precisely where we sat.

—Put you to sleep, I see, Dut said. —As a teacher, I'm accustomed to this.

When we woke, our group had grown. There had been just over thirty boys the night before, and now there were forty-four. By the time we had walked through the day and settled again that night, there were sixty-one. The next week brought more boys, until the group was almost two hundred. Boys came from towns we passed and they came from the brush at night, out of breath from running. They came as groups merging with our group and they came alone. And each time our ranks grew, Dut would unfold his piece of river-green paper, write the new boys' names on it, and fold it again and slide it into his pocket. He knew the names of every boy.

I became accustomed to the walking, to the aches in my legs and in the joints of my knees, to the pains in my abdomen and kidneys, to picking thorns out of my feet. In those early days it was not so difficult to find food. Each day we would pass through a village, and they would be able to provide us with enough nuts and seeds and grain to sustain us. But this became more trying as our group grew. And it grew, Michael! We absorbed boys, and occasionally girls, every day we walked. In many cases, while we were eating in a given village, there began negotiations between Dut and the elders of the town, and by the time we had eaten and were on our way, the boys of that village were part of our group. Some of these boys and girls still had parents, and in many cases it was the parents themselves who were sending their children with us. We were not, at the time, fully aware of why this would be, why parents would willingly send their children on a barefoot journey into the unknown, but these things happened, and it is a fact that those who were volunteered by their families for the journey were usually better equipped than those of us who joined the march for lack of other options. These boys and girls were sent with extra clothing, and bags of provisions, and, in some cases, shoes and even socks. But soon enough these inequities were no more. It took only a few days before any member was as bereft as the rest of us. After they had traded their clothes for food, for a mosquito net, for whatever luxuries they could afford, they were sorry. Sorry that they did not know where we were walking, sorry that they had joined this procession in the first place. None of us had ever walked so long in one day but we continued to walk, every day walking farther, none of us knowing that we would never return.

XI.

There are keys in the door. Michael, I am afraid you are in trouble now, because Achor Achor is home and there will be a reckoning for all this. If only I could see this scene through his eyes! He will handle you and your cohorts without much mercy.

The lock is relieved and the door opens. I see the hulking figure of Tonya.

"Look who's awake!" she says, staring down at me. "Michael!" she barks. She has changed her clothes, into a black satin suit. Michael bursts from my room. He begins to apologize but she stops him short. "Get your ass ready," she snaps, "we got the mini-van." Michael goes to the bathroom and returns with his sneakers, which he begins to tie. I cannot fathom why he left his shoes in the bathroom in the first place.

Now there is another man, not Powder, in my kitchen. He is smaller than Powder, with long loose fingers, and he is sizing up the television set, staring at it as if guessing its weight. He unplugs the cable and sets the cable box on the counter. Gathering the electrical cord in one long-fingered hand, he squats before the TV and tilts it against his chest. He is out the door in seconds.

Tonya walks past me, smelling strongly of a strawberry perfume, and goes to my bedroom again. She is looking through my drawers once more, as if she lives here and has forgotten something. My stomach tightens again as I imagine her, too, finding my pictures of Tabitha. The thought of her handling those photographs makes me instantly nauseous.

Michael is near the door, with his shoes on and his Fanta in his hand. He will not look at me. I spend a long moment with my mouth open, ready to say something, but finally decide against it. I could ask to be untied, but that would only remind them that leaving a witness might be more dangerous than disposing of one.

Tonya appears again and in seconds is with the new man at the door. She scans the room one more time, without looking at me. She pushes Michael out the door; he does not look back to me. Now satisfied, Tonya closes the door. They are gone.

The finality and suddenness of their departure is startling. This time, they were in my apartment no more than two minutes, though her scent lingers.

I am alone again. I detest this city of Atlanta. I cannot remember a time when I felt otherwise. I need to leave this place.

What time is it? I realize it might be a full day before I see Achor Achor again. If I'm lucky, he'll come home before he goes to work. But he has been gone for days before, at Michelle's; he keeps a toothbrush and an extra suit there. He will not be back tonight and will likely go directly from her house to work. If so, I will be here, on the floor, until, at the earliest, six-thirty p.m. tomorrow. No, eight-thirty—he has class after work tomorrow.

I try to yell, thinking that though my voice might be muffled, it might yet be loud enough to attract a neighbor. I try, but the sound is pitiful, dull, a quiet groan.

Soon I will be able to moisten the tape enough that my lips will be free, but with the tape wrapped around my head, it will be difficult for my tongue to maneuver it low enough. I must make myself heard, I must alert a neighbor, bring someone to my door. The police need to be called, the burglars apprehended. I need water, food. I need a change of clothes. This ordeal needs to end.

But it is not ending. I am on the floor, and it could be twenty-four hours or more before Achor Achor returns. He has been gone three days at a stretch. But never without a call. He will call and when I don't answer and don't call back, he will realize something is wrong. And until then there are other options. There are people in this building and I will make myself known.

I can kick the floor. I can raise my feet enough that the kick, even through the wall-to-wall carpet, might be audible below. The neighbors below, to whom I have spoken only once, are decent people, three of them, two women and a man, all white, all over sixty. They are not prosperous, living three to an apartment precisely the size of this one I share with Achor Achor. One of the women, very sturdy and with a tight helmet of silver hair, has a job that requires a security-guard uniform. I am not sure whether or where the other two work.

I know they are Christians, evangelicals. They have placed literature under my door, and I know they have discussed their faith with Edgardo. Like me, Edgardo is a Catholic, but still these neighbors have tried to move us toward their sort of rebirth. Their proselytizing has not offended me. When Ron, the older man who stays at home, approached me once as I was leaving for class, he first wanted to talk about slavery. An earnest-looking man with the face of an overfed infant, he had read something about the persistence of slavery in Sudan; his church was sending money to an evangelical group that was planning to travel to Sudan to buy back slaves. "A few dozen," he said.

This is a fairly booming business, or was a few years ago. Once the evangelical circles became aware of the slavery-abduction practices in the region, it became their passion. The issue is complex, but like many matters in Sudan, it is not as complex as Khartoum would want the West to believe. The murahaleen began abducting again in 1983, once they were armed and could act with impunity.

Christian neighbors below, where are you tonight? Are you home? Would you hear me if I called? Would it be enough to simply bang the floor? Will you hear me kicking? I lift my legs, still tied tightly together, from the knee down, and strike the carpeted floor with as much force as I can muster. The sound is undramatic, a muted thump. I try again, harder now. I kick for a full minute and am winded. I wait for some reaction, perhaps a broomstick banging back in response. Nothing.

Christian neighbors, because it interests you, I will tell you about the slave raids, the slave trade. The slave trade began thousands of years ago; it's older than our faith. You know this, or might have assumed it. The Arabs used to raid southern Sudanese villages, often with the help of rival southern tribes. This is not news to you; it follows the pattern of much of the slave-raiding in Africa. Slavery was officially abolished by the British in 1898, but the practice of slavery continued, even if it was far less prevalent.

When the war began and the murahaleen were armed, the stolen people—for this is what my father called them, *stolen people*—were taken to the north, and traded among Arabs. Much of what you have heard, Christian neighbors, is true enough. Girls were made to work in Arab homes, and later became concubines, bearing the children of their keepers. Boys tended livestock and were often raped, too. This, I have to tell you, is one of the gravest offenses of the Arabs. Homosexuality is not part of Dinka culture, not even in a covert way; there simply are no practicing homosexuals at all, and thus sodomy, particularly the forced sodomy upon innocent boys, has fueled the war as much as any other crime committed by the murahaleen. I say this with all due deference to the homosexuals of this country or any other. It is simply a fact that the thought of boys being sodomized by Arabs is enough to drive a Sudanese soldier to acts of incredible bravery.

It must be said that in this war, almost all of us Dinka have grown to vilify all the Arabs of Sudan, that we have forgotten the friends we have known from the north, the interdependent and peaceful lives we once lived with them. This war has made racists of too many of them and too many of us, and it is the leadership in Khartoum that has stoked this fire, that has brought to the surface, and in some cases created from whole cloth, new hatreds that have bred unprecedented acts of brutality.

The strangest thing is that the so-called Arabs are not so different in any way, particularly in appearance, from the peoples of the south. Have you seen the president of Sudan, Omar el-Bashir? His skin is almost as dark as mine. But he and his Islamicist predecessors look down on the Dinka and Nuer, they want to convert us all, and leaders in Khartoum have in the past attempted to make Sudan the world center of Islamic fundamentalism. All the while, there are plenty among the Arab peoples of the Middle East who do have their own prejudices against dark-skinned Bashir and his proud Sudanese Muslim friends. There are many from within and without Sudan who don't consider them Arabs at all.

But still, the black-skinned Arabs of northern Sudan advocated the enslaving of the Dinka of southern Sudan, and what is Khartoum's defense, Christian neighbors? First they say all of this belongs in the realm of centuries-old "tribal disagreements." When pressed further, they claim that these are not abductions, but are consensual work arrangements. Was that nine-year-old girl abducted on the back of a camel and brought four hundred miles north, forced to work as a servant in the home of an army lieutenant—was she a slave? No, Khartoum says. The girl, they say, is there by choice. Her family, facing hard times, made an arrangement with the lieutenant, whereby he would employ her, feed her and give her a better life, until such time as her biological family could support her once more. Again, the brazenness of the leaders in Khartoum is breathtaking: to deny that slavery existed for the last twenty years, insisting that the people of southern Sudan chose to be the unpaid and beaten and raped servants in Arab households. All this while the Arabic word too many Arabs use for the southern Sudanese means slave.

It is almost comical. This is what they claim, I tell you! And they have convinced others, too. Tribal skirmishes and cultural practices particular to the region, they say. An American diplomat sent to Sudan to investigate the prevalence of slavery returned with this sentiment. They fooled him, and he should have known he was fooled. I have seen the slaves myself. I have seen them abducted—they took the twins, Ahok and Awach Ugieth during the second raid—and friends of mine have seen them. Now, when villages try to repatriate former slaves, children and women, there are problems. Some women were taken when they were so young, six and seven years old, that they remember nothing about their homes. They are now eighteen, nineteen years old, and because they were so young when they were abducted, they speak no Dinka, only Arabic, and are familiar with none of our customs. And they have, many of them, left children in the north. A good deal of them have had children by their captors, and when the women are discovered by abolitionists and then freed, these children have to be left behind. It is a very difficult life for these women, even when they have returned home.

It is criminal that all of this has happened, has been allowed to happen.

In a furious burst, I kick and kick again, flailing my body like a fish run aground. Hear me, Christian neighbors! Hear your brother just above!

Nothing again. No one is listening. No one is waiting to hear the kicking of a man above. It is unexpected. You have no ears for someone like me.

XII.

One afternoon in the first hopeful weeks of walking, we reached a village called Gok Arol Kachuol. On the outskirts, the women gathered along the path to watch our group, now over two hundred and fifty boys.

—Look how sick they are, the women said as they watched us pass.

—Their heads are so big! Like eggs sitting on top of twigs!

The women laughed theatrically, covering their mouths.

—I have it, said another, an older woman, as old and twisted as an acacia. —They're like spoons. They look like spoons walking!

And the women tittered and continued to point at us as we passed, picking out boys who looked particularly peculiar or hopeless.

As soon as the first of our group entered the village, we knew we were not welcome. —No rebels here, the chief said, walking quickly out to the path. —No, no, no! Walk on. Keep going. Go!

The chief, with a pipe in his mouth, was blocking access to the village with his arms, waving his hands as if the wind he generated would blow us to some other place.

Dut stepped forward and spoke with a firmness I had not heard before.

—We need to rest and we'll rest here. Otherwise you *will* hear from the rebels.

—But we have nothing to give you, the chief insisted. —We were raided by the rebels just two days ago. You can sit here and rest, but we can't feed you.

His eyes swept over the line of us, still pouring into the town from the path, boys upon boys appearing from the forest and filling the village. He switched his pipe from one side of his mouth to the other.

—No one could feed so many, the chief said.

Dut was unfazed. —I want you to know the implications of what you're saying.

The chief paused and produced a loud, resigned snort. A second snort was more conciliatory. Dut turned to us.

—Sit here. Don't move until I get back.

Dut followed the chief into his compound. We rested on the grass, hungry and thirsty and angry at this village. The meeting of Dut and the chief lasted far longer than it should have, and the sun rose high over us, examining and punishing us. None of us had shade, and we were afraid to leave. But soon we could not sit still. Some of the boys moved a few hundred yards to sit under a tree. Other boys, older boys, took it upon themselves to retrieve some food on their own. We watched as they crawled into a nearby home and found a calabash of nuts, with which they fled.

The scene that followed was chaos. First the screaming of women. Then a dozen men giving chase. When they could not catch the three thieves, they came after the rest of us, spears in hand. We ran, all two hundred and fifty of us, in every direction, finally settling on a path out of the village, the same way we had entered. We ran for an hour, as the men chased us and caught some of the slower boys and punished them as we retraced most of the path that we had spent all day walking. This is why our walk took longer than it might have: it was not a straight route, it was anything but.

When we stopped running, Kur gathered and counted us. There were six missing. —Where is Dut? he asked.

We had no idea. Kur was the oldest boy there, so everyone looked to him for answers. He didn't know where Dut was and this was troubling.

—We'll stay here until Dut comes back, he said.

Five boys were injured. One had been stuck in the shoulder with a spear. This boy was carried by Kur to a place under a tree, where he was given water. Kur did not know how to help the boy. The only place where he could be helped was the village that had done this to him. We had nothing and no one with us to help anyone with any injury whatsoever.

Three boys were sent with the most injured boy back to the village for treatment. I am not sure what happened to these boys, for we never saw them again. I like to believe that they were taken in by the villagers who felt regretful for what they had done to us.

These were bad days. Dut did not rejoin us for a full day, leaving Kur in charge. This was not in itself a disadvantage; Kur's sense of direction seemed more assured than Dut's, his uncertainty about the journey less overt than Dut's. But Dut was our leader, even though he often brought bad luck with him. Shortly after he returned, a lion leapt across our path in the dark and took two boys, devouring them in the high grass. We did not pause for long to listen.

When we passed other travelers, they warned us of murahaleen in the area. Always we were ready to run; every boy had a plan if the militias came. Every new landscape we encountered we first had to examine for places to hide, paths to follow. We knew that these rumors of their nearness were correct because Deng was wearing one of their headdresses.

We had been walking one day, our limbs leaden but our eyes alert, when he saw it in a tree. A piece of white material, stuck in the branches, flapping in the wind. I lifted Deng up enough so that he could retrieve it, and Kur confirmed that it had been worn by a Baggara; we could not guess at how it had ended up in a tree.

—Can I wear it? Deng asked Kur.

—You want to wear it like an Arab wears it?

—No. I'll wear it differently.

And he did. He arranged it loosely atop his head, looking absurd but claiming that it kept him cool. The effort he had to expend to keep it out of his eyes and from falling to the ground surely negated any immediate benefits, but I said nothing. I knew a piece of sturdy cloth like that might come in handy at some point.

But it was soon over and I was home. I was home and was helping my mother with the fire. My brothers were playing just beyond the compound, and my father was sitting on his chair, outside, with a cup of wine resting at his feet. Far off in the village, I could hear singing—the choir practicing that same hymn they sang four hundred times a day. Chickens chirped and roosters wailed, dogs howled and tried to eat through baskets to get at the humans' food. A round bright moon hung over Marial Bai, and I knew the young men of the village would be out, making trouble. Nights like this were long nights, when the activity all around would make sleeping difficult, so I rarely made any effort to sleep. I lay awake, listening, imagining what everyone was doing, what each sound meant. I guessed at voices, at the distance between myself and each sound. For my mother's benefit I kept my eyes closed most of the night, but at least a few times on these nights, I had opened my eyes to find my mother's open, too. On these occasions, we had shared a sleepy smile. And it was this way tonight, when I found myself again warm in my mother's home, close to her yellow dress, the heat of her body. It was good to be home, and when I had told my family of my adventures, they were greatly intrigued and impressed.

—Look at him, a voice said. —Dreaming of his mother, the voice said. It sounded like Deng. I had told him about my family; I had told him so much.

I opened my eyes. Deng was there but we were not inside my mother's home. In an instant everything warm inside me went cold. I was outside, sleeping in the circle of the boys, and the air was sharper than at any other night of our walking.

I did not move. Deng was above me, behind him not the warm crimsons and ochres of my mother's home, but only the burnt black of the moonless sky. I closed my eyes, wishing, stupidly I knew, that I could will myself back into the dream. How strange that a dream could make you warm when your body knew exactly how cold it was. How strange it was to be sleeping there with all of these boys, in this interlocking circle, under a lightless sky. I wanted to punish Deng for not being my mother and brothers. But without him I could not live. To see his face each day—that was the only tether I had.

In the group there were many boys who became strange. One boy would not sleep, at night or during the day. He refused to sleep for many days, because he wanted always to see what was coming, to see any threats that might befall us. Eventually he was left in a village, in the care of a woman who held him in her lap, and within minutes he was asleep. There was another boy who dragged a stick behind him, making a line in the dirt so he would know his way home. He did this for two days until one of the older boys took his stick and broke it over his head. Another boy thought the walking was a game and jumped and ran and teased the other boys. He played tag with them and found no one willing to play along. He stopped playing when he was kicked hard in the back by a boy who was tired of watching him prance about. A boy named Ajiing was stranger: he saved all the food given to him. He saved the food—groundnut paste, mostly—in a shirt he had brought with him. He would only dip into the shirt once a day, to retrieve enough of the gummy mixture to cover his first three fingers. He would lick these clean and then tie his shirt back again. He was preparing for many weeks without food. But most of the boys only walked and spoke little because there was nothing to say.

—The blue dog!

Four days after we were driven out of the village by the men and their spears, we came upon the blue dog again. Deng saw him first.

—Is it really the same one? I asked.

—Of course it is, Deng said, kneeling down to pet him.

The animal was far fatter than when we last saw her. We could not understand how the dog could have made it so far from its home. Had it been following us these days, staying out of sight but keeping pace with us? Ahead of us we heard commotion, the voices of boys. We went to the voices and the blue dog followed us reluctantly.

The blue dog, it turned out, was not far from its home. I saw that the trees in this place were familiar. Soon we realized that it was the happy village. We had been walking in a circle; we had retraced our steps for many days and now we were again at the bustling village we had seen not long ago, the village where the boys had taunted us with their new white shoes and where the women fed us and sent us on our way. They had denied the threat of the murahaleen but now they were gone. Where the village had been, there was nothing. The homes had been lifted into the sky. There were only black rings where the structures had stood. The thoroughness of the erasure was complete.

And then I saw the bodies. Arms and heads in bushes, in the remains of huts. And far off, the blue dog was chewing on something. We then knew how she had grown so plump.

Out of the tall grass a woman ran to our group. She was carrying a baby in a sling around her torso. As she got closer, the baby became two babies, twins, and the woman began to wail and scream uncontrollably. Her hand was wrapped in pink cloth, soaked through with blood. Now our boys were everywhere in the village, inspecting the damage and touching things I would never touch.

—Get back here! Dut yelled.

But he could not control the boys and their curiosity. Not all of them had seen the murahaleen or their work firsthand. They spread out, some of them also finding and eating abandoned food, and as they plunged into the village, survivors began to emerge from hiding: women, old men, children, more boys. The woman with the two babies in the sling could not stop wailing, and Kur sat her down and tried to calm her. I sat and turned myself from the woman and from the women that came after her. I put my fingers in my ears. I knew it all already and I was tired.

We spent the night there. There was still food in the village, and it was decided that it was the safest place we could be, the site of a recent attack. As we rested, many more came from the forest and grass. They talked to Dut and shared information, and in the morning we left the village with eighteen new boys. They were very quiet boys, and none wore cloud-white shoes.

—My stomach hurts, Deng said. —Achak.

—Yes.

—Does your stomach hurt like this? Like something is inside, moving around? Do you have this?

It was many days later and I had no patience for this. Everyone's stomach hurt; the stomachs of us all were growing hard and round and we were accustomed to the pains of hunger. I said something to this effect, hoping it would assuage Deng's fears and quiet him.

—But this is a new pain, Deng said. —It feels lower than before. Like someone's pinching me, stabbing me.

I had difficulty mustering sympathy for Deng when I was so hungry myself. My own hunger would ebb and flow and when it came to me I felt it everywhere. I felt it in my stomach and chest and arms and thighs.

—I miss my mother, Deng said.

—I want my home, he said.

—I need to stop walking, he said.

I walked ahead in the line so I would not have to hear Deng's bleating. Most of us were stoic, accepting of the futility in complaining. Deng's behavior was an affront to the way we walked.

In the afternoon sky, a jagged blast. We stopped. Again the sound came; it was now clear that it was a gun. Again and again the blasts came, five times. Dut stopped the group and listened.

—Sit. Sit and wait, he said.

He ran ahead. When he came back he was grinning.

—They've killed an elephant. Come now! Everyone will eat meat today.

We began to run. No one knew all that Dut had said but they had heard the word meat. We ran after Dut and Kur Garang Kur.

I ran and the ground beneath my feet flew because I ran so fast, jumping over rocks and brush. We all ran, boys laughing. It had been weeks since we had eaten meat of any kind. I was happy but while running my head was conflicted. I was so hungry, my hunger splitting me everywhere, but in my clan the elephant was sacred. None of my people in Marial Bai would ever contemplate killing, much less eating, an elephant, but still I ran to the animal. No other boy seemed to hesitate; they ran like they were not sick, like they had not been walking so long. We were not dying boys at that moment, we were not those who were walking. We were hungry boys who were about to feast on fresh meat.

When we got close we saw a small grey mountain, and everywhere around the mountain were boys. There were hundreds of boys, ten deep around the elephant. One boy was tearing the elephant's ear. He had climbed onto the head of the beast and was ripping the elephant's ear from its skull. Another boy was standing against the elephant, with his hand and wrist missing, and his shoulder red with blood. A moment later the boy's hand had been restored, but was covered in blood. It had been inside the elephant; he had thrust it in where the bullet had created an opening. He had grabbed whatever meat he could and was eating it, raw, his face dripping with the animal's blood.

Near the elephant were two men wearing uniforms, carrying guns. As the boys tore into the animal, I watched the men.

—Who are they? I asked Kur.

—That's your army, he said. —That's the hope of the Dinka.

I watched as Dut and Kur and one of the soldiers helped to cut into the elephant's hide. They opened a long slice at the top of the elephant and then the boys, ten at a time, would peel the skin back, ripping it down, pulling it to the ground. Underneath, the elephant was as red as a burn. The boys leapt into the animal, biting and ripping flesh, and when each boy had a handful of meat, they ran off like hyenas to gnaw under trees.

Some boys began to eat immediately. Others did not know if they should wait to cook the meat. It was morning, and many boys were not sure how long they would stay here, with the elephant, and if they would be allowed to take meat with them.

The SPLA soldiers had started a large fire. Dut ordered five boys to gather wood in order to grow the flames. Kur started another fire on the other side of the elephant, and we who had not already eaten our meat roasted it on sticks.

The soldiers were pleased to see us eating and they talked to us in a friendly manner. I sat next to Deng, watching him eat. It felt so good to see Deng eating, though Deng ate without smiling, and did not enjoy the meat as the others did. His eyes were yellowed at the rims, his mouth cracked and spotted white. But he ate as much as he could. He ate until he could eat no more.

When the eating was done, we took full notice of the group of rebels sitting around a giant heglig tree. We gathered around the men and stared.

Dut quickly interfered.

—Give them room to breathe, boys! You're like mosquitoes.

We took a few steps back but then slowly closed in again. The men smiled, appreciating the attention.

—We had some trouble in Gok Arol Kachuol, Dut said.

—What sort of trouble? one of the rebels asked.

Dut brought one of the injured boys forward. His leg had been cut with a spear.

—Who did this? the rebel demanded.

The man was named Mawein, and he was suddenly standing, enraged. Dut explained what had happened, that we had walked peacefully to the village, had been refused food and then chased from the town by men throwing spears. He left out the part involving the theft of the nuts, and no boys thought it necessary to bring it up. We were filled with pride and anticipation, watching Mawein's anger grow.

—They did this to Red Army boys? Boys with no weapons?

Dut could taste the revenge and added to their sins. —They chased us for half a day. They wanted no rebels. They called us rebels and cursed the SPLA.

Mawein laughed. —This chief will see us soon. Was it the man with the pipe?

—Yes, Dut said. —Many of the men had pipes.

—We know this place. Tomorrow we'll visit this village and discuss with them the treatment of the Red Army boys.

—Thank you, Mawein, Dut said. He had adopted a tone of great reverence.

Mawein nodded to him.

—Now eat some more food, he said. —Eat while you can.

We ate while staring at the men. Each soldier had around him twenty boys who ate without taking their eyes from him. The men seemed huge, the biggest men we had seen in months. They were very healthy, their muscles carved and their faces confident. These were the men who could fight the murahaleen or the government army. The men embodied all of our rage and spoke to every hope we could conjure.

—Are you winning the war? I asked.

—Which war is that, jaysh al-ahmar?

I paused a moment. —What is that word you used?

—Jaysh al-ahmar.

—What does that mean?

—Dut, you don't teach these boys anything?

—These boys are not yet jaysh al-ahmar, Mawein. They're very young.

—Young? Look at some of these kids. They're ready to fight! These are soldiers! Look at those three.

He pointed to three of the older boys, still cooking meat over the fire.

—They're tall, yes, but very young. The same age as these here.

—We'll see about that, Dut.

—Are you winning the war, Mawein? Deng tried. —The war against the murahaleen?

Mawein looked to Dut and then back at Deng.

—Yes, boy. We are winning that war. But the war is against the government of Sudan. You know this, don't you?

As many times as Dut explained it to me, it still confused me. Our villages were being attacked by the murahaleen, but the rebels left the villages unattended to fight elsewhere, against the government army. It was baffling for me then, and was for many years to come.

—You want to hold it? Mawein said, indicating his gun.

I did want to hold it, very much.

—Sit down. It's very heavy for you.

I sat down and Mawein made some adjustments to the gun and then rested it on my lap. I worried that it might be very hot but when it rested on my bare legs it was very heavy but cool to the touch.

—Heavy, right? Try carrying that all day, jaysh al-ahmar.

—What does that mean, jaysh al-ahmar? I whispered. I knew that Dut didn't want us to know the answer to this question.

—That's you, boy. It means Red Army. You're the Red Army.

Mawein smiled and I smiled. At that moment, I liked the idea of being part of an army, of being worthy of a warrior's nickname. I ran my hands over the surface of the gun. It was a very strange shape, I thought. It looked like nothing I could think of, with its points everywhere, its arms going every direction. I had to look over it carefully to remember which side the bullets exited. I put my finger into the barrel.

—It's so small, the opening, I said.

—The bullets are not wide. But they don't need to be big. They're very sharp and fly fast enough to cut through steel. You want to see a bullet?

I said I did. I had seen casings, but had never held an unfired bullet.

Mawein sifted through a pocket on the front of his shirt and retrieved a small gold object, holding it in his palm. It was the size of my thumb, flat on one end and pointed on the other.

—Can I hold it? I asked.

—Of course. You're so polite! he marveled. —A soldier is never polite.

—Is it hot? I asked.

—Is the bullet hot? he laughed. —No. The gun makes it hot. Now it's cold.

Mawein dropped the bullet onto my palm and my heart sped up. I trusted Mawein but was not certain the bullet wouldn't go through my hand. Now it rested in my palm, lighter than I expected. It was not moving, was not cutting my skin. I held the bullet in my fingers and brought it close to my face. I smelled it first, to see if it had an odor of fire or death. It smelled only like metal.

—Let me smell it!

Deng grabbed at it and the bullet dropped to the ground.

—Careful, boys. These are valuable.

I slapped Deng's chest and found the bullet, brushed the dirt from its surface and polished it with my shirt. I handed it to Mawein, ashamed.

—Thank you, Mawein said, taking the bullet back and replacing it in the pocket of his shirt.

—How many bullets did it take to kill the elephant? Deng asked.

—Three, Mawein said.

—How many does it take to kill a man?

—What kind of man?

—An Arab, Deng said.

—Just one, Mawein said.

—How many Arabs can that gun kill? Deng asked.

—As many as there are bullets, Mawein said.

Deng had as many questions as Mawein would answer.

—How many bullets do you have?

—We have a lot of bullets, but we're trying to get more.

—Where do you get them?

—From Ethiopia.

—That's where we're going.

—I know. We're all going to Ethiopia.

—Who is?

—You, me, everyone. Every boy from southern Sudan. Thousands are going now. You're one group of many. Didn't Dut tell you this? Dut! he yelled over to Dut, who was attempting to pack some of the elephant meat. —Do you educate these boys or not? Do you tell them anything?

Dut looked worriedly at Mawein. Deng had more questions.

—Is it easier for the Arabs to kill a Dinka, or for a Dinka to kill an Arab?

—With the same bullet both men will die. The bullet doesn't care.

This was disappointing to both me and Deng but he pressed on.

—Why don't we have guns? Could we shoot this gun?

Mawein threw back his head and laughed.

—See, Dut? These boys are ready! They want to fight now.

We asked questions until we had eaten all we could of the elephant and until Mawein tired of us. The sun dropped and night came. The soldiers slept in an empty hut nearby while we slept in a circle, all of us resting soundly, feeling safe near the rebels, our heads wild with thoughts of vengeance.

I slept next to Deng, and I knew that in the days to come we would find more food like this. I imagined that we had entered a territory where there were many rebels who hunted. Wherever there were hunters there would be elephants dead, waiting to be eaten, and the elephants were perfect to eat: they were big enough to provide meat for hundreds of boys and the meat was fortifying. I didn't care anymore what my ancestors would think. We were the Red Army and needed to eat.

* * *

In the morning I rose quickly, feeling stronger than I had in many weeks. Deng was next to me and I let him sleep. I looked around the camp for the soldiers but saw none.

—They've already left, Dut said. —They've gone to visit the chief of Gok Arol Kachuol.

I laughed. —That'll be a nice visit!

—I'd like to be there, Dut said.

Action! It was satisfying just to think about. My imagination was afire with guns, the power of the gun, of setting things straight with the village of Gok Arol Kachuol. For the first time in weeks, I was hungry for adventure again. I wanted to walk. I wanted to see what would be ahead of us that day on the path. I pictured the other groups of boys like ours, all on their way to Ethiopia. I gained strength from the thought of the rebel soldiers, their guns and their willingness to fight for us. It was the first time I felt we had any strength at all, that the Dinka could fight, too.

The sun was my friend again, and I was ready to see things and make progress and be alive. I looked around at the other boys, waking up and gathering their things. Deng was still asleep, and I was so happy to see him sleeping comfortably, without complaining, that I did not wake him.

I walked to the hut where the soldiers had slept. They were gone, but I could see the shadows of other boys inside, searching for food, for anything. There was nothing. When we left the hut, we found that most of the boys were sitting in their groups, ready to walk. I took my place with my group, and then remembered Deng.

—Dut, I said. —I think Deng is still asleep.

But Deng was not where I had seen him last. Some of the boys near me were acting strangely. They were avoiding my eyes.

—Come here, Achak, Dut said, his arm around my shoulder.

We walked for a short while and then he stopped and pointed. Off in the distance, I could see Deng sleeping, but now in this different place, and with the Arab's white headdress on his face.

—He's not asleep, Achak.

Dut rested his hand on my head for a moment.

—Don't go to him, Achak. You don't want to get sick like he did.

Dut then turned and addressed a group of older boys.

—Go and gather leaves. Large leaves. We'll need lots of them if we want to cover him properly.

Three boys were chosen to carry Deng's body to the broadest and oldest tree in the area. They rested Deng's body under the tree and leaves were placed upon him to appease the spirit of the dead. Prayers were spoken by Dut and then we began to walk again. Deng was not buried and I did not see his body.

When Deng died I decided to stop talking. I spoke to no one. Deng was the first to die but soon boys died frequently and there was no time to bury the dead. Boys died of malaria, they starved, they died of infections. Each time a boy died, Dut and Kur did their best to honor the dead, but we had to keep walking. Dut would take out his roster from his pocket, make a notation of who had died and where, and we would continue walking. If a boy became sick he walked alone; the others were afraid to catch what he had, and did not want to know him too well for he would surely die soon. We did not want his voice in our heads.

As the number of dead boys rose to ten, to twelve, Dut and Kur grew scared. They had to carry boys every day. Every morning a new boy would be too weak to walk, and Dut would carry this boy all day, hoping that we would come upon a doctor or a village that could take the boy. Sometimes this happened, usually it did not. I stopped looking at where Dut buried or hid the dead, for I know he became less careful as the journey continued. Everyone was weak, far too weak to think clearly when we needed to react to dangers. We were nearly naked, having traded our clothes for food in villages along the way, and most of us were barefoot.

Why would we be of interest to a high-altitude bomber?

When I saw it, all of the boys saw it. Three hundred heads turned upward at once. The sound was not at first different from the sound of a supply plane, or one of the small aircraft that occasionally moved through the sky. But the sound rumbled deeper in my skin, and the plane was bigger than any I could remember seeing so high.

The plane passed once over us and disappeared, and we continued to walk. When helicopter gunships would come our way, we were told to hide in trees, in the brush, but with the Antonovs the only stated rule was to remove or hide anything that might reflect the sun. Mirrors, glass, anything that could catch the light, all were banned. But those items were long gone, and few boys, of course, had had anything like that in the first place. So we walked, not imagining that we would be made a target. We were hundreds of near-naked boys, all unarmed and most under twelve years old. Why would this plane take interest in us?

But the plane returned a few minutes later, and soon after, there was a whistle. Dut screamed to us that we needed to run but did not tell us where. We ran in a hundred different directions and two boys chose the wrong direction. They ran for the shelter of a large tree and this is where the bomb struck.

It was as if a fist punched through the earth, from the inside out. The explosion uprooted the tree and threw smoke and soil fifty feet into the air. The sky was filled with dirt and the day went black. I was thrown to the ground, and stayed there, my head ringing. I looked up. Boys were everywhere splayed on the dirt. The tree was gone and the hole in the earth was big enough to fit fifty of us. For a moment, the air was quiet. I watched, too dazed to move, as boys rose and approached the crater.

—Don't go near! Dut said. —They're not there anymore. Go! Go hide in the grass. Go! The boys still walked close to the crater and looked inside. They saw nothing. Nothing was left there; the two boys had been eliminated.

I did not consider the possibility that the bomber would return. But soon it did. The whine again pried through the clouds.

—Run from the town! Dut screamed. Run from the buildings!

No one moved.

—Get away from the buildings! he yelled.

The plane came into view. I ran away from the crater but some boys ran toward it. —Where are you hiding? I asked them and found them unable to speak; we were just bodies and eyes running. Boys ran every way.

Behind me I heard another whistle, this one quicker than the last, and another punch came from inside the earth and the day again went black. There was a moment of silence, of quiet calm, and then I was in the air. The ground spun upward around my right ear and struck the back of my head. I was on my back. A pain spread through my head like cold water. I could hear nothing. I lay for some time, my limbs feeling disconnected. Above me there was dust but in the center before me, a round window of blue. I stared through it and thought it was God. I felt helpless and at peace, because I could not move. I could not speak or hear or move, and this filled me with a strange serenity.

Voices woke me. Laughter. I rose to my knees but could not put my feet on the ground. I no longer trusted the earth. I vomited where I knelt and lay down again. The sky was growing light when I tried again. I first rose to my knees and my head spun. Pinpricks of white leaped before my eyes, my limbs tingled. I knelt for some time and regained my vision.

My head cleared. I looked about me. There were boys milling, some sitting, eating corn. I put my feet under my body and stood slowly. It felt very unnatural to stand. When I gained my full height, the air spun around me, hissing. I spread my legs wide and my hands left and right. I stood until the vibrations in my limbs ceased and after some time I was standing and felt human again.

Five boys had been killed, three immediately and two others, whose legs had been shredded by the bombs, were alive long enough to watch the blood leave their bodies and darken the earth.

When we walked again, few boys spoke. Among the living, many boys were lost that day; they had given up. One such boy was Monynhial, whose nose had been broken years ago in a fight with another boy. His eyes were close-set and he did not smile and rarely spoke. I had tried to talk to him, but Monynhial's words were brief and put a quick end to conversations. After the bombing, Monynhial's eyes were without light.

—I can't be hunted like this, he told me.

We were walking at dusk, through an area that was once populated but was now empty. The light that evening was beautiful, a swirl of pink and yellow and white.

—You aren't being hunted, I said. —We're all being hunted.

—Yes, and I can't be hunted like this. Every sound from the woods or the sky crushes me. I shake like a bird caught in someone's fist. I want to stop walking. I want to stay still, at least I'll know what sounds to expect. I want to stop all the sounds, and the chance that we'll be bombed or eaten.

—You're safer with us. Going to Ethiopia. You know this is true.

—We're the target, Achak. Look at us. Too many boys. Everyone wants us dead. God wants us dead. He's trying to kill us.

—Walk a few days longer. You'll feel better.

—I'm leaving the group when I find a village, Monynhial said.

—Don't say that, I said.

But soon he did. The next village we passed through, he stopped. Though the village was deserted, and though Dut told him the murahaleen would return to this village, Monynhial stopped walking.

—I'll see you some other time, he said.

In this village, Monynhial found a deep hole, created by an Antonov's bomb, and he stepped down into it. We said goodbye to him because we were accustomed to boys dying and leaving the group in many ways. Our group walked on while Monynhial stayed in the hole for three days, not moving, enjoying the silence inside the hole. He dug himself a cave in the side of the crater, and with thatch from a half-burned hut, he created a small door to cover the entrance, hiding himself from animals. No one visited Monynhial; no animal or person; no one knew he was there. When he became hungry the first day, he crawled out of his hole and through the village, to a hut where he took a bone from the ashes of a fire. Clinging to it were three bites of goat meat, which were black outside but which sated him that day. He drank from puddles and then crawled back to his hole, where he stayed all day and night. On the third day he decided to die in the hole, because it was warm there and there were no sounds inside. And he did die that day because he was ready. None of the boys who walked with me saw Monynhial perish in his hole but we all know this story to be true. It is very easy for a boy to die in Sudan.

XIII.

Lying here, on my floor, kicking for my Christian neighbors, I vacillate between calm and great agitation. I find myself at peace with the predicament, knowing that it will end when Achor Achor arrives, but once an hour I feel a rush of urgency, of blind fury, and I twist and thump and try to break free. Invariably these movements tighten my bindings and bring tears, stabs of pain to the heel of my skull.

But something comes of this latest burst of frustration. I realize that I can roll. I feel stupid for not realizing this sooner, but in a second I have turned myself around, perpendicular to the front door. I roll on my side, my chin scuffed by the carpet, five revolutions until I brush against the front door. I turn myself like a wheel and bend my knees. I take a breath, giddy with knowing that I have come upon the solution, and I kick the door with my bound feet.

Now, if I don't knock the door down, I will surely bring the attention of people outside. I kick and kick, and the door, heavy and lined with metal, rattles against the frame. The sound it makes is satisfyingly loud. I kick again and soon find myself in a rhythm. I am loud. I am, I am certain, being heard. I am kicking with a smile on my face, knowing that everyone outside is waking to the sound of someone in trouble. There is someone in Atlanta who is suffering, who has been beaten, who came to this city looking for nothing but an education and some semblance of stability, and he is now bound in his own apartment. But he is kicking and is loud.

Hear me, Atlanta! I am grinning and tears are flowing down my temples because

I know that soon someone, perhaps the Christian neighbors, perhaps Edgardo or a passing stranger, will come to this door and say Who is there? What is the matter? They will feel the guilt in knowing that they could have done something sooner had they only been listening.

I begin to count the kicks to the door. Twenty-five, forty-five. Ninety.

At one hundred and twenty-five, I take a break. I cannot believe that the clatter has not brought anyone to the door. My frustration is worse than the pain of the bindings, of being struck with the side of a gun. Where are these people? I know that people are hearing me. It is not possible that they are not hearing me. But they see it as beyond their business. Open the door and let me stand again! If I have my hands I can stand. If I have my hands I can free my mouth and tell you what happened here.

I kick again: One hundred and fifty. Two hundred.

This is impossible, that no one would come to this door. Is the noise of the world so cacophonous that mine cannot be heard? I ask only for one person! One person coming to my door will be enough.

For most of the Lost Boys in America, Mary Williams was one of the first people they knew, the conduit to all available assistance and enlightenment. Liquid-eyed and with a voice always close to breaking, Mary was the founder of the Lost Boys Foundation, a nonprofit organization designed to help the Lost Boys in Atlanta adjust to life here, to get into college, to find jobs. Achor Achor brought me to her after I had been in Atlanta for a week. We left the apartment in the rain and took the bus to her headquarters—two desks in a squat glass-and-chrome building in downtown Atlanta.

—Who is she? I asked him.

—She is a woman who likes us, he said. He explained that she was like an aid worker from one of the camps, though she was unpaid. She and her staff were volunteers. It seemed a strange concept to me, and I wondered what would drive her, or her associates, to do favors for us, for free. It was a question I asked often, and the other Sudanese often asked it, too: what is wrong with these people that they want to spend so much time helping us?

Mary was short-haired, soft-featured, with warm hands she put on either side of mine. We sat down and talked about the work of the foundation, about what I needed. She had heard that I was a public speaker, and asked if I would be willing to address local churches, colleges, and elementary schools. I said I would. All around her desk were small clay cattle, much like Moses had made when we were very young. The Sudanese men in Atlanta had been making them, and Mary would be auctioning them off to raise money for the foundation, which was operating with the support and office space of Mary's mother, a woman named Jane Fonda. I was told that Jane Fonda was a well-known actress, and because people would pay more money for objects with her signature upon them, Jane Fonda had signed some of the clay cows, too.

I remember getting a tour of the office after talking briefly with Mary that day about my needs and plans, and I remember being confused. I was shown a very large and elaborate display case that held hundreds of glimmering statues and medals awarded to Jane Fonda. While moving slowly down along the case, my eyes dry— I couldn't blink; I admit I like to look at trophies and certificates—I saw many pictures of a white woman who did not resemble Mary Williams. Mary was African-American but I slowly surmised that Jane Fonda was a white woman, and I knew I would have more questions for Mary after I finished inspecting the contents of the glass case. In so many of the pictures around the office, Jane Fonda was in very small outfits, exercise clothing, in pink and purple. She seemed to be a very active woman. As we left the office, I asked Achor Achor if he could explain all this.

"Don't you know about her?" he said.

I knew nothing, of course, so he told me her story.

Mary was born in Oakland in the late sixties, into the world of the Black Panthers; her father was a captain, a prominent member, a brave man. She had five siblings, all of them older, and the family was poor and moved around frequently. Her father was in and out of prison, his charges related to his revolutionary activities. When he was free, he struggled with drugs, working odd jobs. Her mother, at one time the first African-American woman in the local welder's union, eventually succumbed to alcohol and drugs. Amid all this, Mary was sent to a summer camp in Santa Barbara for inner-city youth, owned and operated by the actress Jane Fonda. Jane Fonda came to know Mary well over the course of two summers, and eventually took her away from her crumbling home and adopted her. She moved from Oakland to Santa Monica and grew up there, with Jane Fonda's other, biological children. Fifteen years later, after college and human-rights work in Africa, and after her sister, who had become a prostitute at age fifteen, was murdered on an Oakland street, Mary read newspaper articles about the Lost Boys, and formed her organization soon after. The seed money was provided by Fonda and Ted Turner, who I was told was a sailor and an owner of many television networks. I later met both Jane Fonda and Ted Turner, separately, and found them to be very decent people who remembered my name and held my hand warmly between theirs.

This was not the only time the Lost Boys in Atlanta found themselves in contact with high-profile people. I cannot understand why it is, but I suppose it was the work of Mary, who tried everything she could to bring attention to us, and by extension to raise money for the Foundation. It did not, in the end, work, but along the way I shook the hand of Jimmy Carter and even Angelina Jolie, who spent an afternoon in the apartment of one of the Lost Boys in Atlanta. That was an odd day. I was told a few days before that a young white actress would be coming to talk to some of the Lost Boys. As always, there was much debate about who would represent us, and why. Because I had led many youth in Kakuma, I was among those chosen to be present, but this did not sit well with the rest of the young Sudanese. I did not care, though, because I liked to be present, to make sure the correct picture of our lives was presented, and that not too many exaggerations were made. So twenty of us crowded into the apartment of one of the Lost Boys living longest in Atlanta, and then Ms. Jolie walked in, accompanied by a grey-haired man in a baseball cap. The two of them sat on a couch, surrounded by Sudanese, all of us trying to speak, trying to be heard while also attempting to be polite and not overloud. I must admit that when I met her, I had no idea who she was; I was told she was an actress of some kind, and when I met her, she did look like an actress—she had the same careful poise, the same flirtatious eyes of Miss Gladys, my extremely attractive drama teacher in Kakuma, and so I liked her immediately. Ms. Jolie listened to us for two hours, and then told us that she intended to visit Kakuma herself. Which I believe she did.

There were so many interesting things happening in those first months in the United States! And all the while, Mary Williams was calling me and I her, and we had a very productive relationship. When I was having trouble receiving treatment for my headaches and my knee—it had been damaged in Kakuma—Mary called Jane Fonda and Jane Fonda brought me to her own doctor in Atlanta. This doctor eventually operated on my knee and improved my mobility greatly. She was very generous, Mary was, but she had already been hurt by the attitudes of some of the Sudanese she served, and I could see in her eyes, which always seemed on the verge of tears, that she was exhausted and would not last long in service to our cause. I remember first understanding how difficult it was for her, how little gratitude she received for the work she did, at a birthday party. She had arranged it all—a party with food, tickets to an Atlanta Hawks game, a private speech given by Manute Bol, the most famous Sudanese man in history, a former NBA player who diverted a large portion of his earnings to the SPLA. But still, there was grumbling and speculation about the job Mary was doing with the Lost Boys Foundation. Was she misusing donations? Was she ineffective in getting Lost Boys into college?

I had only been in the country a few months, and there I sat, in a suit, courtside at a professional basketball game. Picture it! Picture twelve refugees from Sudan, all of us wearing suits, all of these suits one size too small, donated by our churches and sponsors. Picture us sitting, trying to make sense of it all. The confusion began before the game, when a group of twelve young American women of many skin colors, well-built and wearing leotards, fanned out over the empty basketball court, and they performed a hyperactive and very provocative dance to a song by Puff Daddy. We all stared at the gyrating young women, who put forth an image of great power and fierce sexuality. It would have been impolite to turn away, but at the same time, the dancers made me uncomfortable. The music was the loudest I have heard in my life, and the spectacle of the stadium, with its 120-foot ceiling, its thousands of seats, its glass and chrome and banners, its cheerleaders and murderous sound system—seemed perfectly designed to drive people insane.

Shortly after, a different group of cheerleaders began shooting T-shirts far into the stands, using devices designed to look like submachine guns. I stared at the guns, which stored ten rolled-up T-shirts in their barrels, and were capable of launching the shirts forty or fifty feet into the air. These young people, cheerleaders for the Atlanta Hawks, were trying to inspire the crowd, giving away clothing and miniature basketballs, though their task was a difficult one. The Atlanta Hawks team was playing the Golden State Warriors, and because neither team was winning that season, there were only a few hundred people occupying the stadium's seventeen thousand seats.

A good percentage of the attendees that night were Sudanese—one hundred and eighty of us—and twelve had been chosen to sit right near the court with Manute Bol. There we were, watching the basketball game next to one of the tallest men ever to play professional basketball. It was a strange thing, this night in my life, and it should have been positive, all of it, but it was not, and the first sour note was sounded when one of the Lost Boys, who had not been given a courtside seat, found his way to us, and began complaining loudly, even to Manute, about the unfairness of it all. And while this young man, whose name I will not mention, railed about this injustice, it was Mary's name that came up, again and again, as the source of the trouble.

"How can she do this?" he demanded. "What right does she have?"

I had a very low opinion of this man on this night. Finally he was asked by an usher to return to his seat, and, embarrassed, we turned our attention back to the court. As the dancers continued, a few of the Atlanta Hawks players, all of whom looked far larger in person than on TV, jogged in their enormous shoes over to Bol to shake his hand. Bol remained seated, for it was evident that standing was not as easy for him as it once was. We all watched Bol speak to the American players, most of whom said a few words to accompany a quick handshake, and went back to their teams. A few of the Hawks players let their eyes wash over us, Bol's guests, and they seemed to deduce immediately who we were.

It was at once heartening and shaming. We were, as a group, healthier than we had ever been before, but next to these NBA players, we looked frail and underfed. Even our leader, Manute Bol, with his small head and huge feet, resembled an oversized twig pulled from a tree. Everyone from Sudan, our group's appearance implied, was starving, was poorly built. No suits could be made to give us the illusion of ease and comfort in this world.

This game was the beginning of a celebratory evening in honor of our collective birthdays, all organized by Mary and her volunteers. After the game, we celebrated our birthdays in the CNN Center next door. Mary had pulled strings with Ted Turner and we were given space, and the sponsors brought fried chicken, beans, salad, cake, and soda. The Lost Boys Foundation had held a similar party for everyone the previous year, before I had arrived. Why were we all celebrating our birthdays on the same day? This is a good question, and the answer is fascinating in its banality. When we were first processed by the office of the United Nations High Commissioner for Refugees, at Kakuma, we were assigned an age as accurately as aid workers could determine, and were all given the same birthday: January 1. To this day, I do not know why this is the case; it seems like it would have been just as easy for the UN to pick different dates at random for each of us. But they did not do this, and though many boys have chosen their own, new, birthdates, most of us have accepted January 1 as our date of birth. It would be too difficult, anyway, to alter it in all of our official documents.

At the party, we men, some of whom had come from as far as Jacksonville and

Charlotte, talked among themselves and with our sponsoring families. For each of us refugees, there were one or two American sponsors. The sponsors and sponsor-families were almost uniformly white, though they were nevertheless socioeconomically diverse: there were young professional couples, older men wearing trucker hats, senior citizens. But the majority of the Americans present cleaved to a certain type of woman, between thirty and sixty, capable and warm, the sort one expects to find volunteering at a school or church.

To see all these men there—it was tremendous. I could glance across the crowd and see a pair of brothers I had coached in soccer when we were teenagers. There were boys I knew from English classes, another from my Kakuma theater group, another who sold shoes in the camp. This was the first time I had gathered with more than a dozen or so boys from Kakuma, and it almost knocked me over. That we had all survived, that we were all wearing suits, new shoes, that we were standing in a cavernous glass temple of wealth! We greeted each other with hugs and open smiles, many of us in shock.

There was one group among us who were dressed differently than the rest, wearing sweatsuits, visors, baseball hats and basketball shirts, accentuated with gold watches and chains. These men we called Hawaii 5-0, for they had just returned from Hawaii, where they were working as extras in a Bruce Willis movie. This is true. Apparently one of the Lost Boys Foundation volunteers knew a casting director in Los Angeles, who was looking for East African men to serve as extras in a movie directed by an African-American man named Antoine Fuqua. The volunteer sent a photo of ten of the Atlanta-based Sudanese men, and all ten were hired. At the party, the ten had recently returned from three months on the islands, where they stayed at a five-star hotel, had all of their necessities taken care of, and were paid generous salaries. Now they were back in Atlanta, determined to make clear that they had been somewhere, were now of a different caste than the rest of us. One of the them was wearing a half-dozen gold chains over a Hawaiian shirt. Another was wearing a T-shirt bearing a screened photograph of himself with Bruce Willis. This boy wore this shirt every day for a year, and had washed it so many times that the face of Mr. Willis was now threadbare and ghostly.

As Hawaii 5-0 preened and postured, the rest of us were strenuously trying to appear unimpressed. At best, we were happy for them, or could laugh with them at the absurdity of it all. At worst, though, there was jealousy, plenty of it, and again the blame came down to Mary. It was she, it was rumored, who engineered the selection of those who had gone to Hawaii, and who was she to wield such power? The seeds of the demise for the Lost Boys Foundation were sown that night. From that date forward, Mary could do nothing right. I do not think that the Sudanese are particularly argumentative people, but those in Atlanta seem, too often, to find reason to feel slighted by whatever is given to any other. It became difficult to accept a job, a referral. Any gift, from church or sponsor, was received with a mixture of gratitude and trepidation. In Atlanta there were one hundred and eighty pairs of eyes upon us all at any point, and there seemed never to be enough of anything to go around, no way to distribute anything equitably. It was safer, after a time, to accept no gifts, no invitations to speak at schools or churches, or to simply drop out of the community altogether. Only then could one live unjudged.

Later there was dancing, despite there being only four eligible women present, and only two Sudanese among them. After the dancing, Manute Bol made his address. Towering over us, he was stern and pedantic, giving his speech first in Dinka and then in English, for the benefit of the Americans assembled. He urged us to behave while in the United States. He insisted that we become model immigrants, working hard and seeking a college education. If we conducted ourselves with dignity, restraint, and ambition, he said, we would be well-liked by our American hosts, and our success would encourage the U.S. government to bring more Sudanese refugees to America. It was up to us, he explained, to be the light from which hope sprung for the Sudanese still in the camps and suffering in Sudan.

"Remember that time is money!" he urged.

He paused for effect.

"You cannot be late in America!"

Another long pause.

Manute spoke in bursts, beginning each sentence with a few loud words, which then gave way to a quieter tumble of afterthoughts. As he spoke, we all stood, silent, nodding. Our respect for Manute Bol was enormous; he had done everything he could to bring peace to Sudan. He had been, just a few years earlier, encouraged by the government to come to Khartoum, where he would be installed as Minister of Sports and Culture. Being loyal to his country and seeing this as an opportunity to bring more of his people's interests to the attention of the Islamic government, Manute accepted and flew to Khartoum. Once there, he was told the job would not be his unless he renounced Christianity and converted to Islam. He refused, and this proved disastrous. It was an embarrassment for his hosts, and according to legend, he barely made it out alive. He bribed his way out of the country and returned to Connecticut.

"You're not longer on African time! Those days are over!"

We were not being told anything new. In conversations with any of us, it would have been clear to him that we were hell-bent on getting a college degree and being able to send money back to Sudan.

"Make your ancestors proud!" he barked.

Mary watched all of this while busily unwrapping food, thanking sponsors, cleaning up, shaking hands. It was the last time I remember her seeming somewhat happy while working on our behalf. I came to know Mary well in the following months—it was she who joined me in watching *The Exorcist*—and she confided in me about her difficulties with the other Sudanese she sought to serve. They yelled at her; they questioned her competence, often invoking her gender as explanation for her ineptitude; a fallback for many Sudanese men, I admit. With every new charge leveled against her—that she squandered the donations she received, that she played favorites, on and on—she retreated further, and of course had no choice but to favor those Sudanese who were not actively trying to discredit her. I remained supportive of her, for I saw that much of what the Sudanese had in Atlanta had come through her work. I admit that I benefited from the patience and compassion I showed her. The principal gift she directed my way was named Phil Mays.

Though there were many sponsors like yourselves, Christian neighbors—well-meaning churchgoers who had been moved by the plight of the Lost Boys—after a few months in Atlanta, I had no sponsor, and the three months of rent provided by the U.S. government was about to expire. I suffered under constant headaches and often could barely move; the pain could be blinding. I wanted to begin a life, and needed help with countless things: a driver's license, a car, a job, admission to college.

"Phil will help with all that," Mary said as we waited one rainy day at the Lost Boys Foundation office. She patted my knee. "He's the best sponsor I've found."

Most of the sponsors were women, and I knew much antipathy would come my way once it became known that one of the very few men available was being handed to me. But I didn't care. I needed the help and had already given up on the politics of the young Sudanese in Atlanta.

I was very nervous about meeting Phil. I am not joking when I tell you that we all believed, all of us Sudanese, that anything could happen, at any time. In particular, I allowed the possibility that I might arrive at the office of the Foundation the morning of our meeting and be immediately turned over to immigration officials. That I would be returned to Kakuma or perhaps some other place. I trusted Mary, but thought that perhaps this Phil Mays was an agent of some kind who disapproved of our conduct thus far in the U.S. Phil told me later that he could see it in my posture: supplicating, tense. I was grateful for any hour in which I was welcomed and not in danger.

I waited in the lobby, wearing blue dress pants, which I had been given by the church. They were too short, and the waist was far too wide for me, but they were clean. My shirt was white and fit me nicely; I had ironed it for an hour the night before and again in the morning.

A man stepped out of the elevator, wearing jeans and a polo shirt. He was pleasant looking, in his thirties, appearing very much like the average white man of Atlanta. This was Phil Mays. He smiled and walked toward me. He took my hand between his two hands, and shook it slowly, staring into my eyes. I was even more certain that he intended to deport me.

Mary left us alone, and I told Phil a brief version of my story. I could see that it affected him deeply. He had read about the Lost Boys in the newspaper, but hearing my more detailed version upset him. I asked about his life and he told me something of his own story. He was a real-estate developer, he said, and had done very well for himself. He was raised in Gainesville, Florida, the adopted son of an entomology professor who left academia to become a mechanic. His adoptive mother left the family when he was four and his father reared him alone. Phil had been an athlete, and when he could not perform at a college level, he became a sportscaster, a job he held when he graduated. Eventually he went to law school and moved to Atlanta, married, and opened his own office. When he was a teenager, he discovered he had been adopted, and eventually went looking for his biological parents. The results were mixed, and he had always had questions about his life, his origins, his nature, and the nurturing he received. When Phil read about us and the Lost Boys Foundation, he was determined to donate money to the organization; he and his wife, Stacey, had decided on $10,000. He called the LBF and spoke to Mary. She was thrilled with the prospect of the donation, and asked Phil if he might like to donate more than money, that perhaps he'd like to come down to the office and possibly donate his time, too?

And now he was sitting with me, and it was obvious that he was struggling with the predicament we both found ourselves in. He had not originally planned to become my sponsor, but within minutes he knew that if he left that day and simply wrote a check, I would be exactly where I had been before—lost and somewhat helpless. I felt terrible for him, watching him struggle with the decision, and in any other situation would have told him that money was enough. But I knew that I needed a guide, someone who could tell me, for instance, how to find treatment for my headaches. I stared at him and tried to look like someone with whom he could spend time, someone who would be appropriate to bring into his home, to meet his wife and twins, then under a year old. I smiled and tried to seem easygoing and pleasant, not someone who would bring only misery and trouble.

"I love childrens!" I said. For some time I could not remember to leave the *s* off the end of the plural for child. "I am very good with them," I added. "Any help you might give me, I will repay you in child care. Or yard work. I will be happy to do anything."

The poor man. I suppose I put it on too thick. He was near tears when he finally stood up and shook my hand. "I'll be your sponsor. And your mentor," he said. "I'm going to get you working, and get you a car and an apartment. Then we'll see about getting you into college." And I knew he would. Phil Mays was a successful man and would be successful with me. I shook his hand vigorously and smiled and walked him to the elevator. I returned to the LBF offices, and looked out the window. He was emerging from the building, now just below me. I watched as he got into his car, a fine car, sleek and black, exactly beneath where I stood against the glass. He sat down behind the wheel, put his hands in his lap and he cried. I watched his shoulders shake, watched him bring his hands to his face.

Eating dinner at Phil and Stacey's house was a very significant event; I had to make the proper impression. I had to be pleasant, thankful, and had to make sure that their young children liked me. But I could not go alone. I did not have my own car at the time, and so I asked Achor Achor to give me a ride to the house on his way to a meeting with some other Lost Boys. I washed and ironed the same shirt I had worn when I met Phil—it was the only appropriate shirt I had at that time—and I ironed my khakis. When Achor Achor and I got into the car, he informed me that he would be picking up two other Sudanese refugees, Piol and Dau, on the way.

"What?" I said, angry. I had planned for Achor Achor to walk me to the door, because I did not feel I could make it alone. And now I would be escorted by three Sudanese men? Would Phil and Stacey even open their door?

"Don't worry," Achor Achor said. "We'll leave after we drop you off."

We parked the car on the street and walked up the footpath. The house was enormous. It was the size of a home reserved for the most exalted dignitaries of Sudan— ministers and ambassadors. The lawn was lush and green, the hedges trimmed into cubes and orbs.

We rang the bell. The door opened and I saw the shock on their faces. It was Phil and Stacey, each holding one of the twins.

"Heeeey," Stacey said. She was petite and blond, her voice clear but uncertain. She looked to Phil, as if he had neglected to tell her there would be four Sudanese for dinner, not one.

"Come in, come in!" Phil said.

And we did. They closed the door behind us.

"I hope barbecue is okay with you guys," Stacey said.

I turned to Achor Achor, to give him a look that would urge him to leave, but he was too busy marveling at the house. It was obvious that Achor Achor and Piol and Dau had already forgotten about whatever meeting they had planned. They were staying for dinner.

Inside, the house was more impressive than from the exterior. The ceilings seemed thirty feet high. There was a light-filled living room, and a staircase that wound to the right and to the upstairs rooms, with a balcony overlooking the living room. The bookshelves led high up the walls, and there was a gigantic television in the corner, imbedded into the shelving. Everything was white and yellow—it was a bright and happy place, full of air. On a peninsula of marble extending from the kitchen, there was a silver bowl, shimmering and full of fresh fruit.

We walked to the back porch, where Phil inspected the grill, on which six hamburgers were laid, darkening. I tried to smile at the babies, but they were not immediately smitten with me. They looked at me, with my eggplant skin, my oddly shaped teeth, and they wailed.

"It's okay," Phil said. "They cry around everyone they meet."

"You've had hamburgers before?" Phil asked us all.

Achor Achor and I had eaten at restaurants before, and had had hamburgers in our time in Atlanta.

"Yes, yes," I answered.

"And you know what's inside a hamburger?"

"Yes, of course," Achor Achor said. "Ham."

It sounds like an easy joke, as do so many of our mistakes, the many holes in our understanding, and they were often funny to Americans. We did not know how the air conditioning worked when we first moved into our apartment; we didn't know we could turn it off. For a week we slept with all of our clothes on, covered in blankets and towels, every linen we owned.

We told this story to Phil and Stacey, and they liked it very much. Then Achor Achor told him the story of the tampon box. There was a different pair of Lost Boys, who had recently been taken shopping for the first time, at an enormous grocery store. They had fifty dollars to spend, and had no idea where to start. Along the way, they had picked out a very special box and put it in their cart. Their sponsor, a woman in her fifties, smiled and tried to explain what was in the box, which was in fact tampons. "For women," she said, not knowing how much they knew about women's anatomy and cycles. (They knew nothing.) She thought she had accomplished her task, only to find that the men wanted the package anyway. "It is beautiful," they said, and they bought it, took it home and displayed in on their coffee table for months.

We tried to be polite about our eating, but there were many new foods on the Mays's table, and we could not know what was a danger and what was not. The salad seemed different than the salad we had eaten before, and Achor Achor would not touch his. The vegetables looked familiar, but had not been cooked, and Achor Achor and I preferred ours cooked. All fresh vegetables and fruits were problematic for us; we had not been fed such things in our ten years in Kakuma. I drank the milk placed before me. It was my first-ever glass of Western-style milk, and it caused a good deal of problems for me in the ensuing hours. I did not know then that I had become lactose-intolerant. I was at war with my stomach for my first year in America.

Finished with his dinner, Phil dropped his cloth napkin on the table.

"So do you guys have expressions that you use, like, Dinka words of wisdom?"

I looked at Achor Achor and he at me. Phil tried again.

"Sorry. I'm just interested in proverbs, you know? For instance, I might say, 'a stitch in time saves nine,' and that would mean..." Phil paused. He looked to Stacey.

Stacey offered no help. "Well, I don't know what that one means. But do you know what I'm asking for? Like something your parents or elders would say to you?"

The four of us Sudanese shot each other glances, hoping one among us would have a satisfactory answer.

"Excuse me," Achor Achor said, and walked to the bathroom. Once down the hall, he cleared his throat loudly. I looked to him; he was gesturing for me to join him. I excused myself, too, and soon Achor Achor and I were whispering furiously in the Mays's bathroom.

"Do you know what he wants?" he whispered. There was an urgency to this matter, just as there was always an urgency to matters in those early days. We thought our whole world might hinge on every question, every answer. It seemed possible to us both that if we didn't please Phil here, he might change his mind about me, and refuse to help me at all.

"No," I said. "I thought *you* would. You're better at Dinka than I am." This was true. Achor Achor's command of the language and its dialects and idioms has always been far greater than my own.

In five minutes together in the bathroom, we gathered two proverbs that we thought might fulfill Phil's needs.

"Here is one," Achor Achor said, sitting down to the table. "It was spoken by an important official in the Sudan People's Liberation Movement: 'Sometimes the teeth can accidentally bite the tongue, but the solution for the tongue is not to find another mouth to live in.'"

Achor Achor smiled and we all smiled. No one but Achor Achor knew what the proverb meant.

After the plates were cleared, Achor Achor, Piol, and Dau left, and Phil asked me to stay so we could talk. Stacey brought the babies to their room, and said goodnight. Phil and I walked up their grand staircase, to the babies' playroom. I had never seen so many toys in one place. It looked like a day-care center or preschool, but for dozens of children, not just two. The walls were painted with murals, pictures from children's books—fairies and flying cows. There were stuffed animals, three-dimensional puzzles and a dollhouse, everything in white and pink and yellow. At the far end of the room was a large adult's desk, on which sat a laptop computer, a phone, and a printer. "Home office," Phil explained. He told me it was mine to use whenever I needed it.

There was only one chair in the room, so we sat on the floor.

"So," he said.

I didn't know what to do so I said what I wanted to say, which was, "It is God's way that we have met."

Phil agreed. "I'm glad."

I asked about the pictures that had been painted on the walls, and Phil told me about Alice in Wonderland, Humpty Dumpty, the Big Bad Wolf, and Little Red Riding Hood. As the room darkened, Phil turned on a lamp, the light flowing through a slowly turning series of silhouettes. Salmon-colored horses and lime-green elephants galloped across the walls and windows.

"So I think you should tell me the whole story," he said.

Since I had arrived in Atlanta, I had not told it all to anyone, but I did want to tell Phil Mays. He was a very good man, it seemed, and I knew he would listen.

"You don't want to hear it all," I said.

"I do. I really want to," he reassured me. He was holding a stuffed horse and he put it down on the floor next to him, standing it carefully on its legs.

I was satisfied that he was serious so I began to tell him the story, from those first days in Marial Bai. I told him about my mother in her sun-yellow dress, and about my father's shop, about playing with the hammers-as-giraffes, and the day the war came to Marial Bai.

It became a ritual. Every Tuesday, I would come to dinner, and after dinner, Stacey would take the twins to bed, and Phil and I would sit on the floor of the playroom and talk about the war in Sudan and the journey I had made. And on the days we did not do this, Phil helped me with everything else.

Within a month we had set up a bank account for me and I was given an ATM card. He arranged driving lessons for me, and promised to co-sign on a car loan when I was ready. With Stacey and the twins, we went to the grocery store, and they explained what sorts of food I should be eating at each meal. Before that trip, I had never eaten a sandwich. Achor Achor and I were not exemplary cooks, and we had eaten only one meal each day; we knew no other way, and worried constantly that the food would run out. It continually amazed Phil, I think, how little we knew, and how he could not assume that we knew any of the things he took for granted. He explained the thermostat in the apartment, and how to write a check, and how to pay a bill, and which buses took you where. Eventually he did cosign for my Toyota Corolla, which greatly eased my commuting time. I was able to get to the furniture showroom, and then to Georgia Perimeter College, in less than a third of the time I had been spending on the bus. I did not miss taking that bus.

All along, with Phil, the learning curve was steep but I stayed with him and Phil seemed not overly burdened; he appeared genuinely pleased to explain the most basic things, like boiling water on the stove or the difference between the freezer and the refrigerator. He approached each problem with the same careful and serious tone of voice, and seemed only frustrated by the fact that he could not do more. In particular, he was troubled by Achor Achor. Achor Achor had no such sponsor—he shared one, a woman in her sixties, with six other Sudanese, and it was not the same as the concentrated attention I was getting. Achor Achor never said a word about it, and I said nothing, but it was obvious to all of us that he sorely needed Phil's help, too, and it was just as clear that Phil could not do it.

Achor Achor had been in the United States eighteen months longer than me, of course, and was far more advanced in his adjustments to life here. He had a car, and a regular job, and was taking classes at Georgia Perimeter College. He was also a leader among the Sudanese in Atlanta and was constantly on the telephone, mediating between disagreeing parties and organizing and attending gatherings, in Atlanta and elsewhere. After I had been in Atlanta for some time, I attended my first major gathering, this one held in Kansas City, and this is where I met Bobby Newmyer.

The conference had been dreamed up and organized by Bobby Newmyer, and the point of it was twofold: he was a movie producer who wanted to make a film about the Lost Boys experience, and to talk to us about the project. Secondly, he wanted to establish a national network for the Sudanese in America, whereby we could exchange information and resources, lobby the Sudanese and U.S. governments, and send funding and ideas home to southern Sudan.

Thirty-five of us were brought to Kansas one weekend in November 2003, and it was something to see. We were each given our own rooms at the Courtyard by Marriott, and there was a detailed schedule of events over the course of three days, culminating with a large gathering in the events room of the nearby Lutheran church. But being faithful to the schedule proved impossible. Everyone arrived at different times, different days, and a good portion of the attendees could not find the hotel. And when everyone was finally gathered, there was too much catching up necessary. We had been given a conference room at the hotel, and it took us two hours simply to become reacquainted with each other. There were Sudanese there who had been resettled in Dallas, Boston, Lansing, San Diego, Chicago, Grand Rapids, San Jose, Seattle, Richmond, Louisville, so many other places. I knew most of the men from Kakuma or Pinyudo, if not personally, then by reputation. These were prominent young Sudanese men; they had been speaking out and organizing since they had been teenagers.

When we had caught up and settled into our seats that first morning, we met Bobby Newmyer, whom Mary Williams had told me about. Mary was, in fact, the person who first spoke to Bobby about the idea of a feature film about our lives. And now he was greeting all of us, as we sat in a half-circle, all in our best suits. I immediately noticed how unlikely he looked for a powerful man who had arranged this gathering and had produced many popular Hollywood movies. His hair, a mixture of red and brown and blond, was unkempt, and his shirt was untucked, misbuttoned. He spoke for a few minutes, a bit hunched over—he always seemed to walk or stand at an angle—and then seemed eager to hand over the proceedings to one of his associates, a woman named Margaret, who would be writing the screenplay to the movie Bobby intended to make.

She stood and very clearly explained the plot of the story she was trying to tell, and it seemed reasonable enough to me. But not to the other attendees. It became complicated very quickly. There were questions about who would benefit from the movie. There were questions about why one version of the story would be told, and not another. One after another, the Lost Boys representatives stood up and made their case. If you have not heard a Sudanese speech, I must explain that when we stand to speak, our comments are rarely brief. Some say it is the influence of John Garang, who was known to talk for eight hours uninterrupted and still feel like he had not made his point. In any case, the Sudanese of our generation very much like to speak. If there is any topic being discussed, it is highly likely that all the people in the room will weigh in, and that each person might need five minutes each to express himself. Even in a small gathering such as this one in Kansas, comprising only thirty-five of us, that meant that any given subject, no matter how trivial, would be subjected to two hours of speeches. Each speech will be similar in structure and gravity. The speaker will first rise, straighten his suit, and clear his throat. Then he will begin. "I have been listening to this discussion," he will begin, "and I have some thoughts I must express." And what will follow will be part autobiography and will concern points that likely have already been well covered. Because each attendee will feel it necessary to be heard, the same points are usually heard half a dozen times.

Everyone in Kansas was looking to protect their interests. The representative originally from the Nuba region of Sudan wanted to make sure Nuba was properly represented. Those from Bor wanted to make sure there were provisions for the needs of those from Bor. But all of this had to be thoroughly discussed before anything actually got done, and thus in Kansas, as at many of these meetings, very little got done. There was a Lost Girl present in Kansas, and she wanted to know what would be done for the female refugees of Sudan. Lost Boys! she said. Always Lost Boys! What about the Lost Girls? This went on for a while in Kansas, and happened frequently in these conferences. No one disagreed with her, but we all knew that her presence, and our need to factor in the needs of the eighty-nine Lost Girls into everything we touched upon, would greatly impede headway on many matters.

Though the progress was halting in Kansas, I was able to spend time getting to know Bobby, and I came to be one of his advisors on the film and the national network. Eventually I helped as much as I could in the planning of the much larger conference, this one in Phoenix, which took place eighteen months later. This one was organized by Ann Wheat, a sponsor of Lost Boys in that city, and Bobby, who at that point I imagined was as baffled as we were by how deeply he had become involved in every aspect of the Sudanese diaspora. Phoenix was designed to be the largest gathering of Sudanese ever held in America. The city's convention center would host at least a thousand Lost Boys and their relatives, and in some cases their spouses and children. The conference grew beyond all expectations, at one point holding 3,200 Sudanese in one enormous banquet hall.

But it was so very hot in Phoenix that weekend. Complaints came from every attendee. This is worse than Kakuma! we laughed. At least in Kakuma there was wind! we said. It was more than 110 degrees in Phoenix, though we felt it only on those rare occasions when we left the convention center. The action, all of it, was held inside, the one giant box of a room, unadorned but for a simple stage and thousands of chairs. The goal was to assemble, to meet on a large scale, and to engineer some sort of congress of young Sudanese refugees here in the United States. We wanted to elect a leadership council, the members of which would keep the rest of our thousands organized and would be the international voice of the displaced youth of Sudan. The weekend would culminate with a visit by John Garang himself. For most of us, it was the first time we had seen him since we were ten, twelve years old, in Pinyudo.

It was astonishing to see so many of the men of Kakuma there in Phoenix. And suits! Everyone was dressed for business. It was good to see the men, and the Lost Girls, too, who were represented in large numbers—probably three-fourths of the eighty-nine in America were in Phoenix that weekend, and each spoke louder than any three of their male counterparts. The Lost Girls are not to be trifled with, never to be underestimated. They are beautiful and fierce, their English invariably better than ours, their minds more agile and ready to pounce. In the U.S. at least, in that sort of context, they demand and get full respect from all.

The order of events was logical and august. The mayor of Phoenix greeted us to start the day. John Prendergast, of the International Crisis Group, spoke about the world's attitude toward Sudan, and what was likely to happen. We had seen Prendergast in Pinyudo in 1989, and at least a few of the men remembered him. Bobby and Ann spent much of their time trying to stay invisible, making clear that the convention, while facilitated by their efforts, was ours, in which we could fail or triumph.

I am not sure which was the outcome. I believe the triumph was muted by our usual sort of controversy. There were nominations for a national council, and these nominees, about forty of them, were brought to the stage, and each gave a brief speech. Later in the day, these candidates were voted on by the attendees, and when the results became known, there was anger and even a brief melee. It turns out that the majority of those elected were from the Bahr al-Ghazal region, my region, and that those from Nuba felt underrepresented. The controversy was still raging through the evening's barbecues and the entertainment provided by an array of Sudanese groups, and even through the second and last full day of the convention, when the doors were locked, guards were posted at regular intervals, and we were told to sit and stay seated.

That was when John Garang entered. This was the man who more or less began the civil war that brought war to our homes, the war that brought about the deaths of our relatives, and set in motion our journey to Ethiopia and later to Kenya, which of course led to our resettlement here in the United States. And though there were many people in that room with mixed feelings about John Garang, the catalyst and driving force behind the civil war and prospective independence walked into the room amid much ecstatic cheering and many bodyguards, and stepped onto the stage.

He looked absolutely thrilled to be there among us, and when he took the podium, it was obvious—perhaps I imagined this but I bet not—that he considered himself our most important influence, our spiritual teacher, and that he was beginning where he had left off, fifteen or so years earlier, when he last spoke to us at the Pinyudo camp for refugees.

After the conference, as I tried to untangle all of the demands of and obligations to the various groups, and as I tried with Achor Achor and others to broker an acceptable compromise that would allow the national council to go forward, I worked closely with Bobby on options to salvage the conference. As we talked, we ventured into more personal subjects: how my life was in Atlanta, how school was progressing, what I was doing the upcoming summer. And because he had been so fair with all of us, and because I badly wanted to leave the city for any amount of time, I asked him if I could come to Los Angeles and spend a summer with him, working in whatever capacity he saw fit. I surprised myself by asking this. And he surprised me by saying yes. So I came to stay with him, in his comfortable home, living with him and Deb, his wife, and their family. There were four children, from seventeen years old to three-year-old Billi, and I like to think that I fit in very well and pulled my weight. I swam in their pool, attempted to learn the game of tennis, assisted in the cooking and grocery shopping, and watched the younger children when I was asked to. I learned the limits, too, of what I was allowed to do. I slept on the bottom bunk in James's room, and one morning I woke up late—I always slept well at this house—and saw that I was alone. Everyone was at breakfast, so I made my bed and James's, in the manner I had been taught by Gop Chol. When Deb later saw both beds made, she wanted to know why I had done this. I told her that James was my little brother, and that the room looked better with both beds made. She accepted this, but told me never to do it again. James is twelve, she said, and should make his own bed.

The Newmyers' generosity was, I believe, irrational, reckless even. It was difficult to understand. They welcomed me into every family activity, including a road trip, in a recreational vehicle, with their family and friends, from Los Angeles to the Grand Canyon. It was then that I acquired, from Bobby's teenage son Teddy and his friends, the nickname V-Town, and it was then that I almost drove the RV off a cliff. Such was the faith that Bobby had in me. He did not ask me whether or not I had a driver's license. I had not driven in his presence since I had arrived to stay with him. He did not ask me about my driving skills, nor did he ask me whether I felt comfortable commanding such a large machine. One day in Arizona, he simply handed me the keys, the family piled into the back, and I was left in charge. Bobby sat next to me, grinning, and I started the vehicle.

When I mistook the accelerator for the brake, he laughed uproariously. When the road was straight and clear, there was not much difference in principle to my Toyota, but when there were turns to make, and cars to avoid, there was a good deal of difference indeed. I do not like to remember how close we were to the edge of the cliff when I finally righted the vehicle, but I can say that Bobby barely uttered a word. He simply kept his eyes on me and when I found my way back onto the road, he went back to sleep.

I left Los Angeles that summer with plans to return for Thanksgiving, and still spoke to Bobby frequently on the phone. He and Phil together were assisting me with my college applications, and there was much work to do. I have almost completed the credits necessary to receive my associate's degree from Georgia Perimeter College, a junior college in Atlanta, and Bobby was helping with a transition to a four-year college. We talked almost daily about it; he sent me brochures constantly.

But this past summer and fall was not so good after all; it seemed that much of what I had built and that which had been built around me fell apart. Phil and Stacey moved back to Florida, the move necessitated by his work. We still talk on the phone and we send letters over the internet, but I do miss their home, I miss the Tuesday dinners and the twins. The Lost Boys Foundation was disbanded in 2005. Mary could no longer handle the stress, and because there was so much speculation about her handling of the organization, donations had evaporated. Today the foundation administers no scholarships, connects no sponsors to refugees, and assists no Sudanese. Mary still helps a few Lost Boys with their college tuition, but she has moved on. She is currently on a cross-country bicycle trip; when she finishes that, she will leave Atlanta, too, to work as a ranger in the national parks.

John Garang died in July of 2005, a year after brokering the peace agreement between the Sudan People's Liberation Movement (now the political arm of the SPLA) and the government of Sudan, and just three weeks after being named vice president of Sudan. He was traveling via helicopter from Uganda to Sudan when the machine fell in the jungle and all aboard were killed. Though there was initial speculation that this was some sort of assassination, no evidence has yet supported this, and it has been accepted by most Sudanese, here and around the world, that his death was accidental. We can be thankful only that the peace agreement was signed before his death. No other leader in southern Sudan had the power to broker it.

Bobby died in the winter of 2005. He was forty-nine years old and his children were still the same ages they were when we shared our summer—seventeen, twelve, nine, three. He was in Toronto producing a film and was exercising in the hotel's gym. I believe he was on the stationary bicycle when he felt a flutter, a stab of pain in his chest. He left the treadmill and sat down. When the pain subsided, he did not do what he might have done, which was to leave the gym and perhaps seek medical attention. Because he was who he was, he got back onto the treadmill and minutes later collapsed again. The heart attack was massive and he did not stand a chance.

And after all this, I am still in Atlanta, and I am still on the floor of my own apartment, tied with telephone cord, still kicking the door.

XIV.

It should not have taken so long to cross the Nile. But there were hundreds, perhaps thousands, of us on the riverbank, there were only two boats, and it was too far to swim. At first, some boys tried to make it across, paddling like dogs, but they underestimated the river's power. The current was fast and the river was deep. Three boys were taken downriver and were not seen again.

The rest of us waited. Everyone waited. We had been on our journey to Ethiopia for perhaps six weeks and at the river, our group mixed with other travelers—adults, families, elderly men and women, babies. This was the first time I became aware that it was not only boys who were walking to Ethiopia. There were hundreds of adults and younger children on that riverbank, and we were told that there were thousands ahead of us and thousands behind.

There was tall grass on the bank of the river, and in the grass so close to the water, insects thrived. We had no mosquito nets. We slept outdoors, and we built fires with kindling and bamboo. But that did not help us with the mosquitoes. At night, there was crying. The adults moaned, the children wailed. The mosquitoes feasted, a hundred eating from each person. There was no solution. There can be no doubt that dozens contracted malaria while we waited to cross the water. It took four days to get from our side to the other.

Once we were across, there was a village, and in that village, we were welcomed. The inhabitants lived close to their sandy shore, and they cultivated maize. They shared their food with us and I thought I might faint from their generosity. We sat in our groups and the women of the village brought us well water and even stew, each bowl with one small piece of meat. Within minutes of finishing the food, boys were everywhere sleeping, so sated they could not stay awake.

When I woke the orange sun had fallen toward the treeline and I heard a voice.

—You!

In front of me I saw nothing but boys, some of them bathing in the water. Behind me there was nothing but darkness and a path.

—Achak!

The voice was very familiar. I looked up. There was a shadow in a tree. It looked very much like a leopard, its silhouette all length and sinew.

—Who is that? I asked.

The shape jumped from the tree into the sand beside me. I flinched and was ready to run, but it was a boy.

—It's you, Achak!

—It's not you! I said, standing.

It was him. After so many weeks, it was William K.

We embraced and said nothing. My throat tightened, but I could not cry. I no longer knew how to cry. But I was so thankful. I felt it was God giving me this gift of William K after taking away Deng. I had not seen him since the murahaleen came to Marial Bai and it seemed impossible that I would find him here, along the Nile. We smiled at each other but were too excited to sit. We ran to the river and then walked along the sand, away from the other boys.

—What about Moses? William K asked. —Did he come with you?

It had not occurred to me that William K would not know the fate of Moses. I told him that Moses was dead, that he had been killed by the horseman. William K sat down quickly in the sand. I sat down with him.

—You didn't know? I asked.

—No. I didn't see him that day. They shot him?

—I don't know. They were about to get him. I looked away.

We sat for some time, looking at the smooth rocks by the riverside. William K picked up a few stones and threw them into the brown water.

—Your parents? he asked.

—I don't know. Yours?

—They told me they'd see me back at home during the rainy season. I think they're waiting to come back. So I just have to go back home once the rain comes.

This sounded very wishful to me, but I did not comment. We sat for some time, quietly, and I felt like the trip to Ethiopia now would not be very difficult. Walking with my good friend William K would make it tolerable. I'm sure he felt the same way, for more than once he looked at me out of the corner of his eye, as if checking to make sure I was real. To make sure that all of this was real.

It took us a surprising amount of time to remember to ask how we had arrived here at the river with the groups traveling east. I told him my story and then he told me his. Like me, he had run that first day, all through the night and the next day. He was lucky enough to come upon a bus taking people to Ad-Da'ein, where he had relatives. He knew that Ad-Da'ein was in the north, but all of the Dinka on the bus were sure that there they would be safe there, for Ad-Da'ein was a large town and had long had a mixed population of Dinka and Arabs, Christian and Muslim. Like the group of elders with whom I had walked at the beginning of my running, they felt that being in a government-controlled town would be most secure.

—It was safe for a while, William K said. —My uncle and aunts lived there, and he worked as a bricklayer, working for the Rezeigat. It was a decent job and he was able to feed us all. We lived near many hundreds of Dinka, and we were able to do as we wanted. There were about seventeen thousand Dinka there, so we felt safe.

—The Rezeigat, Arab herders, held the power in the town, but there were also people there from the Fur, the Zaghawa, Jur, Berti, and other tribes. It was a busy town, peaceful. Or that's what my uncle said. Things changed not long after I got there. Bad feelings developed. Militiamen were in the town more and more, and they brought bad feelings toward the Dinka. The Muslims in the town began to act differently toward the non-Muslims. There was a Christian church in the town, which had been built a long time ago, with the help of a Rezeigat sheikh. This church now became a problem for the Muslims. The people were angry at the Dinka and the Christians because of the SPLA. Every time they heard about the SPLA winning some battle, they got angrier. In the spring, the Rezeigat came to the church and they burned it down. There were many people inside worshiping, but they burned it anyway. Two people were burned inside. Then the Rezeigat went to where the Dinka homes were, and they burned many of those, too. Three more people died there.

—We were scared. The Dinka knew this was not a good place for them anymore.

My uncle brought us to the police station one morning, where many hundreds of Dinka had gone for safety. The police helped us, and told us to gather in Hillat Sikka Hadid, an area near the railway station. We stayed there all night, all of us huddled together. Everyone among us decided that in the morning we would begin to walk back to southern Sudan, where we could be protected by the SPLA.

—In the morning, government officials, with the police, moved all of us to the railway station. They told us that we would be safest there, and they would transport us away from the town on the train. We would be carried away from the town and would be safe to go back to southern Sudan or wherever we wished to go.

—So they helped load everyone onto the train, onto the cars where they keep cattle. There were eight cars, and most of the people were happy to be leaving, and that they would not have to walk. They told us that they wanted the men and boys on one car, so they could watch them, to make sure they were not SPLA. I was worried about this development, but my uncle said not to worry, that it was natural that they would want to make sure the men were not armed. So my uncle and cousins boarded one of the cars for men.

—I boarded a different train car with my aunts and younger cousins, all girls. My uncle was on the first car, and we were on the fifth car. We were very cramped inside the cars. There were almost two hundred women and children in the car with us. We could barely breathe; we pushed our mouths to the slits that were open to the outside, and we took turns inside the car, getting close to the air. Many children were crying, many were getting sick. A girl near me vomited all over my back.

—After two hours, we heard a lot of yelling close to the first car, where my uncle was. Then gunfire. We couldn't see anything from where we were. We didn't know if the army was fighting SPLA or what was happening. Then we heard the sound of burning, the whooshing and crackling. And then, like a wave, the yelling of hundreds of Dinka men. Rezeigat men were yelling, too, screaming things at the Dinka. "They're burning!" someone screamed inside our car. "They're burning the men!" Everyone started screaming. We were all screaming then. We screamed for a long time but we were trapped.

—I don't know how our car was opened, but the door opened and we ran out. But it was too late for most. A thousand had been burned. My uncle was gone. We ran from the town with hundreds of others, hiding in the woods until we got to an SPLA town. Eventually my aunts thought I should join the walking boys.

William K had been at the river for days before we arrived, having been brought by bus for part of the way, and then joining another, larger group of boys walking. Most of them had walked on while William had stayed at the river, enjoying the hospitality of the women at the riverside. He was healthier than most of us, and seemed optimistic about what was to come.

—Did you hear we're very close to Ethiopia? he asked.

I had not heard this.

—It's not far from here, I heard. Only a few days, and then we're safe. We just have to cross some desert and if we run we might make it in one day. Maybe you and I should run ahead to get there first. And then we'll go home once the rains come. If your parents aren't in Marial Bai, you can have my parents, and we can be brothers.

For the first time in my life, I welcomed the fabrications of William K. He told many that afternoon, about how he knew that his parents had already made it to Ethiopia, because he had been asking people along the way if they had seen people like his parents, and they had all readily agreed. Though his strength might have only recently been restored, it was nevertheless wondrous to hear a boy talk with such enthusiasm about anything at all. For weeks, the rest of us had been barely able to speak.

—Is this a new boy, Achak?

Dut had found us sitting by the riverside.

—This is William K. He's from our village.

—Marial Bai? No.

—Yes, uncle, William K said. —My father was assistant to the chief.

Dut seemed immediately to know that William was a fabricator, though a harmless one. He nodded and said nothing. He sat with us, watching the passage of the people over the Nile. He asked William K how he, the son of the assistant to the chief of Marial Bai, had come to join us at the river, and William K told him a truncated version of his story. In response, that afternoon Dut told a story stranger than the one he had told about the Baggara and their new guns.

—I'm not surprised you had trouble in Ad-Da'ein, William K. The history of the southern peoples and the northern peoples is not a very happy one. The Arabs have always been better armed than us Dinka. And they have been smarter, too. This is why in Ethiopia we will reverse this imbalance. Have you heard of the people of England, boys?

We shook our heads. Ethiopia was the only other country we were aware of.

—These are people from very far away. They look very different from us. But they are very powerful, with more and better weapons than any Baggara you could find. Can you imagine this? The most powerful people you can think of.

I tried to imagine this, thinking of the murahaleen, but larger versions of them.

—The British people became involved in southern Sudan, in this land we're walking through, in the 1800s. A long time ago. It was they who helped bring Christianity to the Dinka. Someday I will tell you about a man named General Gordon, who tried to abolish slavery in our land. But for now I will tell you this. Are you following me so far?

We were.

—The other part of the history of this land is the country of Egypt. Egypt is another powerful country, but their people are somewhat similar to the people of northern Sudan. They are Arabs. The Egyptians and the British both had interest in Sudan—

I interrupted. —What do you mean when you say that, they had interest?

—They wanted things here. They wanted the land. They wanted the Nile River, the river we just crossed. The British controlled many countries in Africa. It's complicated, but they wanted influence over a lot of the world. So the British and the Egyptians made a deal. They agreed that the Egyptians would control the north of the country, where the Arabs lived and still live, while the British would control the south, the land we know, where the Dinka and other people like us live. This was good for the people of the south, because the British were enemies of the slave raiders. In fact, they said they would get rid of the slave trade, which at the time was quite active. They were taking many more than are taken now, and they were being sent all over the world. The British ruled southern Sudan with a very light hand. They brought schools to Sudan, where the children were taught Christianity and also English.

—That is why they are called English? William K asked.

—Well... sure, William. In any case, the English were good for this land, in one way, because they kept the spread of Islam in check. They made us safe from the Arabs. But in 1953, a long time ago, before I was born, near the time your father was born, Achak, the Egyptians and the British signed an agreement to leave Sudan alone, let it govern itself. This was after World War II and—

—What? I asked.

—Oh Achak. I can't begin to explain. But the British had been involved in a war of their own, a war that makes our current conflict look very small by comparison. But because they had extended themselves all over the world and could no longer maintain their hold, they decided to grant control of the country to the Sudanese. This was a very important time. There were many who assumed that the country would be split into two, the north and the south, because the two regions had been fused under the British, after all, and because the two sides shared so few cultural identities. But this is where the British sowed the seeds for disaster in our country, which are still being harvested today. Actually, look at this.

Dut pulled a small batch of papers from his pocket. We didn't know until then that he kept other papers, in addition to the roster of boys under his care. But he had many papers, and he flipped the pages quickly and came upon a crumpled yellow page, which he unfolded and presented to me. The print upon it looked like nothing I had ever seen. I could as soon read it as I could fashion wings from it and fly away. Remembering that I could not read, he snatched it back.

—It took me a long time to translate so I'll give you the benefit of my hard work. Yes, now:

"The approved policy of the Government is to act upon the fact that the people of the southern Sudan are distinctly African and Negroid, and that our obvious duty to them is therefore to push ahead as far as we can with their economic development on African and Negroid lines, and not upon Middle-Eastern Arab lines of progress which are suitable for the northern Sudan. It is only by economic and educational development that these people can be equipped to stand up for themselves in the future, whether their lot be eventually cast with the northern Sudan or with eastern Africa, or partly with each."

William and I understood almost nothing Dut said, but he seemed very satisfied.

—That was written by the British, when they were trying to decide how to handle their departure from Sudan. They knew it was wrong to have the country as one unified Sudan. They knew we were anything but unified, and could never be such a thing. They were very conflicted about this. They called it the Southern Sudan Question.

I was unsure what that meant.

—Your fate, all of our fates, were sealed fifty years ago by a small group of people from England. They had every ability to draw a line between north and south, but they were convinced by the Arabs not to. The British had an opportunity to ask the people of southern Sudan whether they wished to be separate from the north, as one with the north. It's impossible that the chiefs of the south would want to be as one with the north, right?

We nodded, but I wondered if this was true. I thought of the market days in Marial Bai, of Sadiq and the Arabs in my father's shop, the harmony that existed between the traders.

—But they did, Dut continued. —They were tricked by the Arabs, they were outsmarted. Chiefs were bribed, were promised so many things. In the end, they were convinced that there would be advantages to living as one nation. This was folly. Anyway, all of this will change now, Dut said, standing up. —In Ethiopia, there will be schools, the best schools we've ever had. There will be the greatest teachers of Sudan and Ethiopia, and you will educated. You will be prepared for a new era, when never again will we be outwitted by Khartoum. When this fighting is over, there will be an independent nation of southern Sudan, and eventually you boys will inherit it. How does that sound?

I told Dut that it sounded good. William K, though, was asleep, and soon I joined him. Dut walked off, and I wanted to simply rest and be near William K. It seemed his arrival, his resurrection, came at a time when I was unsure if I could have gone on without him. Would I have gone into a hole like Monynhial? I don't know. But without William K, I would have forgotten that I had not been born on this journey. That I had lived before this. Without William K, I could have imagined myself born here in the tall grasses, paths broken by the boys before me, that I had never had a family, had never had a home, had never slept under a roof, had never eaten enough warm food to fill my stomach, had never fallen asleep feeling safe and knowing what could and could not happen when the sun rose again.

I closed my eyes and felt happy there, by that river that day, reunited with William K, as the clouds came in perfect intervals, keeping the day cool, bringing forgiving shade over my eyelids as I slept.

But in the evening this life ended with the coming of thunder.

—Get up!

Dut was yelling at us. The war was coming, he said. He did not tell us who was fighting who or where, but we could hear distant guns, the rumbling of mortar fire. And so we did not linger in that village, which I am certain did not stand upon the earth long after the coming of the sound of the guns. We left as the sun reddened and dropped and we directed ourselves to the desert. We had been told by the villagers that we were close to Ethiopia, that all that was left was to cross the desert, that in a week's time we would find the end of Sudan.

First we left everything we had. We would be more secure, Dut said, from bandits, if we had nothing anyone wanted. We ate the food we had found or saved, we left any possessions we could not wear. I ate a small bag of seeds I had kept tied to my wrist, and many boys even removed their shirts. We cursed Dut for this directive but had no choice but to trust him. We always trusted Dut. At that time, we were boys and he was God.

We walked all that night, to distance ourselves from the fighting, and in the early morning we rested for a few hours before beginning again.

Those first few days we walked with some confidence and some speed. The boys thought we would be upon Ethiopia in a matter of days, and the proximity of our new life awakened the dreamer in William K, who filled the air between us with the beautiful lacework of his lies.

—I heard Dut and Kur talking. They say we'll be in Ethiopia very soon, a few days. We're going to have problems with food, though. They say there's so much food that we'll have to spend half of every day eating it. Otherwise it'll go rotten.

—You're lying, William, I said. —Shh.

—I'm not lying. I just heard them.

William K was not within half a mile of Dut and Kur. William K had not heard anyone saying anything like this. He continued.

—Dut said that we'll have to choose between three homes each. They show us three homes and we have to pick one. We'll have floors made of rubber, like shoes, and inside it's always very cool and clean. We will have to pick between blankets, and different colors for shirts and shorts. Most of the problems in Ethiopia are because of all this choosing we'll have to do.

I tried to block out his voice, but his lies were gorgeous and I listened secretly.

—Also our families are there. What Dut said was that there were airplanes that came to Bahr al-Ghazal after we left, and the planes took everyone to Ethiopia. So they'll all be there when we get there. They're probably very worried about us.

His lies were so exquisite I almost wept.

But there was no water and there was no food. Dut had been told, by whom I am unsure, that in the desert we would find food and could make do with a limited amount of water, and he was wrong on both accounts. Within a few days, our pace became sluggish, and boys began to go mad.

On the morning of the fourth day, I woke to find a boy named Jok Deng peeing on me. He was among the first boys to lose his head in the desert. The heat was too strong and we had not eaten for three days. When I woke to the peeing of Jok Deng, I pulled his leg until he fell over, his penis still shooting urine in lassos. I walked to the other side of the sleep circle and lay down again, smelling everywhere of the urine of Jok Deng; he peed on people each day. There was also Dau Kenyang, who could not answer to his name and whose eyes retreated so far into his skull that they lost their light. He opened his mouth but said nothing. We all began to know the quiet popping of his lips opening, closing, nothing coming out.

William K was next. His madness began with his inability to sleep. He stayed up all night, in the middle of the sleep circle, kicking everyone around him. This we found annoying but it didn't, alone, seem to indicate that William was slipping from the grip of his faculties. But then he began throwing sand at all of the boys. He seemed always to be carrying a handful of sand, and would throw it in the faces of any boy who spoke to him, sometimes referring to them by the name of his arch-enemy in Marial Bai, William A.

I was first to receive William K's gift of sand. I asked him if I could borrow his knife, and he threw the sand. It filled my mouth and stung my eyes. —Enjoy your meal of sand, William A, he said.

I was too tired to be angry, to react in any way. My muscles were weak, cramps came and went. I felt constantly dizzy. We all did our best to walk straight, but our collective equilibrium was so poor that we looked like a line of drunkards, swaying and stumbling. My heart felt like it was beating faster, irregularly, fluttering and shivering. And most of the boys were far worse off than I.

We ate only what we could find. The most-sought treasure was a fruit called abuk. It was a root that could be extracted if the hunter saw its single leaf protruding from the ground. Some of the boys were expert at this hunting but I saw nothing. A boy would rush off in some direction and begin digging, while I had not seen anything. When there was enough, I tried the abuk. It was bitter, tasteless. But it contained water and so it was prized.

Each day Dut sent us into the trees, if there were trees, to find what we could. But not too far, he warned.

—Stay close and stay close to each other, Dut said. In the region, he said, dwelled tribes that would rob boys like us. They would kill boys or kidnap boys and make them tend their livestock.

We ate, if we were fortunate, a spoonful of food each day. We drank as much water as we could keep in our cupped hands.

The dying began on the fifth day.

—Look, William K said that day.

He was following the pointed fingers of the boys in the line ahead of us. Everyone was looking at the shrunken corpse of a boy, our size precisely, not twenty feet from the trail we were following. This dead boy was from another group, a few days ahead of us. The boy was naked but for a pair of striped shorts and was positioned against a thin tree, whose boughs bent over him as if trying to shield him from the sun.

Kur soon took a position between our walking line and the dead boy, making sure everyone continued walking and did not investigate the corpse. He feared any diseases the dead boy might have carried, and every moment was too precious in those most difficult days. When we were awake we needed to walk, he said, for the more we walked the sooner we would be somewhere where we could find food or water.

But it was only a few hours after passing the corpse of the boy that a boy of our own line stopped walking, too. He simply sat on the path; we saw the boys ahead of us walking around him, stepping over him. William K and I did so, too, not knowing what else we could do. Dut finally heard about the boy who had stopped walking and came back for him; he carried him for the rest of the afternoon, but later we heard that he was dead much of that time. He died in Dut's arms and Dut was only looking for an appropriate place to put him to rest.

By the next afternoon, we had seen eight more dead boys along the path, those from groups ahead of ours, and we added three more of our own. On that day and in the days to come, when a boy was going to die, he would first stop talking. His throat would be too dry and to speak required too much energy. Then his eyes would sink deeper, circled in ever-darker shadows. He would no longer answer to his name. His walk would slow, his feet shuffling, and he would be among the boys who would rest longer. Eventually a dying boy would find a tree, and he would sit against the tree and fall asleep. When his head touched the tree, the life in him would fall away and his flesh would return to the earth.

Death took boys every day, and in a familiar way: quickly and decisively, without much warning or fanfare. These boys were faces to me, boys I had sat next to for a meal, or who I had seen fishing in a river. I began to wonder if they were all the same, if there was any reason one of them would be taken by death while another would not. I began to expect it at any moment. But there were things the dead boys might have done to aid their demise. Perhaps they had eaten the wrong leaves. Perhaps they were lazy. Perhaps they were not as strong as me, not as fast. It was possible that it was not random, that God was taking the weak from the group. Perhaps only the strongest were meant to make it to Ethiopia; there was only enough Ethiopia for the best of the boys. This was the theory of William K. He had regained his senses and was talking more than ever before.

—God is choosing who will make it to Ethiopia, he said. —Only the smartest and strongest of us can make it there. There is room for only half of us, actually. Only one hundred boys, actually. So more will die, Achak.

We could not mourn the dead. There was no time. We had been in the desert ten days and if we did not make it through very soon we would not make it at all. At the same time, the war was coming to us with increasing frequency. During the day we would see helicopters in the distance and Dut would do his best to help us hide. Thereafter, we would walk at night. It was during one of our night walks, as we rested for a few hours, that we thought a tank had come to kill us all.

I was asleep when I felt a rumbling in the earth. I sat up and found other boys also awake. Out of the darkness two lights ripped open the night.

—Run!

Dut was nowhere to be found but Kur was telling us to run. I trusted his commands so I found William K, who had begun to sleep again and was far away in slumber. When he stood and was awake, we ran, stumbling through the night, hearing the sounds of vehicles and seeing distant headlights. We ran first toward the lights then away from them. Three hundred boys were running in every direction. William K and I leapt over boys who had fallen and boys who had stopped in bushes to hide.

—Should we stop? I whispered as we ran.

—No, no. Run. Always run.

We continued to run, determined to be the farthest boys from the lights. We ran side by side and I felt we were going in the correct direction. The sounds of boys and rumbling were growing more distant and I looked to my right, where William K had been, and William K was no longer next to me.

I stopped and whispered loudly for William K. In the dark I could hear the wails of boys. It would be morning before I knew what had happened this night and who was wailing and why.

—Run, run! They're coming!

A boy flew past me and I followed. William K had chosen to hide, I told myself. William K was safe. I followed the boy and soon lost him, too. It is difficult to describe how dark the dark is in the desert these nights.

I ran through the night. I ran because no one had told me to stop. I ran listening to my breathing, loud like a train, and ran with my arms outstretched to protect me from trees and brush. I ran until I was seized by something. I had been running at top speed and then I was stopped, stuck like an insect in the silk of a spider. I tried to shake free but I had been punctured. Pain seared me everywhere. There were teeth in my leg, in my arm. I lost consciousness.

When I woke I was in the same place and the light was beginning to push the roof from the sky. I was caught on a fence of parallel steel wires with thorns shaped like stars. The fence had hold of my shirt in two places and one star had lodged deep within my right leg. I disentangled my shirt and held my breath as the pain in my leg began to clarify itself.

I freed myself but my leg bled freely. I wrapped it with a leaf but could not walk while holding the wound closed. The sky was growing pink and I walked in what I thought to be the direction of the boys.

—Who is that?

A voice came out of the thicket.

—It's a boy, I said.

No person was visible. The voice seemed to come from the pink air itself.

—Why are you walking that way, with your hand on your leg like that?

I did not want to carry on a conversation with the air so I said nothing.

—Are you an angry boy or a happy boy? the voice asked.

A man emerged, round bellied and wearing a hat, a blue shadow against the pulsing sky. He approached me slowly, as he might a trapped animal. The round-bellied man's accent was strange, and I could barely follow his words. I didn't know which answer was correct so I answered a different question.

—I am with the walking boys, father.

Now the man was upon me. His hat bore a camouflage pattern, like the uniform of the soldier Mawein. But this man's camouflage was superior: it blended perfectly into the landscape, its tans and greys. He was of an indeterminate age, somewhere between the age of Dut and the age of my father. In some ways he resembled my father, in his slender shoulders, the fluid and upright way he moved. But this man's stomach was full, overfull. I had not seen a stomach so large since my village's Fatman contest, an annual rite abandoned with the coming of war. In the event, men from all over the region would gorge themselves on milk for months, living as sedentary a life as possible. The winner would be the man who was largest, whose belly was the most impressive. This contest was not possible during civil war, but this man before me seemed like a viable contestant.

—Let me see why you're holding your leg, he said, crouching at my knee.

I showed him the wound.

—Ah. Hmm. The barbed wire. I've got something for that. In my home. Come.

I went with the round-bellied man because I was too tired to plan an escape. I now saw the man's hut ahead, looking well-made and standing amid absolutely nothing else. There was no sign of humans anywhere.

—Should I try to carry you? he asked.

—No. Thank you.

—Ah ah ah, I understand. You have your pride. You're one of the boys going to Ethiopia to become soldiers.

—No, I said. I was sure he was mistaken.

—The jaysh al-ahmar? he said.

—No, no, I said.

—The jaysh al-ahmar, the Red Army? Yes. I've seen you passing.

—No. We're just walking. We're walking to Ethiopia. For school.

—School, then the army. Yes, I think this is for the best. Come inside and sit for a moment. I'll fix your leg for you.

I paused for a moment outside the man's sturdy home. He did not know who I was, but he thought he knew something about me. He had been seeing boys my age passing through and he was calling them Red Army, just as Mawein had. There was something slippery about the man, and I thought that entering his home was a questionable idea. But when one is invited into a home in Sudan, particularly as a traveler, one expects food. And the prospect of being fed far outweighed any concerns I had for my safety. I ducked into the darkness of the man's large hut and saw it. My lord it was the bicycle. It seemed to be precisely the same bicycle. I swear that it was the same one—silver, shimmering, new, the same model brought to Marial Bai by Jok Nyibek Arou. This one, though, had been freed of its plastic, and was far more remarkable because of it.

—Ah! You like the bicycle. I knew you would.

I could not speak. I blinked hard.

—Take this.

The man gave me a rag and I dabbed at my wound.

—No, no. Let me, he said.

The man took the cloth and tied it tightly around my leg. The screaming of the wound was muffled and I almost laughed at the simplicity of his solution.

The man gestured for me to sit down and I did. We sat for a moment assessing each other, and now I saw that he had a feline face, with high, severe cheekbones and large eyes that seemed constantly amused. His palms, resting in his lap and open to me, gave foundation to fingers of remarkable length, each with six or more joints.

—You're the first person who has been here in a very long time, he said.

I nodded seriously. I assumed the round-bellied man had lost his wife and family. There were men like this everywhere in Sudan, men of this age, alone.

In a quick movement, he pushed his carpet from the floor, and under it was a door made of cardboard and string. He lifted it and I saw that he had a deep hole underneath, full of food and water and gourds of mysterious liquids. The man quickly closed the hatch again and replaced the carpet.

—Here, he said.

He put a small mound of groundnuts on a plate.

—For me?

—Ah ah ah! The boy is so shy. Can you be so shy? You must be too hungry to be so shy! Eat the food when it's within reach, boy. Eat.

I ate the nuts quickly, first one at a time and then filling my mouth with a handful. It was more than I had eaten for weeks. I chewed and swallowed and felt the paste of the nuts fortifying my chest and arms, clarity returning to my head. The man filled the plate again with nuts and I ate them, now slower. I felt the need to lie down and did so, still eating the nuts, one by one.

—Where did you get it? I asked, pointing to the bicycle.

—I have it, that's what matters, Red Army boy. Have you ridden a bicycle?

I sat up and shook my head. His eyes grew more amused.

—Oh no! That's a shame. I would have let you try it.

—I know how! I insisted.

He laughed at this, his head thrown back.

—The boy says he knows how though he's never done it before. Eat something with me and we'll learn more about what you can and can't do, little soldier.

I could not explain why, but I was very comfortable in the man's home. I worried that the group would be walking on when the sun rose higher but I was eating here and having my wound cared for here and I considered the idea of staying with this man because here it seemed very likely that I would not die.

—Why are you here? I asked.

The man grew serious for a moment, as if reading the question for hidden meanings, and then, finding none, softened.

—Why am I here? I like that question. Thank you for it. Yes.

He sat back and grinned at me, seeming in no way interested in answering the question.

—I was so rude! He threw the carpet aside again and retrieved a plastic container and brought it out and handed it to me. —To give you nuts without a drink to wash it down! Drink.

I took the container and the cold of its surface startled my hands. I turned its white cap and placed it in my lap and tilted the vessel to my mouth. The water was so cold. So fantastically cold. I could not close my eyes, I could barely swallow. I drank from the cool water and felt it flow down my throat, wetting me just under my skin, and then inside my chest and my arms and legs. It was the coldest water I had ever tasted.

I tried a different question. —Where are we?

The man took the vessel from me and replaced it underground.

—We are close to a town called Thiet. That's where your group was passing. Many groups have been passing through Thiet.

—So you live in Thiet?

—No, no. I live nowhere. This is nowhere. When you leave here you won't know where you came from. I insist that you forget where you are already. Do you understand me? I am not anywhere and this is nowhere and that is why I am alive.

A few moments before, I was thankful to the man, and was considering asking him if I could stay with him indefinitely. But now I decided that the man had lost his mind and that I should leave. It was strange, that a man could speak normally for a certain time, and then reveal himself to be mad. It was like finding rot underneath a fruit's unblemished skin.

—I should go back to the group, I said, rising.

Alarm took over the man's face.

—Sit. Sit. I have more. Do you like oranges? I have oranges.

He reached into his hole yet again, his arm this time disappearing up to his shoulder. When his hand emerged, he held an orange, perfectly round and fresh. He gave me one and as I devoured it, he replaced the carpet over his underground cavity.

—I don't live anywhere, and you should learn from this. Why do you think I'm alive, boy? I'm alive because no one knows I'm here. I live because I do not exist.

He took the water from me and replaced it under the ground.

—Out there everyone is killing each other, and those who don't kill each other with guns and bombs, God is trying to kill with malaria and dysentery and a thousand other things. But no one can kill the man who's not there, correct? So I am a ghost. How can you kill a ghost?

I had no comment on this for it seemed the man did indeed exist.

—By this contact alone, me with you, I'm making a great deal of trouble for myself. I have fed you and I have seen your face. But I feel safe only in knowing that no one is likely looking for a boy like you. How many of you are there? Thousands?

I told them that there were as many of us as he could imagine.

—So you won't be noticed. When we're done talking, I'll send you back toward them but you must never tell where you found me. Are we in agreement?

I agreed. I do not remember why it occurred to me to ask this man about the What but it seemed that if any man might have an answer, even a guess, it would be this strange man who lived alone and had saved so much, had even thrived, amid a civil war. So I asked him.

—Excuse me? he said.

I repeated the question, and I explained the story. The man had not heard this story but he liked it.

—What do *you* think is the What? he asked.

I didn't know what I thought. —The AK-47?

He shook his head. —I don't think so, no.

—The horse?

He shook his head again.

—Airplanes? Tanks?

—Please stop. You're not thinking right.

—Education? Books?

—I don't think this is the What, Achak. I think you need to keep looking. Do you have any other ideas?

We sat in silence for a moment. He could sense my deflation.

—Would you like to try the bicycle? he asked.

I could not find the words for how I felt about it.

—You didn't expect that, did you, listening boy?

I shook my head. —Are you serious?

—Of course I am. I didn't know I would offer this to you until I already had done so. I never thought I would offer my bicycle to anyone else but since you are headed for Ethiopia and you might die on the way, I'll let you use it.

The man saw my face fall.

—No, no. I'm sorry! I was telling a joke. You won't die on the way. No. You are many boys, and you'll be safe. God is watching over you. You're strong now with a belly full of groundnuts. I was only joking because it would be so absurd if you were in danger. It is absurd. You'll be fine! And now you will ride the bicycle.

—Yes please.

—But you have never done so.

—No.

The round-bellied man sighed and called himself crazy. He rolled the bicycle out of his home and into the sun. The spokes shimmered, the frame shone. He showed me how to sit on the seat, and while I arranged myself upon it, he held the bike upright. It was the most astonishing bicycle ever seen in Sudan, and I was sitting on its luxurious black leather seat.

—Okay, now I'll push the bike so it moves. You have to start pushing on the pedals when I begin. Understand?

I nodded and the wheels started moving. Immediately it was too fast but the man was holding onto it so I felt steady. I pushed the pedals, though they seemed to be moving on their own.

—Pedal, boy, pedal!

The man was running alongside me and the bike, huffing and heaving and laughing. I pushed on the pedals and my feet swung low and then rose up again. My stomach was in turmoil.

—Yes! You're doing it, boy, you're riding!

I smiled and looked ahead and tried to calm my stomach, which threatened to send its contents onto the dust. I swallowed and swallowed and looked straight ahead and told my stomach to be still. It obeyed and allowed me to think. I was riding the bicycle! It was very much like flight, I thought. The wind in my face felt so strong. I had the unexpected thought that I wanted Amath to be able to see me. She would be so impressed!

—I'm going to let go, the man said.

—No! I said.

Still, I thought I could do it.

—Yes! Yes, the man said. —I will let go.

He let go and laughed.

—I let go! Keep going, Red Army! Keep it straight!

I could not keep it straight. In seconds the bicycle tilted and the tire turned slowly and I fell like the horseman had in Marial Bai, caught under the bike. My leg struck a hard patch of dirt and roots and my wound opened up, wider than before. In a few minutes I was back in the round-bellied man's hut and he was nursing the wound again. He apologized many times but I assured him the fault was mine. He told me I rode well for my first time, and I smiled. I was certain that I could ride it successfully if I tried again. But I knew that if I did not find my way back to the group I would lose them forever and might have to live with this man until the end of the war, whenever that came. I told him I had to leave. He was not overly sad to see me go.

—Please don't tell anyone about the bicycle.

I told him I would not.

—Do you promise me this? he said.

I promised.

—Good. Bicycles are secret in this war. Bicycles are secret, listening boy. Now let's return you to your army. I will take you back to them. Which way did you run from?

It had seemed like hours that I had run the night before, but we walked back to the group in a far shorter time. I saw the mass of boys not far from the man's secret home. Dut was not to be seen, and it did not seem that morning that anyone else cared that he was gone, or that I had been missing. I asked what was the matter and learned that a dozen boys were missing from last night's run. Three boys had fallen into wells; two were dead. The hundreds of boys were scattered and listless. I said goodbye to the round-bellied man and found William K, who had found a large sheet of plastic and was trying to fold it to fit in his pocket. The plastic, even after folded a dozen times, was as big as his torso.

—Which way did you run? William K asked.

I pointed the way I had just come. William K had run the opposite way but had stopped after a short time, hiding in the roots of a baobab tree.

—Did you hear what happened? What the rumbling was, the lights? he asked.

I shook my head.

—It was us. It was nothing.

There had been no attack in the night. There were no guns, no shots. It was only a Land Rover driving through the night. No one knew whose car it was, but it was not an enemy's. It might have even been an aid truck.

When Dut arrived, later in the morning, and gathered us, he was exasperated.

—You can't simply run every which way at every sound in the night.

We were all too confused to argue.

—We lost twelve boys last night. We know three are dead because they fell in those two wells. Too many boys have fallen into wells. This is a bad way to die, boys. The others have run to God knows where.

I agreed falling into a well was a bad way to die, but I was sure that it had been his deputy, Kur, who had sent us fleeing during the night. But at that point nothing was clear. After an hour away from the round-bellied man and his bicycle, I was no longer sure if he himself had been real. I told no one about him.

The food I had eaten gave me strength, as had the secret of the round-bellied man, and yet I was relatively certain that I was dying. The cut on my leg, the bite the barbed wire had ripped from my shin, was very large, a diagonal slash from my knee to the bottom of my calf. It bled slowly all day, and even William K acknowledged this could mean that I would die. In our experience, most boys who had large wounds eventually died. The boys that day and in the coming days did not like to stay close to me, because they saw my wound and guessed that disease had already taken root and was festering within me.

William K knew I was worried and he attempted to assuage my fears.

—In Ethiopia they'll cure that wound quickly. The doctors there are the best. You'll look down at your leg and you'll say, What happened? Wasn't there a wound there? But it'll be gone. They'll erase it.

I smiled, though looking at William K caused me concern. He looked very ill, and he was my only mirror. We could not see ourselves so I relied on the appearance of the other boys, William K in particular, to know something of my own health. We ate the same food and were built in a similar way, so I watched him to see how thin I had become, how my eyes were growing more sunken. On this day I did not look good.

—They actually don't get sick in Ethiopia, William continued, —because the water and air are different there. It's weird, but it's true. People don't get sick, unless they're very stupid. And those people get help from the doctors anyway. The doctors say, You're so stupid to get sick in a place where no one gets sick! But I'll cure you anyway because this is Ethiopia and that's how things are here. I heard this from Dut the other night. You were asleep.

William was a hopeless liar, but it pleased me.

—Can we rest a second? he asked.

I was glad to stop for a moment. Usually we could sit long enough that we felt better, while keeping the line of the group within sight. After a few minutes, watching the other boys shuffle past, William and I were stronger and began again.

—I feel different today, he said. —Dizzier, I think.

My bones shook with each step and there was an odd tingling in my left leg, a shooting bolt of cold every time my heel touched the ground. But he made me feel good and so I allowed him to talk, about my wound and Ethiopia and also about how strong he would be when he grew older. It was one of his favorite subjects, and he talked about it in great detail and scientific precision.

—I'll be a very big man. My father is not so tall, but my brothers are very tall so

I'll be like them, but taller. I'll probably be one of the tallest men ever in Sudan. It'll just be this way. I'll have no choice. And so I'll be a great warrior, and I'll hold many guns at once, and I'll also drive a tank. People's eyes will pop out of their heads when they see me. My mom will be proud when we're all there, back at home, to stand guard against the Baggara. It'll be easy to defend the area when we have some guns. My brother Jor is a huge man. He already has two wives and he's still very young so he'll have more wives when he has more cattle but he will have more cattle because he's very smart and knows cattle and breeding—

I had been walking with my head down, following William's footsteps and listening to his words, and so it was not immediately that I noticed that all the boys were running off the path and into the trees. I looked left and right and everywhere they were running into the trees and climbing. Those who could climb climbed. Those who were too weak stayed below the trees, hoping that something would drop to them.

The trees were full of birds.

I ran to an empty tree and climbed it, finding that the climbing took far longer than it once did. William K ran to the tree, too, and now was under me.

—I can't climb, he said. —Not today, I don't think.

—I'll drop them to you, I said.

In the middle of the tree I found a nest and in it, three small eggs. I didn't wait. I ate two of the eggs while still in the tree. I ate everything, the shell, the feathers inside, I ate it all before I could think. I ate another and finally remembered William K. below me. I jumped down and found William K lying on his side, his eyes closed.

—Wake up! I said.

He opened his eyes.

—I got so dizzy after the running, he said. —Tell me not to run next time.

—You shouldn't run next time.

—No, no. Please don't joke, Achak. I'm so tired.

—Eat an egg. They taste terrible.

Other boys had found nests full of baby birds, and they ate them, after pulling off the feathers that had already formed. They too ate the birds whole, their heads and feet and bones. Kur was spitting out a beak when I saw another tree, unexplored.

—I'll get you one. Stay here, I said to William, and I felt stronger already. I ran to the next tree and once up in its boughs, feasting on another egg, I heard the chopping. It was the chopping and dividing sound of a helicopter. In seconds we were out of the branches and on the ground, running wildly. But there was nowhere to run. There were only the low trees we were in, whose branches were nearly bare and offered no cover, and elsewhere only the desert. Some boys stayed where they were; in some trees there were ten boys hidden. We held onto the branches, spread ourselves against the bark to seem part of it; held it with our arms and faces pressed against its rough surface. The chopping came closer and the helicopters, three of them, came into view, black and low to the ground. The machines split the air and raged over our trees but the helicopters did not fire.

Soon the chopping grew quieter and the helicopters were gone.

This was, to Dut and to all of us, more confusing than the bombing from the Antonovs. Why come so close and see so many targets and not fire at all? We never could understand the philosophy of the Sudanese army. Sometimes we were worth their bullets and bombs, and other times we were not.

Dut decided again that we should walk at night. At night there were no helicopters, so that night we did not rest. Dut felt that we were strong enough, since we had eaten so well from the eggs and birds. And so we walked that night, all night, and the next day we would sleep until the night came again.

—There is more news about Ethiopia, William K began.

—Please, I said.

—Yes, the rumor is that there, the Sudanese are very wealthy. Our people are respected by all, and we are given everything we want. Every Dinka becomes a chief. This is what they say. So we'll all be chiefs, and we get to have what we want. We each have ten people who help us in the ways we need. If we want food, we say "Give me this food" or "Give me that food" and then they have to run and get it. It's not that hard, because there is food everywhere. But they especially worship people like us. I think it matters how far you've come. Because we have come the farthest, we get to choose where we live and we get more servants. We get twenty of them each.

—You said it was ten.

—Yes, it's ten usually. But for us there are twenty, because we've come from so far. I just told you this, Achak. Please listen. You'll need to know these things or else you'll insult the people in Ethiopia. I'm only sad that Moses won't see this with us.

Or maybe he will. Maybe Moses is already there. I bet he's already there. He found a way there and he's waiting for us there, that lucky boy.

As much as I could accept some of what William K said, I knew that Moses was not in Ethiopia and never would be. He was chased down by the man on horseback and his fate was certain.

—Yes, William K continued, —Moses is already getting all the things we'll be getting, and he's laughing at us. What's taking you guys so long? he's saying. We better hurry, right, Achak?

William K did not sound good. I was glad that it was night and that I didn't have to look into William K's sunken eyes, his bloated stomach. I knew I looked this way, too, and so it was doubly troubling to see William and see myself in William. In the black night of the desert we saw no suffering and the air was cooler.

—Look at this, William K said, grabbing my arm.

In the distance, the horizon rose up and drew a jagged line across the sky. I had never seen a mountain range before but there it was. William K was sure that we were upon our destination.

—That is Ethiopia! he whispered. —I didn't expect it so soon.

William K and I were far back in the line and could not ask Dut or Kur where we were. But William's explanation made sense. Before us was a great black silhouette, far bigger than any landmass we had seen before. It could contain as many elephants as walked the earth. William K now walked with his arm around my shoulder.

—When we reach that mountain we're in Ethiopia, he said.

I could not disagree. —I think you're right.

—This was not so bad, Achak. This was not so much to walk to reach Ethiopia. Do you think? Now that we are so close, it was not so bad, was it?

We were close but all was getting worse. We did not reach Ethiopia that day, and we did not reach Ethiopia the next. We slept all times of day and night, because now we were barely walking; our feet were leaden, our arms feeling disconnected. The wound on my leg was infected and I had no friends but William K. No one else wanted to be near me, especially after the vulture. After an early-morning nap I had woken up to a shadow blocking my vision, blocking out the sun. I first thought I was in trouble with Dut, that I had overslept and was about to be kicked awake. But then the figure raised his arms suddenly and turned its head, and I knew it to be a vulture. It hopped onto my good leg and began inspecting my bad leg. I leapt back and the vulture squawked and jumped forward again, toward me. He had no fear of me.

This became a problem for all the boys. If we stayed in one place too long, the vultures would become more interested. Sleeping for more than an hour in the sun was sure to bring carrion birds, and we had to be vigilant, lest the birds begin to feast while we were alive.

It was this day, after I chased off the bird who wanted to eat me, that William K began to look different. There were marks on his face, circular designs in a lighter tone than his skin. He complained of cramps and dizziness but then again, I also had cramps and dizziness. William K continued to talk and because he continued to talk I figured he was as strong as any of us.

—Look, William K said.

I followed William K's finger to a dark lump ahead of us. A vulture flew away from it as they approached. It was the body of a boy, a bit older than us.

—Dumb, said William K.

I told him not to talk about the dead in this way.

—But it *is* dumb! To come so far and to die here.

Now there were bodies all along the trails. Boys, babies, women, men. Every mile we would see bodies, of boys and men, under trees, just off the path. Soon the bodies were wearing SPLA uniforms.

—How can a soldier die like this? William K asked Dut.

—He was not wise about his water, Dut said.

—How close are we, Dut?

—We're getting there. We're close to being close.

—Good, good. The word *close* is a good word.

We walked that day, through the most desolate land we'd crossed yet, and the heat grew in surges. Before noon the air was like something with skin or hair. The sun was our enemy. But all the while, my own dreams of the splendor of Ethiopia increased in vividness and detail. In Ethiopia I would have my own bed, like the bed the chief of Marial Bai had, stuffed with straw and with a blanket made from the skin of a gazelle. In Ethiopia there would be hospitals and markets where all foods were sold. Lemon candies! We would be nursed back to our former weights, and wouldn't have to walk each day; on some days we would not have to do anything at all. Chairs!

We would have chairs in Ethiopia. I would sit on a chair, and I would listen to the radio, because in Ethiopia there would be radios under all the trees. Milk and eggs—there would be plenty of these foods, and plenty of meat, and nuts and stew. There would be clean water where we could bathe, and there would be wells for each home, each full of cool water to drink. Such cool water! We would have to wait before drinking it, because of its coolness. I would have a new family in Ethiopia, with a mother and father who would bring me close and call me son.

Up ahead we saw a group of men sitting under the shade of a small heglig tree. There were eleven men, sitting in two circles, one within the other. As we got closer, we saw that two of the three men were very ill. One appeared to be dead.

—Is he dead? William K asked.

The man closest to William K lunged at him, hitting him in the chest with the back of his large bony hand.

—You will be too unless you keep walking!

The man's yellowed eyes shook with rage. The other soldiers ignored us.

—What happened to him? William K asked.

—Go away, mumbled the soldier.

William persisted. —Was he shot?

The man glared at him. —Show some respect, you ungrateful bug! We're fighting for you!

—I *am* grateful, William K protested.

The man snorted.

—Please believe me, William K said.

The man softened, and after a moment, believed that William was sincere.

—Where are you from, Red Army? he asked.

—Marial Bai.

The man's face relaxed.

—I'm from Chak Chak! What's your name?

—William Kenyang.

—Aha, I thought I would know your clan. I know Thiit Kenyang Kon, who must be your uncle.

—He *is* my uncle. Have you seen him?

—No, no. I wish I had news for you, but I've been gone longer than you. You're not far now. A few days more and you're in Ethiopia. We just came from there.

We sat with the soldiers for some time, and some of the boys were cheered by seeing them, but their presence was troubling. The men had guns and were part of a unit called The Fist, which to me sounded very capable. But then, the men of The Fist were starving, dying. What kind of place were we going to, if grown men with guns had left there and were starving on their way back to Sudan?

The dead soldier disturbed me more than any death of any boy along the way, and when my belief in our journey wavered my steps became reluctant and slow.

In the mirror of William K, I did not look well that day. My cheeks were sunken, my eyes ringed in blue. My tongue was white, my hipbones were visible through my shorts. My throat felt lined with wood and grass. Attempting to swallow caused enormous pain. Boys were walking with their hands on their throats, trying to massage moisture into them. I was quiet and we continued to walk. The afternoon was a very slow one. We could not walk at a pace near to what we had when the walk began. We were covering so little ground. This day, William K asked to stop frequently.

—Just to stop and stand for a moment, he said.

And we would stop and William would lean on me, resting his hand on my shoulder. He would take three breaths and say he was ready again. We did not want to fall behind.

—I feel so heavy, Achak. Do you feel heavy this way?

—I do. I do, William. Everyone does.

The afternoon cooled and the air was easier to breathe. Word came down the line that someone had found the carcass of a dik-dik. They had chased away the vultures and they were trying to find some edible meat on the bones of the animal.

—I need to rest again, William K whispered. —We should sit for a while.

I did not agree that we should sit, but William K was already making his way to a tree, and soon was sitting beneath it, his head against the trunk.

—We need to walk, I said.

William K closed his eyes. —We need to rest. Rest with me, Achak.

—They've found a dik-dik.

—That sounds good.

He looked up to me and smiled.

—We need to get some of the meat. It'll be gone in seconds, William.

I watched as William K's eyes flickered, his eyelids closing slowly.

—Soon, he said. —But sit for a second. This is helping me. Please.

I stood above him, giving him shade, allowing him a few moments of peace, and then said it was time to go.

—It's not time, he said.

—The meat will be gone.

—You get some. Can you get some and bring it back to me?

God forgive me, I thought this was a good idea.

—I'll come back, I said.

—Good, he said.

—Keep your eyes open, I said.

—Okay, he said. He looked up to me and nodded. —I need this. I feel like this is helping me.

His eyes slowly closed and I ran to get our share of the animal. While I was gone, the life in William K fell away and his flesh returned to the earth.

It was easier to die now. With Deng, there had been a night between the living Deng and the departed Deng. I had assumed that dying always took place over those many hours in the dark. But William K had done something different. He only stopped walking, sat under a tree, closed his eyes, and was gone. I had returned with a finger's worth of meat to share with him and found his body already cold.

I had known William K since he was a baby and I was a baby. Our mothers had placed us in the same bed as infants. We knew each other as we learned to walk and speak. I could not remember more than a handful of those days that we had not been together, that I had not run with William K. We were simply friends who lived in a village together and expected to always be boys and friends in our village. But in these past months, we had traveled so far from our families, and we had no homes, and we had become so weak and no longer looked as we had before. And now William K's life had ended and his body lay at my feet.

I sat next to him for some time. In my hand his hand became warm again and I looked into his face. I kept the flies at bay and refused to look up; I knew the vultures would be circling and I knew that I could not prevent them from coming to William K. But I decided that I would bury him, that I would bury him even if it meant that I would lose my place with the group. After seeing the dead and dying of the lost Fist, I no longer had any faith in our journey or in our guides. It seemed only logical that what had begun would continue: that we would walk and die until all boys were gone.

I dug as best I could, though I needed to rest frequently; the activity made me lightheaded and short of breath. I could not cry; there was not the water in my body to spare.

—Achak, come!

It was Kur. I saw him in the distance, waving to me. The group had assembled again and was leaving. I chose not to tell Kur or anyone that William K was dead. He was mine and I did not want them touching him. I did not want them telling me how to bury him or how to cover him or that he should be abandoned where he lay. I had not buried Deng but I would bury William K. I waved back to Kur and told him I would come soon and then returned to my digging.

—Now, Achak!

The hole was meager and I knew it would not cover William K. But it would keep the carrion birds at bay for some time, long enough so that I would be able to walk far enough that I wouldn't have to see them descend. I placed leaves on the bottom of the hole, enough that he had a cushion for his head and there was no dirt visible. I dragged William K into the hole and then placed leaves over his face and hands. I bent his knees and folded his feet behind his knees to save space. Now I needed to rest again, and I sat, feeling small satisfaction in knowing that he would fit inside the hole I had made after all.

—Goodbye, Achak! Kur yelled. I saw that the boys had already left. Kur waited a few moments for me, and then turned.

I did not want to leave William K. I wanted to die with him. I was so tired at that moment, so bone-tired that I felt that I could fall asleep as he did, sleep until my body went cold. But then I thought of my mother and my father, my brothers and sisters, and found myself invoking William K's own mythic visions of Ethiopia. The world was terrible but perhaps I would see them again. It was enough to bring me to my feet again. I stood and chose to continue walking, to walk until I could not walk. I would finish burying William K and then I would follow the boys.

I could not watch the first dirt fall on William K's face so I kicked the first layer with the back of my heel. Once his head was covered, I spread more dirt and rocks until it bore some resemblance to a real grave. When I was finished, I told William K that I was sorry. I was sorry that I had not known how sick he was. That I had not found a way to keep him alive. That I was the last person he saw on this earth. That he could not say goodbye to his mother and father, that only I would know where his body lay. It was a broken world, I knew then, that would allow a boy such as me to bury a boy such as William K.

I walked with the boys but I would not talk and I thought frequently about quitting this walking. Each time I saw the remnants of a home, or the hollow of a tree, I was tempted to stop, to live there and give all this up.

We walked through the night, and in the late morning we were very close to the border with Ethiopia, and the rain was a mistake. There should not have been rain in that part of Sudan at that time but the rain came heavily and for most of the day. We drank from the raindrops and we collected the water in all the vessels we had among us. But just as soon as the rain was a boon, it became our curse. For months we had prayed for moisture, for wet earth between our toes and now all we wanted was dry solid ground. By the time we reached Gumuro, there was virtually no piece of land that had not been drenched, reduced to swamp. But there was one elevated patch of land and Dut led us to it.

—Tanks!

Kur saw them first. We stopped and crouched in the grass. I did not know if the SPLA had their own tanks, so at first I assumed the tanks were those of the government of Sudan and were there to kill us.

—This should be SPLA territory, Dut said, walking toward the village.

Three military trucks stood in the center of the town. The town was burned everywhere but we were happy to see three SPLA soldiers step out from the husk of a bus. Dut stepped carefully.

—Welcome boys! one of the soldiers said to us. He wore fatigues and boots but no shirt. We smiled at him, sure that we would be fed and cared for.

—Now please leave, he said. —You need to get out.

Dut stepped forward, insisting that we were on the same side and that we needed food, to rest on dry land until the rains let up.

—We have nothing, a weary voice said. It was another soldier, wearing only shorts. He looked much like us, malnourished and defeated.

—This is SPLA land? Dut asked.

—I guess it is, the second soldier said. —We hear nothing from them. They've left us out here to die. This is a war run by fools.

The soldiers, eleven of them waiting at Gumuro, were from another lost battalion, this one without a nickname like The Fist. These men had been left in Gumuro without supplies and with no means of communicating with their commanders in Rumbek, or anywhere else. Dut explained that he did not want to add to the woes of the soldiers, but he had more than three hundred boys who could not walk through the night and would like to rest.

—I really don't care one way or another, the second soldier said. —Just don't take anything. We have nothing to take. Do what you want.

Thus Gumuro was chosen as the day's place to rest, and we spread out under the trucks and in the shadow of the tank, anywhere where the rain was deflected. It was not long before some of the boys wanted to look for food, or for fish in the swamps. The first soldier, whose name was Tito, urged them to stay put.

—There are mines here, boys. You can't wander off. The Sudanese army left mines all over here.

The message was not getting through to the boys, so Dut stepped in.

—Does everyone know what a mine does to a person?

Everyone nodded, though Dut was not convinced. So he led a demonstration. He knelt on the ground, and asked a volunteer to pretend to step onto his hand. When he did, Dut made the sound of a great blast, and he took the boy's foot and threw the boy onto his back; he landed with a slap. The boy, his eyes tearing with anger and pain, got up and returned to his spot under a bus.

It was not long before boys disobeyed. Dozens of boys walked off in all directions. Many were hungry, and were determined to find food. Three boys went into the grass. I asked them where they were going, hoping that they would be fishing and that I might join them. They did not answer me and walked down the hill. I sat under a truck, my head between my knees, and thought of William K, about the carrion birds who might be curious about him. I thought of Amath and my mother and her yellow dress. I knew that I would die soon and hoped that perhaps she was dead, too, and that I could join her. I did not want to wait in death to see her.

The sound was like the popping of a balloon. Then a scream. I did not investigate. I did not want to see. I knew the boys had found a mine. The movement of many men followed, those coming to help the boy. It emerged that one boy had lost his leg;

two others had been killed. These were the boys who I had asked to join. The boy who had lost his leg died later in the evening. There were no doctors in Gumuro.

Some boys rested but I decided that I would not sleep. I would not close my eyes until I reached Ethiopia. I did not feel like living, and I was very sure that I was dying, too. I had eaten the eggs in the tree, and the nuts from the bicycle man, and so had eaten more than some boys, but the wound on my leg would not heal, and each night I felt the insects explore its crevices. When we walked, the boys in front of me were a blur and their voices, when they came to me, no longer made sense. My ears were infected, my vision unreliable. I was a very good candidate to be taken next.

After the soldiers had helped Dut dispose of the dead boys, one of the soldiers saw me under the truck and crouched before me. The rains had abated.

—Come here, Red Army, he said.

I did not move. I am not rude this way by nature, but at that moment I did not care about this soldier or what he wanted me to do. I didn't want to help bury bodies or anything ideas he might have for me.

—That is an order, Red Army! he barked.

—I'm not in your army, I said.

His arm was quick and his grip was immediate. In one quick motion he had taken me from under the truck and lifted me to my feet.

—You're not part of us? Of this cause? he asked. Now I saw that it was the soldier named Tito. His face was heavily scarred, his eyes yellow, ringed in red.

I shook my head. I was not part of anything, I decided. I was not even part of the walking boys. I wanted to return to the man with the bicycle, to his oranges and cold hidden water.

—So you'll just die here? Tito demanded.

—Yes, I said. I was even then ashamed at how insolent I was acting.

Tito took me roughly by the arm and led me across the village to a pyramid of logs and kindling, and behind it, the legs of a man. The rest of the man's body was hidden under the leaves. His feet were pink, black, white, covered in grubs.

—You see this man?

I nodded.

—This is a dead man. This was a man like me, a man my age. A big man. Strong, healthy. He had shot down a helicopter. Can you imagine this, Red Army, a Dinka man shooting down a helicopter? I was there. It was a great day. But he's dead now, and why? Because he decided not to be strong. Do you want to be like the dead man?

I was so tired that I didn't react at all.

—This is acceptable to you? he barked.

—Everyone is dying, I said. —We passed dead soldiers coming here.

This seemed surprising to Tito. He wanted to know where we had seen them, and how many there were. When I told him, he was changed: it became clear to him that his was not the only group of soldiers alone in the desert, forgotten in the war. This news, I believe, gave Tito strength. And watching him run back to the bus to tell his comrades, I felt stronger, too. I realize it was not rational.

In the early evening, as the sky's blue grew black, we were settling in to sleep when a figure broke the horizon. Dut saw him and stood on the edge of the village, squinting into the distance. The figure became a boy.

—Is that one of ours? Dut asked.

No one answered. Tito was asleep in the shadow of the tank.

—Kur, could that be one of ours? Dut asked.

Kur shrugged.

I squinted and saw that the boy on the horizon became many boys, then hundreds of figures. I sat up. Dut and Kur stood, their hands on their hips.

—My God, who is that?

Dut woke Tito and asked if he knew anything about a group of boys coming to Gumuro.

—We didn't know about *you*, Tito said wearily. He was unhappy to be woken but was interested in the mass of people approaching.

The group in the distance grew closer. All of the boys of our group were watching as this other, larger, line of boys approached. The line did not end. The line grew to four boys wide and soon there were women visible, very small children, armed men. Tito was agitated.

—What the hell is this?

This was a river of Sudanese and they were coming into Gumuro. They looked stronger, and they walked briskly, with purpose. They carried bags, baskets, suitcases, sacks. And then the most incredible thing: a tanker.

—Water, Tito said. —That's the SPLA water tanker.

—A tanker? Dut whispered. —We have a tanker?

The group emerging from the drenched horizon was eight hundred strong, perhaps a thousand. They were accompanied by fifty soldiers or more, armed and healthy and guarding the walkers. The first of them began to enter the town. Dut was elated. He saw their food and their water and gathered us.

The first of the new soldiers stepped up to Dut and Tito.

—Hello uncle! Dut said, now exuberant, almost in tears.

—Who are you? the new soldier said. He wore a baseball hat and a full uniform.

—We're some of the walking boys, Dut said. —Like you. We just arrived earlier today. It's so good to see you here! We're so hungry! And we have no clean water. They're drinking from puddles, from the swamps. When I saw that tanker I thought God himself had sent it to us. We really could use some of that. We're dying here. We've lost so many. How should we—

—We'll feed the soldiers, the new rebel said, —but you shouldn't be here.

—In this village? Dut was incredulous. His voice cracked.

—We have to take this village. We've got a thousand people.

—Well, we're only three hundred. I'm sure there's room. And we really need assistance. We lost nineteen boys in the desert.

—That may be the case. But you have to leave now, before the rest of my group arrives. These are important people and we're escorting them to Pinyudo.

Dut watched the people arriving. There were families and adults in fine clothing but there were among them many boys, small boys, looking very much like us. The only difference was that the new group was better fed. Their eyes were not shrunken, their bellies not bloated. They wore shirts and shoes.

—Uncle, Dut tried. —I have respect for you and your position. I only ask that we share this land tonight. It's already getting dark.

—Then you better move now.

Dut was sputtering now, as the reality of the soldier's resolve became clear.

—Where? Where will we go?

—I won't draw you a map. Move. Get these mosquitoes out of our way.

He cast a disgusted look over all of us, our protruding bones and eyes and cracked skin, our mouths circled in white.

—But uncle, we're the same! Aren't we the same? Are your goals different than mine?

—I don't know what your goals are.

—I can't believe this. It's absurd.

The crack at that moment was very similar to that when my father was struck in his shop. I turned away. Dut lay on the ground, his temple bleeding from the blow of the butt of the gun. The soldier stood over him.

—It *is* absurd, doctor. Good choice of words. Now get the hell out of here.

The soldier raised his gun and shot into the air. —Get out of here, you insects! Move!

The new soldiers chased us from the village, beating whomever they could. Boys fell and bled. Boys ran. We ran and I ran and I had never felt the rage I felt at that moment. My anger was more intense than it had ever been toward the murahaleen. It was born of the realization that there were castes within the displaced. And we occupied the lowest rung on the ladder. We were utterly dispensible to all—to the government, to the murahaleen, to the rebels, to the better-situated refugees.

We settled on the edge of Gumuro, in a marsh, where we rested in ankle-deep water and tried to sleep. We were alone and in a circle again, listening to the sounds of the forest, watching the lights of the tanker in the distance.

It was two days more before we reached Ethiopia. Before Ethiopia we had to cross a tributary of the Nile, the Gilo River, wide and deep. The people who lived by the water owned boats but would not allow us to use them. Swimming was our only choice.

—Who'll be first? Dut asked.

On the riverbank there were three crocodiles drying themselves. When the first boys stepped into the river, those crocodiles chose to enter the water, too. The boys leapt from the water, crying.

—Come, look, Dut said. —These crocodiles won't attack. They're not hungry today.

He waded into the river and then began to swim, gliding easily, his head above water, his glasses never getting wet. Dut seemed capable of anything. Some boys cried anew, watching him in the middle of the river. We expected him to disappear in an instant. But he swam back to us untouched.

—Now we must go. Anyone who wants to stay here, can do so. But we are crossing this river today, and once we do, we will be very close to our destination.

We squinted to see what lay ahead on the opposite bank of the river. From our perspective, it looked very much like the side of the river we were on, but we had faith that once across the water, all would be new.

Few among us could swim, so Kur and Dut, and the boys who could swim, pulled across those who could not. Two swimmers would take one boy at a time, and this took quite some time. Each boy was courageous and quiet as they were brought to the opposite shore, keeping their legs from dangling too deep. No one was attacked in that river that day. But these same crocodiles would grow accustomed to eating people at a later time.

As I waited for my turn, hunger came to me like I had not experienced in weeks. Perhaps it was because I knew that in the riverside village there was real food, and that there must exist some way to get it. Alone, I walked from house to house, trying to conceive of a plan to trade for or steal food. I had never stolen in my life but the temptation was becoming too great.

A boy's voice spoke to my back. —You, boy, where are you from?

He was my age, a boy who looked not dissimilar to us Dinka. He spoke a kind of Arabic. I was surprised to find that I could understand the boy. I told him that I had walked from Bahr al-Ghazal, though this meant nothing to him. Bahr al-Ghazal did not exist here.

—I want your shirt, the boy said. Soon another boy, looking like the older brother to the first boy, approached and commented that he, too, wanted my shirt. In a moment a deal was struck: I told them I would sell them my shirt in exchange for a cup of maize and a cup of green beans.

The older boy ran into their hut and returned with the food. I gave them the only shirt I had. Soon I rejoined the walking boys at the water; others had traded with the villagers and were cooking and eating. Naked but for my shorts, I boiled my maize and ate quickly. As we waited to be brought over the water, those boys who had not eaten now went about bartering what they had. Some sold extra clothes, or whatever else they had found or carried: a mango, dried fish, a mosquito net. None of us knew that only one hour away would be the refugee camp where we would settle for three years. When we arrived there, at Pinyudo, I would curse my decision to trade my shirt for a cup of maize. One boy traded all of his clothes, leaving him naked completely, and he would remain naked for six months, until the camp received its first shipment of used clothes from other parts of the world.

*   *   *

In the late afternoon, it was finally my turn to cross the river. I had eaten and felt sated. Dut and Kur, however, seemed very tired. They spent much of my crossing on their backs, mistakenly kicking me, splashing slowly backward. When we reached the far bank, I sat with the other boys, resting and waiting for our hearts to settle. Finally, as night fell, Dut and Kur finished crossing the river with boys. We thanked them for pulling us over and I kept close to Kur as they led us up from the river, through a thicket of trees, and upon a clearing.

—This is it, Kur said. —We are now in Ethiopia.

—No, I said, knowing he was making a joke. —When will we reach it, Kur?

—We've reached it. We're here.

I looked at the land. It looked exactly like the other side of the river, the side that was Sudan, the side we left. There were no homes. There were no medical facilities. No food. No water for drinking.

—This is not that place, I said.

—It is that place, Achak. Now we can rest.

Already there were Sudanese adults spread out across the fields, refugees who had arrived before us, lying on the ground, sick and dying. This was not the Ethiopia we had walked for. I was sure we had farther to go.

We are not in Ethiopia, I thought. This is not that place.

BOOK II

XV.

First I hear his voice. Achor Achor is close. Talking on his cell phone, in English. His wonderful high-pitched voice. I look up to see his form pass through the window. Now the scratching of his keys against the door and finding their place in the lock.

He opens the door and his hand falls to his side.

"What are you doing?" he asks in English.

To see him is too much. I had a secret fear that I would never see his face again. I manage to make a few grateful squeaks and grunts before he kneels and removes the tape from my mouth.

"Achak! Are you okay?"

It takes me a moment to compose myself.

"What the hell is this?" he asks.

"I was attacked," I finally say. "We were robbed."

He spends a long moment taking in the scene. His eyes rest on my face, my hands, my legs. He scans the room as if a better explanation will reveal itself.

"Cut me loose!" I say.

He is quick to find a knife and kneels next to me. He cuts through the phone cord. I give him my feet and he unties the knot. He switches to Dinka.

"Achak, what the hell happened? How long have you been here?"

I tell him it has been almost a full day. He helps me stand.

"Let's go to the hospital."

"I'm not injured," I say, though I have no way of knowing.

We walk to the bathroom, where Achor Achor inspects the cut under the bright lights. He cleans the cut carefully with a towel soaked in warm water. As he does, he takes in a quick breath, then corrects himself.

"Maybe a few stitches. Let's go."

I insist on calling the police first. I want them to be able to begin the case; I'm certain they will want the warmest trail to follow. The assailants could not be far.

"You pissed your pants."

"I've been here for a day. What time is it? Is it past noon?"

"One-fifteen."

"Why are you home?"

"I came to get money for tonight. I was going to Michelle's after work. I'm supposed to be back at the store in ten minutes."

Achor Achor looks as concerned about getting back to work as he does about me. I go to my closet for a change of clothes. I use the bathroom, showering and changing, spending too long on basic tasks.

Achor Achor knocks. "Are you okay?"

"I'm so hungry. Do you have food?"

"No. I'll go get some."

"No!" I say, almost leaping off the toilet. "Don't go. I'll eat whatever we have here. Don't leave."

I look in the mirror. The blood has dried on my temple, on my mouth. I finish in the bathroom and Achor Achor gives me half a ham sandwich he has retrieved from the freezer and microwaved. We sit on the couch.

"You were at Michelle's?"

"I'm so sorry, Achak. Who were they?"

"No one we know."

"If I had been here it wouldn't have happened."

"I think it would. Look at us. What would we have done?"

We discuss calling the police. We have to quickly review anything that could go wrong if we do. Are our immigration papers in order? They are. Do we have outstanding parking tickets? I have three, Achor Achor two. We calculate whether or not we have enough in checking accounts to pay the tickets if the police demand it. We decide that we do.

Achor Achor makes the call. He tells the dispatcher what has happened, that I was attacked and we were robbed. He neglects to mention that the man had a gun, but I figure it will not matter for now. When the police cars arrive I will have plenty of time to describe the events. I will be taken to the station to look at pictures of criminals who resemble those who assaulted me. I briefly imagine myself testifying against Tonya and Powder, pointing at them across an outraged courtroom. I realize I will know their full names, and they will know mine. Making them pay for this will be satisfying, but I will have to move from here, because their friends will also know my address. In Sudan a crime against one person can pit families against each other, entire clans, until the matter is thoroughly resolved.

Achor Achor and I sit on the couch and it grows quiet between us. Having the police in this apartment causes growing anxiety. I have little luck with cars or police. I have owned a car for three years and have been in six accidents. On January 16, 2004, I was in three accidents in one twenty-four-hour period. All of the incidents were small, at stoplights and driveways and parking lots, but I had to wonder if I was being toyed with. Now, this year, has begun the ordeal of near-constant towing. I have been towed for parking tickets, have been towed for an out-of-date car registration. This happened two weeks ago and began when I passed a police car leaving a Kentucky Fried Chicken. He followed me, turned on his lights, and I pulled over immediately. The man, very tall and white, his eyes hidden behind sunglasses, quickly told me that he might take me into jail. "You want go to jail?" he asked me, suddenly, loudly. I tried to speak. "Do you?" he interrupted. "Do you?" I said I did not want to go to jail, and asked why I would be going. "Wait here," he said, and I waited in my car as he returned to his. Soon enough I learned that he had pulled me over because the sticker on my license plate had expired; I needed a new, different-colored sticker. For this he saved me—he used the words "I'm gonna stick my neck out and save you here, kid"—from jail, instead simply forcing me to leave the car on the highway, from which it was towed.

"I think I have to go back to work," Achor Achor says.

I say nothing. I know he is just thinking through his options. I know he will come with me to the hospital but needs first to assess how difficult it will be to call his supervisor. He feels he could be fired any day for any reason, and taking an afternoon off is not a decision easily arrived upon.

"I could tell them what happened," he says.

"There's no need," I say.

"No, I'll call them. Maybe they'll let me work the weekend to make it up."

He makes the call, though it does not go well. Achor Achor, and most of us, have learned various and conflicting rules of employment here. There is a strictness that is new, but it also seems shifting and inequitable. At my fabric-filing job, my coworker seemed to operate under vastly different rules than I. She arrived late each day and lied about her hours. She did not seem to work at all while I was present, allowing me—she called me her assistant, though I was no such thing—to do all the day's work. Short of reporting her poor work ethic, I had no recourse but to work twice as hard as she, for two-thirds her pay.

"I wonder if they turn on the sirens for something like this," Achor Achor mused.

"I think so."

"Do you think they catch people like them?"

"I bet they will. These two seemed like criminals. I'm sure the police have pictures of them."

Thoughts of Tonya and Powder being pursued, being caught, fill me with great satisfaction. This country, I am sure, does not tolerate things like this. It occurs to me that this is the first time an officer will act on my behalf. The thought gives me a giddy strength.

Ten minutes pass, then twenty. We've made a list of the major items, but now, with more time than we expected to have, Achor Achor and I begin to catalog the lesser things stolen. We gather all of the user manuals for the missing appliances, in case the police need the model numbers. The information will likely help them recover the stolen items, and the insurance companies, too, will expect this information.

"You'll have to reprogram all the birthdays into your phone," Achor Achor notes.

He is one of my few friends who did not laugh when he knew I was recording the birthdays of everyone I knew. To him it seemed logical enough, providing as it did a string of stopping points along the path of a year, sites where you could appreciate who you knew, how many people called you friend.

Achor Achor is now righting the apartment—the table, the lamp, the couch cushions that are still on the floor. Achor Achor is exceedingly practical, and effortlessly organized. He finishes his homework one day before it's due, because when he does, it affords him that extra day to recheck it. He brings his car in for an oil change every twenty-five hundred miles and drives as if his DMV tester were with him at all times. In the kitchen, he uses the proper equipment for each task. Anne and Gerald Newton, who spend a good deal of time cooking, watching television shows, and reading books about cooking, gave us a vast array of utensils and potholders and other kitchen objects. Achor Achor knows what each is for, keeps them well organized, and tries very hard to find occasion to use each one. Last week I found him cutting onions while wearing goggles, the strap of which said ONIONS ARE FOR WEEPERS.

After half an hour, Achor Achor has the idea that the police might have written the address down incorrectly. He opens the door to see if there is a squad car in the lot; perhaps an officer is checking the other apartments. I tell him about the officer that was there for forty minutes the day before, though I can tell that it is too strange a concept for him to begin to understand. Instead, Achor Achor calls the police again. The response is perfunctory; they tell him a car is on its way.

"I'm cursed," I say. It is the thought on both of our minds. "I'm sorry," I say.

He doesn't immediately relieve me of this burden.

"No, I don't think so," he lies. There can be no other explanation for the things that have happened to me since moving to the United States. Only forty-six refugees were scheduled to fly to New York on September 11, and one of them was me. I have lost my good friend Bobby Newmyer and Tabitha is gone and now this. It is the sort of thing that causes one to laugh, frankly. And at the instant this thought occurs to me, Achor Achor begins to laugh. I smile and we know what we're smiling about.

"They even took the clocks," he says.

Achor Achor chose poorly when he chose me. Yes, there are far worse men, young Sudanese who enjoyed themselves too much, who involved themselves in any mess a young man can find, and I am not that, and neither is Achor Achor. But I have not brought him much good fortune. As we sit, I find it difficult to look at him. We have known each other for too long, and being with him here is perhaps the saddest of all of the situations in which we have found ourselves. We are pathetic, I decide. He is still working in a furniture store, and I am attending three remedial classes at a community college. Are we the future of Sudan? This seems unlikely. Not with the way we attract trouble, not with how often we are victims of calamity. We bring it upon ourselves. Our peripheral vision is poor, I think; in the U.S., we do not see trouble coming.

It has been fifty-two minutes when there is a knock on the door.

I begin to stand but Achor Achor gestures me to sit. He grabs the knob and turns it.

"Wait!" I yell. He doesn't hesitate; I believe for a moment it could be Tonya again. Instead he opens the door and finds a small Asian woman with a ponytail, dressed in half of a police uniform. She has no hat, and her pants do not match her shirt. Achor Achor invites her in, looking at her with unmasked curiosity.

"I heard you had an incident here," she says.

Achor Achor invites her in and closes the door. She sweeps her eyes around the living room without seeing the blood stain. Her toes are touching its outline on the carpet. Achor Achor stares at the stain for a moment, and she follows his eyes.

"Ha," she says. She steps back from the stain.

"Which one of you is the victim?" she asks, her hands on her waist. She looks at me and then Achor Achor. I am sitting four feet from her, dried blood on my mouth and temple. She returns her attention to me.

"Are you the victim?" she asks me.

Achor Achor and I say yes at the same time. Then he gets up and points to my face. "He has been wounded, officer."

She smiles, tilts her head, and sighs loudly. She begins to ask me questions, about how many and when.

"Did you know the perpetrator?" she asks.

"No," I say.

I recount the events of the night and morning. She writes a few words down in a leather-bound notebook. She is thin, miniature everywhere, with dark hair and high cheekbones, and the movements of her hands are the same—tidy, small.

"You sure you didn't know these people?" she asks again.

"No," I repeat.

"But then why did you open the door?"

I explain again that the woman had needed to use my telephone. The officer shakes her head. This doesn't seem to her a satisfactory answer.

"But you didn't know her."

I tell her I did not.

"You didn't know the man, either?"

"No," I say.

"Never seen them before?"

I tell her that I saw the woman on the way up to my apartment. This is of interest to the officer. She writes something in her notebook.

"Do you have insurance?" she asks.

Achor Achor says he has insurance, and finds his card. She takes the card and frowns down at it. "No, no. Renter's insurance," she says. "Something that covers theft like this."

We have nothing of the kind, we realize. I tell her that the woman made at least one phone call from my cell phone.

"That should be helpful, Mr. Achor," she says to me, but does not write this in her notebook.

"I'm Achor Achor," Achor Achor says. "He is Valentino."

She apologizes, pointing out how interesting our names are. She sees this as a segue into the inevitable question of our origin. She asks where we're from, and we tell her Sudan. Her eyes come alive.

"Wait. Darfur, right?"

It is a fact that Darfur is now better known than the country in which that region sits. We explain the geography briefly.

"Sudan, wow," she says, half-heartedly inspecting the locks on our front door. "What are you doing here?"

We tell her that we're working and trying to go to college.

"So were you part of the genocide? Victims of that?"

I sit down, and Achor Achor tries to clarify things for her. I allow him to expound, thinking that perhaps she'll open her notebook again and take down more information about the assault. Achor Achor explains where we came from, and our relationship with the Darfurians, and it's only when he mentions that some from that region have come to Atlanta to live that she seems interested.

They arrived one day at our church in Clarkston, officer. Our priest, Father Kerachi Jangi, turned our attention to the guests at the back of the church, and when everyone turned, our eyes set upon eight newcomers, three men, three women, and two children under eight, most dressed in suits and other formal clothing. The young boy was in a Carolina Panthers jersey. We greeted them then and after church, surprised to see them among us, and curious to know what they had planned. It was not customary for Darfurians, most of whom were Muslim, to be mixing with Dinka, and unprecedented for them to be attending a Christian church on a Sunday. The Darfurians historically had identified more with the Arabs than with us, even though they resembled us far more closely than the ethnic Arabs. Our feelings about them had long been complicated, too, by the fact that many of the murahaleen raiders who terrorized our villages were from Darfur; it took us some time to know that those who were suffering in this new stage of the civil war were not our oppressors, but were victims like ourselves. And so we let them be, and they us. But all is different now, and alliances are changing.

When Achor Achor is finished, the officer sighs closes her notebook.

"Well," she says, and looks once more at the stain.

She hands me a piece of paper the size of a business card. It says COMPLAINT CARD. Achor Achor takes it.

"Does this mean that what happened to him is a complaint?" Achor Achor asks.

"Yes," she says, almost smiling. She then recognizes that he is taking issue with this way of naming the crime. "What do you mean?"

I tell her that having a gun pointed to my head seems more than a complaint.

"This is the way we define a matter like this," she says, and closes her notebook. She has written no more than five words inside.

"You guys take care now, okay?"

She is leaving, and I cannot bring myself to care. The sense of defeat I feel is complete. I had, for the fifty minutes while we waited for the officer's arrival, mustered so much indignation and thirst for vengeance that now I have nowhere to put the emotions. I collapse on my bed and let everything flow through the sheets, the floor, the earth. I have nothing left. We refugees can be celebrated one day, helped and lifted up, and then utterly ignored by all when we prove to be a nuisance. When we find trouble here, it is invariably our own fault.

"I'm sorry," Achor Achor says. He is sitting on my bed. "We should go to the hospital, right? How does it feel, your head?"

I tell him that the pain is severe, that it seems to be traveling throughout my body.

"Then we'll go," he says. "Let's go."

Achor Achor brings me to the hospital in Piedmont. He drives my car, and at his suggestion, I ride in the back seat. I lie down, hoping that doing so will ease the pain in my head. I watch the passing sky, bare trees spidering across the window, but the pain only grows.

XVI.

I have been to this hospital. Shortly after I arrived in Atlanta, Anne Newton brought me here to get a physical. It is the finest hospital in Atlanta, she told me. Her husband Gerald, who I do not know as well—he is a money manager of some kind and is not always home for dinner—came here for surgery on his shoulder after a water-skiing accident. It is the finest we have, Anne said, and I'm happy to be there. In hospitals I feel palpable comfort. I feel the competence, the expertise, so much education and money, all of the supplies sterile, everything packaged, sealed tight. My fears evaporate when the automatic doors shush open.

"You can go home," I tell Achor Achor. "This might take a while."

"I'll stay," he says. "I'll wait till they treat you. Then you can call me when you need to be picked up. I might try to go back to work for an hour or so."

It is four o'clock when we step into the reception area. An African-American man, about thirty years old and wearing short-sleeved blue scrubs, is at the receiving desk. He looks us over with great interest, a curious grin spreading under his thick mustache. As we approach, he seems to register the injuries to my face and head. He asks me what happened, and I relay a brief version of the story. He nods and seems sympathetic. I feel almost irrationally grateful to him.

"We'll get you fixed up quick," he says.

"Thank you so much, sir," I say, reaching over the counter to shake his hand between my two hands. His skin is rough and dry.

He hands me a clipboard. "Just fill in the blanks and—" Here he cuts his hand horizontally through the air, from his stomach outward to me, closing his eyes and shaking his head, as if to say, This will be easy, this will be nothing.

Achor Achor and I sit and fill out the forms. Very quickly I arrive at the line asking for the name of my insurance company, and I pause. Achor Achor begins to think.

"This is a problem," he says, and I know this is true.

I had insurance for about eighteen months, but have been without it since I started school. I am making $1,245 a month, and school fees are $450, rent $425, and then food, heat, so many things. Insurance was not an expense I could work into the equation.

I complete the form as best I can, and bring the clipboard back to the man. I notice his nametag: Julian.

"I can pay you in cash for whatever you do," I say.

"We don't take cash," Julian says. "But don't worry. We'll treat you whether you have insurance or not. Like I said—no sweat." He makes the horizontal gesture again and again it puts me at ease. He must be able to pull whatever strings are necessary. He will personally make sure this is done quickly and done well. Achor Achor is sitting down when I return from the desk.

"He said I'll be treated either way. You can go now," I say. "You should get back to work."

"It's okay," Achor Achor says, not looking up from his magazine; for some reason he is reading *Fish and Game*. "I'll wait till you go in."

I open my mouth to object, but then catch myself. I want him here, just as he wanted me with him when he got his driver's license, and when he applied for his first job, just as we have wanted each other near on dozens of other errands when we felt stronger and more capable as two rather than one. So Achor Achor stays, and we watch the TV above us, and I flip through a basketball magazine.

When fifteen minutes pass, I suppress my disappointment. Fifteen minutes is not long to wait for high-quality medical care, but I did expect something more from Julian. I feel the disappointment, hard to justify but impossible to ignore, in knowing that my injury does not impress Julian or this hospital enough that they throw me onto a gurney and send me swiftly through hallways and doors, barking orders to each other. I have the fleeting thought that perhaps Achor Achor and I can find a way to get my head to bleed again, if only a small amount.

Twenty minutes, thirty minutes pass, and we become engrossed in a college basketball game on ESPN.

"Do you think it's because of the insurance?" I whisper to Achor Achor.

"No," Achor Achor says. "You told him you would pay. They just want to make sure you can pay. Did you show him a credit card?"

I had not done that. Achor Achor is annoyed.

"Well, show him. You have a Citibank."

Julian has not moved from the desk since we arrived. I have been watching him as he fills out forms and organizes files, answers calls. I approach him, removing my wallet as I arrive at his station.

He preempts me. "It shouldn't be too long," he says, looking down at my clipboard. "How do you say your name, anyway? Which is first? Deng?"

"Valentino is my first name, Deng the last name."

"Ah, Valentino. I like that. Just have a seat and—"

"Excuse me," I say, "but I was wondering if the delay in treatment is due to a question about my ability to pay."

I see Julian's mouth begin to open, and decide I need to finish before he misinterprets me. "And I wanted to make sure that it is clear that I can pay. I know that you cannot take cash, but I also have a credit card—" now I remove my new Gold Citibank card from my wallet—"which will cover the costs. It is guaranteed and my credit limit is $2,500, so you should not worry that I will leave without paying."

The look on his face indicates that I've said something culturally indelicate.

"Valentino, we've got to take care of everyone who comes in here. By law, we do. We can't turn you away. So you don't need to show your credit cards. Just relax and watch the Georgetown game and I'm sure you'll get stitched up soon. I'd do it myself but I'm not a doctor. They don't let me near the needle and thread." Here he smiles a generous smile, which slips quickly into a tighter grin, one that indicates that our discussion is finished for now.

I thank him again and return to my seat and explain the situation to Achor Achor.

"I told you," he says.

"You told me?"

A phone rings and Achor Achor's raised finger tells me to stop talking. He is a truly exasperating person. He answers the call and begins to talk quickly in Dinka. It is Luol Majok, one of us, now living in New Hampshire and working as a concierge at a hotel. It is said, mainly by Luol Majok, that Luol Majok knows Manchester better than anyone born or raised there. The conversation is animated and full of laughter. Achor Achor catches my stare and whispers, "He's at a wedding."

Normally I would care about whose wedding it was—I soon gather that it is an all-Sudanese wedding, there in frozen Manchester—but I cannot muster the enthusiasm to hear more details. Achor Achor begins to explain to Luol that he and I are at the hospital, but I wave my hands in front of his face to cut him short. I don't want Luol to know. I don't want anyone to know; it would ruin the celebration. The phone calls would not end. Within minutes, the rumors would have me comatose or dead and no one would feel right dancing. Soon Achor Achor is finished and puts his phone back into his belt holster. Overnight, it seems, every Sudanese man in Atlanta has acquired a belt holster for his cell phone.

"You remember Dut Garang?" he asks. "He's marrying Aduei Nybek. Five hundred people there." In Sudan, weddings are without limit; no one is excluded, whether a guest knows the bride and groom or not. All can attend, and the expense, the speeches, the festivities, they do not end. Sudanese weddings are different in the United States than in Sudan, of course. There are no animals sacrificed, for instance, no checking for blood on the immaculate sheets. But the spirit is similar, and the weddings will be coming quickly from now on. The first of the Lost Boys will soon get their citizenship, and when they do, the brides from Kakuma and Sudan will come flooding over, and the Sudanese population in America will double quickly, and then double again. Most of the men are ready to have families, and they will get no argument from their new wives.

Achor Achor continues his conversation for some time, and greets any number of the Lost Boys I have known. I have no appetite for conversation with them. Talk of weddings brings Tabitha to mind, and the wedding we might have had, and I would rather not have that on my mind on the day when I have been beaten and robbed.

It is six o'clock, Julian. We have been in the waiting room for two hours. The pain in my head has not diminished, but is less sharp than before. I expected help from you, Julian. Not because you are of African descent, but because this hospital is very quiet, the emergency room virtually devoid of patients, and I am one man sitting in your waiting room with what I hope are minor wounds. It would seem to be easy to help me and send me home. I cannot imagine why you would want me here staring at you.

"No point in trying to go back to work now," Achor Achor says.

"I'm sorry," I say.

"It's okay."

"Should we call Lino? I was supposed to see him tonight."

We agree to call Lino and only Lino. Achor Achor does so, and before he tells Lino where I am, he insists that our present location be kept secret.

"He's coming over," Achor Achor says. "He's borrowing a car."

I cannot see the point in him coming here, really, given that I am sure I will be treated any moment, and Lino lives twenty minutes' drive from the hospital. And it is almost assured, I tell Achor Achor, that Lino will get lost along the way, doubling his commute. But in the unlikely event that the wait does continue, Lino's presence will brighten the room. He has begun dating women he has met through eHarmony.com, and he has stories. These stories of dating, all of them unsuccessful, are invariably entertaining, but soon enough the talk will return to weddings, and then to Lino's plans to return to Kakuma, to find a wife. Lino is about to undertake such a trip, and his hopes are high, though the process is protracted and costs a stunning amount of money.

Lino's always-grinning brother Gabriel recently took such a trip. It was not easy. Gabriel came to the U.S. in 2000, spent one year in high school, and is now working at a bottling plant outside Atlanta. He decided, last year, that he wanted a wife. He chose to find his bride at Kakuma, an increasingly popular method for Sudanese in America. He put word out through his contacts still at the camp—he has an uncle, former SPLA—that he was looking to marry. His uncle began to look for him, periodically sending him pictures over the internet. Some of the women were known to Gabriel, some were not. Gabriel preferred a woman from his own region, the Upper Nile, but there were not so many of that kind, his uncle reported. Gabriel soon narrowed his choices down to four women, all of them between the ages of seventeen and twenty-two. None were attending school; all were working in households with relatives in Kakuma. And all would leap at the chance to move to the United States as the wife of one of the Lost Boys.

The Sudanese in America are considered celebrities in Kakuma, and are presumed to possess indescribable wealth. And relatively speaking, we are prosperous. We live in warm and clean apartments, and we own TVs and portable CD players. The fact that most Lost Boys now own cars is something almost beyond comprehension to those still in Kakuma, so it follows that the opportunity to be married to such a man would be enormously attractive. But now there are obstacles. Even ten years ago, it would seem impossible that a woman would insist on seeing a picture of a prospective groom. The women are inspecting the men!

This is happening now, and it makes me laugh and laugh. Gabriel, being a very decent man but not handsome in a conventional sense, lost two of his bride choices once his picture was distributed. The final two women, both of them eighteen and friends with each other, each seemed content to marry Gabriel, though he was unknown to them and their families. At that point it came down to bride price. One of the women, named Julia, lived with about fifteen family members, and she was quite attractive— tall, well shaped, long necked, and with very large eyes. Her father had been killed by a grenade in Nuba, but her uncles were all too happy to negotiate her price, for they would be the beneficiaries. Under Sudanese custom, no woman can receive a dowry, so if a father is dead, it is the uncles who take possession of any cattle.

So this girl's uncle-consortium had long known that they had a beauty on their hands, and expected a very high price for her. Their first offer was one of the highest ever heard of in Kakuma: two hundred and forty cows, which translates to approximately $20,000. As you can imagine, a man like Gabriel, who is being paid $9.90 at a beef-processing plant, is lucky to have saved $500 over the course of two years. So Gabriel waited to hear the asking price of the lesser bride choice, a very sweet young woman though less stunning in appearance. She was shorter than her rival, less statuesque, but very appealing, and said to possess many domestic skills and a good disposition. She lived with her mother and stepfather, and their demands were more reasonable: one hundred and forty cows, or about $13,000.

From there, Gabriel had some thinking to do. He could not afford this price, either, but rarely does a man pay the bride price alone; it is a family matter, assisted by many uncles, cousins, and friends. Gabriel went to his relatives and friends, in the United States and in Kakuma, and found that together, he could could account for one hundred cows, about $9,000. Having settled on the less-expensive bride, through representatives, Gabriel relayed the offer to the girl's people in Kakuma. It was rejected, and no counteroffer was made. He would have to come up with the thirty remaining cows, or have no bride choices at all. He now appealed to the only person he could think of who might be able to make the difference—a prosperous uncle still living in Sudan. Gabriel made a satellite call to Rumbek, a large village about a day's walk to the smaller village where this particular uncle lived. The message was relayed to the uncle: "It is me, Gabriel, son of Aguto, and I want to marry a girl at Kakuma. Will you help me? Can you provide thirty cows?" The message was delivered to the uncle two days after it was sent to Rumbek, and three days later, a return message was brought from Rumbek, and a call was made to Gabriel, in Atlanta: the answer was yes; this rich uncle would be glad to provide the cows, and by the way, was Gabriel aware that his uncle had just been named a member of parliament representing the district? There was good news traveling in all directions.

So the match was agreed upon, and now all Gabriel had to do was this: translate the cattle price in Kenyan shillings; finalize the arrangement; find a flight to Nairobi and passage to Kakuma; spend three months arranging a visa and permit to travel to Kenya; once in Kakuma, meet his bride and her family; visit all of his own relatives at Kakuma, bringing each of them money, gifts, food, jewelry, sneakers, watches, iPods, Levi's from America; arrange a wedding; conduct the wedding while in Kakuma (it would be held at the tin-roofed Lutheran church); then, upon returning to Atlanta, begin the process of bringing his bride to America. For starters, he would have to wait two more years, until he was a naturalized citizen, and after that, the paperwork would begin; while waiting, pray that his bride was not tempted by other Sudanese men in Kakuma or raped by Turkana while getting firewood, for if either happened, she would no longer be desirable, and he would be out one hundred and thirty cows. It was always difficult to get cattle returned once a marriage was dissolved.

Julian, at the time I found Tabitha again, I had not begun to think of marriage. I needed to graduate from college first, and to graduate from college, I needed to save money while I attended English classes at the community college. I was, I calculated, about six years from being ready to marry anyone, Sudanese or otherwise. Thus, when Tabitha said she was busy with another man in Seattle, a former SPLA soldier named Duluma Mam Ater, I was not heartbroken.

Nevertheless, we began to talk. We talked the day after that early conversation, and from there, the calls did not abate. She announced herself into my life with great aplomb. She called me three, four, seven times a day. She called in the morning to say good morning and often called to say goodnight. It seemed in many particulars that we were involved in some sort of romance, but then much of the time, when we talked on the phone, we talked about Duluma. I had never known this man in Kakuma. I knew of him, he was a basketball player of some renown, but otherwise the only things I knew I learned from Tabitha, who called me with complaints about him, worries, alternate plans. He was abusive, she said. He wanted to treat her in the Sudanese way, she said. He held no job and borrowed money from her. I listened and counseled and tried not to appear too anxious to see her leave him.

But I was anxious, because very quickly I had fallen very deeply in love with Tabitha. It was impossible not to. All those hours on the phone, with that voice—I tell you, it is hard to describe. The deep music of it, the intelligence and wit. I talked to her in my bedroom, in the kitchen, in the bathroom, on the deck of our apartment building. It seemed impossible that she could still be seeing Duluma, for we seemed to be talking on the phone six hours a day. In what hours did she fit this Duluma?

"Would you like me to come visit?" she asked me one day.

And then I knew she was testing me. She was ready to jump from Duluma to me and she first wanted to see if she could love me in person.

Two weeks later, she was in Atlanta. It was so strange to see her, to see the woman she had grown into. She was a woman in every particular, a very dramatically shaped woman. She opened her door, not expecting me, and at first, even though she had come to see me, it seemed that for a moment, she did not recognize me. It had been three years since we had last seen each other, in Kakuma. More than three years, and many thousands of miles. After this moment of doubt, the reality of me seemed to settle upon her.

"You've gained weight!" she said, grabbing my shoulders. "I like it!" She noted my new muscles, the thickness of my neck. Many who knew me in the camps comment on the fact that my body no longer resembles an insect's.

The moment she took my shoulders in her hands, when we faced each other square—so close it was difficult to look straight into her perfect face—we were as man and wife. The fact that Tabitha was spending the night was a source of great fascination among the Sudanese in Atlanta. At that time, it was not common for men like us to entertain women, Sudanese women in particular, in our homes for days and nights. This was before Achor Achor met his Michelle, and he stayed in his room much of the weekend, unsure how to deal with the situation. For me, too, it was a transformative weekend. With Tabitha so close for so many hours, awake and asleep, I felt that I had everything that I had ever wanted, and that I had begun to live the life I was intended to live.

On my couch on the second day, as we watched *The Fugitive*—she wanted to see it; I was seeing it for the third time—she told me she had left Duluma. He had been very upset at first, she said.

Indeed, he called me that weekend. He was very agitated. He told me that he needed to confide with me, from one man to another. Tabitha was a whore, he said. She had slept with many men, and would continue to do so. And while he said these things, none of which I believed, I was staring at Tabitha, who was lying on my bed, reading a copy of *Glamour* she had bought when we had gone out for breakfast. She had been pregnant, he said. Pregnant with his child, and she had aborted it. She didn't want the baby and she would not listen to him. She had killed the baby over his objections, he said, and what sort of woman would do that? She is ruined, he said, barren. All the while, I watched Tabitha on her stomach, turning the pages slowly, in her pajamas, her feet crossed in the air. I loved her more with every false and conniving word Duluma said about her. I hung up and went back to Tabitha, to our lazy and luxurious morning together, and I never told her who had called.

Achor Achor is rifling through the magazines on the end table. He finds something of interest and shows me a newsmagazine with a cover story about Sudan. A Darfurian woman, with cracked lips and yellow eyes, looks into the camera, at once despairing and defiant. Do you know what she wants, Julian? She is a woman who had a camera pushed into her face and she stared into the lens. I have no doubt that she wanted to tell her story, or some version of it. But now that it has been told, now that the countless murders and rapes have been documented, or extrapolated from those few reported, the world can wonder how to approach Sudan's violence against Darfur. There are a few thousand African Union troops there, but Darfur is the size of France, and the Darfurians would much prefer Western troops; they are presumed to be better trained and better armed and less susceptible to bribes.

Does this interest you, Julian? You seem to be well-informed and of empathetic nature, though your compassion surely has a limit. You hear my story of being attacked in my own home, and you shake my hand and look into my eyes and promise treatment to me, but then I wait. We wait for someone, perhaps doctors behind curtains or doors, perhaps bureaucrats in unseen offices, to decide when and how I will receive attention. You wear a uniform and have worked at a hospital for some time; I would accept treatment from you, even if you were unsure. But you sit and think you can do nothing.

Achor Achor and I glance through the Darfur article and see some passing mention of oil, the role oil has played in the conflict in Sudan. Admittedly, oil is not at the center of what has happened in Darfur, but Lino can tell you, Julian, about the role oil played in his own displacement. Do you know these things, Julian? Do you know that it was George Bush, the father, who found the major oil deposits under the soil of Sudan? Yes, this is what is said. This was 1974, and at the time, Bush Sr. was the U.S. ambassador to the United Nations. Mr. Bush was an oil person, of course, and he was looking at some satellite maps of Sudan that he had access to, or that his oil friends had made, and these maps indicated that there was oil in the region. He told the government of Sudan about this, and this was the beginning of the first significant exploration, the beginning of U.S. oil involvement in Sudan, and, to some extent, the beginning of the middle of the war. Would it have lasted so long without oil? There is no chance.

Julian, the discovery of oil occurred shortly after the Addis Ababa agreement, the pact that ended the first civil war, that first one lasting almost seventeen years. In 1972, the north and south of Sudan met in Ethiopia, and the peace agreement was signed, including, among other things, provisions to share any of the natural resources of the south, fifty-fifty. Khartoum had agreed to this, but at the time, they believed the primary natural resource in the south was uranium. But at Addis Ababa, no one knew about oil, so when the oil was found, Khartoum was concerned. They had signed this agreement, and the agreement insisted that all resources be split evenly... But not with oil! To share oil with blacks? This would not do! It was terrible for them, I think, and that is when much of the hard-liners in Khartoum began thinking about canceling Addis Ababa and keeping the oil for themselves.

Lino's family lived in the Muglad Basin, a Nuer area near the border between north and south. Unhappily for them, in 1978 Chevron found a large oil field here, and Khartoum, who had authorized the exploration, renamed this area using the Arabic word for unity. Do you like that name, Julian? Unity means the coming together of people, many peoples coming together as one. Is it too obviously ironic? Extending the joke, in 1980 Khartoum tried to redraw the border between the north and south, so the oil fields would be in the north! They didn't get away with that, thank the lord. But still, something needed to be done to cut the Nuer who lived there out of the process, to separate them from the oil, and to ensure that there would be no interference in the future.

It was 1982 when the government got serious about dealing with those, like Lino's family, living above the oil. The murahaleen began to show up with automatic weapons, precisely as they later did in Marial Bai. The idea was that they would force the Nuer out and the oil fields would be protected by Baggara or private security forces, and thus would be inoculated against any kind of rebel tampering. So the horsemen came, as they always come, with their guns and with their random looting and violence. But it was mild this first time; it was a message sent to the Nuer living atop the oil: leave the area and do not come back.

Lino's family did not leave their village. They didn't get the message, or chose to ignore it. Six months later, Sudanese army soldiers visited the village to clarify their suggestion. The Nuer were told to leave at once, to cross the river and move to the south. They were told that their names would be registered, and they would later receive compensation for their land, homes, crops, and whatever possessions they needed to abandon. So that day, Lino's family, and all those in the village, gave their names to the soldiers, and the soldiers left. But even then, Lino's family didn't leave. They were stubborn, Julian, as so many Sudanese are stubborn. You have no doubt heard of the thousand Sudanese in Cairo, those who were trampled? This was not long ago. A thousand Sudanese, squatting in a small park in Cairo, demanding citizenship or safe passage to other nations. Months pass, they will not leave, they cannot be appeased until their demands are met. The Egyptians don't see it as their problem, and the park where the Sudanese are squatting has become an eyesore, and unsanitary. Finally Egyptian troops move in to destroy the shantytown, killing twenty-seven Sudanese in the process, including eleven children. A stubborn people, the Sudanese.

So Lino's family remained. They and hundreds more decided to simply stay where they were. One month later, as might have been expected, a regiment of militiamen and army soldiers rolled into the village. They very calmly strolled into the town, as they had when they took the names. They said nothing to anyone; once positioned, they began to shoot. They shot nineteen people in the first minute. They nailed one man to a tree, and dropped an infant into a well. They killed thirty-two in all, and then climbed back onto their trucks and left. That day, the survivors of the village packed and fled, traveling south. By 1984, Lino's village and the villages near it, all of those sitting atop the oil, were all cleared of Nuer, and Chevron was free to drill.

"Hey sick man!"

Lino has arrived, wearing a blue pinstriped zoot suit, and three gold chains around his neck. There is a store in Atlanta, God help us, where too many Sudanese are buying their clothes. Julian looks up from his reading, amused by Lino's outfit, interested in the three of us speaking quickly in Dinka. I catch his eye and he returns to his book.

It is seven o'clock. We have been here well over three hours.

Lino throws himself onto one of the chairs next to us, and grabs the remote control. While speeding through the channels, he asks what is taking so long. We try to explain. He asks if I have insurance and I say no, but that I offered to pay with cash or credit card.

"That won't work," Lino says. "They don't trust you. Why would they? They don't think you can pay, and they'll wait till you leave, I think. Or you need to figure out a way to ensure that you'll pay."

I don't know that Lino has any insight that might trump my own, but he has me again doubting Julian, this hospital, and my ability to receive treatment here.

"Call Phil. Or Deb," Achor Achor says, referring to Deb Newmyer, Bobby's widow. I have been thinking the same thing. I could have called Phil, but calling Phil at night, with his small children, is not an option; I know the twins go to bed at seven, I have put them to bed myself. I could call Anne and Gerald Newton, but the thought gives me pause. They would over-worry. They would instantly appear at the hospital, bringing Allison, disrupting their lives, and I don't want that. I want only a phone call. I want someone who knows the rules in such situations to make a phone call and explain things to Julian and to me. Deb lives in California, and is likely at home. I dial her number; the Newmyers' youngest, Billi, answers.

"Valentino!" she says.

"Hello my young friend!" I say. I ask her about her swimming lessons. I drove her to the pool a few mornings, and sat on the concrete while she made her first attempt at freestyle. She was scared to put her face straight down, staring at the pool's refracted floor. I smiled at her, attempting to exude confidence, but it did not work. She cried all through the lessons and does not want to talk about them tonight.

Seconds later Deb is on the line. I tell her a longer version of the story. Deb, who has worked in Hollywood for many years and has been involved in a television series called *Amazing Stories*, is incredulous. I am, she says, like the boy who cries wolf, except that each time I cry wolf there is actually a wolf. Deb asks to speak to the man at the desk. I take a certain pride in handing the phone to Julian. He registers it with with a half-lidded glare.

"Who is this?" he asks me.

"She is one of my sponsors. She is calling from Los Angeles and would like to inquire about the care I am receiving."

Julian grimaces and brings the phone to his ear. He and Deb talk for a few minutes, during which time his face contorts into many expressions of dissatisfaction and amusement. When they are finished talking, the phone is returned to me.

"He says they're short-staffed," Deb says. "I yelled at him, but I don't know what else to do. I wish I could come to you and fix this, Val."

I ask her how long she feels that I should wait.

"Well, the guy says it should be any minute. How long have you been there?"

I tell her almost four hours.

"What? Is it busy? Is it some kind of madhouse there?"

I tell her it's been quiet, very quiet.

"Listen, call me in half an hour if you're not treated by then. If you haven't seen a doctor, I'll get serious with these guys. I know some tricks."

I thank Deb, feeling that she has made a great difference. She sighs the weary sigh I have heard many times before. Deb is an energetic woman, but dealing with me has, she says, challenged her optimism.

"Valentino, I just don't know what God has against you," she says.

We sit with that thought for a moment. We both know that there is a question there that has not yet been answered.

"Call me after you get a diagnosis," she says. "If it's anything serious we'll fly you out here and we can see my doctor. But I think you'll be okay. Call me soon."

This is Deb's country, and if Deb says that I will be treated, that it is not about money or insurance, I believe her.

I return to the waiting room, to Lino and Achor Achor, who are on the phone again, talking to various attendees of the Manchester wedding. Between the loud chatter from them and his having to explain himself to Deb, Julian is now visibly unamused. I do not want to be a bother to him, to Deb, to anyone. I want to be independent and move through this world without having to ask questions. But for now I still have too many, and this is frustrating to one such as Julian, who feels he knows the answers and knows me. But Julian, you know nothing yet.

XVII.

The walk to Ethiopia, Julian, was only the beginning. Yes we had walked for months across deserts and wetlands, our ranks thinned daily. There was war all over southern Sudan but in Ethiopia, we were told, we would be safe and there would be food, dry beds, school. I admit that on the way, I allowed my imagination to flower. As we drew closer to the border, my expectations had come to include homes for each of us, new families, tall buildings, glass, waterfalls, bowls of bright oranges set upon clean tables.

But when we reached Ethiopia, it was not that place.

—We are here, Dut said.

—This is not that place, I said.

—This is Ethiopia, Kur said.

It looked the same. There were no buildings, no glass. There were no bowls of oranges set upon clean tables. There was nothing. There was a river and little else. —This is not that place, I said again, and I said it many times over the coming days. The other boys tired of me. Some thought I had lost my mind.

I will admit that when we did cross into Ethiopia, there was a measure of safety, and some rest. We were able to stop, and this was strange. It was strange not to walk. That first night, we slept again where we sat. I was accustomed to walking every day, to walking at night and at the first light of morning, but now, when the sun rose, we stayed. There were boys spread all over the land, and all that was left to do, for some, was to die.

The wails came from everywhere. In the quiet of the night, over the hum of the crickets and frogs, there were the screams and moans, spreading over the camp like a storm. It was as if so many of the boys had been waiting to rest, and now that they had settled at Pinyudo, their bodies gave out. Boys died of malaria, of dysentery, of snake bites, of scorpion stings. Other illnesses were never named.

We were in Ethiopia and there were too many of us. Within days there were thousands of boys and soon after the boys arrived, there were adults and families and babies and the land was crowded with Sudanese. A city of refugees rose up within weeks. It is something to see, people simply sitting, surrounded by rebels and Ethiopian soldiers, waiting to be fed. This became the Pinyudo refugee camp.

Because so many had lost or bartered their clothing along the way, only half of us wore any garments at all. There sprung up a class system, whereby the boys who had shirts and pants and shoes were considered the wealthiest, and next were those who had two of the three. I was lucky to be considered upper-middle-class, with one shirt and two shoes and a pair of shorts. But too many boys were naked, and this was problematic. There was no protection from anything.

—You wait, Dut said to us. —It will improve.

Dut was busy now, and moved to and from the camp, always meeting with elders, disappearing for days. When he returned, he would visit us, the boys he had brought here, and would reassure us that Pinyudo would soon be a home.

For some time, though, finding food was a task left to each of us; we fended for ourselves. Like many boys, I went to the river to fish, though I had no experience fishing at all. I came to the water and everywhere there were boys, some with sticks and string, some with crude spears. My first day fishing, I brought a twisted stick and a piece of wire I had found under a truck.

—That won't work, a boy said to me. —You have no chance that way.

He was a thin boy, as thin as the stick I was holding; he seemed weightless, bending leftward with the gentle wind. I said nothing to him, and threw my wire into the water. I knew he was probably right about my chances, but I couldn't admit it to him. His voice was strangely high, melodic, too pleasing to be trusted. Who was he, anyway and why did he think he could speak to me that way?

He was named Achor Achor, and he helped me that afternoon to find an appropriate stick and piece of string. Together that day and in the days that followed, we waded into the water with our fishing poles and a spear Achor Achor had carved himself. If one of us saw a fish, we would try to triangulate it, while Achor Achor thrust the stick into the water, attempting to spear it. We were not successful. Occasionally a dead fish would be found in a shallow swamp, and that fish we cooked or sometimes ate raw.

Achor Achor became my closest friend in Ethiopia. At Pinyudo he was small like me, very thin, scrawnier than the rest of us even, but very smart, cunning. He was expert at finding things we needed before I realized we needed them. He would locate an empty can one day, full of holes, and save it. He would bring it to our shelter and clean it and patch it until it was an excellent cup—and only a few boys had cups. He eventually found fishing line, and a large undamaged mosquito net, and sisal bags large enough to tie together and use as a blanket. He shared with me always, though I was never sure what I brought to our partnership.

Some food was provided by the Ethiopian army. Soldiers rolled drums of corn and vegetable oil to the camp, and we ate one plate each. I felt better, but many of the boys overate and fell ill soon after. We traded anything we had for corn or corn flour in the nearby village. Soon we learned to recognize the wild vegetables that were edible and common, and we went on expeditions to harvest them. But as the days went on, and more boys came, the vegetable hunters were too many, and the vegetables were soon scarce and then exhausted entirely.

More boys arrived every day, families too. Every day I saw them crossing the river. They came in the morning and they came in the afternoon and when I woke up more had come in the night. Some days one hundred came, some days many more. Some groups were like mine, hundreds of emaciated boys, half of them naked, and a few elders; some groups were only women and girls and babies, accompanied by young SPLA officers with guns tied to their backs. The people came without end, and each time they crossed the river, we knew it meant that the food we had would need to be further divided. I came to resent the sight of my own people, to loathe how many of them there were, how needful, gangrenous, bug-eyed, and wailing.

One day a group of boys threw rocks at a group of new arrivals. The rock-throwing boys were beaten severely and it never happened again, but in my mind, I threw rocks, too. I threw rocks at the women and the children and wanted to throw rocks at the soldiers but I threw rocks at no one.

* * *

235

When order came to the camp, life improved. We were organized, divided, groups were created: Group One, Group Two, Group Three. Sixteen groups of boys, each group with over a thousand boys. And within the groups were groups of one hundred, and within those, groups of fifty and then of twelve.

I was put in charge of a group of twelve, eleven boys and me. We were twelve and I called them The Eleven. Achor Achor was my deputy and we all lived together, ate together, and divided tasks among ourselves—fetching food, water, salt, repairing our shelter, our mosquito nets. We had been thrown together because we were from the same region and spoke similar dialects, but we convinced ourselves that our group was one of all-stars. We came to consider our group superior to all others.

Beyond Achor Achor, there was Athorbei Chol Guet, outspoken and fearless. He would approach anyone, and quickly made allies; he knew Pinyudo's refugee chairman, the UN aid workers, and Ethiopian traders. Gum Ater was preposterously tall and perilously thin and was a distant cousin of the camp's second-in-command, Jurkuch Barach. Akok Anei and Akok Kwuanyin each had light, copper-colored skin, and were feared by many boys because they were older and fiercer than the rest of us. Garang Bol was a great catcher of fish and was highly skilled at finding edible fruits and vegetables. He had replaced a nameless boy who was part of the Eleven for only a few days, a boy who had sipped from a puddle to quench his thirst and died of dysentery shortly thereafter. I suppose there are too many boys to mention, Julian.

But there was also Isaac Aher Arol! He was the only boy of the Eleven who had traveled as far as I had. The boys who came to Ethiopia had walked from all over southern Sudan, but the majority came from a place called Bor, which is not far from the Ethiopian border. I had walked months, whereas many of the boys walked mere days. So Isaac Aher Arol was from my region, Bahr al-Ghazal, and he called me Gone Far and I called him Gone Far, and everyone called both of us Gone Far. To this day, when I see certain boys from Pinyudo, they use this name for me.

But I have many other names, too, Julian. Those who knew me in Marial Bai called me Achak or Marialdit. In Pinyudo I was often Gone Far, and later, in Kakuma, I was Valentino, and sometimes Achak again. Here in America I was Dominic Arou for three years, until last year, when I changed my name, legally and after much effort, to a combination of my given and appropriated names: Valentino Achak Deng. This is confusing to the Americans who know me but not to the boys who walked with me. Each of us has a half-dozen identities: there are the nicknames, there are the catechism names, the names we adopted to survive or to leave Kakuma. Having many names has been necessary for many reasons that refugees know intimately.

In Pinyudo, I missed my family, I wanted to be home, but we were made to understand that there was nothing left in southern Sudan, and to return would mean certain death. The images they painted for us were stark, the destruction complete. It was as if we were the sole survivors, that a new Sudan would be created from us alone, when we returned to a barren land ready for regeneration. We settled in at Pinyudo, and found a way to be thankful for what we had there: a measure of safety, of stability. We had what we had sought: regular meals, blankets, shelter. We were, to the best of our knowledge, orphans, but most of us held out hope that when the war ended, we might find our families again, or portions thereof. We had no basis on which to believe this, but we slept on this hope every night and woke up with it each morning.

For those first weeks and months at Pinyudo, it was only boys and duties, attempts to make order of the camp. Most of my group, being among the youngest, became water boys. My duty was to go to the river to bring back water for drinking and cooking, and each day I trekked down to the riverbank with a jerry can to fill and return to camp. I was told that the water at the bank of the river was not suitable, that I needed to wade into the middle of the river to find the cleanest water.

But I could not swim. I was no more than four feet tall, maybe less, and the river could exceed that on any day, and moved with a rapid current. I had to ask others, taller boys and young men, to help me find the highest-quality water. Four times a day I had to go to the river, and four times a day I had to ask another boy to wade into the river to fill the jerry can. I badly wanted to learn how to swim but there was no time and no one to teach me. So with help, I retrieved the water twice in the morning and twice in the afternoon, carrying the six-liter jerry can back to camp. The weight was significant for an insect like me. I had to rest every ten steps, small steps I hurried together.

Sometimes I would encounter local boys—of a river people called the Anyuak— playing by the water, building houses in the sand. I would hide my jerry can in the tall grass and crouch with the boys, helping to dig trenches and construct villages from mud and sand and sticks. We would jump in the water afterward, laughing and splashing. During these times, I would remember that only months before, I had been a boy like this, too.

One early morning, the light still golden, I played with the Anyuak boys and then returned to the camp. Immediately I was confronted by one of the elders.

—Achak, where is the water? he asked.

I didn't know what he was talking about. I was a forgetful boy, Julian, though I like to think it had something to do with malnourishment.

—We sent you to the river to get water. Where is your jerry can?

Without saying anything, I turned and ran back to the river, jumping over logs and holes along the way. I had seldom run so fast. When I reached the water, I found the riverbank empty; the boys were gone. I slid down the bank with my jerry can, and when I arrived at the bottom, my foot met a large stone. Immediately I drew back. It was a large rock, and covered in a sort of dark moss. It was difficult to see in the shadows, so I crouched down to see if there were any creatures underneath. When I brought my face closer, a smell assaulted me. The rock was a man's head. It was a man's body, dead for some time, floating in the river. The rest of the corpse had been hidden in the grass at the river's edge. The man's eyes faced the river's bottom, arms at his side, his shoulders moving slightly with the current. There was a rope around his waist, and the torso was bloated, seeming about to burst.

Later, the body was identified as that of a young Sudanese man, an SPLA recruit. He had been stabbed three times. The Sudanese elders surmised that the dead man had been killed by the Anyuak; he had likely been caught stealing. They used the dead man as a lesson: if the Sudanese steal, they will be killed by the river people.

After that day, I didn't want to return to the river. I thought of the man all day and particularly at night. Though life in Ethiopia was not comfortable in any way, there was a measure of safety there, so much so that I believed that I would not live so close to violent death. But evil could happen at Pinyudo; of course it could. I spent the next day sleeping, hiding from the elders' voices that called me to work, to eat, to play. Nothing was over. Nothing was safe. Ethiopia was nothing to me. It was no safer than Sudan, and it wasn't Sudan, and I wasn't near my family. Why had we come so far? I did not have enough strength, enough life in me for this.

The elders told me that I would not see another man stabbed, that this would not happen again. But this was not the case. More SPLA were killed, and more Anyuak were killed in vengeance, and relations between the Anyuak and us, the interlopers, deteriorated quickly. There were charges that SPLA soldiers had raped Anyuak women, and Sudanese were killed and lynched in return. The SPLA, better armed, escalated the conflict, burning homes and killing resisters. When, much later, the Anyuak shot a pair of SPLA soldiers along the riverbank, it brought on what was known as the Pinyudo-Agenga Massacre. The Agenga village of Anyuak people was torched, women and children and animals murdered. Thereafter, the Agenga Anyuak left for safer surroundings, but many of its men remained in the area, forming gangs of snipers whose goal was simple and frequently successful: to shoot SPLA soldiers, or any Sudanese, really. When we Sudanese were finally chased from Ethiopia, two years hence, the Anyuak heartily joined in firing shots at our backs as we crossed the river Gilo, its water thick with our blood.

But for a time, there was relative peace between the Sudanese and the Anyuak, and there was even a sense of security at that refugee camp. When, after some months, the international aid community recognized Pinyudo, there were new sources of food for the Anyuak, and trade between our camp and the riverside villages was brisk and agreeable to all involved.

Though we were told not to visit the riverside villages alone, Achor Achor and I did anyway; he was bold and we were bored. In the villages, we were watched by everyone, all eyes suspecting that we came to steal. We explored daily, though, investigating the life along the water, peeking into huts, smelling the food and hoping someone might feed us without our solicitation. One day this very thing happened, though Achor Achor was not with me; he had gone to the airfield to watch a landing that was expected that afternoon.

—Come here, you.

A woman cooking in front of her home spoke to me in Anyuak. One of my stepmothers in Marial Bai was half Anyuak, so I knew enough of the language to understand the woman. I stopped and stepped toward her.

—Do they feed you at that camp? she asked. She was an older woman, older than my own mother, almost like a grandmother, her back bent and her mouth a loose, toothless cavern.

—Yes, I said.

—Come inside, boy.

I went inside her hut and smelled its smells of pumpkins, sesame, and beans. Dried fish hung from the walls. The woman busied herself cooking outside and I settled against the wall of the hut, resting my back against a bag of flour. When she returned she poured a dish of flour and water into a bowl. When I was finished with that, she took a bowl of corn foo-foo and into it poured a cup full of wine, a concoction I had never seen before. When I ate that, she smiled a sad toothless smile. Her name was Ajulo and she lived alone.

—Where are you people going? she asked.

—I don't think we're going anywhere, I said.

This surprised her.

—You're not going anywhere? Why would you stay here?

I told her I didn't know.

—There are too many of you here, she said, now deeply troubled; this was not the information she expected. No one along the river had seen the Sudanese as permanent guests. —Until your people leave, you can come here any time. Come alone and you can eat with me any day, Achak.

When she said that, Julian, she touched my cheek as a mother would, and I crumpled. My bones fell away and I lay down on her floor. I was in front of her, heaving, my shoulders shaking and my fists trying to push the water back into my eyes. I was no longer able to know how to react to kindness like this. The woman brought me close to her chest. I hadn't been touched in four months. I missed the shadow of my mother, listening to the sounds inside her. I had not realized how cold I had felt for so long. This woman gave me her shadow and I wanted to live within it until I could be home again.

—You should stay here, Ajulo whispered to me. —You could be my son.

I said nothing. I stayed with her until evening, wondering if I could indeed be her son. The comfort I would know could not be approximated while living with half-naked boys at the camp. But I knew I couldn't stay. To stay would mean I would abandon the hope of returning home. To accept this woman as my mother would be to deny my own, who might yet be living, who might wait for me the rest of her years. And then, lying in the lap of the Anyuak woman, I wondered, What did she look like, my mother? I had only a shifting memory, as light as linen, and the longer I was with this woman Ajulo, the more distant and indistinguishable my vision of my mother would become. I told Ajulo I could not be her son, but she fed me still. I came

240

once a week and helped how I could, bringing her water, portions of my rations, things she could not otherwise procure. I went there and she fed me and let me lie in her lap. During those hours I was a boy with a home.

After a month, my stomach was no longer wailing and my head ceased spinning. I felt good in many ways, I felt like a person the way God had intended a person to feel. I was almost strong, almost whole. But then there were jobs for healthy boys.

—Achak, come here, Dut said one day. Dut was a high-ranking leader at the camp now, and because we had walked together, he made sure my needs and those of those of the Eleven were addressed. But he expected things in return.

I followed him and learned we were going to the hospital tent, set up by the Ethiopians. Inside were those wounded in the fighting in Sudan, and those sick and dying at Pinyudo. I had never been in the tent and only knew it by its smell, which was rancid, piercing when the wind passed through.

—There is a man inside who has died, he said. —I want you to help carry him and then we'll bury him.

I could not object. I owed Dut my life.

Inside the tent, the light was blue-green and there was a body wrapped in muslin. Around the body were six boys, all of them older than me.

—Come here, Dut said, directing me to the dead man's feet.

I carried the man's left foot, and the other six boys each took a region of the man's cold hard form. We followed the path, Dut holding the man's shoulders and facing away. I looked to the clouds, to the grass and the brush—anywhere but at the face of the dead man.

When we arrived at a great twisting tree, Dut told us to begin digging. There were no shovels, so we clawed at the ground with our fingernails, throwing rocks and dirt to the side. Most of us dug like dogs, scratching the dirt between our legs. I found a rock with a bowl-like edge that I used to scoop dirt to the side. In an hour, we dug a hole six feet long and three feet deep. Dut directed us to line the hole with leaves, and we gathered leaves and made the hole green. Dut and the larger boys then lifted the body into the hole, the man's face turned to the east. We weren't sure why this was the case, but we did not ask when Dut told them to do this. We were directed to place leaves over the body, and once that was done, we dropped dirt onto the body of the dead man until he disappeared.

This was the beginning of the cemetery at Pinyudo, and the first of many burials in which I participated. Boys and adults were still dying, for our diet was too limited and the dangers too many. Most days, we were given just one meal, yellow corn grains and a few white beans. We drank water from the river and it was impure, rife with bacteria, so the deaths came from dysentery, diarrhea, various unnamed afflictions. There was very little medical expertise at Pinyudo, and the only patients who were brought to the Pinyudo One General Health Clinic were those who were already too close to death to save. When a boy would not rouse himself from bed, would refuse food, or fail to recognize his name, his friends would wrap him in a blanket and bring him to the clinic. It was a well-known fact that any patients admitted to the clinic did not leave, and so that tent became known as Zone Eight. There were seven zones at the camp, where the boys were housed and worked, and Zone Eight became the last place one went on this earth. "Where is Akol Mawein?" someone might ask. "He's gone to Zone Eight," we would answer. Zone Eight was the hereafter. Zone Eight was the end of ends.

Burying Zone Eights became my job. With five other boys, we buried five to ten bodies a week. We took the same parts of the bodies each time; each time, I was the carrier of the deceased's left foot.

—You're a burial boy, Achor Achor said one day.

I smiled, at that time thinking it was a job holding some prestige.

—That's not a good job, I don't think, Achor Achor said. —I think this could be bad for you in some way. Why are you doing that job?

It was not as if I had a choice in the matter. Dut had asked me, and I had to agree. He had promised benefits for being a burial boy, including extra rations, and even another shirt, which meant that soon I had two—an extravagance at Pinyudo.

Soon, though, Dut's role as overseer of the burials was ceded to a cruel and nervous man we called Commander Beltbuckle. Each day, over his fatigues, he wore a silver-and-red belt buckle so large and ridiculous that it was almost impossible to face him without laughing. But he was very proud of it, its size and sparkle; it was never unshined and he was never seen without it. He employed a certain boy named Luol who was in charge of shining it each night, at which point he put it back on. Rumor had it that the commander slept on his back each night because he would not take off the pants that held the buckle, and to sleep on his side or stomach would drive the buckle into his abdomen. We did not have a high opinion of Commander Beltbuckle or his clothing accessories.

Commander Beltbuckle had a series of rules about carrying bodies and burying them, some of which were sensible and some of which were utterly divorced from any logic or purpose. When we carried the bodies, for the dignity of the person who had passed, we were to keep the body as stiff as possible; someone had to walk below the body, crouching, keeping the back from dragging on the ground. When we dug the graves, they were to be given perfect ninety-degree corners on all sides. When we lay the bodies down, their hands were to be placed atop their waists, and their heads turned slightly to the right. Then they were covered in a blanket and the graves filled with earth. No one questioned these rules. There was no point in doing so.

I had gotten accustomed to the burials, and was helping to bury at least one body each day. Some days there were two, three, four people, mostly boys. Burying boys was both blessing and curse—blessing because they were lighter than the grown men and women, but more difficult when we were aware of or even knew personally the boy we were burying. But such instances were thankfully rare. Commander Beltbuckle knew enough to cover the faces of the Zone Eights. We did not ask their identities, even though we could often guess. We did not want to know who was who.

The boys we could carry with just four members of the burying team; adults took six or more. The only burying I refused to do myself was that of babies. I told Commander Beltbuckle that I preferred not to bury infants and thereafter I did not have to bury babies. The babies were rare, for the parents preferred to bury them themselves. The babies that were put to rest by the burial boys were those whose mothers were dead or lost. The cemetery grew too quickly, grew in every direction, and the quality of the burials began to vary.

One day we were bringing a dead boy from the hospital to the cemetery when we saw a hyena fighting with something in the ground. It looked like it was trying to pull a squirrel from the ground, and I threw rocks at it to scare it away. It would not leave. Two boys ran closer to it, with sticks and rocks, yelling at it. Finally it turned and ran off, and then I saw what the hyena was chewing on: the elbow of a man. It was then that my team knew that other burying teams were not burying their dead very well. We reburied that man and afterward Dut gestured to me, and I came to see him. He lived in a sturdy house that could sleep four.

—Sit down, Achak.

243

I obeyed.

—I'm sorry you have to do such work.

I told him that I had become accustomed to it.

—Yes, but you shouldn't. This isn't the way I had imagined this camp, and our trip to Ethiopia. I want things to be better for you here. I want you to be in school.

Dut stared out at the camp with his small enfolded eyes, and I wanted to reassure him. —It's okay, I said. —This is temporary.

He opened his mouth to speak, but then said nothing. He thanked me for my hard work and gave me a pair of dates he retrieved from a sack on his bed. I left Dut's tent, worried for him. I had seen him lost before, but this despondence was something new. Dut was a faithful man, an optimistic man, and seeing him this way fostered doubt within me. I had no particular expectations that the long-promised schools would be created, but I did imagine that our time in Ethiopia was temporary. I lived with the assumption that the day would come when the group I arrived with would walk back to Sudan together, when the fighting was done, and at each village we would drop off whoever lived there, until our line of boys dwindled down to the Gone Fars, who would return home last. I would walk the longest but I would find a way home soon enough and would have many stories to tell.

I had many curious thoughts during the day. Dreams appeared before me. When I stood or turned quickly, I felt a dizziness that numbed my limbs and brought white flies to my eyes, and occasionally with this disorientation came people I once knew. I would see my father, or the baby of my stepmother, or my bed at home. I often saw the head of the dead man in the river, though in my visions I saw his face, which had been stripped like the faceless man's.

I often woke in the morning thinking I was in my own bed, and it would take me a moment before I realized that I was not at home, that I would not be at home again for some time, if at all. I had become accustomed to the visions, the way these faces from my home appeared before me. They frightened me at first, but soon they became a kind of comfort; I knew they would come and fade in a few moments. There were ghosts all around me and I had come to accept them and accept the sort of shadow world I lived in during those days.

But one day a certain vision, this one of Moses, would not leave me. I was washing my extra shirt in the river when he appeared next to me, smiling like he had a fantastic secret. It was not the first time I had seen Moses; I often imagined him with me, there to protect me with his strength and willingness to fight. But this day at the river the picture of Moses was moving slightly, his eyes wide open and his head tilting, as if he wanted me to acknowledge that he was real. But it had been a long time since I had been fooled by one of these visions, of him or anyone.

—Did you lose your mouth, Achak?

I went back to my washing, expecting the vision to disappear any moment. That this one was speaking to me was disconcerting, but not unprecedented. I had once woken up to my baby stepbrother Samuel talking to me about horses. Had I seen his new horse? he wanted to know. He accused me of stealing his new horse.

—Achak, don't you know me?

I knew the boy in front of me to be Moses, but the real Moses had been killed by the murahaleen. I had seen him in the moment before his death.

—Achak, talk to me. Is it you? Am I crazy?

I gave in and spoke to the vision.

—I won't talk to you. Go away.

And with that, the vision of Moses stood up and walked away. This was something I had never seen a vision do before.

—Wait! I said, raising myself and dropping my shirt.

The vision of Moses kept walking.

—Wait! Moses? Is it you?

As I ran closer to the vision of Moses, he seemed more and more a real Moses and not a vision of Moses, and my heart jumped around, as if looking for a way to exit my body.

And finally the vision of Moses turned to me and it was really Moses. I hugged him and patted him on the back and looked in his face. It was Moses. He was older, but was still shaped the same way, a muscular man in miniature. It was surely Moses.

I explained the visions and the real and not-real, and Moses laughed and I laughed and then punched Moses softly on the arm. Moses punched me back, harder, on the chest, and I returned the blow and soon we were punching each other and wrestling in the dust with more intensity than either of us had planned. Finally Moses threw me off of him, squealing in real pain.

—What? What hurts?

And he turned and lifted his shirt. His back was striped with deep crimson scars.

—Who did that? I asked.

—My story is so strange, Achak.

We walked under a tree and sat down.

—Have you seen William? he asked.

I did not expect him to ask about William at that moment.

—No, I said.

We were very far from home so I thought it was acceptable to tell a lie like that. I didn't want to think about William K. Instead, I asked Moses to tell his story and he did.

—I remember the fire, Achak, do you? It wasn't orange anywhere, though. Did you see that, when the village burned? The sun was directly above and the fire was clear or grey. Did you see this, how the fire was clear?

I could not remember the color of the fire on the day our village burned. In my mind the fire was orange and red, but I trusted that Moses was correct.

—I remember breathing slowly, Moses continued. —I was breathing in the smoke. It became so hard to breathe in our hut. I would take in a little air and would have to cough, but I did it anyway. I kept breathing, and soon I felt weak. I was so tired! I was going to sleep, but I knew it wasn't sleep. I knew what was happening, I knew I was dying. My mother was dead, I knew, just outside the hut. I knew all this but I don't remember how I knew it all. Maybe I didn't know it all and am guessing now that I do know.

I remembered seeing Moses's mother. Her torso was uncovered and her face had been burned on one side, burned beyond recognition, but the rest of her was untouched.

—So I ran. I ran through the door and I jumped over my mother and I ran. I didn't want to look at her because I knew she was dead. And I was mad at her for leaving me in the hut. I thought she was stupid, to leave me where she knew I would suffocate. I was so angry with her for just dying and leaving me inside. I thought she was so weak and stupid.

—Moses, stop.

I remembered Moses standing over his mother, yelling at her. I did not tell Moses I had seen this. I was ashamed I had not come to save him sooner.

—I'm sorry, Achak. This is just what I thought. I prayed for her and asked forgiveness for how I thought. I ran and I saw the school in the distance.

—But they burned the school, too, I said.

—I didn't think the school would protect me, but I thought that other people might be there, and that they would help me know what to do. I ran through the village, still coughing. There was smoke everywhere. So many screams, screams from people fallen and bleeding. I jumped over two more bodies, old men in the middle of the path. The second man grabbed my ankle. He was alive. He grabbed me and told me that I should lie with him and play dead. But he was bloody everywhere. One of his eyes was burned closed and blood flowed from his mouth. I didn't want to lie down with the bloody man. I ran again.

—That was the old drunk man from the market.

—It was, I think.

—I saw him, too.

—He died.

—He died, yes.

—I didn't see any murahaleen, and for a while I thought they were gone. But then I heard the hooves. There were many of them moving around the village, saying God is great! God is great! Did you hear them yelling that?

—Yes, I heard that, too.

—I looked to my right, toward the market, and saw two men with their horses. They were far enough away. I was sure I would make it to the school. But I wasn't running very fast. I was so weak and disoriented. The hooves got closer. It was so loud, the sounds of the horses—the violence of the hooves filled my head. I thought the horses would run over me, that any moment their feet would crush my back and head. Something struck me, and I was sure it was the foot of a horse. I fell and landed on my face; dust filled my eyes. I heard the sound of a man landing from his horse and some shuffling. Then I was in the air. I had been lifted by the man, whose hand was gripping my ribs, the other hand my legs. For a few seconds I expected death. I expected a knife or a bullet to end my life.

Again I wanted to tell Moses that I saw him being chased by the horseman but I did not and soon it was too late to tell him. And my memory of the pursuit was different than Moses's memory. I stayed quiet and replaced my memory with his.

—Then my face was against the leather. He had put me on his saddle and he tied me onto it. I felt a rope against my back, digging into my skin. He was tying me to the horse in some way. It took him a few minutes, and he kept tying more and more knots, each one bringing more rope cutting into my skin. Finally we began to move. He had caught me. I was then a slave, I knew.

—Did you see Amath?

—I didn't at first. Later I saw her for a moment. We began to ride, and I vomited immediately. I had never been on a horse. I could see the ground underneath me, and the dust overwhelmed my eyes. The movement of the ride was like being thrown around inside a sack of bones. Have you been on a horse?

—Not while it was moving.

—It was terrible. It didn't get better. I didn't get used to it, though we rode for many hours. When the horse finally stopped, I stayed on the horse. I was tied to it and could feel it breathing beneath me. I could hear the men eating and talking, but they never removed me from the saddle. I slept there, and after a while began to sleep more and more. I couldn't stay awake. I awoke and saw the ground racing under me. I awoke and it was night, it was noon, it was dusk. Two days later I was thrown onto the ground and told that that was where I would be sleeping, under the hooves of the horse. In the morning I dreamt that my head was being pressed into the sun. In my dream, the sun was smaller, the size of a large pan, and my head was being pressed against it. The heat was so strong, it seemed to be melting my hair and skull. I awoke to the smell of something burning. It smelled like flesh on fire. Then I realized that the dream was not a dream: the Arab was putting a burning metal rod to my head. He was branding me. In my ear he branded the number 8, turned on its side.

Moses turned to show me. It was a very rough marking, the symbol raised and purple, scarred into the flesh behind his ear.

—Now you will always know who owns you, this man said to me. The pain was so intense that I passed out. I woke when I was being lifted. I was thrown on the saddle again and he tied me down again, this time tighter than before. We rode for two more days. When we stopped, we were at a place called Um el Goz. It was some kind of military camp for the government army. Hundreds of boys like me were there, all under twelve, Dinka and Nuer boys. I was put in a huge barn with all of these boys, and we were locked inside. There was no food. The barn was full of rats; everyone was being bitten by them. There were no beds in the barn, but at night we didn't want to be lying on the ground, because the rats weren't afraid of us, and would come to bite us. Have you been bitten by a rat, Achak?

I shook my head.

—We decided to make a sleeping circle to guard against the rats. We carried sticks and the boys outside the circle would scare off the rats. This is how we slept. Do you know a circle of sleep, Achak?

I said I had learned this way of sleeping.

—The next day we were taken into a building and they laid us on cots. It was some kind of medical building. There were nurses there, and they inserted needles into our arms and took our blood. I threw up again when I saw the blood coming out of another boy's arm. The nurses were very understanding, though. It was very strange. They cleaned up my vomit and then gave me some water. Then they put me back on the cot and another nurse came to hold me down. She leaned over me, holding one arm and with her other hand on my chest. They put the needle in my arm and that way they took two bags of blood from me. Have you had a needle in your arm, Achak?

I told him I had not.

—It's this long, and hollow.

I wanted to hear no more about the needle.

—Fine. But it was huge. Its point is at an angle. They stick it in you like that.

—Please.

—Okay. Afterward the nurse gave me some sweet lemon juice, and then sent me back to the barn. In the barn, I learned that some of the boys had been there for many months, and that they had been giving blood once a week or more. They were being used as a blood supply for government soldiers. Every time there was a battle with the SPLA, the boys would be brought out from the barn and made to give blood.

—So that's where you stayed?

—For a while. But then it was quiet for a while. There were no more wounded, I don't think. We weren't needed. Not all of us at least. So after four days at Um el Goz I was put onto the horse again and we rode with about a hundred other murahaleen, this time very far. It was while riding that I saw Amath. I heard the screaming of a young girl, speaking my language, and saw her on another horse, very close to me. The man who was holding her was striking her with his gun, and laughing. I caught her eye for a second and then I lost sight of her. I didn't see her again. That was strange, to see her so many hundreds of miles from home.

The strings inside me snapped again but I said nothing.

—We rode for many days. We stopped at a house, a very well-built house. It was the house of an important man. His name was Captain Adil Muhammad Hassan. The man who brought me there was somehow related to this man. I heard them talking, and I learned that I was being given to Hassan as a gift from this man. Hassan was very thankful and the two of them went inside to eat. I was still tied to the horse outside. They were gone inside all evening and I stayed on the horse. I stared at the ground and tried to think about where I might be. Finally I was untied and brought into this man's house. Have you ever seen the house of a man like this, a commander in the Sudanese government army?

I shook my head.

—It's a house like you could not imagine, Achak. Very smooth floors and everything clean. Glass for the windows. Water running inside the house. I became this man's servant. The man had two wives, and three children, all the children very young. I thought that the kids would be decent to me, but they were crueler than their parents. The kids were taught to beat me and spit on me. To them, I was one of the animals. For four months I had to watch the goats and sheep in the yards, and I cleaned the house. I washed the floors, and I helped with the making of meals and serving at meals.

—You were the only servant?

—There was another Sudanese there, a girl named Akol, the age of your sister Amel. Akol worked in the kitchen, mostly, but she was also Hassan's concubine. She was pregnant with Hassan's baby so his wife hated her. The wife would find Akol crying for her mother and she would scream at her, threatening to slit her throat with a knife. She called her bitch and slave and animal. I learned many Arabic words, and these were the ones I heard most often. She only called me *jange*—dirty infidel, uncultured person. They gave me another name, too: Abdul. They sent me to Koranic school and renamed me Abdul.

—Why would they send their slave to school?

—Men like this want everyone to be Muslim, Achak. So I pretended to be a good Muslim. I thought they would be kinder to me, but this didn't happen. They beat me more than was necessary. The kids especially liked to whip me. The oldest boy, smaller than us, when he was left alone with me, would whip me without pause. I couldn't retaliate at all, so I had to run from him, run around the yard until he got tired. I wanted to murder that boy and I made many plans to do that.

I could not take my eyes off of the 8 on the side of Moses's head. Its color changed in the light of the sun.

—I stayed there for three months before I decided I would try to escape. I told Akol I was going to escape and she thought I was mad. I planned to run away at night. The first time I tried, I was caught almost immediately. I ran into the next yard and a dog began barking. Its owner came out of the house with a torch and caught me. I was gone for a very short time. Hassan laughed a lot at me. Then he took me into the yard and he made me squat. I squatted in the yard like a frog, and he brought his children out and told them to jump on me. They sat on my back and pretended that I was a donkey, and they laughed, and Hassan laughed. They called me a stupid donkey. And the kids fed me garbage. They said I had to eat it, so I ate it—anything they gave me. Animal fat, tea bags, rotten vegetables.

—I'm so sorry, Moses.

—No, no. Don't be. No, this was the key to my escape. After eating all the garbage, I began to vomit. I vomited for hours that night, and I was sick for two days. I couldn't stand. I couldn't work. Akol helped me, and I began to feel better. But when I was recovering I had an idea. I decided to be sick all the time.

—This is how you escaped?

—It was easy. I forced myself to be sick always. Whenever I ate I thought of anything I could to make myself vomit. I thought of eating humans. I thought of eating zebra hides and the arms of babies. Then I would vomit and vomit. Soon Hassan decided he didn't want me around anymore. He said I was a bad gift, and that he would be selling me. One day two men appeared, each on camels. They were dressed in white, white covering their faces and feet. They threw me onto the back of the camel and I was taken many days away, to a town called Shendi. Again I was put in a barn with other Dinka and Nuer boys, this barn smaller than the one before. A few of the boys had been there for a week or more. They told me that this was a town where slaves were traded. They said that traders bought slaves here for people in many different countries—Libya, Chad, Mauritania. I stayed in that barn for two days without food, and only one bucket of water for fifty of us.

—Were you sold?

—I was, Achak! I was sold twice. First I was sold to a Sudanese Arab. He was an older man and he had his son with him. They seemed to be very strange people. They bought me and I went with them, simply walking out of the village without any bindings or leash or anything. They had a camel with them but the three of us just walked away. We traveled for many days, on foot and all three of us on this camel. It was very uncomfortable but they were not cruel men. They barely said a word, and I did not ask questions. I knew we were going south because of the direction of the sun and I planned to see how far we would go, and eventually I would find my chance and escape.

—And you escaped where?

—I didn't need to, Achak! I told you I was bought twice, and the second time was how I became free. We camped in this one forest for three days, and did almost nothing all day. They had me gather wood during the day, but otherwise we only sat and they slept in the shade. On the second day, another Arab man came to visit them, and they exchanged some information, and the man left. On the third day, we rose at dawn and walked until midday, until we reached an airfield, and there I saw twenty other Dinka—boys like me, women, girls, and one old man. Around them were ten Arabs, some on horseback, some armed. They seemed to be a mixture of traders and murahaleen, and the Arab pair who had bought me brought me to the rest of the group and I felt so scared, Achak! I thought that they had brought me all this way to kill me with the rest of the Dinka. But this wasn't their plan.

—They killed no one?

—No, no. We were valuable to them! It was such a feeling! An airplane came to that landing strip and from the plane came two people with the white skin. Have you seen any people like this, Achak?

I said I had not.

—There was a man, very fat, and a very tall woman. Their pilot looked like these Ethiopians here. And then the white people spoke for some time to the Arabs who held all of the Dinka. They had a sort of bag that I found out later was full of money. This was how I was bought again, Achak!

—These people bought you? Why?

—They bought all of us, Achak. It was very strange. They paid for all of us, and then they told us that we were free. All twenty of us were free, but we had no idea where we were. The Arabs turned and walked off, heading west, and then we waited. The white people waited with us, for most of the afternoon. Finally two Dinka men, dressed very well and with clean shirts, appeared in a large white vehicle. It seemed to be very new. And so many of the former slaves got inside the vehicle and some walked alongside, and I rode on top with one other boy. We drove for many hours, until it was dark and we came to a Dinka village. I ate and slept there for a few weeks, until I was told to join the walking boys.

—And you walked with a big group?

—It was not a bad walk, Achak. I even got to ride on a tanker.

I was very jealous of Moses at that moment, but I didn't tell him this. I thanked God for granting Moses this small act of mercy. Then I told Moses about William K, and afterward and we sat by the river for the rest of the day. Moses said nothing at all.

More stories like Moses's began to be told at Pinyudo, as boys who had been abducted were occasionally freed or escaped and found their way to the camp. But Moses was the only boy I knew who had been aided by the white people, and thus information about their deeds was scarce. I personally doubted that the people Moses had seen were actually white until I saw my first of the species. This was perhaps three months after we had been in Ethiopia, and after Moses had become part of the Eleven. By then the rest of the world, or some portion of the humanitarian-aid world at least, had become aware of the forty thousand or so refugees, half of us unaccompanied minors, living just over the Ethiopian border.

I was woken by excited talk outside the shelter.

—You haven't seen him?

—No. You're saying he's a white man? His hair is white?

—No, his skin, every part of him. He's white like chalk.

I sat up and crawled outside, still not alert enough to think much of what the three of the Eleven were discussing. When I stood and peed, I saw clutches of boys everywhere in the camp talking intensely, in groups of ten or more. Something was happening, and it was somehow related to the gibberish my tentmates had been uttering. As I began to piece together their conversation, I looked up to see the heads of hundreds of boys turning simultaneously. I followed their stares and saw what seemed to be a man who had been turned inside out. He was the absence of a man. He had been erased. An involuntary shudder went through my body, the same reaction I had when I saw a burn, a missing limb—a perversion or ruination of nature.

I began to walk toward the erased man before I realized I had not lifted my pants after urinating. I fixed myself and followed the crowd of boys who were herding in the direction of the erased man. I looked for Moses, to ask him if this was the sort of person he had seen, but Moses was nowhere to be found. The white man was a few hundred yards away, and the murmuring among the boys was getting quieter as we drew closer. An older boy burst in front of us.

—Stop! Don't bother the khawaja. He'll run away if you get too close. A hundred boys running to him will scare him off. Now get away.

We returned to our shelters, to our chores, but over the course of the day, theories about the new man abounded. The first theory held that he had been sent by the Sudanese government to kill all of us—that he would count all of the boys, and then he would decide how many weapons he would need to exterminate us. Once he had done so, the killing would come at night. This theory was quickly debunked when we discovered that the elders did not fear him; in fact, they were talking to him and shaking his hand. Naturally, then the pendulum swung and the next notion posited that he was a god, that he had come to save all of us, and would lead us back to southern Sudan, to triumph over the murahaleen. This idea gained currency throughout the day, and was undermined only when we cataloged the activities in which the god engaged. He spent most of his time with a few of the elders, building a storage shed for food, which seemed like work too pedestrian for a god or even a minor deity. Thereafter, some of the older boys offered more nuanced views.

—He works for the government, but in secret. That's why he hides in the white skin.

—He's turned inside out, and is in Sudan to find out how to become right again.

Finally I had had enough of the theories, and went to ask Dut.

—You've never seen a white man? he laughed.

This interested Dut. I didn't know where I would have seen a white man. I didn't think it was funny. His face softened and he sighed.

—The white people come to Sudan for many reasons, including their desire to teach us about the Kingdom of God... I know there weren't any white people in Marial Bai, but they didn't have white missionaries in your church in Aweil, either?

I shook my head.

—Well, okay. They also come for the oil, and this has been a source of much trouble for people like us; that is a story for another time. For now we'll talk about another reason they come, which is to help people when they're being attacked, oppressed. Sometimes the white men who come to inspect things here represent the armies of the white men, which are the most powerful armies on earth.

I pictured the armies of the murahaleen, only with white men on white horses.

—So which reason brought this white man to Pinyudo? I asked.

—I don't know yet, Dut said.

I decided to wait for a few days, until there was more information available, to get closer to the inside-out man. The next day, the facts were clearer: the man had a name, it was either Peter or Paul, he was French, and he represented something called the UNHCR. He was here to help the elders build food-storage containers. If he liked the people he met, it was said, he would bring food to fill the containers. This information was accepted by most of the boys, though many of us still eyed the man warily, expecting anything from him: death, salvation, fire.

When interest in the man had plateaued, I got close enough to observe him more closely. His skin was remarkable. Some days it was indeed as white as chalk, and others it was pink, like that of a pig or the underbelly of a goat. His arms and legs were covered in tangles of dark hair, again like a pig's, only these hairs were longer.

The man produced more sweat than any man I had ever seen. He would wipe the sweat from his face every few minutes; it seemed to be the primary occupation of his day. I found myself feeling sorry for the white man, for his sweating and because he resembled a pig in so many particulars. He was unsuited to the heat of Pinyudo, and I feared that he would burn up. He seemed fragile, oppressed by the sun; he carried a water bottle with him always, which he attached to his back with some kind of belt. He would sweat, and then wipe the sweat, and then drink water, and soon after, he would sit under the fig tree, alone.

I visited Ajulo and asked her about him. She had heard about the white man, too. I asked her if the presence of the inside-out man was a good thing, what it might mean. She thought about this for a long moment.

—The khawaja is an interesting thing, son. He is very smart. He has things in his head that you would not believe. He knows many languages, and the names of villages and towns, and can fly airplanes and drive cars. The white men are born knowing all of these things. He is powerful in this way, and very useful, very helpful to us. When you see a white man, it means things are going to improve. So I think this man is good for you.

After church, I asked the priest the same question.

—It is a very good thing, Achak, he said. —The white man is a close descendant of Adam and Eve, you see. You have seen the pictures of Jesus in your books, have you not? Adam and Eve and Jesus and God all have such skin. They are fragile, their skin burning in the sun, because they are closer to the status of angels. Angels would burn in a similar way if placed on earth. This man, then, is here to deliver messages from God.

I began to circle closer to the man named Peter or Paul, and soon, it seemed, the man noticed me. One day Moses and I were walking close to the man, pretending not to be looking at him as he sat under his fig tree.

—The khawaja smiled at you! Moses said.

At first this troubled me. I had decided that it would be bad if the white man set his eyes upon me, so whenever the man turned toward me, I looked away and then walked quickly home. I preferred to watch, from a safe distance, as the man worked, to observe the man as he rested, always alone, under the giant fig tree. It made sense that the white man would rest alone, because he needed to receive messages from God. In crowds of noisy people such messages would be difficult to hear. I imagined the messages as delicate things, too. This seemed appropriate in the case of the white man, for he seemed like a very mild sort of man, a quiet god, if he was indeed a god or messenger for gods.

For many nights I lay awake in my shelter, the mosquito net close around my face, the night and its noises crowding close, and I wondered if I should ask Peter or Paul whether he knew anything about Marial Bai and my family, their fates. If the man was a close descendant of Adam and Eve, and spoke to God from under the fig tree, surely he would know about my relatives—whether they were alive, and where they were now. Perhaps he would even be able to transport me back to Marial Bai. If my parents had been killed, he could bring them back to life, and restore the town to its state before the murahaleen's dark cloud arrived. And if he could do that, and it seemed likely enough, could he not also stop the war in southern Sudan? Perhaps he could not do this himself, but by calling upon his God and the other gods, why couldn't they intercede, and for the sake of all of the boys at Pinyudo, allow us all to go home? I decided that I would, if it came to it, compromise, and ask at the very least, the man might spare Marial Bai. If it was necessary for the war to continue, and I knew that gods often allowed men to fight, then perhaps Marial Bai could be excluded. I lay awake for too long each night, the Eleven falling off to sleep around me, planning how I might approach the white messenger, and how I might ask these favors without seeming burdensome. But one day Peter or Paul was gone and was never seen again. No one had an explanation.

It was not long, though, before more white people, and aid workers from all over Africa, began to descend upon Pinyudo. From a distance I could see the delegations walking through the camp briskly, always guided carefully by one of the Sudanese elders. We were sometimes made to sing for the visitors, or to paint vast banners of greetings. But that was as close as we got to them. The visitors never made it deep into the camp, and usually left the same day they arrived.

Supply trucks soon came three times a day; we began to eat at least twelve meals a week—it had only been seven before. We gained weight, and projects were underway all over the camp: new wells were dug, medical facilities opened, more books and pencils arrived. With relative contentment and full stomachs came thoughts of return. Moses was one of the first boys to suggest going back to Sudan.

—We have food here, and things are stable, he said. —This means things are safe at home. We should go home now. Why should we stay? It's been a year since we left.

I didn't know what to think. The thought seemed mad, but then again, just as Ajulo had questioned our existence in this place, I began, too, to wonder why we were not on our way to some other place, or home.

—We won't have any elders with us, though, I said. —We'd be killed.

—We know the way now, Moses said. —We'll get twenty of us. That's enough. Maybe one gun. Some knives, spears. Put some food in bags. It won't be like before, like coming here. We'll have all the supplies we need.

Indeed, there was much talk among the boys of whether or not the war was over. Many thought it was time to return, and they were dissuaded only when the rumors of our plans reached the elders. An enraged Dut came to our shelter one night. He had never come inside our home.

—This war is not over! he barked. —Have you lost your minds? Do you know what awaits you in Sudan? It's worse there than ever before, you fools. Here you are safe, you're well-fed, you'll soon be educated. And you want to leave this, so you can walk through the desert alone? Some of you boys are no bigger than cats! Already we've heard of two boys who have left the camp in the dark of night. What happened to them, do you suppose?

We knew the boys who had left, but did not know their fate.

—They were killed by bandits just over the river. You kids wouldn't even make it past the Anyuak!

He was gesticulating wildly. He paused to collect himself.

—If any of you are thinking of leaving, leave, because you're too stupid to remain here. I don't want you. I want only the boys with brains. Leave now, and when school begins in the fall, I expect only the boys who are smart enough to know what they have here and what they don't have in the desert. Goodbye.

He strode quickly from the shelter, still stammering as he walked away. Some of the Eleven didn't believe the story about the bandits, because they could not imagine what the bandits would want from small boys, but after Dut's outburst, our general restlessness diminished dramatically. The prospect of school actually beginning was a fantasy that we wished dearly to believe. Moses, though, was not convinced. There was an anger growing within him and it would drive him to adventures worse than the one that brought him to Shendi and back.

—Valentino!

I was walking to Mass one day, always held under a certain tree near where the Ethiopians lived, when someone threw this name to the sky. I had not heard that name in so long. I turned and a familiar man, a priest, came toward me. It was Father Matong, the priest who had baptized me in Marial Bai. He had been visiting other camps in Ethiopia, he said, and was now checking on the boys at Pinyudo. He was the first person I had seen at this camp, outside of Dut and Moses, who I had known from my life at home. I stood for some time, silent, staring at him; it felt, for a moment, that the world in which I had first known him, my hometown and all it held, could regenerate itself around him.

—Son, are you okay? He placed his hand on my head. It felt wonderful. Still I could not manage words.

—Come with me, he said.

I walked with Father Matong on this day and other days, during the two weeks he stayed at Pinyudo. I don't know why he spent time with me alone, but I was grateful for the time with him. I asked him questions about God and faith; perhaps I was unique in the attention I gave to his answers.

—Who was Valentino? I asked one day.

We were on one of our walks, and he stopped in his tracks.

—You don't know?

—No.

—I never told you? But he's my favorite saint!

He had never told me this. Nor had he told me why he had given me this name.

—Who was he? I asked him.

We were walking past an airfield. A group of soldiers were unloading enormous crates from a cargo plane. Father Matong stood for a moment, watching, then turned and we walked back in the direction of the camp.

—He was alive so long ago, son. Before the grandfather of your grandfather. Before his grandfather and his grandfather. Before more grandfathers than there are stars. He was a priest like me, an ordinary priest named Valentino. He worked in Rome, in a place now called Italy, far north from here, where white people live.

—So he was a white man? I asked. The thought had not occurred to me.

—He was. And a selfless man. He preached to his flock but also took a particular interest in prisoners. At the time, many men in Rome were imprisoned under questionable circumstances, and Father Valentino did not want to deprive them of the gospel. So he went to these captives and he spoke the word of the Lord, and these men were converted. The jailers did not appreciate this. They resented his presence and the light he brought to lives of the prisoners. So he, too, was punished. He was jailed, he was beaten, he was sent away. But again and again, he found ways to speak to the prisoners, and soon he even converted the blind daughter of the jailer himself.

As we had been walking, we hadn't realized that we were so close to the barracks of the Ethiopian troops. We heard voices, and were soon upon a group of soldiers crowded together, watching a struggle on the ground before them. It seemed like some sort of wrestling, though only one of the participants was in uniform, and only one seemed to be moving. One of the wrestlers wore a garment of an Anyuak color, and let out a womanly cry. Again we altered our course.

—He visited the girl often; she was no older than you, my son. They prayed together and they spoke of her blindness. She had been blind since she was very small.

Again he put his palm on my head and again it felt like home.

—But when the jailer found out about the priest's efforts, he was furious. His daughter brought the word of God into her father's house and that was the end of Valentino. He was jailed, he was tortured. But the daughter knew where he was being held, and she came to visit the priest. He was chained to the floor, but still they prayed, and she slept just outside his cell for many nights. And it was on one of those nights, when they were praying together before sleep, that a brightness came into the cell. It blasted through the bars and swirled around Valentino and the girl. The priest was not sure if it was an angel but he held the jailer's daughter close and after the brightness flew about the cell, circling like a swallow, it finally left through the barred window whence it came. The priest and the jailer's daughter were again in the dark.

—What was it? I asked.

—It was an envoy of God, my son. There is no other explanation. The next morning, the girl awoke and she could see again. Her eyes had not worked since she was a baby but now she could see again. For this miracle, Father Valentino was beheaded.

I asked Father Matong why this man was his favorite saint, and why he gave me his name. The answer was not yet clear to me, though I believe Matong expected by that point that it would be. He took his hand off my head.

—I think you will have the power to make people see, he said. —I think you will remember what it was like to be here, you will see the lessons here. And someday you will find your own jailer's daughter, and to her you will bring light.

XVIII.

Most prophecies go unfulfilled. It's just as well. The expectations Father Matong put upon me took many years to fade from the forefront of my mind. But thank God they did. Free of this pressure, my head was, for a time, clearer than it had been in years.

It is just past midnight and Lino is asleep. Julian, no doubt tired of seeing our faces and being unable or unwilling to bring help to us, has retreated to an office behind the desk. Achor Achor is watching a documentary about Richard Nixon on the overhead television. He will watch anything about American politics, or any politics at all. He is certain to hold office in a new southern Sudan, should it really become independent. There are plenty of southern Sudanese in the Khartoum government now, but Achor Achor insists that he will only return to Sudan if the south votes to secede in 2011, which the Comprehensive Peace Agreement allows. Whether the National Islamic Front or Omar al-Bashir, the president of Sudan, actually allows this to occur remains to be seen.

Achor Achor's phone begins to vibrate on the table between us, turning slowly clockwise. As he is looking in his pockets, I lift the phone and hand it to him. Given the hour, I am reasonably sure it is a call from Africa. Achor Achor flips his phone open and his eyes grow round.

"It what? In Juba? No!" Achor Achor stands suddenly and walks away, past Julian. Lino does not stir. I follow Achor Achor and he hands me the phone.

"It's Ajing. He's going nuts. You talk to him."

Ajing is a friend of ours from Kakuma who now works for the new government of southern Sudan. He lives in Juba and is training to become an engineer.

I take the phone.

"Valentino! It's Ajing! Call CNN and tell them that the war is on again!"

He's out of breath. I beg him to slow down.

"A bomb just went off. Or a mortar. They just bombed us. Huge explosion. Call CNN and tell them to send a camera. The world needs to know. Bashir is attacking us again. The war has returned! I'll call you back—call CNN!"

He hangs up, and Achor Achor and I stare at each other. There had been chaotic sounds in the background of the call, sounds of machinery and movement. Ajing, being in Juba, certainly should know what was happening there. My stomach drops to my feet. If the war were to begin again, I don't know that I could live through it, even safely here in the United States. I doubt any of us could. We live only knowing that rebuilding has been possible in southern Sudan, that our families are safe. But this, a return to blood and madness—I am quite sure I will not be able to bear the burden.

"Should we call CNN?" Achor Achor asks.

"Why us?" I ask.

"We live in Atlanta. You've met Ted Turner."

This is a good point. I decide I will first call Mary Williams and proceed from there. I am dialing her number when Achor Achor's phone rings again. I answer.

"Valentino, I'm sorry. I was wrong. What a relief!" Ajing is still breathing heavily and seems to have forgotten the rest of his explanation.

"What?" I yell. "What happened?"

It was a false alarm, he says. There was an explosion within the barracks, but it was an accident from within, a mistake, a nothing.

"Sorry to scare you, friend," Ajing says. "How are you, by the way?"

Lino is sleeping with his head tilted back, resting against the wall behind us, and I watch as it slowly begins to slide rightward, until the weight of his head is too much. It falls to his shoulder and he wakes with a start, sees me and seems momentarily surprised to see me. He smiles drunkenly, then goes back to sleep.

It has been an hour since Ajing called, and Julian has been replaced by an older white woman with a great cloud of yellow hair that sweeps up from her forehead and rolls down her back. I catch her eye. As I am about to approach her, in hopes of appealing to her, she gets up and finds something urgent she must do in the next room. We are no longer considered patients here. No one knows what to do with us. We are furniture.

And so I sit with Achor Achor.

With Tabitha, even hours of sitting in a waiting room would be electric. Like many couples in the first months of love, we were content in the most mundane situations. We did very little that might be considered glamorous or even imaginative; neither of us had money to spend on restaurant dinners or shows of any kind. We usually stayed in my apartment and watched movies or even sports on television. One summer night when my Corolla was being fixed by Edgardo, we spent the night waiting for and riding city buses. It was a night of waiting and fluorescent lighting, and yet it was a night of near-rapture. While waiting for a bus home from downtown, where we had took a walk in Olympic Park, she nuzzled my neck and whispered to me how badly she wanted to kiss me, to take off my shirt. Her voice was seductive on the phone, overpowering in person, explosive when hot in my ear. In the bus shelters of Atlanta there has never been such romance.

But when we were apart, she could be flighty and moody. She would call me seven times in one day, and if I was unavailable that day, her messages would become more agitated, suspicious, even cruel. When we finally would mend our relationship, and our phone conversations would again be enjoyable, she would disappear for days. Her absence would go unexplained, and when she reappeared, I was forbidden to dwell on why or where she had gone. I often struggled to keep up with and decipher her signals. "Are you stalking me?" she would ask one week, while the next, she would wonder if she herself was the stalker. I was so puzzled by her behavior that I asked Allison Newton, my teenage friend, about it. "Sounds like she has another flame," she said, and I did not believe her. "Standard behavior for that situation—she hides, she overcompensates when she returns, she suspects you of the things she's doing herself." That was the last time I asked Allison for advice on these matters.

Hoping to find food of some kind, I leave the waiting room and walk the salmon-colored halls, passing photographs of the hospital's past administrators and the artwork of young people. There are watercolors and pastels done by students at a local high school, each work for sale. I inspect every one. There are many renderings of pets, four of Tupac Shakur, and two paintings of rickety piers extending out over placid lakes. The line of artwork ends at a long window looking into the waiting lounge. The room is dark, the patterns of the furniture a plaid of burgundy and blue. I see two vending machines, and am tempted to open the door. But there is a family there, asleep on the couch together. A young father is on the end, his head resting against a duffel bag he has placed on the couch's arm. Next to him are three small children, two girls and a boy, all under five, lying one against the other. Small pink backpacks lie at their feet, the remnants of dinner on the end table. It is likely their mother who is sick here. Beyond them, in the parking lot, a single tree is illuminated from below, giving its leafless branches a rose-colored glow. From where I stand, the sleeping family appears to be lying below this tree, protected by its great outstretched boughs.

Though I wish I could enter and buy something to eat, I do not want to wake them. Instead I sit outside their room and read words from Tabitha. I open my wallet and remove the page I keep there, three of Tabitha's emails. I printed them one night in advance of a phone date we had planned. I wanted to talk to her about her moods, her conflicting signals, and planned to cite the emails, all three written in the span of one week. That night I lost my nerve to confront her, but nevertheless I keep the page folded in my wallet, and I read the messages to punish myself and to remember the way Tabitha expressed herself to me when she wrote—far more effusively than when we were together. Rarely did she say "I love you" to my face, but in her emails, written in the dark hours, she felt she could.

The first message:

My Val:

I just wanted to say that I love you. May the spirit of God keep our love lively and sweet. I love you dear, and my heart always watches you smiling at me. I love your beautiful smiles; I don't know if I can get enough of them. I am so much in love with you and I can't stop thinking about you because you are so darling, sweet, touchy, smiley, lovely, respectful, and wonderful. I missed you so badly this week. The little talk we had wasn't enough for the week.

I thought you were going to call me but I didn't receive any call. I don't know if you did call me or not.

Love love love,

Tabitha

The second message, two days later:

Hi Val,

I don't know if you called me yesterday or not. Just to let you be aware, my cell phone, makeup, and lotion got stolen yesterday during my PE period. I disconnected the line for a while till I replace it. I don't know how long it will take me to replace it.

I am doing fine, just feeling confused about everything. I'm puzzled also because I don't know if we should be together. Atlanta is so far away and sometimes I feel that if you really cared for me you'd move here. You know I can't move to you, with college and my brothers in Seattle. But if you really loved me like you say you do…

I guess we'll just email until my phone is replaced. Maybe it'll be good for us to take this break.

With affection,

Tabitha

And a week later, when she got her phone back, there was this:

Honey,

I was thinking about you yesterday, just before I fell asleep. Then I dreamt sweet warm dreams about you and me. Don't ask me what happened in the dream. I want to tell you on the phone, I want to whisper it to you when we're both on our pillows. Could you please not go to bed early today so I can call you? The latest I'll call will at be at 10 to 11 your time.

Am I sending too many messages to you? Please let me know. Where have you been? Are you avoiding me? Please don't play games with me. I need to know that you love me because life is dramatic enough right now without being uncertain about important things, like love.

Desperate and wanting,

Tabitha

I believe that Tabitha liked very much to be pursued, to know that I was so far away but that I waited for her, that I pined for her. I imagine her telling her friends that I was "a nice boy" while she kept her eye open for new opportunities. This is not to say I believe she was otherwise involved. Only that she was a desirable young woman, new to the possibilities of this country, and she needed attention as much as she needed love. Perhaps more so.

In any case, Tabitha was not the first woman to confuse me, to confound me. In Ethiopia there were four such girls, sisters, and it was remarkable to find such girls in a refugee camp like Pinyudo. I was not alone in my obsession with them, though in the end I would be alone in my success with them. Anyone who was at my camp in Ethiopia knows of the Royal Girls of Pinyudo, but it was a surprise that Tabitha knew of them, too.

We were talking one day about my name; Tabitha had just told an older American friend that she was seeing a man named Valentino, and her friend had explained the implications of such a name. Tabitha called me immediately after hearing the stories of Rudolph Valentino, and, newly jealous, demanded to know if I was as successful with women as my name implied. I did not boast, but I could not deny that certain women and girls had found me pleasant enough to be around. "How long has this been going on, this success with ladies?" she asked, with an uncomfortable mixture of mirth and accusation. I told her it had been this way as long as I could remember. "Even at Pinyudo were you meeting girls?" she asked, expecting the answer to be no.

"There were girls there, yes," I told her. "There were these four girls in particular, sisters named Agum, Agar, Akon, and Yar Akech, and..."

She stopped me there. She knew these girls. "Were they from Yirol?" she asked. I told her they were indeed from Yirol. And only then did I make the connection myself. Of course Tabitha would have known these girls. She not only knew them, she went on, she was related to them, she was their cousin. And knowing them made Tabitha temporarily less jealous, then, as I told her the story of the Royal Girls, more so.

This was 1988. We had been at Pinyudo for a few months when something strange happened: they opened the schools. There was a new chairman of the camp, named Pyang Deng, a man we all considered compassionate, a man of integrity, a reasonable man who listened. He played with us, he danced with us, and, with the help of the the Swedish arm of Save the Children and the United Nations High Commissioner for Refugees, he opened schools for about eighteen thousand refugee children. He called an assembly one day, and because the camp had no chairs or microphones or megaphones at that time, we sat on the dirt and he yelled as best he could.

—Schools will be yours! he roared.

We cheered.

—You will be the best-educated Sudanese in all of history! he yelled.

Bewildered, we cheered again.

—Now we will build the schools!

We cheered again, but soon the cheering died down. It dawned on us that the task would come down to us. And it did. The next day, we were sent into the forests to cut trees and collect grass. We were told that the forests were dangerous. There were animals in these forests, they said. And there were local people who considered the forests their own, they said, and were to be avoided. The dangers were many but still we were sent into the forests and almost immediately boys were lost. On the first day, a boy named Bol went into the forest and one part of his leg was found eight days later. Animals had eaten the rest of him.

But the materials were extracted by that time, and the schools went up: four poles for each roof and thatch laid on top, sometimes with plastic sheeting when available. We built twelve schools in one week, named simply: School One, School Two, School Three, and so on. When we finished building the schools, we were called to the open field that became the parade grounds and site of major announcements. Two men spoke to us, one Sudanese and one Ethiopian, the joint educational directors for the camp.

—Now you have schools! they said.

We cheered.

—Each day, first you will march. After you march, you will attend your classes. And after classes, you will work until your dinner.

Again, our enthusiasm dampened.

But other aspects of life at the camp were improving. With the advent of the UN came clothing, for example, and this development was greeted with great relief by all the boys, especially those too old to be naked, who had gone without since we had arrived in Ethiopia. Whenever there was a shipment, the older boys would retrieve the large bags, stuffed with garments and labeled *Gift of the UK* or *Gift of the United Arab Emirates*, and would bring them back to the smaller groups. When our first share arrived, it came down to me to distribute the clothing to the Eleven, and to prevent arguing we sat in a circle and I handed out the contents of the bag, one piece at a time, in a clockwise system. That the clothing rarely fit the recipient didn't matter.

I knew trading would ensue within the Eleven and elsewhere, and this was necessary, as half of our first shipment was women's clothing. This would have been humorous if we had been less desperate to be looking again like we had been raised, with shirts and shoes and pants. Without clothes we could not hide our wounds, our protruding ribs. Our nakedness, our rags, spoke too bluntly about our sorry state.

By the time school began, most of us had bartered successfully enough to have clothed ourselves, and when we sat down that first day, we really felt like students, and the school really seemed like a school. The classrooms were thatched rooms, roofs without walls, and on the first morning of classes, the fifty-one boys sat on the ground and waited. Finally a man strode in, and introduced himself as Mr. Kondit. He was a tall man, very thin, with an extraordinarily small skull. He wrote his name on the chalkboard and we were greatly impressed. Only a few among us could recognize any letters at all, but still we stared at the white marks on the board and blinked, happy to watch whatever might happen next.

The first day's lesson covered the alphabet. Mr. Kondit's voice was loud and harsh, sounding impatient at having to explain these things to us. It felt that first day as if he wanted the lesson, all of the lessons of the alphabet and writing and language generally, to be finished in one sweeping hour. He wanted simply to gesture at the alphabet and be done with it.

A B C

He wrote the three letters and read them aloud, demonstrating the sounds they denoted. Because we had no pencils or paper, Mr. Kondit sent us outside. There, we copied the letters into the dirt with sticks or our fingers.

—Make your letters neat! he barked from his chalkboard. —You have three minutes. If you make a mistake, erase your letter and draw it again. When you have three letters that are to your satisfaction, raise your hand and I will inspect your work. Hands were raised and Mr. Kondit began to make his rounds.

I had never written before; the first time I tried to write a letter B in the dirt, Mr. Kondit came behind me and clucked disapprovingly. He leaned over and grabbed my finger roughly, then guided it through the dirt to make the proper B, pushing my forefinger so hard into the ground that my fingernail cracked and bled.

—You must do better! he yelled to the crowns of our heads. —You have nothing now, nothing but education. Don't you see this? Our country is in shambles, and the only way we can reclaim it is to learn! Our independence was stolen from us due to the ignorance of our ancestors, and only now can we correct it. Many of you no longer have mothers. You have lost your fathers. But you have education. Here, if you are smart enough to accept it, you will be educated. Education will be your mother. Education will be your father. While your older brothers fight this war with guns, when the bullets stop, you will fight the next war with your pens. Do you see what I'm telling you?

He was hoarse by now and he grew quiet. —I want you to succeed, boys. If we are ever to have a new Sudan, you must succeed. If I'm ever impatient, it's because I cannot wait for this godforsaken war to end, and for you to assume your role in the future of our ruined land.

On our way back to our shelters, Mr. Kondit was the subject of fascination and debate.

—Did you hear that crazy man? we said.

—Education is your mother? we said.

We laughed and did imitations. We thought Mr. Kondit, like more than a few of the men and boys who had crossed the desert to get to Ethiopia, had lost his mind along the way.

Not long after the schools opened, another strange thing happened: they brought girls to class. There were very few girls at Pinyudo in general, and there were no girls in any of the schools at all, as far as I could tell. But one morning, as the fifty-one boys in Mr. Kondit's class settled onto the ground before the blackboard, we noticed four new people, all of them female, sitting in the front row. Mr. Kondit was squatting before these new people, talking to them, placing his hands on their heads in a familiar way. I was baffled.

—Class, Mr. Kondit said, rising to his full height, —we have four new students today. Their names are Agar, Akon, Agum, and Yar Akech. They should be treated with respect and courtesy, because they are all very good students. They are also my nieces, so I expect that you will be that much more careful about your behavior around them.

And with that, he began the lesson. I was three rows behind the girls and spent all of that day's hours looking nowhere but at the backs of their heads. I studied their necks and their hair, as if the secrets of the world and history were discernible in the twists of their braids. I glanced around to see if the other boys were having a similar problem and found that I was not alone in this. Nothing academic was learned that day and yet we boys felt, cumulatively, that the focus of our lives and all earthly pursuits had changed. These four sisters, Agar, Akon, Agum, and Yar Akech, each of them graceful, well-dressed and so attractively aloof, were far more worthy of study than anything that could be written on a blackboard or in the dirt surrounding the classroom.

We did not eat or sleep as we had before. Dinner was made and consumed but was not tasted. Sleep came when the morning light had already begun to leak from the other side of the earth. We had been awake all of those dark hours, discussing the sisters. At first, no one knew which sister was which; Mr. Kondit's introduction was too quick and cursory. Only through much sharing of information did my Eleven come to remember all four names, and through the same system of information sharing we amassed a dossier on each of the four. Agar was the oldest, that seemed clear. She was very tall and wore her hair in braids; her dress was a striking pink with white flowers. Akon was the next oldest, her face round and her eyelashes very long; she wore a dress with red and blue stripes, with matching barrettes in her hair. Agum could be the same age as Akon, for she was the same height but much thinner. She appeared the least engaged in the goings-on at school, and seemed perpetually bored or frustrated, exasperated even, by everyone and everything. Yar Akech was the youngest, it was clear, a few years behind Agum and Akon, and perhaps one year younger than me and my Eleven. Nevertheless, she was taller than us, too, and this fact, that we were all shorter and far less mature than the nieces, rendered the girls far more fascinating and unattainable in every way.

After the night had been filled with the dissection of every known detail of the sisters, one question lingered among us and seemed unanswerable: Would the girls really be there the next day? And the day after that? It seemed too good for me, for Moses and the Eleven, or for the fifty-one. Could we really be this fortunate? It would mean the complete upending of the school and world we knew.

All of us, the Eleven and I, walked to school that morning in a fog. None of us had slept enough to facilitate effective thinking. We encountered the nieces as we walked in. The girls were seated in the back, on chairs. We took our seats in front.

—Okay, Mr Kondit began. —It is obvious that you all are of an age that makes concentration difficult when in the presence of young women.

We said nothing. How had he known? Mr. Kondit was a smart man! we thought.

—I have made a few adjustments to the seating arrangements to help you all in your concentration. I trust that today the lesson will be more captivating to you students. Now, today we will continue with the consonants...

We had no choice but to watch and listen to Mr. Kondit. But we had not planned to. We had, each boy, come to class with other plans. We had, in fact, already divided up the tasks, with two or three boys assigned to each of the girls, to obtain the maximum possible amount of information through close observation. Unless we wanted to turn entirely around, observing the sisters was now impossible. Fact-finding, thereafter, became possible only when we were all writing outside, before the lesson had begun or after it was finished.

Through our reconnaissance before school, after school, and during our writing exercises in the dirt, by the end of the first week, more was known about the sisters' clothes, their hair, their eyes and arms and legs, but they had spoken to no one. They did not speak in class and they made no conversation with any boy. What was known was that they were uniformly beautiful and very smart and dressed far better than the unaccompanied minors like me had any chance to. The nieces' clothes were clean, without tears or holes. They wore the most brilliant reds and purples and blues, their hair always fixed with the utmost care. I had never had any particular interest in girls as playmates, because they cried too quickly and didn't typically want to wrestle, but each night for many weeks, after the talk of the Eleven had faded to whispers and sleep had overtaken us, I lay in the shelter and found myself wondering why I should be so blessed, to have these spectacular royal sisters in my class. Why should I be so fortunate? It seemed, then, that God had had a plan. God had separated me from my home and family and had sent me to this wretched place, but now there seemed to be a reason for it all. There was suffering, I thought, and then there was light. There was suffering and then there was grace. I was placed in Pinyudo, it was clear now, to meet these magnificent girls, and the fact that there were four of them meant that God intended to make up for all the misfortune in my life. God was good and God was just.

I found myself raising my hand more often. Usually my answers were correct. I was, improbably, smarter than I had been days earlier. I sat in the front. Though I was farther from the girls, I needed to be where I would be noticed by Mr. Kondit, and by extension, by his nieces. I answered every question asked of me, and I studied with great diligence at night. I had to get myself noticed by the girls, and if classtime was the only time I could see them—and it was, since they lived on the far side of the camp, where the more essential people lived—then that was when I would have to shine.

Each time I was correct in my answers, Mr. Kondit would say "Good, Achak!" and if I could do so undetected, I would glance back at the nieces, to see if they had noticed. But they rarely seemed to do so.

The Eleven, though, had certainly noticed, and they hassled me without end or mercy. My new success at school was dulling the sheen on the rest of them, and this caused some concern. Would I, they wanted to know, always be this much of a pain?

—Why are you suddenly so interested in school, Achak? they asked.

—Is education your mother and father, Achak? Moses said.

Their hounding forced me to admit my strategy.

—I don't give a goddamn about education is my father! I said.

The Eleven fell down laughing.

—You know why I'm raising my damned hand. Now shut up.

But I had not finished what I had begun. The more I tried, and the longer the nieces seemed unimpressed, the more extreme my efforts became. I helped after class, wiping the board clean and organizing Mr. Kondit's papers and books. I took attendance at the beginning of class, which was both boon and curse. As I called out the names, I had to face the knowing stares of the Eleven, each of them grinning maniacally at me, some batting their lashes in mock-flirtation. When I was done with them, though, I was able to call out the names Agar, Akon, Agum, and Yar Akech, and in this way, I became the only boy the girls looked directly at, the only boy to whom they spoke. Here, the sisters said. Here, here, here.

They were the Royal Nieces of Pinyudo. One of my roommates named them and the girls were immediately known this way—or alternately as the Royal Girls—in the class of fifty-one and elsewhere in the camp, too. There were other families, other sets of sisters, yes, but none so uniformly exceptional. It was unlikely that these four girls were unaware of their nickname, and no one doubted that they found it agreeable. They were aware of the reverence we had for them, but still, they seemed oblivious to me in particular.

As the semester wore on, I began to doubt my strategy. I was the best student in the class, but they paid me no mind. I began to worry that they didn't care much about the academic achievement of me or any boy. It was likely that they wanted nothing to do with someone of my status, an unaccompanied minor. It was very different than being the niece of Mr. Kondit. The unaccompanied minors were the lowest rung of the ladder at Pinyudo, and we were reminded of it constantly. Our clothes were few and tattered and our homes looked like they had been built by boys, which of course they had. When I arrived here in the U.S., one of my old friends from the camps bought me a gift, a set of Tinker Toys. The thin dowels were so like the sticks we used to construct our first shelters in Pinyudo that I had to laugh. Achor Achor and I built a facsimile of our Group Twelve home on our coffee table and then we laughed some more. It was so similar it stunned us both.

It took the entire semester, but finally my efforts toward the Royal Girls bore fruit. With one week left before classes let out for a month, as I was leaving school one day, Agum positioned herself in front of me and said something. It was as likely as a zebra appearing before me and whistling. What had Agum said? I had to piece the words together. It was all so sudden, the changing of one life into another. I was so jarred I heard nothing. I had been looking at her eyes, her lashes, her mouth that was so close to mine.

—Achak, my sister has something to ask you, she had said.

Agar, the eldest and tallest, was suddenly next to her.

Her sister stomped on her foot and was punched in return. I didn't know what was happening, but it seemed good so far.

—Do you want to come to lunch at our house? Agar asked.

I realized at that moment that I had been standing on my tiptoes. I righted myself, hoping they had not noticed.

—Today? I asked.

—Yes, today.

I thought a moment. I thought long enough to think of the wrong thing to say.

—I cannot accept, I said.

I could not believe I said that. Can you believe this is what I said? I had refused the Royal Nieces of Pinyudo. Why? Because I had been taught that a gentleman refuses invitations. The lesson had been explained by my father, one warm night as I was helping him close the shop, but the context was not applicable here, I would later learn. My father had been talking about adultery, about a man's honor, about respect for women, about the sanctity of marriage. He was not, I would later remember, talking about the refusal of an invitation to lunch. But at this moment, I thought I was acting like a gentleman, and I refused.

The sunny faces of Agum and Agar clouded over.

—You cannot accept? they said.

—I am sorry. I cannot accept, I said, and backed away.

I backed away until I walked into one of the poles that held up the classroom. It threatened to collapse on me, but I spun from it, righted the pole, and then ran home. For an hour I was happy with myself, by my unerring grasp of my emotions, my impulses. I was a model of restraint, a true Dinka gentleman! And I was certain the Royal Nieces now knew this. But after my hour of reflection, the reality of it struck me. I had refused a lunch invitation from the very girls I had spent the semester trying to impress. I had been offered everything I wanted: to spend time with them alone; to hear them speak casually, to know what they thought of me and of school and Pinyudo and why they were here; to eat a meal cooked by their mother—to eat a meal, a real meal, cooked by a Dinka woman! I was a fool.

I went about trying to recover. What could I do? I had to take the invitation, now dust, and somehow reconstruct it. I would make fun of myself. Could I act as if I had been kidding? Would they believe that for a moment?

The end of the semester was upon us, and with it final exams. When school let out there would be a month without school, and if I did not salvage the situation, I would not see them until school began again in the spring. I found the youngest, Yar, under a tree, reading her textbook.

—Hello Yar, I said.

She said nothing. She stared at me as if I'd stolen her lunch.

—Do you know where your sisters are?

Without a word, she pointed to Agar, who was walking toward us. I straightened myself and presented her a smile that begged forgiveness.

—I shouldn't have said no, I said. —I wanted to go to lunch.

—Then why did you say no? Agar said.

—Because...

As we spoke, as I hesitated, Agum joined us. And under that sort of pressure, I had a blessed and fortuitous thought. In a week of obsession I could not come up with a suitable excuse but here, in a desperate moment, I came up with the perfect solution.

—I was concerned about what your mother would think of me.

Now Agar and Agum were interested.

—What do you mean?

—I'm from the Dinka Malual Giernyang. I don't speak your dialect. My customs are different. I wasn't sure if your mother would accept me.

—Oh! Agar said.

—For a while, Agum said, —we thought you were brain-damaged.

Agar and Agum and even Yar shared a giggle that offered ample evidence that the two of them had discussed me and my mental state at great length.

—Don't worry about being Dinka-Malual, Agum said. —She won't care where you're from. She'll like you.

Then Agar whispered something urgently into Agum's ear. Agar corrected herself. —But just to be safe, maybe we won't tell her you're Dinka-Malual.

There was another moment of whispering.

—And we'll tell her you're from Block 2, not from the unaccompanied minors' group.

I stood quiet for a second.

—Is that okay? Agar asked.

I could not have cared less. I only cared that my gambit was working. I had played the victim a bit, pretending that as a Dinka-Malual, I felt inferior, unworthy of their company. And it had worked. They were able to feel generous in accepting me, and I appeared all the more honorable for having refused in the first place. I congratulated my brain for its success under pressure. Still, I could not seem overanxious. I had to remain cautious, aware of the risks involved.

—That's best, I said, nodding gravely. —What about your uncle?

—He works late, they said. —He won't be home until dinner.

At that moment, the two older girls seemed suddenly to take notice anew of the youngest, Yar, and they looked upon her like a thorn stuck to their collective heel.

—You won't say anything, Yar.

The little girl, her eyes narrowed, gave them a defiant stare.

—Nothing, Yar. Or else you won't sleep in peace again. We'll move your bed into the river while you're dreaming. You'll wake up surrounded by crocodiles.

Yar's round little face was still defiant, though now fringed with fear. Agar stepped closer, throwing a crisp shadow over Yar's tiny body. The smallest sister's consent came out in a whimper. —I won't.

Agar turned her attention back to me.

—We'll meet you at the coordination center after school.

I knew the place. It was where the kids who didn't have to march loitered between classes and after school. At the coordination center, I would be among the kids with parents, those whose parents were in the camp—the wealthier children, the sons and daughters of teachers and soldiers and commanders.

When classes ended, I ran home. Once there, I realized I had no reason to be home. I paused a moment in the shelter, wondering if there was anything I could do. I changed into my other, light-blue, shirt, and ran to the coordination center.

—Why did you change? Agar said. —I like your other shirt better.

I cursed myself.

—I like *this* one better, Agum said.

Already they were fighting over me! It was bliss.

—You ready? Agum asked.

—To eat lunch? I asked.

—Yes, to eat lunch, she said. —You sure you're okay?

I nodded. I nodded vigorously, because I was indeed ready to eat. But first we had to walk through the camp, and this was—I knew it before it began and it fulfilled every expectation, every fear and dream I had concocted over three months of planning—the most extraordinary walk I have ever undertaken.

So we walked. There were two Royal Nieces on my left, two on my right. I was between these highly regarded sisters, and we were walking to their home. Yes, the camp took notice. It is safe to say that everyone in my class died of envy and shock. With every step, as we passed through one block and then another, more boys and girls gaped at our procession, which was obviously, to them, some kind of date, something significant, far more than a casual stroll. It was a parade, a procession, a statement: The Royal Girls of Pinyudo were proud to have me with them, and this was fascinating to all. Who is that? the parade-watchers wondered. Who is that with the Royal Sisters of Pinyudo?

It was me, Achak Deng. Successful with ladies.

I glanced at Moses, whose eyes, William K would have been happy to know, burst from his face. I grinned and suppressed a laugh. I was loving it all, but at the same time I was a jumble, my body an assemblage of unfamiliar parts. I was forgetting how to walk. I almost tripped on a hose, and then found myself thinking too much about my feet and legs. I was lifting my legs slowly but higher than necessary, my knees almost hitting my stomach. Agum noticed.

—What are you doing? she asked. —Are you making fun of the soldiers?

I smiled shyly.

—Achak! she said, clearly approving. —You shouldn't do that.

Hearing her laugh eased my legs and I walked again like a person in control of his limbs. But just as soon, my arms lost their connection to my nervous system. I was no longer moving my arms. They felt limp, heavy. I gave up.

But I didn't give a goddamn. I was with the Royal Nieces of Pinyudo! We passed Block 10, Block 9, Blocks 8, 7, 6, and 5, and the girls asked me questions I was hoping they would not ask.

—Where are your parents? Agum asked.

I told them I didn't know.

—When did you get separated from them?

I told them a very brief version of my story.

—When you will see them again? Yar asked, and for this received a punch on the shoulder from Agar.

I was tired of this line of questioning. I told them I didn't know when or how I would see my family again, hoping this, spoken to the ground, would encourage the nieces to seek other subject matter. It did and they did.

The house was one of the most impressive at the camp. There was a stone wall around it, a path leading to the front door, and inside, four different rooms—a living room, a kitchen, two bedrooms. It was the biggest house I had seen since I had left home. It was not a hut like we lived in in Marial Bai and elsewhere in southern Sudan. This was a brick building, a sturdy-seeming structure, permanent.

Standing at their door, my legs went limp and I found the wall in time to support myself. The door opened.

—Hello girls, their aunt said. She stood over us, so beautiful, looking like all of her nieces but in woman form. She turned her attention to me. —Is this the boy you were talking about, the star student?

—This is Achak, Agar said, walking past her aunt and into the house.

—Hello, Achak. My husband says you are an exemplary young man.

—Thank you, I said.

I was invited inside, and given a chair. A chair! I had sat in a chair only one other time since arriving at Pinyudo. Soon there was food, a rich and spicy meat broth. There was fresh bread and milk. It surpassed my most fevered dreams. I was still finishing the last of my milk when Agar grabbed me by the hand and lifted me from my seat.

—We're going to study science, Agar said. And with that, she pulled me into the bedroom the four girls shared. The door was kicked closed, and Yar was left on the other side. She pounded it once and walked off.

I was alone with the three older girls in their bedroom. They each had a bed; two were bunks. The walls were white, and decorated with pictures of oceans and cities. Agum and Akon sat down on the single bed, leaving me standing face to face with Agar. It took all of my power in order to keep myself from evacuating my bowels at that moment. And this was before any of the things that were about to happen happened.

Agar took my right hand in hers and spoke. The eyes of Agum and Akon were upon us. They seemed both expectant and familiar with the script we would follow.

—Now we'll play hide and seek, Agar said. —First, you have to find something that I hid here.

Agar pointed to her chest. I took in a quick breath. Even thinking of it now, I cannot believe it happened, that I was chosen for these experiments. But this happened, exactly as I say it did, and next she said the words that I still hear today, when I close my eyes and lay my head to rest.

—You have to look for it. With your hand.

I glanced to the other girls for help. They nodded at me. They were all in on this! I felt as able to put my hand under her shirt as I might make fire from earwax. I stood, smiling dumbly. My nervous system had ceased functioning.

—Here! Agar said, quickly taking my hand and putting it under her shirt.

Can I feel, to this day, the heat of her skin? I can! Her skin was very warm, and taut as a drum, with the thinnest layer of perspiration upon it. I felt her hot skin and held my breath. Her skin surprised me. It didn't feel different than my own, or that of the boys, but still I thought I might explode.

—You have to look!

I forced my hand to make cursory explorations around Agar's torso. I didn't know what was what. —Okay. That was a good try, she said. —I think you found it.

—Now we have to find something on you, Agum said.

—I think it's in there, Agar said, pointing to my shorts.

This was a very different step, and I could not watch. Yes, there were hands in my shorts. As they reached and prodded, I stared at the wall over Agar's shoulder, unsure if God would strike me down at that moment or within the day.

In seconds, all three girls had looked for the missing thing in my shorts, and, satisfied that they had found it, informed me that something was now lost under their dresses. I obliged, looking under Agar's dress, then under Akon's. Agum, for whatever reason, decided that nothing was hidden in her dress.

At some point they decided that we would go swimming. The girls brought their towels to the door, one for me. I feigned delight at the idea, but was stricken as we walked. I worried about a certain something, and then found a solution, and put it out of my mind. The girls brought us to a secluded part of the river, at a bend and in the shade, and there, the girls quickly pulled their dresses over their heads and were naked. The three Royal Nieces were in their underwear and standing in the shallow water. My throat felt as dry as it had during our desert journey. This was all so uncommon. Never in Marial Bai, before the war, would such a thing happen, would a boy of my age—maybe eight, maybe nine or even ten—be invited to swim naked in the river accompanied by three girls such as these. But so much was different here, and my thoughts about my situation were deeply conflicted. Would I have suffered as I had suffered, would I have left my village and walked as I had walked, would I have watched boys die, stepped over the chalk-white bones of rebel soldiers, if I knew that this would be my reward? Would it have been worth it? Because the truth is, such a thing would not likely have happened in my village. The rules there were stricter, the eyes were everywhere. But in this camp, while we were in Ethiopia and our country was at war and we were divorced from so many customs, things like this, and the searchings in the bedroom of the Royal Girls, became possible and happened many times, the experiments varied and plentiful. My pleasure in this particular moment at the river, watching the girls play in the shallow water, was diminished, to a degree, by what happened next.

—Take off your shorts, Achak, Agar said.

I stood rigid in disbelief, in terror.

—Achak, why are you standing there?

—I'll swim with them on, I stammered.

—No you won't. You'll be wet all day. Take them off.

—I'll just watch you swim, I said. —I like it here, I said, pointing to a patch of sand, on which I promptly sat. I did my best to look thrilled with where I was and with the general state of things. I even covered my legs in sand, to further connect myself with the earth and imply that a foray into the water was unlikely.

—Get in here, Achak! Agum demanded.

This continued for some time. I insisted that the shorts should remain on, and the girls could not understand why. Why would I swim with my good shorts on? Their aunt looked at me curiously, too. My strategy was not working.

I needed some chance to explain my predicament, but this was not the place. I am not like the boys you're used to, I would say. You didn't notice when you searched my shorts, I don't think. My clan practiced circumcision on its males, and I knew that the Dinka from their district did not. I was sure that when the Royal Nieces of Pinyudo saw me, the anguala—a circumcised boy—they would flee the water squealing.

Finally Agar ran out of the water and strode directly to me. She stood before me for a moment wearing a grin of sheer menace. Then she pulled my shorts down to my ankles. I did not resist. There was no time and they were too determined. And so I stood before them, my penis naked and unsheathed.

The girls stared for a very long time. Then we all went back to normal, or pretended this was possible. The girls and I continued to play, though for the next hour, anytime they had the opportunity, they peeked between my legs, having no idea what had happened to my penis. They had never seen anything like it.

—So this is what the Dinka-Malual look like? Agar muttered.

Agum nodded. I heard the exchange but pretended I had not.

We continued to play, but I knew everything had changed. Afterward, I went back to Group Twelve and the Royal Nieces of Pinyudo returned to Block 4. I assumed that I would never socialize with them again. I was asked to recount every detail to the Eleven, and decided I would not. For I knew that if I did, the story would make its way around the camp in hours, and the Royal Girls would no longer be considered Royal. They might be considered of easy virtue, and it is no exaggeration to say that out of the tens of thousands of people in that camp, there surely would be one man, perhaps more, willing to risk his life to despoil one of these girls. I told the Eleven only of having a delicious lunch with the Nieces, and of the fine decorating of their home. This was enough for the boys; even these details were sumptuous to them. That night, I lay in bed, not expecting to sleep, recounting every moment, committing all of it to memory, never expecting to speak to any of them again.

But the next day, they asked me to lunch. I was shocked and overwhelmed and said yes without hesitation. Their invitation, and our friendship, was a victory over the petty prejudices between clans, between regions, and a defeat to the caste system of the Pinyudo refugee camp. So I returned to their house, to the meat stew, to the bedroom—even at this moment I can describe every object in that room, the location of every nick on their floor, every knot in the plywood of their bunks—so many times I returned to play hide and seek, at which, thankfully, our abilities never improved. I was very bad at looking for things, so I had to look and look! This was my life for many of the days that year in Ethiopia. It was not the worst of my years.

XIX.

"Let's go, Valentino."

Julian is standing in front of me. He has returned.

"MRI. Follow me."

I stand up and follow Julian out of the emergency room and down the hallway. The floor smells of human feces.

"Homeless guy shat in here," Julian tells me, his walk surprisingly nimble. We reach the elevator bank and he pushes the button.

"Sorry you got mugged, man," he says.

We step into the elevator. It is 1:21 a.m.

"Happened to me, too. A few months ago," he says. "Same kind of thing. Two kids, one of them had a gun. They followed me home from the store and got me in the stairwell. Stupid. They were about two hundred pounds, both of them put together."

I glance again at Julian. He's powerfully built, not the sort of man one would expect to be targeted for a mugging. But if he were wearing his hospital uniform, perhaps they considered him a peaceful man.

"What did they take?" I ask.

"Take? They took nothing, man. I'm a vet! I was back from Iraq five weeks when they tried that shit on me. The whole way home I knew they were following me. I had plenty of time to decide what to do, so I made a plan: I was gonna break one of their noses, then take that guy's gun and shoot his friend with it. The one I didn't kill

I'd hold till the cops came. He'd spend the rest of his life scared straight. Hey, what's your middle name, anyway—how do you say it?"

"Achak," I say, skipping quickly over the first syllable. In Sudan, the "A" is barely audible.

"You heard of Chaka Khan?" Julian asks.

I tell him that I haven't.

"Forget it," he says. "Dumb reference."

This man makes me ashamed that I didn't do more against my attackers. I, too, have been in a war, though I suppose I never was trained the way this man Julian was. I glance at his arms, which are carved and tattooed, at least three times the size of my own.

The elevator opens and we arrive at the MRI unit. There is an Indian man waiting for us. He says nothing to either of us. We walk past him and into a large room with a circular tomb in the center. A flat bed extends from the hole in the center.

"You ever done one of these?" Julian asks me.

"No," I say. "I've never seen a machine like this."

"Don't worry. It doesn't hurt. Just don't think of cremation."

I lower myself onto the white bed. "Do I keep my eyes open or closed?"

"Up to you, Valentino."

I decide to keep my eyes open. Julian leaves my side and I hear his footsteps, almost silent, as he leaves the room. I am alone as the bed glides into the chamber.

The ring above me whirs and rotates around my skull and I think of Tonya and Powder and remember that they are free and will never be caught. By now they are selling my possessions to a pawn shop and have deposited Michael at whatever place he considers home. They believe they have taught me a lesson and they are correct.

Above me, the smaller ring begins to turn inside the larger ring.

I have high hopes for this test. I have heard of the MRI; its name was invoked many times, by Mary Williams and Phil and others who sought to discover why my headaches persisted. And now I will finally know what is wrong with me, I will receive the answer. At Pinyudo one day, under a striped white ceiling of clouds, Father Matong taught us about the Last Judgment. When boys such as myself made clear we were scared of being so judged, he allayed our fears. Judgment is relief, he said. Judgment is release. One walks through life unsure if he has done right or wrong, Father Matong said, but only judgment from God can provide certainty about the way one has lived. I have thought about his lesson many times since. I have been unsure about so many things, chief among them whether or not I have been a good child of God. I am inclined to think that I have done so much wrong, for otherwise I would not have been punished so many times, and He would not have seen fit to harm so many of those I love.

The noise of the machine above me is steady, a mechanical murmur that sounds at once reassuring and utterly certain of itself.

I know that the MRI is not the judgment from above, but still, it promises to release me from so many questions. Why does my head still ache so many mornings? Why do I so often dress with a piercing pain in the back of my head, its tendrils shooting from the back of my skull into the very whites of my eyes? I have hope that if I know the answer to questions like these, even if the diagnosis is dire, I will have some relief. The MRI might explain why I continue to receive occasionally mediocre grades at Georgia Perimeter College, even though I know I should be and can be excelling there. Why have I been in the United States for five years now and seem to have made so little progress? And why must everyone I know die prematurely, and in increasingly shocking ways? Julian, you know of only a small portion of the death I have seen. I have spared you the details of Jor, a boy I knew in Pinyudo, who was taken by a lion only inches from me. We had gone to fetch water at dusk, walking through the high grass. One moment I could feel Jor's breath on my neck, and the next I could smell the animal, its dark-smelling sweat. I turned and saw Jor limp, dead in its jaws. The lion was looking directly at me, emotionless, and we stared at each other for days and nights. Then he turned and left with Jor. Julian, I do not want to think of myself as important enough that God would choose me for extraordinary punishment, but then again, the circumference of calamity that surrounds me is impossible to ignore.

The inner ring has performed a full revolution and now stops. The quiet in the room is absolute. Now footsteps.

"Not too bad, right?" Julian is at my side.

"Yes, thank you," I say. "It was interesting."

"Well, that's that. Let's head back downstairs."

I stand and need a moment to steady myself against the machine. It is warmer than I had expected. "What happens now?" I ask. "Do you read the results?"

"Who, me? No, no. Not me."

We pass the operator behind the glass and I see, in the dark room, screen images of a cross-section of a head—mine?—colored in greens, yellows, reds. Like satellite pictures of weather systems from another planet.

"Is that me?"

"That's you, Valentino."

We stand for a moment at the glass, watching as the screen changes to what I assume are different sections of my brain, different ways of seeing it. It is a violation, that this stranger can examine my head without knowing me.

"Does that man examine the results?" I ask.

"No, not him, either. He's just the technician. Not a doctor."

"Oh."

"Pretty soon, Valentino. Right now there's no one here who knows how to read the scans. That doctor doesn't come in for a while. You can wait where you were before. You hungry?"

I tell him I am not, and he gives me a doubtful look.

We ride the elevator back up. I ask him if he killed one of the boys.

"That's the one thing I didn't do. The second they called me bitch, I turned on them, threw one of their heads against the wall, and kicked the second guy in the chest. He hadn't even pulled his gun yet. The one kid was unconscious against the wall and the one I kicked, he was on the ground. I put my knee on his chest, took the gun and played with him for a few minutes. Put the gun in his mouth, all that. He pissed his pants. Then I called the cops. Took them forty-five minutes to get there."

"This is the same with me," I say. "Fifty-five minutes."

Julian puts his arm around my shoulder and squeezes my neck in an apologetic way. The elevator doors open and I can see Achor Achor and Lino across the way.

"Makes you wonder what sort of problem gets the cops running, right?"

Because Julian is smiling, I force a chuckle.

"Anyway," he says. "What do you want, right?"

I turn my head quickly. "What did you say?"

"Aw, nothing, man. Just running my mouth."

My body has a current shooting through it.

"Please. What did you just say?"

"Nothing. I just said, What do you want? Like, what are you gonna do? What'd you think I said?"

And like that, the current dies.

"Sorry," I say. It would not be surprising to me to hear Julian ask about the What. The What, I think, has something to do with why he and I waited for almost an hour, after being held at gunpoint, to be visited by police. It has something to do with why it took nine hours for me to get an MRI, and why I am now being brought to a bed in the ER—passing Achor Achor and Lino, who begin to stand up—to wait for a doctor who, at some point, will judge my results.

"I wish I could expedite this process, Valentino," Julian says.

"I understand," I say.

I sit on the bed, and Julian stands there with me for a moment.

"You'll be okay here?"

"I will. Can you tell my friends where I am?"

"I will. Sure. No sweat."

Julian leaves me on the bed, pulling the curtain, attached to a track on the ceiling, around my area of the room. I have little doubt that Julian would prefer having me here, where he does not have to see me, to me sitting in front of him in the waiting room. But when he gets back to his desk, how will he make Achor Achor and Lino disappear?

"Excuse me Julian?" I say.

He returns. The curtain squeals and Julian's face appears.

"I'm sorry," I say. "Can you tell my friends to go home now, that I'm fine?"

He nods and smiles broadly. "Sure. I'm sure they're ready. I'll tell them." He turns to leave me but then remains. He stares at his clipboard for a long moment, then looks at me through the corner of his eye.

"You fight in that war, Valentino, the civil war?"

I tell him no, that I was not a soldier.

"Oh. Well good, then," he says. "I'm glad."

And he leaves.

XX.

I was almost a soldier, Julian. I was saved by a massacre.

Pinyudo changed slowly and I felt the fool for not knowing what had been planned. I believe now that they, the SPLA leadership, had conceived it all from the beginning. If they are guilty of this foresight, I am split between awe and horror.

My awareness of the architecture of it all began one day, at the beginning of summer, when boys were everywhere dancing, celebrating. I was with the Eleven; we were eating our dinner under the low ceiling of a humid grey sky.

—Garang is coming! boys sang, racing past our shelter.

—Garang is coming! another boy, a teenager, roared. He skipped like a child.

—Who's coming? I asked the passing teenager.

—Garang is coming!

—*Who?* I asked. I had forgotten many of the details of Dut's lessons.

—Shh! the teenager scolded, looking around for listeners. —Garang, the leader of the SPLA, fool, he hissed. And then he was gone.

Indeed John Garang was coming. I had heard the name, but knew very little about him. The news of his arrival was delivered after dinner in an official manner by the elders. They visited all the barracks—we were now living in brick buildings, grey and cold but sturdy—and subsequently the camp fell into a state of pandemonium. No one slept. I had heard very little about John Garang before this time, only what Dut had told me long ago, but in the days leading to his visit, information flowed freely and unfiltered.

—He is a doctor. —Not a medicine doctor, he's a farming doctor. He went to school in the United States. In Iowa. —He has an advanced degree in Agriculture from a university in Iowa. —He is the most intelligent Sudanese man alive. —He was a decorated soldier, the most commended Dinka. —He is from Upper Nile. —He's nine feet tall and built like a rhino.

I checked with Mr. Kondit and found that most of this information was correct. Garang had received a doctorate in Iowa, and this seemed to me so exotic that immediately I had the utmost faith that this man could lead a new southern Sudan to victory and rebirth.

In advance of his visit, we were made to clean our dwellings, and then those of the teachers, and finally the road leading into Pinyudo. It was decided that the stones lining the road should be painted, and thus paint was distributed and the stones were made white and red and blue, alternating. On the day of the visit, the camp had never looked so beautiful. I was proud. I can remember the feeling still; we were capable of this, the creation of a life from nothing.

On the day of the visit, the residents of Pinyudo were frantic. I had never seen the elders so nervous and wild eyed. Garang's visit was to take place in the parade grounds, and everyone would be there. As Moses and I gathered in the morning with the rest of the camp, the crowd grew far beyond my imagining. This was the first time I had seen the camp's entire human volume, perhaps forty thousand of us, in one place, and the sight was impossible to take in. SPLA soldiers were everywhere—hundreds of them, from teenage boys to the most battle-hardened men.

The sixteen thousand or so of us unaccompanied boys were seated directly in front of the microphone and while we waited for John Garang, the forty thousand assembled refugees from Sudan sang songs. We sang traditional songs of southern Sudan, and we sang new songs composed for the occasion. One of the unaccompanied boys had composed lyrics for this assembly:

Chairman John Garang,
Chairman John Garang,
A chairman as brave as the buffalo, the lion, and tiger
In the land of Sudan
How would Sudan be liberated if not by the mighty power we possess?

The immense power the Chairman possesses
Look at the Sudan! It resembles the ruins of the Dark Ages

Look at the Chairman—the Doctor!
He's carrying a sophisticated gun
Look at John Garang,
He's carrying a sophisticated gun

All the roots are uprooted
All the roots are uprooted
Sadiq El Mahdi remaining a single root
And John will uproot him in our land

We will struggle to liberate the land of Sudan
We will! With the AK-47
The battalions of the Red Army will come
We'll come
Armed with guns in the left hand
And pens in the right hand
To liberate our home, oh, ooo!

When the song was sung it began again and once more and finally the guards arrived, the advance guards who heralded the arrival of Garang himself. Thirty of them strode into the parade grounds and surrounded the staging area, all of them armed with AK-47s and looking with suspicion and displeasure at us.

I did not like those guards. There were too many guns, and the men looked reckless and unkind. My mood, which had been euphoric with the songs and cheering, clouded over. I told Isaac, the other boy called Gone Far, of my feelings.

—They are here to protect Garang, Gone Far. Relax.

—From who? From us? This is wrong, the men with guns everywhere.

—Without the guards someone would kill him. You know that.

Finally the leadership entered: Deputy Commander William Nyuon Bany, Commander Lual Ding Wol, and then Chairman Garang himself.

He was indeed a large man, broad chested and with a strange grey beard, unkempt and wayward. He had a great round forehead, small bright eyes, and a prominent jaw. His presence was commanding; from any distance it would be obvious that he was a leader of men.

—That is a great man, Moses whispered.

—That man is God, Isaac said.

Garang raised his hands triumphantly and the adults, the women in particular, whipped themselves into a furor. The women ululated and raised their arms and closed their eyes. We turned and the adults and trainees were dancing, waving their arms wildly. More songs were sung for his approval.

We'll adjust the Sudan flag
We'll alter the Sudan flag
For Sudan is confused herself

Sadiq El Mahdi is corrupted
Wol Wol is corrupted
SPLA has a knife—fixed at the barrel tip of an AK-47
Courageous men who fear nothing
These are the men that will liberate us through bloodshed

Red Armies—soldiers of the Doctor
We'll struggle till we liberate Sudan
The man who suffers from mosquito bites, thirst, and hunger?
He is a genuine liberator
We'll liberate Sudan by bloodshed

Then John Garang began.

—I seize the opportunity to extend my revolutionary greetings and appreciation to each and every SPLA soldier in the field of combat who, under very difficult conditions, has been and is scoring giant, convincing victories one after the other against the various governments of exploiters and oppressors.

A roar came up through the forty thousand.

—Half-naked, barefooted, hungry, thirsty, and confronted by a swarm of many other due hardships, the SPLA soldier has proved to the whole world that the trappings of life can never sway him from the cause of the people and the justice of their struggle. The SPLA soldier has once again validated the age-old human experience concerning the infiniteness of the human capacity for resilience and resolve against challenges to dignity and justice.

He was a brilliant speaker, I thought, the best I had ever heard.

I listened to Dr. John Garang while carefully watching the soldiers surrounding him. Their eyes roamed over the crowd. Garang spoke of the birth of the SPLA, of injustices, of oil, land, racial discrimination, sharia, the arrogance of the government of Sudan, their scorched earth policy toward southern Sudan, the murahaleen. Then he spoke of how Khartoum had underestimated the Dinka. How the SPLA was winning this war. He spoke for hours, and finally, as the afternoon gave way to evening, he seemed to wind down.

—To the SPLA soldier, he boomed, —wherever you are, whatever you are doing now, whether you are in action or in camouflage, however you are challenged, however you feel, whatever your present condition, I salute and congratulate you, the SPLA soldier, for your heroic sacrifices and steadfastness in pursuit of your single-minded objective to build a new Sudan. Look at us! We will build a new Sudan!

The roar was like the earth ripping open. The women ululated again and the men yelled. I threw my hands to my ears to block out the sound but Moses slapped my hands away.

—But there is much work to do, Garang continued. We have a long road ahead of us. You boys—and here Garang indicated the sixteen thousand of us boys sitting before him—you will fight tomorrow's battle. You will fight it on the battlefield and you will fight it in the classrooms. Things will change at Pinyudo from here on after. We must get serious now. This is not just a camp for waiting. We cannot wait. You young boys are the seeds. You are the seeds of the new Sudan.

That was the first time we were called Seeds, and from that point forward, this is how we were known. After the speech, everything at Pinyudo changed. Hundreds of boys immediately departed to begin military training at Bonga, the SPLA camp not far away. Teachers left to train, most of the men between fourteen and thirty had gone to Bonga, and the schools were reorganized around the missing students and teachers.

Moses, too, thought it was time.

—I want to train.

—You're too young, I said.

I was too young, I believed, and thus Moses was too young, too.

—I asked one of the soldiers and he said I was big enough.

—But you'll leave me here?

—You can come. You should come, Achak. Why are we here, anyway?

I didn't want to train. There were so many aggressive young boys at Pinyudo, but I have never had this aggression in my blood. When boys wanted to wrestle, to fist-fight to pass the time or prove their worth—and at Pinyudo, once we had all gotten our strength up, boys would want to spar for no reason at all—I couldn't find the inspiration within me. If the wrestling wasn't done among friends and out of affection, I couldn't bring myself to care about such contests. I wanted to be in school, wanted only to see the Royal Girls and eat lunches cooked by their mother and find things hidden under their clothes.

—Who will fight the war if not men like us? Moses said.

He thought we were men; he had lost his mind. We were no more than eighty pounds, our arms like bamboo shoots. But nothing I said could dissuade Moses, and that week he went off down the road. He joined the SPLA, and that was the last I saw of him for some time.

The summer was awash in work and upheaval. Shortly after the departure of John Garang, another charismatic young SPLA commander came to Pinyudo, and he came to stay. His name was Mayen Ngor, and he was on a mission. Like Garang, he was an expert in agricultural techniques, and made it his task to irrigate the land that abutted the river. We watched him one day, tall and swan-like in a white shirt and pants, trailed by four smaller, duller ducklings—his assistants, in tan uniforms, who busily demarcated vast swaths of uncultivated land. The next day he returned, with Ethiopians and tractors in tow, and with incredible speed they turned over the soil and created dozens of neat rectangles extending from the water. Mayen Ngor was a man of great efficiency, and he liked very much to talk about about his knack for efficiency.

—Do you see how quickly this is happening? he asked us. He had assembled about three hundred of us by the river to explain his plans and our role in them.

—All of this land you see before you is potential food, all of it. If we can work this land wisely, all the food we'll ever need can be provided by this land, by this river and the care we invest in it.

We thought this was a fine idea, but of course we knew that the most difficult aspects of working the land would be left to the unaccompanied minors, and indeed they were. For weeks, Mayen Ngor instructed us in the use of hoes, spades, wheelbarrows, axes, and sickles, and we went about doing the manual labor after the large Ethiopian machinery was long gone. While we worked and eventually planted seeds for tomatoes, beans, corn, onions, groundnuts, and sorghum, Mayen Ngor, his eyes alight with visions of the bounty of the land, walked among us, proselytizing.

—What is your name, jaysh al-ahmar? he asked me one day.

The Eleven, who worked close to me, all took notice of the great man's presence among us. I told Mayen Ngor my name. He chose not to use it.

—Jaysh al-ahmar, do you have a sense of what this land will look like when you're finished? Do you see that all this earth is potential food?

I told him that I did, and that the thought excited me greatly.

—Good, good, he said, standing and looking out at the rows of hundreds of boys beyond, all bent over their hoes and spades. The sight of these emaciated boys working under the summer sun gave him much pleasure.

—All of it! he exclaimed. —All of it, potential food!

And then he strode on, down the row.

When he was out of earshot, the laughter broke out all around me, with the Eleven unable to contain themselves. That was the day Mayen Ngor became known as Mr. Potential Food. For months afterward, we would point to anything—a rock, a shovel, a truck—and say "Potential food!" Achor Achor did the best imitation, and took his performance the farthest. He would point at random objects and, while gazing out at the horizon, proclaim: "You see that tree, jaysh al-ahmar? Potential food. That tire? Potential food. That lump of manure, that pile of old shoes? Potential food!"

When the fall came, the transformation of the camp grew more complete—it was now a militarized place, with rigid rules, more constant and varied chores for us all, and far more intimations that we were there for one primary purpose: to be fed and fattened such that we might fight once we were large enough to do so, or the SPLA was desperate enough to use us—whichever came first. Many teachers had returned from their training at Bonga, and the marching began. Each morning, we were brought to the parade grounds and we were lined up in rows, and made to do calisthenics, counting with the elders. Then, using our farm implements to simulate AK-47s, we marched up and down the parade grounds, all the while singing patriotic songs. When the marching was done, we were given the announcements for the day, and were informed of any new rules and regulations. There seemed to be no shortage of new guidelines and prohibitions.

—I know that most of you boys are learning English now, said a new teacher one day. He was fresh from Bonga, and he came to be known as called Commander Secret, —and a few of you are becoming proficient. I need to warn you, though, that this does not mean you can use your English to speak to any of the aid workers here. You are not permitted to talk to any non-Sudanese, whether they're black or white. Is that understood?

We made clear that this was understood.

—If for any reason you do find yourself asked a question by an aid worker, observe these guidelines: first, you should act as shy as possible. It is better for this camp and for you personally if you do not talk to an aid worker, even if they ask you a question. Is that understood?

We told Commander Secret that it was understood.

—One last thing: if you're ever asked anything about the SPLA, you are to say you know nothing about it. You do not know what the SPLA is, you have never seen a member of the SPLA, you don't know the first thing about what those letters stand for. You are merely orphans here for safety and schooling. Is that clear?

This was less comprehensible to us, but the dichotomy of the UN and the SPLA would become clearer as the months went on. As the UN presence grew, with new facilities and more equipment arriving each month, the SPLA influence on the camp grew, too. And the two factions evenly divided up the day. Before nightfall, the camp was dedicated to education and nutrition, with us attending classes and eating healthfully and in all ways seeming to the UN observers a mass of unaccompanied minors. But at night, the camp belonged to the SPLA. It was then that the SPLA took their share of the food delivered to us and the other refugees, and it was then that operations were undertaken and justice meted out. Any boy who had shirked or misbehaved would be caned, and for many of these boys, skeletal as they were, canings could prove debilitating, even fatal. The canings, of course, were done at night, out of sight of any international observers.

The boys at the camp were split in their opinions about our rebel leaders. Among us were plenty, perhaps even a majority, of boys who could barely wait to leave for

Bonga to train, to be given a gun, to learn to kill, to avenge their villages, to kill Arabs. But there were plenty like me, who felt apart from the war, who wanted only to learn to read and write, who waited for the madness to end. And the SPLA did not make it easy to fight with them, for their army. For months I had been hearing rumors of hardship at Bonga, about how difficult the training was, how harsh and unforgiving. Boys were dying over there, I knew, though the explanations were shifting and impossible to confirm. Exhaustion, beatings. Boys tried to escape and were shot. Boys lost their rifles and were shot. I now know that some of the news from Bonga was false, but between what was hidden and what was exaggerated there is some truth. Those who had gone to fight the Arabs had to fight their elders first. Still, every week, boys willingly left the relative safety and comfort of Pinyudo of their own accord to train at Bonga. We lost four of the Eleven that way, between the summer and winter, and all of them were eventually killed. Machar Dieny fought and was killed in southern Sudan in 1990. Mou Mayuol joined the SPLA and was killed in Juba in 1992. Aboi Bith joined the SPLA and was killed in Kapoeta in 1995. He was probably fourteen years old. Boys make very poor soldiers. This is the problem.

Our days were now entirely reconstituted. Where before there had been studying and soccer and simple chores like water-fetching, now there was manual labor—in addition to the farm work—and jobs we were much too young to be expected to do.

Each morning, when we were lined up on the parade grounds, the elders would indicate one group: —You will help Commander Kon's wife build a pen for her goats. Another group: —You will find firewood in the forest. Another: —You will help this elder build a new house for his cousins. When school was over and lunch had been eaten, we would know where to go.

I spent two weeks building a house for a friend of my biology teacher. We were hired out for any task, no matter how great or small. We planted seeds in gardens, we built outhouses. We did the wash for any elder who demanded it. Many SPLA members had brought their families to Pinyudo to live while they trained nearby at Bonga. So we did their wash in the river, and brought water to the officer's wives, and performed whatever task they could concoct. There was no payment for our work, and we could not ask for or expect even a glass of water from the beneficiary of our labor. I asked once for a drink, after me and the Eleven—ten of them, actually; Isaac was playing sick—had completed the home for the family of a newly arrived officer. We

295

came to the door of the hut, a door we had just installed, and the officer's wife stepped through it, looking angrily at us.

—Water? Is this a joke? Get out of here, mosquitoes. Drink from a puddle!

Often the work lasted until dark. Other times, we were released in the late afternoon, and could play. Soccer was played everywhere at Pinyudo, in games that often had no discernible boundaries or even goals. One boy would take the ball—there were always new soccer balls available, gifts of John Garang, it was said—and dribble off with it, and would soon be trailed by a hundred boys, who wanted only to touch it. Even then, though, in the late afternoon, an elder might have an inspiration.

—Hey you! he could call out to the mass of barefoot boys chasing the ball across the dust —You three, get over here. I have a job for you.

And we would go.

No one wanted to enter the forest, for in the forest, boys disappeared. The first two who died were well-known for having been devoured by lions, and thus hunting in the forest for building materials became the job everyone chose to avoid. When our number was called for forest duty, some boys went mad. They hid in trees. They ran away. Many ran to Bonga, to train as soldiers, anything to avoid having to enter the forest of disappearing boys. The situation became worse as the months wore on. The forest's bounty was depleted daily, so boys searching for grass or poles or firewood had to venture further every day, closer to the unknown. More boys failed to come back, but the work continued, the construction spread wider and wider.

The winds came one day and blew down the roofs of dozens of the elders' homes. Six of us were assigned the task of reconstructing the roofs, and Isaac and I were busy with this assignment when Commander Secret found us.

—Into the forest with you two. We have no kindling.

I tried to be as formal and polite as I could when I said:

—No sir, I cannot be eaten by a lion here.

Commander Secret stood, outraged. —Then you'll be beaten!

I had never heard such delicious words. I would take any beating over the risk of being devoured. Commander Secret took me to the barracks and beat me on the legs and backside with a cane, with force but without great malice. I suppressed a smile when it was over; I felt victorious and ran off, unable to hold off a song I sung to myself and to the night air.

Soon after that, no boys would enter the forest, and the beatings multiplied. And when the beatings multiplied, so did the methods to reduce the impact of each. An extensive system of clothes-borrowing was instituted for those anticipating a caning. Usually the recipient would have a few hours' notice at least, and could borrow as many pairs of underwear and shorts he could convincingly wear. The canings usually took place at night; we thanked God for that, because our additional padding was that much less detectable.

After a few weeks, the teachers, out of sloth or an interest in instilling a sort of military discipline in us, ordered us to cane each other as punishment for whatever offense arose. Though initially a few boys actually followed through with the beatings—they paid in the end for their enthusiasm—overall a system was devised whereby the caner struck the ground, not the victim's backside, and caner and canee still made the expected sounds of effort and pain.

The new military strictness was an annoyance, but otherwise we felt strong and no one was dying. Most of us were still gaining weight, and could work and run. There was enough food, and the food, in fact, provided the one reliable excuse for avoiding the afternoon work. In our groups of twelve, we were each assigned one cooking day, on which that boy was allowed to skip school and the work detail afterward, because that boy busy was ostensibly cooking for the other eleven others. Food was distributed once a month, by truck. We were sent to carry it back to the camp, where we stored it in a series of corrugated sheds. The bags, full of corn flour, white beans, lentils, and vegetable oil, were as big as many of us, and often had to be carried by pairs.

Every twelfth day was my free day, and that was a good day. In the nights leading up to it I fell asleep smiling, and as the day approached my mood bubbled closer and closer to giddiness. When it arrived, I slept in after the Eleven had gone to the parade grounds and to school, and once awake, I thought about what I would cook. I thought about it on the way to the river to fetch water, and I thought about it on the way back. Soup was just about all we could make for lunch, but when it was my turn, I tried to make a soup that was not lentil. Lentil soup was the everyday soup, and most of the Eleven were content to cook it and eat it, but being the leader of the group, I tried to do something better on my cooking days, something that would make the Eleven feel extraordinary.

I would check the supplies we had to see if there was an extra portion of something that could be traded. If we had an extra ration of rice, for example, I might be able to trade it for a fish by the river. With a fish, I could make fish soup, and the Eleven very much liked fish soup. While they were at school, I would be busy, preparing the soup and thinking about the evening meal. But preparing soup doesn't require all the hours of the day, and allowed for some leisure. Even if an elder found me lounging, I could tell him, "I'm a cook today," and the elder would be silenced. Being a good and responsible cook was essential.

I was an excellent cook, but serving the soup was difficult at first. When the camp began, there were no plates or utensils, so the food, and even the soup, was served on the bags that had held the grain. The bags were sturdy and made of woven plastic, so the food would stay on its surface without soaking through. After many months, we were given utensils, and some months later, plates were distributed, one aluminum plate per boy. No one ate breakfast in all the time we were at Pinyudo, but after a time, we began to drink tea in the morning, though tea was not distributed. We would have to trade part of our food ration in the town for the tea and sugar. When we had nothing to trade for sugar, or there was no sugar in the shops, we learned how to hunt bees and extract honey from their hives.

I was cooking one day when one of my neighbors, a round-faced boy named Gor, rushed toward me. It was obvious he had news, but he and I weren't friends, and he was visibly disappointed that because no one else was around, I would have to be the recipient.

—The United States has invaded Kuwait and Iraq!

I didn't know what Kuwait or Iraq were. Gor was a smart boy, but I was stung by his knowledge of world affairs. I had assumed we were getting the same education at Pinyudo, and yet there were inequities that were difficult to account for.

—They're rescuing Kuwait from Saddam Hussein! They're bringing five hundred thousand troops and are taking back Kuwait. They'll get rid of Hussein!

Finally, after feigning understanding for a few minutes, I swallowed my pride enough to ask for a thorough explanation. Saddam Hussein was the dictator of Iraq, Gor told me, and had been supplying guns and planes to the Sudanese army. Hussein had given Khartoum money and nerve gas. It was Iraqi pilots who flew some of the helicopters that strafed our villages.

—So this is good, I asked, —that the United States is fighting him?

—It is! It is! Gor said. —It means that soon the Americans will fight Khartoum, too. It means that they will remove all the Muslim dictators in the world. This is def-

298

initely what it means. I guarantee this. God has spoken through the Americans, Achak.

And he went off, in search of more boys to educate.

This was the prevailing theory for some time, that the war in Iraq and Kuwait would lead, inevitably, to the toppling of the Islamic fundamentalists in Sudan. But this did not happen. The fortunes of the SPLA were not promising that year. Battles and territory had been lost and the rebels, as might be expected, began to eat their own.

One morning at ten o'clock, an assembly was announced. School was called off and we poured out of the classrooms.

—To the parade grounds! the teachers ordered.

I asked Achor Achor what the assembly was all about, and he wasn't sure. I asked another elder, who snapped at me.

—Just get to the parade grounds. You'll enjoy it.

—Do we have to work this afternoon?

—No. This afternoon is education.

Achor Achor and I walked to the grounds, our moods buoyant. Anything was better than work in the afternoon, and very soon we were sitting in the front row of a growing throng of boys. There was an SPLA commander, Giir Chuang, at the camp that week, and we assumed the assembly was called to honor him.

Commander Secret was there, as was Commander Beltbuckle and Mr. Potential Food and Mr. Kondit and every other elder at the camp. I looked for Dut, but didn't find him. His presence at the camp had been sporadic for many months, and the boys who had walked with him concocted theories about him: that he was now a commander in the SPLA, that he was in college in Addis Ababa. In any case, we missed him, all of us, that day. I looked around and saw that most of the boys assembled were close to me in age, somewhere between six and twelve. Very few were older. All the boys were grinning and laughing, and soon they were singing. Deng Panan, the best-known singer of patriotic songs and a celebrity among the rebels, stood before us with a microphone. He sang of God and faith, of resilience and the suffering of the southern Sudanese at the hands of the Arabs. A cheer rose up as he began to sing the words written by one of the boys in Pinyudo.

We will struggle to liberate the land of Sudan
We will! With the AK-47

The battalions of the Red Army will come
We'll come!
Armed with guns on the left hand
And pens in the right hand
To liberate our home, oh, ooo.

Meanwhile a platoon of fifteen soldiers marched into the grounds and assembled themselves in a straight line, shoulder to shoulder, facing us. Next, a line of men, bedraggled and tied together by rope, were pushed into the parade grounds. Seven men, all of them looking malnourished, some bleeding from abrasions on their heads and feet.

—Who are they? Achor Achor whispered.

I had no idea. They were now kneeling in a line facing us, and these men were not singing. The SPLA soldiers, in clean uniforms, stood behind them, AK-47s in hand. There was a man, one of those tied to the rest, sitting directly in front of me. Quickly I caught his eye, and he stared back at me with a look of unmitigated fury.

When Deng Panan finished his song, Giir Chuang took the microphone.

—Boys, you are the future of Sudan! That is why we call you the Seeds. You are the seeds of a new Sudan.

The boys around me cheered. I continued staring at the tethered men.

—Soon Sudan will be yours! Giir Chuang yelled.

The boys cheered more.

The commander spoke of our potential to repair our beloved country once the war ended, that we would return to a ruined Sudan, but one waiting for the Seeds—that only our hands and backs and brains could rebuild southern Sudan. Again we cheered.

—But until there is peace in Sudan, we must be vigilant. We cannot accept weakness within our ranks, and we cannot accept betrayal of any kind. Do you agree?

We all nodded.

—Do you agree? the commander repeated.

We said that we agreed.

—These men are traitors! They are deviants!

Now we looked at the men. They were dressed in rags.

—They are rapists!

Giir Chuang seemed to have expected a reaction from us, but we were silent.

We had lost the thread. We were too young to know much about rape, the severity of the crime.

—They have also given secrets of the SPLA away to the government of Sudan, and they have revealed SPLA plans to khawajas here in Pinyudo. They have compromised the movement, and have tried to ruin all we have accomplished together. The new Sudan that you will inherit—they have spat upon it! If we let them do it, they would poison everything that we have. If we gave them the opportunity, they would collaborate with the government until we were all Muslims, until we begged for mercy under the boot of the Arabs and their sharia! Can we let them do that, boys?

We yelled no. I felt that the men should surely be punished for such betrayals. I hated the men. Then something unexpected happened. One of the men spoke.

—We did nothing! We raped no one! This is a cover-up!

The protesting man was struck in the head with the butt of a gun. He fell onto his chest. Emboldened, the other prisoners began to plead.

—You're being lied to! a tiny prisoner wailed. —These are all lies!

This man was also struck with the butt of a gun.

—The SPLA eats its own!

This man was kicked in the back of the neck and sent into the dirt.

Giir Chuang seemed surprised at their impunity, but saw it as an opportunity.

—See these men lie to you, Seeds of a new Sudan! They are shameless. They lie to us, they lie to us all. Can we let them lie to us? Can we let them look us in the eye and threaten the future of our new nation with their treachery?

—No! we yelled.

—Can we let such treason go unpunished?

—No! we yelled.

—Good. I'm happy you agree.

And with that, the soldiers stepped forward, two of them behind each bound man. They pointed their guns at each man's head and chest, and they fired. The shots went through the men and dust rose from the earth.

I screamed. A thousand boys screamed. They had killed all these men.

But one was not dead. The commander pointed to a prisoner still kicking and breathing. A soldier stepped over and shot him again, this time in the face.

We tried to run. The first few boys who tried to leave the parade grounds were knocked down and caned by their teachers. The rest of us stood, afraid to move, but the crying wouldn't stop. We cried for the mothers and fathers we hadn't seen in years, even those we knew were dead. We wanted to go home. We wanted to run from the parade grounds, from Pinyudo.

The commander abruptly ended the assembly.

—Thank you. See you next time, he said.

Now boys ran in every direction. Some clung to the closest adult they could find, shaking and weeping. Some lay where they had been standing, curled up and sobbing. I turned around, vomited, and ran away, spitting as I ran to the home of Mr. Kondit, who I found already sitting inside, on his bed, staring at the ceiling. I had never seen him so ashen. He sat listless, his hands resting limply on his knees.

—I'm so tired, he said.

I sat on the floor below him.

—I don't know why I'm here anymore, he said. —Things have become so confused.

I had never seen Mr. Kondit express doubt of any kind.

—I don't know if we'll find our way out of this, Achak. Not this way. This is not the best we can do. We are not doing the best we can do.

We sat until the dusk came and I went home to the Eleven, whose ranks had been depleted. We were now Nine. Two boys had left that afternoon and did not return.

After that day, many of the boys stopped attending rallies, no matter what the stated purpose. They hid in their shelters, feigning sickness. They went to the clinic, they ran to the river. They invented any reason to miss the gatherings, and because attendance could not be counted, they were seldom punished.

The stories abounded after the executions. The men had been accused of various offenses, but those implicated with the rape were, according to the whispers in the camp, innocent. One of them had eloped with a woman coveted by a senior SPLA officer, who then framed the groom as a rapist. The woman's mother, who did not approve of the marriage, collaborated with the accusers, and claimed the groom's friends had raped her, too. The case was complete, and the men were condemned. All that was left to do would be to execute the men in front of ten thousand adolescents.

I was very close to the age where I would have been sent to train, Julian, but was saved from that fate when we were forced out of Pinyudo, all forty thousand of us, by the Ethiopian forces that overthrew President Mengistu. This, I learned later, had been in the works for some time, and would drive the problems of Ethiopia for years to come. But it began with an alliance between disparate groups in Ethiopia, with help from Eritrean separatists. The Ethiopian rebels needed the Eritreans' help, and vice versa. In exchange, the Eritreans were promised independence if the coup succeeded. The coup was indeed successful, but thereafter, things got complicated between those two nations.

I was leaving church when the news came. My church was close to the section where the Ethiopian aid workers lived, and when Mass was over we saw them crying, women and men.

—The government has been overthrown. Mengistu is gone, they wailed.

We were told to gather everything we could and prepare to leave. By the time I arrived at our shelter, it was already empty; the remaining Nine had left ahead of me, with a note: *See you at the river—The Nine.* I stuffed what I could of my hoarded food and blankets into a maize bag. In less than an hour, all the boys and families and rebels were gathered at the field, ready to abandon Pinyudo. All of the camp's refugees covered the landscape, some running, some calm and unaffected, as if strolling to the next village. Then the sky broke open.

The rain was torrential. The plan was to cross the Gilo River and to reconvene on the other side, possibly at Pochalla. At the water, it became evident that groups were not well organized. The rain, the grey chaos of it, washed away any sense of order to our evacuation. At the river I couldn't find the Nine. I saw very few people I knew. Off in the distance, I caught sight of Commander Beltbuckle, riding atop a Jeep, carrying a broken megaphone, barking muffled instructions. The area near the river was marshy and the group was soaked, wading through the heavy water. The river, when we arrived, was high and moving quickly. Trees and debris flew with the current.

The first shots seemed small and distant. I turned to follow the sound. I saw nothing, but the gunfire continued and grew louder. The attackers were nearby. The sounds multiplied, and I heard the first screams. A woman up the river spat a stream of blood from her mouth before falling, lifeless, into the water. She had been shot by an unseen assailant, and the current soon took her toward my group. Now the panic began. Tens of thousands of us splashed through the shallows of the river, too many unable to swim. To stay on the bank meant certain death, but to jump into that river, swollen and rushing, was madness.

The Ethiopians were attacking, their Eritrean cohorts with them, the Anyuak doing their part. They wanted us out of their country, they were avenging a thousand crimes and slights. The SPLA was attempting to leave the country with jeeps and tanks and a good deal of supplies that the Ethiopians might have considered their own, so they had cause to contest the conditions of the rebels' departure. When the sky split apart with bullets and artillery fire, all sped up and the dying began.

I had hesitated in the shallows, the water to my stomach, for too long. All around me people were making their decisions: to jump in or to run downriver, to look for a narrower spot, a boat, a solution.

—Just get across the river. Once we cross, we'll be safer.

I turned around. It was Dut. Again I was being led by Dut.

—But I can't swim, I said.

—Stay near me. I'll pull you over.

We found a narrow portion of the river.

—Look!

I pointed across the water, where two crocodiles lay on the shore.

—There's no time to worry, Dut said.

I screamed. I was paralyzed.

—They didn't eat you last time, remember? Maybe they don't like Dinka.

—I can't!

—Jump! Start swimming. I'll be right behind you.

—What about my bag?

—Drop your bag. You can't carry it.

I dropped my bag, everything I owned, and jumped in. I paddled with my hands cupped like paws, only my head above water. Dut was next to me. —Good, he whispered. —Good. Keep going.

As I moved through the water, I could feel the current carrying me downstream. I watched the crocodiles, keeping my eyes fixed upon them. There was no movement from them. I kept paddling. There was a great blast behind me. I turned around and could see the soldiers, kneeling in the grass of the riverbank, shooting at us as we crossed. Everywhere I saw the heads of boys in the river, and around them the white of the water, the debris, the pounding of the rain and bullets. All of the heads were trying to move across the river while hiding their bodies under the surface. Screams were everywhere. I paddled and kicked. I looked again for the spot on the riverbank where I had last seen the crocodiles. They were gone.

—The crocodiles!

—Yes. We must swim fast. Come. There are so many of us. We're at a mathematical advantage. Swim, Achak, just keep paddling.

A scream came from very close. I turned to see a boy in the jaws of a crocodile. The river bloomed red and the boy's face disappeared.

—Keep going. Now he's too busy to eat you.

We were halfway across the river now, and my ears heard the hiss under the water and the bullets and mortars cracking the air. Each time my ears fell below the surface, a hiss overtook my head, and it felt like the sound of the crocodiles coming for me. I tried to keep my ears above the surface, but when my head was too high, I pictured a bullet entering the back of my skull. I would duck into the river again, only to hear the screaming hiss underneath.

Maniacal screaming came from the retreating riverbank. I turned to see a Dinka man with a gun screaming at the river. —Bring me over! he yelled. —Bring me over! There was a man in the river near him, swimming away. Another man dove in and began swimming. Now the armed man was yelling at both of the swimming men. —I can't swim! Bring me over! Help me! The two men continued to swim. They didn't want to wait to help the armed man. The armed man then pointed his gun at the swimming men and began to fire. This was no more than fifty feet away from where I swam. The armed man killed one of the swimming men before his own shoulders exploded red; he had been shot by Ethiopian bullets. That man fell there, sideways, his head landing in the mud of the riverbank.

It is only luck that brought me across that river that day. My feet met the ground and I threw myself onto the riverbank. At that moment, a mortar shell exploded twenty feet ahead of me. There was no sign of Dut.

—Run to the grass!

Who was saying this?

—Come now!

I climbed the riverbank and a man grabbed my arm. Again it was Dut. He lifted me up and threw me to the grass next to him. We both lay with our stomachs upon the grass, looking back across the river.

—We can't move here, he said. —They'll see us and shoot. Right now they're shelling the area beyond the river, so we're safest here.

We lay on our stomachs for thirty minutes as people scrambled up the bank and rushed past. From the high riverbank, we could see everything, could see far too much.

—Close your eyes, Dut said.

I said I would, and I pushed my face into the dirt, but secretly I watched the slaughter below. Thousands of boys and men and women and babies were crossing the river, and soldiers were killing them randomly and sometimes with great care. There were a few SPLA troops fighting from our side of the river, but for the most part they had already escaped, leaving the Sudanese civilians alone and unprotected. The Ethiopians, then, had their choice of targets, most of them unarmed. Amid the chaos were the Anyuak, now joining the Ethiopian army in their war against us. All of the pent-up animosity of the Anyuak was released that day, and they chased the Sudanese from their land with machetes and the few rifles they possessed. They hacked and shot those running to the river, and they shot those flailing across the water. Shells exploded, sending plumes of white twenty feet into the air. Women dropped babies in the river. Boys who could not swim simply drowned. A woman fleeing would be moving one moment, there would be a hail of bullets or a mortar's plume, and then she would be still, floating downstream. Some of the dead were then eaten by crocodiles. The river ran in many colors that day, green and white, black and brown and red.

When darkness came Dut and I left the riverbank. We had not run far when the strangest thing happened: I saw Achor Achor. He was simply standing there, looking left and right, unsure where to go, in the middle of the path. Dut and I nearly bumped into him.

—Good, Dut said. —You have each other. See you at Pochalla.

Dut returned to the river, looking for the injured and lost. That was the last time we saw Dut Majok.

—Where do we go? I asked.

—How would I know? Achor Achor said.

There was no clear direction to go. The grass was still high, and I worried about the lions and hyenas hiding within. We soon found two other boys, a few years older than us. They were strong-seeming boys, neither of them bleeding at all.

—Where are you going? I asked.

—Pochalla, they said. —That's where everyone is now. We stop in Pochalla and see where to go.

We went with them, though we did not know their names. We four ran, and Achor Achor and I felt these were good boys to run with. They were fast and decisive.

We ran through the night, through the wet grass and smelling the smoke of fires in the sky. The wind was strong and threw smoke at us, and threw the grasses around us with violence. I had the sensation that I might always be running like this, that I would always have to run, and that I would always be able to run. I did not feel tired; my eyes seemed able to see anything in the night. I felt safe with those boys.

—Come here! a woman said. I looked to find the source of the voice, and turned to see an Ethiopian woman in a soldier's uniform. —Come here and I will help you find Pochalla! she said. The other boys began walking toward her.

—No! I said. —See how she's dressed!

—Don't fear me, she said. —I am just a woman! I am a mother trying to help you boys. Come to me, children! I am your mother! Come to me!

The unknown boys ran toward her. Achor Achor stayed with me. When they were twenty feet from her, the woman turned, lifted a gun from the grass, and with her eyes full of white, she shot the taller boy through the heart. I could see the bullet leaving his back. His body kneeled and then fell on its side, his head landing before his shoulder.

Before anyone could run, the woman shot again, this time hitting the arm of the other strong boy. The impact spun him around, and he fell. When he raised himself to run, a last bullet, which entered through his clavicle and exited through his sternum, sent the boy swiftly to heaven.

—Run!

It was Achor Achor, running past me. I had not moved. I was still mesmerized by the woman, who was now aiming her gun at me.

—Run! he said again, this time grabbing my shirt from behind. We ran from her, diving into the grass and then crawling and hurtling away from the woman, who was still shouting at us. —Come back! she said. —I am your mother, come back, my children!

Everywhere Achor Achor and I ran, people ran from us. There was no trust in the dark. No one waited to find out who was who. As the night grew darker, the bullets stopped. We guessed that the Ethiopians would not pursue us to Pochalla—that they were only driving the Sudanese out of their country.

—Look, Achor Achor said.

He pointed to two large blades of grass, tied together across the path.

—What does that mean?

—It means we don't go that way. Someone's warning us the path is unsafe.

Whenever we saw the path blocked by the grassblades crossed, we chose a new direction. The night became very quiet, and soon the sky fell black. Achor Achor and I walked for hours, and because we avoided so many routes, we soon suspected that we were walking in circles. Finally we came upon a wide path, which bore the tracks, old and dried, of a car or truck. The path was clear and Achor Achor was sure it would bring us to Pochalla.

We had walked for an hour, the wind wild and warm, when we heard an animal sound. This was not the sound of an adult—we heard much of that on the way, moaning and retching—this was a baby, wailing in a low voice. It scared me to hear a baby making such a sound, guttural and choking, something like the dying growl of a cat. We soon found the infant, perhaps six months old, lying next to its mother, who was splayed on the path, dead. The baby tried to breastfeed on its mother for a moment before giving up, crying out, tiny hands as fists.

The baby's mother had been shot in the waist. At the river, perhaps, the bullet had passed through her, and she had crawled this far before collapsing. There was blood along the trail.

—We have to take this baby, Achor Achor said.

—What? No, I said. —The baby will cry and we'll be found.

—We have to take this baby, Achor Achor said again, crouching down to lift the naked infant. He took the skirt off the baby's mother and wrapped it around the baby. —We don't need to leave this baby here.

When Achor Achor wrapped the baby and held it close to his chest, it became quiet.

—See, this is a quiet baby, he said.

We walked with the Quiet Baby for some time. I thought the infant was doomed.

—Any baby that nurses from a dead person will die, I said.

—You're a fool, Achor Achor said. —That makes no sense. The Quiet Baby will live.

We took turns carrying the Quiet Baby, and it made few sounds as we walked. To this day I do not know if she was male or female, but I think of her as a girl. I held her close to me, her warm head nestled between my shoulder and chin. We ran past small fires and through long stretches of dark silence. All the while the Quiet Baby lay against my chest or over my shoulder, making no sound, eyes wide.

In the middle of the night, Achor Achor and I found a group sitting in the grasses by the path. There were twelve people, most of them women and older men. We told the women about finding the Quiet Baby. A woman bleeding from the neck offered to take her.

—Don't worry about this baby, I said.

—This is a quiet baby, Achor Achor said.

I lifted the baby from my shoulder and she opened her eyes. The woman took her and the baby stayed quiet. Achor Achor and I walked on.

Achor Achor and I found a large group of men and boys, resting briefly along the road, and together we walked to Pochalla. When we got there, we saw those who had fled Pinyudo and survived. Eight of the Nine made it across, we learned; two witnesses were certain that Akok Kwuanyin had drowned.

We attempted to make this information real in our hearts but it was impossible. We acted as if he had not died; we chose to mourn later.

Thousands of Sudanese were sitting all over the fields surrounding a defunct airstrip. Achor Achor and I chose an area of long grasses under trees. We pushed down the grass, flattening it to enable us to sleep there. At the moment we finished flattening the grass, it began to rain. We had no mosquito net but Achor Achor had found a blanket, so we lay down next to each other, sharing it like brothers.

—Are you being bitten by the mosquitoes? I said.

—Of course, Achor Achor said.

All night we pulled at the blanket, yanking it off each other, and neither of us slept. Sleep was impossible when the mosquitoes were so hungry.

—Stop pulling it! Achor Achor hissed.

—I'm not pulling it, I insisted.

I was pulling it, I must admit, but I was too tired to know what I was doing.

In the night, Achor Achor and I asked the elders for sisal bags, and were each given one. We wove them together to make a mosquito net almost big enough for us both. We tied it to the blanket and it seemed sufficient. We were proud of it and looked forward to sleeping under it. We agreed not to urinate near our flattened grass, so as not to attract the mosquitoes.

But soon it rained and our preparations were for naught. The water came under the net and we sat up, lifting the net higher, and when we did, mosquitos flooded in. We spent the night awake, wet and fighting the insects with both hands, flailing, exhausted, soaked and spotted everywhere with our own blood.

It was the rain that killed many boys. The rain made us frail and brought the insects, and the insects brought malaria. The rain weakened us all. It was very much like what the rain would do to the cattle we would make from clay—under the relentless rain, the clay would soften and give, and soon the clay would not be a cow anymore, but would break apart. The rain did this to the suffering people of Pochalla, especially the boys who had no mothers: they broke under the force of the rain, they melted back into the earth.

In the morning, Achor Achor and I lay on our stomachs, watching the people who had come to Pochalla and the people who continued to come. They arrived all day, from first light to last. We watched the field fall away and the trees disappear under the mass of humanity gathered there.

—You think Dut is here? Achor Achor asked.

—I don't think so, I said.

It seemed to me that if Dut were near, we would know it. I had to believe that Dut was alive and leading other groups of boys to safety. I knew that Pochalla was not the only place people were going, and if people were traveling through the night, then surely Dut was leading them.

—Do you think the Quiet Baby is here? Achor Achor asked.

—I think so, I said. —Or maybe soon.

We looked for the Quiet Baby that day, but all of the babies we saw were howling. Their mothers tended to them and to their own injuries. The wounded were everywhere. Only the lightly wounded, though, had made it to Pochalla. Thousands died at the Gilo River and hundreds more died on the way to Pochalla. There was no way to help them.

—I get tired of seeing these people, Achor Achor said.

—What people?

—The Dinka, all these people, he said, nodding his chin toward them.

Close to us, a mother was nursing a baby while holding another child between her feet. Only the mother wore clothing. Three more infants sat nearby, screaming. The arm of one looked like the face of the faceless man I had encountered when I fled Marial Bai.

—I don't always want to be these people, Achor Achor said.

—No, I said, agreeing.

—I really don't want to be one of these people, he said. —Not forever.

The same people that left Pinyudo reorganized themselves at Pochalla. Most had lost everything on the way. The camp was a wretched mess of plastic, small fires, blankets, and filthy clothing. There was no food. Thirty thousand people searched for food in a field where a few dogs would struggle to eat.

Achor Achor and I joined two other boys from northern Bahr al-Ghazal and we trekked into the forests nearby to find sticks and grass. We built an A-frame hut with a grass roof and mud walls, and we spent most of our time inside, keeping dry and warm with a near-constant fire, which we vigilantly maintained so that it was large enough for warmth but not so large that it would jump to the roof and cook us all.

—It's definitely better to die, Achor Achor said one night. —Let's just do something and die. Okay? Let's just leave here, fight with the SPLA or something, and just die.

I agreed with him but still chose to argue.

—God takes us when he wants to, I said.

—Oh shut up with that shit, he snarled.

—So you want to kill yourself?

—I want to do something. I don't want to wait here forever. People are getting sicker here. We're just waiting to die. If we stay, we're just going to catch something and wither away. We're all part of the same dying, but you and I are just dying more slowly than the rest. We might as well go and fight and get killed quicker.

This night, I felt that Achor Achor was probably correct. I said nothing, though. I stared at the red walls of our shelter, the fire dimming until we lay in the dark, our breath growing colder.

XXI.

It is time to leave this hospital. They have made a fool of me. Julian abandoned his promise. He is gone. In the waiting room, Achor Achor and Lino are gone. I approach the new nurse, she with the cloud of yellow hair, at the admitting station.

"I am leaving now," I say.

"But you haven't been treated," she says. She is genuinely surprised that I would consider leaving after only fourteen hours.

"I have been here too long," I say.

She begins to say something but then holds her tongue. This news seems new to her. I tell her I'd like to call back later about the results of the MRI.

"Yes," she says. "Sure..." and on a business card, she writes down a telephone number I can call. Since I was attacked in my home, I have been given two business cards. I have not, I don't think, asked for extraordinary care, or heroics from the police. When everyone wakes up, Phil and Deb and my Sudanese friends, there will be outrage and phone calls and threats to these doctors.

But for now it is time I left this place. I have no car and no money to pay for a taxi. It is too early to call anyone for a ride, so I decide to walk home. It is 3:44 a.m., and I need to be at work at five-thirty, so I prompt the automatic doors, leave the emergency room and the parking lot, and begin walking to my apartment. I will shower and change and then go to work. At work they have some rudimentary medical supplies and I will dress my wounds as best I can.

I set out down Piedmont Road. The streets are abandoned. Atlanta is not a city for pedestrians, let alone at this hour. The cars pass through the liquid night and illuminate the road much as they did in those last days of our walk, before Kakuma. Then, as now, I walked while pondering whether I wanted to continue to live.

I was blind, nearly so, when we finally walked to Kakuma. During that walk, I harbored none of the illusions I had when we traveled to Ethiopia.

This was at the end of the hardest of years. It was a year of nomadic life. After the Gilo River, there had been Pochalla, then Golkur, then Narus. There had been bandits, and more bombings, more boys lost, and finally, one morning, I woke unable to see. Even trying to open my eyes caused immeasurable pain.

One of my friends reached out to touch my eyes. —They don't look good, he said. There were no mirrors in Narus, so I had to take his word that my eyes appeared diseased. By the afternoon, his diagnosis proved correct. I felt as if sand and acid had been poured under each of my eyelids. We were at Narus temporarily; it was about a hundred miles north of Kenya, but the climate was similar, the air carrying red dust.

I waited for my eyes to heal but they only worsened. I was not the only boy to contract what they called *nyintok,* sickness of the eye, but while theirs improved in two or three days, after five days my eyes were so swollen I could not open them. The elders suggested various remedies, and much water was poured upon my eyelids, but the pain persisted, and I became despondent. To be blind in southern Sudan during a war would be very difficult. I prayed for God to decide whether or not he would take my eyesight; I wanted only for the pain to end.

One night, as we all lay under our lean-tos—there were no proper shelters in Narus—we heard the roar of cars and trucks and I knew we would soon be on the move again. The government army was on its way and Narus might soon be overtaken. We boys were to walk to Lokichoggio, in Kenya, under the watch of the UNHCR. I did not want to stand, or walk, or even move, but I was dragged from my lean-to and made to join the line.

I shuffled with bandages over both eyes, held there with what amounted to a blindfold. I found my way by holding the shirttails of whoever walked in front of me. Even though I knew we would soon cross the border into a country without war, this time I had no dreams of bowls of oranges. I knew that the world was the same everywhere, that there were only inconsequential variations between the suffering in one place and another.

When we left Ethiopia, so many died along the way. There were thousands of us together, but there were so many injured, so much blood along the path. This is when I saw more dead than at any other time. Women, children. Babies the size of the Quiet Baby who would not survive. There seemed to be no point. I look back on that year and see only disconnected and miscolored images, as in a fitful dream. I know that we were at Pochalla, then nearby, at Golkur, three hours away. It rained there with a constant grey fury for three months. At Golkur there were again SPLA soldiers and NGOs and food and, eventually, school. There we heard of the rebel split, when a Nuer commander named Riek Machar decided to leave and create his own rebel movement, the SPLA-Nasir, a group that would for some time cause the SPLA as much trouble as Khartoum. This resulting war within the war had Garang's Dinka rebels fighting Machar's Nuer rebels. So many tens of thousands were lost this way, and the infighting, the brutality involved, allowed the world to turn an indifferent eye to the decimation of Sudan: the civil war became, to the world at large, too confusing to decipher, a mess of tribal conflicts with no clear heroes and villains.

We were at Golkur most of that year, and one day, as the conflict devolved and the country fell further into chaos, Manute Bol, the basketball star from America, came to us, flying on a single-engine plane, to greet the boys staying at the camp. We had heard of him only in legend, and there he was, stepping out of the airplane barely big enough to contain him. We had been told he had become an American and were thus surprised when he emerged and was not white. Not long after, we were attacked by militias hired by the government, and were told we would be bombed very soon, and so one day the elders told us it was time to leave Golkur for good, and so we did. We left again and we walked to Narus. Some weeks later, at the urging of the UN, we walked to Kenya. In Kenya, we were told we would be safe, finally safe, for they said this country was a democracy, a neutral and civilized country, and the international community was creating a haven for us there.

But we had to move quickly. We had to get out of Sudan, for the Sudanese army knew our location. During the day we could see the gunships, and when they came overhead, we scattered under trees and prayed into the dust. We walked primarily at night, for two weeks or more, and because we thought we were close to Kenya, and the situation was desperate and the land inhospitable, we walked with more haste and less mercy than ever before. As we got closer to the border, the weather worsened. We were walking into the wind for days, and many among us were sure that the strength and constancy of the wind was meant to repel us, urging us to turn back.

I knew from the smell of the air that this was a dusty place. I took off my shirt and wrapped it around my head, to guard my face from the dust and wind. The infection in my eyes, which had plagued me for days now, allowed me only to make out broad dark shapes split by my lashes.

There were trucks every so often along that walk, carrying the worst-off travelers, sometimes bringing food and water to us. Even with my eyes swollen shut, I was not a candidate for the trucks, for my legs worked and my feet were intact. But I so wanted to be carried. The thought of being carried! I looked at the trucks and thought about how good it would be to be inside, elevated, being carried forth.

When the trucks drove off, each time, boys would try to climb onto the back, and each time, the truck would stop and the driver would throw them off, back onto the gravel. —Wait! a voice ahead wailed. —Wait! Stop!

In this way a boy was run over by one of the aid trucks. By the time I reached the spot where he had been killed, the boy's body was gone, perhaps dragged off the road, but the dark stain of his blood was as clear as the outlines of the mountains ahead.

I turn from Piedmont Road to Roswell Road, which will take me home. This walk through early morning Atlanta is long but not unpleasant. I can see a purple rope of light in the east and I know it will expand as I draw closer.

Each time I find myself giving up on this country, I have the persistent habit of realizing all that I have here and did not have in Africa. It is annoying, this habit, when I want to count and measure the difficulties of life here. This is a miserable place, of course, a miserable and glorious place that I love dearly and of which I have seen far more than I could have expected. I have moved freely about for five years now. I have flown thirty-nine times around this country, and have driven perhaps twenty thousand miles to see friends and family and canyons and towers. I have been to Kansas City, to Phoenix, to San Jose, San Francisco, to San Diego, Boston, Gainesville. I spent only sixteen hours in Chicago, not even venturing into the city; I came to speak at Northwestern University, got lost coming from the airport, and in the end, while standing on a chair, I spoke to about a dozen students as they were leaving the lecture hall. In Omaha, I once watched a minor league baseball game and another time watched as snow dropped on the city like a cloak, covering every surface in minutes. In Oakland I walked underground and could not believe the existence of the subway; still it seems impossible and I won't take it again until its viability is proven to me. I have been to Memphis seven times to see my uncle, my father's brother, and have walked inside a giant green pyramid of glass. In New York City I viewed the Statue of Liberty from a ferry, and was surprised to see that the woman was walking. I had seen pictures perhaps a hundred times but never realized that her feet were in mid-stride; it was startling and far more beautiful that I thought possible. I have been to South Carolina, to Arkansas, New Orleans, Palm Beach, Richmond, Lincoln, Des Moines, Portland; there are Lost Boys in most of these cities. I have been to Seattle, in 2003, to speak at a convention of doctors in Washington State. They hired me to speak to their members about my experiences, and I did so, and while in Seattle, the same friend who handed the phone to Tabitha that one day brought me to her.

It's odd to say this, but I loved Tabitha most from afar. That is, my love grew for her each time I could watch her from a distance. Perhaps that sounds wrong. I did love her when we were together, in my room or on the couch, our legs entwined and her hands in mine. But when I could see her from across a street, or walking toward me, or stepping onto a broken escalator, these are the moments I most remember. We were once at the mall—it seems as if we spent a good deal of time at the mall, and I suppose we did—and she had shopping she wanted to do. I went to the food court to buy drinks for us both. We had agreed to meet at an information kiosk on the first floor. I sat nearby and waited for her for a very long time; being late was not unusual for Tabitha. But when she finally appeared at the top of the escalator, two shopping bags in her hand, her face exploded into a smile so spectacular that all movement everywhere in the mall ceased. The people shopping stopped walking and talking, the children no longer ate and ran, the water stood still. And at that moment, the escalator that she had just stepped onto stopped moving. She looked down, her free hand coming to her mouth, amazed. She looked down to me and laughed. Resigned to the fact that she had caused the escalator to cease escalating, she walked down the steps, descending in a merry way that only someone content and at ease with the world could. She was wearing a snug pink T-shirt and form-fitting black denim pants, and I know I was staring. I know that I stared as she took the twenty-six steps down to me. While I watched her, she saw my unblinking stare and she looked down and away. I know that when she arrived to me, she would slap me playfully on the arm, scolding me for staring the way I did. But I didn't care. I devoured her walk down the steps, and I stored the memory away so I could conjure her always.

When she returned to Seattle, she began to worry about Duluma. He was calling more often, agitated, issuing threats into her answering machine. She would hear noises outside her apartment at night, and once Duluma had left a note under her door, a crazed jumble of accusations and pleadings. When she told me of these developments I urged her to return to Atlanta, to me. She couldn't, she said. She had finals coming up, and anyway, she had her brothers to call upon in case she felt unsafe.

I decided to call this Duluma, to talk about his behavior, and when I did, the results were satisfying. Because I suppose I am always hoping to find a compromise, to find calm and agreement where there is rancor, I spoke to him with empathy and with an eye toward reconciliation for all three of us. And before the conversation was over, I have to say that we were friendly. I felt I could trust him and that he had reached a new equilibrium. He said that he had come to grips with her seeing me— he had called around and asked about me, and now that he knew about me, knew I was a good man, he was content. He was ready to let her go, he said, and I thanked him for being such a good man about it all. It is not easy to let go of a woman you cherish, I said, though I still found him to be a disagreeable and excitable man. We said goodnight as friends, and he asked me to call him again some day. I said I would, though I had no intention of doing so.

I called Tabitha afterward, and we laughed about the twisted mind of Duluma, about how perhaps some nerve gas had depleted his faculties during his SPLA days. I remember wanting so desperately to be with Tabitha that day. She was merry on the phone, and dismissive of Duluma and his wild talk, but she was concerned and I was concerned. I wanted to fly to her, or bring her to me, and I will always curse my hesitance to do so. She was in Seattle and I was here in Atlanta, and we let this distance remain between us. I could have easily left this city for hers; there is little here to keep me. But she was in college, and I wanted to finish the semester's classes, and so we felt compelled to stay where we were. I cannot count the times I have cursed our lack of urgency. If ever I love again, I will not wait to love as best as I can. We thought we were young and that there would be time to love well sometime in the future. This is a terrible way to think. It is no way to live, to wait to love.

I am standing outside the door to my own apartment, and I don't think I will go inside after all. I don't know what I was thinking in going home. In there, my blood will still be on the carpet, and I will be alone. Could I visit Edgardo? I have never been in his home, and it seems a poor time to visit unannounced.

I want to leave, go away from here in my car, but the keys to my car are inside the apartment. I spend a few seconds debating whether I can bear to be in the apartment long enough to get them. I decide that I can, and so I turn the key.

Inside, I can smell the strawberry memory of Tonya, and beneath it, the boy. What is his smell? It is a sweet smell, a boy smell, the smell of a boy's restless sleep. I keep my head high, refusing to glance at my blood on the floor, or at the couch cushions that may still be on the carpet. I find my keys on the kitchen counter, sweep them into my hand, and quickly leave. Even the sound of the door closing is different now.

I get into my car. I decide that I could sleep here, in the parking lot, for an hour, before I need to go to work. But here I am too close to them, the attackers, their car, the Christian neighbors, everyone who participated in or ignored what happened. I stumble through the possibilities. I could drive to a park and sleep. I could find a place to eat breakfast. I could drive to the Newtons' house.

This feels like the right idea. When I began working and studying, I saw the Newtons less, but their door, they said, would always be open. Now, this morning, I know I need to be there. I will knock lightly on their window, the one by the kitchen's breakfast nook, and Gerald, who wakes up very early, will come to the door and welcome me in. I will nap on their couch, the brown modular one in the TV room, for one luxurious hour, smelling the house's aroma of dogs and garlic and air freshener. I will feel safe and loved, even though the rest of the Newtons won't know I was there until I am gone.

I drive to their house, only a few miles away, leaving the disarray I live in, by the highway and amid the chain stores, and entering the shaded and winding roads where the lawns are expansive, the fences immaculate, the mailboxes shaped like miniature barns. When I first came to know the Newtons, I spent two or three days a week at the their house, eating dinner there, spending whole weekends together. We went on outings to Atlanta Braves games, to the zoo, to movies. They were a very busy family—Gerald was on the boards of three nonprofits and worked constantly, Anne was active in their church—and so I began to feel guilt about the time they created for me. But I felt that I was helping Allison to understand certain things, about the war and Sudan and Africa and even Alessandro, so perhaps it was somewhat mutually beneficial. I had known them a few months when we took a picture outside their house, on their lawn, Allison sitting on the grass, me standing with Anne and Gerald.

—For the Christmas card, they said.

Had I heard right? They would put me on their Christmas card? They sent it to me ten days later, the picture we had taken mounted on a green folding card, the four of us smiling in their lush yard. Inside, they had printed: *Happy Holidays and Peace in the New Year, from Gerald, Anne, Allison, and Dominic (our new friend from Sudan)*. I was very proud to have that card, and proud that they would include me in such a way. I kept it on my wall, taped there in my bedroom over my end table. I originally displayed it in our living room, but Sudanese friends visiting me had occasionally felt jealous. It is not polite to show off these sorts of friendships.

Thinking about the card warms me to the idea of walking under the arched doorway of the Newtons' home, but when I arrive at their house, the plan seems ridiculous. What am I doing? It's 4:48 a.m., and I'm parked outside their darkened house. I look for lights on inside, and there are none. This is the refugee way—not knowing the limits of our hosts' generosity. I am going to knock on their door at nearly five in the morning? I have lost my head.

I drive up the street, now a block away, so they won't see me if anyone inside does wake up. I decide I will simply wait here until it's time to go to work. I can get there early, shower, perhaps buy a new shirt and pair of pants in the pro shop. I receive a 30 percent discount on all clothing, and have taken advantage of this before. I will clean myself up and buy the clothes and look presentable and tell no one what happened. I am tired of needing help. I need help in Atlanta, I needed help in Ethiopia and Kakuma, and I am tired of it. I am tired of watching families, visiting families, being at once part and not part of these families.

A few weeks after I spoke to Duluma, and laughed about Duluma with Tabitha, I was with Bobby Newmyer again in Los Angeles. He was holding a gathering of Lost Boys at the University of Judaism. Fourteen Lost Boys from around the United States had flown in to talk about plans for a national organization, a website that would track the progress of all the members of the diaspora, perhaps a unified action or statement regarding Darfur. We were just sitting down to begin the morning's discussions when my phone rang. Because we Lost Boys all seem to have a problem with our mobile phones—we feel that they must be answered immediately, no matter the circumstances—rules had been imposed: no calls during the meetings. So I did not take Tabitha's call. During our first break, I checked the message in the hallway. It had been left at ten-thirty that morning.

"Achak, where are you?" she asked. "Call me back immediately." I called her back, and reached her voice mail. I was going to be busy that day, I told her. I'll call you after the meetings are over. She called again, but by then I had turned my phone off. At four o'clock, when I turned my phone on again, the first call was from Achor Achor.

"Have you heard anything?" he asked.

"Anything about what?"

He paused for a long moment. "I'll call you back," he said.

He called back a few minutes later.

"Have you heard anything about Tabitha?" he asked.

I told him I had not. He hung up again. My only guess was that Tabitha had been trying to reach me through Achor Achor, and that she had gotten upset, perhaps even said some things about my remoteness, callousness. She said such things whenever she wanted to reach me and could not.

The phone rang again and it was Achor Achor.

He told me what he knew: that Tabitha was dead, that Duluma had killed her. She had been staying in the apartment of her friend Veronica, where she had gone to be safe from Duluma. Duluma had found her, called, and threatened to come over. Tabitha was defiant, and despite Veronica's protestations, she dared him to come over. Veronica did not want to open the door but Tabitha was unafraid. Holding Veronica's baby in the crook of her arm, she released the door's lock. "I'll handle this poor man," she told Veronica, and she opened the door. Duluma leapt through it, holding a knife. He stabbed Tabitha between her ribs, sending the baby soaring. As Veronica recovered her child, Duluma threw Tabitha to the floor. Veronica watched, helpless, as Duluma sank his knife into Tabitha twenty-two times. Finally he slowed and stopped. He stood, breathing heavily. He looked to Veronica and smiled a tired smile. "I have to be sure she's dead," he said, and he waited, standing above the body of Tabitha.

After Tabitha was dead, Duluma walked out of the apartment and threw himself off an overpass. I asked Achor Achor if he was dead. He was not dead. He was in a hospital, his back broken.

I left the conference and walked alone for some time, where the campus overlooked the highway. The road was busy with cars, loud with speed and indifference. It was too soon to believe, to feel. I was sure, though, in that hour I spent alone that I was alone completely. I lived without God, even for a time, and the thoughts I entertained were the darkest my mind had ever known.

I returned to the conference and told Bobby and a few other men what had happened. The conference ended that day and they tried to comfort me. I wanted to fly directly to Seattle but was told by Achor Achor not to. The family was too upset, he said, and her brothers did not want to see me. I could not yet contemplate the reality of her death, so on that first day I thought about causes and solutions, vengeance and faith.

"God has a problem with me," I told Bobby. We were driving home from the conference. He said nothing for some time, and his silence meant to me that he agreed.

"No, no!" he finally said. "That's not true. It's just—"

But I was sure that there was a message being directed to me.

"I'm so sorry about all this," Bobby said.

I told him there was no need for him to be sorry.

Bobby fumbled for answers, and urged me not to blame myself, or to read anything about God's intentions into Tabitha's murder. But many times during that drive he banged his steering wheel and yelled, and ran his hands through his hair.

"Maybe it's this stupid country," he said. "Maybe we just make people crazy."

This was four months ago today. Though whispered doubts have ringed my head and though I have had certain godless hours, my faith has not been altered, because I have never felt God's direct intervention in any affairs at all. Perhaps I did not receive that sort of training from my teachers, that he is guiding the winds that knock us down or carry us. And yet, with this news, as we drove, I found myself distancing myself from God. I have had friends who I decided were not good friends, were people who brought more trouble than happiness, and thus I have found ways to create more distance between us. Now I have the same thoughts about God, my faith, that I had for these friends. God is in my life but I do not depend on him. My God is not a reliable God.

Tabitha, I will love you until I see you again. There are provisions for lovers like us, I am sure of it. In the afterlife, whatever its form, there are provisions. I know you were unsure about me, that you had not yet chosen me above all others, but now that you are gone, allow me to assume that you were on your way to deciding that I was the one. Or perhaps that's the wrong way to think. I know you entertained calls from other men, men besides me and Duluma. We were young. We had not made plans.

Tabitha, I pray for you often. I have been reading Mother Teresa and Brother Roger's book called *Seeking the Heart of God,* and each time I revisit it, I find different passages that seem written for me, describing what I feel in your absence. In the book, Brother Roger says this to me: "Four hundred years after Christ, a believer named Augustine lived in North Africa. He had experienced misfortunes, the death of his loved ones. One day he was able to say to Christ: 'Light of my heart, do not let my darkness speak to me.' In his trials, St. Augustine realized that the presence of the Risen Christ had never left him; it was the light in the midst of his darkness."

There have been times when those words have helped me and times when I found those words hollow and unconvincing. These authors, for whom I have great respect, still do not seem to know the doubts that one might have in the angriest corners of one's soul. Too often they tell me to answer my doubts with prayer, which seems very much like addressing one's hunger by thinking of food. But still, even when I am frustrated, I look elsewhere and can find a new passage that speaks to me. There is this, from Mother Teresa: "Suffering, if it is accepted together, borne together, is joy. Remember that the passion of Christ ends always in the joy of the resurrection of Christ, so when you feel in your own heart the suffering of Christ, remember the resurrection has yet to come—the joy of Easter has to dawn." And she provides a prayer that I have prayed many times in these last weeks, and that I whisper tonight in my car, on this street of overhanging trees and amber streetlights.

Lord Jesus, make us realize
that it is only by frequent deaths of ourselves
and our self-centered desires
that we can come to live more fully;

for it is only by dying with you
that we can rise with you.

Tabitha, these past months without you, when first I wondered where you might be, whether you were in heaven or hell or some purgatory, I have had the most intolerable thoughts, homicidal and suicidal. I have struggled so fiercely with the harm I have wanted to do to Duluma and the futility I have seen, in my darkest minutes, in living. I have found some respite in the nightly consumption of alcohol. Two bottles of beer typically allow me to sleep, if fitfully. Achor Achor has been worried about me, but he has seen me improve. He knows I have been here before, that I have approached the precipice of self-termination and have walked away.

I never told you of those dark days, Tabitha, when I was much younger. Achor Achor does not know, either, and had he and I been together then I might not have fallen so low. We had been separated at Golkur, though both of us were on our way to Kenya, to Kakuma. We were on the same road, but days apart. The last I had seen Achor Achor he was in a Save the Children medical tent, being treated for dehydration. I had been cowardly; I thought he would surely die and I could not bear it. I ran away and did not say goodbye. I left the camp with another group, wanting to be away from his imminent death, from all death, and so I walked with one of the first groups into the wind and desert that awaited us in Kenya.

In those last days of my walk, Tabitha, I walked in the dark. My eyes were nearly swollen shut, and I walked blind, trying to lift my feet to avoid tripping, but finding myself barely able to drag them across the gravel. My head swam with fatigue and disorientation, just as it does this morning, Tabitha, when I have been beaten and I miss you. That night, when I walked as such a young boy, it seemed a good time to die. I could continue to live, yes, but my days were getting worse, not better. My life in Pinyudo worsened as the years went on, and Achor Achor, I feared, was dead. And now this, walking to Kenya, where there were no promises. I remembered my thoughts about buildings and waterfalls in Ethiopia, and my disappointment when, after crossing the border, I found only more of the blight we thought we had left. For many years, God had been clear to boys like us. Our lives were not worth much. God had found innumerable ways to kill boys like me, and He no doubt would find many more. Kenya's leadership could turn over just as Ethiopia's had, and there would be another Gilo River, and I knew that would be too much to bear. I knew that if that came again, I would not find the strength to run or swim or carry a quiet baby.

So that night I stopped walking. I sat and watched the boys shuffle by. Just to stop was such a great relief. I was so tired. I was far more tired than I had realized, and when I sat on the hot road I felt relief greater than any I had known before. And because my body so welcomed this rest, I wondered if, like William K, I could simply close my eyes and pass away. I didn't feel so close to falling from this world to the next, but perhaps William K did not, either. William K had only sat down to rest, and moments later was gone. So I lay my head back on the road and I looked into the sky.

—Hey, get up. You'll get run over.

It was the voice of a boy passing by. I said nothing.

—You all right?

—I'm fine, I said. —Walk on, please.

It was a very clear night, the stars carelessly splashed across the sky.

I closed my eyes, Tabitha, and I conjured my mother as best I could. I pictured her in yellow, yellow like an evening sun, walking down the path. I loved to watch her walk down the path toward me, and in my vision I allowed her to walk the entire way. When she came to me I told her I was too tired to continue, that I would suffer again, and would watch others suffer, and then wait to suffer again. In my vision she said nothing, for I didn't know what my mother would say to all that, so I let her remain silent. Then I washed her from my mind. It seemed to me that to die I needed to clear my mind of all thoughts, all visions, and concentrate on passing on.

I waited. I lay with my head on the gravel, and I waited for death. I could still hear the scuffling of the feet of the boys, but soon no one bothered me and that seemed a blessing. Perhaps they assumed I was already dead. Perhaps, in the dark and the wind, they could not see me at all. I felt on the verge of something, even if only shallow sleep, when a pair of feet stopped. I felt a presence just over me.

—You don't look dead.

I ignored the voice, that of a girl.

—Are you asleep?

I did not answer.

—I said, are you asleep?

It was very wrong, that this voice was so loud in my ear. I stayed still.

—I can see you closing your eyes tighter. I know you're alive.

324

I cursed her with all my heart.

—You can't sleep here on the road.

I continued to try to leave the earth through my closed eyes.

—Open them.

I kept them closed, tighter now.

—You can't sleep when you're so trying so hard.

This was true. I opened my eyes enough to see a face, no more than five inches from my own. It was girl, a bit younger than myself. One of the few girls walking.

—Please leave me alone, I whispered.

—You look like my brother, she said.

I closed my eyes again.

—He's dead. But you look like him. Get up. We're the last people now.

—Please. I'm resting.

—You can't rest on the road.

—I've rested on roads before. Please let me be.

—Then I'll stay here with you.

—I'll be here forever.

She knotted her fist in my shirt and pulled.

—You won't. Don't be so stupid. Get up.

She lifted me up and we walked. This girl was named Maria.

I decided that it was easier to walk with this girl than to argue with her in the dark. I could die tomorrow easily enough; she could not watch me forever. So I walked with her to please her, to quiet her, and at first light, we were in the middle of the desert with ten thousand others. This was to be our next home, we were told. And we stood in that land and we waited that day as trucks and Red Cross vehicles came and left more people there, in a land so dusty and desolate that no Dinka would ever think to settle there. It was arid and featureless and the wind was constant. But a city would grow in the middle of that desert. This was Lokichoggio, which would soon become the staging ground for international aid in the region. One hour south would be Kakuma, sparsely populated by Kenyan herders known as the Turkana, but within a year there would be forty thousand Sudanese refugees there, too, and that would become our home for one year, for two, then five and ten. Ten years in a place in which no one, simply no one but the most desperate, would ever consider spending a day.

You were there, Tabitha. You were there with me then and I believe you are with me now. Just as I once pictured my mother walking to me in her dress the color of a pregnant sun, I now take solace in imagining you descending an escalator in your pink shirt, your heart-shaped face overtaken by a magnificent smile as everything around you ceases moving.

BOOK III

XXII.

When Tabitha was taken, Phil called me often, Anne and Allison called, only to talk, to listen, they said, but I knew they were worried about my health and state of mind. I suspect that they had lost their grasp of me. They knew now that the Sudanese in America were capable of murder, of suicide, and so what, they wondered, might Valentino do? I admit that I spent many weeks largely unable to move. I rarely went to class. I asked for time off from work and spent that time in bed or watching television. I drove aimlessly. I tried to read books about grief. I turned off my phone.

Bobby had suggested that Tabitha's murder was made possible by the madness of this country, and on occasion in those dark weeks after her death I allowed myself to find America complicit in the crime. In Sudan, it is unheard of for a young man to kill a woman. It had never happened in Marial Bai. I doubt that anyone in my clan could remember it ever happening, anywhere or at any time. The pressures of life here have changed us. Things are being lost.

There is a new desperation, a new kind of theatricality on the part of men. Not long ago, a Sudanese man in Michigan, I do not know the town, killed his wife, his innocent child, and then himself. I do not know the full story, but the one that blows through Sudanese society holds that this man's wife wanted to visit her family in Athens, Georgia. He refused. I do not know why, but in traditional Sudanese society, the husband does not need a reason why; held over the woman's head is the possibility of a beating, perhaps months of beatings. So they argued, she was beaten, and he thought he had made his point. But the next day she was gone. She had, weeks before, bought a plane ticket to Athens for her and their daughter, even before discussing it with him. She had either assumed she would have her way, or she simply didn't care. But the man in Michigan cared. While his wife and daughter visited aunts and cousins in Athens, he boiled at home. The loss of face, I tell you, can do awful things to a man. When his wife returned with her daughter, he met them at the door with a knife he bought that weekend. He killed them in the foyer and an hour later, himself.

I cannot help but think that Duluma got the idea from this man, this notion of being able to punish she who left you without having to be punished yourself. That, too, would be impossible in Sudan. A man does not kill his child, does not kill himself. In southern Sudan, too many men abuse their wives; wives are beaten, wives are abandoned. But never this sort of thing.

Some say it is the fault of the women here, the clash of their new ideas and the old habits of men unwilling to adapt. Tabitha may or may not have had an abortion—I did not ask her, for it is not my right—and then she left Duluma on her own accord. Both choices would be unprecedented in traditional Sudanese society, and still quite rare in the relaxed moral context of Kakuma. In southern Sudan, even a sexual relationship before marriage is unusual, and very often precludes that woman being married at all. Virgins are preferred, and for a virgin, the bride's family receives a far higher dowry. Telling Americans about this yields fascinating reactions. They cannot conceive of how one's virginity could even be determined in the absence of a gynecological examination.

The Sudanese way is simple. On the eve of the wedding, two or three members of the bride's family, usually the bride's aunts, bring to the marriage bed the cleanest white sheets. On the first night that the groom is permitted to visit his bride, these women hide inside the home, or just outside the door. When the groom first penetrates his bride, the women ululate, and as soon as they are able, they go inside to inspect the sheets for the blood of a broken hymen, to prove that their niece was indeed a virgin. With this evidence in hand, they return to the relatives of both bride and groom.

But here there has been premarital sex, and there was an assertive young woman who decided to break off a relationship with an angry young Sudanese man. He thought she was leaving him for money. He assumed that because my name was well-known at Kakuma that I was a wealthy man here in Atlanta. And it began to twist his head in knots. He made furious calls to her, during which he gave her terrible names. He threatened her and even warned her that should she choose me over him he would do something drastic, something irrevocable.

This is where I direct some frustration toward Tabitha. She did not take his threats seriously, and this seems, to me, madness. Duluma had been in the SPLA, he had fired a machine gun, he had walked over corpses and through fire. Would he not act on a threat? But she did not tell me of these warnings. I knew that he would act on such a threat, but had been placated by our phone call, assuring me he had accepted that she was no longer interested in him.

When Phil called me, he apologized for what had happened to me in his country, just as Bobby had. Bobby was not a religious man, but Phil is a man of faith, and we talked at length about our beliefs when tested. It was interesting to hear Phil talk about those instances when his faith wavered in times of great crisis or needless suffering. I am not sure if what I've felt is doubt. My inclination is to blame myself: what have I done to bring such calamity down upon myself and those I love? Not long ago, a gathering of Lost Boys in the Southeast was scheduled to take place in Atlanta. On the way, a carload of representatives from Greensboro, North Carolina, spun off the highway, killing the driver and injuring two others. The next day, another Lost Boy of Greensboro, distraught by the accident and other disappointments in his life, hanged himself in his basement. Is the curse upon me so great that it casts a shadow over everyone I know, or do I simply know too many people?

I do not mean to imply that these deaths were simply trials for me, for I know God would not take these people, would not take Tabitha in particular, simply to test the strength of my own faith. I will not guess His motivations for bringing her back to Him. But her death has proven to be a catalyst for me to think about my faith and my life. I have examined my course, whether or not I have made mistakes, whether I have been a good child of God. And though I have tried to remain on course, and I have redoubled my efforts to pray and to attend Mass regularly, I have also realized that it is time to start my life again. I have done this before—each time one life has ended and another has begun. My first life ended when I left Marial Bai, for I have not seen my home or family since. My life in Ethiopia also ran its course. For three years we lived there and I became aware of my place in the grand plan of the SPLA and the future of southern Sudan. And finally, with our arrival at Kakuma, I started again.

After my walk to Kenya, when Maria found me on the road wanting to be lifted back to God, I spent many months thinking about why I should have been born at all. It was a grave mistake, it seemed, a promise that could not be fulfilled. There was a musician at Kakuma, the only musician in those early days, and he would play one song, day and night, on his stringed rababa. The melody of his song was cheerful but the lyrics were not. "It was you, mother, it was you," he sang, "it was you who birthed me, and it is you I blame." He went on to blame his mother, and all the mothers of Dinkaland, for giving birth to babies only to have them live in squalor in northwest Kenya.

There is a perception in the West that refugee camps are temporary. When images of the earthquakes in Pakistan are shown, and the survivors seen in their vast cities of shale-colored tents, waiting for food or rescue before the coming of winter, most Westerners believe that these refugees will soon be returned to their homes, that the camps will be dismantled inside of six months, perhaps a year.

But I grew up in refugee camps. I lived in Pinyudo for almost three years, Golkur for almost one year, and Kakuma for ten. In Kakuma, a small community of tents grew to a vast patchwork of shanties and buildings constructed from poles and sisal bags and mud, and this is where we lived and worked and went to school from 1992 to 2001. It is not the worst place on the continent of Africa, but it is among them.

Still, the refugees there created a life that resembled the lives of other human beings, in that we ate and talked and laughed and grew. Goods were traded, men married women, babies were born, the sick were healed and, just as often, went to Zone Eight and then to the sweet hereafter. We young people went to school, tried to stay awake and concentrate on one meal a day while distracted by the charms of Miss Gladys and girls like Tabitha. We tried to avoid trouble from other refugees—from Somalia, Uganda, Rwanda—and from the indigenous people of northwest Kenya, while always keeping our ears open to any news from home, news about our families, any opportunities to leave Kakuma temporarily or for good.

We spent the first year at Kakuma thinking we might return to our villages at any moment. We would periodically receive news of SPLA gains in Sudan and the optimistic among us would convince ourselves that a surrender from Khartoum was imminent. Some of the boys began to hear about their families—who was alive, who was dead, who had fled to Uganda or Egypt or beyond. The Sudanese diaspora continued and spread throughout the world, and at Kakuma I waited for news, any news, about my parents and siblings. The battles would continue and the refugees arrived without pause, hundreds per week, and we came to accept that Kakuma would exist forever, and that we might always live within its borders.

This was our home, and Gop Chol Kolong, the man I considered my father at the camp, was a wreck on a certain day in 1994. I had never seen him so flustered.

—We really have to get this place in order, he said. —We have to clean this place up. Then we have to build more rooms. Then we need to clean up again.

He had been saying this every morning for weeks. Mornings were the time he worried most. Every morning, he said, he was leapt upon by the snarling hyenas of his many responsibilities.

—You think two more rooms will be enough? he asked me.

I said it seemed like plenty.

—Whatever it is it won't seem like enough, he said.

He could not believe they were coming.

—I can't believe they're coming here! To this rathole!

At that point I had been living in Kakuma, with Gop Chol, for almost three years. Gop was from Marial Bai, and had come to Kakuma by way of Narus and various other stopovers. Kakuma had been born with the arrival of ten thousand boys like me who had walked through the dark and dust, but the camp grew quickly, soon encompassing tens of thousands of Sudanese—families and portions of families, orphans, and after some time, also Rwandans, Ugandans, Somalis, even Egyptians.

After months of living in squat shelters like the ones we customarily built when first arriving at a camp, we eventually were given, by the United Nations High Commissioner for Refugees, poles and tarpaulins and materials to build more presentable homes, and so we did. Eventually many boys like me moved in with families from our hometowns and regions, to share resources and duties and to keep alive the customs of our clans. As the camp grew to twenty thousand people, to forty thousand and upward, as it grew outward into the dry wind-strewn nothingness, and as the civil war continued unabated, the camp became more permanent, and many of those, like Gop, who first considered Kakuma a stopover until conditions improved in southern Sudan, now were sending for their families.

I said nothing to Gop about the prospect of bringing his wife and three daughters to such a place, but privately I questioned it. Kakuma was a terrible place for people to live, for children to grow. But he really did not have a choice. His youngest daughter had been diagnosed with a bone disease at the clinic in Nyamlell, east of Marial Bai, and the doctor there had arranged for her transfer to Lopiding Hospital—the more sophisticated clinic near Kakuma. Gop did not know precisely when the transfer would take place, and so spent an inordinate amount of time searching for information from anyone at Lokichoggio, anyone involved in medicine or refugee transfer in any way.

—Do you think they'll be happy here? Gop asked me.

—They'll be happy to be with you, I said.

—But this place... is this any kind of place to live?

I said nothing. Despite its flaws, from the beginning it was clear that this camp would be different from those at Pinyudo and Pochalla and Narus and everywhere else we had been. Kakuma was preplanned, operated from the start by the UN, and staffed almost entirely, at first, by Kenyans. This made for an orderly enough operation, but resentment festered from within and without. The Turkana, a herding people who had occupied the Kakuma District for a thousand years, were suddenly asked to share their land—to cede a thousand acres in an instant—with tens of thousands of Sudanese and, later, Somalis, with whom they shared few cultural similarities. The Turkana resented our presence, and in turn the Sudanese resented the Kenyans, who seemed to have seized every paying job available at the camp, performing and being compensated for tasks that we Sudanese were more than capable of in Pinyudo. In turn, the Kenyans, in their less charitable moments, thought of the Sudanese as leeches, who did little more than eat and defecate and complain when things didn't go as desired. Somewhere in there were a handful of aid workers from Europe, the United Kingdom, Japan, and the United States, all of whom were careful to defer to the Africans, and who cleared out when the camp erupted into temporary chaos. This did not happen too often, but with so many nationalities represented, so many tribes and so little food and so great the volume and variety of suffering, conflict was inevitable.

What was life in Kakuma? Was it life? There was debate about this. On the one hand, we were alive, which meant that we were living a life, that we were eating and could enjoy friendships and learning and could love. But we were nowhere. Kakuma was nowhere. *Kakuma* was, we were first told, the Kenyan word for nowhere. No matter the meaning of the word, the place was not a place. It was a kind of purgatory, more so than was Pinyudo, which at least had a constant river, and in other ways resembled the southern Sudan we had left. But Kakuma was hotter, windier, far more arid. There was little in the way of grass or trees in that land; there were no forests to scavenge for materials; there was nothing for miles, it seemed, so we became dependent on the UN for everything.

Early in my days at the camp, Moses again appeared in and departed from my life. When Kakuma was still being shaped, I would take daily walks around its perimeter, to see who had made it and who had not. I saw arguments between the Sudanese and Turkana, between European aid workers and Kenyans. I saw families being re-formed, new alliances forged, and even saw Commander Secret talking passionately to a group of boys just a few years older than me. I kept clear of him and any SPLA officers, for I knew their intentions. While walking the camp's borders in the first few weeks, I learned that Achor Achor had made it after all, and that three of the original Eleven were with him.

When I saw Moses, it was not very dramatic. Early one morning in the first months of Kakuma, as I stepped over a group of young men sleeping, sharing one long blanket, their feet and heads exposed, I simply saw him. Moses. With another boy our age, he was attempting to cook some asida in a pan, over a fire in a small can. He saw me just as I saw him.

—Moses! I yelled.

—Shh! he hissed, and came to me quickly.

He turned me away from his companion and we took a walk around the perimeter of the camp.

—Don't call me Moses here, he said. Like many others at the camp, he had changed his name; in his case, it was to avoid any SPLA commanders who might be looking for him.

He was a different boy than the last time I had seen him. He had grown many inches, was built like an ox, and his forehead seemed more stern and severe—the forehead of a man. But in essential ways, in his wide crooked smile and bright smiling eyes, he was still very much Moses. He wanted immediately to tell me about his time as a soldier, and he did so with the sort of breathless excitement one might use in describing a particularly attractive girl.

—No, no, I wasn't a fighter. I never fought. I only trained, he said, answering my first question. I was greatly relieved.

—But the training! Achak, it was so different than the life here, than in Pinyudo. It was so hard. Here we have to worry about food and insects and the wind,

335

but there they were trying to kill me! I'm sure they were trying to kill me. They killed boys there.

—They shot them?

—No, no. I don't think so.

—Not like Pinyudo, the prisoners?

—No, not like that. No bullets, they just drove them to their deaths. So many boys. They beat them, ran them into the ground, chased them back to Heaven.

We walked past a small tent, inside of which a white photographer was taking pictures of a Sudanese mother and her emaciated child.

—Did you get to shoot a gun? I asked.

—I did. That was a good day. Have you shot a gun?

I told him I had not.

—It was a good day when they gave us the guns, the Kalashnikovs. We had waited so long, and finally they had us shoot at targets. Oh man, the guns hurt! They shoot you while you're shooting the targets! They call it kickback. My shoulder is sore right now, Achak.

—Which shoulder?

He indicated his right shoulder, and I punched it.

—Don't!

I did it again. This was hard to resist.

—Don't! he said, and tackled me.

We wrestled for a few minutes and then, because we were tired and underfed, realized we had no energy to wrestle properly. We were hungrier than we had been in Pinyudo. We ate one meal a day, at night, and the rest of the day we tried to conserve our energy. I do not know why it was easier for the UN to feed the refugees of Pinyudo than it was those of Kakuma. We stood and continued walking, past a group of shelters were the SPLA's families lived.

—They gave us five bullets and they held us steady while we shot. We lay down on our stomachs to help keep still. It was very painful but I was happy to see the bullets come from my gun. I hit nothing. I don't know where my bullets went. I never saw them again. They went into the sky or something.

I told him the training sounded good.

—No, no, Achak. It wasn't good. No one thought it was good. And I was singled out for punishment. In their eyes, I did something wrong, Achak. I was late to the parade one day and they thought I was a troublemaker. They had me confused with another Moses, I later discovered. But they thought I was a bad guy so I was punished. They put me in a pen, like the pens where you keep livestock. I had to stay there for two days. I couldn't sit down. I stood for every minute until I slept. They let me sleep from dawn until the sun was up, maybe two hours. It was worse than the Arab's house. When I was with the Arab it was easy to hate him and his family and those kids. But this was so confusing. I came to Bonga to train and fight but they were fighting me. They were trying to kill me, I swear, Achak. They said it was training. They said they were making us men but I know they wanted to kill me. Have you ever felt like people were really trying to kill you, you in particular?

I pondered this question and realized I didn't know for sure.

—We ran all day, Achak. We ran up the hills and then ran down. While we ran, the trainers were hitting us, yelling at us. But the boys weren't strong enough. Those trainers were not very smart. They had their training methods and they were using them but they forgot that these boys were very sick and weak and skinny. Can you start running up hills while being beaten, Achak?

—No.

—So the boys fell. The boys fell and they broke bones. I watched one boy fall. We were running down the hill and one of the trainers started yelling at this boy, whose name was Daniel. He was my size, but thinner. I knew when I saw him that he should not have been at Bonga. He was one of the youngest and he was so slow! He ran slower than you can walk. It was funny to watch but it was real, it was stupid the way he ran. This made the trainers so angry. They didn't want him in the camp, like they didn't want me at the camp. So they yelled at Daniel and they called him Shit. That was his name at Bonga: Shit.

We both laughed for a second about this. We couldn't help it. We had never known someone named Shit.

—We were always running up and down this hill and one time when we did this it was almost dark. The sun was down and we were having trouble seeing. There was a trainer named Comrade Francis who was cruel to everyone, but I had not seen him interact with Daniel before. This night he was everywhere Daniel was. He ran alongside him, he ran backward in front of him, always blowing a whistle. Comrade Francis had a whistle and he just blew and blew it into Daniel's face.

—And Daniel? What did he do?

—He was so sad. He didn't get angry. I think maybe he made himself deaf. He didn't seem to hear anything. He just did his running. Then Comrade Francis kicked him.

—Kicked him?

—The hill was steep, Achak. So when he kicked him it was like he flew. He flew twenty feet I think, because he was already running and had momentum. When he began to fly, Achak—sorry, I mean Valentino—when he was in the air my stomach got sick. I felt so sick. Everything dropped into my knees. I knew this was bad, that Daniel was flying down the hill with all the rocks. The sound was like the snapping of a twig. He just lay there. He lay there like he'd been dead forever.

—He was dead?

—He died right there. I saw the ribs. I didn't know this could happen. Did you know your ribs could come out of your skin?

—No.

—Three of his ribs had come through his skin, Achak. I walked up to him right after it happened. The trainer was doing nothing. He thought the boy would get up, so he was still blowing his whistle but I had heard the sound so I went to Daniel and saw his eyes open, like they were looking through me. They were dead eyes. You know what those look like. I know you do.

—Yes.

—And then I saw the ribs. They were like bones on an animal. When you slaughter an animal you can see the bones, and they're white and have blood around them, right?

—Yes.

—This was like that. The ribs were very sharp, too. They had been broken so the parts coming through his skin were very sharp, like curved knives. I was there and then the trainer yelled at me to keep going. I turned around and there were two other trainers there. I think they knew something was wrong. They beat me until I ran down the hill and I saw them surrounding Daniel. Three days later they told us all that Daniel had died of yellow fever. But everyone knew it was a lie. That's when boys began to escape. That's when I left.

Moses and I had made a circle of the camp and now were back at the site of his fire and companion and asida.

—I'll see you around, Achak, right?

I told him of course I would see him around. But we didn't actually see each other much. We spent a few weeks making journeys together in the camp, talking about the things we had seen and done, but after telling his story, Moses was not very interested in discussing the past. He saw our presence in Kenya as a great opportunity, and he seemed constantly to be thinking of ways to take advantage of it. He became a trader of goods in those early days, silverware and cups and buttons and thread, starting with a few shillings and tripling their value in a day. He was moving faster than I could, and he continued to do so. One day not long after our reunion Moses said he had some news. He had an uncle, he said, who had long ago left Sudan and was living in Cairo, had located Moses at Kakuma and was arranging for him to go to private school in Nairobi. He was not alone in this arrangement. A few dozen boys every year were sent to boarding schools in Kenya. Some had won scholarships, some had located or were located by relatives with means.

—Sorry, Moses said.

—It's okay, I said. —Write me a letter.

Moses never wrote a letter, because boys don't write letters to boys, but he did leave one day, just before refugee-camp school would begin for the rest of us. I would not hear from him for almost ten years, until we found that we were both living in North America—myself in Atlanta and he at the University of British Columbia. He would call once every few weeks, or I would call him, and his voice was always a salve and an inspiration. He could not be beaten. He went to school in Nairobi and Canada and always looked courageously forward, even with with an 8 branded behind his ear. Nothing about Moses could be defeated.

Maria was living with foster parents, with a man and his wife from her hometown, in the area of Kakuma where the more or less intact families had set up their homes. Maria had lived with three other young women and an old man—the grandfather of one of the women—until the man died and the women were either married off or returned to Sudan, leaving Maria available for the claiming. One day I spent a morning looking for her, and finally saw her shape in a corner of Kakuma, arranging men's garments on a clothesline.

—Maria!

She turned and smiled.

—Sleeper! I was looking for you last week in school.

She called me Sleeper and I did not mind. I had so many names at Kakuma and this was the most poetic. I would allow Maria to call me anything she wished, for she had saved me from the road at night.

—What class are you in this year? I asked.

—Standard Five, she said.

—Ooh! Standard Five! I bowed deeply before her. —A very special girl!

—This is what they say.

We both laughed. I hadn't realized she was so extraordinary in her academics. She was younger than I, and to be in Standard Five! She was surely the youngest in the class. —Are these all your clothes?

I pointed to a pair of pants that reached the ground. Whoever owned them was at least six-and-a-half feet tall.

—My father here. He was the bicycle man in my town.

—He fixed bicycles?

—He fixed them, sold them. He says he was close to my father. I don't remember him. Now I'm with them. He calls me his daughter.

There was so much work, Maria said. More work than she'd ever done or heard of. Between the chores and school, after sunset she was too exhausted to speak. The man she lived with expected two sons to join them soon at the camp, and Maria knew her workload would increase threefold when they arrived. She finished hanging the clothes and looked into my eyes.

—What do you think of this place, Achak?

She had a way of looking at me that that was very different than most Sudanese girls, who did not often meet your eye so directly, did not speak so plainly.

—Kakuma? I said.

—Yes, Kakuma. There's nothing here but us. Don't you find that weird? That it's only people and dust? We've already cut down all the trees and grass for our homes and firewood. And now what?

—What do you mean?

—We just stay here? Do we stay here always, till we die?

Until that moment I hadn't thought of dying in Kakuma.

—We stay till the war ends, then we go home, I said. It was Gop Chol's constant and optimistic refrain, and I suppose I had been fairly convinced. Maria laughed loudly at this.

—You're not serious, are you, Sleeper?

—Maria!

It was a woman's voice coming from the shelter.

—Girl, come here!

Maria made a sour face and sighed.

—I'll look for you at school when we start again. See you, Sleeper.

Gop Chol was a teacher loosely affiliated with the SPLA, and was a man of vision and careful planning. Together, we had constructed our shelter, considered one of the better homes in our neighborhood. With the UN-provided poles and plastic sheeting, we built a home, with palm-tree leaves on top, keeping it cool during the day and warm at night. The walls were mud, our beds assemblages of sisal bags. But it was so hot in Kakuma most nights that we slept outside. We slept under the open sky, and I studied outside, under the light of the moon or the kerosene lamp we shared.

Like Mr. Kondit, Gop insisted that I study constantly, lest the future of Sudan be in jeopardy. He too imagined that once the war was over, and once independence for southern Sudan had been achieved, those of us educated in Pinyudo and Kakuma, and benefiting from the expertise and materials of the international community hosting us, would be ready to lead a new Sudan.

But it was difficult for us to see this future, for at Kakuma, all was dust. Our mattresses were full of dust, our books and food were plagued with dust. To eat a bite of food without the grind of sand between one's molars was unheard of. Any pens we borrowed or were given worked sporadically; the dust would clog one in an hour and that was that. Pencils were the standard and even they were rare.

I blacked out a dozen times a day. When I stood up quickly the corners of my vision would darken and I would wake up on the ground, always, strangely, uninjured. Stepping into darkness, Achor Achor called it.

Achor Achor was better connected to the prevailing expressions of the young men at the camp, for he still lived among the unaccompanied minors. He shared a shelter with six other boys and three men, all former soldiers in the SPLA. One of the men, twenty years old, was missing his right hand. We called him Fingers.

There was not enough food, and the Sudanese, an agrarian people, were not allowed to keep livestock in the camp, and the Turkana would not allow the Sudanese to keep any outside the camp. Inside Kakuma, there was no room to grow crops of any kind, and the soil was unfit for almost any agriculture anyway. A few vegetables could be raised near the water taps, but such paltry gardens went almost nowhere in meeting the needs of forty thousand refugees, many of whom were suffering from anemia.

Every day in school, students would be absent due to illness. The bones of boys my age were attempting to grow, but there were not enough nutrients in our food. So there was diarrhea, dysentery, and typhoid. Early on in the life of the school, when a student was ill, the school was notified, and the students were encouraged to pray for that boy. When the boy returned to school, he would be applauded, though there were some boys who felt it best to keep their distance from those who had just been sick. When a boy did not recover, our teachers would call us together before classes, and tell us that there was bad news, that this certain boy had died. Some of us would cry, and others would not. Many times, I was not sure if I had known the boy, and so I just waited until the crying boys were done crying. Then the lesson would continue, with those of us who did not know the boy hiding our small satisfaction that this death would mean that school would be dismissed early that day. A dead boy meant a half day, and any day that we could go home to sleep meant that we could rest and be better able to fight off disease ourselves.

After some time, though, there were too many boys dying, and there was no time to mourn each one. Those who knew the dead boy would mourn privately, while the healthy would hope we would not get sick. Class would go on; there were no more half days.

This made study difficult, and academic achievement near impossible. Frustrated with it all, many boys would simply not go to school. Of sixty-eight boys in my junior-high class, only thirty-eight went on to high school. Still, it was safer than being in Sudan, and we had nothing else. I was hungry, but I was thankful every day that I seemed to be free, for the time being, from the threat of SPLA enlistment. There were fewer canings, fewer reprisals, less militarism in general. We were, for a time, no longer Seeds, no longer the Red Army. We were simply boys, and there was, after a time, basketball.

I discovered basketball at Kakuma, and I quickly came to believe that I was very good, that like Manute Bol, I would be brought to the United States to play professionally. Basketball would never become as popular as soccer in the camp, but it attracted hundreds of boys, the tall ones, the quick ones, those who liked the chance to get more touches than we would in one of the mass herdings that passed for soccer. The Ugandans were good with basketball strategy—they knew the game—the Somalis were quick, but it was the Sudanese who dominated, our long legs and arms simply out-classing the rest. When a pickup game came together, and the Sudanese banded against whatever team could be assembled against us, we invariably won, no matter how good the outside shooting was, no matter how quick the guards were, no matter how much will the opponents could muster. It gave us great pride to think of ourselves as we once had, as the kings of Africa, the monyjang, the chosen people of God.

In the days before his family was to arrive, Gop began to posit various scenarios by which his wife and daughters would not make it to Kakuma. They could be shot by bandits, he would suggest. I would tell him that that was not possible, that they would be coming with many others, would be safe, perhaps even in a vehicle. Gop would be content for an hour or so, and then he would get positively manic, taking apart his bed and putting it together again, and sliding back into crushing doubt. "What if my daughters don't recognize me?" he asked six times each day. To this I could not muster an answer, given that I no longer could remember what my own parents looked like. Worse, the daughters of Gop were younger, far younger, than I had been when I left home. His three daughters had all been under five, and now it was eight years later. None would know Gop by sight.

—Of course they'll know you, I said. —All girls know their father.

—You're right. You're right, Achak. Thank you. I'm thinking too much.

Each day, Gop waited for news about those who were coming to Kakuma. We occasionally received word about a movement of refugees, and would anticipate their arrival and prepare for it. Even after three years, any given week could bring a thou-sand new people, and the camp continued to grow outward by miles, such that I could walk a new avenue each morning. Kakuma grew to encompass Kakuma I, II, III, and IV. It was a refugee city with its own suburbs.

But most of the arrivals came from regions of Sudan, and particularly those vil-lages closer to Kenya. Few were from anywhere near Marial Bai. Most of those I asked had never heard of my village. And when they knew anything of northern Bahr al-Ghazal, they provided sweeping news of its elimination from the planet.

—You're from northern Bahr al-Ghazal? one man said. —Everyone there is dead.

Another man, elderly and missing his right leg, was more specific.

—Northern Bahr al-Gazhal is now the home of the murahaleen. They've taken over. It's their grazing land. There's nothing there to go back to.

One day, news of my region came from a boy I did not know well. I was at the water tap before school when the boy, named Santino, ran to me, explaining that there was a man at Lopiding Hospital who was from Marial Bai. Another boy had been at the hospital for malaria and had begun talking to the man, who mentioned my hometown, and this man said he even remembered me, Achak Deng. So I was obligated to find a way to Lopiding, quickly, I thought, for this was the first time in many years that someone had come to Kakuma from Marial Bai.

But then I thought of Daniel Dut, another boy I knew who had awaited news of his own family, only to learn that they were all dead. For months afterward, Daniel had insisted that he wished he'd never found out, that it was far easier to walk through life in doubt and with hope than knowing that everyone was gone. Knowing your family was dead brought on visions of how they died, how they might have suffered, how their bodies might have been abused after death. So I didn't immediately seek out the Marial Bai man in the hospital. When I heard, a week later, that he was gone, I was not unhappy.

The announcement of the census was made while Gop was waiting for the coming of his wife and daughters, and this complicated his peace of mind. To serve us, to feed us, the UNHCR and Kakuma's many aid groups needed to know how many refugees were at the camp. Thus, in 1994 they announced they would count us. It would only take a few days, they said. To the organizers I am sure it seemed a very simple, necessary, and uncontroversial directive. But for the Sudanese elders, it was anything but.

—What do you think they have planned? Gop Chol wondered aloud.

I didn't know what he meant by this, but soon I understood what had him, and the majority of Sudanese elders, greatly concerned. Some learned elders were reminded of the colonial era, when Africans were made to bear badges of identification on their necks.

—Could this counting be a pretext of a new colonial period? Gop mused. —It's very possible. Probable even!

I said nothing.

At the same time, there were practical, less symbolic, reasons to oppose the census, including the fact that many elders imagined that it would decrease, not increase, our rations. If they discovered there were fewer of us than had been assumed, the food donations from the rest of the world would drop. The more pressing and widespread fear among young and old at Kakuma was that the census would be a way for the UN to kill us all. These fears were only exacerbated when the fences were erected.

The UN workers had begun to assemble barriers, six feet tall and arranged like hallways. The fences would ensure that we would walk single file on our way to be counted, and thus counted only once. Even those among us, the younger Sudanese primarily, who were not so worried until then, became gravely concerned when the fences went up. It was a malevolent-looking thing, that maze of fencing, orange and opaque. Soon even the best educated among us bought into the suspicion that this was a plan to eliminate the Dinka. Most of the Sudanese my age had learned of the Holocaust, and were convinced that this was a plan much like that used to eliminate the Jews in Germany and Poland. I was dubious of the growing paranoia, but Gop was a believer. As rational a man as he was, he had a long memory for injustices visited upon the people of Sudan.

—What isn't possible, boy? he demanded. —See where we are? You tell me what isn't possible at this time in Africa!

But I had no reason to distrust the UN. They had been feeding us at Kakuma for years. There was not enough food, but they were the ones providing for everyone, and thus it seemed nonsensical that they would kill us after all this time.

—Yes, he reasoned, —but see, perhaps now the food has run out. The food is gone, there's no more money, and Khartoum has paid the UN to kill us. So the UN gets two things: they get to save food, and they are paid to get rid of us.

—But how will they get away with it?

—That's easy, Achak. They say that we caught a disease only the Dinka can get. There are always illnesses unique to certain people, and this is what will happen. They'll say there was a Dinka plague, and that all the Sudanese are dead. This is how they'll justify killing every last one of us.

—That's impossible, I said.

—Is it? he asked. —Was Rwanda impossible?

I still thought that Gop's theory was unreliable, but I also knew that I should not forget that there were a great number of people who would be happy if the Dinka were dead. So for a few days, I did not make up my mind about the head count. Meanwhile, public sentiment was solidifying against our participation, especially when it was revealed that the fingers of all those counted, after being counted, would be dipped in ink.

—Why the ink? Gop asked.

I didn't know.

—The ink is a fail-safe measure to ensure the Sudanese will be exterminated.

I said nothing, and he elaborated. Surely if the UN did not kill us Dinka while in the lines, he theorized, they would kill us with this ink on the fingers. How could the ink be removed? It would, he thought, enter our bodies when we ate.

—This seems very much like what they did to the Jews, Gop said.

People spoke a lot about the Jews in those days, which was odd, considering that a short time before, most of the boys I knew thought the Jews were an extinct race. Before we learned about the Holocaust in school, in church we had been taught rather crudely that the Jews had aided in the killing of Jesus Christ. In those teachings, it was never intimated that the Jews were a people still inhabiting the earth. We thought of them as mythological creatures who did not exist outside the stories of the Bible.

The night before the census, the entire series of fences, almost a mile long, was torn down. No one took responsibility, but many were quietly satisfied.

In the end, after countless meetings with the Kenyan leadership at the camp, the Sudanese elders were convinced that the head count was legitimate and was needed to provide better services to the refugees. The fences were rebuilt, and the census was conducted a few weeks later. But in a way, those who feared the census were correct, in that nothing very good came from it. After the count, there was less food, fewer services, even the departure of a few smaller programs. When they were done counting, the population of Kakuma had decreased by eight thousand people in one day.

How had the UNHCR miscounted our numbers before the census? The answer is called recycling. Recycling was popular at Kakuma and is favored at most refugee camps, and any refugee anywhere in the world is familiar with the concept, even if they have a different name for it. The essence of the idea is that one can leave the camp and re-enter as a different person, thus keeping his first ration card and getting another when he enters again under a new name. This means that the recycler can eat twice as much as he did before, or, if he chooses to trade the extra rations, he can buy or otherwise obtain anything else he needs and is not being given by the UN—sugar, meat, vegetables. The trading resulting from extra ration cards provided the basis for a vast secondary economy at Kakuma, and kept thousands of refugees from anemia and related illnesses. At any given time, the administrators of Kakuma thought they were feeding eight thousand more people than they actually were. No one felt guilty about this small numerical deception.

The ration-card economy made commerce possible, and the ability of different groups to manipulate and thrive within the system led soon enough to a sort of social hierarchy at Kakuma. At the top of the ladder as a group were the Sudanese, because our sheer numbers dominated the camp. But on an individual basis, the Ethiopians were the top social caste—a few thousand representatives of that country's middle class who were forced out with Mengistu. They lived in Kakuma I, and owned a good portion of the prosperous businesses. Their rivals in trade were the Somalis and the Eritreans, who found a way to coexist with the Ethiopians, though their countrymen were at odds with each other at home. Meanwhile there was tension between the Somalis and the Bantu, a long-suffering group who had been transplanted from another Kenyan camp, Dadaab. The Bantu had first been made slaves in Mozambique and in the 1800s migrated to Somalia, where they endured two hundred years of persecution. They were not allowed to own land, or given access to political representation at any level. When civil war engulfed Somalia in the 1990s their situation worsened, as their farms and homes were raided, their men killed, and their women raped. There were eventually some seventeen thousand Bantu in Kakuma, and even there they were not always safe, as their numbers brought resentment from many Sudanese, who considered the camp theirs.

Just below the merchants were the SPLA commanders, and under them, the Ugandans—only four hundred or so, most of them affiliated with Joseph Kony's Lord's Resistance Army, a rebel group at odds with the ruling National Resistance Movement. The Ugandans couldn't go back; most were well-known at home and had prices on their heads. Sprinkled around the camp there were Congolese, Burundians, Eritreans, and a few hundred Rwandans who many suspected had been participants in the genocide and were unwelcome in their homeland.

Somewhere near the bottom of it all sat the unaccompanied minors, the Lost Boys. We had no money, no family, and little means to attain either. One step up from this low rung could be gained if one found his way into a family. Living with Gop Chol had afforded me some status and a few privileges, but I knew that once Gop's family arrived, it would be difficult to spread the family's rations around, and the many items necessary—with so many young girls in the home—would mean that there needed to be more income in our home, and an extra ration card was the beginning of the flow of wealth.

—One of us will have to recycle once the girls get here, Gop said one day.

And I knew this to be true. I received my own rations every week, and when his wife and daughters arrived, Gop would qualify for a family ration. But the rations for a family of five would be insufficient, and we knew that the prime time to recycle again would be immediately after the census, when there would be extra vigilance about how much food we would be given.

—I will go, I said, and I was sure of it.

I would go as soon as his wife and girls arrived, I announced. Gop pretended to be surprised by my offer, but I knew he expected this of me. Recycling was always done by the young men at Kakuma, and I wanted to prove my worth to the family, to earn their respect shortly after they arrived.

For the weeks that followed, Achor Achor and I spent many nights lying outside my shelter, doing our homework in the crisp blue light of the moon, plotting my recycling trip.

—You'll need extra pants, Achor Achor said.

I had no idea why I would need pants, but Achor Achor enlightened me: I would need pants because with the pants I would get the goat.

—One pair of pants should do it, he surmised.

I asked Achor Achor why I needed a goat.

—You need to get the goat to get the shillings.

I begged him to start at the beginning.

I needed the pants, he said, because when I left Kakuma, I would be traveling to Narus, in Sudan, and in Sudan, they cannot find the sort of new, Chinese-made pants that were available in Kakuma Town. If I were to bring such pants to Narus, I could trade them for a goat. And I needed a goat because if I were to bring a healthy goat back to Kakuma, where goats are scarce, I would be able to sell the animal for two thousand shillings or more.

—You might as well make some money while you're out there risking your life.

This is the first I had heard of the trip still being dangerous. Or rather, I knew that in the past, if one left Kakuma, and traveled the roads to Lokichoggio and past Lokichoggio, there were bandits one might encounter, Turkana and Taposa bandits, and they would, at best, steal everything you had, and at worst, steal all you had and kill you afterward. I had thought that those dangers were in the past, but apparently not. Nevertheless, the plan continued to develop, and Gop joined in.

—You should bring more than one pair of pants! Gop huffed one night over dinner. Achor Achor was eating with us, which he often did, because Gop knew how to cook and Achor Achor did not.

—More goods, more goats! Gop bellowed. —You might as well really make it worthwhile, since you're risking your life and all.

From then on, the plan expanded: I would bring with me two shirts, a pair of pants, and a blanket, all new or seemingly new, and with all this I would be able to trade for at least three goats, which would bring six thousand shillings in Kakuma Town, an amount that would keep Gop's family in necessities, even in luxuries like sugar and butter, for many months. The money, combined with the extra ration card, would make me a hero in the family, and I dreamed of impressing my soon-to-be-sisters, who all would look up to me and call me uncle.

—You can start your own store, Achor Achor said one night.

This was true. Immediately I liked the idea, and thereafter this too became part of the larger plan. I'd long wanted to start a small retail outfit, a canteen, outside my shelter, where I would sell foods and also pens, pencils, soap, slippers, dried fish, and whatever soda I could get my hands on. Because I was trusted by those who knew me, I was confident that if I offered my goods at a fair price I would do well, and once I had some capital, the stocking of the canteen would be no problem. I remembered lessons from my father's store in Marial Bai, and knew that in such matters customer relations were crucial.

—But you'll need more than the two shirts and pants, Achor Achor noted. —You'll need two pairs of pants, three shirts, and at least two blankets, wool ones.

Finally the plan became real. I would be leaving at the next opportunity, the next time the roads were considered safe. I was given a backpack by Gop's cousin, a sturdy vinyl apparatus with zippers and many compartments. Inside I placed the two pairs of pants, the three shirts, the wool blanket, and a bag of nuts and crackers and peanut butter for the trip. I planned to leave early in the morning, to sneak out from Kakuma IV, and then walk the mile or so to the main road to Loki, which I would follow, avoiding Kenyan police, camp guards, and passing cars.

—But you can't leave during the day! Gop sighed when he heard of this part of the plan. —You leave at night, you dope.

So the plan was altered again. At night I would not be seen by anyone. The official way to leave Kakuma was with an approved refugee travel document. But I had no legitimate business leaving, and even if I did, applying for such a document could take months. If I had connections at the UNHCR, I might be able to get my application expedited, but I knew no one well enough that they would risk anything for me.

That left one remedy, the most popular and speedy, that being the bribing of the Kenyan guards along the road. Kakuma was never a gated camp; the refugees could walk out of the camp if they wished, but very soon, along the main road, they would be stopped by Kenyan police at stations or in Land Rovers, and the traveler would have to present his or her refugee-travel document. It was at that moment that a traveler without a document would have to present an appropriate incentive for the officer to look the other way. Night travel was recommended, for the simple fact that the less upstanding officers were given the night shifts, and there were fewer of them.

So finally I was ready to go. But first we would wait for Gop's family, to make sure there were still three daughters and one wife. Though they had sent word months before that the four of them would be arriving together, there were no such guarantees in Sudan. Gop and I did not talk about this, but we knew it to be true. Anything can happen during so long a trip.

In the end they arrived, everyone intact, though they appeared without warning. One morning, Gop Chol and I walked to the tap to get more water, so that no one would have to retrieve it for a few days. As we approached the tap, we saw, in the distance, a Red Cross van steaming through the dust. We both stood, knowing that it was unusual to see a van in our part of the camp, and at the same time, we both wondered, Could it be? Gop had received word a week earlier that his family might be transferred sometime soon, but there had been no news since. We watched the van slow as it approached our home, and when it came to a stop it was in front of our door and Gop was running. I ran after him. Gop was not a fast runner, so I overtook him quickly. When we were within sight of the van, Gop began yelling. He sounded maniacal and unwell.

—Aha! Aha! You are here! You are here!

They couldn't hear us yet. We were a few hundred yards away.

A tiny girl, frail and in a white dress, stepped out of the van first, followed by two more girls, each taller than the last but both under eight years old, also in white. They stood, squinting in the sunlight, flattening their dresses over their legs. They were followed by a beautiful woman in green, the green of rain-soaked elephant leaves. She stood, guarded her eyes from the sun, and looked around at Kakuma.

—You are here! You are here!

Gop was yelling but wasn't close enough to be heard. He ran, waving his arms wildly. Soon he was near enough for the woman in green to see him, but only as a vague shape in the dust. I had run ahead and could see his family clearly.

—Hello! he yelled.

She turned her head to him and gave him the kind of disgusted look reserved for drunkards and the raving mad. The driver helped them with a few bags he retrieved from the back, and deposited them on the ground in front of the house.

—It's me! It's me! Gop was screaming, and it was evident that his running toward them was making the girls, and their mother, uncomfortable.

Gop was no more than one hundred yards away when he seemed to change his mind. He slowed and then stopped, and then ducked out of the road. I followed him as he dodged between the anarchic maze of homes nearby. We were now out of sight of the road and Gop's family. He leaped over the low fences of the neighboring homes and under the clotheslines and around the sad stringy chickens kept by our neighbors, until he was at the back door of the home we shared. He entered his home and I followed him. I could hear someone at the front door, and guessed it was the Red Cross driver, whose knocking was loud and impatient.

Gop was in his bedroom.

—Don't answer the door! he begged me. —Let me change.

I waited by the door.

—I don't want them to know I was the man screaming down the road.

By now, I had guessed as much. I waited by the door as Gop splashed and straightened and cleaned. In a minute he emerged, freshened and wearing his finest white shirt and clean khakis.

—I'm ready, yes?

I nodded, and opened the door. Gop strode through, his arms wide.

—My wife! My daughters!

And he lifted the girls, one after the other, starting with the oldest and finishing with the youngest and most delicate, a tiny girl he kept on his arm for the better part of the day, as they unpacked and ate. The family had brought many foods from Sudan, and he and I showed the women the house we had constructed for them.

—There was a crazy man running down the road, his wife eventually said, as she arranged sheets on the girls' beds. —Did you hear him?

Gop sighed. —There are all types here, my darling.

I became close with Gop's wife, Ayen, and their daughters, Abuk, Adeng, and Awot. The restructuring of the household, which was extensive, changed my life and worked to everyone's advantage. Because Gop and his wife now needed a bedroom of their own, we built another one, and the girls moved into the one that he and I used to share. Gop and his wife wouldn't have me sleeping in the room with the girls, so a separate bedroom was built for me, and in the middle of building it, we had an idea: it was unusual for a boy my age to have his own room, and Gop and I knew of plenty of boys who would gladly move in with us and would help bring in more income and food, so invitations were extended to Achor Achor and three other boys, all students of Gop's, and my bedroom was built to accommodate five boys. When we were done, the household had grown from two to ten in one week.

There were four shelters now, all of them attached, and a kitchen and common room in the middle and it made for a very large household with many young people moving within it. It was never a question of whether or not all us kids would get along; there was no choice but to become a perfect machine, all of us parts moving in sync, peacefully and without complaint.

Every day, all eight of us kids would wake up at six o'clock and together go to the water tap to fill our jerry cans for our showers. The water would run from the tap starting at six o'clock; it was then that everyone in our region of the camp, about twenty thousand people, had to get their own water for washing; the water for cooking and cleaning was retrieved later. The line at the tap was always long, until years later, when the UN dug more taps. But at that time, there were commonly over a hundred people in line when the taps came alive. At home we would all shower and dress for school. During those years, breakfast was not eaten at Kakuma—it was not until 1998 that there was enough food for morning meals—so if we consumed anything before leaving the house it was water or tea; there was enough for one meal a day, and that came at dinner, together, after school and work.

We all attended the same school, a short walk away, with an enrollment just under one thousand. First there would be an assembly, where announcements would be made, and we all would be given the advice of the day. Often the advice pertained to hygiene and nutrition, an odd subject given how poorly we were fed. Just as often, it would cover malfeasance and punishment. If any students had been misbehaving, there would be retribution then and there, with a quick caning or verbal reprimand in front of the student body. Then there would be prayer, or the singing of a hymn, for all of the students in that school were Christians, at least as far as we could tell. If there were Muslims, they were very quiet about their faith, not protesting then or during the regular sessions in what they called Christian Religious Instruction.

There were sixty-eight students in my class. We stayed in one classroom throughout the day, sitting on the dirt, as our instructors, specialists in English, Kiswahili, Math, Science, Home Science, Geography, Agriculture, and Arts & Crafts & Music moved in and out. I enjoyed school and was well liked by my teachers, but many of my friends had stopped attending classes. They were impatient with it, could not see the point, and went into the markets to make money. They would trade their rations for clothes, sell the clothes in the camp and turn a profit. And of course they continued to leave Kakuma for the SPLA, and we would hear soon enough about who had been shot, who had been burned, who had been separated from his limbs by a grenade.

On the days food was distributed, we kids would be sent to the UN compound, where we would line up. The UN workers or the LWF workers would scoop food from the trucks, first checking the ID cards and ration cards of each recipient. On the way back, we would carry the bags of grain or sorghum the mile home, either on our heads or shoulders, resting frequently. We all complained about retrieving the rations, and on the rare occasions when someone missed the distribution, when they slept late or were late getting into line, the ration would not be brought home and the family would be affected. Backup plans had to be made and carried out, to ensure the family ate. It was time for my recycling trip.

I had my backpack and good shoes and—

—Do you have a hat? Gop's daughter Awot asked me.

—Why would I need a hat?

—What if there's someone at Loki who knows you when you come back?

She was a brilliant girl, this Awot. So I included Achor Achor's prized Houston Astros hat in the backpack and finally I was ready. It was midnight when the family saw me off. Gop did not seem to fear for my life, so I took our goodbye lightly and the girls followed suit. Achor Achor walked me to the border between Kakuma and the great beyond, and when I turned to the leave, he grabbed my arm and wished me luck.

—Did you bring your ration card? he asked me.

And I had indeed brought my ration card, a grave mistake. If I was robbed by the Turkana, or interrogated by the Kenyan police, or asked to empty my pockets by the officials at Loki, my original ration card would be taken, and the entire point of the trip would be lost. So I gave my ration card to Achor Achor, we patted each other on the back like men, and I was off into the night, with no identifying papers on me. I was new, I was no one.

I had been told that if I came upon any Kenyan police along the road, a bribe would be requested and I soon would be on my way. And this is precisely what happened: within a few miles of Kakuma it happened three times. Each set of guards were bought with fifty shillings and were exceedingly polite and businesslike about the transaction. I might as well have been buying fruit from a sidewalk grocer.

I walked through the night perhaps too cheerfully, thinking my trip charmed and knowing I would be successful. With any luck I would be back at Kakuma, with six thousand shillings and another ration card in three days' time.

I arrived at Loki in the early hours, found the dirt roads empty, and slept inside a compound maintained by Save the Children, an NGO we knew well: they had been supplying food to the starving in southern Sudan for years. Loki is dotted with these NGO staging areas, which are in most cases no more than small shacks or adobe houses, surrounded by wooden fences or gates of corrugated steel. Save the Children, back then and still today, works closely with the Sudanese, and their people are always willing to help those of us coming to Kakuma or leaving for Sudan.

When I woke up I saw first the feet of a man standing over me, talking to another man on the other side of the fence. The man almost stepping on me, I learned, was named Thomas. He was a bit older than me, had been SPLA, but left during the split between Garang and Machar. When he was done speaking to the man over the fence, he turned his attention to me.

—So what's your situation? he asked.

I told him a general version of my plan.

—How much money do you have?

I told him I had only fifty shillings left.

—Then how do you intend to get your papers from the SPLM?

I had not been told that these papers would cost money. I knew if I entered SPLA-controlled territory, I would need an SPLA/SPLM-issued identification card, but I thought they would provide it for free. The SPLA/SPLM, I had been told, would put any name you wanted on the document, and I had planned to give them a name similar enough that it would be regionally correct; that way I would be able to answer any questions about clans in my part of Sudan. With the new document, I would ride back to Loki, sell the goats, and, at the Loki immigration office, I would hand them my documents and claim to be in danger if I returned to Sudan. I would be processed as a refugee, and under my new name be granted admission to Kakuma.

—No money left, huh? Thomas said. —You just left last night!

Thomas gave me a curious smile, his head tilted.

—Poor planning, Achak. Do you have a new name chosen? No doubt you'll be glad to be rid of Achak.

I told him Valentino Deng would be my new name.

—Not bad. I like that, Valentino. There are a few other Valentinos around. It won't look suspicious. Listen, here's fifty shillings. You can pay me back next time you come through. I'm here a lot; I do some business here and there. You take the fifty shillings, combine it with yours, you have one hundred. That might be enough if the SPLM takes pity on you. Give me a pitiful face, Valentino Deng.

I turned my mouth downward into a pout, and teared my eyes.

—Wow, not bad, Valentino. Impressive. You have a ride?

I did not have a ride.

—Oh lord. Never have I encountered such an unprepared traveler. If you give me the face again I'll tell you where to get a ride into Narus.

I gave him the look again.

—That is really a pitiful look, son. I congratulate you. Okay. There's a truck coming from Sudan right now. It's down the road and one of the drivers is a friend of mine, cousin to my wife. It's going back to Sudan in a few minutes. You ready?

—I am, I said.

—Good, he said. Here it comes.

And indeed a truck pulled up at that moment, a standard flatbed truck, the sort I was accustomed to seeing full of passengers. It was a dream, it seemed, to have found a direct ride so quickly. I had only been awake five minutes. The truck shook to a halt in front of Save the Children. Thomas spoke to the driver for a few minutes and then gave me the signal. The engine rumbled awake and the tires chewed the gravel.

—Go, fool! Go! Thomas yelled to me.

I gathered my bag and ran after the truck and jumped onto the back bumper. I turned to wave to Thomas, but he had gone inside the compound, finished with me. I threw my bag in and climbed over the back door. My first foot landed on something soft.

—Excuse me! I gasped.

It was then that I saw that I had stepped on a person. The truckbed was filled with people, fifteen or more. But they were grey, white, covered in blood. These people were dead. I was stepping on the chest of a man who made no protestation. I jumped off his chest and onto the hand of a woman who also offered no objection. I stood on one foot, my other foot hovering over the exposed innards of a boy only a bit older than myself.

—Careful, boy! There are a few of us still alive.

I turned to find a man, an elderly man, lying prone and twisted like a root, near the back of the truck. —I'm sorry, I said.

The truck jerked and the old man's head hit the back hatch. He moaned.

We were moving, and the truck quickly picked up speed. I gripped the side of the truck and tried not to look at its cargo. I looked into the sky but then the smell overtook me. I gagged.

—You'll become accustomed to it, the man said. —It's a human smell.

I tried to move my foot but found it stuck; blood covered the truck floor. I wanted to jump but the truck was traveling too fast. I looked forward, wanting to get the attention of the driver. A head emerged from the passenger side of the truck cab. A cheerful man hoisted himself so he was sitting on the window ledge, looking back at me. He seemed to be an SPLA soldier, but it was difficult to tell.

—How are you back there, Red Army?

—I'd like to get out please, I stammered.

The maybe-rebel laughed.

—I'll walk back. Please. Please, uncle.

He laughed until tears filled his eyes.

—Oh Red Army. You are too much.

Then he slipped back into the cab.

A moment later, the truck swerved and I lost my footing, and for a second I found my knee in the broken thigh of a dead soldier, whose open eyes stared into the sun. As I raised myself, I glanced over the contents of truckbed. The corpses were arranged as if they had been thrown. Nothing held them in place.

—It's pitiful, it is, the old man said. —Many of us were alive when we left Sudan. I've been keeping the vultures away. A dog jumped aboard yesterday. He was hungry.

The truck jumped again and my foot slipped on something viscous.

—The dogs now, they have a taste for people. They go straight for the face. Did you know that? It was lucky that one of the men in the cab heard the dog. They stopped the truck and shot it. Now it's just the four of us, he said.

Four aboard were yet alive, though it was difficult to find them, and I was not sure the old man was correct. I glanced to a body next to him. At first it seemed that this man's arms were hidden. But now it was clear, because I could see the white bones of his shoulders, that the man's arms had been removed.

The truck swerved wildly again. My right foot landed on the arm of a teenage boy, wearing a blue camouflage uniform and a floppy hat.

—He's still alive, I think, the old man said. —Though he hasn't spoken today.

I raised myself again and heard wild laughter from the truck cab. They'd swerved on purpose, each time. The cheerful man's head again appeared from the passenger window.

—The driver is very sorry, Red Army, he said. —There was a lizard in the road and he was very concerned about killing such a creature of God.

—Please uncle, I said. I don't want to be here. I want to leave. If you could only slow down a bit, I'll jump off. You don't need to stop.

—Don't worry, Red Army, the maybe-rebel said. His face and tone were suddenly serious, even compassionate. —We only have to drop the wounded at Lopiding Hospital, and then bury the bodies over the hill, and we'll have an empty truck all the way to Sudan. Wherever you need to go.

The truck had taken a bump and the man's head had struck the top of the window frame. Soon he was inside the truck again, yelling at the driver. For a moment the truck slowed and I thought I had a chance.

—Take the ride, boy.

It was the old man.

—How else will you get to Sudan? he said.

He looked at me then, as if for the first time.

357

—Why are you going back, anyway, boy?

I did not consider telling the man the truth, that I was trying to recycle, to get another ration card. It would seem ridiculous to a man struggling to live. The people of southern Sudan had their problems, and by comparison the mechanisms of Kakuma, where everyone was fed and was safe, were not worth mentioning.

—To find my family, I said.

—They're dead, he said. —Sudan is dead. We won't ever live there again. This is your home now. Kenya. Be glad for it. This is your home and it will always be your home.

A sigh came from below my feet. The teenage boy turned over, his hands praying under his ear as if he were comfortably at home on a pillow of feathers. I looked down at him, determined that I should focus on him, for he seemed most at peace. My eyes assessed him quickly—I could not control them, and cursed them for their speed and curiosity—and realized that the boy's left leg was missing. It was now a stump covered with a bandage fashioned from a canvas tarpaulin and rubber bands cobwebbed to his waist.

The ride, I now know, was less than an hour, but it is impossible to convey how long it seemed that day. I had covered my mouth but still I gagged continuously: I felt chills, and my neck seemed numb. I felt sure that this truck represented the devil's most visible deeds, that in every way it symbolized his work on Earth. I knew I was being tested, and I rode until the truck finally slowed upon reaching the driveway to the Lopiding Hospital.

Without hesitation I jumped over the side and tumbled onto the ground. I meant to outrun the truck and find safe haven in the clinic. Upon landing on the hard dirt, I needed a moment to re-engage with the world, to know that I was not dead myself, that I had not been cast into Hell. I stood and felt my legs and arms working and so I ran.

—Wait, Red Army! Where are you going?

I ran from the truck, which was slowly traversing a series of potholes. I ran and outpaced the vehicle easily, aiming myself for a building on the end of the compound.

Lopiding was a series of tents and a few white brick buildings, sky-blue roofs, acacia trees, plastic chairs set outside for waiting patients. I ran to the back of a building and almost knocked over a man holding a false arm.

—Careful, boy!

The man was Kenyan, middle-aged. He spoke to me in Kiswahili. All around him were the makings of new feet, legs, arms, faces.

—Hey Red Army! Come now.

It was the soldier from the truck.

—Take this. Put it on.

The Kenyan gave me a mask, red, too small for me. I sank my face into it. I could see through the holes for eyes and the Kenyan tied it closed.

—Thank you, I said.

He was a constant-smiling man, heavy-jowled and with great sloping shoulders.

—No need, he said. —Are they still looking for you?

I peered around the corner. The two men from the truck were walking toward the building. They went inside for a moment and returned to the truck with a canvas stretcher. They first unloaded the old man, and brought him inside. They returned to the truck and retrieved the teenage boy with the missing leg, and he lay on the stretcher just as he had in the truck, looking as comfortable as could be. These were the only two passengers who disembarked at Lopiding. The rest were dead or would soon be dead. The men threw the stretcher into the back of the truck and the driver climbed into the cab. The other man, maybe-rebel who taunted me, stood with one hand on the door handle.

—Red Army! Time to go! You can ride in the cab this time! he yelled.

Now I was unsure. If I did not take this ride I would probably not get another. I stepped out from the building. The maybe-rebel looked directly at me. He dropped his hand from the truck, and tilted his head. He was staring into me, but made no movement, and neither did I. I felt safe behind the mask. I knew he would not know me. He turned from me and yelled up into the trees, looking for the boy who had been in the truck.

—I'm sorry, boy! the man yelled. —I promise we'll take you to Sudan. Safe and sound. Last chance.

I stepped forward, toward the truck. The Kenyan grabbed my arm.

—Don't go. They'll get a price for you. The SPLA would be happy to have a new recruit. Those guys would be paid well for delivering you.

It was an impossible decision.

—I'll get you back to Sudan if you need to go, the Kenyan said. —I don't know how, but I will. I just don't want you getting killed over there. You're too skinny to fight. You know what they do, right? You train for two weeks and then they send you to the front. Please. Just wait here a second till they leave.

I wanted so badly to join the men in the truck, wanted to believe their promise to keep me with them, in the cab, to deliver me safely over the border. And yet I found myself trusting the Kenyan, whom I did not know, more than my own countrymen. This happened occasionally and always it was a conundrum.

I was still standing in full view of the man from the truck, and again he fixed his eyes on me. It was so pleasing to wear that mask, to be invisible!

—Final chance, Red Army! he said to the boy he thought he was looking for.

The man shielded his eyes from the sun, still trying to figure out why this boy with a mask seemed so familiar. And still I stood, emboldened, until he finally turned back to the truck, lifted himself into it, and left in a cloud. The Kenyan and I watched the truck disappear into the orange dust.

I didn't want to remove the new face. I knew that the Kenyan would not give it to me, and I wondered briefly if I could escape with it at that moment. Perhaps the mask would make it possible to run—back to Kakuma or into Sudan—undetected. I luxuriated in the thought of presenting this new face to all the world, a new face, without marks, blemishes, a face that told no tales.

—Doesn't fit you, boy, the Kenyan said. His hand was on my shoulder, his grip strong enough that I knew escape was impossible.

I took the mask off and handed it to the Kenyan.

—Where will they bring the bodies? I asked.

—They're supposed to bring them back to Sudan, but this is not done. They'll drop them in the creek and take paying passengers back to Sudan.

—They'll bury them at the creek?

—They won't bury them. Does it make a difference? They get buried, they're eaten by worms and beetles. They don't bury them, they're eaten by dogs and hyenas.

The man was named Abraham. He was a doctor of sorts, a maker of prosthetics. His shop was behind the hospital, under a yawning tree. He promised me lunch if I could wait an hour. I was happy to wait. I did not know what doctors ate for lunch but I imagined it was extravagant.

—What are you making now? I asked.

He was fashioning something like an arm or shin.

—Where do you live? he asked.

—Kakuma I.

—Did you hear an explosion last week?

I nodded. It had been quick, a pop, like the sound of a mine coming alive.

—A soldier, SPLA, a very young one, was visiting his family in the camp. This was Kakuma II. He had brought some souvenirs home to show his siblings. One of the souvenirs was a grenade, so here I am, making a new arm for the soldier's little brother. He is nine. How old are you?

I didn't know. I guessed that I was thirteen.

—I've been doing this since 1987. I was here when they opened Lopiding. It was fifty beds then, one big tent. They thought it would be temporary. Now there are four hundred beds and they add more every week.

Abraham carved the plastic as it cooled.

—Who is this for? I said, picking up the mask I had worn.

—A boy's face was burned off. There's much of that. The kids want to look at the bombs. One boy last year had been thrown onto a fire.

He held his creation to the light. It was a leg, a small one, for a person smaller than me. He turned it around and around, and seemed satisfied.

—Do you like chicken, boy? It's time for lunch.

Abraham brought me to a buffet line, arranged in the courtyard. Twenty doctors and nurses lined up in their uniforms, blue and white. They were a mixed bunch: Kenyans, whites, Indians, one nurse who looked like a very light-skinned Arab. Abraham helped me with my plate, filling it with chicken and rice and lettuce.

—Sit over here, son, he said, nodding his head to a small bench under a tree. —You don't want to sit with the doctors. They'll ask questions, and you never know where that might lead. I don't know what kind of trouble you're in.

He watched me tear into my chicken and rice; I hadn't had meat in months. He took a bite of a drumstick and stared at me.

—What kind of trouble *are* you in?

—I'm in no trouble, I said.

—How did you get out of Kakuma?

I hesitated.

—Tell me. I'm a man who makes arms. I'm not an immigration officer.

I told him about sneaking away and bribing the police officers.

—Amazing how easy it is still, right? I love my country, but graft is as much part of life as the air or soil. It's not so bad to live in Kenya, right? When you're old enough, I'm sure you'll find a way out of the camp, and to Nairobi. There you can find some kind of job, I'm sure, maybe even go to school. You seem smart, and there are thousands of Sudanese in the city. Where are your parents?

I told him I didn't know. I was dizzy with the taste of chicken.

—I'm sure they're fine, he said, examining his chicken and choosing the location for his next bite. With his mouth full, he nodded. —I'm sure they lived. Did you see them killed?

—No.

—Well then, there's hope. They probably think you're dead, too, and here you are in Kenya, eating chicken and drinking soda.

I believed the words of Abraham, simply because he was educated and Kenyan and perhaps had access to information that we did not inside the camp. The separation of life inside Kakuma and in the rest of the world seemed completely impenetrable. We saw and met people from all over the world, but had virtually no hope of ever visiting any other place, including the Kenya beyond Loki. And so I took Abraham's words as those of a prophet.

We finished our lunch, which was delicious and by volume too much for me to consume; my stomach was not accustomed to this much food in one sitting.

—How will you get back to Kakuma? Abraham asked.

I told him I still intended to try to make my way to Narus.

—Not this time, son. You've seen enough for this trip.

He was right, of course. I had no will left. I was broken for now, and the plan was broken and all I could do now was return to Kakuma, with nothing gained or lost. I thanked Abraham and we promised to meet again, and he put me on an ambulance going to Loki. There, I waited for any trucks going to Kakuma whose drivers would not ask questions. I saw no sign of Thomas and so did not venture into the Save the Children compound. I walked up and down the dirt roads of Loki, hoping an opportunity would reveal itself before nightfall, when I knew that the Turkana would see me as a target.

—Hey kid.

I turned. It was a man, his nose broken and bulbous. He seemed Turkana but might have been anything else—Kenyan, Sudanese, Ugandan. He spoke to me in Arabic.

—What's your name?

I told him I was Valentino.

—What do you have there?

He was very interested in the contents of my bag. I gave him a brief look inside.

—Ah yes! he said, suddenly grinning, his smile as broad as a hammock. He had heard, he said, that there was a very smart young Sudanese man who possessed clothing from Kakuma Town. He seemed a kind and even charming man, so I told him about the trip, the truck, the bodies, Abraham, and the broken plan.

—Well, maybe it's not a total loss, he said. —How much would you take for all of it, the pants and shirts and the blanket?

We volleyed a few prices until we settled on seven hundred shillings. It was not what I had hoped for, but it was far more than I would have gotten in Kakuma, and double what I had paid for the clothes.

—You're a good businessman, the man said. —Very shrewd.

I had not thought of myself as a good businessman until that moment, but certainly this man's comment seemed true. I had just doubled my money.

—So seven hundred shillings! he said. —I have to pay it, you've got me over a barrel. I haven't seen pants like this here in Loki. I'll bring you the money tonight.

—Tonight?

—Yes, I have to wait here for my wife. She's at the hospital, too, having an infection checked on. She's with our baby, who we fear has some kind of dangerous cough. But they said she'll be back in a few hours and then we return to Kakuma. Will you be around at eight o'clock?

The man was taking the bag from my hands and I found myself saying yes, of course, that I would be there at eight o'clock. There was something trustworthy about him, or perhaps I was just too tired to be sensible. In any case, I wished the man well, sent my blessings to the man's wife and baby, improved health to the three of them. The man walked away with my clothes.

—Don't you need to know where I live? I asked him as he shrank into the crimson light of one of the shops.

The man turned and did not seem at all flustered.

—I assumed I would ask for the famous Valentino!

I gave him my address anyway, and then went out to the road leading back to Kakuma. After walking for a short while, I realized that I had been swindled, and that the man would never come to Kakuma. I had just given my clothes to a stranger and had sent to the wind the only commodity I had. I walked the entire distance back to Kakuma, watching trucks pass; I did not ask for a ride and did not have bribe money. I moved only in shadows, for I knew if I were caught all would be lost, and I would lose all my benefits, such as they were, as a refugee. I darted from bush to bush, ditch to ditch, crawling and scraping and breathing too loudly, as I had when I first ran from my home. Each exhalation was a falling tree and my mind went mad with the noise of it all, but I deserved the turmoil. I deserved nothing better. I wanted to be alone with my stupidity, which I cursed in three languages and with all my spleen.

XXIII.

The dream came to me once a month, with startling regularity. Usually it arrived on Sunday afternoon, when I had a chance to nap. All week would be work and school but on Sunday I had no responsibilities at all and it was then that I read and roamed the camp and, in the late afternoon, lay with my head in the shade of my shelter, my legs naked to the sun, and I slept a deep and satisfying sleep.

But the river dream kept me from my rest. When I dreamt it, I woke up troubled and I woke up driven.

In the dream I was many people in the way in a dream one can be many people at once. I was myself, I was my teacher, Mr. Kondit, and I was Dut. I knew this in the dream as one always knows who one is and isn't in a dream. I was a combination of these two men and I was floating in a river. The river was partly the river of my home, Marial Bai, and partly the river Gilo, and in the river with me were dozens of boys.

They were young boys I knew. Some were the boys under my charge at Kakuma, some of them born in the camp, and there were boys who had never left boyhood: William K, Deng, the boys taken back to God along our walk. We were all in the river, and I was trying to teach my students in the river. All of the students, about thirty boys, were treading water in the river, and I was treading water, too, shouting lessons about English verb forms to the boys floating in the river. The water was rough, and I was frustrated with the difficulty of trying to teach these boys under such circumstances. The boys, for their part, were trying their best to concentrate while also treading water and ducking the waves that periodically upset the calm of the river. The boys periodically disappeared behind a wave and then reappeared when the wave was gone. And all the while I knew the water was cold. It was so wonderfully cold, like the water given to me by the man who did not exist in the desert of the barbed wire.

I would float high on a wave of cold water and was then able, for a few moments, to see the heads of all of my students as they tried their best to see me and hear me, but then I would descend into the wave's valley, and could see only a wall of coffee-colored water. Always at this point in the dream, when the waves had become walls, I would return to be myself again, and from here on, the dream would take place largely under the coffee-colored water. I would find myself on the river's bottom, among the green tentacles of the underwater plants, and there at the bottom were bodies. Those boys who were trying to listen to me were at the river's bottom now, and it was my job to send them again to the surface. I knew it was my job and I performed it with a workmanlike efficiency. I would find a boy underwater, not dead, but sitting on the floor of the river, and I would put my hands under his arms and then send him upward. It was simple work.

I would see a boy and would position myself under him, placing my hands under his arms and then I would lift him upward. I did this knowing that once I did so, that boy would be safe. He would live and breathe the air above again once I had sent him to the surface. While I did this, a part of me worried that I would tire. There was so much sending-up to do, and I was underwater for so long—surely I would tire and some boys would be lost. But my worries were unfounded. In the dream I never tired, and I did not need to breathe. I moved under the water, from boy to boy to boy, and I lifted them to the air and the light.

—Achak, they whispered to me, and I pushed them to the surface.

—Valentino, they whispered, and I pushed them up.

—Dominic! they whispered, and I pushed them up and up.

I was now eighteen years old. I had been at Kakuma six years. I was still living with Gop Chol and his family, and during that time I had dreamt this dream perhaps a hundred times, and its message was clear to me: I was responsible to the next line of boys. We were all treading water together, and I was meant to teach. So at Kakuma camp, I became a teacher, and at the same time, I became Dominic.

The name Valentino had been supplanted, at least in the minds of many, by the name Dominic, and though I did not prefer this nickname, it stuck to me tenaciously. It was my association with Miss Gladys, my own teacher and by all accounts the most desirable woman at Kakuma, that brought the name Dominic upon me, and so I made no complaints. Miss Gladys was my drama instructor and later my history teacher, a young woman of extraordinary light and grace. It was Miss Gladys who brought me in touch with Tabitha, and it was Miss Gladys who brought me to the lights of Nairobi and to the potential for escape from the winds and drought of Kakuma. It was while holding the hand of Miss Gladys that I listened to Deborah Agok, a traveling midwife who knew the fate of my family and my town. This was an eventful time for me and for so many young men at Kakuma, even though that year in southern Sudan, the Dinka who remained would know a horrible famine, created by God and helped along by Khartoum.

El Niño had brought about two years of drought, and aid was desperately needed in the south. Hundreds of thousands in Bahr al-Ghazal faced starvation, and Bashir took this opportunity to ban all flights over southern Sudan. The region was effectively cut off from relief, and when it did make its way through, it was first intercepted by the SPLA and local chiefs, who did not always see to its equitable distribution. All this made the prospect of living at Kakuma even more attractive, and the camp's population swelled. But once a person had escaped the mayhem of Sudan, and once that person was legitimately recognized as part of Kakuma, entitled to its services and protection, there was little to do but pass the time. Besides school, this meant clubs, theatrical productions, HIV-awareness programs, puppetry—even pen pals from Japan.

The Japanese were very interested in Kakuma on many levels, and it started with the pen pal project. The letters from the Japanese schoolchildren were written in English, and it was difficult to know whose English was worse. Just how much information was actually transmitted from Kenya to Tokyo and Kyoto was debatable, but it was important to me, and to the hundred others who participated. After a year of letters, the Japanese boys and girls who had been writing arrived at Kakuma one day, blinking in the dust and shielding their eyes from the sun. They stayed for three days and visited our classrooms and watched traditional dancing from the Sudanese and Somali zones of the camp, and I was not sure how much stranger the camp could become. I had seen Germans, Canadians, people so white they looked like candles.

But the Japanese continued coming, and continued giving, with a particular interest in the youth at the camp, which of course accounted for about 60 percent of Kakuma's residents. The Japanese built the Kakuma Hospital, which could treat the cases that couldn't wait for Lopiding. They built the Kakuma community library and donated thousands of basketballs, soccer balls, volleyballs, and uniforms so the youth might play these sports with a degree of dignity and panache.

The Lutheran World Federation was the primary administrator of many of the cultural projects, and found their instructors among the Kenyans and the Sudanese. I first joined the LWF's public speaking and debating club, hoping it would help with my English. Soon after, I joined the Youth and Culture program, and this would grow into a job for me. In 1997 I became Kakuma I's youth leader. This was a paying occupation, something very few of my friends, and none of the children in my Kakuma family, possessed. Youth was considered anyone between seven and twenty-four years old, so in our part of the camp, this was six thousand youths. I was the liaison between the UNHCR and these kids, and Achor Achor was more impressed by this job than he had been years before, when I was a burial boy.

—I'll be here if you need advice, he said.

Achor Achor had just acquired glasses, and looked very studious and far more serious than before. Everything that left his mouth seemed suddenly to carry the weight of deep contemplation and far-reaching intellect.

—I will, I said.

As the youth leader and coordinator of Kakuma I's youth activities, I came into contact with Miss Gladys, who soon every boy at Kakuma would know and would think about often at night and alone.

She was assigned to be the instructor for the Drama Club, of which I was a member and the ostensible student director. Twelve members of the group were present on our first day, ten boys and two girls, and for this one meeting I was the director. We were told by the LWF that the group's adult sponsor and instructor would arrive for our second meeting. It was because I was the director by default that I could try to convince Maria to attend. I went to visit her one afternoon after school, two days before the first meeting. I found her hanging the laundry behind her adoptive family's shelter. —Hello Sleeper, she said.

She did not hide her foul mood. She never did. When she was down, her shoulders slumped, and her face frowned almost comically. She had not been to school in weeks; the man acting as her father had decided it was too problematic for her to both attend classes and properly help with the chores at home. His wife was pregnant, and he insisted that Maria be on hand should she need anything. As the baby grew within the womb of his wife, he said, she would need more help as the weeks and months went on. School, he said, was a luxury an orphan girl like her could not afford.

Neither Maria nor I had hopes that she would be a long-term member of the drama group, but I convinced her to come to the first meeting. We arrived together and, with the other members, we read aloud the first few scenes of a play Miss Gladys had written. Maria, playing the lead, a woman beaten by her husband, took to it immediately. I knew she was a spirited person, for she had saved my life on the night of the spilled stars. But I did not suspect she had the soul of an actress.

Maria attended the second meeting of the group, but I do not remember much about what she said or did, for this heralded the arrival of Miss Gladys. When Miss Gladys emerged, I ceded all authority and thereafter barely spoke at all.

Miss Gladys was a young Kenyan, long necked and favoring floor-length skirts that swished flamboyantly as she walked. She immediately admitted that she did not have vast theatrical experience, and yet was in every way a performer, a woman who knew the power of every word she breathed and gesture she made. In her mind and in reality, there were no moments when she was not being watched.

She was very adept at writing, we learned, having been educated for two years in England, at the University of East Anglia, where she had polished the English she'd learned in Nairobi's best private schools.

—What is that accent? we asked each other later.

—It sounds very well-educated.

—One day she will be my wife, we said.

We could not understand why someone as regal and clean as Miss Gladys—she did not perspire!—would spend her time with refugees such as us. That she actually enjoyed our company, and she really seemed to, was too much to contemplate. She smiled at the boys among the group in a way that could only be considered flirtatious, and she clearly appreciated the attention she received. The girls, meanwhile, did their best to like her despite it all.

The purpose of the club under her stewardship was to write and perform one-act plays that would illuminate problems at Kakuma and offer solutions in a non-pedantic manner. If there were misunderstandings, for example, about the risks of HIV infection, it was not possible to print flyers or air public-service announcements on television. We had to communicate first through dramatizations, and then hope that our messages would be entertaining, would be learned, internalized, and disseminated from person to person, mouth to ear.

But Miss Gladys could not remember who, among us boys, was who. Among the ten boys was a boy named Dominic Dut Mathiang, who was by far the most humorous boy at Kakuma. The funniest Sudanese boy, at least; I did not know how humorous the Ugandans were. Very soon, at the first meeting of the club under Miss Gladys's direction, she took to Dominic Dut Mathiang and laughed at every joke he made.

—Your name is what again? she asked.

—Dominic, he said.

—Dominic! I love that name!

And so the fate of the ten boys of our drama company was sealed, for she could not remember the names of the rest of us. She said she was not good at names, and this seemed to be true. She rarely referred to the girls by name, and it seemed the only name she could access readily was Dominic. And so we all became Dominic. At first it was a mistake. One day she absentmindedly referred to me, too, as Dominic.

—I'm sorry, she said. —You both have both Italian names, correct?

—Yes, I said. —Mine is Valentino.

She apologized, but called me Dominic again the next day. I didn't care. I did not care at all. I agreed with her that our names were very similar. I agreed very much with everything she said, though I did not always listen to the words coming from her beautiful mouth. So she called me Dominic, and she called the other boys Dominic, and we stopped correcting her. She began to simply call us all Dominic. Not one of us cared, and besides, she didn't need our names very often. We never took our eyes off her, so she needed only to direct her eyes, guarded by lashes of remarkable length and curvature, to whomever she was speaking.

We boys talked about her during all our available hours. We held special meetings, in the home of the real Dominic, Dominic Dut Mathiang, to discuss her merits.

—Her teeth aren't real, one boy suggested.

—Yeah. I heard she had them fixed in England.

—In England? You're crazy. People don't do that in England.

—But they can't be real. Look at our teeth and then at hers.

Our first play was called *Forced Marriage,* and it sought to dramatize and offer alternatives to the traditional Sudanese way. I played the part of an elder who disagreed with the idea of forcing young women into loveless marriages. In the play, my position was opposed by many other elders, who thought the existing system was best. The majority won in the end, and the girl in the play in question was given away. We left it to our youth audiences to decide that allowing this system to remain was unacceptable.

We performed this first play dozens of times all over Kakuma, and because it was occasionally humorous and in large part because Miss Gladys made an appearance—as the sister to the bride—it was very well liked and we were urged to continue. So we wrote and performed dramas about AIDS and how to prevent it. We wrote a play about anger management and conflict resolution. One play concerned castes and social discrimination in the camp, another covered the effects of war on children. We performed a one-act proposing gender equality—that the boys and girls of Sudan, like those in Kenya, should be treated the same—and to our continual amazement, the plays were appreciated and we received very little resistance, at least overtly, to our message.

But some elders did not appreciate our irreverence, and the man under whose care Maria lived was one of those who did not support our efforts. One day, Maria did not come to rehearsal after school, and when she had missed three days in a row, I went to look for her. I found her at home in the evening, crouching by the fire outside, cooking asida.

—Not now! she hissed, and rushed inside.

I waited for a few minutes, and then left. It was not until many days later that I saw her again, by the water pump.

—He won't let me, she said.

Her caretaker had been outraged, it seemed, when Maria was gone in the afternoons, given that it was that time when the women prepared meals and retrieved all the water for the night and the next morning. Women were not expected to venture out of their homes after dark, so the hours between school and sunset were vital for the performing of Maria's duties.

—I can talk to him, I offered.

I had spoken to other families since I had become a youth leader. If there was a gap in understanding between generations, I was often asked to mediate. "The boy who keeps his hands clean eats with his elders," Gop had taught me, and this lesson informed my behavior every day and served me well. When another girl in the troupe, a rail-thin actress named Adyuei, had been prevented from attending our meetings, I intervened. She first told her parents that I would like to talk to them. When they agreed to see me, I arrived the next evening with a gift of writing pads and pens, and sat with them for some time. I explained that Adyuei was essential to our group, and that she was doing very important work for the youth of the camp. Knowing that her parents, like Maria's, were depending on the windfall of her bride price, I appealed to their mercenary interests. I told her father that Adyuei would be far more attractive to her future husband with the skills of an actress, and that her increased visibility would only bring a more competitive market for her when she was ready to be married. All of my arguments worked on her father; they worked far better than I expected. Adyuei was not only allowed to attend all the rehearsals, but her father came with her occasionally, too, insisting that she receive prominent roles and specialized instruction from Miss Gladys. All this had worked, and so I thought it would work for the man who called Maria daughter, but she would not have it.

—No, no. Forget it. He's not that kind of man, she said.

Nothing would work for this man, she said. She had no plans to defy her caretaker, for she knew she would be beaten. And anyway, she said, being unable to perform in the troupe was the least of her worries. It was evidence of her openness and trust in me that she told me, that day at the water pump, that only three days prior, she had received her first period. As a youth educator, I had access to a good deal of information about health and hygiene, so I knew what this meant physiologically for Maria. More importantly, I knew it meant that in Sudanese society, she was now considered a woman. When Sudanese girls first menstruate, they are considered available for marriage and are very often claimed within days.

—Does anyone know? I asked.

—Shh! she whispered. —Not yet.

—Are you sure? How could your mother not know?

—She *doesn't* know, Sleeper. She asks me about it but she doesn't know. I'm too young to have it, anyway. No one else I know has had it. Now shh. I shouldn't have told you. Forget I said anything.

And she walked off.

That day Maria insisted that I not tell a soul of her status; she had not decided how to keep her discharges secret from her caretakers, but she was determined to do so as long as possible. This was not unprecedented at Kakuma, but it was uncommon. Most girls, even if they plan to fight off the prospect of an arranged marriage, do not conceal their womanhood. Most accept it, and some celebrate it. There are certain clans in southern Sudan who celebrate a girl's first period with a party attended by family and suitors from villages near and far. It serves as a coming-out event, alerting the bachelors of the region that a girl has become a woman. To some men, plucking their bride at that moment is ideal, for it provides for an unquestionable purity.

If I were to guess Maria's age at that time, it would have to be fourteen. But in Sudan it is not the age that is important, but more so the shape and maturity of a woman's body. And even I, who had known Maria since she was a twig of a girl, had taken notice of her signs of womanhood. In another life, one where she was not under the care of an angry man expecting a return on his investment, I might have sought to romance her. There was no girl with whom I had such understanding, no girl who felt so like an extension of my own soul. But unaccompanied minors like me were not considered viable mates for young women like Maria. We only complicated the plans of their caretakers; if there was a young man like me circling a girl like Maria, questions of her virginity inevitably arose. People like Maria and I could be friends only, and even then, friends of occasional meeting.

SPLA soldiers and commanders were among the busiest of those who shopped Kakuma for a desirable young bride. They would sweep through the camp, ascertaining through rumor and sight which young women they might add to their families. The rebels also came to Kakuma, and other camps in the countries surrounding Sudan, looking for recruits. Thousands of potential soldiers lived peacefully at our camp, and this fact created some consternation on the part of the rebels, and no limit of handwringing on the part of men my age.

The Dominics of the drama group had begun to talk seriously about the possibility of joining the SPLA; many felt useless at Kakuma. This happened periodically, especially when there were great advances won or great losses incurred by the rebels. The young men attending school or simply idling at the camp would discuss, with varying degrees of intensity, enlisting, either to bolster the flagging efforts of the rebel army, or to be there when the job was ready to be finished.

As if fully knowing the minds of the men my age, a phalanx of soldiers and commanders arrived in Kakuma one day, looking for as many young men as they could carry to war. Officially, there was not to be an SPLA presence at the camp, but former and current commanders moved through without check. They came with enough troop trucks to carry hundreds of young men away, if they could be persuaded to leave the camp and return to southern Sudan to fight.

A meeting was called for ten o'clock one night, in a building made of corrugated steel and mud. There were five SPLA officers sitting at a table, and before them, two hundred young men who had been asked and coerced to attend this informational meeting. The SPLA had a very bad reputation among many young men, and so many were skeptical of their presence. Some felt betrayed because though the SPLA recruited heavily from northern Bahr al-Ghazal, they had done little to protect the region from attack. Others disapproved of their use of child soldiers, while still others were simply dissatisfied with how long it was taking to win the war against the government of Sudan. And so Achor Achor and I, and all of the young men we knew, came to the meeting that night, in part out of sheer curiosity about what they would say, what angle they might use in trying to persuade us to take up arms and leave the relative safety of the camp. The room was crowded, and though Achor Achor found a seat near the front, I did not, and instead stood by the window. And while the room was full that night, many young men stayed as far away as they could. For many years, the SPLA dictated that deserters were to be executed on sight, and there were certainly a good number of deserters at Kakuma.

The commander in charge that night, a squat and imperious man named Santo Ayang, walked in, sat at the blue wooden table before us, and addressed this particular point first.

—If there are boys here who have left the army, do not worry, he said. —The laws about desertion are different now. You will be welcomed back to the army without penalty. Please tell your friends.

This sent an approving murmur through the audience.

—This is a new SPLA, a united SPLA, Commander Santo said. —And we are winning. You know we're winning. We have won at Yambio, Kaya, Nimule, and Rumbek. We now control the majority of what's important in southern Sudan, and we need only to finish the job. You have a choice, boys… Well, you are not boys any longer. Many of you are men, and you are strong and have been educated. And now you have a choice. How many of you young men would like to stay in Kakuma for the rest of your lives?

None among us raised their hands.

—So then. How do you think you will leave this place?

No one said a word.

—You expect to return home when the war is won, I suppose. But how will this war be won? Who will win it? Who is fighting this war? I ask you. You are here in Kakuma, having your food provided to you, buying expensive shoes...

Here he pointed to a boy standing on a chair in the corner. He was wearing new sneakers, of immaculate leatherette, white as bone.

—And you are waiting here, in safety, until we finish the work. Then you will return and benefit from the shedding of our blood. I take it from your silence that this is indeed your plan. It is a shrewd plan, I admit, but do you think we are an army of rabbits and women? Who is fighting this war, I ask you! *Men* are fighting this war, and I don't care if they call you Lost *Boys* here at this camp. You are men and it is your duty to fight. If you do not fight, this war is lost, southern Sudan is lost, and you will raise your children at Kakuma, and they will raise their children here.

A young man named Mayuen Fire jumped up.

—I will go!

The commander smiled. —Are you ready?

—I am ready, Mayuen Fire shouted.

We all laughed.

—Quiet! the commander barked. The room grew quiet, in part because the commander had demanded it, and in part because we realized Mayuen Fire was serious. —At least there is one man among all these boys, Santo continued. —I'm very happy. We leave in three days. Thursday night there will be trucks outside the west gate. We'll see you there. Bring your clothes and other belongings.

The new recruit, in his excitement, did not know what to do at that point, and so walked out of the building. It was awkward, given the room was so crowded that it took him a few minutes to step over all of us to reach the door. Then, realizing he might miss important information at the meeting, he returned and watched from a window.

—Now, Commander Santo said. —We have a special guest tonight.

A man who had been sitting behind the commander now stepped forward, a twisted cane in his hand. He was a robust old grandfather, grey-haired and toothless, with a frail jaw and tiny eyes. He wore a black suit jacket and light-blue pajama pants, and a camouflage hat on his small wrinkled head. Commander Santo shook his hand and presented him to us.

—This man before you, a chief from Nuba, will illuminate how despicable are the methods of Bashir and his army. Perhaps he will convince the rest of you to follow the courageous young man who has already volunteered. Kuku Kori Kuku was a powerful and respected man. But he made a mistake: he allowed himself to trust the government of Khartoum. He's here to tell us the results of that demonstration of trust.

—Thank you, Commander Santo.

—Tell them the treachery you experienced.

—With your permission, Commander, I will.

—Tell them the deception and the murder you witnessed.

The chief opened his mouth to speak but did not get the chance. Not yet.

—When you're ready, please tell us. Take your time, Santo added.

Finally the chief waited, his hands on his cane, eyes closed. When he was satisfied that Commander Santo would not interrupt him, he opened his eyes and began.

—Boys, I was the chief of a village called Jebel Otoro. As you know, we in Nuba were the victims of repeated attacks from the government and the murahaleen. I lost my son in one of the attacks; he was burned in our home while I was traveling to another village to mediate a dispute. And as you know, thousands of Nubans have been sent to the "peace villages," the internment camps you have heard about.

At this point I took notice of Achor Achor, who was sitting near the front. Watching his face became more interesting than watching the words come from the mouth of Kuku Kori Kuku. Already, from the man's first words, Achor Achor was rapt.

—This way, the government can watch us, and make sure we cannot fight against them. And these camps have attracted many Nubans who want no part of the conflict. There they are kept under the watch of soldiers, and are fed poorly. At these peace villages, the women are repeatedly abducted and raped. The government has made clear that if the people of Nuba do not bring themselves to live in the peace villages, they are therefore taking the side of the SPLA and are thus the enemy. Like you, the people of Nuba had suffered for some time and we longed for a way to end this.

Achor Achor's tongue extended from his lips, as if he were tasting the air for the next turn to the story.

—We were happy, then, when the government asked for a meeting. Bashir was said to have personally requested a meeting with all the chiefs of Nuba. And I must admit that this affected our pride; we were very impressed with ourselves. We were called by Khartoum for a meeting and we went willingly, like fools. We trusted, and we should not have trusted. Will we ever learn a lesson from this war, from the history of this country? We trusted! Our grandfathers trusted, and their grandfathers trusted, and look where it's gotten us.

The chief's voice was rising, and when it did, it cracked and wavered. I remembered the story of the chiefs who had originally agreed to stitch southern Sudan together with the north, a mistake most knew enough to regret.

—So yes, we were proud and so we went. All sixty-eight Nuban chiefs arrived for the meeting at the appointed day. Many of the chiefs traveled many days to get there, some by foot. When we arrived, we realized that we had not been brought to meet with representatives from Khartoum. It had been a trick. All of us, the chiefs of dozens of villages, were herded onto trucks and taken to a new prison, in a former hospital; I had been to the hospital as a young man. They held us in two small rooms for two days, with little food or water. We demanded that they free us. We thought that perhaps this was the action of a rogue group of government soldiers. We imagined that the government, who had organized this conference, would be outraged by this action and would soon intervene on our behalf. But not all of the chiefs were this optimistic.

I looked around me, and the faces of the boys in the room seemed already to know the fate of the assembled chiefs. Already they were ready to fight. Achor Achor's face was twisted into a terrible frown.

—We tried to plead with the guards, explaining that we were tribal chiefs who had committed no crime. You are enemies of the government, and that is crime enough, one guard said. That is when we knew that our future was in question. But we thought the worst they would do would be to keep us in a sort of peace camp for chiefs—perhaps more severe, perhaps just separated from our people. We expected that we might be detained there for years, even, until the end of the war. But the government had different plans. That night in the early hours, they roused us and pushed us out of the hospital prison and into the night. We were loaded onto military transport trucks, and as we sat in the back of these trucks, finally we were scared. They had tied our hands behind our backs, and we felt very helpless. In the truck, we tried to assist each other, tried to undo our bindings. But the truck was traveling up a rough mountain road and it was very dark. We could see nothing in the truck, and we were thrown about by the winding and poorly made road. Also, many of these chiefs were old men, you must remember, and not very strong. So there we were: we were the leaders of Nuba, and we had no way to help each other. It was humiliating.

Achor Achor was shaking his head slowly, tears in his eyes.

—Soon the trucks stopped. Get them out! the officer of the soldiers yelled. We stepped out of the truck one by one, and soon the soldiers lost patience. They threw the last chiefs from the trucks and those chiefs, one very old man, fell hard on the road, for his hands were bound. We all stood on the road and they made us march. The moon was half full and bright. We saw the faces of the soldiers, and among the soldiers saw one Dinka man. I remember looking at him for a long time, trying to see what had happened to him. I assumed he had become a Muslim, and then had been convinced that we were the enemy of his country and his faith. Still, though, I thought I saw him look away from us. I thought that perhaps he was ashamed. But I could be imagining all that. I wanted him to be ashamed but perhaps he was as committed to his task as were the rest of the soldiers.

Achor Achor was the picture of barely suppressed rage.

—We were taken to a ridge on the mountain, and they lined us up. There were twenty soldiers with automatic rifles. One chief attempted to run down the mountain. He was shot immediately. At that point the soldiers began to shoot. They shot each chief, in the back of the head if they could. A few men tried to fight with their feet and they were shot in the chest and face and anywhere else. It was the worst thing I have ever seen, to see such men fighting for their lives, kicking and jumping with their hands bound. This was no way to die. It was a terrible mess, all of it.

—This took some time, the executions? the commander asked.

—No, no. It was all over very quick. It was over in a few minutes.

—But they didn't shoot you. Why not?

The chief snorted. —Of course they shot me! They shot me with everyone else! I was a chief, and I had to die! They shot me in the back of the head, yes, but the bullet went through and came out my jaw.

Some of the boys in the room did not believe this and the chief took notice.

—You don't believe me? Look at this.

He revealed a jagged scar at the corner of his jaw.

—That is where the bullet left me. And here is the bullet.

From his pocket he brought forth a rounded and rusted thing, looking nothing like something that could have penetrated a man's skull.

—It didn't hurt. I thought I was dead, so I felt little pain. I lay on the ground, wondering at the strangeness of my sight and my thoughts. I was dead, but I could still see. I was seeing the body of another man, another chief, and I could hear the boots of the soldiers. I could hear the truck starting again. And all the while I wondered why I was hearing all this. I did not expect to see and hear after death like this.

—I thought that perhaps I was not yet dead. That I was still dying. So I lay there, unable to move, waiting to die. I thought of my family, of the people of my village. Here was their chief, lying among sixty-seven more, all dead. All trusting fools. I thought of the shame of all this, all these chiefs dying in one place, killed by these young government soldiers who knew nothing about life. I cursed our stupidity. We were trusting and foolish, as our ancestors had been fifty years earlier. This would be the end of us, I thought. If it was this easy to kill all the chiefs, then certainly killing our children would be a very easy task indeed.

—I did not realize until later that I was still alive. The light came in the morning and I was still seeing and thinking, and this caused me to believe that I might still be alive. I attempted to move my arms. To my surprise, they moved. It occurred to me that there might be a new group of soldiers coming soon to bury us, the evidence of the massacre, so I rose and I walked away. I simply walked back to my village. It took me three days and I saw very few people along the way. When I reached the first village on my journey, I met the deputy chief there and he greeted me with great enthusiasm. He wanted to know how the meeting had gone. I had to tell him that it had not gone well.

—He and his people nursed me and brought me to a clinic nearby, where they sewed the hole in my face. After a week I walked on, escorted by the deputy, back to my village, where they had heard about what had happened. I wouldn't be safe there, so I was kept hidden until I could escape one week later. Eventually I met others traveling to Kakuma. It was decided this would be the only safe place for me.

—Boys, we can never be one with the north, with Khartoum. We can never trust them. Until there is a separate south, a New Sudan, we won't have peace. We can never forget this. To them we are slaves, and even if we are not working in their homes and on their farms, we will always be thought of as a lesser people. Think of it: the end result of their plan is to make the entire country an Islamic state. They plan to convert us all. They are doing it bit by bit already. Three-fourths of this country is already Muslim. They don't have far to go. So remember: we have independence, or we will no longer exist as a people. They will subsume those they can, and kill the rest. We cannot be one with them, and we cannot trust them. Never again. You promise me?

We nodded.

—Now fight these monsters! he roared. —I beg you.

Twelve others pledged their support that night. Ten of those ended up leaving with the SPLA on Thursday, along with fourteen more who had not been at the meeting—mostly sons, brothers, cousins, and nephews of SPLA commanders. I cannot say that I ever seriously considered joining the SPLA at that time. I was busy in the camp, with my theater projects and Miss Gladys, but Achor Achor spent two days in turmoil, coming to me each night to help with his thinking.

—I think I have to go. Don't I? he asked.

—I don't know. I don't know if it makes a difference, I said.

—You don't think the war can be won.

—I don't know. It's been so many years already. I don't know if anyone would know if the war was won. How would we know?

—If we had independence.

—You really think that would ever happen?

We sat with that thought for a moment.

—I think I need to go, he said. —It's me who should be fighting this war. I'm from Aweil. If I don't go back and fight, then who will?

—They won't station you at Aweil.

—Then I'll get my own gun and go back to Aweil.

—There won't be anyone in Aweil. No one will still be there.

—Commander Santo said the SPLA is different now.

—Maybe it is. Maybe it isn't. But look at you. You've never fought in your life. You wear glasses now. How will you shoot if your glasses break?

I did not really think this argument would work, but it did. It worked immediately, and that was the end of Achor Achor's army career. I am fairly certain that he was simply looking for a good reason not to join, something he could say when or if he were ever asked. He never spoke of the SPLA again.

I do not want to be indelicate but it is important to note that we were not long past puberty, and some of the younger boys in the class were still in the thick of hormonal change and a deeper awareness of the opposite sex. Thus what Miss Gladys did next stirred havoc among us young men at a time when there was already sufficient physiological turmoil. My first hairs had recently appeared in small thickets, a few patches in my underwear, one in each armpit. I was later than many other boys, but we were all developmentally tardy, we were told, due to the trauma we had endured and our ongoing state of malnutrition. But at that juncture of our development, our Miss Gladys had a very strong impact on our lives. With her open and confident sexuality, she was the constant igniter of everything flammable within us. It was enough to see her twice a week with the drama group, but when she walked into our history class she took it too far.

—Ah, Dominic! Good to see you! she said.

This was a semester after she began with the Napata Drama Group. We had not been told that there would be a new history teacher. Our previous instructor, a Kenyan named George, seemed capable and permanent.

—You're teaching this class? I said.

—You sound unhappy to see me, she said with a theatrical pout.

I did not know what to say. Her presence in Napata was manageable, given I could mask my nerves and weak stomach under the guise of my acting. But with her as my history teacher, I knew immediately that I would not be able to concentrate; my grades would drop. All of the inherent problems issuing from her presence were doubled by a new wrinkle to her personality. Something about history brought out the provocateur in her, and this simply destroyed most of the fifty-eight boys who sat on the ground beneath her.

She didn't talk about sex outright, but she seemed to find a way, during her lectures, to include the sexual habits of whomever she discussed, no matter how incongruous the context.

—Genghis Khan was a very harsh dictator, she might begin. —He was cruel to his enemies but he loved women very much. He had a great appetite, it was said. The rumor is that he had impregnated over two hundred women with his seed, and often visited three or more women in one night. He was also known to take certain tools into bed with…

The first day, one boy fainted. We were utterly unprepared for both the discussion of sexual appetites and for such discussion to spring forth from the mouth of the goddess named Gladys. Why was she doing this? She controlled us all, fifty-eight

381

boys, she possessed us utterly and sometimes without mercy. The discussion about the sexual mores of Genghis Khan and his ilk went on for the full period and left us spent.

Our confused and longing faces had an effect on her, and that effect was to spur her on, to the point where she made a point to insert some sexual fact or aside in each day's lesson, and we could count on it, and dressed appropriately. The fainting boy brought with him wads of paper to stuff in his ears when she began expounding on the subject, for his parents were in the camp and he was sure they would know if he returned home with that sort of information in his head.

Among the few girls in the class, there was a broad sort of annoyance with Miss Gladys's antics and the boys' obsession with her. But there was one girl, younger than the rest, who seemed to enjoy Miss Gladys, and laughed at her jokes even when we didn't recognize them as jokes. This girl was Tabitha Duany Aker. I had not seen her for a semester and a summer, since we had been in home economics together, but I was very happy to see her again, and to see that it was only she who laughed when Miss Gladys made the joke about Idi Amin in the sauna. The joke was met by silence by all except for a loud guffaw from the side row. Tabitha covered her mouth and exchanged a long look of mutual admiration with Miss Gladys, and from that day on I took an interest in her, and tried to see her outside of class, at any opportunity at all. In many ways she reminded me of Maria—in her wit, her quick way with words, her heart-shaped face—but she was more girlish than Maria. She had a wild femininity about her that she tamed and mastered, I believe, by studying every movement and gesture of Miss Gladys.

Meanwhile, the rest of the boys, those who had just become acquainted with our new history teacher, spent a good deal of time alone and together thinking about our new teacher, about her various lessons. Miss Gladys became the most famous and sought-after teacher at Kakuma, and with her, the notoriety of us Dominics grew. There were four Dominics in that history class, and because she seemed very familiar with us, the rest of the boys looked at us with murder in their eyes, for we clearly had an inside track to her heart. Whenever Miss Gladys was mentioned, her favorites were also noted, the four Dominics from the Drama Group. Our real names were all supplanted by Dominic only, and our notoriety bound us closer. When we played basketball together, our team was the Dominics. When we walked by, people said, "There go the Dominics." And the numbers of random boys wanting suddenly to study acting—and history, in our class, no matter where in the camp they lived—grew unabated. Miss

Gladys allowed none of them to join, because we did not need more boys.

We had too many boys already, and it was becoming a problem that because the troupe had only two girls, the majority of the women in our plays had to be played by men. In particular, the women's roles were played by one of the Dominics, whose real name was Anthony Chuut Guot. He was fearless about wearing a dress, or any other female clothing, and was unafraid to walk and talk like a woman. It was for his courage that we nicknamed him Madame Zero, after a cross-dressing comic-book spy. This was a name he enjoyed, at least initially. It was when the nickname extended beyond the Dominics that he became less amused, and this led to his and Miss Gladys's insistence that we recruit or somehow find at least one young woman for the club.

Thus, on one glorious afternoon, Tabitha joined the Napata Drama Group.

Tabitha was a friend to Abuk, the oldest of Gop's daughters, so even outside of classes such as home ec and history, I had been able to observe her, and knew certain things about her. I knew first of all that she was permitted to join the group because her mother had been an actress herself, and was an enlightened woman who wanted Tabitha to take advantage of any opportunities in the camp. I also knew that she had a face unsettling in its perfection. When I first knew Maria, I had feelings for her, but looking at her, speaking to her, was not a challenge for me. She seemed as much a sibling as anything else, and I felt when standing before her that she was a young person like me, that we were both refugees, that nothing about her intimidated me.

But Tabitha was not like this. I was not alone in knowing that Tabitha's face was unparalleled in its symmetry. Her skin was without blemish, the lashes on her eyes of a length that defied any precedent. I knew all this from far away, and after observing her more closely I knew that when she walked she walked slowly and deliberately, no part of her body moving with any effort whatsoever. From a distance, it seemed that she floated, her head never bobbing, the movement of her legs barely detectable under her skirts. I knew this and I knew that she touched the forearms of her friends as she spoke. She did this frequently, and when she laughed she would grip the forearm and then pat it twice.

I knew all this, and I knew that I was for some time utterly hoarse and dim-witted in her presence. She was younger than I by a few years at least, and I was far taller than her, and yet near her I felt that I was a child, a child who should be playing with dolls in the shade of her skirt. I alternately wanted to be close to her, to have her always within sight, and then, a moment later, to exist in a world where she did not. It seemed the only way that I might be able to concentrate again.

The first few times she attended the meetings of the drama group, she, like everyone else, was captivated only by the antics of the humorous Dominic. She laughed at everything he said, placing her hand on his forearm repeatedly, even squeezing once or twice. I knew that Dominic's affections were committed elsewhere, but still, it was difficult to watch. If she ever took the hand of another young man, I was sure I would not recover. The only solace I had was in knowing that I would see her every week, in close quarters, as we wrote and produced our plays—whether or not she ever looked directly at me, or spoke to me. She had done neither.

The drama group was thriving, in part due to the efforts of Tabitha and the Dominics and our libidinous teacher, but also due to the generous funding we began to enjoy. Our Youth and Culture Program began to receive direct aid from an organization called the Wakachiai Project, a Tokyo nonprofit. Their goal was to instruct the youth of Kakuma in sports, drama, first aid, and disaster management, but they also found a way to outfit a full refugee marching band with clothes and instruments and a part-time instructor specializing in woodwinds. When the project began, they sent one of their own to Kakuma, a young man of twenty-four named Noriyaki Takamura, who would become one of the most important men I would ever know, and from whom I would learn about trying to love someone who was fragile and very far away.

Soon after the project started, I was chosen as Noriyaki's right-hand man. I had been working for the Youth and Culture Project for two years and was well-known among the Sudanese youth and the NGO workers. It did not seem controversial that I would be given such a position, but my appointment did not sit well then or later with the Kenyans, who, we presumed, wanted every job for themselves. I did not care, and happily accepted the job, which brought higher pay and even an office. For a Sudanese to work in an office! We were given a small office in the UN compound, and in it we had a satellite phone and two computers, one that Noriyaki had brought with him and one that he ordered for me. He did it the first day we worked together.

—So here we are, Dominic, he said.

As I said, the name Dominic had overtaken us all.

—Yes sir, I said.

—I'm not sir. I'm Noriyaki.

—Yes. I am sorry.

—So are you excited?

—Yes I am, sir.

—Noriyaki.

—Yes. I know this.

—So we need a computer for you. Have you used a computer?

—No. I have seen people work on them.

—Can you type?

—Yes, I lied. I don't know why I chose to lie.

—Where did you learn to type? On a typewriter?

—No, I'm sorry. I misunderstood. I cannot type.

—You can't type?

—No sir.

Noriyaki exhaled enough for three lungs.

—No, but I will try.

—We need to get you a computer.

Noriyaki began to make phone calls. An hour later he had reached his project's office in Nairobi and had ordered a laptop computer for me. I did not believe that the computer would come to Kakuma or to me but I appreciated Noriyaki's gesture.

—Thank you, I said.

—Of course, he said.

And that day we did very little outside of talking about his girlfriend at home, a picture of whom was set on his desk. Noriyaki had just unveiled the photo, in which she was wearing a white shirt and white shorts while holding a tennis racket. Her smile was small and brave, as if in defiance of tears she had just dried from her face.

—Her name is Wakana, he said.

—She looks like a very nice girl, I said.

—We're engaged.

—Oh good, I said. I had recently been told, in one of my English texts, that it was rude to say Congratulations in such a situation.

—It's not official yet, he said.

—Oh. Will you elope?

—No, we'll get married in a proper wedding. But I have to propose in person.

I did not know exactly how things worked in Japan, and was only vaguely familiar with the workings of marriage in the Western world.

—When will you do this? I asked.

I was not sure how many questions I was allowed along these lines, but there seemed to be nothing that offended Noriyaki in any way.

—When I go home, I guess. I can't get her to visit me here.

We sat together for a moment, staring at the picture, at the young woman's sad smile.

Already I missed Noriyaki, on that first day. I had not pondered the idea that he would leave Kakuma someday, even though I knew well that no one stayed at Kakuma but the Kenyans, and even they didn't stay for more than a few years. Noriyaki became my good friend on that first day, but he was not only my friend; Noriyaki was loved by all. He was far shorter than any Sudanese men I knew, but he was athletic, very quick, and quite competent at any sport that was played at Kakuma. He joined pick-up games in soccer, volleyball, basketball. He seemed to replace the basketball net once a week; he always had new white nylon nets. And because he kept replacing the net, it was fairly clear to all that the nets were disappearing, to be sold at Kakuma Town, with the knowledge that they would quickly be replaced by the stocky Japanese man whose name everyone knew, or at least attempted.

—Noyakee!

—Noki!

From the start, Noriyaki was always with the Sudanese people, in the camp, walking the paths, asking what we needed. He ate with the refugees, moved among them. When he drove his car, he would stop and pick up anyone who asked. Any person who was going to the compound he would carry, until his truck was overfull with smiling riders who all loved Noriyaki, or however one interpreted his name.

—Nakayaki!

—Norakaka!

None of it mattered to Noriyaki, who walked through Kakuma with a shy grin, happy because he was doing essential work and because, I imagined, he knew that in Kyoto there was a very beautiful young woman waiting for him.

* * *

One week after Noriyaki arrived and ordered the computer for me, something interesting happened: the computer arrived. There was an air shipment that day from Nairobi, primarily emergency medical supplies, but on the plane there was also a box, its corners perfectly square, and in that box, there was a laptop that had been ordered for me. It was rare in Kakuma to find a box that well-formed, with corners so crisp, but there it was, on the floor of the office, and Noriyaki grinned at me and I smiled back. I always smiled when I looked at Noriyaki; it was difficult not to.

The box arrived when we were both in the office, eating our lunches, and when Noriyaki opened it for me—I did not trust myself not to damage it—I wanted to hug Noriyaki or at least shake his hand, which I did, with a good deal of enthusiasm.

Noriyaki opened two orange Fantas, and we toasted the arrival of the computer. Toasting with Fanta became a tradition between us, and that day we drank our Fantas slowly, looking down on the box and its extraordinary contents, wrapped in plastic and encased in black foam. The laptop computer was worth perhaps ten times the value of all of my possessions and those of my Kakuma siblings combined. To entrust me with such a thing gave me a feeling of competence that I had not known since I was perhaps six years old, allowed to hold my father's Chinese rifle. I thanked Noriyaki again, and then pretended to know how to operate the computer.

—Take it home and practice, Noriyaki said finally.

—Take it where?

—Take it home and practice.

Noriyaki had noticed, in the days since the laptop came, that I had no idea what I was doing. I spent an hour one day attempting to turn the machine on. When I did turn it on, typing took me an extraordinary amount of time, and my work was made more difficult because the nervous sweat coming from my forehead and arms and fingers was drenching the laptop's keys. This made any kind of training, much less work, impossible.

—We'll send you to train, he said. —You can take computer classes.

—Where?

—Nairobi. We'll write it into the budget.

Noriyaki was a magician. Nairobi! Write it into the budget! I did not understand why Noriyaki would come to Kakuma, and why he stayed in Kakuma, especially when he had a family and a ladyfriend in Japan. For a very long time, I tried to figure out what exactly was wrong with him, what might have prevented him from getting an actual job in Japan. What would have caused him to travel so far for such a poor-paying and difficult position as he had here, with us? But I knew that Noriyaki did everything well, so it did not follow that he would be forced to take a job in a refugee camp. He was skilled on the computer, was personable, and got along famously with the Kenyans, the Europeans, the British and Americans, and especially the Sudanese, who seemed uniformly to adore him. He had no physical deformities that I could discern. I discussed Noriyaki with Gop's family one night over dinner. I had brought the laptop home, and Gop had insisted on having it within view as we ate dinner together. It was indeed a strange object to see in the sort of place we lived. It was like a bar of solid gold resting in a mountain of dung.

—He could be some sort of criminal in Japan, Ayen offered.

—Japan is very competitive, Gop mused. —Maybe he got tired of that life.

But they did not want to spoil it and I did not want to spoil it. It was an odd thing: there were few jobs for adult Sudanese with the UNHCR and NGOs, but they needed someone young who would understand the needs of the youth, so I was getting one of the best NGO salaries of any refugee at Kakuma. The project purportedly only had funding for a certain amount of time, but Noriyaki always talked about extending it.

—The Japanese government has plenty of money, he said.

He said that he and I would have to make sure to use the existing funding well, though, to involve refugees in the planning and stretch every dollar.

I asked him why he came to Kenya in the first place. Why the Sudanese? I asked.

—When I was growing up, my teacher had us do a report on a country in Africa. He was very interested in the continent, so he spent probably too much time on Africa. I wasn't this teacher's favorite student, I have to say. So he went around the room, asking everyone which country they wanted to research, and he called on me last. By then, only Sudan was left.

I would have suspected as much, but still, this fact hurt my heart. I thought of it many times over the next years, that Sudan was not wanted by any of these Japanese schoolchildren.

—There wasn't too much information about your country, I have to say. It was a very short report, he said.

He laughed, and I managed to laugh. It was a goal of his, it seemed. He walked in the office every day, I am sure, determined to get me to laugh, no matter the subject matter. He talked about his family and about his girlfriend—his fiancée. Wakana he missed with an agony that was tangible. Many days I arrived at work to find him under his desk, on the phone. I am not sure why he chose to talk to her under his desk, but usually he did. After he was finished, I often found notes on the floor, as if he were consulting lists of things to say to her. When he would pine for her, I would listen until I could not listen any more.

—Your *girlfriend?* I would say. —You're complaining about missing your girl-friend? I don't have a family!

He would laugh and say, —Yeah, but you're used to it.

We found this very funny, and it became a refrain between us: —Yes, but you're used to it. And though I laughed about it, it also caused me to wonder whether this was a truth. It did seem to be true, that he missed his fiancée more than I missed my family, because he was certain she was alive. My feelings for my own family were more distant and vague, for I could not picture them, and did not know if they were alive or dead, in Sudan or elsewhere. Noriyaki, though, had his mother and father and two siblings, and he knew every day where they were.

—My family is your family now, he said one day.

They knew all about me, he said, and wanted very much to meet me. He added a picture of his parents and younger sister to the desktop, and he insisted I think of them as mine. It was a strange thing that his plan worked; I did grow to think of his family as people who were watching over me, expecting good things from me. I stared at the picture of his parents—his mother and father both in black, their hands clasped before them, standing before a giant statue of a charging soldier—and I believed that some day we would meet in their home, perhaps just before Noriyaki married Wakana, when I visited Japan as a prosperous man. I was not confident this day would come, but it pleased me to think about it.

One day a man came to Noriyaki. The man was a Sudanese elder, an educated man, respected among the Dinka. He had finished three years at the University of Khartoum, and his opinion was sought on any number of matters, political matters in particular. Today, though, he was agitated, and asked to speak to Noriyaki imme-diately. Noriyaki asked him inside, and gave him a seat.

—I would like to stand, he said.

—Okay, Noriyaki said.

—I need to stand because what I have to say is very important and upsetting.

—Okay. I'm listening.

—You need to talk to your people, your government, Mr. Noriyaki. It is the Chinese and the Malaysians who are making this war worse. These two countries alone own 60 percent of the oil interests in Sudan. You know how much oil they take? Millions of barrels a year, and it's growing! China plans to get half its oil from Sudan by 2010!

—But sir...

—And we all know that the oil is what is driving the war. Bashir wants only to keep the south in chaos and the SPLA away from the oil fields. He does this with weapons from where? From China, Mr. Noriyaki. China wants the south insecure, because this keeps out other countries who don't want their hands dirty with the human-rights abuses around this oil extraction! Your government is providing arms that are used against civilians, and they are also buying the oil that is ill-gotten and is the reason hundreds of thousands have died. I have come here to appeal to you, as a representative of your government, to speak out against these injustices!

When Noriyaki finally had a chance to speak, he told the man he was not Chinese. The man spent five minutes digesting this information.

—I do not mean to be rude, but you have the look of a Chinese.

—No sir. I'm Japanese. We're not such great friends of the Chinese, either.

The man left, confused and disappointed.

There was blame everywhere for what was happening to the Sudanese. And the more we understood how we were connected to so many of the problems of the world, the more we understood the web of money and power and oil that made our suffering possible, the more we felt sure that something would be done to save southern Sudan. And a series of bombings brought us, we thought, to the forefront of the world's mind.

I was refereeing a youth soccer game when I heard the news from a pair of boys passing on a bicycle. —They bombed Nairobi! And Dar es Salaam!

Someone had bombed the U.S. embassies in Kenya and Tanzania. The camp ceased all activity. The Kenyans stopped working. Wherever there were televisions or radios, and there were not many of the former, they were surrounded. Hundreds dead, the reports said, five thousand injured. We watched for days as bodies were pulled from the rubble. The Kenyans at Kakuma raged for answers. When it was learned

390

that it was the work of Islamic fundamentalists, there was trouble at Kakuma. It was not a good time to be a Somali or an Ethiopian. The Muslims of any nation kept themselves hidden those days, and made sure to be clear about their opposition to the work of these terrorists, to Osama bin Laden. This was the first I had heard his name, but soon everyone knew of him, and knew that he was living in Sudan. Gop spent every moment next to the radio, and lectured me at dinner.

—This is bin Laden's work. And it's Sudan that will pay for this crime. They helped him, and they will pay. And it's about time they did.

Gop seemed almost happy about this development. He was sure that bin Laden's bombings would turn the world's attention to Sudan, and that this could only be good for us.

—Finally they'll get this man! He's been everywhere. He was at the center of the Islamist revolution, Achak! He provided so much money to Sudan! This man funded everything—machinery, planes, roads. He was involved in agriculture, business, banking, everything. And he brought thousands of al Qaeda operatives to Sudan, to train and plan. The companies he set up in Sudan were used to get money to all the other terrorist cells all over the world. This was all because of the cooperation of Khartoum! Without a government sponsoring these things, it's much more difficult for someone like bin Laden, who is not satisfied with blowing up travel offices. So he owns a construction company in Sudan, and so he can buy explosives from anyone he wants, in whatever quantities he needs. It seems legitimate, right? And then with Khartoum's help, he can ship these explosives to Yemen or Jordan or anywhere else.

—But he wasn't the only terrorist in Sudan, right? I asked.

—No, there were groups from everywhere. Hezbollah had people there, Islamic Jihad, so many groups. But Osama is the worst. He claimed to have trained the guys in Somalia who killed the American soldiers there. He had issued a fatwa there against any Americans in Somalia. And then he financed the bombing of the World Trade Center in New York. You know this building?

I shook my head.

—A huge building, as high as the clouds. Bin Laden paid to have a man drive a truck into the basement of the building to blow it up. And then he tried to kill Mubarak in Egypt. All the men involved in that plot were from Sudan, and bin Laden paid for everything. This man is a big problem. Terrorists could not do so much before him. But he has so much money that things become possible. He brings more terrorists into the world, because he can pay them, gives them a good life. Until they kill themselves, that is.

A few days later, Gop's expectations came true, or seemed to. Again I was refereeing a soccer game when a UN truck drove by with two Kenyan aid workers in the back, bringing the good news.

—Clinton bombed Khartoum! they yelled. —Khartoum is under attack!

The game stopped amid wild celebrating. That day and that night there was considerable excitement in the Sudanese regions of Kakuma. There was talk about what this might mean, and the consensus was that it indicated that the United States was clearly angry at Sudan, that they were being blamed for the bombings in Kenya and Tanzania. It proved, everyone thought, beyond any doubt, that the United States sided with the SPLA, and that they disapproved of the government in Khartoum. Of course, some refugee pundits were more ambitious in their thinking. Gop, for example, who thought that independence for southern Sudan was imminent.

—This is it, Achak! he said. —This is the beginning of the end! When the U.S. decides to bomb someone, that is the end. Look what happened to Iraq when they invaded Kuwait. Once the U.S. wants to punish you, there is trouble. Wow, this is it. Now the U.S. will overthrow Khartoum in no time at all, and then we will return home, and we will get money from the oil, and the border between north and south will be established, and there will be a New Sudan. I think it will all happen within the next eighteen months. You watch.

I loved and admired Gop Chol, but about political matters—about any matters concerning the future of Sudan—he was invariably wrong.

But in smaller ways, a great deal of change was afoot among the people of southern Sudan, and there were developments that might be considered hopeful. Sudanese customs were bent and broken at Kakuma with more frequency than they would have been had there been no war, had eighty thousand people not been in a refugee camp run by a progressive-minded international consortium. My own attitudes and ideas certainly would not have been as liberal as they became, but because I was a youth educator, I became well-versed in the language of health and the human body, of sexually transmitted diseases and prophylactic measures. Often I spoke too informally with young women, and confused the language of health class with the language of love. I once ruined my chances with a young woman named Frances by asking if she was developing correctly for her age. My exact words were:

—Hello Frances, I have just been to health class, and I was wondering how your feminine parts were developing.

It's one of the things that one says when young, and from which there is no escape. After that, she and her friends had a very low opinion of me, and the words have haunted me for many years after.

I learned many important lessons, first among them the fact that making forward statements in English was considered more acceptable than in Dinka. Because our grasp of English was tenuous, tone and precise meaning in that language was amorphous and shifting. I could never say "I love you" to a new girl in Dinka, for she would know exactly its meaning, but in English, the same words might be considered charming. Thus I used English a good deal, always in the interest of appearing charming. It did not always work.

But I spent a good deal of time calibrating my approach to girls, and when I was ready to inquire about Tabitha's interest in me, I was anything but bold. I knew by then that Tabitha was that rarest of girls who was still allowed to go to school, whose mother was at Kakuma and was enlightened enough to afford her a range of opportunities, academic and even those related to friendships with boys like me.

There was a certain day each year called Refugee Day, and I am quite sure it was the day that half of all youth relationships at Kakuma began or ended. On this day, June 20 each year, from morning to dusk, all the refugees of Kakuma celebrated, and there was less adult supervision, and more mingling of nationalities and castes, than at any other time of year. They celebrated not the fact that they were refugees or were living in northwest Kenya, but instead the simple existence and survival of their culture, however tattered. There were exhibitions of art, demonstrations of ethnic dances, there was food and music and, from the Sudanese, many speeches.

This was my opportunity to speak to Tabitha, who I was tracking all day. When she watched a traditional Burundian dance, I watched her. When she sampled food from Congo, I watched her from behind a display of Somali arts and crafts. And when the day was waning, and there was only a few minutes before she and all the girls would be expected to retreat to their homes, I strode to her with confidence that surprised even me. I was four years older than she was, I told myself. This is a young person, someone around whom you should not feel like a child. And so I walked to her with a serious face and when I stood behind her—she had had her back turned to me during my approach, which made it far easier—I tapped her on the shoulder. She turned to me, very surprised. She looked to my left and right, surprised to find me alone.

—Tabitha, for a long time, I said, —I have tried to talk to you about something, but the opportunity never presented itself. I was not sure how you would react to what I wanted to propose.

She stared up at me. She was not very tall at the time. Her head barely reached my chin. —What are you talking about? she said.

There is no lonelier feeling than when a proposal you have rehearsed is rejected out of hand. But through adrenaline and plain stubbornness, I continued.

—I like you and would like to go on a date with you.

This was how we said things at that time, but it did not mean that a real date would ever take place. It was unacceptable for a young man and woman to go off alone together, to a restaurant or even for a walk. A date, then, might mean a meeting at church, or in another public setting, where it would be known only to Tabitha and myself that a date was taking place.

Tabitha looked at me and smiled as if she had been only trying to cause me suffering. She did this often, in those days and in the future—all the years I've known her.

—I'll let you know at a later time, she said.

I was not surprised. It was not customary for a girl to give her answer immediately. Usually, a time would be arranged, a few days later, when the answer would be given either in person or through an emissary. If no appointment was made, it would mean the answer was no.

In this case, the next day, I learned through Abuk that the answer would come at church on Sunday, at the south entrance, after Mass. Those intervening days were torturous but tolerable, and when the time came, she was exactly where she said she would be.

—How was the homework that you gave to yourself?

This was my attempt at charm.

—What do you mean?

What I meant was that it might be considered humorous that instead of answering my first question, about a possible date, when I asked it, she went home to think about it for five days. But this was not very humorous, at least not the way I put it.

—Nothing. Sorry. Forget it, I said.

She agreed to forget it. She forgot a lot of what I said. She was merciful that way.

—I've been thinking about your question, Achak, and I have come to a decision. She was always spectacularly dramatic.

—And I've asked around about you… and I haven't heard anything bad. She had not talked to Frances, apparently.

—So I accept the date, she said.

—Oh thank God! I said, taking the Lord's name in vain for the first time in my life, but not at all the last.

I am not sure what might be considered our first date. After that day at church, we saw each other often, but never alone. We spoke at church and at school and, through my stepsister Abuk, I sent messages detailing the extent of my admiration for her, and how often I was thinking of her. She did the same, and so the volume of the messages kept Abuk busy. When the messages were deemed urgent, she would come running across the camp to me, her arms flailing and out of breath. She would finally regain herself and then relay the following:

—Tabitha is smiling at you today.

There could be little private contact between young people like ourselves, even if madly in love, as Tabitha and I were. Like most of the courtship, any interaction at all was done in plain sight, so as to draw no questioning eyes or murmuring among the elders. But even in plain sight, in daylight and in public, we were able to do quite enough to satisfy our modest desires. Those who knew me at Pinyudo, and suspected what happened in the bedroom of the Royal Girls, were surprised by the chaste courtship that Tabitha and I shared. But what had happened in Pinyudo seemed, now, outside of time. It was done by children who did not invest meaning in such explorations.

The first time I was able to hold Tabitha against me was one Saturday morning, amid many dozens of people, during a volleyball match. I was on a team with the Dominics, and we were playing against a group of overconfident Somalis this particular morning, and were being cheered on by a dozen Dinka girls our age and younger. There were no official cheerleading squads at Kakuma, and though many girls participated in sports, on this day Tabitha was there both to cheer for me and to hold herself against me. In any culture, there are certain loopholes that can be exploited by hormonally desperate teenagers, and at Kakuma we realized that under the auspices of the girls cheering us on, giving congratulatory hugs after a winning point was somehow acceptable.

There were five Dominics playing volleyball that day, and four of us had notified our ladyfriends that if they rooted us on, we would be able to hold each other between games or after successful points. So this is how I first held Tabitha. She had not done this cheering and hugging before, but she took to it immediately and very well. The first time I spiked a winning shot past the face of a certain overconfident Somali, Tabitha cheered as if she might explode, and came running over to me, jumping and hugging me with abandon. No one took notice, though Tabitha and I savored those jumping and hugging moments as if they were sacred honeymoon hours.

When it became more widely known that such hugs were available to athletes, the less romantically successful boys altered their priorities. "I have to learn some sports!" they said, and then tried. The enrollment in intramural sports grew dramatically for a time. Of course, there was a crackdown, soon enough, on the cheering and hugging, when the ratio between sports and hugging became too close to 1:1. But it was very good, indescribably good, while it lasted.

—Tell me!

Noriyaki's appetite for details was insatiable.

—Tell me tell me tell me!

It was puzzling, because I had never asked him about the physical aspects of his relationship with Wakana—to whom he had recently become engaged—but he felt no shame in asking me to recount every meeting with Tabitha. I obliged, to an extent. There was a stretch of several weeks when I worried about the youth of Kakuma, because the two employees of the Wakachiai Project were doing little but discussing my meetings with Tabitha. Thankfully, he did not push me for smells and other sensations.

But they were extraordinary. After three months or so, Tabitha and I had mustered enough courage to visit each other in our respective homes on the rare occasions that they were empty. These opportunities were exceedingly rare, given her household held six people and mine eleven. But once a week we might find ourselves alone in a room, and hold hands, or sit on a bed together, our thighs touching, nothing more.

—But all this will change on the drama trip, right? Noriyaki prodded.

—I hope so, I said.

Did I really hope so? I was unsure. Did I want this sort of unsupervised time alone with Tabitha? The thought made me nauseous. Already I wondered if we had too much time alone, even in public. Her touch was more powerful than she knew. Or perhaps she knew it well, and was reckless with her touching; they sent every part of me into turmoil, and perhaps it was this control she found amusing and intoxicating.

But we would be going to Nairobi, and I would not and could not miss such an opportunity. The computer classes Noriyaki had suggested had not yet been manageable, with the schedule of the camp, and the permits necessary. I had never seen a city, had not left Kakuma for five years, and had no sense of being part of the real Kenya. Kakuma was, in a way, a country of its own, or a kind of vacuum created in the absence of any nation. For many of us at Kakuma, the desire to return to Sudan was replaced by a more practical plan: to go to Nairobi and live there, work there, establish new lives, become citizens of Kenya. I cannot say that I was close to achieving this, but I had more of a chance than most.

Our troupe had conceived of a play called *The Voices,* and we had performed it in Kakuma for many weeks. A theater writer from Nairobi, visiting a cousin who worked at the camp, saw the play and immediately invited us to perform the play in the capital, as part of a contest involving the best amateur theater groups in the country. We were to travel to Nairobi to represent the refugees in Kakuma; it would be the first time in the history of the competition—quite a long and robust history, we were told—that any refugees had participated in the contest. And so we would all go, Tabitha would be there, and with us only one chaperone, Miss Gladys.

Tabitha and I barely spoke about the trip in the weeks leading up to our departure. It was simply too much to think about, that we would have time alone together, that we would perhaps find the place for our first kiss. I believe we were both overwhelmed by the possibilities. I slept poorly. I walked around the camp fidgeting and smiling uncontrollably, all the while my stomach in a constant uproar.

—First Kiss! Noriyaki began to call me. I walked into work each day and these were his first words: Hello, First Kiss! To anything I would ask, he would answer, Yes, First Kiss. No, First Kiss.

I had to beg him, with the utmost seriousness, to stop.

Abuk, serving as the messenger of Gop Chol, came to our office one day with the urgent news that I was to come to dinner directly after work. I told her I would, but only if she told me what the occasion was.

—I can't tell you, she said.

—Then I can't come, I said.

—Please, Valentino! she wailed. —I had to *swear* I wouldn't tell. *Please* don't get me in trouble! They'll *know* if I *told!*

Abuk was passing through a period of great drama in her life, and emphasized far too many words, with far too much emphasis, than was necessary.

I let her leave without an answer, and I walked home that evening, attempting not to think about what awaited me there. I was fairly certain Gop would give me a lecture about being careful with Tabitha, given the time we might have together unsupervised. He had not yet given me such a talk.

When I arrived at home, Gop and Ayen were there, as were all the members of my Kakuma family, and a handful of neighbors, from the smallest children to the most senior adults. And among them all were two people who seemed particularly out of place in our shelter: first of all, Miss Gladys. It was a shock to see her standing in the room where we ate our meals. And though her beauty might be expected to suffer in such environs, she only radiated that much more powerfully. She was talking to a new woman, a sophisticated Dinka woman who held a small girl in her arms. This was, Ayen told me, Deborah Agok.

She was an important woman, I was told by Adeng, and would be bringing with her news that would change our lives. Adeng had insisted that these were the words her father had given her, but because Gop was not a stranger to this sort of hyperbole, I did not spend much time pondering just what the news might be. Gop had once gathered us all, atop a similar pedestal of unspeakable significance, to announce that he had acquired new sheets for his bed.

In any case, it was overwhelming to see all these people in one place. It was also somewhat difficult to move, as our shelters were not made for so many. I still had no idea what the occasion was that would bring all of these people to our home, but was immediately distracted by a familiar smell. It was a certain food cooking, the name of which I had long forgotten.

—Kon diong! Ayen said. —Don't you remember?

I did remember. It was a dish I hadn't tasted, or heard of, in years. Kon diong is particular to my region, and is not an everyday dish. It's a hard porridge made from white sorghum flour, cheese, and skimmed sour milk; these are not things easily attained. It's a dish favored by prosperous families, and only during the rainy season, when the cows produce milk in abundance.

—What's this all about? I finally asked. My Kakuma sisters were looking at me in a peculiar way, and everyone seemed to be stepping around me, being solicitous and overly deferent. I was not sure I liked the atmosphere.

—You'll learn soon enough, Gop said. —First, let's eat.

I still had not spoken to Miss Gladys, who was being quizzed and fussed over by the elderly women in the house. And Deborah Agok, our guest, would not look at me. She spent her time speaking to my sisters and attending to the girl now in her lap, who I learned was her daughter, Nyadi. She was a bone-thin girl wearing a pale pink dress, her eyes seeming far too large for her face.

Dinner was consumed at an impossibly slow rate. I knew that the purpose of the dinner, and of Deborah Agok's visit, would not be revealed until after dinner, until after the adults drank araki, a wine made from dates. All this is not uncommon among the Dinka, this sense of drama, but that night I felt that this sense of drama was perhaps overly precious.

Finally the food had been eaten, the wine had been drunk, and Gop stood. He looked down at Deborah Agok, sitting on the floor with the rest of us, and he insisted that she be given the home's one proper chair. Miss Agok refused, but he insisted. An elderly neighbor was moved from the chair to the spot on the ground previously occupied by Miss Agok, and now Gop continued.

—Most of you do not know Deborah Agok, but she has become a friend to our family. She is a respected midwife, trained in both the Sudanese and more technological birthing methods. She has been working at the Kakuma hospital, where she met the esteemed Miss Gladys, whom we have all heard about from Achak, who has been so grateful for her… instruction.

Everyone laughed, and my face burned. Miss Gladys glowed more than ever before. This was, it was clearer than ever, the sort of attention she relished.

—Miss Agok was recently sent by the International Rescue Committee into southern Sudan to teach new birthing techniques to the village midwives. Now, as it happens, one of the villages she visited was called Marial Bai.

All eyes fell upon me. I was not sure how to react. My throat shrunk; I could not breathe. So this was it, this was the reason for all the mystery, the special dish from my region. But the idea of receiving any news of my home this way seemed immediately wrong. I did not want to know anything about my family in the midst of such an audience. Deborah would be the first person in all my years at Kakuma with accurate and recent information about Marial Bai, and my mind spun with possibilities. Did the river still flow the same way as before? Had the Arabs cleared the region of its rich pastures and trees? Did she know anything of my family? But for this to be part of the theater of the evening! It was unacceptable.

I looked for the exit. There were twelve bodies I would have to step over to make my way to the door. Leaving would require too much effort, would create a scene unbecoming to me and disrespectful of my adoptive family. I stared hard at Gop, hoping to convey my displeasure with this sort of ambush. Though the atmosphere had been buoyant thus far, it seemed perfectly possible that this Miss Agok had tragic news of my birth family, and Gop had gathered everyone I knew to lift me up after the news knocked me to the ground.

Now Deborah Agok stood. She was a tall and muscular woman whose face gave away no answers about her age. She might have been a young woman or a grandmother, such were the crossed signals given by her taut skin, bright eyes encircled by hair-thin wrinkles. She remained sitting in the chair, her hands in her lap, and thanked Gop and Ayen for their hospitality and friendship. When she spoke, her voice was hoarse and low. By her voice, one might guess she had lived three lifetimes without rest.

—My friends, I have traveled throughout Bahr al-Ghazal, visiting Nyamlell, Malual Kon, Marial Bai, and the surrounding villages. I bring a heartfelt greeting from the people of Marial Bai, including Commander Paul Malong Awan, the senior-ranking SPLA officer there.

All the attendees of the dinner looked to me, as though it was a great honor to me in particular that Commander Paul Malong Awan had sent greetings.

—Yes, she continued, —I have been to your village, and I have seen what has become of it. Of course there have been the assaults from the murahaleen and the government army. And related to those attacks I found rampant malnutrition and a rash of deaths caused by controllable diseases. As you know, hunger is at its peak; hundreds of thousands will starve in Bahr al-Ghazal this year.

The Sudanese way of speaking was in full glory—the roundabout way to any given point. How could she do this to me? All I wanted to hear about was my family. This was cruelty, no matter how good her intentions.

Sensing my anxiety, at that moment a shape appeared in front of me, and then

400

filled the space next to me. It was Miss Gladys, with her smell of fruit and flowers and a woman's perspiration, and before I could assess this new situation—it was the closest she had ever been to me—she was holding my hand. She did not look at me, but only at Deborah Agok, but she was with me. She would be there whatever the news was. The timing for this most intimate contact with the object of my innumerable daydreams could not have been less appropriate.

—Because I am a midwife, Deborah continued, and I tried to listen, —I came to know a midwife in Marial Bai, a very strong woman who wore most days a dress of faded yellow, the yellow of a tired sun.

All eyes were upon me again, and I struggled to keep mine dry. I was being pulled with such force in two directions. My hand was already soaked with sweat entwined within the fingers of the divine woman by my side, and at the same time, my ears had heard that my mother might be alive, that Deborah had met a midwife who wore a yellow dress. My eyes were wet before I could prevent it. With my free hand, I pulled at the skin below my eyes to drain the water back into my body.

—This midwife and I spent a good deal of time together, comparing stories of bringing babies into the world. She had assisted in the birth of over one hundred babies, and had had great success in avoiding untimely deaths for these infants. I shared with her new advances in the science and techniques of midwifery, and she was a very quick and willing learner. We quickly became good friends, and she invited me to her home. When I arrived, she cooked for me the dish we had tonight at Kakuma, and she told me of life in Marial Bai, about the effect the famine was having on the village, about the latest attacks by the murahaleen. I told her of the world of Kakuma, and in talking about my life here, I mentioned my good friends Gop and Ayen, and the boys they had taken in. When I mentioned the name Achak to this woman, she was startled. She asked what this boy looked like. How big is he? she asked. She told me she had known a boy with that name, so long ago. She asked if I might wait a moment, and when I said I would, she left her home in a hurry.

Now Miss Gladys held my hand tighter.

—She returned with a man she identified as her husband, and he explained that she was his first wife. She asked me to repeat what I had told her, that I had known a family in Kakuma who had adopted a boy named Achak. What is the name of this man in the camp? the husband asked. I told him his name was Gop Chol Kolong. The man was very interested in this information, insisting that this man was from Marial

Bai, too. But they had no way to confirm that the Achak who I knew of in Kakuma was the same Achak who was their son. It was not until I returned to Kenya and told this story to Gop that it all became clear. So now I must ask you some questions, to know the answers for sure. What is the name of Achak's father? she asked, directing her query to Gop.

I don't know why she did this. She had yet to meet my eye.

—Deng Nyibek Arou, Gop said.

—His mother? she asked.

—Amiir Jiel Nyang, I answered.

—Was Achak's father a businessman in Marial Bai? she asked.

—Yes! almost everyone in the room responded.

Her theatrics were insufferable.

—Tell us! Were these people Achak's parents? Gop finally asked.

She paused, annoyed to have her spell broken.

—They are the same. Achak's parents are alive.

In the next few days, before my scheduled trip to Nairobi, much effort was expended by Gop, Ayen, Noriyaki, and others in keeping me at Kakuma. Now that I knew my parents had survived, it seemed impossible to remain apart from them. Why wouldn't I simply go back to Marial Bai and join my father in his business? The purpose of all my journeys was to keep me safe and educate me, and now that I was both safe and educated and I was grown and healthy, how could I not return to them? The most recent raid of Marial Bai had been just months before, but this didn't matter to me, not at all.

I spent my hours contemplating my arrival at home, crossing the river, parting the grasses, emerging from the brush and into the village, striding into my parents' compound as they emerged from their homes to see me. They would not immediately recognize me, but as they moved closer they would know it was their son. I would be twice the size I was when I ran from Marial Bai, but they would know it was me. I could not picture them, my mother or father. My siblings were also faceless to me. I had formed an approximation of all of the members of my family, drawn from people I knew at Kakuma. My mother's face was Miss Gladys's, but somewhat older. My father's was that of Gop, plus many years of deprivation and decline.

Once we had embraced and my mother had wept, we would sit together all day and all night, talking until I knew about every day, every week since I had been gone. Did you think I was dead? I would ask. No, no, they would say, We always knew you would find a way to survive. Did you think I would come back? I would ask. We knew you would come back, they would say. It was right for you to come back.

—Are you forgetting that the country is in the middle of a famine? Gop asked.

Gop knew my plans too well, and threatened to tie me to my bed, to cut off my feet to prevent me from walking out of Kakuma.

—Are you forgetting that you would have to pass through land held by Riek Machar's Nuer forces, who would not like to see a Dinka boy of army age? You're leaving comfort and education and a job here to go back to what?

I could not remember a time that Gop was so agitated. He followed me all the hours of the day; he amassed allies—other teachers, elders at the camp—in his quest to keep me from leaving. I was watched at all times, with friends and strangers both congratulating me on the news from home, and at the same time urging patience, a prudent course, to wait until the time was right to return.

—At the very least, give it time, Ayen said one night at dinner. —Think it over. Go to Nairobi and think about this. Remember, on the Nairobi trip you will be with both Tabitha and Miss Gladys.

When she said this, and I did not immediately respond, I saw her exchange a quick glance with Gop. They knew they had captured my interest.

—Why not go to Nairobi, and then decide? Ayen added. —Then if you do go home, you can tell your parents all about your trip to the city.

Ayen was a very convincing woman.

When the day of the trip finally arrived, seeing Tabitha on that UN vehicle was devastating. I approached the bus as it idled and Tabitha's heart-shaped and symmetrical face was there, by the window, ignoring me. She was sitting with another Sudanese girl, and she finally glanced at me, made no sign she even knew me, and then returned to her conversation. This was according to plan, I should note. We had decided to make no outward signal of our feelings, though a few on the bus knew our intentions. I played my part, climbing aboard the bus and sitting with the humorous Dominic, knowing he would help pass the time on the ride, which had been described as very long and punishing.

—Hey, Madame Zero, will you be shopping for new dresses in Nairobi? he asked.

Everyone laughed, and Anthony smiled a barely tolerant smile.

It is hard to communicate how momentous it was, after seven years in that camp, to be on the way to Nairobi. It is impossible to explain. And most of those in the group were worse off than me. I lived with Gop Chol, and had a paying job with an NGO, but most of the other members of the drama group—twenty-one of us, all Sudanese and Somalis, all between twelve and eighteen—had nothing. Besides Tabitha, there were eight girls, most of them Sudanese, and this made the trip particularly enjoyable, and not at all punishing, for the rest of the Dominics. We rode on a standard blue UN staff bus, the windows open, the two days of driving buoyed by cool wind and constant songs.

The scenery was astonishing, the peaks and valleys, the mist and the sun. We passed through the Kapenguria area of Kenya, much of it mountainous and cool with rain. We saw birds with bright plumage, we saw hyenas and gazelles, elephants and zebras. And corn! So many crops, everything growing. Seeing this part of Kenya made it all the more depressing and inconceivable that our refugee camp had been placed where it had. We pressed our faces to the glass and wondered, Why couldn't they put Kakuma there? Or there, or there? Do not think it was lost on us that the Kenyans, and every international body that monitors or provides for the displaced, customarily places its refugees in the least desirable regions on earth. There we become utterly dependent—unable to grow our own food, to tend our own livestock, to live in any sustainable way. I do not judge the UNHCR or any nation that takes in the nationless, but I do pose the question.

As the land passed by, I saw my parents, my approximated visions of them, on every hill and around each bend. It seemed as logical as anything else that they would be there, on the road ahead of us. Why couldn't they be here, why couldn't we will ourselves together again? Surely my father could find a way to live and thrive in Kenya. Just the thought of my mother here, walking with me along these green paths, along that river, near those giraffes—it felt so very possible for a few hours of that drive.

We stayed in Ketale, in a hotel with beds and sheets and electricity and running water. Though this town was not the size of Nairobi, still it left us astounded. We were unaccustomed to the sky's black being punctured by lights. Some of the Somalis had experienced these things before, but those of us from southern Sudan had seen none of this; even in our homes, in our villages before the war, there was no plumbing, and any of these amenities, bedsheets and towels, were rare and coveted. At that hotel in Ketale, we ate at their restaurant, drank cold drinks from an icebox, swishing the ice cubes—which at least a portion of the group had never touched—around in our mouths. If we had turned around the next day, just that one night in Ketale would have made for the most spectacular of journeys. In all of the time at Ketale, Tabitha and I barely spoke, saving any interaction for a later time. The opportunity would arise, we knew, and we needed only to wait and watch.

We drove on in the morning, through the afternoon and through the night, and by the morning after, were in Nairobi. I have to attempt to communicate the awe that comes over a group of young people like us, after spending many years in a camp at the edge of the world, upon seeing something like Nairobi, one of the largest cities in Africa. We had nothing with which to compare it. On the bus there was a hush. You might imagine a bus full of teenagers loudly pointing at buildings, at cars and bridges and parks. But this bus was utterly silent. Our faces were pressed against the windows but no one said a word. Some of what we saw was impossible to understand. Houses upon houses, windows upon windows. The tallest building I had seen before that day was precisely two stories tall. And knowing that these buildings faced no threat, that they would stand untouched—the sense of permanence was something I had not known for many years.

When we arrived at Nairobi that morning, we were dropped off at a church and there we met our sponsors. Each of us was assigned a host family, most of whom were in some way affiliated with the national theater. I was assigned to a man named Mike Mwaniki, an extraordinarily handsome and sophisticated man, I thought. He was perhaps thirty years old, and was one of the founders of the Mavuno Drama Group, based in the city; they performed original plays by young Kenyan playwrights.

—This is the man, eh? he said to me. —You're our guy!

He shook my hand heartily and slapped me on the back and gave me a slice of cake. I had never had cake, and in retrospect it doesn't make much sense that he would greet me at nine-thirty in the morning with cake, but he did, and it was delicious. A white cream cake with stripes of sunflower orange.

The other members of the group went with their sponsors, and Tabitha went off with hers, an older couple dressed extravagantly and driving a Land Rover. Miss Gladys quickly disappeared with a very handsome and wealthy-looking Kenyan man—we did not see her again until the performance two days later—and I went with Mike. He shared an apartment with his girlfriend, a diminutive and luminous woman named Grace, and together they lived in a part of the city called BuruBuru Phase 3. It was a mad neighborhood, busier than any place I had ever known. Kakuma held eighty thousand people, but there was very little traffic, few cars, no horns, scant electricity, very little bustle. But in Nairobi, in BuruBuru Phase 3, the hum of the streets was inescapable. The motorcycles, the cars and buses run at all hours, and the sweet toxic smell of diesel is everywhere. Even in their apartment, where the floors and glass were so clean, the street was there, the smell of the roads and sounds of people passing under their windows. The cars were so many colors, an array I didn't know existed. In Kakuma all the vehicles were white, identical, all bearing the UN symbol.

I was given the bedroom Mike and Grace shared; the mattress was enormous and firm, and in that first moment in that room the sheets were so white that I had to turn away. I put my bag down and sat on a small wicker chair in the corner. I had a crippling headache. I thought I was alone in the room so I dropped my head to my hands and tried to massage my skull into some kind of agreement that all this was good. But my head frequently was overwhelmed, and the best times of my life were often accompanied by migraines of inexplicable origin.

—Are you set? Mike asked.

I looked up. He was standing in the doorway.

—I'm fine, I said. —I am very good. I am very happy.

I forced a smile that would convince him.

—We're seeing a movie tonight, he said. —You'll come?

I said I would. He and Grace had to go to work. They worked at an automobile dealership down the road, but they would be back at six to pick me up. Mike showed me the TV and the bathroom and gave me a key to his front door and to the apartment building, and he and Grace jogged down the steps and were gone.

To be alone in that place! They had given me the key and I sat for some time, watching the people move below the window. This was the first time I had been on the second story of a building. It was quite disorienting, though not so much unlike sitting in a tree over Amath's house with Moses and William K, trying to listen in to the conversations she would have with her sisters.

After an hour of watching the street, the path below the window, I tried the television. I had seen only scattered bits of TV by that point, and so, left to my own devices, alone with twelve channels, this was a problem. I did not move for three hours, I am ashamed to admit. But the things I saw! I watched movies, the news, soccer, cooking shows, nature documentaries, a movie where the sky held two suns, and an examination of the last days of Adolf Hitler. I found a learning channel, directed to students my age, where the hosts were teaching the same book I was studying at Kakuma. This filled me with a certain pride, knowing that what was good enough for refugees was good enough for the Kenyans of Nairobi.

In the afternoon, after far too much TV, I heard the students returning from school. I used my key to lock the door and I walked out to see all the boys and girls in their uniforms, and they looked at me and whispered.

—Turkana!

—Sudan!

—Refugee!

They pointed and giggled but they were not unkind, and I loved them for not being unkind. Here the students walked freely and wore clean white shirts with plaid skirts and scarves to match. It was too much. I wanted to wear a uniform, too. I wanted to be one of them, to know what to wear every day, and to be Kenyan, to go to school along paved roads and laugh about nothing. To buy some candy on the way home and eat it and laugh! That was what I wanted. I would have walls where I slept, and I could turn a faucet and water would come and wash over my hands, as much as I wanted, cold as bone.

The film Mike, Grace, and I saw that night, I remember distinctly, was *Men in Black*. I knew to some extent what was going on in the movie, but wasn't sure what was real and what was not. It was the first time I had been in a theater. The film was confusing but I did my best to follow the reactions of the audience. When they laughed, I laughed. When they seemed scared, I became scared, too. But all the while the separation of the real from the not-real was very difficult for me. After the movie, Mike and Grace took me for ice cream, and they asked me what I thought of *Men in Black*. There was no possibility that I would admit that I had no idea what was happening much of the time, so I lavished the film with praise and otherwise agreed with all their assessments. They were fans of Tommy Lee Jones, they said, and had seen *The Fugitive* four times.

We walked along the streets of Nairobi that night, on the way back to their apartment, and I thought of this life. To have ice cream! We actually had to choose between two ice cream vendors! I remember being conscious of the fleeting nature of that night, how in two days I would be back at Kakuma. Though I tried to disguise it, I slowed our pace as we walked. I wanted so badly to make the evening last. It was a lovely night, the air warm, the wind civilized.

Back at the apartment, Mike and Grace bid me goodnight and encouraged me to take what I wanted from the refrigerator, to watch television if I liked. This might have been a mistake. I did not take any food from them, for I was overstuffed anyway, but I did take advantage of the second part of their offer. I am not sure when I fell asleep. I spun the channels until my wrist was sore. I know that light had begun to bleach the sky when I finally went to bed, and I was dazed for most of the next day.

In the morning, I found Grace on the couch, crying. I tiptoed quietly into the living room. She held a newspaper in her hand.

—No no no! Grace said. —No! I can't believe it!

Mike came to see what Grace was reading. I stood, timidly, for fear that something like the bombing of the embassy had happened again. As I got closer to the newspaper, I saw the image of a white woman in a car. She was very pretty, with sandy brown hair. There were pictures of the same woman handing flowers to an African child, stepping off airplanes, riding in the back of a convertibles. I guessed that this woman, whoever she was, was dead.

—This is terrible, Mike said, and sat with Grace, holding her shoulder against his. I said nothing. I still did not know what had happened.

Grace turned to me. Her eyes were wet, swollen.

—Don't you know her? she asked.

I shook my head.

—This is Princess Diana. From England?

Grace explained that this woman had given a great deal of money and assistance to Kenya, that she worked for the ban on land mines. She was a beautiful person, she said.

—A car crash. In Paris, Mike said. Now he was behind Grace, wrapping his arms around her. They were the most loving couple I had ever seen. I knew my father loved my mother, but open affection like this was not part of life in my village.

All day, people were crying. Ten of us, Tabitha and the Somalis and most of the

Dominics, walked through the city and wherever we went, we found people weeping—in the markets, outside the churches, on the sidewalks. It seemed the whole world knew this person named Diana, and if the world knew her, the connection between the peoples of the earth was tighter than I had imagined. I wondered if the people of England would mourn if Mike and Grace died. At that time, confused as I was, I imagined that they would.

My sleep-deprived state dulled my senses, and perhaps this was helpful. After lunch we went to the theater to rehearse for the next night's show, and had I been more alert I might have fainted. The theater was enormous, a lavishly decorated space. The last time we performed the play we had done so on the dirt of Kakuma, the audience sitting on the ground before us. There were no proper stages in our camp, and now we were standing on real boards of cherry wood, looking out at the plush seats, twelve hundred of them. We rehearsed that day, though the mood was somber. The members of our group had all been informed of Diana's death, and who she was, and they feigned or adopted sadness.

When the troupe was alone that day, in whole or in part, we talked about staying. We all wanted to remain in Nairobi, to live there forever. No one wanted to go back to Kakuma, even those of us with families, and we theorized about how we might stay. There were plans to run away, to disappear into the city, to hide until they'd given up on us. But we knew at least some of us would be caught and punished severely. And if anyone did run, it would mean the end of any trips to Nairobi for anyone else at Kakuma. In the end the only solution, we knew, was a sponsorship. If a Kenyan citizen agreed to sponsor any of us, or any refugee in Kakuma, one could live with that sponsor, go to a real Kenyan school, and live as the Kenyans did.

—You should ask Mike to sponsor you, one of the Dominics urged me. —I bet he would.

—I can't ask him that.

—He's young. He can do it.

The idea was not a good one, I didn't think. It was the habit of so many I knew, in Kakuma and later, to take the generosity of a person and stretch it to breaking.

But in a few weaker moments I thought, *I could ask him, couldn't I?* I could ask him the night before I was to leave. Then no harm would be done; if he said no, it would not be uncomfortable.

So that became my plan. Until the last day, I would be cavalier and happy, showing how appealing I was, and then, the last night, I would mention to Mike that a
young man like myself would be helpful in Nairobi, would be able to do just about
anything for Mike and Grace and the Mavuno Drama Group.

After rehearsal, Mike and Grace offered to take me and one friend out for dinner
at a Chinese restaurant. I chose Tabitha, but was ready to have my selection rejected
as inappropriate. But as it was not unusual in Kenya for people like Tabitha and me
to date, Mike and Grace accepted and welcomed her. My selection intrigued them,
I believe, for they asked many questions on our walk to pick her up. *Which one was she
again? Did we see her yesterday? Was she wearing pink?*

We ate at a restaurant with clean ceramic floors and pictures on the wall of past
dignitaries of Kenya. Tabitha and I ate lamb and vegetables and soda. I gained weight,
everyone did, so quickly those few days. We had never eaten so well. All during dinner Mike and Grace watched us eat, smiling sadly, and as we became sated and could
talk undistracted by our food, Mike and Grace, I am sure, noticed that we were in love.
They looked from Tabitha to me and back again and they grinned knowingly.

We walked from dinner to a shopping mall, four stories tall and filled with stores and
people, so much glass, a movie theater. Tabitha and I pretended to be familiar with a
place like this, and tried not to seem overly impressed.

—Oh lord, we're tired, Grace said, forcing an extravagant yawn. Mike laughed
and squeezed her hand. He stopped outside a photo-processing shop. A potbellied
man stepped out and he and Mike and Grace greeted each other warmly.

—Okay, Mike said to Tabitha and me. —I'm guessing you two would like some
time alone, and we're willing to allow this. But first we'll make an arrangement. This
is my friend Charles.

The potbellied man nodded to us.

—He'll be working here till ten o'clock. We will allow you two to stay here at
the mall together, unchaperoned, so long as at ten o'clock, you meet Charles back here
at his shop. He'll close up and take you both home.

It was a very good deal, we thought, and so we accepted immediately. Mike
handed me a handful of shillings and winked at me conspiratorially. When I held that
money in one hand and Tabitha's hand in the other, I felt sure that I was living the
best moment of my life. Tabitha and I had almost two hours alone together, and it

did not matter that we needed to stay inside the mall.

—Be back here at ten, Charles said, looking at Tabitha.

—You'll be okay? Mike asked me.

—Yes sir, I said. —You can trust us.

—We do trust you, he said, and then winked at me.

—Now go, you're free! Grace said, and shooed us with the back of her tiny hand.

Mike and Grace left the mall and Charles returned to his film-developing machines. Tabitha and I were alone and the choices were too many. I began to think where might be the most appropriate spot to hold her against me, to hold her face in my hands. Gop had instructed me to hold a woman's face in my hands when I kissed her, and I was determined to do it this way.

I knew nothing about the mall, but I had the presence of mind to know that in such a situation, the man should appear decisive, so I first led Tabitha up two flights of stairs and into the biggest and brightest of the mall's stores. I did not know what was inside. When I finally realized it was a grocery store, it was too late for me to change my mind. I had to feign great pride in my choice.

When I look back on this, it seems very unromantic, but we spent most of our two hours in this grocery store. It was enormous, brighter than day, and filled with as much food as all of Kakuma could eat in a week. It was also something of a variety store and a drug store, too—so many things in one place. There were twelve aisles, some with freezers stuffed with pizzas and popsicles, others stacked with home appliances and cosmetics. Tabitha examined the lipsticks, the hair products, false eyelashes, and women's magazines; she was very much a cosmetics girl even then. At Kakuma Town the stores were wooden shacks stuffed with ancient-seeming products, nothing packaged brightly, nothing so pristine and delectable as the contents of that Nairobi grocery-variety store. We walked up and down each aisle, showing each other one wonder after another: a wall of juices and sodas, a shelf of candy and toys, fans and air conditioners, an area in the back where bicycles were lined up and gleaming. Tabitha let out a little squeal and ran to those made for the smallest riders.

She sat on a tiny tricycle built for a toddler and honked the horn.

—Val, I need to ask you an important question, she said, her eyes alight.

—Yes? I said. I was so worried that she wanted something of me that I was not prepared to give. I had feared for a long time that secretly Tabitha was well-versed in the ways of love, and that the moment we were alone, she would want to move too

411

quickly. That it would be clear I had no experience at all. Seeing her on that tricycle provoked strong and inexplicable feelings in me.

—Let's run, she said.

This wasn't what I had expected.

—What? Run where? I said.

—Run away. Stay here. Leave Kakuma. Let's not go back.

I told Tabitha that she had lost her mind. She said nothing for a minute and I thought she had regained her senses. But she was far from finished.

—Val, can't you see? Mike and Grace expect us to leave tonight, together. That's why they left us alone.

—Mike and Grace don't expect us to leave.

—You heard Grace! She said *shoo!* We can go off and be like them. Wouldn't you like to live like them? We can, Val, you and me.

I told Tabitha I could not do it. I did not agree that Mike and Grace expected us to leave that night. I believed that they would be greatly troubled by our disappearance, that it would bring them a lot of trouble from police and immigration officials. Our defecting would also, I reminded Tabitha, put an end to all sanctioned refugee excursions from Kakuma. Our trip to Nairobi would be the last any youth from Kakuma would ever make.

—C'mon, Val! We can't think of that, she said. —We have to think of what you and I can do. We have to live, don't we? What right do they have to tell us where we can live? You know that's not living, how they have it at Kakuma. We're not humans there and you know it. We're animals, we're just penned up like cattle. Don't you think you deserve better than that? Don't we? Who are you obeying? The rules of Kenyans who know nothing about us? Everyone will understand, Val. They'll cheer us from Kakuma and you know it. They don't expect us to come back.

—We can't, Tabitha. This isn't the right way.

—You're put on this Earth just once and you're going to just live as these people make you live? You're not a person to them! You're an insect! Take control.

She stomped her foot onto mine.

—Who are you, Valentino? Where are you from?

—I'm from Sudan.

—Really? How? What do you remember from that place?

—I'll go back, I said. —I'll always be Sudanese.

—But you're a person first, Val. You're a soul. You know what a soul is?

She truly could be condescending, exasperating.

—You're a soul whose human form happened to take that of a boy from Sudan. But you're not tied to that, Val. You're not just a Sudanese boy. You don't have to accept these limitations. You don't have to obey the laws of where someone like you must belong, that because you have Sudanese skin and Sudanese features you have to be just a product of the war, that you're just part of all this shit. They tell you to leave your home and walk to Ethiopia and you do. They tell you to leave Ethiopia, to leave Golkur, and you do. They walk to Kakuma and you just walk with them. You follow every time. And now they tell you that you have to stay in a camp until they allow you to leave. Don't you see? What right do all these people have to draw boundaries around the life you can live? What gives them the right? Because they happened to be born Kenyan and you Sudanese?

—My parents are alive, Tabitha!

—I know that! Don't you think it would be more likely to get to them from Nairobi? You could work and earn money and get to Marial Bai far more easily from here. Think about it.

I can look back and see the wisdom in what she said that night, but at the time, Tabitha was frustrating me greatly, and I had a low opinion of her views and of her. I told her that her rhetoric would not convince me to break laws or to diminish the quality of life for thousands of young people at Kakuma.

—I have no right to make life harder for anyone else, I said.

And that was the end of our talk. I wandered through the store for some time, not sure if I wanted to be with Tabitha then or ever again. She was a different person than I had previously assumed. She seemed selfish to me, irresponsible and short-sighted and immature. I decided I would simply go to Charles's shop at ten o'clock, hoping Tabitha would be there. But I did not want to be the one to prevent her from fleeing if she so chose. I hoped so dearly that she would not run away but I did not want to tell her not to. I did not have that right. I was sure that this night would be the end of our romance. She would see me as timid and overly obedient; this was something I feared from the beginning, that Tabitha favored more dangerous men than me. I was then, like I was on so many days, at war with my law-abiding personality. Over the years, my eagerness to please those in authority got me into far too much trouble.

It was, however, too soon to admit this to myself or to Tabitha, so I remained among the bicycles, reminded of the man in the desert who kept fresh food in a hole in the ground. I thought of this man and found myself unconsciously touching my shin where the barbed wire had made a meal of me. It was then that I saw that Tabitha had returned. She was storming down the aisle to me, past the electric fans and the coffee makers and towels, and she was soon in front of me, standing inches away.

—Stupid boy! she yelled.

I had no answer for that accusation, for it was certainly true.

—Now kiss me, she demanded.

She was as angry as I had ever seen her, her forehead making use of muscles I did not know a face possessed. Her lips, though, were pursed, and she closed her eyes and tilted her head up to mine. And immediately all of my opinions about her fell away. My stomach and heart collided but I leaned down to Tabitha and kissed her. I kissed her and she kissed me until a clerk in the grocery store asked us to leave. They were closing, he said, pointing to his watch. It was ten o'clock. We had been kissing for forty minutes there among the bicycles, her hands on the handlebars and mine on hers.

I remember nothing from the next day. Tabitha was obligated to spend the day with her sponsors, and because Mike and Grace were working, I spent much of the day in their apartment. Occasionally I walked around the neighborhood, attempting to think, even for a second or two, of anything beyond the kiss we shared. But it was futile. I relived that long kiss a thousand times that day. In the apartment I kissed the refrigerator, I kissed every door, many pillows and all of the couch cushions, all in the effort to approximate the sensation again.

I should have been concerned about Tabitha, about whether or not she would appear that day at the rehearsal, but I had not yet processed the night before. When Tabitha arrived that afternoon at the theater, I was so entranced by memories of the night before that I barely noticed the real Tabitha, who was purposely ignoring me. Sometime in the night she had decided to be mad at me again. She would continue to fume for weeks to come.

On the night of our performance, the theater was full. There were eighteen different groups performing, from all over Kenya. Ours was the only troupe of refugees. I thank the Lord that we performed well that night; we remembered our lines and under the lights, with all those seats, we still found a way to be present in the words and drama of the play we had written. We did well, we knew we did well. When we finished, the audience cheered and some people stood and clapped. Our group placed third overall. We could not have asked for more.

Afterward, there was a celebratory dinner, and then we all went to our sponsors' homes. Even on the walk there the struggle was evident on my face.

—What's the matter? Grace asked. —You look like you ate something sour.

I told her it was nothing, but I was a wreck. I knew that I had only this night to speak to Mike and Grace about the possibility of his sponsoring me.

But I said nothing to Grace, and nothing to either of them as they washed up before bed. Grace went to sleep and Mike did, too, before he returned to the living room. —Couldn't sleep, he said.

We sat on the couch that night watching television for hours more, and while I asked him questions about what we saw—who are the men in the curved hats? who are the women wearing feathers?—all I could think was *Could I? Could I really ask him such a thing?* I could not ask such a thing of Mike. It was far too much, I knew. Mike was too busy to be burdened with a refugee. But then again, I thought, I *could* be such a help. There were so many things I could do to earn my keep. I could cook and clean and certainly help in any way the theater needed me. I was organized, I had proven that, and I was well liked, and I could clean the theater after it closed, or clean it before it opened. I could do either or both, and afterward, could come home and turn down the bed for Mike and Grace. Certainly Mike would know all the things that I would be willing to do. He knew that I would be willing to work for my room and board, to make it advantageous to have me around.

I cursed my stupidity. Mike did not need or want someone to help with all that. He wanted to be a young man unencumbered by the plight of a gangly Sudanese teenager. This was his good deed, this week of hosting me, and that was enough. If my mother knew I was even contemplating imposing on someone in such a way, she would be so ashamed.

—Well, this is the end of the night for me, he said, and stood.

—Okay, I said.

—You staying up again? he asked. —I don't know when you sleep.

I smiled and opened my mouth. A tumble of words, obsequious and needful words, were so close to leaving my mouth. But I said nothing.

—Good night, I said. —Your hospitality has meant everything to me.

He smiled and went to bed, to join Grace.

We went home the next morning, all of us refugees from Kakuma. Everyone was tired; I was not the only one who had developed a taste for television. I did not sit near Tabitha, and did not speak to her the entire ride back. It was just as well. I was drowning in so many thoughts and needed a rest from her, from any reminder of the choices I had not made. I rested my head on the glass, trying to sleep it all away. We did not stop at Ketale this time, instead driving straight through to Kakuma. I slipped in and out of consciousness, watching the lush parts of Kenya pass by, its great green hills and sheets of rain drenching far-off farms. We flew past all that and back to the howling mess of Kakuma.

XXIV.

I am in the parking lot of the Century Club and there are twenty minutes before the gym opens. There is not enough time to nap, even if I were able, so I turn on the radio and find the BBC World News. This program has been a part of my life for so long, since Pinyudo, when the SPLA commanders would blast its reports from Africa across the camp. In the past few years, it seems that no BBC World News broadcast has been complete without an item on Sudan. This morning there is first a predictable story about Darfur; an expert on African affairs notes that seven thousand African Union troops patrolling a region the size of France have been ineffectual in preventing continued janjaweed terror. Funding for the troops is about to run out, and it seems that no one, including the United States, is ready to put forth more money or come up with new ideas to stop the killing and displacement. This is not surprising to those of us who lived through twenty years of oppression by the hands of Khartoum and its militias.

The second Sudan story is more fascinating; it concerns a yacht. It seems that the African Union was to meet in Khartoum, and el-Bashir, the president of Sudan, wanted to impress the heads of state with an extravagant boat, which would be docked in the Nile and would carry the dignitaries up and down the river during their stay. The vessel was ordered from Slovenia, and Bashir paid $4.5 million for it. It goes without saying that $4.5 million would be useful in feeding the poor of Sudan.

The yacht was transported from Slovenia to the Red Sea, where it sailed to Port Sudan. From Port Sudan, it needed to be transported overland to Khartoum in time

417

for the conference. But getting it to the capitol proved far more difficult than antici-
pated. The 172-ton boat challenged the bridges it had to be driven over, and the overhead electrical wires along the way were problematic; 132 of them had to be cut down
and reassembled after the yacht had passed. By the time the yacht was within sight of
the Nile, the leaders of Africa had come and gone. They had somehow managed without the yacht and its satellite TVs, fine china, and staterooms.

But before the boat reached Khartoum, it had become a symbol for how decadent
and callous Bashir is. The man has enemies from all sides—it is not only the southern Sudanese who despise him. Moderate Muslims do, too, and have formed a number of political parties and coalitions to oppose him. In Darfur it was a non-Arab
Muslim group, after all, who rose up against his government, with a variety of
demands for the region. If genocide does not incite the people of Sudan to replace this
madman, and the whole National Islamic Front that controls Khartoum, perhaps the
boat will.

As I have been listening to the radio report, I have been staring across the parking lot
to a pay phone, and now I see it as an invitation. I decide that I should call my own
number, to ring my stolen phone. I have nothing to lose in doing so.

I use one of the phone cards I bought from Achor Achor's cousin in Nashville. He
sells $5 phone cards that in fact give the user $100 worth of international long distance.
I don't know how it works, but these cards are bought by all the refugees I know. The
one I have is very strange, and was probably not made by Africans: it bears an unusual
montage: a Maori tribesman in full regalia, spear in hand, with an American buffalo in
the background. Over the images are the words AFRICA CALIFORNIA.

It takes me a moment to remember my own number; I have not called it often.
When I do remember it, I dial the first six digits quickly and pause for a long
moment before finishing the cycle. I often cannot believe the things I do.

It rings. My throat pounds. Two rings, three. A click.

"Hello?" A boy's voice. Michael. TV Boy.

"Michael. It is the man you stole from last night."

A quick small gasp, then silence.

"Michael, let me talk to you. I just want you to see that—"

The phone is dropped, and I hear the sound of Michael speaking in an echo-giving
room. I hear muffled voices and then "Gimme that." A button is pushed and the call ends.

I gave the police officer this number and now I know that they did not try to call it even once. The phone is still in possession of the people who stole it, those who robbed and beat me, and this phone is still working. The police did not bother to investigate the crime, and the criminals knew the police would do nothing. This is the moment, above any other, when I wonder if I actually exist. If one of the parties involved, the police or the criminals, believed that I had worth or a voice, then this phone would have been disposed of. But it seems clear that there has been no acknowledgment of my existence on either side of this crime.

Five minutes later, after I have returned to my car to catch my breath, I return to the pay phone to try my number again. I am not surprised when the call goes directly to voicemail. Out of habit, I type in my access code to listen to my own messages.

There are three. The first is from Madelena, the admissions officer at a small Jesuit college I visited months ago and which all but promised me entry at that time. Since then, they seem to have arrived at a dozen or more reasons why my application is incomplete. First, they said, my transcript was not official enough; I had sent a copy, when they needed a certified original. Then I had failed to take a certain test that earlier they told me was unnecessary. And all the while, every time I have tried to reach Madelena on the phone, she has been gone. Periodically, though, she calls me back, always at an hour when she knows I will not pick up. I am not sure how she does it. She is a master at this. This message is more informative than any other:

"Valentino, I've talked to my colleagues here at the college and we think you should get some more credits under your belt from the community college"—and here she fumbles with her papers, finding the name—"Georgia Perimeter College. The last thing anyone wants to happen is for you to come all the way out here only to be unsuccessful. So let's get back in touch after a few more semesters, and see where you're at..." This continues for a while, and when she hangs up I can hear the relief in her voice. She will not have to deal with me, she assumes, for another year.

In much the same way as happened at Kakuma, people have been astonished by my difficulty achieving some objectives that they imagine would be easy for me to reach. I have been in the United States five years and I am not much closer to college than I was when I arrived. Through assistance from Phil Mays and the Lost Boys Foundation, I was able to quit my fabric-sample job and study full-time at Georgia Perimeter College, taking the classes I had been told that I would need to apply to a four-year college. But it has not gone as planned. My grades have been inconsistent, and my teachers not always encouraging. Is college really for me? they asked. I did not answer this question. My Foundation money ran out and I had to take this job, at the health club, but I am still determined to attend college. A respected college where I can be a legitimate student. I will not rest until I do.

This fall it seemed I had finally reached a place where I was ready. I had four solid semesters of community college under my belt and my grades were on the whole fine. They dipped after the death of Bobby Newmyer but I did not think these few missteps would hamper my applications. And yet they did. I applied to Jesuit colleges all over the country and their response was confusing and conflicted.

First I toured. I visited seven colleges and always did my best to take notes, to make sure I knew exactly what it was that they were looking for in a prospective student. Gerald Newton had told me to ask them point-blank, "What will it take to make sure I am a student here in the fall?" I said exactly those words at every school I visited. And they were very encouraging. They were friendly, they seemed to want me. But my applications were rejected by all of these schools, and in some cases the admissions officers did not respond at all.

When I finally spoke to an admissions officer at one school, a man who agreed to be candid with me, he said some interesting things.

"You just might be too old."

I asked him to explain. He represented another liberal arts college with a small undergraduate population. I had visited this school, its manicured topiary, its buildings looking much like the catalog we had passed around while waiting for the plane to take us away from Kakuma.

"Look at it this way," he said. "There are dorms here. There are young girls, some of them only seventeen years old. You know what I mean?"

I did not know what he meant.

"Your application says you're twenty-seven years old," he said.

"Yes?"

"Well, picture some white suburban family. They're spending forty thousand dollars to send their young blond daughter to college, she's never been away from home, and the first day on campus they see a guy like you roaming the dorms?"

In his opinion, he had explained everything he needed to. He was trying to give me frank and final advice; he imagined I would quit. But I refuse to believe that this is the end of my pursuit of a college degree, though it seems to me now that I might have to be creative. At Kakuma we could invent a new name for ourselves, a new story for whatever purpose, whenever the pressures and obligations necessitated it. —You have to innovate, Gop said many times, and he meant that there were few unbendable rules at Kakuma. Especially when the alternative was deprivation.

There is a message on my phone from Daniel Bol, who I have known since Kakuma. He was in the Napata Drama Group, and though he does not say it outright, I know that he needs money again. "You know why I'm calling you," he says, and exhales dramatically. Normally I would not consider calling him back, but something occurs to me, a way I might solve my problem with Daniel once and for all. I call him back.

"Hello?" It is him. He is awake. It is 3:13 a.m. where he is. We chat for a few minutes about general things, about his new marriage and his new child, born three months ago. Her name is Hillary.

Daniel is not a particularly graceful man, and I take some pleasure in hearing how clumsily he arrives at the purpose of his call.

"So..." he says. Then he is silent. I am supposed to glean from that that he needs my assistance, and now I am expected to be asking him which Western Union is the closest to his home. I decide to have him explain his situation a bit more clearly.

"What's the matter?" I ask.

"Oh Achak, as you know, I have a new child at home."

I remind him that we were just speaking about her moments ago.

"Yes, and she was sick last week, and then I did a dumb thing. I am very ashamed of what I did but it is done. So..."

And again I'm supposed to infer the rest and then wire the money. But I will not make it so easy for him. I put on a bit of theatrics for old time's sake.

"What is done? What happened? Is your baby still sick?"

I know that his baby isn't sick at all, and was not sick, but I am surprised when he drops this part of his gambit.

"No, this isn't about the baby. She's fine now. This is about something stupid I did over one weekend. Two weeks ago. You know what I'm talking about."

It is always curious how he prefers not to say the word *gambling,* as if he doesn't want to pollute our conversation with the word. But I push him one step further and finally he explains what I knew to be the case when I first heard his voice on my answering machine. Daniel leaves his wife and child for days at a time and travels forty-five minutes to the Indian reservation, where there is a casino he favors. There he has lost a total of $11,400 over the last six months. All of us who know him have attempted various methods of helping him, but nothing has worked. For some time, many of us made the mistake of simply giving him money. I gave him $200, all I could manage, and only because he told me that he had no insurance coverage for his child and had to pay the birthing expenses out of pocket. Americans from his church, and Sudanese all over the country sent him money at that time, and only later did we learn that he had been insured all along, and that every cent of the $5300 or so provided to him, from twenty-eight of us, went back to the casino. Since that time, he has been gingerly feeling out those among us who might still be tapped for donations. His approach this morning is to claim a new direction, and salvation.

"This is the end of it for me, Dominic. I'm finally free of this habit."

He still will not say the words *gambling* or *blackjack*. I listen to him for ten minutes and he refuses to say the words.

"If I can't pay this off," he says, then drifts off for a moment. "I just might have to... end it. Just give it up, dammit. Everything."

For a moment I don't understand what he's saying. An end to the gambling? But then I understand. But I know this threat to be hollow. Daniel is perhaps the last person I know who would ever take his life. He is too vain and too small. We sit with his threat for a few moments, and then I decide that it is time to play the card I have been holding all along.

"Daniel, I wish I could help in your time of need, but I was attacked last night."

And so I tell him the entire story, the ordeal from the beginning. Though I know him to be a self-centered man, I am nevertheless surprised by how little he seems to care. Along the way, he makes curt sounds that he hears what I'm saying, but he does not ask how I am doing, or where I am now, why I am awake at 5:26 a.m. But it is clear that he knows he cannot continue to ask me for money. He only wants to get off the phone, for he is wasting time with me when he must think of who to call next.

By many we have been written off as a failed experiment. We were the model Africans. For so long, this was our designation. We were applauded for our industriousness and good manners and, best of all, our devotion to our faith. The churches adored us, and the leaders they bankrolled and controlled coveted us. But now the enthusiasm has dampened. We have exhausted many of our hosts. We are young men, and young men are prone to vice. Among the four thousand are those who have entertained prostitutes, who have lost weeks and months to drugs, many more who have lost their fire to drink, dozens who have become inexpert gamblers, fighters.

The story that broke everyone's will was widely told and unfortunately true: One night not long ago, three Sudanese men in Atlanta, all of whom I knew here and in Kakuma, were out carousing. They drank in no-name bars and later in the street, and eventually were awake and intoxicated while the rest of the city had found reasons to sleep. Two of the men began to argue about money; there was $10 at issue, which had been loaned and not repaid. Soon there was a fight between two of them, clumsy and seemingly harmless. The third man tried to break it up but all three of them were sloppy and blurred and one of the men attempted a kick to the chest of his debtor, and lost his balance, landing on his head. That effectively ended the dispute for that night. The three dispersed, and the third man helped the kicker home, where his head swelled. Half a day later, the friend called an ambulance but by then it was too late. The kicking man fell into a coma, and died two days later.

Does this sort of thing happen to Americans? A man tries to kick another and then dies? Could anything be more pitiful? Did it need to be over $10? I find myself cursing the third man, the friend, for not bringing the kicker to the hospital sooner, and for telling everyone that the dispute was over so little. The Sudanese, anyone can now say, will kill each other over $10.

I send money to many. Because everyone at Kakuma knew I had a job there, they assume I am wildly successful in America. So I receive calls from acquaintances in the camp, and in Nairobi, Cairo, Khartoum, Kampala. I send what I can spare, though most of my money goes to my younger brothers and stepbrothers, three of them in school in Nairobi. They were so small when I left Marial Bai that I can remember little about them from that time. Now they are grown and have plans. Samuel, the oldest and shortest, just graduated from high school, and is applying to business schools in Kenya. Peter will graduate from a British-run preparatory school in Nairobi; Phil helped to pay for his tuition. Peter is perhaps the most like myself; at school he is very involved—he is a prefect, he plays basketball and is a black belt in karate. He is quiet but is respected by his peers and his teachers. Because he is the most reliable of my brothers, I send funds through him for distribution to Samuel and to Philip, who is sixteen and wants to be a doctor. I am happy and proud to send them money, sometimes as much as $300 a month. But it is never enough. There are so many others for whom I cannot do what I would like to. My father's sister lives in Khartoum with three children, and has very little means of taking care of herself. Her husband was killed in the war, and his brothers are dead, too. I send her money, perhaps $50 a month, and I wish I could send more.

The last message is from Moses. Moses of Marial Bai, Moses who was brought north as a slave, Moses who was branded and escaped and later trained to be a rebel. Moses who went to private school in Kenya and college in British Columbia and now lives in Seattle. I have not seen him since Kakuma and I am so grateful when I hear his voice. His is a voice so unwavering, always bright, lunging forward with hope.

"Gone Far my man!" he says in English. He always liked this nickname for me. He switches to Dinka. "Lino called me and he told me what happened. First of all, don't be mad at Lino. He said I was the one and only person he would call. And I won't tell anyone else. I promise. He also said that you're doing okay, and that the injuries weren't so bad. So I send you my best wishes for a quick recovery."

Every time I wonder about where we're going and who we are, if I speak to Moses, I feel assured. If only you were with me now, Moses! You would be strong enough to carry us both through this horrible morning.

"Now, I know this sounds like a bad time to bring this up..." he says, and I catch my breath. "But I'm organizing a walk..." I exhale. He says he is organizing a walk to bring attention to the plight of the Darfurians. He plans to travel from his home in Seattle to Tucson, Arizona, by foot.

"Achak, I want to do this and I know it will make a difference. Think of it! What if we all walked again? What if we could all get together and walk again, this time on roads and in view of the whole world? Wouldn't people take notice? We'd really be able to get people thinking about Darfur, about what it means to be displaced, chased, and walking toward an uncertain future, right? Call me back when you can. I want you to be part of this."

There is a pause, when it seems that Moses has put down the phone. Then he picks it up again in a clattering rush.

"And I'm so sorry about Tabitha. Achak, I am so very sorry. You'll find another girl, I know. You're a very desirable man." He pauses to correct himself. "That is, to women, not to me. I do not find you desirable that way, Gone Far."

He is laughing quietly when he hangs up.

XXV.

"There he is!"

I push through the front door to the Century Club and am met by Ben, the club's maintenance engineer. He is a thin man, with small hands and huge empathetic eyes and a great dome of a forehead.

"Hello, Ben," I say.

"Whoa, you look wasted, son." He rests his clipboard on the counter and comes to me, holds my face in his hands. "Where have you been? You look like you haven't slept in weeks. And this!" He touches the cut on my forehead. "And your lip!"

He holds my face and examines every pore.

"You get in a fight?"

I sigh, and he assumes this means yes. He drops his hands from my face and adopts a dissatisfied expression.

"Why are you Sudanese always fighting?"

I touch his shoulder and walk past. I don't feel like explaining everything that happened. I need to wash myself.

"Talk to me after you get cleaned up, yeah?" he calls out.

In the locker room I am alone. I take a clean white towel from the pile by the door and open my locker. Taking off my shoes is a miracle. My feet breathe, I breathe. Immediately I feel better. I throw them into the locker and undress slowly. I am sore everywhere; my body seems to have aged decades overnight.

The water is a shock at any temperature. As it becomes warmer, my limbs and bones grow more limber. I ease my head under the rain and watch the blood slip down my body and across the tile. There is not much, a tidy rose-colored thread that dashes for the drain and is gone.

In the mirror I do not look much different. My bottom lip is cut, and there is a sickle-shaped abrasion from my cheek to my temple. A small red spot now occupies the corner of my left eye, just one small drop in the center of the white.

I put on a T-shirt that is nearly clean, and the sweatpants and sneakers I keep at the club. Once the club's shop opens, I will buy another tennis shirt and wear it today. Though I have not slept, simply changing my clothes has created a dividing point between that day, those events, and today. I take a deep breath from the room and am overtaken. I collapse on the cushioned chair they keep in the corner. My neck has given out, and my chin hits my chest. For a moment, I am defeated. My eyes are closed, and I see nothing—no colors, nothing. I can't envision getting up again. My spine seems to have left me. I am an invertebrate, and there is comfort in this. I sit with this idea, following a course that would allow me to remain collapsed on this chair forever. It is attractive for a moment, and then seems less compelling than simply going to work.

I close my locker and soon regain myself. I have to be at the front desk in one minute; my shift begins at five-thirty.

When I get to the desk, I am relieved that Ben is gone. He feels he is more helpful, with his advice and opinions, than he actually is. If he knew what happened to me yesterday, he would have hours of suggestions about what to do, whom to call, where to file complaints and lawsuits. I sit down, alone in the foyer, and turn on the computer. My job is to check in members as they arrive and hand out brochures to prospective members. My shift is only four hours long on Mondays, and the club is not busy at this hour. There are regulars, though, and I know their faces if not always their names.

First is Matt Donnelley, who often walks in the same time I do. He runs on the treadmill from 5:30 to 6:05, does two hundred sit-ups, showers, and leaves. Here he is, a few minutes late, sturdily built, with a thin purple slash of a mouth. When I started at the club, he spent some time one morning talking to me, asking about the history of the Lost Boys and my life in Atlanta. He was well-read and sincerely

427

interested in Sudan; he knew the names Bashir, Turabi, Garang. He was a lawyer, he said, and told me to call him if ever I needed any help or legal advice. But I couldn't think of a reason to call him, and since then we have exchanged only compulsory greetings.

"Hey Valentino," he says. "What's the good word?"

The first few times he said this, I thought he was actually looking for a certain word, something appropriate for that particular day. "Blessed," I said the first time he asked. He explained the expression to me, but I still don't know how to answer.

Today I say hello to him, and he hands me his membership card. I swipe it and his picture appears, twelve inches tall and in garish color, on the computer monitor in front of me.

"Gotta get me a new picture," he says. "I look like they dug me up, right?"

I smile and then he is gone, into the lockers. But his picture remains. It is a quirk of the computer system that the members' pictures linger on the screen until the next member passes through. There is probably a way to remove them from the monitor but I don't know it.

So I look for a moment at Matt Donnelley.

Matt Donnelley, at first it was a rumor. In the winds of Kakuma, people were talking about America. On a certain day in April of 1999, in the morning people talked about so many different things—soccer, sex, a certain aid worker who had been removed for touching a young Somali boy—and by sunset no one spoke of anything but America. Who would go? How would they decide? How many would go?

It started with one of the Dominics. He had been in the office of the UNHCR when he heard someone talking on the phone. The person had said something akin to "That's very good news. We're very happy, and the boys will be very happy, I'm sure. Right, the Lost Boys. When you know how many you will take, please let me know."

In days, those words had been repeated hundreds of times, maybe thousands, among the unaccompanied minors of Kakuma. No one could concentrate on anything, no one could play basketball, school was a disaster. Everywhere groups of boys, twenty or fifty in a cluster, were huddled around whoever had new information. One day the news was that all of the Lost Boys would be taken to America. The next day it was America and Canada that would take us, and then Australia. No one knew much about Australia, but we imagined that the three countries were close together, or perhaps three regions of the same nation.

Early on, Achor Achor appointed himself an authority on the matters of resettlement, though he had no unique expertise.

—They will take only the first in each class, Achor Achor said. —I think I'll go, but most of you will be left behind.

This view was contradicted by most of the boys, and soon enough by the facts. The United States planned to resettle hundreds, perhaps thousands of the young men of Kakuma. It became the sole occupying thought in my mind. Resettlement was known to happen to refugees from camps like ours, but the conditions were always extreme and rare, reserved for well-known political dissidents, victims of rape, others whose safety was continually threatened. But it seemed that this undertaking would be something very different, a plan whereby most or all of us unaccompanied minors would be taken and brought across the ocean to America. It was the most bizarre idea I had ever heard.

It took days of discussion to conjure an explanation for why the United States would possibly want us all. It is a fact that this country did not have an obligation to resettle four thousand young men living in a camp in Kenya. It would be an act of generosity without any material benefit for them. We were not scientists or engineers, we did not have valuable expertise or education. Nor were we from a country, like Cuba or even China, that would be embarrassed by our defection. We were penniless young men who would do our best to go to college and become better men. Nothing more. These considerations increased the strangeness of it all.

We did not know much about America, but we knew it was peaceful and that there we would be safe. We would each have a home and a telephone. We could finish our educations without worrying about food or any other threat. We conjured an America that was an amalgam of what we had seen in movies: tall buildings, bright colors, so much glass, fantastic car crashes, and guns used only by criminals and police officers. Beaches, oceans, motorboats.

Once the possibility became real in our minds, I expected to be taken at any time. We had been given no timetable, so it seemed possible that one morning I would be in class and the next moment I would be sitting on a plane. Achor Achor and I talked about how at any moment we had to be ready, because there would likely be a bus one day, and it would be going directly to the airport and then to America. We had ironclad agreements that ensured we would not forget each other.

—If you're in school when the bus comes, I'll run to tell you, I said.

—And you'll do the same for me? Achor Achor said.

—Of course. And if I'm at work, you'll find me?

—I will, I will. I won't leave without you.

—Good, good. I won't leave without you, either, I said.

In class, I tried to concentrate but found it impossible. I was constantly watching the roads, looking for the bus. I trusted Achor Achor but feared that we both might miss our ride. It occurred to us both that there might be only one bus, and whoever made it on that bus would reach America—no one else. This made our day-to-day existence difficult, with the two of us on the lookout every hour of every day. For weeks, our only relaxation came at night, when we were sure the bus could not or would not come. The planes could not fly at night, we reasoned, so the bus would not pick us up at night. We also came to the conclusion that the bus would not come on a weekend, so we relaxed on those days, too. This was all very odd, of course, because no one had told us about any bus, let alone its schedule. We had conjured our theories and plans based on no facts whatsoever. But in those days everyone had their own theory, each as plausible as the next, for nothing seemed impossible anymore.

It was very surprising for me, for Achor Achor and the rest of us when, after two weeks, the bus had not come. We wondered if there were obstacles, and what exactly they were. Outside of the unknown and uncontrollable factors, there were those we knew quite well. The Sudanese elders of Kakuma, a good portion of them, did not want to allow us boys to go to the United States.

—You will forget your culture, they said.

—You will get diseases, you will get AIDS, they warned.

—Who will lead Sudan when this war is over? they asked.

Because many of the unaccompanied minors assumed that it was these elders who were holding up the process, a meeting was called between our leadership and theirs. Hundreds attended, even though only a fraction could fit inside the church where the meeting was held. A crowd twelve deep surrounded the little corrugated-steel building, and when Achor Achor and I arrived—we were to be among the youth representatives—there was no chance of finding a space inside. So we listened from the outer ring of those gathered outside. From the church came yelling and arguing, and the standard fears were expressed: of our losing sight of our customs and history;

doubts that the emigrations would ever really occur; and what the loss of four thousand young men would mean.

—How can our country recover when we lose the youth? they said.

—You are the hope of the country, you boys. What will become of our country if there is peace? We risked our lives to have you educated in Ethiopia, we brought you here to Kakuma. You speak many languages now, you can read and write and are being trained in other trades, too. You are among the best educated of our people. How can you leave when we're so close to victory, to peace?

—But there *is* no peace and there *will be* no peace! a young man said.

—You have no right to hold us back, said another.

And so on. The meeting went late into the night, and Achor Achor and I left after standing for eight hours, listening to the rhetoric circling and spinning off in a dozen directions. Nothing was settled that night, but it became clear to the elders that they could not control these four thousand young men. There were too many of us and we were too hungry to move. We were a small army of our own now, we were tall and healthy and hell-bent on leaving the camp with or without their blessing.

The first step in leaving Kakuma was the writing of our autobiographies. The UNHCR and the United States wanted to know where we had come from, what we had endured. We were to write our stories in English, or if we could not write adequately in English, we could have someone write it for us. We were asked to write about the civil war, about losing our families, about our lives in the camps. Why do you want to leave Kakuma? they asked. Are you afraid to return to Sudan, even if there is peace? We knew that those who felt persecuted in Kakuma or Sudan would be given special consideration. Maybe your family in the Sudan had done something to another family and you feared retribution? Perhaps you had deserted the SPLA and feared punishment? It could be many things. Whichever strategy we applied, we knew that our stories had to be well told, that we needed to remember all that we had seen and done; no deprivation was insignificant.

I wrote my story in an examination booklet, its small pages lined in blue. It was the first time I told my story, and it was very difficult to know what was relevant and what was not. My first draft was only one page long, and when I showed it to Achor Achor, he laughed out loud. His was already five pages long and he hadn't reached Ethiopia yet. What about Gilo? he asked. What about Golkur? What about the time

431

we ran to the planes, thinking they would drop food, and instead they dropped bombs, killing eight boys? What about that?

I had forgotten that, and so many things. How could I put everything down on paper? It seemed impossible. No matter what, the majority of life would be left out of this story, this sliver of a version of the life I'd known. But I tried anyway. I tore up my first version and began again. I worked on it for weeks more, thinking of every last thing I had seen, every path and tree and pair of yellowed eyes, every body I buried.

When I finished, it was nine pages long. When I turned it in, the UN took a passport picture of me to attach to my file. It was the first such picture of me I had ever seen. I had been in group pictures before, my head a blur in a crowd, but this new picture, of only me, staring straight ahead, was a revelation. I stared at this photo for hours and held the folder close for days, debating with myself whether or not this picture, these words, were truly me.

I now see it as a mistake, but I brought the picture to Maria one day. I wanted her to see it. I wanted everyone to see it. I wanted to talk and talk about who I was now, the young man who had had his picture taken and was on his way to the United States. I found her outside her home, hanging laundry.

—I've never seen you smile like that, she said. She held the picture for a long time; such photographs were rare in those days. —Can I keep it? she asked.

I told her no, that it was necessary for the file, that it was crucial to my application. She gave it back to me.

—Do you think we'll be taken, too? The girls?

I was not prepared for this question. I had not heard any mention of girls being taken for this round of resettlements. It did not seem a possibility to me.

—I don't know, I said.

Maria smiled her hard smile.

—But I'm sure it's possible, I said, almost believing my words.

—I was only kidding, she said. —I would never want to go, anyway.

She was an awful liar, always transparent.

I was determined to find out if girls were applying, and a few days later I learned that it was indeed possible, that many girls, dozens of them, had begun their applications. I ran to tell Maria, but she was not at home. Her neighbors said she was at the water tap and when I found her there, I told her what I knew: that girls were invited to apply, too, that they simply had to prove that they had no family and were unmarried. When I told her this, a light came to her eyes, for a moment, before flickering out.

—Maybe I'll see what I can do, she said.

—I can take you there tomorrow, I said. —We'll get an application.

She agreed to meet me at the UN compound in the morning. But the next day, when I arrived, she was not there.

—She's at the water tap, her sister said.

I found her in line again, sitting again with her two jerry cans.

—I'll see what happens with all of you first, she said. —I'll go next time.

—I think you should apply now. It might take a while.

—Maybe next week, then.

She seemed unmotivated to begin the process. Perhaps it was the nature of the day, too warm and windy, a day that kept many inside. Maria did not look at me that day, did not entertain notions of escape. I had a low opinion of her attitude that day, and I left her there, sitting in the dust. The line moved. Maria picked up her empty containers and moved them a few feet forward, and sat down again.

—What's happening with your application? Noriyaki asked me. —Any news?

Many months had passed since the initial wave of excitement about the resettlements. We had all turned in our stories, and since then, many young men had been asked to come to the UN compound for interviews. But I had not been called upon. I told Noriyaki there was no news, that I had not heard anything since I turned in my papers. He nodded and smiled.

—Good, good, he said. —That's good. That means things are on track.

Noriyaki was a sorcerer at convincing me of the most implausible things, and on that day he persuaded me that despite hearing nothing from the UN, I would be scheduled for the first airlift to America. I should begin to plan accordingly, he said— I should begin deciding which NBA team I preferred, for there would be no doubt that I would be asked to play professionally. I laughed, but then wondered if I could indeed play basketball for a living. Maybe I could play for whatever college I eventually attended? Every decent player at Kakuma imagined the day that he would be discovered and lifted up, as Manute Bol had been, and brought to glory. That day, I, too, allowed myself a moment of self-delusion.

433

—I should tell you now, Noriyaki said that day, —I'm leaving Kakuma, too. In two months. I wanted you to know first.

It had been long enough, he said. He needed to be home with his fiancée. And with me gone, he had decided, it would be the right time to hand the Wakachiai Project over to the next team. It seemed the right thing to do, I thought. We were both happy for each other, that we would finish this stage of our lives and move on together, albeit on other sides of the earth. We talked all that day about how we could keep in touch, how easy it would be with our new, more opulent lifestyles. We could call or email each other each day, send jokes and memories and pictures. We opened two Fantas, clinked them together, and drank them down.

—You'll come to my wedding! he said suddenly, as if the plausibility of the idea suddenly occurred to him.

—Yes! I said. Then I asked, —How?

—Easy. You'll have the proper immigrant status. You'll be able to travel wherever you want. It's one year from today, Valentino. We've set a date. You'll come to Japan and you'll be there when I marry Wakana.

—I will! I said, believing it completely. —I'll definitely be there.

Drinking our Fantas, we savored that thought for an afternoon, the luxury and goodness of it all: airplanes, cities, cars, tuxedos, cake, diamonds, champagne. The day when we would meet again as prosperous men, comfortable and accomplished men of means, seemed very close.

In those days there was euphoria in the camp for so many reasons, among them the Vatican's first-ever canonization of a Sudanese martyr. Josephine Bakhita, who had been enslaved herself, died as a Canossian Sister in Italy in the late 1940s, and now she was a saint. This was a source of fascination and pride for us all, many of us having no idea that it was even possible for a Sudanese to be sanctified. Her name was invoked at church every day, and was on the tongues of every proud Dinka Catholic at Kakuma. It was an unusual time for us all, a time when for the first time in years the Dinka felt strong, felt wanted by God and faraway nations. A woman of southern Sudan could be a saint, and the Lost Boys could be flown across the ocean to represent Sudan in America. If one event was possible, so was the other. Nothing was out of the question.

When the first resettlement flights departed, there were celebrations all over

Kakuma, and I went with Achor Achor to the airfield to watch the planes disappear. I was overjoyed for these young men, fully believing that I would soon join them in America. As the flights continued, though, as the near-constant news of the good fortune of this boy and that boy, I became numb to their happiness, and could only question my own inadequacies. Perhaps five hundred young men left, and as the months passed and I received no word from the UN, I became less happy for those who had been chosen. Parties broke out with every posting. Families celebrated, groups of young men dancing together when their names appeared. Each week there was incalculable joy for them and devastation for the rest of us.

I was not close to leaving. I hadn't even been given an interview. The interview was the first step, long before one's name could be posted. Something seemed very wrong.

—I'm very sorry, Achor Achor said one day.

I had already heard. Achor Achor's name had appeared that morning.

—When do you leave? I asked.

—One week.

The news was always quick like this. One's name was posted, and then that person was gone, it seemed, within days. We all had to be ready.

I managed to congratulate him, but my pleasure in his good fortune was tempered by the bewilderment I felt. I had done everything right, I thought. Through my job, I even knew some of the same UN staff members who were helping with the resettlement process. Nothing seemed to give me an advantage. I had not been a soldier, I had an exemplary record at Kakuma, and I was not the only one baffled by the fact that so many were sent to America before me. No one understood it, but theories abounded. The most plausible among them held that there was a prominent SPLA soldier named Achak Deng, and that the two of us were being confused. This fact was never confirmed, but Achor Achor had his own theory.

—Maybe they don't want to lose you here.

This did not cheer me.

—You're too valuable to the camp, he joked.

I did not want to be so valuable to the camp. I wondered whether I should be less responsible for a while. Could I shirk my duties, seem less competent?

—I'll say something to the UN people when I see them next, he said.

All of the boys who lived in the household of Gop had been lifted up and transported—to Detroit, San Diego, Kansas City. Soon I was among only a few men of my age left at the camp. The others whose applications had been ignored or rejected were known SPLA commanders or criminals. I was the only one I knew who had an unblemished background but who had not yet even been interviewed. I had been scheduled for interviews, yes, but each time the day approached, something would happen and the date would be pushed back or canceled. One day there were clashes in the camp between the Sudanese and the Turkana, one killed from each side, and Kakuma was closed to visitors. Another time the American lawyer who was present at all the interviews had to go home to New York at the last minute. He would return three months later, they told us.

There is no feeling like rejection coupled with abandonment. I had read about the Rapture, wherein sixty-four thousand souls would be taken to heaven before the End Days, when the Earth would be engulfed in flames. And over the next six months of 2000, it felt very much like I was being left at Kakuma while all those I knew were pulled from our purgatory and lifted up to the Kingdom of God. I had been examined by the powers that be, and was deemed deserving of eternal hellfire.

Achor Achor left one morning and we did not allow drama into our goodbye. He was wearing a winter coat, because someone had told him Atlanta would be very cold. We shook hands and I patted his puffy shoulder, both of us pretending we would see each other again, and soon. He left with another of the Eleven, Akok Anei, and as I watched them walk down the road to the airfield, Achor Achor looked back at me with eyes that betrayed his sadness. He did not think I would ever leave the camp.

After Achor Achor, hundreds more left. Dozens of planes took to the sky, full of Lost Boys like me, so many whose names I never knew.

Everyone found my continued presence at Kakuma very amusing.

—They'll reschedule you till you're the last guy! the humorous Dominic said. He was the last of the Dominics to remain with me, but he had been interviewed already and so was buoyed by confidence. —Gone Far, you're not going anywhere! he laughed. He didn't mean to be cruel, but he had lost the power to make me laugh.

Noriyaki tried to remain positive.

—They wouldn't keep rescheduling you if they didn't want you to go.

He had extended his stay at Kakuma, citing various organizational technicalities and directives issued by his superiors in Japan. But I had a terrible feeling that he was waiting for me to leave before he left himself. I eventually learned this was indeed his plan.

—Maybe they're waiting for *you* to leave first, I told him. I badly wanted him to go home to his fiancée. She had waited too long for him.

—I'm afraid that's out of my hands, he said, grinning. —I have my orders.

Finally, a tornado of a day. I had prayed for such a day, and then it came. In one morning I received word both that I would be interviewed and that Tabitha and her brothers had been accepted for resettlement. It was a wild sort of a day that began, with Tabitha arriving at my door just after dawn.

—We're going! she squealed.

I had not yet opened my door. It was unheard of for her to appear at my door alone before the daylight was whole. I told her this in an urgent whisper. We would risk the disapproval of the community; we had already stretched their tolerance, I was sure.

—I don't care! she said, now louder. —I don't care I don't care!

She danced and squeaked and jumped.

When I stood and awakened enough to hear and, later, to process her news, she was already off to wake up whoever she planned to tell next. I was not surprised that she delivered this news to me in such a cavalier way. It is a fact that no love fostered in Kakuma could compete with the prospect of leaving that place. Later I learned that her departure date was scheduled for two weeks from that day, and I knew then that I would not see her again in the camp—not in any meaningful way. I knew from watching the departures of so many hundreds of others that the days between notice of departure and the day itself, there was little time for anything, let alone romance. I would see her in groups, walking quickly to and fro with her brothers or friends, taking care of so many details. I suppose we did find a few moments alone, but she was not with me anymore. All romances ended in those days, when so many were leaving Kenya. Even while sitting together in her empty house or mine, Tabitha would talk only about the United States, about Seattle, about what she would find there—Nairobi multiplied many times over! Oh, she would laugh, the kaleidoscopic possibilities!

The morning she gave me her news, I received news of my own. Tabitha's scent was still in the air when another voice came from the other side of my shelter.

—Achak!

There were only a few people who still called me Achak.

—Who is it?

It was Cornelius, a young neighbor of mine, a boy of eight, born on a rainy day at Kakuma, who always seemed to know everything before any other soul. Months earlier, he had known which refugee had impregnated a Turkana girl, and on this day, he told me that he had heard that I had been scheduled for an IOM interview. It was well-known that Cornelius's information was invariably correct.

And so it was. It was July of 2001, eighteen months after the resettlements began, and finally I sat in a white cinderblock room, before two people: one white American and a Sudanese interpreter. The American, round in the face and with cold blue eyes, introduced himself as a lawyer, and then apologized.

—We're so sorry, Dominic. We know you've been puzzled by the delay in your application. You probably wondered what the heck was going on.

I did not contradict him. I had almost forgotten that I had used the name Dominic on my application.

Their questions swung from very simple questions about my name and hometown to more involved investigations of the dangers I had faced. I had been briefed by many other Lost Boys about what questions to expect, but the ones they asked me varied slightly. There was a majority of the Sudanese who insisted that one embellish as often as possible, to be sure to claim the deaths of all of one's family and known relatives. I had decided, against the advice of many, to answer all the questions as truthfully as possible.

—Are your parents alive? the lawyer asked.

—Yes, I said.

He smiled. It seemed to him a new kind of answer.

—Your brothers and sisters?

—I don't know, I said.

From there the questions went deeply into my experiences as a refugee: Who were the groups that wanted to kill you and what made them want to kill you? What kind of weapons did they carry or use? Before you left your village, did you see people killed by these attackers? What motivated you to leave Sudan? Which year did you leave Sudan? When did you arrive in Ethiopia and by what means? Did you ever fight in the wars of Sudan? Do you know of the SPLA/SPLM? Where you ever recruited by the rebel army? What security issues do you face in Kakuma? And finally: Have you ever heard of the country called the United States of America? Do you know anyone there? Do you prefer to be resettled in a country other than the U.S.?

I answered all of the queries without distortion, and it was over in twenty minutes. I shook their hands and left the room, puzzled and depressed. Certainly that was not the sort of interview that would decide whether or not a man traveled across the world and became the citizen of a different nation. As I stood, dazed, the interpreter opened the door and caught my arm.

—You did very well, Dominic. Don't worry. You look worried. I'm sure this'll be straightened out now. Smile, friend. And get used to the idea of leaving this place.

I didn't know what to believe. Everything had been delayed so long that I felt uneasy about expecting anything. I knew that nothing was real until one's name was posted on the board, that in the meantime I had to keep working and going to school.

Noriyaki, though, was more certain.

—Oh, you're going.

—Really? I said.

—Oh yeah, it'll be weeks now. Days. No time.

I thanked him for his encouragement, but I made no plans. He, however, did. Finally he made arrangements to leave the camp. He was almost a year late, but now he would finally be going home. The relief I felt was enormous. He had been at Kakuma long enough on my account, and every moment he remained there was taking a toll on me. I wanted him to resume his life, I wanted him to finally make a happy woman out of his long-suffering fiancée. We toasted his imminent departure with orange Fanta and marked the remaining highlights on our calendar. There was little of consequence left to do—only the standard games and classes and deliveries of equipment, and one trip into central Kenya with the youth basketball team. We would be chaperones and coaches, and this, we decided, would be the final hurrah of the Wakachiai Project, at least under our administration.

This was late July and the day was clear. Noriyaki and I were in the cab of a converted truck, the two of us in front and in back the youth basketball team, twelve Sudanese and Ugandan boys, who were to travel four hours to Lodwar to play a team representing a Kenyan high school.

The day was so bright. I remember distinctly feeling God's presence that morning. It was a day that many women, waking and beginning their chores, were calling glorious, a morning for which we gave thanks.

We left the camp very early, about five a.m. All of the boys, and Noriyaki and I, were euphoric to be on the road; Kakuma's refugees were always happy to leave the camp for any amount of time, for any reason. In fact, there were delays in leaving this particular day, because as was customary, there was a good deal of pleading from a variety of Kakuma's characters who attempted to argue their way onto the basketball team. Soon enough, though, we were an hour away from Kakuma, fourteen of us, and the sun was rising. I was in the cab of the truck with Noriyaki, with the twelve players, all of them under sixteen years old, riding in the back, sitting on benches, bouncing in the truckbed with every bump of the crumbling road. Lodwar was about 190 kilometers away, and the drive would take more than four hours, given the rough roads and checkpoints. Everyone was in a good mood, though, singing traditional songs and songs of their own creation.

The second of the early-morning regulars enters.

"Valentino, mon amour! How are you?"

This is Nancy Strazzeri, an elegant woman in her mid-fifties with short white hair and a blood-red velvet sweatsuit. She once brought me coffee cake she had made herself.

"Fine, thank you," I say.

"Broken any hearts lately?" she asks while handing me her card.

"I don't think so," I say.

I swipe her card, replacing Matt Donnelley's face with hers.

"See you in an hour, mon frère," she sings, and is gone. Her face, a tired face with eyes that speak of past mischief, remains.

Nancy, the road to Lodwar was dotted with potholes and cut everywhere with cracks that had become small winding canyons. Noriyaki did his best with the truck, which he had driven only once before, and never this far. It was a stick shift, and the trucks he had driven around Kakuma had automatic transmissions. I had never been in the front seat of any vehicle, and tried to remain calm, though Noriyaki's control of the vehicle seemed tenuous.

The passage of time was slow as we turned a corner and saw the obstacle. There was a large mound of dirt in the right lane. It should not have been there. There was no reason that that dirt should be there.

Noriyaki yelled in Japanese, swerving left to avoid it.

The truck tilted heavily, and bodies flew past my window. The players in the truckbed were thrown onto the road. Noriyaki swerved again, now to the right, but he had lost control. The truck tilted onto two wheels.

Noriyaki again screamed a word I didn't know. Screams from the truckbed. Three more players were tossed. The truck groaned and slid slowly off the road, down the berm, and rolled onto its roof. The breaking of glass, the squeal of machinery. It was not fast, our decline, but it was irreversible, and when it was clear that the truck would crash, Noriyaki threw his arm across my chest. But then he was gone.

The truck came to a stop on its side. I was still inside the cab, and through the broken windshield I could see two boys lying on the dirt. I looked over to Noriyaki. He had fallen out of the truck, and when the truck rolled, it had landed on his chest. Blood left his head like water. There were fragments of glass in his cheek and fore-head, shards everywhere around him, pink with his blood.

—Oh! he said, and then closed his eyes.

—Noriyaki! I said, my voice far weaker than I could have wished. I reached through the window and touched his face. He did not respond.

Now there was someone on my side of the truck, pulling at me. It was then I was reminded of the rest of the world. That I was alive.

I was helped out of the truck, and stood for a moment. There were now people all around the road, new people. Kenyans from another truck, a food truck. They had seen the accident. The basketball boys were strewn everywhere, all over the road and embankment. How many were dead? Who was alive? Everyone was bleeding.

—Dominic! a boy's voice said. —What happened?

This boy seemed to be fine. Who was he? My limbs felt loose, disconnected. My neck was sore, my head felt detached. I stood under the sun, my eyes stinging with sweat, everything so heavy, and I watched.

—One, two, three! The Kenyans were moving the truck off of Noriyaki. They rocked the truck one way and then the other, and when the truck was tilted away from Noriyaki, one of the men was able to slip in and push Noriyaki out. The truck was dropped again where Noriyaki had lain. The men carried Noriyaki up to the road, his body limp, blood no longer leaving his head.

That was what I saw before I fell.

I was loaded onto the food truck and taken to Kakuma. I awoke on the road.

—He lives!

—You see this, Simon?

—Ah, good! Good! We were not sure about you, Sudan.

—You would have died if we had not been driving by.

—Stay awake, boy. We have an hour to go.

—Pray, Sudan. We are praying for you.

—He doesn't need to pray. God spared him today.

—I think he should pray. He should say thanks and keep praying.

—Okay, Sudan, pray. Pray, pray, pray.

Two more people, a couple, enter the club. I do not remember their names. They smile at me and say nothing, his hand on the small of her back. They are in business attire, and they hand me their membership cards. Jessica LaForte. Malcolm LaForte. They smile again and they are gone.

I look at the face of Malcolm LaForte, wishing I had swiped them in reverse order. His wife is dark-eyed and dark-haired and her face is soft and forgiving, but he is a severe-looking man. An impatient man. Impatient men have made my life much more difficult than it might otherwise have been. He gives me a terse smile he thinks passes for sincere, and enters the club.

Malcolm LaForte, in the camp, I was dead. For many days, among many hundreds of people, I was considered deceased. The casualties reported from the truck accident varied hour to hour, day to day. At first, all aboard the truck were presumed killed. Then the basketball players themselves began arriving at Kakuma, and it became clear that none of these young boys had died. Everyone agreed it was miraculous.

But I was dead, most were certain. Valentino Achak Deng was dead.

Gop and his family heard this and they wept and screamed. Anyone who knew me cursed Noriyaki, they cursed Kakuma and basketball and the broken Kenyan roads. My coworkers at the UNHCR were despondent. The Napata Drama Group held a ceremony in my memory, led by Miss Gladys with speeches from Dominic and Madame Zero and all the members. Tabitha wailed and did not leave her bed for three days, rising only when she heard that I was not, in fact, dead.

I woke up at Lopiding Hospital. There was a nurse with her hand on my forehead. She said something to me while looking at her watch.

—Do you know what happened? she asked.

—Yes, I said, though I wasn't sure.

—None of your friends are dead, she said.

At this I was relieved. I had a memory of Noriyaki looking grey and covered with glass, but this woman seemed to be saying that he had survived.

—But the Japanese driver is dead, she said, standing.

She left and I was alone.

Noriyaki's family! I thought. Oh, Lord. This was too much. I had seen senseless death, but it had been so long since I had seen something like this.

I was responsible for Noriyaki's death. It was boys like me who had forced the creation of Kakuma. If there was no Kakuma, Noriyaki would not have come to Kenya. He would be at home, with his family and fiancée, living a normal life. Japan was a peaceful country, and people from peaceful countries should not be involved in the business of countries at war. It was absurd and wrong that this man should come so far to die. To die while bringing some refugees to play basketball? To die because he wanted to see me leave the camp? It was a wretched thing my God had done this time. I had a low opinion of my Lord and a lower opinion of my people. The Sudanese were a burden upon the Earth.

Having seen the death of Diana mourned around the world, I reserved some expectation that Noriyaki's death would provoke tributes and despair throughout the camp, throughout Kenya and the world. But I heard of nothing of the kind. I asked the nurse if there had been television reports about the accident; she said she had not seen any. The aid workers at Kakuma were distraught, to be sure, but there was no worldwide outpouring, no front-page obituaries. Within two days of his last breath, Noriyaki's body was taken to Nairobi, where he was cremated. I do not know why.

—What are you doing here?

A man was standing over me, his face silhouetted by the sun through the low window. He stepped closer and it was Abraham, the maker of new legs and arms. Immediately tears fell down my face. I had been in the hospital for days, in and out of sleep.

—Don't worry, he said. —Your limbs are intact. I'm here only as a friend.

I tried to talk but my throat was too dry.

—Don't talk, he said. —I know about your head, the drugs they have you on. I'll just sit here with you for a while.

443

And he did. He began to sing, quietly, the song he had hummed that day, long before. I fell back asleep and did not see him again.

I was at the hospital nine days. They tested my head, they examined my hearing and vision and bones. They put stitches in my head and bandaged my limbs. I slept much of each day, and Tabitha left while I stumbled through the fog of my painkillers.

I suppose in the back of my mind I knew the day was fast approaching, but I was not certain until a note was delivered to me one day after breakfast. I do not know how Tabitha was able to find a pink envelope in that camp, but somehow she did. It even smelled like her. The note was written in English; she had employed the help of a Kenyan writing instructor, I suppose, to make the note as formal and eloquent as possible.

> Valentino my dear,
>
> I was so worried when I heard about the accident. And when I believed that you perished on the roadside, I was devastated. Imagine my joy when it was not true, when I knew that you had survived and would be fine. I tried to visit you, but they were not admitting people who could not claim to be your caretakers. So I waited for news of your health, and was encouraged when I knew you would make a full recovery. I am so very sorry that Noriyaki has passed away. He was well loved and will surely go to Heaven.
>
> As you know, my flight could not wait. I am dictating this letter just hours before my plane leaves for Nairobi. My heart is heavy, but we know that I had to leave. This camp cannot tell us where we should live. I could not miss the opportunity to fly away. I know you understand me on this point.
>
> I will see you again, my dear Valentino. I don't know what our lives will be like in America but I know that we will both be successful. The next time I see you we will both drive cars and meet at a clean and expensive restaurant.
>
> Your loving friend,
> Tabitha

A stream of new people bursts into the club at ten to six. First, two women in their seventies, both wearing baseball caps. Now a very large woman with corkscrew hair shooting in every direction, followed by a pair of younger women, sisters, very fit and with their hair in ponytails. There is a pause in the flow, and I look to the parking lot, where I see the gold sun rising in the reflection of the cars. A white-haired man enters the club, walking with his body angled forward. He is the last of the bunch: Stewart Goodall, with close-set eyes and a crooked smile.

Stewart Goodall, can you imagine a letter like that? Everyone I knew had left for a place expected to be paradise many times over, and I remained behind, and now even Tabitha was gone, having slipped away while I slept.

After a week recuperating, I went back to the Wakachiai Project. Because it was a two-person staff, if I did not return quickly, the project would wither. Most of Noriyaki's possessions were still there—his letters, his sweatsuit, his computer, his picture of Wakana in her white tennis dress. I was not prepared for the reality of being there without him. I put all of his things in a box but still the room spoke his name all day. I knew I would have to leave very soon.

I was charged with finding a replacement for Noriyaki. The Japanese wanted to continue funding the project, and to keep it running, I had to pick a new officer. I interviewed many candidates, most of them Kenyan. It was the first time a Sudanese refugee had interviewed a Kenyan for a job at Kakuma.

I found a Kenyan man named George and he became my assistant. We continued to plan activities for the youth of Kakuma, and soon after my return we received a large shipment of soccer balls, volleyball uniforms, and running shoes from Tokyo. Noriyaki had been trying to find the funding for this shipment for months, and now seeing all of it spread around the office, so many new things—it was so difficult.

The doctor checked on my progress once a week. I was sore in my bones and joints, but the symptoms the doctor had worried about—dizziness, blurred vision, nausea—did not occur. It was only the headaches, of varying severity throughout the day, that affected me, and they were worst at night. I lowered my head to my pillow and as I did, the pain grew. My friends and family checked on me and watched me warily. I had lost ten pounds at Lopiding, so they gave me extra rations and anything they could find to distract me—a handmade chess set, a comic book. When I did fall asleep, I fell deep, and my breathing was hard to detect. More than once I woke up to Gop poking me in the shoulder, making sure I was alive.

After a month, my body had recovered and mentally I had reached a certain numbness that was hard for me to define or for others to detect. Outwardly I performed my duties at work and at home, and my appetite had returned to normal. I alone knew

445

that I had decided on a change. A few days earlier, I decided definitively, though against the advice of virtually everyone, to return to Sudan to rejoin my family. There was no reason to stay at Kakuma, and remaining there was a daily punishment. It was God and the earthly powers that be saying this was the best I deserved, that this life was good enough for the insect known as Valentino Achak Deng. But Tabitha's letter had ruptured something inside me, and now I did not give a damn about Kakuma, about my duties, about what was expected of me. I decided I would go first to Loki, then buy my way to Marial Bai. I had enough money, I surmised, to bribe my way onto an aid flight. I had heard of this being done before, and with less money than I had already saved.

Gop inadvertently reinforced my way of thinking about leaving the camp. He had been making many remarks at that time about imminent peace in the south of Sudan. He pointed to many positive developments, including the 2000 Libyan/Egyptian Joint Initiative on the Sudan. Though it was later invalidated, it provided for the establishment of an interim government, power-sharing, constitutional reform, and new elections. And just a few days earlier, President Bush had designated John Danforth, a former senator, as Presidential Envoy for Peace in the Sudan. He would, they said, certainly see that peace was necessary, and with American might, make sure it was achieved.

—You look better today, my new assistant George said one day. We were on our way to replace the nets on the basketball courts, and George was wearing a whistle tied around his neck. He loved to wear his whistle.

When I told George my plan to leave, he almost punched me. He raised his hand to me and then stopped, his whistle in his mouth.

—Are you crazy? he said.

—I have to.

Now he blew the whistle in my face.

—Sudan's still a war zone, man! You said yourself that the murahaleen were still active in your region. How are you going to fight them? Are you going to read to them? Write a play for them? No one in the world, not one person in southern Sudan, would leave this place to go there. And I'll personally see to it that you don't. I'll tie you up with these nets. I'll cut off one of your feet.

I smiled, but George had not changed my mind. People still went back to Sudan. Strong young men like me could do so, and I was older and smarter than I was when

I attempted my recycling. Staying at Kakuma was an untenable idea. Everyone would see me as having been rejected—four thousand are taken to America and I was deemed not worthy. It would be too difficult to live with that stigma.

George blew his whistle again, this time to get my attention.

—Listen. I bet Wakachiai will hire you full-time if you want it. You'll make ten thousand shillings a month, be able to eat at the UN restaurants, drive one of their Land Rovers. Pick a nice bride and live pretty well here.

—Right, I said, and smiled.

—Don't be crazy.

—Okay, I said.

—Don't be stupid.

—I won't, I said.

—This is your home, he said.

—Fine.

—Accept it and thrive here.

I nodded and we installed the new nets.

Six-thirty is when the real crush begins at the Century Club. The rooms become crowded, the exercise machines are all occupied, people become tense. The members are determined to work out and it is frustrating to them when they cannot do it on the timetable they have planned. I check in a dozen people within a five-minute span. They are all working people, professional-looking people. They smile at me and some exchange a few words. One middle-aged man, who has told me he teaches high-school history, asks me how my classes are coming. I lie and tell him they're all fine.

"Headed to college?" he asks.

"Yes sir," I say.

The last woman of the rush is Dorsetta Lewis, one of the few African-American women who works out at this club. She is about forty, very appealing, at once confident but with a shy way of carrying her head, a perpetual rightward tilt.

"Hey there, Valentino," she says, and hands me her card.

"Hello, Dorsetta," I say, and swipe it. In her photograph, she seems to be in the middle of a belly laugh. Her mouth is open wide, all of her teeth visible. I have never heard her laugh and have occasionally thought of trying a joke on her.

"Still hanging in there?" she asks.

"I am, thank you," I say.

"All right then," she says, "that's what I like to hear."

She disappears into the locker room.

The truth is that I do not like hanging in there. I was born, I believe, to do more. Or perhaps it's that I survived to do more. Dorsetta is married, a mother of three, and manages a restaurant; she does more than hang in there. I have a low opinion of this expression, Hang in there.

The club goes quiet again for a spell, and instinctively, I find myself checking my email. There is a note from my brother Samuel.

"Will you call her yet?" he asks. "Here is a picture."

Samuel has recently taken a trip from Nairobi to Khartoum, and joined my father there. They planned the trip so my father could buy goods to reconstitute his business in Marial Bai. Phil Mays had sent my father $5,000, and with this money he planned to buy enough goods to open his shop again. While in Khartoum, Samuel heard about a certain young single woman—she was from a prosperous family and was currently studying English and business in Khartoum. Samuel went to see her and thought immediately that she was meant for me. I have no doubt that he first pursued her himself, but nevertheless, he has been pestering me since, insisting that I call her, so she and I can realize we're meant to be married. I look at the picture he has attached, and she certainly is attractive. Very long hair, an oval face, a V-shaped smile, remarkable teeth. This woman, Samuel assures me, would jump at the chance to move to the United States to be my wife.

Now that I'm online, I decide that I should send an email to those whose addresses I can remember. I would call, but my stolen phone contains all of my phone numbers; I have memorized only a few. I conjure the email addresses of Gerald and Anne, of Mary Williams and Phil, and Deb Newmyer, and Achor Achor; he will forward the message to everyone else. At this point I do not care who knows.

> Hello friends,
>
> I am writing to inform you that I have recently been assaulted by two danger-ous persons in my apartment. The attackers asked me to let them use my phone and when I opened the door, they held me at a gunpoint, kicked me in the cheek, forehead, and back, until I lost consciousness. They took my cell phone, digital camera, checkbooks, and over five hundred dollars in cash. Thank God

they didn't shoot me. For some time, I was guarded by a boy who I believe to be their son, Michael.

As I write to you, I do not have a cell phone and do not have your contact information. Please send me your numbers and I will call you tomorrow. I need to get all my information back.

Have a blessed day.

Sincerely,

Valentino Achak

P.S. Please remind me of your birthday.

Dorsetta, I pretend that I know who I am now but I simply don't. I'm not an American and it seems difficult now to call myself Sudanese. I have spent only six or seven years there, and I was so small when I left. I can return to Sudan, though. Perhaps I should. The country has been very vocal about needing the Lost Boys to return to southern Sudan. "Who will rebuild this country if not you?" they ask. It is the most incredible turn of events that we boys, who were shuffled from camp to camp and who lost half our ranks along the way, are now considered the hope of the nation. Though we are working jobs such as this, hovering near $8.50 an hour, we are far wealthier than most of the residents of our country. We live in apartments and houses that would be reserved only for rebel commanders and their families. And as fraught with peril as our journeys were, in the end, we have become the best-educated group of southern Sudanese in history.

My friends who have returned to Sudan, to visit their families and find a bride, uniformly gape at the primitive nature of life there. A life without cars, roads, television, air conditioning, grocery stores. There is very little electricity in my hometown; most of the power, when they have it, is provided by generators or solar devices. Certain amenities like satellite phones are becoming more common in the larger towns, but on the whole the country is many hundreds of years behind the standard of living to which we are now accustomed. One man I know drank the water from the river, as all of the people do, and he was in bed for a week, vomiting a year's worth of meals. We have been weakened by our time in America, perhaps.

Dorsetta, what was I doing getting on another vehicle, again heading to Kitale, so soon after my accident? My bones still ached everywhere and I had no desire to get on that road again, but there had been a trip planned for many months, and I could not disappoint the boys. Thirty of them, two squads of nine-year-olds, were traveling to Kitale to play against the local boys' teams. Usually such games were exhibitions only; our kids were roundly defeated by any of the Kenyan squads. But the score never mattered, only leaving the camp mattered, so there I was, just weeks after the accident, on September 5, getting on the bus again.

I stood by the vehicle, a closed-top UN bus this time, with George, and we watched the boys run from all sides of the camp. They were good boys, smiling boys—about a third of them had actually been born here, in this camp. To be born here! I never would have thought it possible. The others had come from many regions of Sudan, many brought here as infants, starving and barely alive. I occasionally wondered if one of them could be the Quiet Baby, now grown. Perhaps the Quiet Baby was a boy. It was possible, of course it was. In any case, I loved all of the boys equally.

As they boarded, each of them giddy and touching every inch of the bus, I checked their names against the team roster.

Two were missing.

—Luke Bol Dut? I called out.

The boys laughed. On a day like this, they laughed at anything.

—Luke Bol Dut?

I looked out the window. The day was bright, light as linen. Two boys were running toward the bus. It was Luke and Gorial Aduk, the other missing boy. They were in their uniforms and were racing toward us as if reaching the bus would save them from certain death.

—Dominic!

It was Luke. He leaped onto the bus, almost hysterical. He couldn't get his next words out. —Dominic! he said again.

Another fifteen seconds as he caught his breath.

—What is it, Luke?

—Your name is on the board!

I laughed and shook my head. It was not possible.

—Yes it is! And not just on the board! Your name's on the list for cultural orientation. You got it! You're going!

Cultural orientation was the final step. But before that step were so many others: first a letter, then another interview, then the name on the board. Then another notice for cultural orientation. All of this usually took months. But this wild boy was telling me that the board was telling me all this at once.

—No, I said.

—Yes! Yes! yelled Gorial. He was trying to pat my back.

—Wait, I whispered.

I asked the bus driver to wait, and I told the boys to stay with the bus. I turned to George. I stammered for a second, asking him to wait a moment while I...

He blew his whistle. —Go!

I ran toward the board. Could this be true? Noriyaki had been right! They really wanted me! Of course they did! Why wouldn't they want me? They would not have waited so long if they didn't want me.

I ran.

Halfway there, I caught myself. What was I doing? I stopped. I looked like a fool, running to the board because some nine-year-olds told me my name was listed. False reporting had become a joke; it happened all the time, and was never funny. I slowed down and considered turning around.

The moment I slowed my pace, I heard screaming. I looked up to see Luke and Gorial, trailed by a mass of other boys, running toward me.

—Go! they screamed. —Go to the board!

They looked like they would knock me down if they reached me. I turned again and ran, the boys close at my heels. We all ran, the boys skipping and jumping and laughing along side me. Gop Chol, coming back from the tap, saw us running down the road.

—Where are you going? he yelled.

His face again restored me to my senses. Should I tell him what the boys said, tell him where I was running?

I smiled and continued running. I ran with an abandon I hadn't known since I was very small.

—It's on the board! Gorial screamed to him. —Dominic is on the board!

—No! Gop gasped. —No!

He dropped his jerry can and ran with us. Now there were fifteen of us running.

—You really think it's on the board? he huffed alongside me.

—It is, it is! yelled Luke. —I know how to read!

We ran, tears streaming down our faces because we were laughing and maybe crying and maybe just delirious. Finally we were at the board, the Lutheran World Federation's information kiosk, where they displayed refugees' arts and crafts.

I ran my eyes over the names. Gop was doubled over, holding his side. There were so many names, and the light was too bright, the ink so faint.

—There it is! Gorial yelled. His finger was stuck on the board so I couldn't see. I swept his little finger away and read my name.

DOMINIC AROU. SEPTEMBER 9. ATLANTA.

Now Gop was reading with me.

—September 9? he said. —That's Sunday. Four days away.

—Oh my God, I said.

—Four days! he said.

The boys made a song of it. —Four days! Four days! Dominic's gone in four days!

I hugged Gop and he said he would tell the family. He ran off and I ran off, back to the bus. —I'm going! I told George.

—No! he said.

I told the boys.

—Where? With us?

—No, no. To America. My name is on the board!

—No! they all yelled. —No it isn't, never!

—You're really leaving? George asked.

—I think I am, I said, not quite believing it.

—No! You're here for life! the boys joked.

But finally the news sunk in. I would not be going on their trip that day, and probably wouldn't see them again. Some of the boys seemed hurt, but they found a way to be happy for me. George shook my hand and they leapt over the seats and crowded around me and patted me on the back and the head and hugged my waist and legs with their small arms and tiny bony hands. I was not sure if I would see them again before I left. I hugged all the boys I could reach and we cried and laughed together about the insanity of it all.

It was Wednesday night and I was leaving Sunday. I had hundreds of things to do before my flight to Nairobi. My head ran through all the tasks necessary. There was no time. I knew everything that had to be done, having seen all of my friends leave before me. I had to be at cultural orientation two of the next three days, leaving no time for anything. I would say goodbye to my Kakuma family and friends on Saturday, but before then, it would be madness.

That night I went back to the board, to see my name again. It was indeed my name. There could be no error now. They could not remove my name from that list. Actually, I knew they could—they could do anything, and often did—but I felt at least I had grounds to fight if they tried to rescind their promise. While I was looking at the board that night, I saw also my name on the list for INS letters. They had not sent the letter; I only had to pick it up, and that was the last part of my release. It was all happening at once. I didn't know what to make of the logic of the UN, but it didn't matter. I was leaving in three days and soon everyone knew.

I was telling any person I could see, and they each told ten or twenty more. There was rejoicing in all quarters but there was also concern. Gop's family, and many of my friends, though expressing happiness to my face, worried for me: what did this mean, that I should go on this trip so soon after the accident? This could not be good, they thought. It seemed to be tempting fate to take such a trip so soon after a near-death experience. No one said anything to me. I was too happy and unworried and they didn't want to dampen my optimism. Instead, they prayed. I prayed. Everyone prayed. And amid it all, I thought, This is not right. I've just found out my family is alive. How can I travel across the world? How can I not at least wait in Kakuma until Sudan is safe again? I had waited fifteen years to see my family, and now I was voluntarily taking myself even farther from them. Nevertheless, this was God's plan. I could not believe otherwise. God had placed this chance in front of me, I was certain, and I became convinced of his presence in the sequence of my life when I learned of the possibilities offered by Mr. CB.

There was at that time a brand-new development at Kakuma: through the ingenuity of a Somali entrepreneur, it became possible for those with means to reach, or try to reach, relatives in war-torn areas of East Africa. The Somali, who became known among the English-speaking refugees as Mr. CB, knew how to contact NGOs working throughout the region, and could occasionally arrange to have those living nearby brought to the radio to speak to family members at Kakuma. To reach someone in southern Sudan, we could visit Mr. CB, and for four minutes of radio time, pay him 250 shillings—quite a lot for most of the camp's residents. He would then try to ascertain how best to reach the relative in question. If there was an SPLA radio outlet in the area, he could start there. If there was an NGO in the area, he could go about negotiating with them. This was more difficult, given the NGOs typically had restrictions against using their radios for personal communications. In any case, if all hurdles were cleared, Mr. CB or one of his operatives—for he had employees representing all the nations of Kakuma—would say, We are looking for such and such a person, can you bring them to the radio? And on the other end of the line, someone would be dispatched in whatever village or camp or region to find this person. Sometimes that person would be a hundred yards away, sometimes a hundred miles.

I had the money to pay for a connection to Marial Bai, where I learned there was a cooperative NGO worker at the International Rescue Committee. I knew that it was necessary, now more than ever, for me to reach my father, to tell him about the developments in my life, that I had been chosen for resettlement to the United States. So very soon after Mr. CB opened his operation, I arrived, with 250 shillings in hand.

Mr. CB's place of business, a rectangular room of mud walls and thatched roof, was always crowded. Wives were attempting to reach husbands, children looked for their parents. The Somali's primary clientele was Dinka, but when I arrived that day there was a Rwandan teenager looking for her aunt, her only surviving relative, and a Bantu woman seeking her husband and children. I sat between two other Lost Boys, younger than I, who had come only to watch the process, to test its reliability before they went about raising the money for their own phone call.

We all sat on log benches on either side of the long room, and at the front, Mr CB sat on a chair, the radio on a rough-hewn table before him, two assistants flanking him, one Dinka, one Ethiopian, ready to translate when needed.

After two hours of listening only to static and disappointment, it was my turn, and by this time my hopes were realistic. As I waited, no one had been connected that day, so my expectations were low. I sat down before the table and listened as Mr. CB and his helpers contacted the IRC operator in Marial Bai. Much to everyone's surprise, the connection was made within minutes. The Lost Boys behind me gasped to hear a Dinka voice on the other end. But it was far too soon. I wasn't ready.

Mr. CB, using basic Arabic, explained that he was looking for my father, Deng Nyibek Arou. The Dinka assistant translated, and I heard the NGO worker say that he had seen my father just that day, at the airfield. There had been an Operation

454

Lifeline supply plane that morning, and virtually the entire village had turned out to see what comprised the shipment. Mr. CB asked that my father, Deng Nyibek Arou, be summoned to the radio, and that he would call back in one hour. The man in Marial Bai agreed. I sat back on the log bench, the Lost Boys congratulating me, both of them electric with anticipation. I was absolutely numb. I was sure I had lost the power of speech. It seemed utterly impossible that I would be speaking to my father in one hour. I had not even planned what I would say. Would he remember me? He had so many children by now, I knew, and he was growing older... It was a horrible hour, that hour of waiting in that narrow room and that Somali barking into his radio.

A Burundian couple went ahead of me, attempting to reach an uncle they thought might send them money, but they had no luck. And soon it was my turn again. Mr. CB, with a certain swagger in knowing that at least this one connection, my connection, worked, took my money and contacted the Marial Bai operator again.

—Hello? he said. —Is he there? Okay.

The microphone was handed to me. I stared at it. It was as dead as a stone.

—Talk, boy! the Dinka assistant urged.

I brought the microphone to my mouth.

—Father?

—Achak! a voice said. The voice was not at all recognizable to me.

—Father?

—Achak! Where on Earth are you?

The voice broke into a loud belly-laugh. It was my father. To hear my father say my name! I had to believe it was him. I knew it was him. And just as I became sure, the connection ended. The Somali, his pride at stake, called again. In a few minutes, my father's voice again burst through the box.

—Achak! he barked. —Speak if you can! Be quick like a bunny!

—Father, they want to send me to the United States.

—Yes, he said. —I heard they were sending boys there. How is it?

And the connection died. When Mr. CB found Marial Bai again, I continued where I had left off.

—I'm not in America. I'm at Kakuma. I want to ask you what I should do. I want to see you. I'm not sure I want to travel so far away from you, now that I know you and my mother are alive. I want to come home.

The radio cut out once more. This time the Somali took twenty minutes to regain the IRC operator, and the connection was now far more faint.

When my father and I could hear each other again, he was still talking, as if he had never been interrupted. He was lecturing now, far from amused, his voice raised.

—You have to go, boy. Are you crazy? This town is still ashen from the last attack. Don't come here. I forbid it. Go to the United States. Go there tomorrow.

—But what if I never see you again? I said.

—What? You'll see us. The only way you'll see us is if you get to the United States. Come back a successful man.

—But father, what—

—Yes, the What. Right. Get it. This is it. Go. I am your father and I forbid you to come to this place—

The connection snapped closed for good. The Somali could not regain it.

So that was that.

In those last few days before leaving, I ran everywhere. The next day was my first day of orientation, and my last day of work at the Wakachiai Project. I ran to class and sat with fifty others, mostly younger boys who I did not know; everyone my age was gone. There were two teachers, an American and an Ethiopian, the American withering in the heat. This classroom, the best in Kakuma, was indoors, in the International Organization for Migration center. It had a real roof and floor and we sat in chairs. We listened, but were too excited to pay attention properly, to process the information in a useful way.

They talked about life in the United States. About how to get a job, how to save money, how to arrive on time for work. They talked about apartments, about buying food and paying rent. They helped us with the math—most of us, they said, would be making $5 or $6 an hour. This seemed like a great deal of money. Then they told us about buying food, and paying rent on an apartment. They had us do the calculations, and we realized we could not afford to live on $5 or $6 an hour. No particular solution was offered, I don't think, but we were too high to dwell on the details. We tried to listen to all the words, but we were so excited. Trying to learn numbers and facts that first day was like catching bats leaving a hollow. They managed to seize our attention when the American brought out a cooler and passed around a large cube of ice. I had seen ice before, though in smaller form; none of the other boys had seen ice at all, and they laughed, and squealed, and passed it hand to hand as if it might change them forever if they held it too long.

At work that day, I attempted to impart everything I knew to George, who would have to take over the project entirely. He was very attentive, but we both knew that leaving so quickly would be problematic. The operation had lost its two primary staff members in the space of a month.

—Maybe they'll send another Japanese person, George said.

—I hope they don't, I said.

I wanted no more people coming to Kakuma unless they had no other choice. I wanted us to take care of ourselves, and to solve all this on our own, and to bring no innocents into the hole we had dug. It seemed a sensible plan, that day at least, and after we locked up the office that afternoon, I felt the satisfaction of having settled another of my affairs at the camp.

As I walked home, the afternoon still bathed in harsh light, I saw my stepsister Adeng walking quickly toward me. Her arms were wrapped around her torso, a strange expression on her face.

—Come quickly, she said.

She took my hand in hers. She had never held my hand before.

—Why? What is it? I asked.

—There is a car, she said. —Outside our house. For you.

A car had only once before stopped at our shelter, when Abuk had arrived.

We walked quickly toward home.

—See? she said.

When we arrived, I saw four cars, UN cars, black and clean, dust everywhere around them. I stood with Adeng. The car doors opened and a dozen people stepped out at once. There were two white people, two Kenyans. The rest were Japanese, and all were wearing formal clothing—jackets and ties, clean white shirts. A young Japanese man, tall and wearing a tan suit, stepped forward and introduced himself as the translator. And then I knew.

—These are the parents of Noriyaki Takamura, the man said, sweeping his arm toward a middle-aged couple. —This is Noriyaki's sister. They have come from Japan to meet you.

My legs almost gave way. This was such a difficult world.

His parents greeted me, holding my hand between theirs. They looked very much like Noriyaki. His sister took my hand. She looked like Noriyaki's twin.

—They say they are sorry, the translator said, —but Wakana, Noriyaki's fiancée, is not well. She wanted to meet you, but she is finding all this very difficult. She is in bed, in the UN compound. She sends her good wishes for you.

Noriyaki's father spoke to me and the man in the tan suit translated.

—They say that they are sorry for the pain in your life. They have heard much about you and they know you have suffered.

—Please tell them that this is not their fault, I said.

The translator related this to the Japanese. They spoke to me again.

—They say they are sorry to add to the tragedy of your life.

Noriyaki's mother was crying now, and soon I was, too.

—I am so sorry that you have lost Noriyaki, I said. —He was my good friend. He was loved by everyone in this camp. I beg you not to cry for me.

Now everyone was crying. Noriyaki's father was sitting on the ground, his head in his hands. The man in the tan suit had stopped translating. Noriyaki's mother and father cried and I cried there, in front of my shelter, in the heat and light of Kakuma camp.

I had two more days before I left for Nairobi, then Amsterdam, then Atlanta. I slept without peace that night and woke early, hours before the second day of orientation class. In the inky blue light before dawn I walked around the camp and felt sure I would never see any of it again. I had never seen Sudan again, had never seen Ethiopia again after we fled. In my life up to that point, everything moved in a single direction. Always I fled.

There were too many things to do in those last forty-eight hours. I knew I would do few of them well. The orientation class ended at two o'clock and with the remaining daylight I had to cancel my ration card, pack and then see hundreds of people who I would never see again.

I knew I would give away most of my things, for when someone is leaving the camp, that person is descended upon; he becomes very popular. Custom requires that he leave all of his possessions to those remaining in the camp. First, though, there is the practice of booking, wherein anyone close to a departing refugee will claim whatever they would like to have upon the person's departure.

Within a day of knowing I would be leaving, everything I owned was booked. My mattress was booked by Deng Luol. My bed was booked by Mabior Abuk. My bike was booked by Cornelius, the boy from the neighborhood. My watch was booked by Achiek Ngeth, an elderly friend who had commented many times on how much he liked it. I used some of the money I had saved to buy new clothes, some pants with side pockets, lightweight and stylish.

I rushed from place to place on my bicycle, that night and the next morning, and when people saw me, they could not believe that I was leaving.

—Are you really leaving? they asked.

—I hope so! I said. I really had no idea if any of this was real.

It was Saturday and I would be gone the next afternoon. I was still not so sure I would be leaving, because the false starts had been many and all of them cruel. And besides, when I spent time thinking on it, I had no business going to the United States; none of it made sense. It was logical, much more so, that the whole affair would be called off. As I raced through the camp, shaking hands with people I knew, it began to seem more possible that I would leave—likely even. With every person who knew about my leaving and wished me well, I began to believe. So many people could not be deceived.

When I arrived home, to sleep one last night at Kakuma, I ate a very sad and joyful dinner with Gop and the family I had adopted. Ayen and her daughters cried because I was leaving. These adopted sisters of mine, every one of them as worthy as I was, cried also because they themselves had no chance of leaving, unless they were married off to prosperous men in Sudan. They were not considered by the UN for resettlement because they were a family, and thus were in no danger. None of the resettlement countries wanted families, it seemed, so Gop and his wife and daughters are still at Kakuma today.

After dinner, I packed the few belongings I would be taking: the new pants I had bought, and the many documents I had kept—my grade reports, proof of completion of a course in refereeing, my CPR certification, my drama-group membership card—twelve papers in all. I found two perfectly sized pieces of cardboard, and I taped them inside, to make sure the documents would not be damaged during any portion of my trip. Then the strangest thing happened: Maria came into my room. I had planned to say goodbye to her tomorrow but she was here now.

I don't know how she was able to leave her home in the evening. I don't know what she said to Gop and his wife that they allowed her into my shelter. But now she stood tentatively in the doorway, her arms roped together over her chest.

—I don't think you should go.

I told her that I was sorry to leave her, that I would miss her, too.

—It's not that I'll miss you. I mean, I will, Sleeper. But I think there's something God is doing. He took Noriyaki and I think he has a plan for you. I have a premonition.

I held her hand and thanked her for worrying about me.

—I sound crazy, I know, she said. She shook her head then, as if tossing aside her concerns, the way she dismissed any hopes and ideas of her own. But then her face hardened again and she looked into my eyes with a new fierceness.

—Don't go tomorrow, she said.

—I'll see you in the morning, I said. —I'll come visit and if you think I shouldn't leave, we'll consider a new plan then.

She agreed, though she only half-believed me. She slipped away from my shelter that night and I did not see her again. I didn't tell her that I shared the same worries, that my own fears were far more immediate and vivid than hers. I told no one, but I was fairly certain that something would go wrong with this trip. But I could not live in that camp anymore. I had been at Kakuma for almost ten years and would not live out my life there. Any risk, I felt, was acceptable.

The lobby of the Century Club is stone quiet after eight a.m. The members are working out beyond the glass, stepping and running and lifting, and I watch them and think of adjustments I might make to my own regimen. Two months ago I began to work out sometimes after my shifts. The manager, a petite and muscular woman named Tracy, told me that I could get a 50 percent discount on a partial membership, and I have been using that opportunity. I've gained four pounds in those two months, and have, I think, increased the size of my chest and biceps. I don't ever again want to look in the mirror and see the insect that I was.

A new woman enters the club, someone I have never seen. She is white, very large, exceedingly graceful. She looks startled to see me.

"Hello," she says. "Haven't seen you before. What a wonderful smile you have."

I try to frown, to seem hardhearted.

"I'm Sidra," she says, and extends her hand. "I'm new. I've only been here twice before. I'm, you know, making some changes." She looks down at her girth shyly, and I immediately feel that I should say something. I want to make her feel better. I want her to feel blessed. I want her to know that she has been blessed. To be here now, to be alive as she is, to have lived always in this country, Sidra, you are blessed.

She gives me her card and I swipe it. Her picture appears, her smile sad and tilted, and she enters the gym.

Sidra, on that last morning I woke at four a.m. to make sure I could avoid any line at the water tap. When I arrived, there was no line, and I saw this as a good omen. I brought water home and took a shower. As I was stepping out of the shower enclosure, Deng Luol, who had booked my bed, was standing at the doorway.

—It's not even dawn, I said.

—I've never had a mattress, he said. —I have a wife, and she would dearly appreciate one. With this, I will be her hero.

He wished me a safe trip and left with the mattress on his head.

I dressed in my crisp new clothes and packed my things in a plastic bag. I had only my toiletries, one change of clothes, and my documents. There was nothing else.

Everyone in my house began waking up, and all were crying.

—Make the Sudanese proud, Gop said.

—I will, I said. At that moment, I believed I could.

I said goodbye to each of my Kakuma sisters, and to Ayen, who had been my mother for many years at the camp. It was a swift parting; it was too confusing to stay any longer. I left so quickly that I forgot one of my new shirts, and left my new shoes. I realized this later, but did not want to go back.

When I walked outside, I found Cornelius, the neighbor boy who had booked my bike. It was a good bike, a Chinese-made ten-speed, and Cornelius was already sitting on its clean vinyl seat, with the kickstand down, practicing riding it, pushing the pedals forward and back.

—Ready? Cornelius said.

—Okay, let's go.

There would be unblemished blue skies all day. I was willing to walk to the compound—I would catch the bus to the airfield there—but Cornelius, with his new bicycle, insisted on chauffeuring me. So I sat on the small seat over the back tire, my bag on my lap.

It took him some time before he steered the bike competently with me aboard.

—Pedal, boy, pedal! I said.

Soon he was steady and we got onto the main road to the compound. When we joined the road, we saw the other people. Hundreds. Thousands. It seemed half of Kakuma was walking on that road, to see off the forty-six boys leaving that day. For each person leaving, there were hundreds of friends walking with them. You could not tell who was going and who were the friends. It was a great procession, the women all so sad, the colors of their dresses blooming all over the cracked orange road to the airfield.

Cornelius was now taking us with great speed through the crowd. He rang the bell on my handlebars, parting the throng before us.

—Look out! he yelled. —Move aside, move aside!

Those leaving were sorry for those staying and those staying were sorry to be staying. But I could not stop smiling. My headache cleared momentarily during that bike ride and when we passed through the camp, riding on the back of my own bike, people stepped out of the way of the bike and yelled to me.

—Who is that leaving? they said.

—It's me, I said. —Valentino! It's me!

Cornelius rode faster and faster. The thousands of those I knew at Kakuma were now a blur painted in every color. They stepped out of their homes and ran after me, wishing me well in all my names.

—Who is that leaving? It can't be! they said. —Is it you? Is it Achak?

—Yes! I yelled, laughing. —I'm leaving! Achak is leaving!

And they waved and laughed.

—Good luck to you! We'll miss you Achak!

—Goodbye to you, Dominic!

—Don't come back to this dirty place, Valentino!

And I looked at their faces as I passed, sitting over the rear tire of my bouncing ten-speed, and hoped that those people would leave the camp, though I knew that few would. The sun was strong when we reached the compound. Cornelius slowed and I leapt off. He had already turned the bike around and was heading home when he remembered to say goodbye. He shook my hand and was off. A boy so young with a bike like that? It was unprecedented at that camp.

I passed through the gate. Inside the compound, the other leaving boys leaving had gathered and were sitting in the yawning shade of the biggest tree in Kakuma. The flight was to depart at two p.m., but we who were leaving on that plane were already gone, already thinking, planning; mentally, we had already left Kakuma, left Kenya, left Africa. We were thinking of the kind of work we would do in the United States. We thought of school there, many of us imagining that we would, within weeks, be studying at American universities. One of the boys had a catalog for a college, and we passed it around, admiring the beautiful campus, the students of many ethnicities walking under the canopies of trees, past the buildings of raw-cut stone.

—I thought Jeremiah Dut was coming, one of the boys said.

—He wasn't approved. They found out he'd been a soldier.

The boys talked about that for some time, quietly, and we compared the lies we had told. Many of the boys had said their parents were dead, when only some of the boys were sure either way. After an hour of sitting in the shade, a plane came over the hills, looking very small and very fragile.

—That's the plane? someone said.

—No, I said.

At that moment, as it circled closer and finally landed, I was very sure that this was the plane that would take me to my death.

We stepped onto the plane, piloted by a Frenchman no larger than a teenage girl. There were forty-six of us on the flight, all of us having walked more or less the route I had walked. I knew none of them well; all of my friends were long gone. As soon as the plane's engines started, one boy vomited on my shoes. The boy ahead of me, smelling the vomit, expelled his breakfast on the seat in front of me. When the plane lurched forward, three more boys vomited, two of them finding the air-sickness bags in time. Beyond the retching, no one made a sound. Those of who could see out the windows were flabbergasted.

—Look at that building! A bridge?

—No, that's a house!

And inside the plane it was so bright. We had to lower the shades to rest our eyes.

The plane landed late on Sunday. No one had been to Kenyatta International Airport before, and all were astounded. The size of it all. It was much larger than the airfield at Kakuma, larger than any settlement we had ever seen; it seemed to have no end.

As evening came, we waited at the airport for a bus to take us into Nairobi, to Goal, a refugee processing center run by the International Organization of Migration. We would wait there until the next day, for our flight to Amsterdam and beyond.

In the dark around the airport it was impossible for young men like us to know what we were seeing. What were the lights? Were they disembodied lights or attached to structures? At night, most of Kakuma is dark, for there is little electricity. But here at Kenyatta everyone was still awake. No one slept at all.

—And the cars!

In all of Kakuma there were only a few at one time.

—Man, this is big! one of the men said.

Everyone laughed because it was what we were all thinking. As we drove from the airport into Nairobi, the awe grew. None but I had been in a city.

—These buildings! one of the boys said. —I don't want to walk under them.

None of the others had seen buildings over three stories, and they had little faith that those throwing shadows over the roads would stand.

At Goal we checked in, were given our itineraries and a buffet dinner of beans, maize, and marague, a mix of corn and beans and cabbage. We were shown to our rooms, six boys in each, sleeping on three sets of bunks.

—Ooh, look at these!

Most of the boys with me had never slept on clean white sheets. A boy named Charles threw himself onto the bed and pretended to swim. Then others joined in, and I did it myself. We all swam on the white sheets and laughed until we were sore.

I slept fitfully that night, listening to my roommates talk without end.

—Where are you going again?

—Chicago.

—Oh yes, Chicago. The Bulls!

And we would all laugh again.

—Is it cold in San Jose?

—No, no. I think it's warm.

—Too bad for you, Chicago!

Again we laughed.

In the morning, on a clear and humid Monday, there was breakfast and afterward nothing at all to do. No one was allowed to leave the hotel. It was fenced in and guarded by Kenyan soldiers. We were not sure why.

Again that night, no one slept. The room was dark but jokes were told, and the same questions asked.

—Who's going to Chicago again?

—Me. I am the bull.

It's hard to explain why this was so funny, but it was at the time. The other favorite joke of the night concerned San Jose. Three of the boys in the room were going there, but no one could pronounce that place.

—We're going to Saint Joe's! they said.

—Yes, San Joe's will be the place to be.

The next day we were finally going to the airport to board the real plane, the one that would make it to Amsterdam and then New York. From New York we would be sent to twelve different cities—Seattle, Atlanta, Omaha, Fargo, Jacksonville, so many places.

Once on the bus, exhaustion finally overcame us. It was Tuesday, we had been at Goal thirty-six hours, and no one had slept more than a few minutes. Finally we were going to the airport, each of us wearing matching IOM T-shirts, and every window of the bus bore the weight of someone's resting head. A pothole just before the entrance to Kenyatta woke everyone up and again there was merriment. I tried to stay still and quiet, for my head was so heavy, the pain so acute that I wondered if something was truly wrong with me. I briefly contemplated saying something to the Kenyan who had guided us onto the bus, to ask him for medicine of some kind, but then decided against it. It was unwise to make oneself noticed in such situations. Make a noise and the opportunity might be taken away. Complain about anything and get nothing.

There were thousands at the airport this day, a bewildering mix of Kenyans and lighter-skinned blacks, and a hundred or more white people, most of them sunburned a raw pink. We saw a group of whites, perhaps fifty—more white people than we ever had seen in one place—all gathered together with their extensive luggage, all of them looking for their passports. I wanted to speak to them, to practice my English, to tell them that soon I would be part of their world. I had no idea where they were from but I was caught up in the idea that I was leaving one world and entering another, that the American world was a white one and all whites, even these people in Nairobi, were part of it.

We waited near the gate, trying not to attract attention. There was concern among everyone that if we were noticed by the police or airport authorities, we might be taken directly back to the camp. Thus no one wandered from their seats. No one went to the bathroom. We waited an hour, our hands in our laps, and then it was time. We boarded a plane five times the size of the one we had taken to Nairobi, and more luxurious in every way. We buckled our seatbelts. We waited. The pain in my head grew every minute.

We sat until everyone had boarded, and then sat for thirty minutes more. We were all seated in a swath in the middle of the plane, and we stayed very quiet. An hour passed. We said nothing, because we had no idea how long it took for planes to leave for Amsterdam and then New York. But the other people onboard, whites and Kenyans, had begun to ask questions, and there were a series of assurances over the intercom. —We are awaiting clearance from the tower. —We're ready to go, and are waiting for instructions. —Please bear with us. Thank you for your patience. Please stay seated with your seatbelt on.

Another thirty minutes passed. The intercom came alive again.

—There has been an incident in New York. This plane cannot go there.

Silence for a few minutes more.

—Please deplane in an orderly fashion. There will be no aircraft leaving Nairobi at this time. Go back to your gate and await further instruction.

Our bus was the second to reach the hotel, and in the lobby, a hundred people, the Sudanese and the Kenyan hotel staff, even the cooks and maintenance workers, were all gathered around the TV, watching the towers burn like chimneys and then fall. Then images of the Pentagon. None of us Sudanese had ever seen the buildings that were under attack, but we understood that the United States was at war and that we would not be going there.

—Who is the enemy? I asked a Kenyan porter.

He shrugged. No one knew who had done this.

We ate and slept as best we could; we were stranded at Goal while the world decided what to do. As I had foreseen, as Maria had foreseen, I was being sent a message from God. I did not belong on this or any plane.

We expected to be sent back to Kakuma immediately, but that first day we were not sent back to Kakuma. The next day, we were not sent back to Kakuma. We knew nothing about our situation, what plans they had for us, but as the days passed, we became more encouraged about our fates. Maybe we would be resettled in Nairobi. One boy had the idea that we would work at the hotel at Goal, or at least those among us who had applicable skills might. He claimed to be a very good cook.

Some among us did not want to go to America now. To them, Sudan seemed safer than New York. Things would only get worse, they surmised, as retaliation was undertaken and led to a larger conflict. It was generally agreed that any war the United States would be engaged in would be the biggest war the world has ever known. I took what I had seen of explosions in films and extrapolated. The coming war would look like that, fire filling the sky, covering the world. Or perhaps the buildings, all of the buildings in America, would simply continue to fall in on themselves as they had in New York. A smoldering, then collapse.

There was no news from the IOM or anyone on Wednesday, Thursday, or Friday, and on Saturday something unfortunate happened: more refugees arrived from Kakuma. Another plane had flown from the camp to Nairobi, and now the hotel had another forty-six Sudanese boys. Another group followed that evening. And on Sunday, two more planes brought a hundred more passengers. These were regular flights, like the one we had taken, and they had not been rescheduled. Soon there were three hundred refugees at Goal, a facility designed for of third of that number. We slept two per bed. Mattresses were brought into the hotel from surplus stores and hospitals, and soon there were only narrow paths carved where people could walk. The rest of the floors were covered with blankets and sheets, and we slept upon them at all hours, whenever we could.

It was from one of the new arrivals that I heard about Maria. Shortly after I saw her that night, when she had urged me not to leave, she had attempted to take her own life. She had swallowed a mixture of cleaning solution and aspirin, and would have died had it not been for her caretaker, who found her in her bed, a tendril of white liquid descending from her mouth. She was taken to Lopiding and was now in stable condition. I was wrecked by this news on this day, but Sidra, thank God, her story ends well. In the hospital she met a Ugandan doctor, a woman who listened to her story and took it upon herself to guarantee that Maria would not return to the man who wanted to gain from her the best bride price. This particular doctor cared for her and eventually arranged for her to go to school in Kampala, to a school with pens and pencils, uniforms and walls. Maria is now in college in London. We are in touch via email and text-message and now I can call her Sleeper, too, for she attempted to sleep forever but now seems content to be awake.

On the second day at Goal, hot rain soaked Nairobi, and the hotel passed quickly into fetid. The bathrooms were unclean. There was not enough food. We wanted to use the money we had—and many among us had brought savings—to buy food in Nairobi, but security was now tighter than before. No one could come or go. Competition for the food served at Goal fostered ugly behavior. On the rare occasion there was meat, it brought arguments and bitterness; only a small percentage of us tasted it.

There was nothing to do. We prayed in the morning and at night, but I was helpless and dizzy. I had felt powerless for most of my life, but there was nothing like this. Some of the boys blamed the driver of our bus, saying that he had driven too slowly— had he been quicker, they claimed, we would have reached the plane sooner, and would have left the airport before the flights were grounded. This was the thinking of desperate minds. But few of us believed it was likely that we would still go to the United States. Australia perhaps, or Canada—but not this nation under attack. We were sensitive to the tenuousness of our acceptance into the United States, we did not take it for granted and were aware of how quickly and justifiably their minds could be changed. Why would a country under attack need people like us? We were added trouble for a troubled country.

The rain stopped the afternoon of the eighth day and Nairobi warmed under cloudless skies. I sat on the bed I shared with yet another Daniel and stared at the walls and ceiling.

—I wish I'd never known about America, a boy in the bunk under me said.

I wondered if these were my thoughts, too. I do not remember doing anything that day. I don't think I moved.

The three hundred of us waited. We learned that the flights carrying Lost Boys just before us had been diverted to Canada and to Norway. Travelers were stranded all over the earth. —The world has stopped, said one of the Kenyans. Everyone nodded.

Soon the flights from Kakuma stopped, but refugees continued to arrive at

Goal. A group of seventy Somalis from the other Kenyan camp, Dadaab, were now at Goal, and the center's administrators were forced to allow everyone to spend more time outside. We took turns breathing the air of the courtyard.

With all the other young men at Goal, I watched the news, hoping to hear the American president say something about war, about who the enemy was. We were heartened somewhat that as the days passed, no more attacks occurred. It seemed impossible, though, that there was simply one day of attacks and no more. It was not the kind of war we were accustomed to. We stayed close to the television, expecting only bad news.

—You Sudanese want to go to America!

A Somali man, as old as any Somali I had ever seen, was speaking to us from across the room. He was standing, watching us watch the news. No one knew anything about him, but someone said they had seen him at Kakuma.

—Where will you go? They're at war! the Somali said.

I had heard of this man. The others at Goal called him the Lost Man. The Lost Man made me very angry very quickly.

—You thought it would be better there? he yelled, as the television presented a new angle of the planes breaking through the black glass of the buildings.

No one answered him.

—It'll be no better! he continued. —You thought you'd have no problems? Just different problems, stupid boys!

I didn't listen to the man. I knew he was broken, mistaken. I knew that in the United States, even with attacks such as these, we would live lives of opportunity and ease. I had no doubt. We were prepared to surmount any obstacles put before us. We were ready. I was ready. I had succeeded at Kakuma and I would find a way to succeed in America, whatever state of war or peace that country found itself in. I would arrive and immediately enroll in college. I would work at night and study during the day. I would not sleep until I had entered a four-year college, and I was sure I would have my degree in short order, and would then move on to an advanced degree in international studies, a job in Washington. I would meet a Sudanese girl there and she would be a student in America, too, and we would court and marry and form a family, a simple family of three children and unconditional love. America, in its way, would provide a home for us: glass, waterfalls, bowls of bright oranges set upon clean tables.

The Lost Man was still ranting, and one of the men who had been on my flight from Kakuma could take the old man's taunting no longer.

—But you're going there, too, fool! he yelled.

This is what was strange about the Lost Man: he was going to America, too.

We were familiar with the attacks on the embassies in Tanzania and Nairobi, and as the days wore on, the world became more certain this was the work of the same man. As the days produced no more attacks, though, we realized that America was not at war, that it was relatively safe to go there. We decided we wanted to go more than ever.

After nine days, I organized a contingent of young men, four of us, Sudanese and Somali, to plead for our deliverance. I requested a meeting with the IOM representative I had seen moving in and out of Goal every few days. Incredibly, the meeting was granted.

He was a South African man of mixed race. When he arrived, before he could speak, I launched into my plea. We will fight! I said. We will do whatever is asked of us if you only send us to America, I said. We have waited so long! We have waited twenty years only to know that something good will happen! Can you imagine? Do not deprive us of this. You must not. We will do anything, everything, I said. My companions looked at me warily, and I suspected I was doing more harm than good. I was overtired and perhaps sounded desperate.

The man walked out of the room, having said nothing. He left a piece of paper, and on it was printed an IOM directive: the flights were to continue as soon as the airports were reopened in the United States. In the mythology of Goal, my speech became the deciding factor in the resumption of flights. I was celebrated for days, no matter how many times I denied responsibility.

The postings began on September 19. Every day, a list of twenty refugees was taped to a window by the television set, and those people would be picked up the same afternoon and taken to the airport. On the first day, the men whose names were on the list packed, unbelieving, and got on the bus at two-thirty. The bus left and that was that. The rest of us could not fathom how simple and quick the process had become. When the first three groups did not return, we became relatively certain that if we got on an afternoon bus, we would indeed leave Goal for good.

I have never been so happy to see Sudanese people disappear. Each day there were fewer people at Goal—first 300, then 260, then 220. On the fourth day I was placed in a new room, a small room with one window, high above and striped with steel bars. I had a bed to myself but shared the room with fourteen others. Every night that I knew I would not be leaving the next day I slept well, hearing the planes leaving from Nairobi.

On the fifth day my name appeared on the sheet taped to the window. I would be on the bus the next afternoon. That night I lay in bed staring at the other young men in the room, all of them shadows, only a few asleep. Half were leaving the next day with me, and those who were leaving could not rest. The mood was very different than it had been eight days earlier. The Sudanese, as far as we knew, were now spread all over the world, stranded, redirected; some who were meant for one country were now staying, indefinitely, in another. But we would be flying into all of this the next day. None of us were sure we would ever see the earth again. To fly from Africa, over the ocean, in an airplane, bound for the city where planes were flown into buildings? It wasn't just about a country at war. We were leaving everything we knew, or thought we knew; each of us had only one small bag of possessions, and no money at all, no family where we were going. This journey was an act of reckless faith.

It was dark in our small room, the fan above us unmoving. The youngest among us, a young man named Benjamin, had turned to the wall, awake and shaking.

—Don't be frightened, I said to him.

I was the oldest of the group and I felt it was my responsibility to calm him.

—Is that Valentino? he said.

—It is. Don't fear tonight, Benjamin. Or tomorrow.

The men in the room murmured their assent. I slipped out of my bed and down to Benjamin's bunk. Now that I saw him close-up, he looked no more than twelve.

—Already we've seen more than most of our ancestors. Even if we disappear while flying to our destination, Benjamin, we should be thankful. Do you remember the flight to Nairobi? We had to close every window it was so bright. We've seen the earth from the sky, we've seen the lights of Nairobi and all the people of the world walking through its streets. This is more than an our ancestors could have dreamed.

Benjamin's breathing slowed, and the men in the room agreed that this was true. Emboldened, I continued to speak to Benjamin, and to the shadows of these men. I told them that the mistakes of the Dinka before us were errors of timidity, of choosing what was before us over what might be. Our people, I said, had been punished for centuries for our errors, but now we were being given a chance to rectify all that.

471

We had been tested as none before had been tested. We had been sent into the unknown once, and then again and again. We had been thrown this way and that, like rain in the wind of a hysterical storm.

—But we're no longer rain, I said, —we're no longer seeds. We're men. Now we can stand and decide. This is our first chance to choose our own unknown. I'm so proud of everything we've done, my brothers, and if we're fortunate enough to fly and land again in a new place, we must continue. As impossible as it sounds, we must keep walking. And yes, there has been suffering, but now there will be grace. There has been pain but now there will be serenity. No one has been tried as we have been tried, and now this is our reward, whether it be heaven or something less than that.

When I was done talking, Benjamin seemed pleased, and words of agreement were sent up into the dark from all of the room's men. I climbed back into my bed but felt as if I was floating above it. Every part of my body felt electric. My chest ached and my head throbbed with the great terrible limitless possibility of the morning, and when it came, the sky was washed white, everything was new, and I hadn't slept at all.

XXVI.

When the morning ends and my work is done at the Century Club, I leave, knowing I am leaving this job and I am leaving Atlanta. I walk outside; it's an unremarkable day. I know that I will not miss the sky that guards over this city. The heavens here have been a hammer to me, and I will be moving, as soon as I am able, to a quieter place. A place where I can spend some time thinking. I need to make some new plans without the eyes of these clouds over me.

My plans are a jumble for now, but I do know certain things that I will and will not do. I will not file fabric samples again. I will not haul television sets or sweep tinsel from the floors of a Christmas-themed shop. I will not butcher animals in Nebraska or Kansas. I have no prejudice against these jobs, for I have done most of them. But I won't go back to that kind of work. I will reach upward. I will attempt to do better. I will not be a burden upon those who have helped me too much already. I will always be grateful for what pleasures I have enjoyed, what joys I have yet to experience. I will take opportunities as they come, but at the same time, I will not trust so easily. I will look at who is at the door before opening it. I will try to be fierce. I will argue when necessary. I will be willing to fight. I will not smile reflexively at every person I see. I will live as a good child of God, and will forgive him each time he claims another of the people I love. I will forgive and attempt to understand his plans for me, and I will not pity myself.

At the beginning of this unremarkable day, I will first drive home. Achor Achor and I will cover the floor that bears my blood with a plant, a lamp, perhaps a table, and we will replace the things that were stolen. I will tell Achor Achor that I am leaving the apartment, and he will understand. It will take him very little time to find a new roommate. There are plenty of my brethren in Atlanta who will appreciate that apartment, and the next man will not care about what happened there.

Today I have options. There is a friend of mine who has a new baby. He's one of the Dominics, actually; he and his wife live in Macon. Maybe I'll drive there, bring greetings and a gift. I could go to Macon, hold the newborn for a time, and then, if I felt strong, I could drive on to see Phil and Stacey and their twins in Florida. The ocean would be cold at this time of year but still I would try to swim. Or should I drive the other way? I could drive all day and night and find Moses in Seattle, stay with him and eventually join his walk. I dearly want to walk with Moses again, and will do so, I promise I will do so, unless he plans to walk barefoot. Would he do such a thing, walk barefoot to Arizona to make some sort of point? In that case I would not join Moses; that would be madness.

I look across the roofs of cars and into the field that spreads out beyond. I close my eyes against the white sky and see the yellow of a falling sun. I can see her clearly now, moving swiftly down the path toward me, walking her tall gangly walk. I should be home. It seems wrong that I am not home with her. I could leave this struggle here behind and be with her, with my father and in the cradle of the vast family I have in Marial Bai. To stay here, struggling and with my head aching so with the pressure, is, perhaps, not my destiny. For years I have vowed to return home, but not until I had finished my college education. I saw myself stepping off a plane, wearing a suit, carrying a suitcase, my diploma entombed in leather inside, and into the embrace of the town and my family. I told my father this plan, too, and he liked it very much, though he insisted that I wait until he, too, had regained the ground beneath him. He did not want me to see him again until his business was rebuilt, and not before our compound was again as it was when I came into the world.

I believe this day will come. It is, though, taking longer than expected.

Whatever I do, however I find a way to live, I will tell these stories. I have spoken to every person I have encountered these last difficult days, and every person who has entered this club during these awful morning hours, because to do anything else would be something less than human. I speak to these people, and I speak to you because I cannot help it. It gives me strength, almost unbelievable strength, to know

474

that you are there. I covet your eyes, your ears, the collapsible space between us. How blessed are we to have each other? I am alive and you are alive so we must fill the air with our words. I will fill today, tomorrow, every day until I am taken back to God. I will tell stories to people who will listen and to people who don't want to listen, to people who seek me out and to those who run. All the while I will know that you are there. How can I pretend that you do not exist? It would be almost as impossible as you pretending that I do not exist.

ACKNOWLEDGMENTS

The author and Valentino Achak Deng would like to thank the following people and organizations for their support, analysis and encouragement, and the following texts for inspiration and guidance: Lueth Mou Mou and Bol Deng Bol; Deng Nyibek Arou, Amiir Jiel Nyang, Adut Kuol, Achol Liai, Fatuma Osman, Atak Mayuol, Adeng Garang Ngong, Amath Dut, Aguil Apath, Amin Deng and Ayen R. Lonyo; all Arous, Adims, Gurtungs, Achaks, Dengs, Piols, Agouds, Achols, Aduts, Jors, Nyijurs, Nyibeks, Ahoks, and Mayens; Mary Williams; John Prendergast of the International Crisis Group; Simon Kuot; Malual Geng; Isaac Mabior; Tito Achak; Akoon Ariath; Kuek Mzee; William Kuol Bak; Deng Kur; Leek Akot; Manut Kon; Tong Achuil; Mabior Malek; Francis Piol Bol; Monynhial Dut; Ayuen & Lual Deng; Lual Dau Marach; Bol Deng; Lino Diadi; Luach Luach; James Alic Garang; William Kolong Pioth; Deng Colobus; Yai Malek; Boll Ajith; Garang Kenyang; James Dut Akot; Kenyang Duok; Santino Dut Akot; Joseph Deng Akon; Katherine Kuei; Manyangdit; Mador Majok; Madame Zero; Gat-kier Machar; Sam Rout; Helena A. Madut; Akuol Nyuol; Ajok Geng; Matter Machar; Angok Agoth Atem; Achol Deng; Anne Ito; Lual Thoc; Dominic Dut Mathiang; Isaac Chol Achuil; Angelo Uguak Aru; Awak Kondok; Awak Ring; David Nyuol; William Machok; Sisimayo Faki Henry; Angelo Ukongo; Anthony Ubur; Ferew Demalesh; Faith Awino; George Chemkang Mabouch; Hannington Nyamori; Tutbang; Machien Luol; Abraham Telar; Mangor Andrew; Kumchieng; Kon Alier; Garang Dhel; Garang Aher; Garang Kuot; Aluel Akok; Yar Makuei; Adeng Maluk; Rebecca Ajuoi; all at the Nairobi office of the SPLM; Jason Mattis in Nairobi; Peter Moszynski in Nuba; Peter Dut Adim in Marial Bai; Daniel Garang Deng (Marial Bai); Dierdre O'Toole and Joseph Kalalu of CONCERN; John Dut Piol; Aweng Aleu and Gisma Hamad; Geoffrey Beaton; William Anei Mayep; Joseph Deng Akoon; Simon Wol Mawein; Akaran Napakira, Veronica Mbugua, George Omandi, Maurice Onyango, Augustus Omalla, Jackson Karugu, Gillian Kiplagat, Thomas Agou Kur, Dominic Dut Mathiang, Khamus Philip Paulino, Cosmas Chanda (UNHCR) in Kakuma; Janie, Robert, Wesley, Anne and Wes French; Harper, Colton, Stacey and Phil Mays; Billi, James, Teddy, Sofia, Deborah and the late Robert Newmyer; Barb Bersche, Eli Horowitz, Jordan Bass, Andrew Leland, Heidi Meredith, Angela Petrella; Mac Barnett, Jim Fingal, and Jess Benjamin; Ayelet Waldman; Sarah Vowell; Brian McGinn; Marty Asher, Jennifer Jackson, and all at Vintage; Simon Prosser, John Makinson, Juliette Mitchell, Francesca Main, and all at Penguin Books; Guisseppe Strazzerri and all at Mondadori; Andrew Wylie; Sally Willcox; Debby Klein; Devorah Lauter; Evany Thomas; Peter Ferry; Christopher Oram; Erika Lopez; Peter Orner; Lala, Sophia, Steven, Susan and

Fred Sabsowitz; Jane Fonda; Dan Moss; Jane Bilthouse; Randy Grizzle; Gary Mann; Princess Swann; Peg James; Susan Black; Peggy Flanagan; Gerry, Bradford, and Jessica Morris; John Jose; Noel and Daris McCullough; Jermane Enoch; Andrew Collins; Justin Springer; Michael Glassman; Kelly McGuire; Dough Calderwood; Andrew Collins; Mike Glassman; Justin and Linsey Springer; Luke Sandler; *War of Visions* by Francis Deng; *War and Slavery in Sudan,* by Jok Madut Jok; Gayle Smith of the Center for American Progress; *Emma's War* by Deborah Scroggins; *Acts of Faith* by Philip Caputo; the International Rescue Committee; Save the Children; the International Crisis Group; The Red Cross; *A Problem from Hell,* by Samantha Powers; Amnesty International; Human Rights Watch; Manute Bol; Ann Wheat; Andrew O'Hagan; Kevin Feeney; Nicholas Kristof; *They Poured Fire on Us from the Sky,* by Benson Deng, Alephonsion Deng, Benjamin Ajak and Judy Bernstein; Thiep Angui; Arab Studies Quarterly; Martha Saavedra, U.C. Berkeley Department of African Studies; *Sudan Mirror;* SPLM Today.com; *Sudan Monthly; Sudan Update; Al-Ahram Weekly;* Refugees International; *The Sudan: Contested National Identities,* by Ann Mosely Lesch; AllAfrica.com; *Making Peace and Nurturing Life,* by Julia Aker Duany; *The Root Causes of Sudan's Civil Wars,* by Douglas H. Johnson; *Politics of Liberation in South Sudan: An Insider's View,* by Peter Adwok Nyaba. And to Vendela and Toph and Bill.

All proceeds from this book will go to The Valentino Achak Deng Foundation, which distributes funds to Sudanese refugees in America; to rebuilding southern Sudan, beginning with Marial Bai; to organizations working for peace and humanitarian relief in Darfur; and to the college education of Valentino Achak Deng.

For more information visit www.valentinoachakdeng.com

About the author: Dave Eggers is the author of three previous books—*A Heartbreaking Work of Staggering Genius, You Shall Know Our Velocity!,* and *How We Are Hungry.* He is the editor of McSweeney's, a quarterly magazine and book-publishing company, and is co-founder of 826 Valencia, a network of nonprofit writing and tutoring centers for young people. As a journalist, his work has appeared in *The New Yorker, Esquire* and *The Believer.* In 2004 he co-taught a class at the UC Berkeley Graduate School of Journalism, out of which grew the Voice of Witness series of books, designed to illuminate contemporary human crises through oral history. The first in the series, *Surviving Justice: America's Wrongfully Convicted and Exonerated,* was published in 2005. *Voices from the Storm,* about the residents of New Orleans who survived Hurricane Katrina, will appear in fall of 2006. The next in the series will give voice to former slaves in Sudan. He lives in the San Francisco Bay area with his wife and daughter.